Promise You'll Come Back

Written by
JESSICA JASPER-RING

abbott press®
A DIVISION OF WRITER'S DIGEST

The characters and names in this novel are fictional, but portray the heroic individuals who carried out incredible actions in the wars in Iraq and Afghanistan. I found it necessary to use my own interpretations and imagination in some of the battle scenes. In telling this story, I have taken small liberties with the facts. Several individuals have been referred to by pseudonyms or nick names to protect their privacy. In recalling conversations and incidences that took place, twelve years or more ago in the past, some of the dialogue and the situation have both been reconstructed and edited. This novel is fictional but based on fact.

Abbott Press books may be ordered through booksellers or by contacting:

Abbott Press
1663 Liberty Drive
Bloomington, IN 47403
www.abbottpress.com
Phone: 1-866-697-5310

ISBN: 978-1-4582-1210-8 (sc)
ISBN: 978-1-4582-1208-5 (e)

Library of Congress Control Number: 2013918226

Printed in the United States of America.

Abbott Press rev. date: 11/26/2014

Acknowledgments

I EXPRESS MY sincere gratitude to those whose support, confidence, and encouragement in me and my writing has never faltered. This novel has been a huge part of my life and now that it is finished, I owe a lot of people tribute, for without them and their encouragement, I wouldn't have finished it. I want to thank those closest to me for always being truthful and for giving me the criticism I needed.

There are so many people I would like to single out and thank. First, I would like to thank God. Without him, I would be lost. I would not be where I am in life if it weren't for my amazing Savior Jesus Christ. He is my light, my strength, and my counselor. Thank you Lord, for giving me this amazing passion, and allowing me to use it to help others and to give you praise. You command my destiny. When I stumbled, you picked me up. When I cried, you wrapped your arms around me and comforted me. Thank you for all the unanswered prayers. I only thought I knew what I wanted, but I decided to trust you and you've led me where you wanted me to go. Thank you for the many blessings I've received in my life, my husband, my children, my family and my friends. I give you all the glory, Lord, thank you for holding my hand as I wrote this.

To my husband, Rowdy, I love you very much and I know God must love me a great deal because he sent you to me. I'm so appreciative of you and all your input and support. I couldn't have found a better man to be my husband and to be the father to our children. I'm very blessed to have you in my life. And no matter how long you're gone, I'm always here waiting on you.

To my father, you are the greatest father, the best teacher, and the biggest patriot I know. It's because of you that I am such a patriot and a strong, independent, woman. I love you. You instilled the moral compass in me and taught me to stand up for what's right, even if I stand alone. I know Mom would be proud of who we've become.

To my Pop, my late grandfather, he was such an inspirational man in my life. He led by example. He taught me many things. He taught me how to kneel before God and humble myself. He taught me how to confide in him and to trust him, especially when times were bleak. He baptized me. He co-officiated my wedding ceremony. He blessed my first born. He encouraged me to write. I know if he were here, he'd fight everyone for the first copy of this. Pop, you're in my heart and I'll miss you dearly, but I'm happy you're with our Lord and my mom. You received your reward for being His messenger. I love you so much. I know Heaven's improved immensely now that Lord has one of his fiercest warriors with him.

To my Meme, you are so special to me. There aren't words to express how thankful I am that I have you in my life. I know I'm the closest to you. I confide to you like a daughter would to her a mother. You are my mother and there isn't anything anyone could say to refute that. I love you so much. We're closer than I ever hoped to be. I honestly would be lost if I didn't have you. You've always been that constant in my life. I know I could tell you anything and you'd hold my hand and we'd get through it.

To the rest of my family, I love you all so much. You all mean so much to me.

To Cleoria Parris-Smith, my best friend for the last twenty years, you are so very dear to my heart. I don't know where I'd be without you. I know I can always count on you for support, your insight and honesty, and you always encouraged me to keep writing. I know you must still have the many notebooks full of the stories I wrote when we were kids. I know I could always count on you for everything.

To the rest of my close friends, Summer, Andrea, Danielle, Shannon, Ashley, Christina and Carrie and so many more, I want you all to know I love you all and I appreciate you so much.

To my English teachers, Mrs. Kelli Tomblin-Hudgins and Mr. Frank Tragni, I always considered writing to be just a hobby that is until you both inspired me to turn my passion into a career. You both convinced me that I had talent as a writer. I never dreamed it possible, but thank you for inspiring me and believing in my work.

To author Steve Newman, your kind words and encouragement to keep going regardless of what others said about my work was inspiring and profound. I appreciate you helping me with my combat scenes. It's not every day a retired Green Beret is impressed with my work. I not only consider you a mentor, but a good friend.

Many people have helped me by talking to me on the phone, replying to my emails, and by reading and correcting drafts of my book. For their patience, frankness and cooperation, I especially thank all of those people.

To the management and staff of Briggs Auto Dealership in Manhattan, Kansas, thank you so much for allowing me to use one of your beautiful trucks for the cover. I really appreciate it.

To photographer Joe Geske of Joseph Geske Photography, your work is absolutely stunning and I'm happy to have had the opportunity to work with you.

To photographer Rebecca Mounce of Rebecca Mounce Photography, thank you for your stunning work for my author picture. I was happy to work with you.

To Mrs. Kasi Roberts, thank you so much for editing my work. I appreciate it and I'm glad you loved the story!

To the staff and production managers here at Abbott Press, thank you so much. It was such a pleasure to work with you.

Disclaimer

THE CHARACTERS AND names in this novel are fictional, but portray the heroic individuals who carried out incredible actions in the wars in Iraq and Afghanistan. I found it necessary to use my own interpretations and imagination in some of the battle scenes. In telling this story, I have taken small liberties with the facts. Several individuals have been referred to by pseudonyms or nick names to protect their privacy. In recalling conversations and incidences that took place, twelve years or more ago in the past, some of the dialogue and the situation have both been reconstructed and edited. This novel is fictional but based on fact.

Dedicated To...

My mother
Karen Lynn McBride- Jasper
June 16, 1967-
December 1, 1988
A beloved daughter, wife, mother, sister and a United States Marine

My Pop
Billy Wayne McBride
December 18, 1940- November 21, 2012
A beloved and respected pastor, son, husband, father, grandfather,
a great grandfather, and a friend.

ET1 Brian Anthony Moss
United States Navy
& the Moss Family in
Sperry, Oklahoma

The passengers and crew of:
American Airlines **Flight 11**
United Airlines **Flight 175**
American Airlines **Flight 77**
United Airlines **Flight 93**

The 2,749 people killed in the World Trade Center on September 11, 2001 & their families

The 343 New York Firemen
The 84 Port Authority employees and the 37 Port Authority Police officers
The 23 New York City Police officers
The fallen Emergency Responders

The 189 people killed at the Pentagon
To all who fought, died and were wounded that day

ET1 Brian Moss was killed in the Pentagon on September 11, 2001. He had just
begun working for the Chief Naval Operations in a fancy office on the building's
west side, the nightmare of rubble. He was sailor of the year in 2000. He was a

husband and a father of two. He was a loving son, husband, father, brother, and friend. He embodied the Navy's motto of honor, courage, and commitment.

Meeting his parents', Billy and Pat, his sisters Angela and Tina of Sperry, Oklahoma, has changed me forever. They are extraordinary people, with hearts bigger than Texas. I think of you often and I think of Brian every time I see the flag flying proudly. I thought of him frequently throughout writing this.

For our fallen U.S. and Coalition troops who fought and died in
Operation Enduring Freedom (Afghanistan)
Operation Iraqi Freedom (Iraq)

For our 1,000,000 plus veterans of
Operation Enduring Freedom (Afghanistan), Operation Iraqi Freedom, and Operation New Dawn
Your service was honorable and words cannot express how grateful I am, how proud
I am of all of you and your faithful service. Thank you for a job well done.

For U.S. military spouses,
Though we do not wear the uniform, or serve in combat, we do serve.
We serve by waiting.

1

TUESDAY, SEPTEMBER 11, 2001, joins December 7, 1941, the attack on Pearl Harbor as days that will live forever in infamy. No one will ever forget where they were or what they were doing on those mornings. The American sky over New York had never been so blue or so dark.

On a quiet, calm morning, it was normal, busy day for America, air traffic controllers and the military. It was 8:09 a.m. when **American Airlines Flight 11** bound from Boston to Los Angeles was hijacked. The passengers onboard were terrified, sprayed with mace, and two people were stabbed. Flight attendants called the FAA seeking advice. The captain and co-pilots were killed.

At 8:33, the North Eastern Air Defense Sector (NEADS) and Otis Air Force Base in Massachusetts were contacted. The FAA requested F-16s to be launched to tail the aircraft. Ironically, on this morning, NEADS and the Air Force were preparing for an operation and were confused whether this was training or real world. Once confirmed this was not a training exercise, the order of "SCRAMBLE" was given and F-16 pilots sprinted to their jets.

With the fighters at their battle stations, they flew up into the sky looking for the hijacked aircraft, but there were over three thousands flights in the air, international and domestic flights that morning. **Flight 11's** transponder was disabled. They were unable to track the aircraft.

With the Air Force on full alert, the aircraft was in a rapid descend and flying erratically over New York. The calls between flight attendants and air traffic controllers were disconnected when **Flight 11** crashed into the North Tower of the World Trade Center. The world watched in disbelief as black smoke billowed up from the tower against that clear blue sky. As far as the world was concerned, this was just a horrible accident, but to the U.S. military, this was war.

Army Green Berets Master Sergeant Jack Hamilton was asleep in his apartment after doing a four day extensive training mission in the woods outside Fort Bragg, North Carolina. His cell phone was on silent, but rang continuously. He rolled over, hearing the buzzing. He saw it was his commanding officer Colonel Gavin Mitchell. He answered quickly. "This is Alpha 1."

"Report in now." He could hear the seriousness in his voice. "A hijacked aircraft just hit the World Trade Center in New York. Report in immediately. We're on standby."

"Yes sir." He hung up. He jumped out of bed, turned on his TV as he quickly got dressed. Seeing the North Tower in flames with black smoke billowing up into the iconic New York City skyline, he knew this was war. Judging by the gaping hole and the inferno, he knew it had to have been a commercial airliner filled with jet fuel and passengers. He grabbed his keys, wallet, and sunglasses and drove onto Fort Bragg.

In Dallas, Texas, Katherine Johnson, a labor and delivery nurse is at work. It was a sunny picturesque morning. She noticed many others in the nurse's lounge watching the TV. She walked in and saw the North Tower in flames. "What happened?" she asked fellow nurse and good friend, Angie.

"A plane hit the World Trade Center in New York." Kate stirred her coffee as she listened to the news reports. After her break, she went back to work checking on her patients.

Jack made it to the Special Forces compound. He hurried to the private secure briefing room where team members were briefed and debriefed. He found his team, all ten men, staring at the TV in their lounge. Bravo and Charlie Teams were there also. Colonel Mitchell was in charge of three Green Berets teams, Alpha, Bravo, and Charlie. Each team had twelve men.

"Did you hear a plane hit the World Trade Center?" his best friend, Tom asked.

"Yeah, what the hell is going on?" They sat watching the T.V. All thirty-six Green Berets were on leave until Thursday.

Jack was the non-commissioned officer in charge (NCOIC) of Alpha Team. He was a weapons sergeant, capable of operating and maintaining a wide variety of U.S. allied and foreign weaponry. He was the warrior's warrior, a decorated soldier with no wife or children, only the Army. He was from Dallas, Texas. He was twenty-six years old. He was tall, six foot, with blondish-brown hair, green eyes and tanned skin. He had a fit and sculpted body, due to running ten miles a day, lifting three hundred pound weights, and doing one hundred push-ups and sit-ups daily. At the age of eighteen, he enlisted right out of high school. He went to Ranger School and graduated with honors. Then he was recruited by the Green Berets after seeing him successfully force fifteen of his fellow Rangers to "tap out" in the Army Combative School. He was an excellent leader of soldiers.

Colonel Mitchell stormed in. "We're at DEFCON 3. Your leave is revoked and we are hereby on immediate standby to deploy. The following information is all the information that I have at this time. At approximately 0809 this morning, a 737, **Flight 11** departing from Boston was hijacked by an unknown group of men. The passengers and crew reported them as possibly Middle Eastern. They made no demands. They sprayed mace at passengers and the crew and they killed the captain and co-captain."

Minutes later, at 9:02, just as the Colonel stood in front of his men briefing them, the team analyst rushed in. The commanders at NEADS were immersed in a real world crisis and were getting reports of a second hijacking. "Sir, there's another hijacking heading for New York City."

Colonel Mitchell ran to the TOC and was given the phone. Alpha, Bravo, and Charlie Teams looked up at the T.V. screen. At 9:03, the world watched as **United Airlines Flight 175** struck the South Tower of the World Trade Center. The men were completely stunned and ready for vengeance. America was under attack. They watched it utter disbelief as the massive fireball consumed the top floors of the tower. Black smoke billowed up from the large hole into that cloudless blue sky. Both towers were on fire and downtown Manhattan was now the center of a disaster. Police evacuated the civilians and the buildings around the World Trade Center. The civilians were in shock, fear, and disbelief. They couldn't take their eyes away from the disaster. Paper and debris fell from the towers into the street. Firemen were gearing up for the near impossible task of putting out fire 110 stories up and evacuating thousands trapped inside.

Colonel Mitchell stormed in. He slammed the door in anger. "We're under attack. We're going to war gents." They continued to watch the TV. They were sickened watching the desperate people, trapped inside the burning towers, jump 110 stories to their deaths. Though they did not know their enemy, the Green Berets were already itching to fight.

Suddenly at 9:21 a.m. NEADS got a call that another hijacked aircraft, **American Airlines Flight 77** carrying passengers was hijacked and headed to Washington D.C.

As Colonel Mitchell and his men were watching the scene unfold, the analyst again rushed into the room. "Colonel, another hijacked aircraft is inbound to Washington D.C."

"Are the fighters from Andrews in the air?"

"I'm not sure, sir."

Colonel Mitchell ran to the TOC and spoke to someone at Andrews Air Base. Unfortunately the fighters went the wrong direction. They were supposed to go north, but they went out over the Atlantic. The threat was from domestic planes, not international. They turned around and headed towards Washington D.C. but it was too late. **American Airlines Flight** 77 had slammed into the Pentagon, U.S. military headquarters.

The United States was officially under attack by an unknown enemy. They had made no demands. A declaration of war had not been given, but it had been carried out senselessly and cowardly, murdering thousands of innocent civilians and military personnel, using aircraft as weapons of war.

Minutes later, Colonel Mitchell walked back in with an expression of distress on his face. He was pale. Jack noticed the look on his face. "Colonel, what's happened?"

"The Pentagon was just hit." The teams were ready to fight.

At the Pentagon, newly appointed Army Chief of Staff Matthew "Matt" Johnson had successfully evacuated the Pentagon. He had just been in an important meeting with other senior military advisors for the President when the building was hit. They felt the building sway and saw the lights flicker.

Surveying the damage, he, a former Green Beret, couldn't sit still knowing there were more people still trapped inside. He had to do something. He was a husband of twenty-five years and a father to two beautiful, smart young women, but there was one fact he could not refute: he was a soldier first.

Together with a band of young and seasoned Army Rangers, they rallied together and decided to go back in to bring out their brothers and sisters-in-arms. They went back in through a gaping hole. They carried out dozens of injured men and women, some military and some civilian. Dozens of EMTs and ambulances were on the scene tending to the wounded.

In Dallas, Texas, Kate overheard from a patient's TV that the Pentagon had been attacked. She stood frozen in shock at the images of the Pentagon. She was worried especially since her father Army Chief of Staff Johnson worked at the Pentagon. She quickly excused herself to the restroom and frantically dialed her father's cell phone number, but there was no answer.

After getting her father's voicemail several more times, she prayed silently and desperately. She dialed her mother's cell phone number. Her mother, Carole, was an English Literature professor at the University of Texas at the Dallas campus. She and her class were watching the news, same as Kate.

Mom answered her cell phone immediately. "Kate?"

"Mom, have you heard about what's going on in New York and D.C.?"

"Yes, sweetie, my class and I are watching it now. It's deplorable what's happening."

She could hear the fear and worry, yet the determination to remain calm in her mother's voice. Her father always taught them that panicking was never good. "Have you heard from Daddy yet?" Kate asked frantic.

Mom could hear the fear in her voice also. "No sweetie, I've been trying to call him since the first plane hit the World Trade Center."

"How are you not freaking out right now?"

"Because I have faith that he's okay, I know he is just trying to help the wounded, look for survivors and get everyone accounted for. You know your father. He is strong."

Kate was twenty-one years old. She had just graduated from the University of Texas with a Bachelor of Science degree in nursing that May. She had just landed her dream job as a labor and delivery nurse at a Dallas hospital. She was petite and in shape. She was athletic, a starting guard for the University of Texas women's basketball team. She ran five miles every morning or evening, depending on her shift. She was average height, soft spoken with a Southern drawl. She had a natural tan, and long curly, dark brown hair and big brown eyes. She was engaged to a man named Kyle

Mowery. He was an architect for a firm in Dallas. He and Kate met through a mutual friend. They were set to marry in January.

The FAA grounded all planes in the air, over four thousand aircraft, were forced to land at the closest airports in the United States. All remaining planes in the air were considered hostile. The fighter pilots were ready to defend the nation from anymore destruction and senseless murder.

United Airlines Flight 93 was flying over Cleveland, Ohio. The air traffic controllers were very concerned. The hijackers claimed to have a bomb onboard. Suddenly the aircraft turned and sped toward Washington D.C. The air traffic controllers requested military action, in the form of fighter jets.

The Air Force pilots still had not been given clearance to fire on any civilian or hijacked aircraft. 90 minutes after the first hijacking, at 9:59 a.m, the world watched as the unthinkable happened. The South Tower, though hit second, was the first to collapse. The thirty six Green Berets were silent as they watched civilians, police, fire, and EMTs run for their lives as a huge dark cloud of debris and dust swallowed everything in its path. The incensed Green Berets were already hungry for vengeance.

With New York and Washington D.C. devastated and in chaos, America was facing the largest most severe terrorist attack in history, but it wasn't over yet. It was unbelievable that downtown Manhattan, one of the largest cities in the world, was the center of a war zone. The word 'war zone' evokes pictures of a distant battleground far away from U.S. cities and towns, certainly not downtown Manhattan. It had been a normal American city with citizens going about their normal daily routines. Never again will it be a normal city.

At 10:14, NEADS received word that hijacked aircraft, **United Airlines Flight 93** was down. The heroic passengers onboard overpowered the hijackers and forced the plane to crash in Shanksville, Pennsylvania. After **Flight 93** was down, the U.S. military received word that use of deadly force was now authorized. The order came too late.

Colonel Mitchell and his men were watching both TVs in the briefing room. They were watching what was going on in both Manhattan and Washington D.C. His secretary walked in with more disturbing news. "Excuse me, Colonel. The fourth plane inbound for Washington D.C. is down."

"It landed?" he asked surprised.

"No sir. It's down."

"Did the Air Force shoot it down?"

"No sir. It crashed."

"Where did it crash?"

She looked to her note. "**United Flight 93** has crashed in a field in Pennsylvania."

Colonel Mitchell looked to his men. He saw the anger and the eagerness to fight in their eyes. He walked to the podium at the front of the room. "This is the largest and deadliest attack on America since Pearl Harbor. That was our granddaddies war, this is our war. This is our Pearl Harbor and we're going after whoever did this. We're now at war, gents. Kiss your wives and children goodbye. Your country needs you now more than ever." The teams geared up and readied for the mission to commence war.

The members of Alpha Team were Jack, Tom, Brad, Luke, Marcus, Jamal, Eric, Jake, Sam, Mark, and Casey. Jack, Tom, and Brad were weapons sergeants. Jamal and Casey were medical sergeants. Jake and Luke were communications sergeants. Sam and Mark were intelligence officers. Marcus and Eric were operations sergeants. The leader of Bravo Team was Trevor and the leader of Charlie Team was Brett.

Back in Dallas, Kate and her friends stood, watching the T.V. She was still frantically trying to get her dad on the phone. Kyle called her phone. "Hello?"

"Hey babe, what are you doing?"

"I'm watching the news." As she talked with Kyle, her younger sister, Lauren came out of the elevator. She was now a freshman at the University of Texas at Dallas, but she was too distraught to go to class.

She approached Kate's friends, Angie, Tess, and Marci. "Where's Kate?"

Angie rushed her to Kate. She was surprised to see her. "Kyle, I'll call you back." She hung up. "Hey, what are you doing here? You're supposed to be in class." she asked.

"I've been trying to get ahold of Daddy and I can't. Something's happened to him, I just know it." Lauren said, sobbing.

Kate saw how upset her sister was. She hugged her. "We can't think like that, Lauren. I'm sure Daddy is making sure everyone who needs help gets it and trying to secure the area. You know how he is. We have to have faith."

Lauren proceeded to cry. "Why is this happening?" she asked. Kate continued to hug her. They were very close. She took off early that day to be with her mother and sister. They were all terrified that he would never be coming home.

Back at the Pentagon, dozens of Pentagon workers, including Matt and a handful of Navy SEALS, Army Rangers, Green Berets, and Pentagon workers were determined to get back inside the inferno to rescue their fellow comrades, but the firemen would not let them advance past them.

Matt was listening to the fire chief tell the mob of determined, adrenaline filled military men that it was too dangerous for them to go back inside. He was frustrated. In his mind, this wasn't a building fire, this was a war zone. There were people still trapped, soldiers, sailors, marines, and airmen as well as Department of Defense civilians. He lived by that philosophy: **never leave a comrade wounded on the battlefield, never leave him behind.**

"Where are you going?" a fireman stopped him and the group of America's warriors.

"We're going in there." Matt replied, with his adrenaline and testosterone pumping.

"Oh, no you're not, the building isn't secure."

"It's best if you just get the hell out of our way." Matt said. He was in combat mode. He was driven by his code of honor to get to them.

Surrounded by Navy SEALs, Green Berets, Marines, and Rangers, the fireman threatened, "I will shut you down if you and your men try to come through here."

"Give us your best shot." one Ranger yelled. The face-off between firemen and soldiers was coming to a heated head. That sense of loyalty and duty was creating a battlefield chaos. Among the soldiers, the frustration was turning into anger. The firemen knew something the eager soldiers didn't. The building was minutes away from collapsing.

Minutes after the confrontation, the building began to collapse. All five floors of the damaged Pentagon wall came crashing down and was reduced to rubble. The soldiers realized that the firemen saved their lives. Had they pushed through the firemen like they wanted, they all would've been killed. Matt thanked the fire chief and resumed with helping those they did save.

The Secretary of Defense was even out there on the Pentagon lawn, helping those that needed help. His expensive business suit was stained with the wounded's blood.

Later that night, Kate, her mother, and sister were at the house watching the news and waiting anxiously by the phone for him to call. At this point the news began to keep repeating all that they had heard all day. No new reports were coming in. The mood was tense. The house was dark, except for the lamps in the living room. Mom was sipping a tall glass of wine to calm her nerves, but it wasn't helping. Lauren was lying on the sofa with Holly, the family's Irish terrier, on her lap. Kate was sitting on the sofa, nervously. She had repeated the same prayer for her father's safety fifteen times. Neither of them had much of an appetite.

Finally, around 9:00 pm, the telephone rang. The echo rang through the quiet house. Mom quickly jumped to answer it. "Hello?" she answered, frantically.

It was Matt. He smiled listening to her voice. "Hi sweetheart, how are you and the girls?" he asked.

She breathed a sigh of relief, smiled, and cried out of elation and joy. She smiled at Lauren and Kate. "We're much better now that we know you're alright. Where are you?"

Relieved, Lauren and Kate hugged.

"I'm still in D.C. I won't be home until possibly next week."

"Are you hurt?"

"No, I'm fine." he lied. He was in a D.C. hospital receiving treatment for second degree burns from pulling burning debris off trapped people inside the Pentagon, but he would never tell his family that. "I love you. I'll be home in a few days. Tell the girls I love them, and don't let them worry." he said.

"Okay, we love you." she said.

"I love you all too." Matt and Carole had been married for twenty-five years and had two daughters, Kate, twenty-one and Lauren was eighteen. Her father had been in the Army for nearly thirty years.

With the tenseness and fear of the day, Kate felt she could only handle a light salad with her mother and sister. After eating, she drove back into the city to her apartment. She lived in a very nice apartment building in uptown Dallas. She had a roommate. Her name was Morgan Brown. She and Kate have known each other since college. Morgan was an event planner for one of the biggest event coordinators in town.

On September 11, 2001, the world seemed to stop turning. Millions of Americans from all walks of life, all different backgrounds, ethnicities and religions, united together. The terrorists thought they could bring America to its' knees, and they did for a brief moment, but what they didn't account for was how Americans are a determined people, we banded together by donating blood, raising money, or volunteering.

All stared somber and exasperated at the sight of where the World Trade Center once stood proudly. The iconic New York skyline would never be the same. Millions around the world were in disbelief as well. The United States' allies, such as Britain, France, Germany, and Italy held silent memorials for the United States, in prayer for those lost and the families left behind. The Royal Guard honored America and the victims by playing the National Anthem at Buckingham Palace. Dozens of Americans in London stood outside the gates proudly waving American flags. There was not a dry eye in the crowd.

The world wondered who could carry out this horrific attack. The answer was Al-Qaeda and Osama Bin Laden.

"Freedom was attacked this morning by a faceless coward and freedom will be defended. Today, our nation saw evil, the very worst of human nature. We responded with the best of America. Make no mistake, the United States will hunt down and punish those responsible for these cowardly acts..." President George W. Bush.

In late October 2001, Colonel Mitchell and his Green Berets were deployed and were to set up camp at the Karshi-Khanabad Air Base in Uzbekistan. This area had very rugged terrain and a long history of tribal battles. The soldiers would fight the Taliban alongside a group of Afghanistan rebels, the Northern Alliance. The Northern Alliance had been at war with the Taliban for many years.

Alpha, Bravo, and Charlie Teams were aboard a MC-130 Combat Talons aircraft, in route to Uzbekistan. Each wore their camouflage Kevlar gear, high powered sniper rifles. During the long flight, many team members slept, listened to music, looked at pictures of their wives and children, or read books.

Jack looked at his best friend Sergeant First Class Tom Merritt. They had made it through Special Forces selections and qualifications, Airborne School, and SERE training together. They both went to John F. Kennedy Special Warfare Center and School (SWCS[1]) together.

"How are Paige and the boys? I haven't seen them in a while." Paige was Tom's wife. They had been married for ten years. They had two sons, Michael, who was seven and Sam, who was five.

"They're good. We signed Mike up for football, and Sam was playing tee-ball before I left."

Jack smiled. "I'll convince Mike to go to OU when he's ready to go to college. They have an excellent football program." He was a passionate *University of Oklahoma* football fan.

Tom laughed. "Na, you won't. If he goes anywhere for football, it'll be to Alabama." Jack grinned. Tom was a passionate, die hard, *University of Alabama* football fan. He was from Birmingham.

"How are you and Chelsea?" Tom asked. Chelsea was Jack's 'girlfriend' who lived near Fort Bragg. They were semi-serious.

Jack shook his head. "I'm going to end it when we get back."

"Why?"

"When I first met her, she seemed to be everything I wanted, but the more I've gotten to know her, she just really aggravates the hell out of me. She's the laziest person I've ever met. She doesn't clean, cook, do laundry, pay bills, or anything. If the trash is overflowing, she'll just continue to try to shove trash into the can until it's literally impossible to fit anything else inside, but she's too lazy to take the trash out and to put a new trash bag in it. Don't get me wrong, she's beautiful, but she's just a slob."

Tom laughed. "If she wasn't a slob, would you still stay with her?" he asked.

"No, I'm just physically attracted to her. Her attitude turns me off. She's insanely jealous. She overreacts, and is overly dramatic. I've got to end it with her or I'm going to go insane."

Tom laughed. "Hopefully when you break things off with her, she doesn't stalk you."

"Well I've already changed the locks on my apartment and my cell phone number."

Arriving in Uzbekistan, they deplaned. They were briefed more on the mission objectives. Colonel Mitchell and his Green Berets received their biggest assignment yet. They were to work with the key resistance leaders of the Northern Alliance to fight the Taliban. For soldiers who've served several years in the Army, like Jack and Tom, this was the moment they've been waiting for.

The Green Berets took a helicopter into Afghanistan, in a valley, known as the 'Valley of Caves'. They landed in a flat river wash.

The next afternoon, Colonel Mitchell met with his new Afghan General counterpart, a tough war lord. The Taliban forced him to leave the country in the late 1990s. Now, he led over two thousand men, fiercely devoted to defeating the Taliban.

The Northern Alliance and Special Forces soldiers planned a strategic strike. They would take a key northern Afghan city, Masra Sharif, where this war lord once ruled. The Green Berets were hesitant to fully trust the Northern Alliance rebels. Colonel Mitchell had to frequently remind the General that the U.S. did not want Afghanistan, they were only there to avenge September 11th.

---

[1] John F. Kennedy Special Warfare School and Center is one of the Army's premier education institutions, managing and resourcing professional growth for soldiers in the Army's three distinct special operations branches: Special Forces, Civil Affairs and Military Information Support. Soldiers educated through SWCS programs use cultural expertise and unconventional techniques to serve their country in far flung areas across the globe.

As the men approached their assignment, B-52 Bombers pounded away at Taliban targets. The Taliban didn't know what to do, so many retreated.

November 10, 2001- Green Berets entered the liberated city of Masra Sharif, the first major Afghan city to fall. As they drove through the city, the citizens were chanting happily. They were waving and smiling at the troops. They were happy that the Taliban had finally been driven out.

The Northern Alliance General turned to Colonel Mitchell, "Why don't you put up an American flag?"

Colonel Mitchell smiled, "No, this is your victory, not ours,"

The Taliban regime was crumbling away. Three days after the liberation of Masra Sharif, the country's capital, Kabul also fell. The Green Berets rolled in and were greeted happily by the citizens. They saw people dancing, crowding the sidewalks to wave, chant and cheer for the Americans and the Northern Alliance troops. The Taliban could not put up with that level of force and fire power.

Around the globe in Dallas, Texas, Kate was just getting off work. It was 7:15 p.m. She worked a twelve hour shift. She called Morgan from her cell phone. "Hey, are you at the house?"

"No, I'm at the store. Do you need anything?"

"No, I think I'm good. See ya later."

They hung up. Kate pulled in and parked in the parking garage to her apartment building. She called Kyle's cell phone for the fourth time in an hour. Getting his voicemail, she was annoyed and left him a message.

She grabbed her purse and walked to the elevator. Unlocking the door to her apartment, she noticed his keys, his wallet, and cell phone lying on her entry table. She grabbed a bottle of water from the refrigerator. Suddenly, she heard noises coming from the back of her apartment, specifically her bedroom. She walked back toward the bedroom and saw the door was partially opened. Pushing the door open, she saw Kyle and Courtney, one of her bridesmaids, in her bed, having sex!

She was stunned. Her eyes were staring and her mouth fell open, as she dropped her bottle of water on the floor. The noise startled the occupied couple. "Kate, this isn't what it looks like!" he proclaimed as they scrambled to get untangled from the bed sheets.

"Oh really, it looks like you and Courtney are having sex in my bed! Get out! GET OUT!" she screamed. She grabbed both sets of their clothes and tossed them out of the fifth story window. She threw the woman's purse and cell phone out also. People on the street were watching and laughing.

"Please don't do this. I love you." he pleaded.

She laughed, trying to keep the tears at bay. She did not want him to see that he had hurt her. "You love me? If this you loving me, then I am better off without you!" she screamed.

"I love you very much. I'm so sorry." he professed, hoping she had gathered her thoughts and would see it from his side, even though he had no defense.

"I agree with you there, *you* are sorry. But hey, at least you found someone as low as you." she referred to Courtney, the bridesmaid, who hadn't said a word to her. She was too frightened. "I'm going to be just fine without you." she stated.

They were standing in the doorway of her apartment with only the sheet and mattress cover around them. "Where are our clothes?" he asked.

"They're waiting for you in the street!" she said, as she slammed the door in their faces. She turned and saw his cell phone, wallet, and keys. Finding her apartment key on his key ring, she took it off and walked to the window and threw those things out. She saw people watching her, down below.

"You go girl!" a few women below shouted in support of her. Kyle and Courtney were in the street picking up their clothes and belongings, with Kate's bed sheets still wrapped around them. The people on the street were laughing at them and taking pictures. Morgan was just pulling into the building and saw them in the street. She was stunned and very curious.

Kate closed her window, turned and finally broke down and cried. She was so hurt and humiliated. She went through her apartment, throwing away pictures of her and Kyle together, and the gifts he had given her.

Morgan opened the door and found her throwing pictures and presents away. "Looks like I missed one heck of a party. What happened?" she asked, laying her purse and keys on the bar.

"I caught him and Courtney having sex in my bed."

Morgan was stunned. "I have a bottle of wine in the refrigerator. It hasn't been opened yet."

"Go get it." Morgan opened a bottle of red wine, poured them each a glass, and sat down with her on the sofa. They talked for a while.

She called her mother and told her that the wedding was off and why. After hearing her mother's assurance that everything would work out and that God had something greater in store for her, she continued to sit on the sofa sipping her glass of red wine. She knew her mother would ease that burden of explaining to their guests for her.

Early the next morning, she woke up early around four-thirty to run her usual five miles before work. Morgan was still asleep in her room. She loved to run at dawn. It always made her optimistic to watch the sunrise. It reminded her that the day was fresh. As she ran, she tried to think of other things beside her broken engagement and her broken heart. Arriving back to her apartment, she quickly took a shower, applied her makeup, and styled her hair. She threw on a pair of royal blue scrubs and tennis shoes. Her shift began at 7:00 am, and was now 6:00. Grabbing her thermos of freshly made coffee, a blueberry muffin, and her purse, she left for work.

Arriving at the hospital, she acted as if nothing was wrong. She could've taken a few days off, but she didn't want to be left alone with her thoughts. In the beginning minutes of her shift, she was taking care of a young mother, who was close to being fully dilated. She walked out to the nurses' station when her close nurse friends Angie, Tess, and Marci approached her.

"Hey, so we've got your bachelorette party all planned out." Angie said.

She looked at them. "Uh, I don't need one."

"We've talked about having a bachelorette party for weeks now, why don't you want one?" Marci asked.

"Kyle and I broke up."

Her friends' were stunned. "What, when?"

"Last night, I caught him and Courtney in my bed."

They were dumbfounded. "Oh Kate, we're so sorry, honey. Is there anything we can do?" Angie asked.

"Oh girls, I'm fine. I'm over him. He obviously wasn't the right man for me." she said optimistically. She was a very private person. She hated to feel vulnerable. She forced herself to act happy and fine, but on the inside, she was a complete mess. Her friends were stunned she was not upset. They were easily fooled by her façade.

In the treacherous mountains of Afghanistan, Colonel Mitchell and his Green Berets with his Northern Alliance counterpart launched an unrelenting bombing campaign on the city of Kunduz. On the outskirts of the city, the Green Berets coordinated air strikes with the help from an Air Force team aboard an AC-130 gunship. The target was a safe house, harboring two hundred Taliban fighters.

After two weeks of airstrikes, Kunduz falls. Over 600 enemy combatants surrendered to the Northern Alliance General. The prisoners demanded to be taken back to Masra Sharif. The General agreed to take them. The Green Berets quickly noticed there was not a confinement facility large enough to house over six hundred enemy prisoners. So after careful consideration, the Green Berets and the Northern Alliance took the prisoners to Qala I Jangi. It was a 19th century fortress, just west of Masra Sharif. The prisoners were in the courtyard with two CIA agents, who interrogated them.

They came across an American man in the group of prisoners. He was from Washington D.C. who had converted to Islam. He flew to Afghanistan and actively sought after Al-Qaeda and the Taliban to join with them. The U.S. military had dubbed Osama Bin Laden with the code name "Geronimo"

As he was being questioned by the CIA agent, the enemy combatants staged a riot in the courtyard. The fighters were able to take control of the fortress. The American troops rushed to the fortress. Many enemy fighters took refuge in a pink house in the middle of the courtyard.

Three hundred yards away, Jack called in airstrikes. The pink house was obliterated, but the enemy fighters were undeterred. The U.S. suffered its first casualty of the war, the CIA agent inside the courtyard, questioning the American man. He was killed by the rioting prisoners. It took six days to put down the uprising of enemy fighters.

Just two months on the ground, the U.S. and the Northern Alliance had driven the Taliban from their strongholds and toppled their regime. Hundreds of Al-Qaeda fighters, including "Geronimo" were on the loose. They regrouped at the Pakistan border in the Shah-I-Kot Valley.

Jack and every member of the team could speak Arabic. His call sign was Alpha 1. Tom was Alpha 2. Sergeant First Class Jake Brigham was Alpha 3. He was from Denver, Colorado. Sergeant First Class Jamal Fields was Alpha 4. He was from Tulsa, Oklahoma. Sergeant First Class Casey Sears from Biloxi, Mississippi, he was Alpha 5. Staff Sergeant Brad Roberts was Alpha 6. He was from Laguna Beach, California. Sergeant Luke Richards' was Alpha 7. He was from Fayetteville, Arkansas. Sergeant Marcus Wills, from Knoxville, Tennessee, was Alpha 8. Sergeant Eric Davis, from Las Vegas, Nevada, was Alpha 9. Sergeant First Class Sam Motts, from Austin, Texas, was Alpha 10. Sergeant Mark Briggs', from Kansas City, Missouri was Alpha 11.

Trevor, the leader of Bravo Team's call sign was Bravo 1. Brett, the leader of Charlie Team was Charlie 1. Trevor, Brett, and Jack were good friends. They hung out together when they were home from deployment. Trevor was from Wichita, Kansas. Brett was from Macon, Georgia. They were also weapons' sergeants.

Each man had a specific job; Jack, Tom, Brett, Trevor and Brad were weapons' sergeants. They could operate any U.S. allied or foreign weaponry. Jake and Luke were communications sergeants. They monitored the radios and were able to listen in on Taliban radio transmissions. They could operate every kind of communication gear from encrypted satellite to old style, high frequency Morse key systems. Jamal and Casey were medical sergeants. They were the best chance the team had for trauma on the battlefield. Marcus and Eric were operations sergeants. They were specialists across a wide range of trades from demolitions to field fortifications. Sam and Mark were intelligence sergeants. They could hack into anything and operate any type of electronic equipment.

In Dallas, Kate was at work trying to get through the day, but her friends were very curious and also very worried about her. "You still don't feel up to talking about what happened with you and Kyle?" Angie asked nicely.

She sighed. "There's nothing to talk about other than it's over and I hope I never see him again."

"I'm so sorry this happened to you, but I need to know, did you really throw their clothes, her purse, his cell phone, and keys out the window?" Marci asked.

She remembered tossing everything out the window and couldn't help but laugh out loud. "Yeah, I did."

They all laughed together. She felt some of the tension release, laughing with her friends.

"I personally would've taken a baseball bat to his car." Marci said.

"I would've keyed it." Tess said.

"Making them leave my apartment with nothing but my sheets around them was enough justice for me. I imagine they were pretty embarrassed riding down the elevator and then picking up their stuff and their clothes in the street."

"Well sweetie, you deserve someone a lot better than him." Angie said supportively.

She shook her head. "They're all the same, so consider me off the dating circuit for good. No fix ups or blind dates." she said strongly.

"No, they're not all the same. You'll find someone great when you least expect it. Don't give up." Tess encouraged.

In Afghanistan, the Special Forces soldiers embarked on a mission called Operation Anaconda. On March 2, 2002, just before dawn, Chinook helicopters delivered more than two hundred U.S. Green Berets into the valley. The soldiers glanced out at the terrain and were in awe of how beautiful the scenery was, but were quickly reminded how deadly and perilous it was.

"This would almost be a great place to go hunting and camping." Tom said.

"We are hunting and camping." Jack joked. They laughed.

"Yeah, you're right. I guess in a way we are."

U.S. Special Forces and Afghan forces were to drive the enemy toward Army blocking positions in the Southeast, giving the enemy nowhere to run. As they reach their landing zone, Jack and his men came under heavy enemy fire from AK-47s.

"We're in a dogfight, men. Stay calm, don't panic." he reminded them. They were so close to the enemy. Many soldiers were eye to eye with an Al-Qaeda fighter. An enemy fighter, dressed in black with long black hair and a black beard, charged Jack. Jack took aim and fired at him. He shot him three times, but the fighter would not go down. Tom grabbed a grenade launcher and shot him and killed him.

"That guy was either brave or crazy." he said to Tom.

Tom laughed, "I prefer him to be crazy,"

Mortar rounds hit, and soldiers' would go flying through the air from the blast. Shrapnel from incoming mortar rounds sliced through the soldiers. Casey and Jamal were running from one injured soldier to the next. Army infantrymen and Special Forces were in their first major ground fight of the War on Terrorism in Afghanistan.

The U.S. had badly underestimated the number of enemy forces in the Shai-I-Kot Valley. Instead of fighting only two hundred enemy fighters, they were fighting one thousand. The fighting was so intense that the MED-EVAC helicopters couldn't get to the wounded. It fell on Army medics and Green Berets medical sergeants to protect their fallen comrades on the battlefield.

An RPG nearly clipped a MED-EVAC helicopter. The boots on the ground were relieved that the helicopter barely missed it. Under heavy cover fire from Apache gunships, the MED-EVAC and the Chinook helicopters were able to land. The wounded were quickly boarded and the ground force left the valley.

"Whew! …Our first big firefight!" Luke said to Marcus.

"I don't know what you're so excited about, that was intense," Marcus said.

Using the cover of night, U.S. air power turned the war in U.S. favor. Operation Anaconda raged on for two weeks, but eight Americans were killed. The projected casualty rate for the enemy was over 800. It's a decisive victory against the Taliban.

The Green Berets returned to their established outpost, Firebase Scorpion, in the Shai-I-Kot valley. The firebase was just on the border of Afghanistan and Pakistan. Surrounded by thick mud walls, high barbed wired fences, the firebase was closely guarded by a handful of Green Berets soldiers armed with high powered rifles. It was equipped with a tactical operations center (TOC), a weight room, a TV room, a landing pad for the Blackhawks, Apaches, Chinooks, a shower area, and they had private bunks.

As Jack settled into his bunk, he laid his rifle down on his bed and checked his email on his laptop computer. Seeing he had ten emails from Chelsea, he opened the most recent one and read.

> *"Jack,*
>
> *I've thought about this a lot, and I don't want to see you anymore. Sure, you're hot and absolutely phenomenal in bed, but there just isn't anything more between us. I've met someone else. His name is Brian. I thought I wanted a military man, but I've changed my mind. We had fun, but let's just go our separate ways. Please don't call me again, just delete my number from your phone.*
>
> *Chelsea"*

Sitting in the chair, he felt relieved. He was relieved that he didn't have to break things off with her. He deleted the email and walked into the weight room to lift the three hundred pound weights and do push-ups and sit-ups.

Tom, Trevor, and Brett walked into the weight room and saw how hard he was pushing himself. "What's going on?"

He quickly stood up, shirtless with his dog tags dangling. Sweat beads ran down his strong arms and raised chest. He looked at Tom. "Chelsea and I are done."

"Did you end it?"

He laughed out of embarrassment. "No, she did. She sent me a 'Dear John' letter, or shall I say email. She met someone else."

"Ouch!" Brett said.

"She did me a favor. Now, I don't ever have to see or talk to her again. On the upside she did say I was phenomenal in bed." he said and they laughed.

"When an ex-girlfriend tells you that, it's a very good thing." Trevor said.

He laughed. "If I had broken things off with her, she would've turned psychotic on me. I'd rather be dumped any day of the week than have to break up with a girl and then deal with all of that. My pride can take it."

"Have you guys ever seen this movie, I can't think of the name of it. It's where this married guy has an affair and when he tries to end it, she goes psychotic. She kills the family pet, kidnaps his daughter from school?"

"You're talking about *Fatal Attraction*," Trevor said.

"Yes that's it!"

"I think that movie scared every man in America." Jack said as they laughed.

"But Jack, Paige has a lot of single friends if you're interested." Tom encouraged.

Jack laid back on the bench press, lifting the three hundred pound weights. Tom stood behind him to spot him. He shook his head. "No thanks, if the Army wanted me to have a woman, one would've been issued to me with my tags and rifle." Tom laughed.

"Yeah, we know you ain't the marrying kind." Trevor said with a laugh.

"I'm never getting serious with a woman or getting married. I don't have to worry about a woman taking care of my business. I pay my bills, I have my truck, I have my savings and I can do what I want when I want. I don't have to worry about anything. Thank God I didn't give Chelsea a POA[2] like she wanted me to, or I'd be up shit creek without a paddle." They continued to work out and talk.

On Kate's day off, she took her engagement ring to a jewelry dealer and sold it. She bought a new mattress. She stopped by a bed and bath store and bought a new comforter set. The mattress was delivered. The delivery guys took her old one away for her at no extra charge.

Her friends were quickly finding out about hers and Kyle's break up. She and Morgan drove to Christi's home. Christi was Kate's best friend and teammate from college. She was married to a Dallas Maverick's guard, Jonah Hamilton. They had a five year old son named Jackson David, but everyone called him JD or Bubba. They lived in a beautiful home in Highland Park, an affluent Dallas suburb. Kate parked in the driveway and rang the doorbell.

"I wish everyone would stop worrying about me. I'm fine." she said to Morgan.

"You just caught your fiancé cheating on you and you just called off your wedding, how are you fine?"

"It could be worse, I could've not found out he was cheating and then I married him."

Jonah answered the door. "Hey Kate, hey Morgan, how are y'all doing?"

"We're good."

Jonah hugged Kate out of sympathy. "How are you doing?"

She laughed confidently. "I'm fine."

"Do you want me to go beat him up?" he teased.

She laughed, "The thought is tempting, but I'll let you know."

He smiled and hugged her, like an older brother would do. "Alright, but the offer is always on the table."

"Thanks, Jonah. Where's Christi?"

"She's in the kitchen." Walking into the kitchen, they saw Christi baking a batch of chocolate brownies as comfort food to ease the heartbreak. Kate was putting on a great façade for her friends and family. She looked great considering. She wore a nice pair of jeans, a casual sweater and boots. Her hair and makeup looked flawless. Though she seemed fine, happy and bubbly, she was really angry, hurt, and humiliated.

"Hey…" she said cheerfully.

"Hey, how are you doing?" Christi asked her. "Your momma and I are really worried about you." she said softly as she walked across the room to hug her.

"I'm fine. Y'all don't need to worry about me. I'm so glad I didn't marry him. Right now, I'm just going to enjoy being with my family and friends."

"So, are you over him?"

Kate smiled. "Yes, I guess. I never want to see him again."

"Are you ready to start dating again?" Morgan asked.

---

[2] POA- is a Power of Attorney. In today's military, the service member has to have a POA on record appointing someone to act on his/her behalf while absent. Otherwise, the appointed person cannot access anything with the service members' name, such as military orders, moving, shipping or receiving of household goods, vehicle registration, bank accounts etc. It is the single most important legal document a military member could have.

"Morgan!" Christi scolded. "She just cancelled her wedding!"

"The quickest way to get over a man is to start dating someone else." Morgan said.

"No, I'm not dating again."

"Yes you will. You're just hurting right now." Morgan encouraged.

"No, I'm serious."

Christi smiled, "Just remember, what doesn't kill you makes you stronger."

As she tried to hide her misery, finally her true emotions surfaced. She began to cry. "I never thought this would happen. Do y'all know how humiliating it will be to send out announcements that the wedding is called off?"

Christi handed her a Kleenex. "No, we don't, but we're here for you. We'll take care of everything."

She sighed, trying to stop herself from crying. "Men suck don't they?"

Christi laughed. "Not all of them. A good man will come in your life that would never do this to you. You deserve to be happy." she said, as she continued to comfort her.

"You never know, tomorrow or the next day you might find the man God wants you to be with." Morgan said.

She dabbed her eyes with a Kleenex. She was angry, hurt, and humiliated. She regretted ever knowing Kyle Mowery. Christi hugged her. "We're so sorry you're going through this. We're here for you."

"We got your back." Morgan said.

She dried her tears with a Kleenex. "I hate crying. I'm going to get over him and never give him another thought. I'm not going to cry over him anymore. I'm going to move on and be happy." She, Christi, and Morgan continued to talk. They planned to go out and have a good time at a honkytonk club in Dallas.

Jack and the other Green Berets were still in Afghanistan at their outpost, Firebase Scorpion. The sun rose in the cold mountain region, as the team prepared for a long day outside the wire. The team gathered in the Tactical Operations Center (TOC) for the intelligence briefing. Enemy fighters from Pakistan were wandering into Afghanistan looking for U.S. soldiers to kill.

Inside the TOC, the team sat around in their favorite worn ball caps, with their water bottles. Colonel Mitchell stood to address his team. "Alright men, we're going back on patrol. Watch your six and that of the man next to you. Our goal is to complete the mission and get back home alive. In the words of General Patton, we aren't dying for our country today. We're going to make those poor bastards die for theirs[3]."

As Alpha, Bravo, and Charlie Teams departed by Humvees through the heavily guarded main gate, Taliban spotters reported their every move as they drove through the rugged terrain. Jack and Tom were overhearing chatter from the Taliban's radios courtesy of Jake and Luke.

Sergeant Taylor Deveraux, a member of Bravo Team, was the gunner on one of the Humvees. He saw a man perched on a ridge, smiling at him. He was immediately on-edge and knew something was going to happen. A rocket propelled grenade was launched. It smashed through the window of the Humvee. It hadn't detonated.

He noticed an object sticking out of this leg. His first thought was it was shrapnel. "Hey man, I have some shrapnel in my leg." he said.

"Alpha 1, Bravo 9 up here thinks he has some shrapnel in his leg."

---

[3]   "No poor dumb bastard ever won a war by dying for his country. He won it by making the other poor dumb bastard die for his country."- General George S. Patton, Jr., War As I Knew It

"Roger…" he said over the radio. The convoy of Humvees stopped. Jack, Casey, and Jamal and the others hurried to the lead Humvee. When they opened the door to the Humvee, they were stunned by what they saw. It wasn't shrapnel that was embedded into the soldier's leg. It was the unexploded rocket propelled grenade (RPG). It was sticking out of his hips.

"Master Sergeant, it's just shrapnel, right?"

Jack looked down at Jamal and Casey. Casey looked up at him. "It's not shrapnel, buddy." he said to him.

"What is it?"

"It's an RPG. It's sticking out of your hips, but we're going to get you to the aid station and you'll be alright," Casey said.

"You're going to make it," Jack said. The soldier's name was Taylor Deveraux. He was just twenty-five years old and a native of New Orleans, Louisiana.

As a weapons sergeant, Jack knew the RPG could still explode inside the soldier and kill everyone. He radioed for a MED-EVAC helicopter to come to their location. The medics were stunned as well. Explosives experts were on scene assisting the medics to carefully move the soldier and not set it off.

The aid station was twenty miles away. Once arriving to the aid station, the surgeons completely violated protocol by bringing him and the live grenade into the operating room. They carefully removed it. The explosives expert went with the medics to the aid station and was handed the grenade. He walked to a secure area on base and detonated it. The injured soldier survived. His hips and pelvis were completely shattered.

Weeks later, on a ridge in the Chowkay Valley, the Green Berets were engaged in a fire fight on the opposite ridge. "They sound like snappers," Brad said.

"Snappers, what are you talking about?" Luke asked.

"You know snappers? Those things kids pop on the Fourth of July,"

"Anyone got a visual?" Jack yelled.

"They're on top of that ridge!" Mark yelled. Sam hurried down into the line of fire and grabbed the SAW. He fired on the fighters. As an Apache came up on the ridge, Jake spotted an enemy fighter with an RPG. He pointed his rifle, looked through the scope, and pulled the trigger before the enemy fighter could launch the RPG. He killed the enemy fighter with one shot. Air support pushed back the enemy fighters.

Now, April 2002, the Green Berets of Alpha, Bravo, and Charlie Teams were near the Afghanistan-Pakistan border. It was unclear where Afghanistan ended and where Pakistan began. Enemy fighters would fire at the troops from the mountains of Pakistan. The soldiers would chase the fighters into Pakistan. At Firebase Scorpion, they were mortared and rocketed every day. The mortars would hit in the direct part of the firebase or on the outside wall.

The firebase was ten miles from a village. The Green Berets tried to establish communication and acquire friendship with the villagers, but the villagers wanted nothing to do with American soldiers. Arriving at the village, Jack and Tom stepped out of the Humvees. The leader of the village distrusted any Americans and would not allow them to come into his village. He and several armed villagers stood guarding and denying entry to the village.

"Put your weapons down!" Jack commanded in Arabic, pointing his rifle at them.

The leader and his men were not scared of the Americans. Jack did not want to open fire, but if the men did not drop their weapons quickly, he would have no choice.

"You leave now!" the leader shouted back to him.

"Can we just talk? My men and I are not here to hurt you or your people,"

"We have no desire to talk."

Jack looked to his men and then back at the group of nine angry Afghans. "Load up." he said to his team. The soldiers' climbed back in the Humvees and drove away.

Weeks later, they came across a friendly village. The villagers invited the soldiers into the village. The soldiers were still on alert. As the soldiers walked with the leader down the street of his village, the soldiers saw many children running up to them and holding their hands. The village leader invited Jack and Trevor into his home to talk. He turned to Jake. "Stay on alert."

Jake and Luke stood armed at the entrance of the leader's home. "Roger."

Jack and Trevor went into the leaders home to talk with him. Jack assured the leader that the soldiers were not there to hurt anyone, only to hunt Taliban fighters. The meeting between leaders was friendly and helpful.

As Jack and Trevor exited the home, a young girl named Adra and her mother approached them. She was eleven years old. She grabbed Jack's hand and placed two handmade beaded bracelets in his hand. "These will protect you." she said in Arabic.

He kneeled down to her, pulled his sunglasses off and smiled at her. Pulling one of his dog tags off, he placed it in her hand. "I am here to protect you." he said to her in Arabic. The girl and her mother smiled at him.

Jack turned to the village leader and asked him, "My two medical sergeants will be happy to treat anyone who has injuries or who are sick." in Arabic.

The man agreed. Jamal and Casey immunized the children and treated their infections. Luke and Mark kicked a soccer ball around with some of the older kids. Jack, Trevor, and Tom gathered valuable intelligence about the Taliban from the villagers. After a thirty minute stay, he thanked the village leader for allowing him and his men to come into their village and for speaking with them. He rounded up his team. The kids waved goodbye to the soldiers.

Once they made it back to their firebase, they unloaded the Humvees and their gear. Jack and Tom were in the Rec Room. "What are some things you miss from home?"

Jack thought about it. "Hot showers, beer, pizza, women, my momma's cooking and her sweet tea and of course watching my Sooners play. What about you?"

"I miss privacy. I miss my satellite and my sports packages, but I definitely miss hot showers, beer and Paige's cooking, and of course I miss watching my 'Bama boys. What are you going to do when we get back?"

"I'm going to Dallas and spend time with my family. I'm taking my nephew camping and fishing. He loves when I take him to a Rangers game."

"How old is your nephew?"

"He's five. His name is JD."

"What's JD stand for?"

"Jackson David. He's named after me."

"Oh Lord, there's two of you? Just what the world needs." Tom teased. They were close enough friends to laugh and joke with each other about their teams and personal lives.

They walked in to the small lounge room and finally got the chance to sit and eat. They heated up their favorite MREs and enjoyed the somewhat home cooked meal. Throughout the night, the remote outposts' 105 Howitzers pounded away, firing at Taliban targets somewhere beyond the dark horizon.

At dawn, just before the sun had risen over the mountain region, the team readied for a new mission. Each put on their Special Forces Load Carrying System (SFLCS). The SFLCS contained body armor, chest rig and various pouches for grenades and hydration carriers. Each man checked his weapon, packed extra ammunition magazines and fragmentation grenades. Jake filled everyone's canteens.

The sun was shining in the mountain region, but the air was chilly. The Green Berets gathered around Colonel Mitchell and the Humvees. He had a map of the area laid out on the hood of the Humvee.

"Alright, team listen up, we are going into deeply held Taliban territory. We need to be on alert for any confrontation. The most difficult part of this war so far is distinguishing friend from foe. Watch your six and that of the man next to you. Our mission is to get back home alive." He explained the specifics of the mission. The team was motivated to achieve the mission and kill the enemy.

They pushed deep into Taliban held territory until they reached another village. They were eager to show villagers that the United States was not there to hurt them, only to push out the Taliban. As the team's Humvees slowly drove through the village, they could tell something was wrong by the villagers' demeanor.

Jack grabbed the radio and alerted his team. "Be on alert, something is definitely up. Watch your six." They slowly stepped out of the Humvees and approached some of the village elders. As they began to communicate, gunfire rang out. Taliban and local fighters began firing at the team and the civilians talking to them. The village was now a battleground.

Jack looked across the courtyard and saw his best friend, Tom kneeling to reload his rifle. Suddenly a vehicle with one driver was traveling at a high speed and heading directly for Tom. He sprinted towards Tom. "TOM! MOVE!" he yelled. Tom didn't hear him shouting. He ran as fast as he could to get to him and tackled him. They rolled out of the way from the truck. The truck crashed into a building and exploded. It was a Vehicle Borne IED (VBIED).

Shrapnel from the explosion was embedded in his leg and abdomen. He let out a scream. "Are you hit?" Tom asked him, checking him.

"I got shrapnel in my leg and my stomach."

Tom also saw Jack's right arm bleeding and his pant leg quickly soaking up with blood. While he was running to save Tom, a stray round caught him in the forearm. "Let's get you to Jamal."

"No, I'm alright."

"You've been shot in your arm."

Jack looked down at it. "I'll tough it out." he said. Despite these painful injuries, he continued to fight alongside his men. Once the fight was over, Jamal tended to wounded members of the team and wounded civilians. The stray round that struck Jack in the arm, luckily had exited through.

Alpha Team suffered one casualty, medical Sergeant First Class Casey Sears. They loaded Casey's body into the Humvee and drove back to the outpost.

Arriving back to Firebase Scorpion, the Green Berets morale was low. Alpha Team had lost a vital member of their team and good friend. Brad and Tom covered the gurney with an American flag. They carried him off the Humvee, all saluted Casey.

At Firebase Scorpion, all Green Berets soldiers, held a memorial for Casey, with his boots, rifle and helmet. They did roll call. On board a C-130 cargo plane sat a flag draped casket. Alpha Team boarded the plane and said their final goodbyes to Casey. Jamal took his death the hardest. They were best friends. He kneeled, bowed his head, and cried as he placed his hand on the casket. "I'll miss you, brother. I'll take care of Jenna and the girls like I promised."

Casey Sears was a fun guy. He loved to laugh and make others laugh. He was a devout Christian and he often held many prayer and Bible study sessions with his Green Berets brothers. He and his wife Jenna were married for seven years and they had two five year old twin daughters, Amanda and Alyssa. On the day he died, he was only two credits shy of a Master's Degree in criminal justice.

Jack walked very slowly, holding his wounded center. Jamal saw him and knew he was in severe pain. "Let me look at your injuries, Jack." he said.

Jack laid back on the table. Tom, Trevor, Brett, and Jake stood around to make sure he was alright. He took his shirt off. Blood was soaking through the bandage he applied earlier.

Jamal looked at the seriousness of the injury. "I think you should get on the MED-EVAC chopper and go to Bagram. You might need surgery to remove the pieces."

"No, that's not happening. Just dig them out here." he said as he took off his belt.

"Jack, you're going to want morphine for me to dig them out, and if I give it to you, you're going to be in a hospital."

"I don't need morphine. Dig them out." He placed the belt in his mouth, between his teeth. "Y'all don't have any whiskey by any chance do you?" he teased.

Tom laughed, "If I did, buddy I'd give you the whole bottle."

Jamal looked to them, "Y'all might not want to watch."

"We're staying." Tom said. Jamal cleaned the area and rubbed a local anesthetic on his skin. He proceeded to remove the foreign objects from Jack's abdomen. Tom, Jake, Brett, and Trevor were stunned he could tolerate it, but just barely. He bit down on his belt as hard as he could. After several minutes, all the pieces of shrapnel were removed. All were amazed he could handle surgery with no anesthesia, just local. Jamal and a medical sergeant from Bravo Team dug out the shrapnel from his leg. Afterwards, he got through the pain by sleeping.

A week later, Jack was loading his ammunition magazines and placing them in his locker. He was still sore from the injuries he sustained in the village fight, but he was able to withstand it. He looked over to Jamal and saw that he was still grieving Casey's death. They were very close. Jamal looked at his locker and sat down on the bench with a box beside him. Inside Casey's locker were pictures of his wife and their daughters. Jamal stood and slowly pulled the pictures of his family off the locker wall and put them in the box to be mailed to Casey's widow. Members of the team watched Jamal carefully place each object in the box. He looked at pictures of Casey and him together, as well as, other members of the team goofing off at home and in theater.

Back in Dallas, Kate had moved on. She had returned all of the wedding gifts and was enjoying being single and independent. She was happy. Kyle had relentlessly called her, filling up her answering machine with apologies. The constant bombardment of calls forced her to change her number. She had returned all the gifts. Being with friends and family helped her take her mind off everything.

She was visiting Jonah and Christi at their home. She was in the kitchen helping Christi cook. "So, is Kyle still calling you?" she asked curiously.

She sliced the potatoes. "Not anymore, I changed my number today. Here it is." handing her a piece of paper with her new telephone number on it.

Christi laughed, "It's still hilarious that you threw their clothes, cell phone, purse, wallet, and keys out the window. Then kicked them out wearing only your bed sheets, I would've paid to have been there." They laughed together.

"It made me feel better," she said as they continued to talk, while cooking stew for dinner.

Jonah walked in, as they were laughing, with photos he had just picked up from the photo shop. He laid the pictures down on the bar and got a bottle of water out of the refrigerator.

"What are those pictures?" Christi asked, as she stirred the sugar into the tea.

He took a drink of his water. "Oh, they are of me, dad, and Jack, out at Lloyd's ranch the last time he was home."

Kate picked them up and she and Christi looked through them. She smiled at the pictures of Jack. "Why is he never here? Is he still in the Army?" she asked.

"Yes, he's still in. He just doesn't get leave very often. I still can't believe you two haven't met."

She smiled at him posing with an eight point buck and a hunting rifle. "When I know he's home, I just stay away and let y'all have family time. What does he do in the Army?"

He looked around the room as if there were spies listening to them. "If he finds out I told you, he will throw me in Gitmo. It's totally classified, but he's a Green Beret. He has the most awesome job in the world. He gets paid to blow stuff up."

She smiled, "Him being a Green Beret isn't classified. The details of his missions are."

"How do you know?"

"My dad was a Green Beret."

She smiled down at the other photos of Jonah, Jack, and their dad together. They were posing with their fishing rods and strings of fish on a lake in east Texas. There were pictures of them posing with their M-4 assault rifles and Winchester rifles at a ranch in Blue Ridge, Texas, a small town about an hour north of Dallas.

Christi caught her smiling at the picture. "Do you find him attractive, Kate?"

She smiled and laid the pictures down. "Yeah, he is very good looking, unlike you Jonah." she teased, as she and Christi laughed.

Jonah laughed sarcastically. "When he comes back into town, you should come by and meet him." he suggested.

"Don't even think about it, Jonah." she warned. "I'm not looking to start anything with anyone right now."

"Why? He's a good guy. Christi, tell her…"

"He really is, Kate. He's nice, considerate, responsible, respectful…"

"And good looking like me," Jonah added and they laughed at him.

"He loves kids and loves being around family, when he has a chance to. He's charming and easy to talk to." Christi added.

"And he's in the military! I know you women think all military men are so hot." He mocked. Christi and Kate laughed at him.

"I highly doubt he'd be interested in me," she admitted.

"You're his type. He likes athletic, independent brunettes." Jonah said.

JD heard them talking about Jack. He was very close to his uncle. Jack would always take him to the park, to baseball games and to the toy store. "Daddy, when is Uncle Jack coming back?"

"I don't know bubba. Do you think Uncle Jack would like Aunt Kate?" Jonah asked.

"Jonah, you shouldn't ask him that!" Kate said.

JD smiled at Kate. "Yeah, I think so. Aunt Kate is pretty."

Christi and Jonah laughed. "Awe, that's so cute!" she said. She gave him a big kiss on the cheek.

"Sweetie, it's time for bed. Go upstairs and get your pajamas on and brush your teeth." Christi said.

"I can't wait for Uncle Jack to come home!" he said running up the stairs.

She smiled at how excited he was. "He loves him doesn't he?" she asked.

"Yeah, he does. He's named after him. He wants to be just like him."

She looked at the picture of Jack and JD together. "They look so cute together." After JD went to bed; they talked as they ate dessert and played cards.

Weeks went by. Members of both Alpha and Bravo Teams were in the recreation room, where they had TVs and computers. They were watching *"Remember the Titans"* They were laughing and enjoying the very little down time they got.

Intelligence analyst Mike came into the room. "Colonel wants a meeting with all three teams in the TOC." The teams walked to the TOC. Colonel Mitchell stepped in. With him was the newest member of Alpha Team, medical staff sergeant Chase Travers. He was twenty six years old, married, and the father of two young girls.

"I know we're still grieving the loss of Casey, but he would want us to move forward with our mission. We all know how he loved Christ, so we know where he is. He's watching over us, watching our sixes. We'll always miss the brothers we lose out here and we'll always remember them. I know some of you are probably wondering how Jenna and the girls are doing and I've appointed someone back at Bragg to look in on her and the kids…"

"That's my job, Colonel," Jamal said. "I promised him that if anything ever happened to him, that I'd be there for Jenna and the girls."

"I understand that, Jamal, but while we're here, I've appointed someone to look in on them weekly until we get back…" Colonel Mitchell said. He saw the team looking at the man with him. He patted the man on the shoulder. "…This is the newest member of our team. His name is Sergeant Chase Travers from Sioux Falls, South Dakota. He'll be assisting Jamal. Jamal, you keep him under your wing."

Jamal nodded his head. Each team member welcomed him. Jack stood, wearing his favorite but worn OU football ball cap. He shook his hand. Chase noticed his hat. "I see you're an OU fan."

"Oh don't get him started on his Sooners," Jake said.

They laughed. "Yeah, I'm a big OU fan." he said.

"I'm a Nebraska fan." Chase replied. The team sat in the chairs of the TOC as Colonel Mitchell briefed them more on the next village they would be going to. After the briefing, the team loaded up their Humvees and gear. They departed for the next village.

This was a friendly village. The soldiers would hand out bags of candy, mainly Tootsie Rolls and Smarties candies to the kids. They would also play soccer with them. Jamal and Chase immunized the children and treated at the ailments of the adults, while Jack, Tom, and Eric would talk with the men of the village gathering intelligence on their Taliban foes.

Chase looked to Jamal. He knew he had lost his buddy. "Hey man, I'm sorry about your buddy."

Jamal looked at him. "Thanks."

"How long were you two friends?"

"Five years," Jamal told Chase more about Casey, about his family, his hobbies, and funny memories. After a successful visit with the villagers, the team made their way back to their firebase. They arrived in the late hours of the evening.

Kate drove out to her parents' house in Dallas. Her father was in Washington D.C. Her parents' used to live in Washington D.C., but her mother got a professorship to the University of Dallas campus. They moved their daughters back to Dallas and bought a beautiful home. He came home on long weekends and holidays. It wasn't ideal, but they made it work.

She unlocked the door. "Momma?" she called. She took off her light jacket, laid her sunglasses and keys down on the entry table. Holly rushed to greet her.

"Hey sweetie, I'm back here!" Mom called from the office.

She walked to the office her parents' share. "Hey, what are you doing?"

"I'm grading term papers." she said tiredly. "How are you doing, sweetie?"

She braved a smile, "I'm fine."

Mom patted her hand. "I know God has someone incredible for you. You just have to trust Him. God will show him to you when he feels you're ready."

She hugged her. "Thank you, Momma." They talked in the kitchen until Lauren and Baylee, Lauren's best friend walked in.

"Hey sis, how are you?" Lauren asked, hugging her.

"I'm good."

"Are you really? You just called off your wedding, how can you be fine?" Lauren asked.

She rolled her eyes. "I wish everyone would stop worrying about me. I'm fine. If I had married him and then found out he was cheating on me, then you would have something to worry about, but at least I found out before the wedding."

"That's true," Baylee said.

"So are you ready to start dating again?" Lauren asked.

"No. I like being single and able to do what I want, when I want. I don't need a man. I'm happy just by myself."

"I know a lot of cute guys who would like you."

"What makes you think they'd like me?"

"Well they like me, and you're my older sister and we do kind of look alike."

She laughed, "No thanks."

"Oh Kate, come on, just go out with a guy. What could it hurt?" Mom asked.

"At least you'd get a free dinner out of it." Baylee pointed out. She reluctantly agreed.

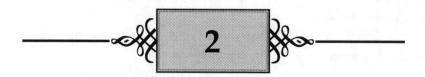

2

I N J UNE 2002, Colonel Mitchell and his Green Berets returned to Fort Bragg, North Carolina, after nine months in Afghanistan. They were given a month of leave time. Green Beret deployments were unusual, not like most Army deployments of a year to fifteen months. Their deployments could last up to nine months and be as short as three weeks. Some had families on post, but most were single and had girlfriends, a lot of girlfriends.

Jack was driving back to Dallas to be with his family the next day. He, his parents, and siblings had a very close relationship, even though he was rarely ever home. He hadn't been to Texas since before September 11th. His parents, William "Bill" and Denise, had been married for thirty years and had three children. Their oldest son, Jonah was twenty-nine. Jack, the middle son was twenty-seven, and their daughter, Meagan was nineteen years old. Jack had just turned twenty-seven on the ninth of June. His dad was a retired major general and former Green Beret. His mother was a pastry chef, trying to open her own restaurant in Dallas.

He drove to his off post apartment in Fayetteville, the neighboring city to Fort Bragg. He rented a one bedroom one bathroom apartment. His rent and other bills were automatically deducted from his pay. He had made a deal with his landlady to check on his place every week. She was in her mid-50s with gray hair. Immediately following his many departures, she kindly held his mail for him and would keep an eye on his place for him. He had been her tenant for three years. Her name was Janet and she thought of him as one of her young sons. He stopped inside the office to say hello and to pick up nine months' worth of mail.

"Hello Jack! It's so good to see you!" Janet said, hugging him. The other office ladies were happy to see him, too.

"How are you and James, ma'am?"

"Oh we're fine. We have a new granddaughter now."

"That's great. I came to pick up my mail."

"You sure have a lot of it." She walked away to pick up the two bins. He quickly took them from her. "When are you going to get married, son?" she asked.

He laughed, "Never…"

"Why not, Jack? You're a handsome young man. I know there must be a line around the block of attractive women wanting to date you."

He laughed. "I doubt that. I'm better on my own. But thank you so much for holding all my mail. I want you to have this as a token of my appreciation."

He gave her a special gift. "Oh Jack, you didn't have to do this."

"Yes, I did. You always take care of things when I'm gone. I don't have to worry about anyone breaking into my apartment and stealing my stuff. I know my truck is secure. Without you, I'd be worrying about that."

"I do that out of gratitude for what you do for us every day." she said quietly.

"I have a job just like everyone else. Now please open it." he told her. He never liked civilians making such a huge deal out of what he did for a living. Of course now they were going to thank him more since September 11th. To him, his 'job' was his mission. A job any person can quit, but a mission had to be seen until its completion. Sure, what he did was very dangerous, demanding, and stressful, but he got paid for it. He didn't do it for the money. It was his true calling. He accepted he'd miss birthdays, weddings, funerals, family reunions, anniversaries, and holidays with his family.

She opened it, blushing. It was one of the colorful, handmade bracelets Adra had made for him. "Jack it's beautiful, thank you so much."

"You're welcome. It's handmade. A little girl named Adra made it for me. We went to her village a lot."

She was stunned to hear that an Afghani child had made this for him. "How was it over there?"

"It was cold." He found talking about combat to civilians was inappropriate and pointless. They would never be able to understand, so it was just easier to avoid the topic. She sensed he did not want to talk about it. "…Well, I'm going to get going. I just stopped in to say hello and to give you that." he said.

"Welcome home, Jack." she said, with a smile. He smiled as he exited the office.

Driving to his apartment, he walked up the stairs and found apartment 1420. He unlocked the door and let out a tired sigh. Finally, he had privacy, his own TV with cable, a real bed with a mattress, a private refrigerator, and his very own shower with hot water. He put the cold pack of beer in the refrigerator and ordered a large pepperoni and sausage pizza from his favorite pizza joint near the base. He turned on his TV and of course, *ESPN Sports Center* was on.

As he waited for his pizza, he opened a beer and enjoyed the cool, crisp taste on his lips. He picked up his cell phone and called his parents. His dad quickly answered seeing it was his name and number on the caller ID. "Jack?" Dad answered, breathing a sigh of relief.

"Hey Dad…"

"Hey, there son, how are you doing?"

"I'm good, how are things back home?"

"We're all good here. I'm so glad you're back, son. Are you heading this way for your leave?"

"Yeah, I plan to head out tomorrow. I get a whole month of leave, I'm excited. How are Momma, Jonah, and Meagan doing?"

"Oh, everyone is good. Jonah and Christi are going through the process of selecting a contractor to remodel their house. They've enrolled JD into tee-ball. His team is called the Warriors…" he said, as they laughed. "You know your mother, she never stops going. She's made a honey-do-list that's about three pages long for me to do. She's taking advantage of my retirement. Meagan is intentionally dating boys she knows I won't like just to make my blood pressure skyrocket."

He laughed. "Well, Dad you know Momma had that list made a long time ago, but I'll help you do everything she wants done when I get there. I don't know what to tell you about Meagan." They laughed and talked for close to an hour.

After talking with his dad, Jack called Jonah. Seeing he was calling, he answered quickly. "Hey, what are you doing, big brother?"

Jonah laughed out of relief. He was happy he was home. "Oh, I'm the butt of Christi and Kate's jokes. I'm trying not to drill a hole in my head."

Jack laughed. "Why are they making fun of you?"

"It's me. Do they really need a specific reason?"

He laughed, "No, you generally do stupid things all the time."

"Shut up, what are you doing?"

"I'm enjoying a pizza and beer, happy to be home."

"Are you still with that Chelsea girl?"

"No, we broke things off months ago. I'm glad that's over." he informed.

Jonah looked over at Kate. He saw an opportunity to introduce Kate and Jack in hopes they would like each other and begin dating. "I want you to talk to Kate. She's single and I think you two would really like each other."

She and Christi were stunned. "Jonah, are you serious?!" Christi scolded.

Kate was embarrassed, while shaking her head no. She didn't know Jack and she certainly wasn't about to talk to anyone she didn't know, over the phone.

"No, Jonah." he said to him. Minutes rolled by. Jonah asked him to hold on for a few minutes, so he could answer another call.

Kate and Christi were in the kitchen talking. He covered the speaker piece of the phone and walked over to her. "It's your mother. She said your phone is dead." he said handing her the phone.

She took the phone to her ear. "Hey momma, I didn't know my phone died. It's in my car."

He was caught off guard and knew exactly what Jonah had done. "Uh, hello?" he said with a laugh. Her voice was soft and pleasant. He thought she had the most adorable Texan accent.

She sat straight up in her chair. "Who is this?"

"Jack…"

She looked at Christi and shook her head. "Your brother is the biggest idiot in the world." she said to him. Christi went to find Jonah. She found him upstairs listening on the other line, like a teenager. She scolded him.

He laughed, hearing Christi scolding Jonah. "I couldn't agree with you more." he replied. His voice was deep, sexy, and commanding. She couldn't help but be attracted to him. There was an awkward silence between them. Neither knew what to say to the other. "So, I've heard a few things about you from Jonah."

"Lord only knows what he's told you." she replied with a nervous laugh. Her body had a reaction to his voice. Her heart began to pound, as if it was going to jump out of her chest and march away. She felt feverish, in a good way. She had butterflies in her stomach.

He laughed. "I promise it's only good things." Seconds slowly crept by. Neither knew what to say to the other. "Has Christi strangled him yet?" he asked.

"I'll go check." she said with a laugh.

"I'm sorry he embarrassed you. I'll deal with him when I get back tomorrow."

She smiled. "Thanks, but I can handle him. I'm used to his practical jokes."

"It was nice talking to you."

"It was nice talking to you too. Goodbye."

Christi made Jonah come downstairs to apologize. Kate handed the phone back to him and gave him a look. "Hello?" Jonah said.

Jack was annoyed with him. "I'm going to put you in a choke hold tomorrow. How could you put her and I on the spot like that?"

Jonah laughed, "I knew you two wouldn't talk to each other unless I gave you a little push."

JD came running through the living room. Jack was still scolding Jonah over the phone. Jonah held the phone out to JD. "Hey bub, Uncle Jack is on the phone. Here talk to him and when you're done, hang up."

Hearing Jonah calling JD to the phone, he scolded Jonah, "No, don't hand him the phone to avoid me yelling at you…"

Jonah gave him the phone. He was so excited. "Hi, Uncle Jack!" he said excitedly.

He smiled, "Hey bubba, what are you up to? Are you behaving for your momma and daddy?"

"Yes, I'm always good."

"What happens when you're not good?"

"I do push-ups and burpies."

Jack laughed, "That's right."

"When are you coming back? I miss you."

"I miss you too, bubba. I'll be there tomorrow."

He was excited, "Can we play catch and go to a Rangers game?"

"You bet. Listen bub, I'll see you in a few days. Is your Dad there? I really need to talk to him."

"No, he ran upstairs. I think he's scared of you."

He laughed, thinking Jonah was too cowardly to talk to him. "Of course he is. Go find him for me."

JD walked upstairs. "Daddy...?"

"What?" Jonah called from the game room.

"Uncle Jack wants to talk to you."

Jonah motioned for the phone while he played video games. "Okay, he'll talk to you."

He laughed, "Okay, thanks bubba. I'll see you in a few days. Be good for your momma." he said.

"I love you, Uncle Jack."

"Love you too, bub." He handed the cordless phone to Jonah and ran downstairs to the kitchen for a snack before bedtime.

"So, why don't you want to meet Kate?" Jonah asked.

"Jonah, it's not that I don't want to meet her, and I certainly hope you're not telling her that I do or I don't want to. I'm happy being single. I don't have to worry about a woman distracting me with her drama. I can't afford to have any distractions."

"Kate isn't like that. She's cool for a woman. She's independent and very...stubborn. Jack, trust me on this. You'll really like her. She's your type, athletic, attractive, and brunette."

"Jonah, she's a woman. All women are dramatic and distracting. Besides, she didn't sound too happy to be talking to me. I sensed maybe she isn't exactly available to date."

"No, she's single."

He laughed at him, "No I meant, maybe she doesn't want to date anyone either."

"I want you two to meet, not run off to Vegas and get married." Jonah said with a laugh.

He took a drink and said hesitating, "I'll think about it." The next morning, he headed out for Dallas just after sunrise. The sky was clear with very few clouds on the hot summer day. The Texas sun beat down and the temperature was near 102 with very little breeze. The weather forecast predicted the temperature would soar to 105 by the end of the week. When he arrived in the Dallas area, it was dusk. It was still a decent 80 degrees in the metroplex.

He pulled in his parents' driveway and parked his black GMC Sierra truck next to his sister's car. He got his bag out of the backseat, looking at the house as he walked up the walkway. His parents' lived in a beautiful two story home in Dallas. There was ivy growing wildly up the side of the house. Mom had planted different colors of pansies on both sides of the walkway. She had many other flowers and plants in her flower beds, in front of the house. The American and Army flags were flying proudly on the flagpole in the middle of the yard. Yellow ribbons were tied around the oak trees out front. He was happy to be home. He smiled when he saw the 'Blue Star Mother's' flag on the inside of the screen door.

He unlocked the door with his key and laid his bags down, in front of the hallway. Hank, the family German Shepard, came dashing towards him and jumped on him. He kneeled down and petted him. "Hey boy, I've missed you. How you been?"

Meagan heard someone playing with Hank. She rushed into the entryway and was shocked to see him kneeling there petting Hank. She laughed, but immediately began crying. "Mom, Dad, Jack is home!"

"Hey sis." he said. He stood and she immediately hugged him tightly. She had tears streaming down her face. "Oh I'm so glad you're back. We've really missed you."

She finally released him. He smiled down at her. He, Jonah, and Meagan were very close. "I've missed y'all too. Why are you crying?"

She laughed as tears ran down her face. "I'm just so happy you're back!" She wiped her tears away.

"Your makeup is smearing," he teased. They laughed, as she playfully swatted his arm.

Mom and Dad came running to him. She had tears of relief and joy in her eyes. He was overwhelmed with pride, as well as relief. "Oh, I'm so glad you're home safe!" she said as she hugged him tightly.

He kissed her on the cheek, "I told you that I would."

He noticed the look on his father's face. "Hey Dad…"

Dad smiled and hugged him. "It's good to have you home, son." They walked into the den. "So, did you see any action over there?"

He smiled at him, "A little…"

"Thank God you came back in one piece."

"Hey I meant to ask you a few nights ago, do you still talk with the Thompsons? I've been trying to get ahold of Mark for months now," he asked curiously.

Dad had a knot in his stomach. "Son, there's something I need to tell you. I didn't want to do it while you were down range, but Mark was killed in the Pentagon on September 11th. They found some of his remains in the rubble this past December."

Mark and Jack had been best friends from high school and they had both enlisted in the Army the same time. He was stunned. He looked at the picture of him and Mark together on the fireplace mantle, just after their high school graduation, "Mark's dead?"

Dad stood. "I'm sorry, son. I know you thought of him like another brother."

He shook his head. "I knew he worked there, but I had no idea he was killed. I sent him an email shortly after it happened asking him if he was alright. I kept wondering why he never emailed me back…now I know why."

"Tommy and Lorraine still live here in Dallas and they ask about you all the time. You should go see them if you feel up to it."

"Yeah, I definitely will. Where is he buried?"

"He's buried at Arlington."

He was feeling different emotions. He was angry, sad, and stunned, but anger was the strongest emotion. "Alright, let's change the subject." He and Dad talked about football. Dad brought him up to speed on college standings and NFL standings. They also talked about the Army.

"So, how's retirement treating you?"

Dad looked at him seriously. "I hate it."

He laughed, "I figured as much,"

Jonah pulled in and parked in the driveway. He was happy to see Jack's truck. He and JD hurried inside. Jack and Dad looked to see who had walked in. "Hey there they are!" he said excitedly.

He and Dad stood as they smiled at them. JD rushed to him. "Uncle Jack!"

Picking him up, he tossed him in the air and caught him. JD laughed. "Hey bubba, wow, you are really getting big."

"Did you bring me anything?"

"As a matter of fact, I did, but it's a surprise. I want to give it to you in front of your mom."

"Is it bugs?"

Jack, Jonah, and Dad laughed. "Maybe we'll see." JD ran to the playroom to play.

Jonah nearly tackled him. "Hey, welcome back!" as they hugged tightly.

"Thanks." They were incredibly close. As kids, they did everything together. If one got into a fight or into trouble, the other was always right alongside him. They looked almost identical but their personalities were very different. They sat on the sofa and talked and laughed with Dad about old times and funny memories.

Mom and Meagan were in the kitchen, making him a sandwich. "I can't believe he's home." Meagan said, as Mom smiled.

"I'm so happy. He looks great." Mom said, as they walked into the den.

Mom and Meagan were happy to see Jonah there. "Hey, when did you get here?" Meagan asked Jonah.

"JD and I just got here."

"Bubba is here?" Meagan asked. She went into the playroom to tickle him, but Jonah and Jack had taught JD how to pester her. JD shot her with a Nerf gun and she retreated back to the living room.

"I see you two made sure to teach him how to pester me. I'm the only one he does it to." Meagan announced as Jack and Jonah laughed.

Jonah picked on and teased her and Jack laughed. Just like old times, he thought to himself. Mom handed him a turkey sandwich, a slice of homemade cherry pie, and a big glass of milk.

"So, what are your plans while you're home? I'm assuming you're going to some ball games with me and Jonah." Dad asked.

"Yeah, definitely, I want to go fishing and camping. We should call Lloyd and have a shoot-out and win this time," he said as he gave Jonah a sarcastic look.

"It's been over a year since we've done that." Dad said, as they laughed together.

"We would've won last time, but Jonah doesn't know how to load a rifle properly." Jack teased.

"That was not my fault," Jonah proclaimed.

"Just admit it, you choked under the pressure," Dad said, as they laughed.

"No, the stupid thing jammed. At least I'm not the one who leaked to Momma that we all went to *Twin Peaks* afterwards, which got ALL of us in trouble!" Jonah said, as they laughed at their dad.

Dad laughed. "I'll admit that one. I'm sorry I messed that one up." he said.

"Yeah, I'll never forget momma's lecture on *Twin Peaks*. It was one of those conversations you avoid having with your mother." Jack said, as Dad and Jonah shook their heads. "By the way, how are Lloyd and his boys doing?" he asked curiously.

Dad smiled, "Oh, he's the same ole Lloyd. Ryan and Jake both enlisted, one in the Marine Corps and the other in the Army. They're having a barbecue for them next weekend. You should come with us, Jack."

"Alright, I'll go. Maybe we can have the shoot-out then. A free steak does sound good," he suggested.

"Yeah, it does, but we just have to make sure Jonah's rifle doesn't 'jam' again." Dad teased, as they all laughed together.

"I'm ignoring both of you." Jonah said, and Dad and Jack laughed at him.

"So Meagan, how was your first year of college? I don't need to scare a few boys straight do I?" Jack asked. She had just completed her freshman year at the University of Texas at Dallas.

She laughed. "No that's the last thing I want to happen. If I were to let you on campus, I'd never get a date again. I remember what you did last time."

"That was funny," Jonah said as he, Jack, and Dad tried not to laugh.

"I just defended myself."

"No, you taunted him into swinging so you could defend yourself."

"That wasn't much of a fight. I mean, he was down and out after only one hit," Jack said as Jonah and Dad laughed.

"This is not funny!" Meagan said.

"Has he tried calling you since that happened?" Jack asked.

"No, he avoids me on campus, thanks to you."

"I did my job. I scared him off."

"So, Jack, when are you going to let us meet the girl you've been seeing?" Mom asked him, as she sat beside Dad.

He was embarrassed to talk about Chelsea. "She met someone else. She sent me a 'Dear John' letter right after I left."

They were all stunned and felt sorry for him. "What a backstabbing little…" Meagan said.

"Meagan Lynn!" Dad scolded sensing she was about to swear. "We're sorry to hear that, son."

He laughed, "No, it's okay, really. We had nothing in common, so it's for the best. I highly doubt I'll ever get serious or get married for that matter. My career will always come first."

"I'm going to pray that God brings a good Christian woman into your life that changes your mind and makes you want a family of your own." Mom said, with a smile.

He looked at her and laughed, "Momma, if the Army wanted me to have a wife and kids, they would've been issued to me with my rifle and tags when I enlisted." he said, as Dad laughed.

"I have a few friends that think you're really good looking, would you like to meet them?" Meagan volunteered.

He laughed out loud, "Meagan, the last type of woman I would consider dating is an annoying sorority girl. No offense, sis. And let's get one thing clear, here. This is not the Hamilton family project, okay? I do not need any of you to find me a woman. I do not want to be set up or anything." he said.

"I want to set him up with one of Christi's friends, but he said no. Meagan, you know Kate?"

"Yeah, I like her." Meagan said. She knew Kate from hanging out with Christi. "You should meet her, Jack. She's very pretty and really nice," she said.

"So Jack, why won't you meet this friend of Christi's?" Mom asked him.

"No, he's too stubborn and doesn't want to meet her." Jonah said.

Jack looked at him. "If I happen to meet her, then I meet her, but I have no intention of starting a relationship with anyone, especially here. I like being single. I like not having to worry about being cheated on or her stealing my money, my things, or wrecking my truck. I like not having those distractions. With my job, I can't afford to have any distractions or worries. Plus, having a long distance relationship with me in North Carolina and her in Dallas would never last."

"Believe it or not Jack, there are women out there that know how to survive and keep busy while their husbands and boyfriends are away on deployment. Don't judge all women by the mistakes and the irresponsibility of the few," Mom informed him.

"Just meet her and see where it goes. Maybe you'll be surprised," Dad suggested.

Running out of excuses, he thought of one more, "I'm sure most of Christi's friends want to date ball players. I don't even make one tenth of the money you do, Jonah."

Jonah smiled, "No, Kate doesn't date ball players, and trust me, many of my teammates have asked her out, but she's always said no."

"I'll think about it, but no promises and no pressure. Agreed?"

"Agreed…" they said. "We won't pressure you." Mom said.

The guys went out into the garage to look at the 1951 Chevrolet 3100 that Dad bought at an auction. The truck needed to be completely restored. He, Jonah, and Jack shared the love for fixing up old cars and selling them, but they fixed them up to look original.

"Wow, where'd you find a 1951 Chevy?" Jack asked, fascinated by Dad's discovery.

"At an auction in Canton, I thought it would be an amazing restoration and a good project for us."

Jack lifted the hood and looked at the original engine. He was like a kid in a candy store. He loved finding and restoring old trucks, especially Chevrolets. They talked about ideas from the color of the body truck to the interior fabric. JD listened to them talk and laugh, as he sat in the drivers' seat pretending to drive.

Across town, Kate was visiting with Christi. It was so hot, they decided to put on their swim suits and lay out by the pool to tan. JD would be sleeping over at Jonah's parents' house that night. "So are there any guys that have made it past the first date I should know about?" Christi asked.

She laughed, "No, the dating world is shallow and almost bare."

"What about that guy your sister set you up with?"

"Oh yeah, I went out with this guy Thomas or something like that last week. I have no idea why I agreed to go…"

"Was it that bad?"

She laughed, "It was so miserable that I'd rather have a root canal. All he talked about was his ex-girlfriend and his business. I couldn't wait to get out of the restaurant. I ended up counseling him on his break-up. It was definitely the longest hour of my life…" she said as they laughed.

"Was he cute?"

She made a face, "He was decent, but not my type on any level. I give up on dating, Chris. It's pointless. Besides, I like being single, I'm independent, able to focus on work, family and friends and not worry about how to balance a guy in the mix. Remember how jealous Kyle would get when I would hang out with you or my sister?" Christi nodded. "I like not having that to deal with. I like being my own person, making my own decisions. Who needs a man?"

"Oh they're useful for some things. Have you ever considered maybe your standards are too high?"

She was lounging in a chair beside her, with her black sunglasses on, sipping her water. "The guys I've gone out with since Kyle do not even come close to my standards, Chris. If anything, I've abandoned my standards just looking for someone somewhat decent,"

"I know you'd like Jack if you met him. You two would really hit it off…" Kate pulled her sunglasses down on her nose a tad bit, looked at her strangely. "…You two would be a perfect match."

"I doubt that."

"I saw the look on your face when you looked at his pictures and when you talked to him on the phone."

"What look did I have on my face?"

Christi laughed at her. She was starting to blush. "The look you have on your face now. Just admit it you are very attracted to him."

She laughed out of embarrassment, "I do think he's very attractive and he has a very sexy voice, but I'm willing to bet my salary he's dating someone."

"No, Jonah told me last night that he and his 'girlfriend' broke up several months ago. She met someone else and sent him a 'Dear John' letter." She was surprised to hear that.

Jack followed Jonah over to his and Christi's home. Pulling into the driveway, he parked behind Kate's black mustang. She had an orange Texas Longhorns sticker on her back window. "Wow, Christi downgraded from a Mercedes to a Mustang? That would've been a historic moment to see." he teased.

Jonah laughed, "No, she would have a panic attack if she had to drive a Mustang instead of her Mercedes," they laughed.

"Then whose car is it?"

Jonah smiled at him, "That would be Kate's."

"Nice try, Jonah."

"Come on, just meet her."

"Who is the woman in all the pictures with Christi in the house? That's who I'd like to meet. She is gorgeous."

Jonah laughed. "Then today is your lucky day."

He smiled. "Are you serious? So Kate is the woman in all those pictures?"

Jonah laughed and nodded. "Why didn't you just say that from the beginning?" he asked, checking his face, teeth, and clothes in the side mirrors of his truck. "How do I look?"

"You look good, man." They joked back and forth as they walked in the house.

"Hey, guess who is home!" Jonah yelled. No one answered. Christi and Kate were by the pool. "Hello, girls?" he shouted upstairs.

Jack walked in the kitchen. Looking out the kitchen window toward the pool and barbecue pit, he noticed two women in black bikinis lounging on lounge chairs, tanning. He looked to Jonah and smiled.

"Want to scare them to death or just mess with them?" Jack asked.

"Let's mess with them. It's good to have my partner in crime back."

They quietly walked out on the patio. Christi was nearly asleep as Kate was reading a magazine.

"Do you have any change?" Jack whispered as they hid behind the bar. The girls were in front of the bar. Jonah handed him three quarters and two dimes. Jack flipped a quarter and it landed in Christi's hair.

Jonah and Jack laughed silently while hiding. Feeling it hit her head, she looked at Kate. "Did you just throw this at me?"

She looked at her strangely. "No, I don't have anywhere to hold change." she replied.

Christi looked at her puzzled, "Then how did it get here?"

"I don't know." They looked at each other curiously. "Your guess is as good as mine."

A few minutes later, Jonah flipped a dime and it landed on Kate's chest. Christi's eyes were closed. "Now I have a dime on my chest," she said. Jonah and Jack were still laughing silently.

"Okay, something is going on. I'm going to check if anyone is here. I may have to call the police." Christi got up and walked around. She didn't think Jonah was home, so she couldn't figure out what was going on. She was afraid photographers had gotten past the gate and onto the property.

Jack and Jonah stealthily snuck back inside the house before she discovered them. She walked into the kitchen and saw Jack getting a beer. "Hey, welcome home!" she said excitedly as they hugged.

"Hey Chris, how are you?" he asked.

"I'm good!" she said happily. "Were you just at your parents'? Did you see JD?"

"Yeah, I did. I can't believe how big he is. I'd like to take him to a Rangers' game this weekend, is it okay with you?"

"Sure, he'll love that. He loves when you're back."

"Yeah, I spend a lot of money on that kid."

"I told you not to start spoiling him you won't be able to stop. It gets worse the older he gets." They laughed. She looked at the window and saw Kate lounging and then looked back at them. "Hey, this may sound weird, but were you two outside flipping change at us?"

"No…" Jonah lied. He was a terrible liar.

She knew he was lying. They had guilty looks on their faces. She folded her arms in front of her chest. "Really, you two want to rethink your answer? You know you're both terrible liars, right?"

"It was us. We're sorry," Jack admitted.

"He wants to meet Kate. He thinks she's gorgeous. Go get her." Jonah announced.

Jack looked to her, "He's going to embarrass me isn't he?" he asked her.

She laughed, "Oh yeah, strap yourself in," she teased. "I'll go get her." She walked outside to Kate.

Kate looked up at her. "Did you find out what was going on?"

"Yeah, I did. It was Jonah. Hey, come in here for a minute, I have something to show you."

She stood up and slipped her gray shorts over her hips and then slipped on her black flip flop sandals. Jack was admiring her from the kitchen window. She had a toned, tanned stomach. Her long dark hair was pulled back in a messy bun. He looked at Jonah. "Wow, she's hot. Do not embarrass me, or I promise you, I will hurt you. Remember the seventh grade?"

"That was an unfair fight, I was sick that day."

He laughed, "How long are you going to lie about that? You're almost thirty and you're still lying about that," he teased.

Kate walked in from the patio and closed the patio door. She saw Jack, Jonah, and Christi and stood frozen. Her sunglasses were still on her face. She only had a thin layer of powder, eye shadow, mascara and liner on. He was captivated by her. She had butterflies in her stomach. He was even more sexy and handsome than his pictures.

Christi turned to him and said, "Jack this is my best friend Katherine Johnson. Kate, this is my brother-in-law, Jack Hamilton."

Taking off her sunglasses, she and Jack shook hands. He found she was even more beautiful in person. "Hi, it's nice to meet you, Katherine." he said.

She couldn't stop looking into his green eyes. "It's nice to meet you too, but you can call me Kate." They stood smiling at each other for a few minutes. His green eyes were mysterious. His sexy smile sent a shiver down her spine. He had perfectly straight, pearly white teeth. Jonah and Christi saw the way they stared at each other.

Forcing herself to break eye contact with him, she looked to Christi, "Well, I better get going. I have that thing tomorrow."

"What thing?" she asked. She knew Kate was embarrassed and very attracted to him.

Jack and Jonah smiled, "You know that thing I told you about earlier?" Kate asked.

"You know you don't have anything to do," Jonah accused.

She laughed out of embarrassment. Knowing Jack was looking at her, she and her voice began to shake. "Yes, I do. I have a lot of things to do. Jack, welcome home, I'm sure I'll see you around here."

He smiled at her, "Thanks, I hope so." He smiled at her. She blushed.

"I'll just see y'all later." She hurried out to her car.

"I think she was shy. I've never seen her like that before," Christi said.

"She was talking so damn fast, like a damn auctioneer," Jonah said as he and Jack laughed.

"Maybe introducing you to her in her bikini top wasn't the best idea. She's very modest," she said to him.

"I think she's gorgeous."

She smiled at him. "I'll be sure to tell her that when I talk to her. She's really nice. You two have a lot in common."

Jack sat on the sofa, watching ESPN highlights as Jonah came walking back in with a couple beer bottles. Handing one to him, he twisted the top off the bottle and took a drink. "So have we found Bin Laden yet?" Jonah asked curiously.

"If we'd found him, you'd know." Seeing a picture of Kate and Christi together on the end table, he picked it up and smiled. "Hey, so what's her story? It's hard to believe she's still single."

Jonah nodded as he took a drink of his drink. "She was engaged."

"What happened?"

"She walked in on him and one of her bridesmaids having sex in her bed."

Jack was dumbfounded, "How can any man cheat on her?"

"The guy was a real idiot and jerk. He tried to control her every move. I wanted to punch him in the face several times. He loved to humiliate her and embarrass her in front of her family and friends. He didn't deserve her and I'm glad she didn't marry him, but I feel bad for how it ended, because she didn't deserve that."

"Why didn't you punch him?"

"I think of Kate as a sister, and I knew it would cause more problems for her, so I just stayed out of it. He really damaged her self-esteem," He noticed him smiling down at the picture. "Wow, you really like her, don't you?"

"I think she's very gorgeous, probably the most beautiful woman I've ever seen."

"I'll give you her number, and you can start talking to her. She needs a good man, just don't hurt her or you and I will have issues." he warned.

Jack looked out the front window. He noticed she was still standing beside her car door, looking frustrated. He watched her through the window trying to open her car door, but it wouldn't open. He smiled at her hanging her head in embarrassment and frustration. He walked out the door. She saw him walking towards her. "Did you lock your keys inside? I can open it for you," he asked.

"No, I ran out of there like a chicken with my head cut off, that I forgot my purse and my keys. Plus it looks like I can't go anywhere, because I'm blocked in," pointing to his truck.

He smiled at her. He adored her Texan accent. "I'll move for you. Are you always this shy, or is it just because I'm here?"

She smiled behind her sunglasses. "You think I'm shy because of you? Wow, you have a pretty big ego," she joked. He laughed. She looked at him and smiled.

Jonah watched them from the window, as they walked back into the house. "Hey, what's up?" he asked her, opening the door.

She smiled, "I forgot my stuff," as she stepped into the entryway.

Jonah, witnessing, their attraction to one another, saw an opportunity to set them up. "So, Jack, are you going to ask her out on a date?" he bluntly asked. Jack was shocked. "…Kate, he thinks you're gorgeous by the way,"

Her face was red from embarrassment, as well as shock. Jack was simply stunned. "Jonah, can I talk to you for a minute?" he asked.

Jonah knew he was embarrassed, "No, I'm trying to set you and Kate up."

She blushed and looked away, avoiding eye contact with Jack. She was just as uncomfortable as he. "Okay, this is certainly the awkward moment everyone talks about, so I'm going to go find Christi," she said, quickly exiting the room. She hurried into the kitchen to talk to Christi.

"Why would you embarrass me in front of her like that?" he demanded, playfully putting Jonah in a headlock.

Jonah laughed, "Hey, calm down. I did you a favor. Now she knows you find her attractive."

"I told you that if you embarrassed me, I'd hurt you." They wrestled, each putting each other in headlocks. Their father taught them self-defense moves when they were growing up, and they always used them on each other. Now, that Jack was a highly skilled warrior, he knew more than Jonah. After a few seconds of being in his arm bar technique, Jonah tapped out.

Kate entered the kitchen. "Hey, I thought you left?" Christi asked.

"I left my purse, towel, and T-shirt here. Jonah just totally embarrassed me and Jack. Why am I surprised? It's who he is." They both laughed.

Christi smiled while shaking her head, as she cooked supper. "What did he do this time?"

"He asked Jack right in front of me, if he was going to ask me out on a date, then he mentioned that Jack thinks I'm gorgeous!" Christi laughed out loud. "It's not funny, Chris. I'm beyond mortified," she said, trying not to laugh.

"I'm sorry he embarrassed you, but Jack told me after you left that he does think you're gorgeous. I think you two should go out and get to know each other."

She playfully rolled her eyes, "Why are you so concerned with my love life? I'm happy."

"How can you be happy going home to a lonely apartment every night? I truly think that you and Jack would hit it off great, if you got to know each other."

"Just because I'm alone doesn't mean I'm lonely…"

"Whatever, I know you. Beneath that hard shell of yours is a lonely woman that needs a good man."

"Okay, if he seems to be this amazing, respectful guy, and obviously extremely attractive, why is he still single?"

"His girlfriend sent him a Dear John letter while he was deployed. She had cheated on him. So, he knows how it feels. Just get to know him. He's really a nice guy." Christi encouraged.

Jonah walked into the kitchen, with his face all red and he was out of breath. "What's wrong with you?" Kate asked him.

"I was having a heated debate with my brother."

"Were you two wrestling?"

"No…" he lied.

"Jonah, did you break anything? Last time you broke two vases from China that my mom bought me," Christi warned.

"We didn't break anything, I promise. Hey, we're going to grill steaks."

"Okay, go for it. Yay, I don't have to cook."

"Kate, will you stay?" he asked.

"Why, so you can embarrass me and Jack even more? No thanks. I just came back in to get my stuff."

"Did I really embarrass you that bad?"

"Yeah, pretty bad. Besides, I can't tonight. I have… laundry to do."

Jonah and Christi rolled their eyes, "Seriously, laundry, you couldn't come up with a better excuse than that?" he asked, laughing.

She had a guilty smile on her face. "C'mon Kate, stay for supper." she encouraged.

She rolled her eyes, "Okay, I'll stay, but y'all better *not* embarrass me again!"

He walked back into the living room and sat on the sofa with Jack. "She's staying for supper."

Jack smiled, "You know what'll happen if you embarrass me again, don't you?" They laughed at each other. They walked into the kitchen to get the steaks and baked potatoes. They walked outside on the patio and began grilling the steaks and the baked potatoes.

Kate and Christi were in the kitchen making Texas style sweet tea and salad. The hot Texas sun was setting. The lavender and orange streaked sky was breathtaking, and the crickets were chirping. "I cannot believe you told me to come in to meet him wearing my bikini top. Do you have any idea how embarrassing that was?"

"It wasn't that bad. Something tells me that you made quite the impression," Christi said. She saw how Jack kept looking back into the window at Kate.

"So, his girlfriend really sent him a 'Dear John' email while he was deployed? Wow, she must've been an idiot and obviously blind."

Jack opened the patio door, "Do y'all want to eat out here?"

"Yes," they both replied, and he closed the patio door. They walked outside, carrying plates, glasses, silverware and the salad bowl. Jack and Kate looked at each other and smiled. Jonah and Christi saw they were attracted to each other. The double date was starting out successfully.

He got another beer out of the cooler filled to the rim with ice. "So, Kate, what do you do for a living?" he asked her, very interested.

She placed a plate down on the patio table in front of him. "I'm a labor and delivery nurse at Medical City hospital."

"Oh wow, so you deliver babies?"

She brought the salad bowl to the table, "Well I help deliver them. I'll either hold the woman's hand or monitor her contractions. I tell her when to push and breathe. I love my job."

He smiled at her, "I hear from a lot of my friends who have kids that childbirth is a very disturbing and dramatic experience."

Jonah cleared his throat loudly. "Yes, and it's incredibly disgusting! Once you watch a woman give birth, you'll never be the same again!" Jack and Kate laughed at him. They all sat down at the table. Jack sat across from her.

"I would probably pass out or throw up if I saw that," he admitted, as they all laughed.

"Many dads throw up and/or pass out in the delivery room. It's pretty common," she said, as she and Christi laughed.

"I couldn't do what you do, Kate. It takes a strong person with a strong stomach to do that job every day," he said.

She smiled at him. "Thank you." She saw his tattoo on the inside of his forearm. It was the Green Beret insignia with "Liberate the Oppressed" in Latin and in black scroll ink. "So you're a Green Beret?" she asked.

"What makes you think I'm a Green Beret?" he asked.

"Well, 'Liberate the Oppressed' is the motto for the Green Berets and you have their insignia on your arm. My dad has the exact same tattoo in the exact same spot, and he's a Green Beret."

He looked down at his arm and then back at her. "What's your rank?" she asked him.

"I'm a Master Sergeant."

Seeing the scar from being shot on this last deployment on his arm, she asked, "Did you receive a through and through gunshot wound there?" pointing to his scar.

He smiled at her and looked down at it. "I don't mean to be rude, but being a nurse I'm naturally curious. I did my clinical rotations in the ER before going up to labor and delivery. I saw so many gunshot wounds."

"You couldn't be rude even if you tried." he said.

"Oh yes she can!" Jonah said. Christi and Kate laughed. "Did you really get shot?" he asked.

"I don't like to parade my battle scars around, so let's change the subject, please."

"Did you bring your rifle?" Jonah asked.

"Yeah, I did. You can't choke on us this time when we go to Lloyd's," he teased as he laughed.

"For the hundredth time, the gun jammed."

Jack laughed, "No, you didn't load the round in the chamber correctly."

"What kind of rifles, Winchesters or Henry rifles?" Kate asked.

They each looked at her in surprise. "You know what those are?" Jonah asked curiously.

She smiled at their facial expressions. "Yes, my dad and I shoot them along with the M-4s all the time. My favorite rifle is the 4590 Winchester Center-fire."

Jack's bottom jaw dropped in shock and he was even more attracted to her. "Okay, that's impressive," he said. He looked at Jonah and smiled.

"My dad and I have an odd hobby for father and daughter. We try to go hunting and fishing when he's home. I have a Colt 1911 pistol."

"Really, that's awesome," Jack said to her. They smiled at each other.

"Okay, for those of us who can barely tell the difference in car models, what's a 4590 or a Colt 1911?" Christi asked curiously.

"The Winchester 4590 is considered the classic American rifle. Many experts say that it is the gun that won the West. Everyone owned a 4590 Winchester," she explained. "And the Colt 1911 is the best pistol in the world. It's my favorite handgun."

Jack and Jonah were dumbfounded. "I never figured you to be the type of woman who's into guns." Jonah admitted.

"Funny, I thought the same about you too," she teased, as they all laughed.

Jack was impressed. He had many Winchester rifles and Colt model pistols. "I'll have to take you to the ranch and let you use my rifle. It's really fun." he said.

"Your M4 rifle or…?"

"Yeah, you can shoot my M4, my SCAR, my Beretta, and my 4590 Winchester. You can shoot every gun and rifle I have."

"Okay, I'd like that," she said, as he smiled.

"So, how old are you?"

"How old do I look?" she asked coyly, giving him a sideways look.

"Uh, oh, Jack. Be careful, guessing a woman's age can be dangerous," Jonah warned, as they laughed at him.

He smiled, studying her, "You're almost twenty-two."

She smiled back at him, "You're correct." He grinned triumphantly at Jonah, as if he won a prize. "How old are you?" she asked curiously.

"I'm twenty-seven. I'm almost an old man," he said jokingly, and they all laughed. He took another drink of his drink. "When are y'all going to have another baby?" he asked Jonah.

Jonah and Christi laughed. "We're talking about having another one," Christi said.

"Good, JD needs a sibling."

"We'll see what happens," Christi said.

"At least JD will have a pet to play with. I brought him one."

"What kind of pet?" Jonah and Christi both asked cautiously.

He laughed, "It's a camel spider."

Christi and Jonah's eyes enlarged. "You brought home a spider?" Jonah asked him, stuttering.

"Yeah, they're real easy to catch and tame. I mean, who needs a dog, when you can have a pet spider from the Middle East?" he teased.

"I've never heard of a camel spider," Jonah said.

He laughed, "It's a spider about the size of your hand, and it chases you." as he scrambled his fingers across the table towards Christi. She nearly jumped out of her chair. They all laughed at her.

He knew Christi had a huge fear of spiders. "Jack that is not funny!" she said. Jack and Jonah laughed again.

"Ewe, I hate spiders. I'm not going to sleep with a spider in my house." she jokingly snapped.

"I didn't really bring home a spider."

"If you had, you could've put it in Meagan's room." Jonah suggested, as they all laughed again.

"Oh that would've been hilarious." he said, as he and Jonah laughed again.

Kate smiled and tried not to laugh at Christi, rubbing her arms as if a spider had crawled on her. "So, Kate, you're being very quiet," Jonah accused.

She smiled at them. "I'm just listening to y'all catch up."

"Are you always this quiet?" Jack asked her. They smiled at each other.

"No she's not, she's quite the talker. I don't know why she's being so quiet," Christi said, as she gave her a look.

Jack smiled at her, "It must be because of me." They made eye contact again. Jonah and Christi watched the two of them talk, smile at each other, and flirt with each other. After supper, she helped Christi clean up as Jonah and Jack sat at the bar eating the chocolate cake Christi had made earlier.

She dried her hands on a dish towel and looked down at her wrist watch. "Well, it's getting late. I better get going. Thanks for supper, Christi."

"Oh, I need to move my truck so you can get out." he said getting up from the bar. They walked to the front door. He walked her to her car and moved his truck. She got her car keys out of her purse, as she waited for him to park his truck.

"You have a nice truck."

"Thanks, I love it." He smiled as he walked towards her. She was now wearing the T-shirt she had forgotten earlier, but he could still see the black bikini top through the fabric. "So, tell your boyfriend that I said he's a very lucky man."

She laughed, "The next boyfriend I have, I'll be sure to tell him you said that."

He smiled at her, "I'd like to be your next boyfriend."

She laughed again. He made her nervous, in a good way. "Wow, you're good. I mean I give you applause for being so suave and confident. Do most women go for this routine?"

He smiled at her, "No, I'm serious. You're gorgeous and I'd like to get to know you, but I'm sure you have a long line of guys chasing after you. So I'm wondering if you could move me to the front of that line, or are you going to make me wait my turn?"

She laughed, "I'm done dating, so that apparent long line of guys will be waiting for a long time. Are you sure you want to wait?"

He smiled, "I'm positive I want to, can I ask why you're done dating?"

His smile made her feel something she never felt before. All she could do was smile up at him. Her attraction to him was very strong, though she tried very hard to ignore it. "Because all men are the same…"

He smiled, "Not all men are the same, just as not all women are the same. Some men don't realize they have something amazing until after they've let it go. I'm not like that. And when I have something amazing, I hang onto it. Let me change your mind. I'll take you out to a nice supper, and I'll prove to you that I'm different…" She smiled as she blushed. He looked down at her. He loved the color of her eyes, how they twinkled in the moonlight like stars. He admired her as the wind swept through her hair. "…You look like you need a good man in your life."

She smiled up at him. "What makes you think I haven't had a good man?"

He smiled, "Your eyes, I see more than you think I do."

She blushed, "And I suppose you're that good man I need?"

He laughed, "Yeah, I am."

"You're pretty arrogant there, master sergeant."

"No, it's not arrogance. I'm confident." They looked at each other, laughing occasionally as they flirted. "So, will you have supper with me? I'll be a perfect gentleman. I won't even expect a kiss goodnight," he vowed, placing his hand on his heart. "And if you don't like me the way I like you, I promise I'll leave you alone and just be your friend."

She looked up into his mysterious green eyes. He smiled at her. His white teeth flashed through his crooked smile. She paused, "I'll have to think about it."

"What could I do to change your mind?"

"I'm sure you'll figure something out."

He laughed, "I can tell you're interested," he said.

"How can you tell?"

"I can read people very well."

She smiled, "I am interested, but I'm also cautious and suspicious."

"That's fair, I can respect that. But I can promise you right now that I'm nothing like the previous men you've dated. I'm mature. I'm a nice guy, and I know a good thing when I see it." She was very attracted to him. Her heart was racing. "So, now that you know that, would you consider having supper with me?" he asked.

She smiled at him. "Hmm…"

"I promise you'll have fun. You'll smile and you'll laugh, I bet you haven't done that in a long time."

She smiled, "Okay, I've considered it, only because you're handsome, very smooth, and you have a gorgeous truck." He laughed, "You better not expect anything, not even a kiss goodnight," she replied.

He smiled, "I won't, but I suspect you'll be the one to kiss me goodnight," he teased.

She laughed, "Very doubtful, I don't kiss on the first date."

"We'll see, won't we? I'm told I'm pretty charming. I'll need your number to give you a call."

"I may not be able to answer right away due to whatever shift I'm working, so you'll need to leave me a message if you want to go out. Can you handle that, Master Sergeant?"

He smiled at her, "Oh I can handle that." he said confidently. She smiled at him. He pulled his cell phone out of his pocket. She gave him her number. He typed the number in, but instead of typing her name in as Kate, he typed in *Beautiful.*

"See what your name is in my phone?" he showed her.

She smiled at the entry of *Beautiful* in his contacts. "How do I know I'm the only one in your phone with that name?"

He smiled, "Here look through my phone." He handed it to her. She looked through his contacts.

Seeing many other women's names in his contacts, she looked at him. "Wow, you're quite the bachelor. Who are these other women?"

"They're not important. I'll delete them all right now." He deleted all the women in his phone except, her and his immediate female family members. "See, now you're the only woman in my phone that I'm interested in."

She couldn't believe he deleted all those numbers. She looked to her car and then back up at him. "Well I better go. It was nice to finally meet you." She stuck out her hand.

He smiled, gently held it and kissed the top of it. "I'm glad we finally met."

"Good night." she said. They smiled at each other.

He opened her door for her. "Good night, beautiful. Drive safe."

She smiled at him and got inside her car. "Thank you." She drove away. Her face hurt from smiling so much. He walked into the house with a big smile on his face.

Walking in the living room, Jonah noticed the smile on his face and says, "Uh, oh, I haven't seen that smile in years. You must really like her."

"What are you talking about? I'm not smiling," he denied.

"Yes you are, go look at yourself in the mirror," he teased. Jack covered his mouth with his hand.

"So, what do you think of her?" Christi asked curiously, looking up from her magazine.

Jonah flipped through the channels on T.V. He sat down on the sofa and took the remote from him. "I think she's nice, interesting, and gorgeous."

"Are you going to see her again?" she asked curiously.

"Maybe, I don't know." He and Jonah fought over the remote again. Though they were grown men, they still acted like kids when they were together.

"I hope you do. I can see that you two are really attracted to each other," Christi said. "But, if you do decide to pursue her, please go easy with her and be considerate. She had a very painful, humiliating break-up with her fiancé."

"Yeah, Jonah told me."

"Ease up, Christi. They just met." Jonah said, skeptically.

"Didn't you see the way they were looking at each other all night, especially when they first saw each other? It was like magic," she pointed out.

They looked at her strangely. "Babe, you've watched too many chick flicks. I'm cancelling the cable." Jonah said, as he and Jack laughed.

Kate smiled as she drove home. She had never seen a man that attractive. He was incredibly handsome, thrilling, and mysterious. His eyes kept her in a trance, where she couldn't look away. She didn't want to look away. His voice thrilled her and made her shiver when he said her name.

She arrived home. Morgan was sitting on the sofa watching TV and eating a bowl of ice cream. "Hey, what's with you?"

"Oh I just met the most attractive man I've ever seen in my life!"

Morgan smiled, "Where'd you meet him?"

"Over at Christi's, he's her brother-in-law."

"What does he look like?"

She smiled, "He's tall, very handsome. He has blondish brown hair and green eyes. He has a sexy smile and great teeth. He's fit and muscular."

"What's his name? What does he do?"

"His name is Jack, and he's in the Army."

"Wow, he sounds really hot."

Jack was out on the patio and sat in a lounge chair looking at the sparkling blue pool water. He looked down at the entry of *Beautiful* and called her. Morgan and Kate were eating ice cream and watching their show together. The phone rang.

She answered the phone, "Hello?"

He smiled, recognizing her voice, "Hi this is Jack."

She smiled, "Hi, wow, you called? I'm surprised to hear from you." Morgan smiled at her.

"Of course I called. Did you think I wasn't going to call you?"

"I wasn't going to get my hopes up, but I'm glad you did."

"I practically had to beg you to agree to go out with me and give me your number, so of course I was going to call you. You don't think I'm desperate for calling you a few hours after getting your number, do you?"

She smiled as she walked back to her bedroom. "Desperate isn't the word I would use."

"What word would you use?"

"Preemptive."

He laughed, "Well I couldn't risk you making a date with another guy. So, I'm calling to reserve my date with the most beautiful woman I've ever seen."

She laughed, "You haven't dated much if you think I'm the most beautiful woman you've ever seen."

"That's where you're wrong, I've dated a lot of women, but none have looked as beautiful as you."

"I can honestly say I've never been pursued by a handsome soldier before."

"I don't know about all that," he said.

She smiled, "Oh, now look who can be modest!" she teased.

He laughed, "I don't mean to come off as arrogant."

"Well you're a Green Beret; you've earned the right to be arrogant now and then." He loved her personality and sense of humor. She was approachable. He loved her adorable Southern drawl. It wasn't annoying or extremely thick, it was adorable and genuine. They continued to talk and laugh. They planned to go out on Friday night.

After talking with him for nearly an hour, she walked back into the living room. Morgan looked up at her, "So, how'd it go?"

She smiled, "We're going out on Friday."

On Thursday afternoon, she was working the 7 am to 7 pm shift at the hospital when a florist delivered two dozen pink roses to her. Her friends were curious who sent her roses. She was very surprised. Looking at the card written in his handwriting, she read:

> *"I'm looking forward to seeing you tomorrow night. These roses are for you to make your day better and to show you I'm different than all the other guys. I can tell by looking at you that you're an amazing woman. I'm excited to see you and get to know you more.*
> *See you tomorrow night, beautiful.*
>
> *Jack"*

Her friends gushed over the breathtaking roses and were curious who Jack was. They saw the look on her face as she read the card. She was very surprised he had already sent her flowers, not just any flowers, but her favorite.

Angie read the card and was very surprised. She and Kate went to a local *Soup or Salad* restaurant on their hour lunch break. "So, who's Jack?" she asked curiously.

"He's Christi's brother-in-law. We're going out tomorrow on a first date. I'm really nervous."

"How'd you meet him?"

"She and Jonah introduced us."

"What is he like?"

She smiled, "He's good looking, funny, and nice."

"What does he do?"

"He's in the Army."

"From the card, he seems to really like you."

She smiled, "When we were talking, I couldn't stop smiling. My face hurts from smiling so much."

Angie smiled, "That's a good sign. What does he look like?"

She smiled, "He's tall, blondish-brown hair, green eyes. He's fit. He has big muscular arms and he's tanned. He has great teeth and a great smile that makes my legs turn into JELLO. He has this incredibly sexy voice that gives me butterflies in my stomach. He's very handsome."

"Wow, can I come with you tomorrow night? I want to see what he looks like." They laughed. "But seriously, Kate, I can tell you're excited to see him. You haven't been this excited about a guy in so long."

"Angie, I'm scared. I think he is extremely good looking and nice, but…"

"You're afraid that you might actually like him and he will want to date you exclusively? Kate, it's almost been a year since you've called off your engagement. And in that year, you haven't dated anyone who has made you this excited or smile like you are now." Kate caught herself smiling again. "My advice is to be open and see where this goes. Just take things nice and slow."

They talked more about the date and other things that were going on at work.

3

I**T WAS FINALLY** Friday evening. The sky was blue and cloudless. The air was cooler. She was just leaving the hospital after a twelve hour shift. He was at his parents' house, sitting outside in a patio chair beside the pool, thinking of her. She had thought of him all day and frequently caught herself looking at her watch. She was excited to see him, but very nervous also. She wondered how she could like him so much already, she barely knew him.

She was just starting her car. She wondered where he was taking her. Looking at the clock on her radio, she saw it was 6:10 p.m. He would be by her apartment at 7:00 p.m.

Driving down her street, she began to think about how she would fix her hair and what perfume to wear. Unlocking her door, she quickly ran to her bathroom to take a shower. She had laid out her favorite brown skirt with a tan tank top with a crème colored, button-up cardigan. She wore her favorite pair of brown cowboy boots. She threw her dark, wet hair up in a towel, and reapplied her makeup. She dried her hair with a hair dryer and put it in hot rollers.

Morgan walked in with the mail. "Wow, you look amazing!"

"You think so?"

"Yes, he'll definitely call you for a second date!"

At his parents' house, he shaved and took a fast shower and got dressed. He put gel in his hair, splashed some after shave on his face and neck, and lightly sprayed cologne on his neck and the front of his shirt. He wore black slacks and a long sleeved, slate-colored button up shirt, un-tucked. He fastened his watch around his wrist.

The dress code for this restaurant was business casual.

Jonah and JD drove up to the house at the same time as Meagan. They all walked in together. Mom sat on the sofa, reading a magazine. Meagan and Christi were going to a movie. Jonah was going out with his friends from the team, so Mom and Dad were babysitting.

Mom and JD walked out in the backyard to find Dad. Jonah walked up the stairs. He reached the top of the stairs. He entered the room and saw Jack. "Where are you going?"

"I have a date tonight with Kate, how do I look?" he asked nervously.

Jonah looked at his outfit. "You look good. Where are you taking her?"

"I'm taking her to *Trulucks Steak & Seafood* on McKinney Avenue, is that a good place?" He checked himself in the mirror one last time.

"Yeah, that's a good place. The steaks are amazing."

"Alright, I'll see you later. I need to run my truck through the carwash before I pick her up," he said. He grabbed his truck keys and hurried over to her apartment. He stopped by an automatic car wash, and then he stopped by a *Tom Thumb* store to buy a bouquet of hot pink roses for her. He drove down Central Expressway and pulled into the parking lot of her apartment building.

He looked in the rear view mirror to make sure that there wasn't anything on his face or in his teeth. He calmly stepped out of the truck, walked up to the building, and pushed the buzzer for 1509.

Morgan was helping her get all of the rollers out of her hair when they heard the buzzer. "Oh, he's here!" she said excitedly and nervously.

"Okay just calm down."

She took a deep breath and walked to the intercom. "Hello?" she answered.

"Hey, it's Jack."

She smiled at his voice. "Hi, come on up. I'm on the fifth floor," she said, allowing him in. He opened the door and stepped in the elevator. The doors opened at the fifth floor. Finding apartment 1509, he rang the doorbell.

She opened the door and smiled at him. He smiled at her, "Wow, you look very beautiful."

Her long, dark hair was curled and flowing around her shoulders. Her makeup was flawless. She looked gorgeous to him. "Thank you. You look amazing. Come on in."

He walked in and closed the door. Seeing the vase of the roses he had sent the day before, he smiled as he handed her the flowers. "These are for you."

She smiled, "Thank you, I'll put them next to the others. Pink roses are my favorite, how did you know?"

He smiled at her, "It was a lucky guess."

Morgan came out of her bedroom. "Hi, how are you?" she asked.

"This is my roommate Morgan. Morgan, this is Jack."

He and Morgan shook hands. "It's nice to meet you." he said.

"It's nice to meet you too. Well, y'all have fun. I'll see ya later, Kate." She walked back to her bedroom.

She smelled the roses and smiled back up at him. "I've never had a man buy me flowers, much less two days in a row."

"See, I've already shown you I'm different than all the others."

She grabbed her clutch purse and they walked down to his truck. He opened the door for her and drove to *Truluck's Steak and Seafood* restaurant on the corner of Maple and McKinney Avenue.

The sun was just starting to set, with beautiful hues of blue, pink, and orange strokes across the periwinkle sky. The evening air was relaxing and calm. Stars were now visible. The freeway was filled with headlights and tail lights, twinkling like gems.

She looked over at him driving in and out of traffic. "So are you enjoying being home?"

"Yeah, I am. I love being back in Texas."

"What do you normally do when you're home on leave?"

He looked at her and smiled, "Jonah and I will go to a few ball games. This weekend, we're going hunting this weekend up north. Normally, we just work on the truck with our dad, go hunting or fishing with him. I take JD to ball games and other stuff."

"Work on the truck?"

"Jonah, my dad, and I are restoring a 1951 Chevrolet. It's a hobby we all get into."

"Oh, that's great. So, what do you do when you're back at Fort Bragg? I'm assuming you don't get a lot of free time."

"I spend most of my free time at the gym, working out and boxing. It keeps the stress down."

"I run five miles every morning or evening, depending on my shift. What else do you do when you're not deployed?

"I'll hang out with my team. Wow, I sound really boring."

She smiled, "I wouldn't go that far."

"How was your day today?" he asked nicely.

"Oh, it was busy. How was yours?"

He looked over to her and smiled, "It's really good now that I'm with you." She blushed. He saw she was blushing. He wanted to hold her hand, but didn't know if she would be comfortable with that on the first date. She could smell his cologne, and that only made her more attracted to him.

They were waiting at a stop light, behind a long line of traffic. "There's no traffic like Dallas traffic on a Friday night."

They finally arrived at the restaurant, parked, and walked toward the doors. He opened the door for her. "Hello, good evening. Do you have a reservation?" the host asked nicely.

"Yes, for two under the name Hamilton," he replied. The host grabbed two menus and seated them by a window. The table had tea light candles flickering on the table, cloth linens, and small rose arrangements. It was a very romantic setting. He pulled out her chair for her. She looked up at him and smiled. She was shocked that chivalry still existed for some men.

"Your server will be right with you," the host said as he handed them the menus.

"This is a really nice place." she said.

They glanced around. "Yeah, it is," he agreed and they looked at their menus. "What are you going to have?" he asked.

"I don't know just yet. Everything looks amazing, what about you?"

"I haven't had a good steak in a long time."

"I bet you haven't, only living off of MREs[4]."

They laughed, "Some MREs are pretty good. When we're outside the wire, we can't heat them up, but when they are heated, they're so good," he said.

"Why can't you heat them up?"

"Because the smell of food would give away our position, I have some out in my truck if you want to eat one," he joked.

She laughed, "No, no thanks. My dad would make my sister and I eat those when we got in trouble," she said, as they laughed.

He smiled at her studying her menu and said, "So, tell me about you."

She looked up at him and smiled, "What do you want to know?"

"I want to know everything about you."

"Well, I'm from here, originally, but being a military kid, I've lived all over, but Dallas is home to me. I am a Christian. You already know that I'm almost twenty-two and that I'm a nurse. I just graduated from the *University of Texas*."

"I'm a military kid too. My dad just retired last year. Wait…did you say you're a Texas graduate? Oh no, we have a big problem here," he teased, as they laughed.

"Yes, I'm a proud *U.T.* graduate," she replied. She was curious to know where he went to college. She feared he was a *Texas A&M University* 'Aggie' graduate. She smiled at him, "Where did you go to college? If you're an Aggie, I'm leaving," she teased.

He smiled. "I enlisted right out of high school, but I'm a diehard Sooner fan."

"Oh no, I'm on a date with a 'Sooner'?" she joked, as they laughed.

"Yes, you are…" and they laughed with each other.

She looked around the restaurant. "I better not say that too loud, or I'll start a riot and probably a hangin'," she joked, as he laughed. "I love the Oklahoma and Texas rivalry. It's the best rivalry in football history. I will argue that until I'm blue in the face. It's so fierce and very intense." she said.

---

[4]   MREs stands for Meals Ready to Eat- a self- contained, individual field ration for the U.S. military to use in combat and other field conditions where organized food facilities are not available.

He was in awe of her. "I agree. It's also one of the oldest. Most people don't know that the rivalry dates back 1900. Oklahoma wasn't even a state then, it was still a territory." he said.

"Really, I didn't realize that."

"Yeah, the first game was October 10, 1900. Texas beat OU, twenty-eight to two."

"Wow, look at you, I have my very own college football historian sitting here with me. Why do they play here in Dallas?"

"Dallas is a neutral location. It's exactly 190 miles from each university. Have you ever been to the game?" he asked curiously.

"Of course, my friends and I go every year. My friends and I love going every year, but we always end up standing in between completely 'wasted' fans, both teams."

He laughed. "Some fans, on both sides, take the game way too seriously. I mean I understand disappointment, but it is just a football game."

"Oh, I agree. My friends and I were in the middle of a huge fight last year. One wasted OU fan actually tried to rip my friend's shirt off because it had a longhorn on it."

He laughed. "Now that's crossing way over the line. What did y'all do?"

"We tossed our drinks in his face and then some sober guys beat him up," she said.

He laughed, taking a drink of his sweet tea, "Did you play any sports in high school or college?" he asked curiously.

"Yes, I've played basketball and fast pitch softball all my life. Christi and I were starters in basketball at UT." He was very impressed. "What about you?"

"I played football, baseball, and wrestling all throughout school."

"Wow, you were quite the jock, huh?"

He laughed. They ordered and handed their menus back to the waitress. He took a drink of his tea. "So is your dad still active or has he retired?"

"No he is still active. I think the President himself will have to force him to retire. What about your dad?"

"My dad retired last year. He was a major general. He hates retirement. He'd give anything to go back to active duty."

"I bet. So, tell me about you," she said, as she folded her hands underneath her chin.

He smiled. "What do you want to know?"

"Everything…" she replied, giving him a flirty grin.

"I'm not that interesting. I'm actually pretty boring, all I do is work or work out at the gym."

"I disagree, you're interesting to me."

He smiled at her. "Well, you already know I'm twenty-seven and a Sooner fan. I love to play sports and be outdoors. I love being in the Army, and I'm also a Christian."

"Being a Green Beret, do you speak any languages?" she asked curiously. She thought that he was very attractive and really funny.

"Yes, I speak Arabic."

"Will you tell me something in Arabic?" she asked, while smiling at him.

He looked around the restaurant. "Kate, you realize we're in Texas, and I could be shot on the spot for speaking Arabic?"

She laughed. "Don't worry, I'll protect you."

He looked around the restaurant. "You know in Texas, you can open carry your weapon?"

She smiled at him. "Yes, but they can't shoot you. Please just one thing."

He just discovered his one and only weakness, her smile. "Okay, one thing just because you have a killer smile."

She smiled at him. "Okay, great. Thank you."

He quietly spoke Arabic. She smiled. "What did you say?"

"I said that you are a very beautiful woman."

She blushed. The attraction and compatibility between them was strong. "Thank you."

"You're welcome." He smiled at her. "So, what does your mom do?" he asked.

"My mom is an English Literature professor at UT here, what about your mom?"

"My mom is a pastry chef. Right now she's trying to open her own restaurant with a bakery inside."

"Wow, let me know when she opens," she said as he laughed.

"I will. She makes the most incredible double fudge chocolate cake, all from scratch."

"Wow, it sounds delicious."

"How many siblings do you have?" he asked.

"I have one sister, Lauren. She's goes to UT at Dallas."

"Jonah and I have a sister, Meagan. She's goes to UT also."

She sipped her tea, "I've met Meagan. She is so funny and very pretty."

"Jonah and I are very protective of her, maybe too over protective," he said.

"You two have your hands full, but I would say you're too overprotective when you beat up her boyfriend," she said, while laughing.

He smiled and then laughed. "You heard about that?"

"Oh yeah, she told me and Christi all about it."

"I wonder if she told you the whole story."

"She told us that you threatened him. Then you punched him three or four times in the face, at your parents' house, in front of everyone. What's your side?"

He grinned. "No, I punched him once and he was out." She laughed. "Well, what happened was I warned him that if he tried anything inappropriate with her, he'd answer to me. He then took a swing at me first, but he missed, so I naturally just reacted."

"Okay, we didn't hear that part. I don't blame you for defending yourself," they laughed. "What are your favorite TV shows?" she asked curiously.

"I'm rarely home to watch TV, but I like to watch sports, boxing, *UFC,* and *MMA* fighting."

"I love to watch boxing and MMA. I have all the *Rocky* movies," she admitted.

He smiled at her in amazement. "You have to be the most amazing and the most attractive woman I've ever met in my life. You like guns, you play sports, and you love boxing. You're beautiful and sweet. I think I hit the lottery."

She laughed. "Blame my father. He always wanted a son, but never got one. My mom says I'm too tomboy. I love going fishing and hunting." she said, as he laughed.

"I'm not going to blame him, I want to thank him. I'm attracted to a woman who isn't afraid to get her hands dirty or to sweat." They smiled at each other. "When is your birthday?" he asked.

"August twenty-third, when is yours?"

He smiled. "June ninth."

Realizing his birthday had just passed, she said, "Oh, Happy belated Birthday."

"Thanks." They talked about their likes and dislikes. They laughed and flirted with each other.

"So, I want to take you up on your offer about shooting your rifle, when can we go?" she asked, giving him a flirty grin.

"I'm free anytime. When you want to go, call me and we'll go out to the ranch."

"That'd be great." she said.

The waitress brought them their check. "That steak was so good. Are you ready to go?" he asked.

She nodded. He stood up and took one last drink of his tea. He paid the seventy-five dollar bill and left a twenty dollar tip. "Thank you for supper," she said as the wind swept through her hair.

He smiled at her. They walked slowly to his truck. "It was my pleasure. Would you want to go see a movie with me?" He opened the passenger door for her.

She smiled at him. "Yeah, I would."

"I haven't been to a movie since before 9/11," he admitted. He drove to the *Landmark's Magnolia Theater.*

She couldn't believe it. "Are you serious?"

"Yeah, the last movie I saw in theaters was *Rock Star.*"

She smiled at him, "Well, it's time we change that. You deserve some down time,"

"You think so?"

"Yes, I do." They smiled at each other. They arrived at the theater and saw that it was fairly busy, the typical Friday night date crowd. They waited in line. "What types of movies do you like?" he asked.

"I like comedies, thrillers, romance, and war movies. I do not like scary movies."

The line slowly moved. "What do you consider scary?"

"Watching or hearing people being tortured and murdered. Do you like scary movies?"

"Yeah, I've always liked them. Meagan is the same way as you, only I don't blame her. When Jonah and I were kids, we'd watch a scary movie and then we'd scare her to death by doing whatever was in the movie. She absolutely freaks out when she sees Jason's hockey mask," he laughed thinking about it.

She laughed. "Y'all are so mean to her, poor Meagan."

"We're her brothers. We're supposed to do that. So, what do you want to see? You pick."

"Are you sure?"

"Yeah, I know absolutely nothing about any of these movies. I trust your judgment."

"Lucky for you, I'm not in a chick flick mood tonight." she teased, as they smiled at each other.

"If there's one you want to see, I'll watch it with you."

She smiled at him. "I'm in the mood for some James Bond." He laughed. He bought two tickets for '*Die Another Day*'. They bought popcorn and drinks and walked into the theater and sitting towards the back. He could smell her perfume. He desperately wanted to hold her hand.

She looked at him. He noticed her looking at him. "Why are you looking at me?"

She smiled. "I'm just trying to figure out how you're still single."

He laughed. "I'm wondering the same thing about you." They talked quietly before the movie started. His hand barely touched hers and she grasped it. As they watched the movie, they held hands and frequently looked at each other and smiled. As the movie ended, they walked slowly up the aisle and threw away their drinks and popcorn. They walked out of the theater to his truck and waited for traffic to clear behind him.

"So, what do you want to do now?" she asked.

"Truthfully, I'm not ready for this night to end."

She looked at the clock. It was almost ten o'clock. "Can you dance?"

He smiled. "If I get to spend more time with you, I'll do anything."

"Good, I was hoping you weren't ready to take me home."

"Have you ever been to Gilley's?"

She smiled. "No, I haven't. I've only been to Red River."

He laughed. "Yeah, I've been there too." He drove to Gilley's Dallas, a legendary country music bar in Dallas. They walked hand in hand. They danced to fast-paced honkytonk music. They held each other and laughed. The live band played a few slow love songs by the legendary Willie Nelson. He held her close as they danced.

Other women noticed him and were walking by him, desperately trying to get his attention, but he ignored each one. He couldn't take his eyes off Kate. At half past midnight, they finally arrived back at her apartment building. They walked inside and rode up in the elevator. "So did you have fun?" he asked.

The elevator doors opened. They walked down the hall to her door. "Yeah, I did. You're a great dancer. Apparently I wasn't the only one that noticed."

"What do you mean?"

"Did you not see how many women tried to get your attention?"

"No, you had my full attention."

She smiled at him. "That was a great line."

"It's not a line, it's the truth." he said. He held her hand in his. She smiled up at him. "I know what you're thinking about," he said.

"You can read minds? Is that a skill they teach you in selections?"

He laughed. "You're thinking about kissing me."

"And what makes you think that?"

"Are you?" he asked, smiling at her.

His smile made her feel something she'd never felt before. She was extremely attracted to him, and she did want to kiss him, but told herself she wasn't going to kiss him. "No." she lied. She kissed his cheek.

"See I told you you'd kiss me first." They laughed. "I had a really great time with you tonight, Kate," he said.

She smiled. "I had a really great time with you too. Thank you for calling me. I haven't laughed or smiled this much in a long time."

He touched her hand. Their fingers inner locked, and they looked in each other's eyes. "I'd really like to see you again," he said, as she smiled.

She looked up into his eyes. She really liked him, his personality, and sense of humor. She was incredibly attracted to him, physically and emotionally. "You would?" she asked.

"Yeah, I would. When are you free?" he asked, holding her hand.

"Well, unfortunately, I work nights the next three nights, but I'm off on Tuesday. Are you free then?"

"I will be, I'll cancel whatever crazy plans Jonah has going on."

"You don't have to cancel plans with him just to see me."

"I'd rather spend time with you."

"Okay, I'll see you Tuesday."

"Good night, Kate."

She smiled at him. "Good night, Jack." He kissed the top of her hand and slowly walked backwards, as they kept eye contact. She unlocked the door, and they looked at each other. She barely opened the door. She was the first to break eye contact. He smiled as he walked to his truck.

She was surprised at how much they had in common and that their first date wasn't 'the awkward first date' most people had. He was surprised that they talked and laughed as much as they did. He had expected to have an awkward time, but they really had a great first date. He thought about her as he drove back to Jonah and Christi's. He could still smell her perfume inside his truck.

She smiled at the two beautiful bouquets of pink roses sitting on the bar. She saw she had three messages on her machine. Pressing the button, she listened to the last message. It was from Kyle.

"Kate, it's me. I really want to talk to you. I miss you and I know you're just dodging my calls. We need to talk. I made a huge mistake cheating on you. Please call me back, I love you."

She wondered how he found out her new number. Deleting the message and the other two he had left, she looked to the roses from Jack and smiled thinking of him. She had officially moved on from Kyle.

Morgan walked out of her bedroom. "Hey you're back? Did you have fun?"

"I did. I haven't had this much fun on a date in well, ever."

"The Loser called several times and left some pretty desperate messages. I wonder how he found out our new number."

"Yeah, I just deleted them." She told Morgan all about their date.

Jack parked in Jonah and Christi's driveway and walked inside. He saw Jonah sitting at the table playing a card game with a few of his teammates. Jonah looked at his watch and saw it was 12:50 a.m. "Hey, you must've had fun since you're getting home after midnight. How did it go?" Jonah asked curiously.

"It went really good. What are y'all playing?"

Jonah shuffled the deck. "Texas Holdem, okay, give me some specifics. I need details. What did you two talk about? Did you flirt with her?"

"Who did he go out with?" one guy asked Jonah curiously.

"Kate, you know Christi's best friend?"

"Hey, wait for me. I want to play. Let me get a beer first," he said, as he walked to the kitchen.

Christi was sitting at the bar, looking through a cook book. JD fell asleep waiting up for him to come home. "Hey, how did the date with Kate go?"

He smiled, as he twisted the top off his beer. "It went good, where's the little man?"

"Oh, he passed out hours ago. So, what did you two do?"

"We went to dinner and a movie, and then we went dancing."

She was stunned. "You went dancing?"

He laughed. "Yeah, it was what she wanted to do."

"Are you going to see her again?" she asked curiously, studying his body language and facial expressions.

He smiled. "Yeah I'd like to."

"Jack, are you coming or not?" Jonah shouted. He walked back in the den and sat next to him. "So, what did you two talk about?" he asked, as he dealt the cards.

"We just talked about the basic things most people talk about on a first date. I didn't propose to her." he said sarcastically, as they laughed.

"I never said propose to her," Jonah said as Jack and the guys' laughed. "Are you going to see her again?"

He smiled as he thought of her. "It's possible."

"Did you at least kiss her?" Jonah asked curiously.

He shook his head. "No I didn't kiss her," as he looked at his hand of cards.

"So, you struck out?" Jonah asked, as they laughed.

"I don't look at it that way." He and the guys continued to talk about the date and their theories about women.

Meanwhile, Christi walked up stairs and called Kate. "Hello?"

"Hey, so how did the date go? What did you think of him?"

She smiled as she thought about the evening. "It went really good. He's really sweet, very attractive, and he's funny. He took me to this amazing restaurant, and we had a great dinner. Then we went to a movie, and I actually talked him into going dancing. We had fun."

"Wow, it's kind of hard to picture him dancing. Do you want to see him again?"

"Yeah, I do."

"What did you two talk about?"

"Oh, we talked about college, our families, our careers, our likes and dislikes. We mainly laughed the whole time. He told me that I was a very beautiful woman in Arabic."

Christi heard the excitement and the happiness in her voice. "Kate it sounds like you really like him. I just hope you're won't be afraid to allow yourself to feel something for him and get close to him. Did he try to kiss you?"

"No, he was a gentleman. He walked me to my door and was very respectful. Did I tell you he sent me a dozen pink roses to the hospital with a cute little note yesterday?"

Christi smiled. "No! Awe, how cute, those are your favorite. I've never seen that side of him."

Kate looked at the two arrangements of roses on her bar and smiled. "And then tonight, he brought me another bouquet of pink roses."

"You should've seen the big smile he had on his face when he came here." They talked more about her and Jack.

The next afternoon, she drove out to her parents' house in Dallas. Her parents' lived in a beautiful two story with a wraparound porch. Her father lived dually in both Dallas and in Washington D.C. It was stressful on her parents to live apart, but with his nearly thirty year career in the Army, Carole was used to having her life, dealing with the demands of his life, and somehow carving out *their* life together, but they were madly in love with each other.

She parked in the driveway and walked in. Holly ran to greet her, as she took off her sunglasses.

"Momma?" she called. She laid her purse and sunglasses on the table in the entryway. Mom was in the kitchen, sitting at the bar grading term papers, still wearing her professional clothes. She walked into the kitchen, and saw her wearing her reading glasses and grading a stack of papers. "Hey momma, what are you doing?"

Mom looked up and smiled at her. "Hey honey, I'm just grading papers. You look nice."

They hugged. "Thanks. What are you grading?" as she sat down at the bar.

"Mid-terms, I'm almost done here, and then would you like to go out for supper?" she asked as she took a drink of her water.

"Sure, I'm starving." she said, while pouring a glass of sweet tea.

"So, what's going on with you? You look really happy." Mom noticed.

She instantly thought of Jack and couldn't help but smile. "I went on an incredible date last night."

Mom looked up at her in surprise and smiled. "Really, that's great! Tell me about him."

"His name is Jack and he is a master sergeant in the Army."

"What is his MOS[5]?"

She smiled as she thought of him. "He's a Green Beret, but please don't tell Daddy. You know how he would be."

---

[5] Military Occupational Specialty, i.e. your job.

"Yes, I do. I won't tell him," she smiled at Kate. "Wow, do you like him?" Kate couldn't hide her attraction to him. "Is he good looking, is he nice?" Mom asked, trying to get her to talk about him.

"Yes, he is very good looking and very nice. He is really funny and so easy to talk to. He has this incredibly sexy voice. You know how first dates are usually awkward and just basic conversations?"

Mom smiled and nodding at her as she listened. "It wasn't like that with him. We laughed and we flirted. We even went dancing. He asked if he could see me again," Kate said, breathlessly.

She was excited for her. "How did you meet him?"

"He's Jonah's brother. They introduced us about a week ago, we had supper at their house." she said smiling. Mom stared at her and smiled. "What? Why are you looking at me like that?"

"I haven't seen you smile like this in a long time," she replied.

"I'm not smiling," Kate denied.

Mom laughed at her. "Yes you are. Go look in the mirror." Kate covered her mouth to hide her smile. "I've never seen that smile," she said.

She playfully rolled her eyes. "You act as if I haven't ever smiled."

"You've never smiled like this, not even when you were with Kyle. When I met your father, I was immediately head over heels, and I smiled like that too."

She shook her head. "So, what does he look like? How old is he?" Mom asked curiously.

The smile on Kate's face reappeared. "He's twenty-seven, tall, and tanned. He's muscular and fit. He has blondish-brown hair and green eyes, great teeth, and a sexy smile. His voice gives me the chills and butterflies in my stomach."

Mom smiled at her and said, "He sounds very… yummy."

She laughed out of embarrassment. "I can't believe you, of all people just said that!"

They laughed. The door unlocked and slammed shut. Lauren walked into the kitchen, and was happy to see Kate sitting there. "Hey sis…" Kate said to her.

"Hey, what have you been up to?" Lauren asked her as she hugged her.

"Have you told your sister your news?" Mom asked excitedly. Kate gave her a look to not talk about it.

"Your news, what's going on?" Lauren asked curiously.

"It's nothing." Kate proclaimed. She downplayed the date with Jack, but she knew her sister and mother were going to make a bigger deal out of it than it was.

"She met a guy and went out on a date last night," Mom announced excitedly.

Lauren smiled at her. "God does work in miraculous ways. It's about time," she teased.

"Thanks Lauren," she said sarcastically, as the smile reappeared on her face.

"Have you ever seen her smile like that, Lauren?"

"No I haven't. Ooh, that's the kind of smile you get after having some really great…" Lauren's voice trailed off.

Mom and Kate looked at her curiously. "Lauren, how would you know?" Mom asked.

"I'm not in-experienced like some people in here." Lauren said, referring to Kate.

"There is nothing wrong with her decision." At fourteen, Kate made a vow to God and to her parents that she would remain a virgin until she was a married woman. Her parents were thrilled and bought her a purity ring; a ring she wore every day on her left hand. When she married a good Christian man, her wedding band would replace the purity ring.

"I'm very proud that one of my daughters' is still a virgin. Sex just complicates things." Mom defended.

"It's a personal choice, the right choice for me," Kate said.

"How could you be engaged and still be a virgin? That's what I don't understand," Lauren asked in disbelief.

"If the man you love truly loves you, he will respect you by waiting for marriage." Mom said.

"What year are you living in? 1776? If a guy says he understands and agrees to wait, he's cheating on you."

"Not all men are cheaters." Mom informed.

"If you don't respect yourself, how can you expect a man to?" Kate asked.

"All I'm saying is maybe that's why Kyle cheated on you. Maybe he just got tired of waiting." Kate rolled her eyes. "…I'm not excusing him from it at all, but in this day and age, how can you expect a man to be celibate?"

"If Kyle really loved me and we were meant to be, he would've been able to, but clearly he wasn't the man for me. And I'm glad I found out what kind of man he really was before I married him."

"Well, Kate I'm proud of you, honey. I know with the pressure these days, it must be hard, but I'm glad that you have kept your vow to us and to God," Mom said.

"Momma, it's healthy to be curious and explore. This is 2002, not 1802. If you're over eighteen and still a virgin, you're considered a freak," Lauren said.

"So, I'm a freak?" Kate asked defensively.

Lauren laughed. "No, sis, you're not a freak, but you just aren't normal."

"Let's change the subject," Kate said sarcastically in an annoyed tone.

"So, this guy you went out with last night, does he know you're still a virgin?" Lauren asked.

"NO! We didn't talk about things that personal."

Lauren laughed. "Maybe you should tell him. That should speed things up a bit."

"If things between us get serious, then I will tell him when I'm ready to tell him."

"What does he look like? What does he do?"

Kate smiled, as she thought about him. "He's tall, muscular, in shape. He has blondish-brown hair and green eyes. He has a great smile. He's nice and funny. He's in the Army."

"He sounds very sexy. What's his rank? How old is he?"

"He's twenty-seven and he's a Master Sergeant."

"What does he do in the Army?"

"He's Special Forces," she explained briefly. She smiled, as she thought of him. "But, yes, he is very handsome."

"Don't tell Daddy you're dating an SF soldier. He'll start obsessing over it."

"Oh trust me, I won't." After supper and talking with her sister and mom, she got her purse, then kissed and hugged her mom bye. She walked out to her car and drove back to her apartment.

Jack and Kate thought of each other quite often, even though they tried not to. While out running errands on Tuesday, she found herself wondering what he was doing and if he was thinking of her. As she was on her way home from the grocery store, her cell phone rang. It was him. "Hello?" she answered happily.

"Hey gorgeous, what are you doing?"

She smiled, his voice made her tingle all over. "I'm running errands, what are you doing?"

"I was just wondering if you had any plans today." He was sitting on the couch in his parents' den.

"No, I don't have any plans. What did you have in mind?"

"I'm going out to a friend's ranch to shoot my rifle, and I was hoping that you would come with me."

She smiled. "Yes, I'd like to, what time do you want to go?"

"I can pick you up in thirty minutes."

"Okay, I'll be home in ten minutes," she replied, looking at the time.

"I'll head that way in ten minutes, okay?"

"See you then." She thought about what she could wear in her closet, as she drove home. She had already fixed her hair and done her makeup since she had started errands early. So she just had to find something that was appropriate to go shooting in.

Hurrying into the apartment, Morgan noticed she was rushing. "What's going on with you?"

"I have a date with Jack."

"Where are y'all going?"

"We're going shooting." She picked a pair of cut off, jean shorts, with a brown belt and buckle. She wore a navy blue and silver *Dallas Cowboys T-shirt* and her favorite pair of brown cowboy boots. She sprayed perfume on her neck, wrists and on the front of the shirt.

"He's really hot. He seems to like you."

She smiled as she put red lipstick on her lips. "So do I look okay?"

"Yes you look amazing!"

She heard the buzzer and briskly walked to buzz him in. In a couple minutes, he rang the doorbell. She opened it and smiled at him. He smiled at her. He admired her tanned legs and her cowboy boots. "Hi, you look amazing." He really liked her. She was even more gorgeous than the last time he saw her.

"Thank you."

"Are you ready?"

"Yeah, I'm ready."

"Hey…" Morgan said to him.

"Hey Morgan, how are you?"

"I'm good. Thanks. Well y'all have fun."

"See ya later, Morgan." she said. They walked down to his truck and stood next to the passenger side. She looked at him and was excited to see his rifle. "Where is it?" she asked.

"I brought my VFC SCAR sniper rifle, my M9 Berretta, and my Glock 9mm pistol. And, I brought your favorite 4590 Winchester Center-Fire."

She smiled excitedly. "Can I see them?" He smiled as he opened the rear passenger door to the back seat. She saw three black cases. He opened the case for the VFC FN SCAR. She smiled. "Oh wow, its beautiful." she said enthusiastically. She touched the barrel of the rifle.

"It's so much fun to shoot." He could see the genuine love she had for rifles. He liked that she was a country girl and wasn't afraid of guns.

"And this is what you use in combat?"

He smiled, "Yeah,"

"I'd hate to be the terrorist shot with this." she said in her adorable Texan accent. He laughed. He liked that she could make him laugh.

"Yeah, he definitely wouldn't be having a good day," He opened and closed the passenger door for her.

"So, where are we going?"

"An old Army buddy of my dad's has a ranch in Blue Ridge."

"Are we shooting paper targets or coffee cans, or what?"

He smiled at her. "No, we have actual human-shaped ballistics gel bodies all set up. It's like shooting an actual human being, with all the effects, except it's not a human," he said with a laugh.

She laughed. "I bet I'm a better shot than you," she challenged him.

He looked over at her, smiling at him. "Okay, you're on."

"What's the wager?" she asked, as he drove out of the city.

He smiled at her. "If I win, I get to kiss you."

She laughed. The thought of kissing him made her nervous and excited at the same time. "And what happens when you lose?"

He laughed. "If I lose, I'll watch any chick flick you want with you."

She smiled at him. "Okay, you're on." They shook hands.

An hour later, they arrived at a beautiful three hundred acre ranch in Blue Ridge, Texas. The driveway was long with lush green pastures on each side with white fences. The home was big and very rustic. There were two flagpoles in the center of the circle driveway with the American flag and the Army flag flying high. He parked in the driveway and they both stepped out.

"Jack!" Lloyd, the ranch owner, yelled excitedly as he and his two sons' walked out on the porch.

"Hey Lloyd, how are you doing?" he asked. They shook hands and hugged.

"I'm great. It's good to see you. Welcome back," Lloyd said.

"Thanks." He shook hands with his sons, Ryan and Jake. He turned to introduce her, but he didn't know what to introduce her as. He didn't know how she would feel if he introduced her as his friend or as his girlfriend, so he just went with his gut instinct. "This is Katherine Johnson, my girlfriend." She smiled at him. "Kate, this is Lloyd Jefferson, an old friend of my father's, and his sons' Ryan and Jake," he said.

"I don't know about *old*, but friend is true enough. How are you, Katherine?" he asked her as he shook her hand.

"I'm fine, but please call me Kate. It's nice to meet you."

He looked at her and then to Jack. "Jack, your woman picking skills have mightily improved. She's absolutely beautiful, you lucky son of a gun," he said slugging him in the arm. Jack became embarrassed, as did she.

"Thank you," she said, blushing. Lloyd could see that they really liked each other.

She and Jack looked at each other. "Yeah, I agree. She is very beautiful," he said.

"Kate, he's a handful I'm just letting you know. I've known him since he was in diapers and boy was he a hellion."

She smiled. She looked up at Jack. He looked completely embarrassed. "Really, Lloyd?" he asked.

"You're not going to find a better man than Jack here. He's a good man. How'd you two meet?"

She smiled. "My best friend is married to Jonah."

"Oh, are you from here?"

"Why are you interrogating her, Lloyd?" he asked, as she laughed.

"I'm just trying to get to know her, is that a crime? She's a very beautiful woman. You should reconsider not getting married before someone else takes her. Besides you need a good woman."

She laughed out of shock. Jack was very embarrassed. He saw she was too. "Okay, Lloyd, we're going to go shoot. We'll be in a little while." he said. He opened the back door to his truck to get the case of the SCAR rifle. He had the M9 Berretta and the Glock 9mm pistols in holsters strapped to his upper thighs as he carried the 4590 rifle and the SCAR.

They walked hand in hand up the gravel driveway to the stables. "I'm sorry if you're embarrassed. He takes pride in embarrassing me."

She laughed. "Oh I'm fine. All the men in my family are the same way. They would embarrass me and interrogate you. My sister and I are the only girls, so imagine how protective they are, but I've never had any of my cousins' beat up any of my boyfriends."

He laughed. "Oh, I see you got jokes?"

"Yeah, just a few," she teased. They walked into the stables. She saw a beautiful black quarter horse and patted it. She had a gentle smile on her face.

He saw her love for horses. "You love horses, huh?" he asked.

She smiled up at the horse and then at him, "Of course, I love horses. I'm a country girl." She lifted the heavy saddle onto the horse and buckled the cinch belt. "My grandparents have a horse ranch just outside of Paris, Texas. As a kid, every summer I'd go there to ride my horses. I still go up there to ride when I have time."

"How many horses do you have?"

"I have three."

They smiled at each other. They got the horses saddled up and rode out on the hillside of the Jefferson's property. "This is such a beautiful ranch." she said admiring the land.

"My dad, Jonah, and I come here to shoot with Lloyd and his sons. We divide into teams, and usually the loser has to buy the winners dinner at *Texas Roadhouse.* The location was originally *Twin Peaks,* but my mom and Mrs. Jefferson found out, so we had to change that."

She smiled at him, as her horse trotted alongside his. The sunlight was gleaming through the trees, as the cool crisp wind swept through her hair. He looked at her admiringly. She was noticeably happy. He watched her hair flutter in the breeze. He had never seen anyone so passionate about something he liked too.

She noticed he was looking at her. "What? Is there something on me?" she asked, thinking a bug was on her.

"No, you're just really beautiful." They smiled at each other.

"Thank you."

"You're welcome."

"I owe you an apology,"

He looked at her strangely. "You do, for what?"

"The other night at Jonah and Christi's; it was incredibly rude and insensitive of me to ask you about your scar, so I apologize."

He smiled at her, "I wasn't angry or annoyed by you asking me about my injuries. I realize that people are curious as to what goes on out there, but I just prefer not to talk about it. If I talk about it, it makes me sound like I'm bragging and I'm not like that. And it's also one of those things, civilians will never understand unless they've been out there."

"I'm sorry you were injured, Jack."

He smiled at her, "They weren't life threatening, all were superficial,"

"So, you were wounded elsewhere?"

"Yes, I received shrapnel to my lower leg and my abdomen,"

"Well I'm happy you came back safe,"

"Thanks," The horses trotted to a hilltop that overlooked a lush green pasture nearly covered in wild flowers, mainly sunflowers, blue bonnets, and buttercups. "Now, are you ready to get your butt kicked?" he asked.

"The question is are you?" she teased as they laughed with each other. They dismounted and tied the horses up to a tree branch. They walked slowly and carefully down the hill. He held her hand down the hill while carrying the cases to the SCAR and the rifle, and Winchester rifle.

She noticed the bracelet on his wrist. "That's a nice bracelet you got there. Did you make it yourself?" she teased.

He smiled at her. "No, this was made by a little girl named Adra while I was in Afghanistan. She said it would protect me."

She smiled at him. "Looks like it did its job."

He smiled at her. He adjusted the sights of the SCAR and loaded the rifle. He was extremely disciplined with his weapons. He never left a weapon loaded with a round in the chamber, due to an accidental discharge. The targets were a good seven hundred yards away. "Okay, which way do you want to do this?"

She looked at him, "I'm a better shot on my stomach."

He smiled at her. "That is called the prone position."

"Just give me the rifle and hush, master sergeant," she teased. He gave her the rifle. She lied down on her stomach in the tall grass of the field, placed the butt of the rifle firmly into her shoulder. She looked through the scope and adjusted the sights. He stood beside her, admiring her tanned legs and rear. She found her target, looking through the scope. He smiled at her precision. She gently squeezed the trigger.

He looked through the binoculars. Seeing that she hit the target between the eyes, he was impressed. "Wow, that's a great shot!"

"I already know what movie I want to watch." She smiled as she stood up.

He laughed. "Yeah, we'll see won't we?" She handed him the rifle. He knelt and firmly held the rifle. Finding the target, he squeezed the trigger. She looked through the binoculars and saw that he hit the same target, an inch above her mark, in the forehead.

They smiled at each other. "What do you think of that?" he asked her jokingly.

"It's pretty good," she admitted. He handed her the rifle. She held the rifle tight into her shoulder. He stood firmly behind her ready to catch her, in case the kick of the rifle knocked her down. She placed the butt of the rifle into her shoulder. Smelling her perfume, he tried to keep his concentration. She smelled of honeysuckle and vanilla. He was very attracted to her, but he tried to ignore it. Squeezing the trigger, the bullet hit the gel body in the chest. He looked through the binoculars.

She smiled at him triumphantly as she handed him the rifle. He raised the rifle up and put the rifle into his shoulder. He looked through the scope, found the target, and squeezed the trigger. He shot the same gel body in the face. He lowered the rifle and smiled at her. She looked through the binoculars. "Show off," as he laughed.

They smiled at each other. "What are you thinking right now?" he asked.

She looked down at the targets and then back at him. "I'm thinking about how much fun I'm having kicking your butt." He smiled at her. "What are you thinking?" she asked.

"I'm thinking about that bet we made in the truck."

"Who's winning?"

"As of right now, we are tied."

She smiled. "Do you want me to win?"

He smiled at her. "No, then I won't get to kiss you," he teased her.

"Aw, you don't want to watch a chick flick with me?"

He smiled at her. He loved her personality and sense of humor, as well as her looks. "I'd rather kiss you."

"We'll just have to see who wins, won't we?"

"I guess so." They shot more, laughed, and joked together. They began to shoot the Berretta 9mm and then the Glock pistols. They were shooting paper targets outlining a man. Over the faces of the targets was Osama Bin Laden's face. He handed her the pistol. She held the gun firmly with both arms extended and her feet firmly planted on the ground. She squeezed the trigger five times. She hit Bin Laden's head and torso.

He smiled at her. "You're an excellent shot."

"Thank you."

An hour later, the sun was setting. The crickets and bull frogs created a melody to match that picturesque sky with strokes of purple and orange clouds across the blue. "Okay, so who's winning?" she asked with a smile.

"I am," he said.

She laughed. "No, you're dreaming!"

"Let's make this interesting, let's shoot the Winchester. We'll move two hundred yards away, but here's the rule, we have to shoot this next target in a major organ causing an instant kill. Whoever has the more fatal shot, wins," he proposed as she laughed and agreed.

She put the gun into her shoulder and found her target. She aimed for the heart and fired. They walked down to the target to see. He saw she hit directly under the breastbone.

He smiled at her as she looked at the mark. "It's not an instant kill."

She smiled. "But eventually he would die, because the lungs would collapse and he'd bleed to death."

"But it has to be an instant kill, not leaving him fatally wounded."

She laughed. "Okay, let's see if you're any better, master sergeant." she teased.

"Are you ready to lose?" he teased as they walked back. Pulling the rifle into his shoulder, he aimed for the head and fired. The target's head exploded like a watermelon. He looked over at her. She was in shock staring at the target. He smiled as he walked towards her. "…I'd say that's an instant kill."

"Yeah, it was a good shot."

"So you know what that means, right?" he reminded her.

They stood face to face, as she smiled up at him. "I lost?" she said.

"Yes and I get to kiss you, but if you don't want me to, I won't."

"I'll honor the bet. After all, we did shake on it," she said, with a smile.

The stars were visible against a periwinkle blue sky and orange sunset. The wind blew through her hair, as lightening bugs blinked around them. He touched her face and gently kissed her lips. At that moment, a flame ignited between them. She wrapped her arms around his neck, as his were wrapped around her waist. They were holding onto each other and kissing in the middle of the field, as her hair fluttered in the summer breeze.

Lloyd and his two sons drove up, with the four wheelers on the ridge, above the field. They saw them kissing.

"Jack!" he yelled, down at them. Jack waved him off, as he continued to kiss her. Lloyd and the boys laughed and whistled.

The hot Texas sun had set. They rode the horses back to the stables and unsaddled them. As they unsaddled the horses, they both kept thinking about that long, incredible kiss in the pasture. She wanted to kiss him again. They walked back to his truck to put his rifles up. He looked at her as he closed the door to his truck. She smiled at him. "Your eyes sure do put those Texas stars to shame," he said.

She smiled. "Are you always this quixotic with all the women you date?"

Moving in closer, he smiled down at her as they stood face to face. The moonlight reflected off her shiny, soft hair. Her eyes sparkled. "Only with you…" She kissed his lips. They kissed for several minutes up against his truck.

He held her hand and they walked to the ranch house to visit with Lloyd and his family. "Y'all had fun didn't you?" Lloyd asked, as Jack smiled at him.

"Yes we did."

"Yeah, it's written all over your faces, especially yours Jack. You got red lipstick on." Jack quickly wiped his mouth, but Lloyd was just giving him a hard time. Lloyd looked to Marie. "We saw them kissing in the field," he whispered, not too quietly.

"Aw, that's sweet. Why were you spying on them?"

"I wasn't spying, Marie, I was just…"

"You were spying…" she scolded him. Jack and Kate laughed. "So, how did you two meet?" she asked. She and Lloyd liked seeing Jack with Kate.

"Jonah and Christi introduced us."

"Kate, what do you do?" Lloyd asked.

"I'm a labor and delivery nurse at Medical City Hospital in Dallas."

He smiled. "Wow, she's beautiful and she has a good job. Jack, you've done well, son!"

Jack and Kate laughed embarrassingly. "Lloyd, stop embarrassing him." Marie scolded. "Where are you from?" she asked Kate.

"I'm from Dallas."

They talked a little. "Jack, I want to show you my newest rifle. Come on." They walked into the rifle room, as Kate and Marie walked into the kitchen. Lloyd took a new rifle down, and showed him. Jack held it and admired it.

"She sure is beautiful and very polite. What do you think of her?" Lloyd asked.

He smiled, as they looked at a rifle. "I think she is gorgeous, very intelligent, and funny. She is an excellent shot too, but if you keep embarrassing me old man, we're going to throw down." he teased, as Lloyd chuckled.

"And I'll knock you down in the dirt."

"Oh we'll see." he said as they laughed.

In the kitchen, Marie poured everyone another glass of tea. "So, what do you think of Jack?" she asked her.

Kate blushed, "I think he is extremely handsome, kind, and very real."

"He's a good boy. I've known him since he was in diapers. He's a sweetheart."

"Yeah he is."

"I remember how all the girls up here would follow him around." Marie said as she laughed. Kate smiled. "But he's never brought a woman he's dating around us."

"Yeah I can tell by the way Lloyd is acting."

"Oh that man. Sometimes, he makes me so mad that I could hit him in the head with my fryin' pan."

Kate laughed. "My momma has done that to my daddy a time or two." she teased.

"I'm sorry he keeps embarrassing you and Jack. We think of Jonah and Jack as our own sons. We watched them both grow up. I'll have to tell his momma how tickled pink I am to meet you."

They walked back into the den, as Jack and Lloyd were walking back from the rifle room. "Jack, I hope you take this beautiful woman out to meet your mother. Denise will absolutely love her. She's so polite," Marie said.

"Your father will be proud that you found a woman so beautiful," Lloyd said.

Jack and Kate looked away from each other. They visited for nearly an hour. Then Jack asked her, "Are you ready to go, Kate?"

She nodded as they stood up. "Kate, honey it was a pleasure to have met you. I hope ole Jack here brings you out again." Lloyd said. He and Marie shook her hand.

"Thank you. It was a pleasure to meet you both. Y'all have a very beautiful ranch," Kate replied.

"Thank you. Jack, you bring her back out here and y'all eat some of my famous black berry cobbler. It's better than your momma's. Kate, do you like cobbler?" Marie told him.

"Oh of course I do." she said.

"Marie, you know if my momma found out I've had some of your black berry cobbler instead of hers, she'll slap the taste out of my mouth! You know how competitive she is."

They all laughed. "Don't tell her," she said to him, as they laughed again.

"Jack, it's always good to see you. Welcome home. Tell your dad he owes me a steak dinner, and you bring this beautiful woman out here anytime."

Jack looked down at her and smiled. "I hope to."

She smiled up at him. "Well we'll see y'all later." he said. They walked out to his truck, hand in hand. He opened the passenger door for her. "Did you have a good time, considering Lloyd's embarrassing behavior?" he asked.

She smiled. "Yes, I did. Did you?"

He drove down the long driveway. "Yeah, it was really fun. I'm glad I won the bet."

"I'm glad you won too," she said, with a smile.

"Be honest, did you let me win?" he asked her.

She looked at him and smiled. "No, I'm very competitive, so I didn't let you, but I wanted you to."

He smiled, and he reached for her hand and held it in his. Arriving back in Dallas, the skyline was lit up and traffic was smooth. They arrived at her apartment building. He walked her up to her door.

She turned towards him. "Thank you for taking me. I had a great time."

They lingered outside her door. "I did too." He touched her hand and looked into her eyes. "I really want to kiss you again."

She smiled up to him. He leaned in and kissed her. They held each other tightly, while kissing outside her front door for several minutes. Feeling she wanted more from him, she made herself break away from him. "Good night," she said.

They were looking into each other's eyes. "Good night. I'll call you tomorrow." He walked down to his truck, with a huge smile on his face. She walked inside and let out a breath of excitement and happiness. She really liked him, but kept telling herself not to get too close or to let things move too fast.

Morgan was sitting on the sofa. She saw the smile on Kate's face. "You look like you had a good time."

"I had the best time with him. Morgan, I've never felt so comfortable with someone. He's funny, he makes me laugh. He's handsome. I love his eyes and his smile. But mostly I love that I can just be me with him."

"Did you kiss him?"

"Yeah, I did."

"And how was it?"

Kate let out a sigh, "Oh it was beyond incredible, like fireworks were setting off. I had to break away from him because I wanted to keep kissing him." They continued to talk.

He reached his truck and could still smell her perfume lingering inside. Driving back over to his parents, he thought about how beautiful she was, and he was impressed with the how she handled the rifles and pistols. He had enjoyed being with her and kissing her. He parked in his parents' driveway and walked up the walkway. He opened the door. Dad was still up watching *ESPN*. Mom was on the phone with his grandmother. Meagan had a date.

Hearing the door close, Dad turned the volume on the TV down. "Hey, how was Lloyd?" he asked.

Jack looked at him in surprise. "How'd you know I was at Lloyd's?" he asked as he sat on the sofa as he and Dad watched *ESPN* together.

"He just called. He told me that you brought this unbelievably beautiful and polite woman named Kate, out there with you."

Jack smiled. "I'm going to kick that old man's butt."

Dad laughed. "He also said that he saw you two kissing in the field. So, naturally I'm very curious to hear about her."

Jack smiled. "Her name is Kate. Yes, she is unbelievably gorgeous. She has a beautiful smile, an amazing, athletic body. She has an incredible personality. She is a Christian, a country girl, and an Army brat."

"Are you two going out again?" Jack smiled and nodded. "I sense a change in you that I've never seen before. Could it be this woman?"

"Maybe, I mean, when I first saw her, I was instantly attracted to her and the more I talk to her and get to know her, the more time I want to spend with her. And the more time I spend with her, I feel more attracted to her."

"What's different about this woman than the previous ones?"

Jack thought about the question. He had asked himself several times, *what is different about Kate than the other women I've dated?* He looked at Dad, who was patiently waiting for an answer. "I can't explain it. This may sound funny, especially coming from me, but it's like God took everything I've ever wanted in a woman, her looks, personality, intelligence, low maintenance, country girl attitude and tomboyish ways and put it all into one woman. She fits every level of what I want in a woman. Dad, I've never met a woman who not only likes to shoot rifles, but she actually knows things about them. She loves to ride horses, likes to hunt, fish, and camp. She loves football and boxing for crying out loud. I'm in awe of her! She makes me laugh; I think about her all the time, and she makes me feel different."

Dad saw the change in Jack. "Who are you? And where is my son?"

Jack laughed. "I don't know. What I'm feeling, saying, and even what I'm thinking is starting to freak me out too, but I can't stop thinking about her, talking to her, or wanting to see her again, even if I wanted to. I think she's the one."

Dad was shocked. "You think she's the one?"

Jack smiled. "Yeah, when you know, you know."

4

THE AIR WAS hot and humid. The sun was high against a cloudless blue July fourth sky. The city was preparing for the huge fireworks display. Flags were everywhere.

Kate and Carole were in the kitchen baking desserts for their annual Fourth of July barbecue and pool party. Kate stirred the Texas style sweet tea as Mom pulled the hot peach cobbler from the oven. Peach cobbler was her father's favorite. He had arrived home from Washington D.C earlier in the week. He was outside marinating the brisket in his homemade, secret barbecue sauce.

"So, have you seen Jack again?" Mom asked.

She smiled as she thought of him while she stirred the batter for a chocolate cake. "Yeah, I saw him yesterday. He took me to a family friend's ranch to shoot his rifle."

Hearing the excitement in her voice, Mom smiled. "Did you have a good time?"

"I had an amazing time. We made this bet and who ever had the more fatal shot won."

"What was the bet you made?"

"If I won, he had to watch a chick flick with me, and if I lost, he got to kiss me."

Mom laughed. "Did you lose?"

"What do you think? He's a Green Beret, of course I lost." They laughed.

"So, how was it?"

She looked at her and smiled, "It was absolutely incredible. It was like setting off dozens of fireworks at once. You know how the first kiss is usually short and sweet? Not this one. It was a long first kiss, followed by even longer second and third. I didn't want it to end,"

Mom smiled. She enjoyed Kate talking about Jack. She saw Kate was happy and excited. "It sounds like you two are falling for each other."

"I'm trying to control how and what I feel for him."

"How's that working out for you?"

"Not well, I'll admit. When I think about him, I get little butterflies in my stomach, and when I hear his voice, I get goose bumps all over. I love the way he looks at me. He really makes me laugh and I catch myself always smiling. I'm surprised at how fast I began to like him. He is extremely good looking. He's funny; he's charming. His voice is so unbelievably sexy. He's a gentleman, but I still have my guard up."

"Honey, not every man is going to treat you like Kyle did." She saw that Kate was still recovering from heartbreak and humiliation and was trying not to get too close to Jack, in fear that he would do the same things to her if she let him in. Kate wasn't about to let her guard down a second time.

"Momma, Kyle hurt me to my soul. I have never felt so low, pathetic, and humiliated in my life and I swore to myself that I would never let another man get that close to me or that I would be that heartbroken again."

"I know he hurt you, baby, but you can't go through life thinking everyone is going to hurt you the first chance they get. From what I've heard about Jack, he sounds like a great man. He sounds like a dream that any mother would want their daughter to date. Don't be afraid to let him in if he's the one for you. I'd hate for you to miss out on real love."

"Yeah, you're right. I shouldn't let what Kyle did to me affect me and how I am with Jack."

At that moment, her cell phone rang. It was Jack. The smile instantly appeared on her face. "It's him isn't it?" Mom asked, seeing the look on her face.

She nodded. She answered the call excitedly, but walked into her parents' office to talk to him privately.

He smiled, hearing her adorable accent. "Hi beautiful, what are you doing?" he asked.

His voice gave her goose-bumps and instantly made her smile. "Hi, I'm just baking with my mom. We're having our annual Fourth of July barbecue this evening. You're more than welcome to come if you'd like."

He laughed. "I would love to, but I am on brisket duty for my parents' barbecue. I haven't seen most of my relatives in a long time."

"So, you're the brisket master?"

He laughed. "Yeah, I cook some really great ribs. I make my own sauce. It's classified above top secret."

"My dad makes his own sauce too, and he says the exact same thing. He says I'll get the recipe in his will."

"I haven't been able to stop thinking about you since I kissed you, so I'm calling to see if I can see you later after our families' barbecues."

She smiled, "I'd love to see you."

"Good, I want to take you to a great place to see the fireworks."

She was excited to see him again. The butterflies in her stomach were flying around and her heart was pounding excitedly. "I can't wait."

They agreed to meet at a park near her parents' house where she would park her car and ride with him. "I'll see you there, beautiful."

She liked that he called her beautiful. Kyle never did that for her. "Okay, bye."

She walked back into the kitchen. Mom saw that she was smiling. "What did he say? You should've seen the smile you had on your face."

"Every time he calls or sees me, he tells me I'm beautiful."

Mom smiled. "I really like this guy already."

"I'm going to watch fireworks with him later." Mom smiled at Kate. She was excited to see him again.

"Yeah, like you'll be watching the fireworks." she said sarcastically.

"We'll pay attention to some." Kate said with a laugh. "He's a really good kisser."

Dad walked in from the backyard. He noticed how happy Kate looked. "How are things with you, sweet pea?"

She smiled as she thought of Jack. "Everything is really good."

"You look really happy."

"I am really happy, Daddy,"

Shortly after talking with Jack, her aunt and uncle, grandparents, cousins, and sister finally arrived to the house. They laughed, talked and shared funny stories over her dad's famous brisket, and her mom's potato salad and delicious peach cobbler.

Nearing seven o'clock, the sun was starting to set. She was sitting with her grandparents, cousins and father. She glanced down at her watch, remembering she had to meet him. "Oh, I have to go. I have a date with Jack," she told Lauren.

"Who's Jack?" Daddy asked. Her two grandfathers and uncle and cousins were very curious to know.

She smiled at him and then at her mother. "He's a guy I've been seeing."

"What's his last name? What does he do? How old is he?"

She blushed feeling all of the male eyes on her waiting on her answers. She kissed her daddy goodbye on the cheek. "I'll see you later, Daddy."

"I'll fill your father in," Mom said, as she gave her a kiss on the cheek and a hug.

"Okay, bye Momma."

"Fill me in on what? Hey, wait who's Jack?" She kissed her grandparents goodbye. She exited out the pool fence door to her car. He sat speechless at the table. "Who's Jack, Carole?" he asked again.

Carole laughed at how curious he was. "She's dating someone new, Matt. Can you just relax?"

"And I take it his name is Jack? Have you met him?" he asked her, as she sipped her iced tea.

"No, but she says that he makes her feel things she's never felt, especially with Kyle."

"I think it's time we do a little recon and find out who this boy is," Grandpa said.

"I agree. We'll scare him to death," Corey, Kate's oldest cousin said. He, Kate, and Lauren were very close.

"Does she even know what this boy does for a living? I don't want any bum taking my daughter out on a date," Matt said.

Carole smiled, as she watched him drink his glass of tea. "As a matter of fact, he's in the Army."

He and her grandfathers were surprised. "Interesting, what's his MOS? Does she know?"

Carole and her mother laughed at how protective he was. "Matt, you are not going to start investigating him. We are going to just sit back and be supportive. She's happy and I hope this guy is the one for her."

"I'm not all that comfortable with her dating a soldier."

"Why aren't you?"

"Because…I know what most young men want from her, especially soldiers, and he ain't getting it from my daughter."

"What if he's a respectful, Christian man?"

"I'm not debating with you anymore, Carole."

She laughed. "Every man in this family is or was in the military. Why isn't it okay for her to date and possibly marry one?"

His eyes enlarged. "Wow, they're thinking about getting married? How long have they been seeing each other?" he asked.

"No, Matt, they are just dating." She and his mother laughed. "You need to see that your little girl is now a grown woman. Let's just see where this goes. My gut says that this is serious."

"Do we know anything more about him?" he asked concerned.

"Matt, she'll tell us more about him when they get more serious. I know that Jonah and Christi introduced them. Can you just relax?"

Matt looked to his two nephews. "Corey, you and Justin find out who this guy is and bring him to the house for a sit down." he ordered.

"You want us to follow her?"

"Yeah, go follow her."

"Matthew James, you know what'll happen when she finds out you're sending Corey and Justin to spy on her." his mother warned.

"That's why we ain't going to get caught." Justin said.

"I just want to scare him with my Carbine rifle and let him know I'll use it if he tries anything," he joked.

"A career soldier won't be scared of your rifle. He probably has his own," she chuckled. He looked at her strangely and continued to eat his food.

Justin and Corey hurried to the truck and followed her. She met Jack at the park. She wore a pair of cut off jean shorts, her brown cowboy boots, and a patriotic tank top. Her hair was curled and flowing, and her makeup was flawless. He smiled at her.

"Wow, you look amazing." he said.

"Thank you. So do you." He wore a pair of shorts with Nike tennis shoes and a T-shirt. His smile excited her. They hugged and kissed. It was dusk, the crickets were chirping and the lightening bugs were blinking.

Corey and Justin watched from afar. "You think she's serious with him?" Justin asked, watching Corey look through the binoculars.

"They look like they're getting serious." They watched her and Jack walk to his truck. They saw Jack open the passenger side door for her.

"At least he opened the door for her." Justin said.

Jack walked around the hood of the truck and saw Corey's truck. He could see them watching them with binoculars. He smiled and waved. "How'd he know we were here?" Corey asked.

She saw him wave. "Who are you waving at?"

"Oh there are these two guys watching us with binoculars."

"What kind of truck is it?"

He looked in his side mirror. "It's a red Chevy 4x4." She rolled her eyes and opened the door to his truck. When Corey and Justin saw her, they immediately threw the binoculars down and quickly tried to start the truck.

"Oh she's gonna kill us when she catches us. Start the truck. GO! GO!" Justin said.

"I'm tryin', it won't turn over." Corey said, trying to turn the key over.

She briskly walked up to them. Jack followed her. "What are you two doing here?" she asked.

"We're just enjoying a summer night in the park." Justin said. "It's a total coincidence that you're here."

She was annoyed and angry. "Uh huh, who sent you, Daddy or Grandpa?"

"No one sent us. We just wanted to come find out for ourselves who you're dating." Corey said.

He smiled. "Friends of yours?" he asked.

"No, they're my nosy cousins, Corey and Justin."

"Who are you?" Justin asked.

"This is Jack, my boyfriend." Justin shook Jack's hand, but Corey didn't. He spit close to Jack's shoe. "Okay, now that you two have seen him and potentially ruined the evening, will you please leave?"

Jack found it amusing. "Good to meet you guys." he said.

She turned to face him, "I'm so sorry if you're freaked out right now, but I know my Daddy sent them to spy on me."

He laughed, "It doesn't bother me. I've done it to my sister a thousand times, but I just never got caught." She smiled. "You look adorable when you're mad."

Justin laughed, "Hopefully you're never on the receivin' end of her temper,"

"Go home!" she scolded. Corey finally got the truck started. As he pulled away, she kicked the bumper. She looked at him and noticed he was smiling and trying not to laugh. "So now what?" she asked.

"How about we pretend this didn't happen?"

She laughed. "I cannot believe they were spying on us." They drove into downtown Dallas. They stopped at the Cheesecake Factory and had a slice of their favorite cake. His favorite was double fudge chocolate cake and hers was red velvet. They sat outside underneath the black umbrellas, laughing and sharing each other's cake. She dared him to try hers.

They were joking, laughing and flirting with each other. As they were talking, a man approached them. "Kate?"

She looked up at him and was stunned to see him. He was Kyle's best friend. "Hi, James," she said hesitantly.

"I thought that was you. So, how have you been? Who is this, a new boyfriend?" he asked, looking at her and then at Jack.

"Yes, this is Jack Hamilton. Jack this is James Monroe."

They shook hands. "Is this another cousin?" Jack asked her.

"No, this is Kyle's best friend, my ex."

"What do you do?" James asked him.

"I'm in the Army," he said.

James was surprised. "I can't wait to tell Kyle that you're dating again. He's not going to be too happy to hear it, especially to hear you're dating a soldier." James said in a threatening tone.

Jack saw how uncomfortable Kate was and he became annoyed. "James, you need to move out," he said to him.

James looked at him and grinned. "Listen G.I Joe, Kate and I are old friends. I'm just trying to have a conversation with her, why don't you just relax and mind your own business?"

He stood up in his face. "I'll give you three seconds to walk away before l escort you and you won't like that. I'm not going to tell you again."

"James, please just leave," Kate pleaded.

He looked down at her. "Okay, Kate. I'll leave. I'll tell Kyle I saw you and your new man," he added as he walked away.

Jack watched him walk away. As he sat down, he noticed the look on her face. "I'm so sorry, Jack. I'm embarrassed that just happened."

He smiled at her. "You don't have any reason to apologize or be embarrassed. He was the one being ridiculous. Are you ready to get out of here?" he asked.

"Yeah, before anyone else interrupts our date." They drove out to Lloyd's ranch in Blue Ridge to watch fireworks. The stars were vividly bright in the velvet sky. The breeze was cool.

Lloyd stepped out on the porch. Many of his former Army buddies were there drinking beer and waiting to start the fireworks. Some were even drinking moonshine. Lloyd smiled at them holding hands. Jack carried a quilt. "Hey how are you two doing?" he asked.

"Hey, what's going on?" Jack asked.

"Oh, nothing much, Marie made homemade Butterfinger ice cream if y'all want some. Kate you sure look pretty," he added.

"Thank you, Lloyd." They walked out back and poured themselves a few drinks. They visited with a few people that knew Jack. Many of them knew his father. Lloyd and a few others loaded the fireworks down into the pasture with everyone sitting far enough away in lawn chairs and sitting on blankets. They had nearly a $1,000 worth of fireworks.

They sat on their quilt, near Marie, but far enough away to have privacy. He picked a pink buttercup flower. He smiled at her as he handed it to her. "Thank you," she put it behind her ear. "How does it look?" she joked.

He smiled. "Gorgeous." They smiled at each other as she held his hand. "I can't believe tonight is my last night here," he said.

She looked at him in surprise. "If tonight is your last night, why are you with me? You should be with your family."

He smiled at her, as they held hands. "I wanted to be with you."

She looked down at their hands. "What are we doing, Jack?"

He looked at her strangely. "We're waiting for the fireworks to start."

She smiled. "No, I know that, but what are *we* doing? Are we just friends, or are we casually dating or are we seriously dating?" He smiled. "I've been jerked around by plenty of men. For once, I want an upfront answer. No BS."

He smiled as he touched her shoulder and twisted a strand of her curled hair around his finger. "We're seriously dating. You're the woman I want. You're real, not afraid to get your hands dirty or sweat. You're independent. I love your country girl attitude. You're stunningly gorgeous, you're sweet, funny, a Christian, family oriented and I love that we have so much in common. When we're together, I like that I can be myself. I have so much fun with you. When we're apart, I can't stop thinking about you and I want to be with you as much as possible. Does that answer your question? That was a no BS answer."

She smiled up at him. "Yeah, thank you."

"How do you feel about me?" The lightening bugs were twinkling around them. She could smell the wild honeysuckle fragrance fill the summer air as she inhaled thinking of her reply.

She smiled at him. She was beginning to blush. "You're everything I've always wanted in a man. You're charming, sweet, and extremely good looking. I love your smile. I love that you're a strong Christian and that your faith means a lot to you. I love that you're family oriented. When I'm with you, I love that I can smile, laugh, feel things I've never felt with anyone else. I think about you all the time and I don't want you to leave tomorrow, but I know you have to."

"I don't want to leave tomorrow either."

"What are your terms in this relationship?"

He laughed. "My terms, uh, I don't know. I didn't know I had to have any."

"Why are you laughing?"

"You make this sound like a business transaction."

"I need to know what you expect from this relationship."

He smiled as he thought about how to answer her. "Okay, I expect you to be strong, unselfish, understanding, faithful and patient. I need you to understand how much my career means to me. I need you to be strong and handle all that comes with my career, the separations, the stress, demands, limitations as well as the rewards. I expect you to not ask me to choose between you and my career. I need you to understand why I do it, respect that I love it, and realize how hard I've worked to get to where I am. I'm hoping you can be faithful and patient, even if I'm gone for a year. Even though I may not be able to see you or talk to you whenever I want, I want you to know I'm always thinking about you. What are your terms?"

She smiled while holding his hand. "I need you to be understanding, patient, respectful, honest and faithful. I need you understand I do not trust easy. I need you to be patient with me while I learn how to trust you. I need you to respect that I will make you work for my trust and I will only give it to you once you've earned it and proved to me that you're not like most of the men I've dated, especially like the man I was engaged to. I'm not just going to hand my heart over to you. It may not be fair, but I need you to respect that. I will not be your consolation prize, so if there is some other girl back at Bragg, you are more attracted to, then please date her because I can't and won't get involved with someone who is just going to lie to me and break my heart like my ex did. I want to be truly loved, appreciated, respected and wanted. I'm tired of feeling empty and hurt. I want to feel safe."

He looked into her eyes. He saw the pain Kyle had caused. He held her hand in his. The warm summer breeze swept through her hair. He moved a strand off her face and tucked it behind her ear. "First of all, you are and always will be safe with me, Kate. I'll never hurt you and I will not let anything or anyone hurt you. Second, you could never be my consolation prize. You're my prize. And thirdly, I have no problem working to earn your trust and your heart. I work for what I earn. But I can promise you right now, that you can trust me. I'll be faithful and honest with you."

They smiled at each other. She laughed, "Your ex-girlfriend was clearly an idiot to let you go."

He smiled. "I have no idea what your ex was thinking when he let you go, but I'm happy he did. Now you'll know real happiness…this isn't going to be a cake walk, Kate. It's going to be very hard. We'll rarely get to see each other and we may not even get to talk to each other for long periods of time. At times we may get frustrated and lonely, are you sure you can handle it? …Because my ex couldn't? I want to be fair to you. I won't be able to be like most boyfriends. I won't be able to take you out every weekend. I may get to see you once every six months and maybe talk to you once a month."

She smiled at him and held his hand tightly. "Jack, I'm not her. I can survive and keep busy while you're gone. I want to be with you. I'd never ask you to choose between me and the Army. Remember, I'm an Army brat? I know the drill. I understand that our relationship will not be normal or ideal, but extraordinary and genuine. I promise you I'll be faithful and I'll be here waiting for you, but I need you to just promise me one thing."

He smiled at her. "I'll promise you anything."

She looked into his eyes. "Just promise me you'll come back."

"I promise." He kissed her lips. They were kissing on the quilt. The fireworks show was beginning. They kissed as red, white, and blue fireworks exploded over them against a velvet summer sky. The stars were twinkling brilliantly.

Marie, Lloyd, and the others saw them kissing. "Hey stop that kissing and watch the fireworks!" Lloyd playfully scolded. "Don't make me call your father, Jack." he teased. Marie swatted him with her flyswatter. "Owe…"

"Leave them alone," Marie scolded. Jack and Kate laughed. They held hands and watched the fireworks. They were both surprised and at times a little scared that they had such strong feelings for each other so fast. Knowing this was their last night together, they kissed like crazy.

The next day, he was at his parents' house packing his bag and saying goodbye to them. He came down the stairs with his bag over his shoulder. His parents, Jonah, and Meagan were sitting in the living room waiting on him. "Do you have everything?" Mom asked him, as her voice began to crack due to crying.

"Yeah, I do. Momma, please don't cry."

She wrapped her arms tightly around his neck. She wiped her eyes with a tissue. "I'm sorry, I can't help it. I just worry about you."

"Be safe out there, son. Keep your head down. Watch your six," Dad said. He and Jack shook hands and then hugged.

"Yes sir, I will."

"Take care of yourself, big brother. I'm going to miss you," Meagan said.

"I'll be alright. You stay out of trouble," he said to her, as he gave her a quick hug.

"I'm never in trouble."

"Right!" he said as they all laughed. "Jonah, I'll see you when I get back."

"Keep your head down, little bub," Jonah said to him. They hugged.

"Yeah, will you do me a favor? Will you watch over Kate for me?"

"Yeah, I will," he said.

"We love you, Jack." Mom said, as she hugged him again.

He kissed her cheek. "I love y'all too." He walked out to his truck. He saw JD sitting in the driver's seat.

"Hey, what are you doing?"

JD looked at him, "I don't want you to leave,"

He smiled and opened the door and picked him up. "I know you want me to stay and I wish I could, but I can't."

JD looked at him seriously. "Uncle Jack, do you kill people?"

He didn't know how to answer him. "There are a lot of bad guys out there and they like to hurt people like you, your mom, and your dad. It's my job to stop them,"

"So you're a superhero, like Batman and Superman?"

He laughed. "I don't think I'm as good as Batman or Superman."

"I'm going to miss you." JD hugged him tightly.

"I'm going to miss you too, bubba. Be good for your momma and daddy."

"Okay, I will."

"You promise?" he asked, tickling him. JD laughed and squealed real loud.

"Yeah, I promise."

"Okay, give me a hug." JD hugged him. They did their secret handshake. JD ran to the porch where the rest of the family stood. He got into his truck and waved goodbye. They all waved back. He drove away.

He drove over to Kate's apartment to say goodbye to her. They were standing outside beside his truck. He smiled at her as they looked in each other's eyes. Her hair danced in the wind. He moved a strand of her hair off her face. They both felt they were starting to fall for each other.

"You are so gorgeous."

She smiled up at him. Their fingers were inner-locked. "Here, I want you to have this…" she said, handing him a photograph of herself. He smiled down at the photograph. "…So you won't forget what I look like."

He smiled. "I could never forget what you look like. You're gorgeous, inside and out." He pulled her towards him and looked in her eyes. "Thank you, I'll look at it every chance I get."

She smiled up at him, with her arms around him. "Do you really have to go?"

He gently touched her face and brushed her hair out of her face. "Yes, I really do. I've never wanted to stay as much as I do now. I've always been ready to get back, but now that I'm with you…I want to stay."

"I'll be here for you when you get back…" She looked up at his eyes. They were mysterious, yet kind, and caring. "…promise me you'll come back?"

Looking down into her eyes, he saw a twinkle of gold in her amber colored eyes. "I promise." They kissed and hugged tightly. Smelling her perfume, he closed his eyes and breathed in her fragrance. Her hair had the familiar scent of honeysuckle and jasmine. That scent would get him through until he returned to her. He looked down at his watch. "I better get on the road." He smiled at her as he sat in his truck.

"Drive safe."

He held her hand and smiled up at her. "I'll call you when I get in." She leaned in and gently kissed him again before he drove away. He watched her in the side mirrors as the distance between them got greater and greater. She stood until she could no longer see his truck.

The next few weeks, they spent much of their free time talking on the phone with each other. They got to know each other really well. Now, August, Colonel Mitchell and his men received orders to deploy back to Afghanistan to hunt down key Al-Qaeda leaders. They deployed within nineteen hours of notification. He usually never called home to alert his family. He just turned his cell phone off. As he was about to shut off his phone, he looked at the entry of *Beautiful* and decided to call her.

She answered happily, "Hello, Master Sergeant…"

.He smiled, hearing her adorable accent. "Hi beautiful, what are you doing?"

"I'm just cleaning, it's my day off. What are you doing?"

"I'm just calling to let you know that my phone will be off for a while. I'm not sure how long, but I'll call you when I can, okay?"

"You're leaving?"

"Yeah…" The smile faded from her face. Suddenly she was nervous for him. She knew he was prohibited from telling her specifics, and at this point she didn't know if she wanted to know the details of this mission. She knew he was headed for danger and the possibility he wouldn't come back was high.

She had tears drizzling down her cheeks. "I'll be praying for you and thinking about you every day. Don't worry about me. I'll be strong for you."

He smiled. "I'll be thinking about you too and looking at your picture every minute I can."

"Well, look at it and think of me when you're safe. Not when bullets are flying all around you."

He laughed. He thought she was adorable. He loved her personality, her voice, the way she was so caring and sincere when she told him that she would think of him. "You take care of yourself, stay gorgeous and I'll come back soon."

She could hear the turbines of the aircraft behind him in the background. "Promise me you'll come back."

"I promise you, Kate."

She smiled. "I'll be here waiting for you." He was falling more and more for her. He loved the way he felt when he saw her, thought of her, and talked to her. He had never felt that way. He had never allowed a woman to get as close to him as Kate had. She had stolen his heart, the heart he thought he had protectively guarded, but the minute he spoke to her, she stole it. Now, he had someone he trusted waiting on him while he was at war and that meant a lot to him.

"I appreciate that, Kate. I really do." He looked back and saw his team waiting on the landing pad. "Okay, baby I need to go. I don't want you to worry about me. I'll be fine."

"It's hard for me not to worry about you. I know you're going somewhere dangerous. I care about you."

He smiled. "I care about you too." They said goodbye to each other. The Green Berets boarded the C-130. The aircraft rolled at an accelerating speed down the runway. He and his team talked about the mission. An hour into the flight, they were quiet. Many were sleeping, getting as much as they could before the mission. He held the picture of her in his hands.

He sat across from Tom. Tom noticed him looking at the picture. "Were you talking to your girlfriend?" he asked him.

He smiled. "Yeah,"

"What does she look like?" He handed the photograph to Tom. He smiled down at the photo. "Wow, she's gorgeous. Congrats. Does she know what you do?"

"Yeah, her dad was a Green Beret."

"Ah, so she comes from a military family? That's one check in the pro column. What does she do?"

"She's a nurse. She works in labor and delivery."

"She has a good job. Another check…" Tom said as he passed the picture to the rest of the team members who were awake. They all thought she was extremely attractive. "…I'm happy for you, man. I hope everything works out for y'all," he said encouraging.

"I have a good feeling it will, because this woman is amazing. She loves boxing, rifles, sports, camping, hunting, and fishing---she is just awesome."

"How did you two meet?"

"My brother is married to her best friend." They talked more throughout the long flight. Twenty hours later, they were in Afghanistan. They landed at the airfield in the Bagram Airbase and unloaded their gear and equipment from the aircraft.

On the Afghanistan and Pakistan border, four Navy SEALS launched a mission to kill the fundamentalist leader who called himself 'Commander Ishmael'. Instead of hunting, they were the hunted. They were ambushed. Taliban fighters recorded the firefight on video.

An enemy soldier said loudly, "If you don't fight, we don't kill you, Allah Akhbar!"

Three of the Navy SEALs were killed in action. The fighters took personal possessions off the bodies, like watches, wedding rings, and boots. Commander Ishmael's men scored a second victory when they managed to shoot down the helicopter heading to the SEALs location. All onboard were killed. When alerted of the helicopter crashing, the Marines and Special Forces soldiers watched the video. They were incensed and looking for retribution. Jack knew those three SEALs that were killed, as well as the many that were aboard the helicopter.

On a hot August afternoon, Kate was just arriving home from work. She saw Kyle standing by the door to her apartment building. He was holding a bouquet of yellow roses. He saw her and walked towards her. "Hey Kate, how have you been?"

She ignored him and walked past him to unlock the door to her building. "What, you aren't going to talk to me?" he asked pressing his body up against hers. He smelled her hair. "You smell great."

"Kyle, get off of me, now!"

"I bought you your favorite flowers in hopes that we can get talk and get back together. I miss you."

"No, we are done. I want you to leave."

"I need to talk to you. James said that he saw you and this Army guy together and that you two are dating."

She looked at him. "Not that it's any of your business who I'm dating, but yes, I'm dating a soldier. I have no interest whatsoever in talking to you or to getting back together. I do not want your flowers. And besides yellow roses aren't my favorite."

She tried to get by him. He grabbed her arm and squeezed tightly. "I've apologized for cheating on you. You know you still love me and miss me. I really miss you, and I want to get back together."

"No, I'm happy with someone else."

"What does this guy have that I don't?"

She pulled her arm out of his grasp. "He is nothing like you, so that's a start. He has a heart and he's kind. He makes me feel good about myself, and he wants me and only me."

"I'm sure he doesn't just want only you. I bet he knows plenty of hotter girls. It's not like you're the most beautiful woman he's ever met."

"He tells me I'm beautiful every day. Please leave me alone and never contact me again," she tried to walk by him again.

Filled with rage and jealousy, he grabbed her and shook her very hard. "I'm not going to let you go that easy, Kate!"

After a few bystanders saw him, he let her go and walked away. She hurried inside her building. She walked inside her apartment and quickly shut and locked her door. Morgan was at work. She looked at her arms in the bathroom mirror. His finger marks were visible. She wished she could tell Jack, but knew that would cause him to lose focus on his assignment. So she just ignored it and tried not to think about it. Hours later, Christi stopped by the apartment since Jonah was at practice.

She rang the doorbell. Kate answered. "Hey!" she said cheerfully. She immediately noticed Kate's mood.

"Hey," Kate said, as she tried to act like nothing was bothering her.

She saw the red finger marks, now turning blue and purple, on her arms from her sleeveless shirt. "Who did this to you, Kate?!"

"It's not a big deal, Chris."

"Yes, it is a big deal, Kate. Someone grabbed you. Tell me the truth."

She finally confessed what had happened. "When I got home from work today, Kyle was waiting for me outside my apartment building."

"What did he say?"

"He wanted to get back together, and when I refused, he grabbed my arms and shook me really hard. My neck is killing me,"

She was stunned. "Have you called the police?"

"No I don't want to. I just want to forget about it."

"Why not, he assaulted you!"

"You've never seen his temper, Chris."

"You could get a restraining order. Are you going to tell Jack?"

Kate looked at her seriously. "No, I don't even want Jonah to know. This has to be our secret."

"Kate, you need to let Jack know."

"No, it'll just make things worse. I'll file assault charges and let the police handle it if you promise you won't say anything to Jonah or Jack."

"I'll go with you if you need me to. I'm here for you."

They hugged. "Chris, promise you won't say anything to Jonah?"

She shook her head. "Kate, I can't keep something like this a secret."

"Chris, you have to promise me that you will not tell Jack or Jonah. Jack is on a mission right now and I don't want him to worry." she pleaded.

"Well Kate, he has a right to worry. You're psycho ex is hurting you."

"I'll take care of it. Just promise me you won't say anything."

Christi was torn. She was afraid for Kate's safety but also didn't want to cause any more drama in her life. "I promise I won't say anything," she said hesitantly.

"Thank you." They drove to local precinct of the *Dallas Police Department* to file a police report and a restraining order against Kyle. Two officers led her into an empty interview room and took her formal statement on the incident. She explained to them the history of her and Kyle's break-up. She told the officers about the excessive phone calls, threatening messages, and how she had to change her number. They took pictures of her injuries. After writing down her statement and filing the restraining order, they left the station.

Christi was conflicted and angry. While cooking, she began to aggressively pound the meat with the meat tenderizer. Jonah had come home from practice.

Walking into the kitchen, he saw she was bothered by something. He watched at how hard she pounded the meat with the tenderizer. "Babe, did you have a bad day? Is something wrong?" he asked her, as he got a bottle of water out of the refrigerator.

She tried to hide it. "No, I'm just thinking about something."

"You can tell me, if you need to talk."

She smiled at him. "Forget it. I'm fine. How was your practice?" pretending to shrug it off.

He sensed that she didn't want to talk about it. "It was good. What's for supper?"

She smiled at him. "I'm making your favorite: steak, baked potatoes and green beans."

"Great, I'm starving." She resumed aggressively pounding the meat.

As they were sitting at the table with JD, Jonah noticed that she hardly ate. He was concerned and wondered what could be upsetting her. After they were in bed, she tossed and turned about what to do. She wanted to believe Kate that Kyle would leave her alone, but knew if she didn't do anything, that something worse could happen. She looked at Jonah sleeping. She touched his arm. "Jonah, wake up."

He woke up and turned on the lamp. "What's wrong, are you feeling sick?"

"No, I need to tell you something."

"Okay, what's going on?"

"Kate is in trouble, and I don't know what to do."

"What do you mean she's in trouble?"

"Kyle went to her apartment. He got physical with her and left bruises on her arms. I promised her that I wouldn't tell you or Jack, but I'm worried. We went to the precinct to file charges and a restraining order on him."

He hugged her. "I'm sorry that you had to worry about this. I'll take care of it."

"You won't tell Jack will you?"

"Yeah, I have to tell him. He's my brother, and I told him that I'd look after her. I would expect him to tell me if something like this was going on with you."

"She doesn't want him to know; she's afraid this will distract him."

"I have to tell him, Christi. I don't keep things this serious secret from my brother."

The next day was Kate's twenty-second birthday. She was at work, working a twelve hour shift. She was monitoring a patient's contractions when Marci popped in. Her arms were sore, but she was able to hide the bruises.

"Kate you need to come to the front."

"Marci, I'm kind of busy."

"I'll take over for you, just go."

She walked to the nurse's station and saw a delivery man holding three dozen pink roses. "Are you Miss Katherine Johnson?"

"Yes, I am."

"These are for you, could you sign here?"

"They're all for me?" she asked signing the form.

"Yes ma'am. I took the order myself. This guy must really love you. Here's the card."

She opened the card and read:

"Happy Birthday, Beautiful I hope you have a great day. I wanted to deliver these in person, but I'll try to call you when I can. I wish I was able to take you out to celebrate, but I'm thinking about you, missing you, and I can't wait to see you again.

Love, Jack"

She smiled. At that moment she couldn't help but wonder where he was, but she was happy he was still able to send her flowers and a sweet card on her birthday.

Jonah drove to Kyle's architecture firm office building in downtown. He took the elevator up to his office. He saw his secretary on the phone, and Kyle at his desk on the phone with his feet propped up on his desk. He pushed the glass door open and yanked the phone from him.

"You and I need to talk." he said.

Kyle stood and buttoned his sports coat to his suit. "What do we have to talk about?"

"I'm only going to tell you this once. Leave Kate alone, you two are done. You had your shot and you blew it. She's now dating my brother and I promise you don't want him after you."

"Kate and I are done when I say we are. And if your brother wants to find me, here give him my business card."

"If you touch her, call her, or come by her apartment again, I will come back and things will not go well for you."

"Does it surprise you that I'm not scared of you?"

"No, I always knew you were stupid. If you were smart, you would be scared." Jonah turned to walk away.

Summer was officially gone. The September air was cool and crisp. The leaves were starting to turn from green to gold. Fall was Kate's favorite time of year.

Weeks had gone by since Kyle assaulted her and she had filed charges. At home on her day off, she was cleaning, reorganizing, and rearranging her furniture. She was waiting by the phone for Jack to call.

Kyle stood outside her apartment building, waiting for the opportunity to sneak in. He had been drinking and had worked himself into a rage. He had just been released from the county jail for assault. He was violently enraged that she pressed charges on him and had a restraining order filed. He wanted to confront her. He was arrested at his office, in the middle of a meeting.

She was mopping her kitchen floor, when a loud banging at the door startled her. She crept to the peep hole and saw him pounding on her door. She wondered how he had gotten past the main door. She saw how angry he was, and she became terrified. He banged on the door again. "Kate! I know you're home! Answer the door!"

She ran to her bedroom, locked her door, and called 911. "Dallas County 911, what is your emergency?" the operator asked.

"My ex fiancé is breaking into my apartment! Please hurry! I have a gun and I will use it if he tries to hurt me," she told the operator as she tried to reach the lockbox for her pistol at the top of her closet.

"Ma'am, you do whatever you have to do to protect yourself," the operator told her.

She gave the operator her name, address, and telephone number. She had a concealed weapons permit and a Colt 1911 pistol in a lockbox in her closet. The pistol was loaded. Her hands were shaking so bad she could barely grip the key. While on the phone with the operator, Kyle kicked her door open. She heard him throwing her furniture around. She heard glass breaking. Then he banged on her locked bedroom door. He pushed it open and broke the door frame around the door. Finally, with her hands shaking, her heart pounding, she opened the lockbox and grabbed the gun just as he opened her closet doors. As she raised the weapon, he grabbed her hands causing her to pull the trigger twice. The rounds went into the closet wall. She was still connected with the 911 operator.

"Shots fired. We have shots fired inside the apartment," the operator alerted police who were in route.

"No! Kyle, please!" she begged. He knocked the gun away from her and jerked her up by her hair and disconnected the call to 911. He threw her up against the wall. She punched him in the face and tried to get away to grab the gun. Grabbing her again, he backhanded her, busting her lip. Pinning her up against the wall, he wrapped his hands around her throat and squeezed. She clawed at his wrists trying to loosen his grasp.

"You filed charges and a restraining order on me! Are you crazy? I should kill you right now!" he yelled at her, as she gasped for air. He punched her in the stomach. She yelped.

She saw the rage in his eyes as she struggled to breathe. Tears rapidly rolled down her cheeks. She kneed him in the groin, he relinquished his grasp.

Blocking her escape, he eyed her like prey. He had the pistol in his hand and rushed towards her. She fought him by punching him and scratching him in the face with her fingernails. He punched her in the face, just below her eye. Her face felt as if it were on fire. He kicked her hard in the ribs. She spat out blood. He picked her up and threw her on the bed. He climbed on top of her and applied all his weight on her. With her arms pinned beneath him, she couldn't move. He covered her mouth so she wouldn't scream.

She shook her head, trying to catch a breath of air. His fingers were blocking her airflow from her nose. "Where's your soldier? He's not here for you, is he?" She had tears rolling out of the corners of her eyes. "…If I can't have you, then he sure as hell won't…" he said.

She was terrified, seeing the rage, anger, and jealousy in his eyes. She could smell the whiskey on his breath. With all of his weight applied to her, she found it very difficult to breathe. She was beginning to panic. Her heart was racing. Her body was shaking. She squirmed beneath him, struggling to breathe, and beyond terrified. She was desperately waiting for police to arrive, but knew he was hell bent on destroying her.

"You know it makes me sick to think of you and him together. You wouldn't give yourself to me, have you given yourself to him?" He looked down in her eyes. He placed the pistol to her temple and looked down into her terrified eyes. "…Let's find out," as he tore open her buttoned blouse. All of the buttons went flying. He saw her bra.

Her scalp was bleeding from him yanking her hair out. Her lip and nose were busted. Her eye was red and beginning to swell. She was a bloody mess. She had many abrasions to her face. Blood trickled down her cheek to her neck.

"If you scream or move I'll kill you," he threatened. He unbuttoned her jeans with the other hand. He worked the jeans down off her hips.

She was crying and silently praying to God to save her. Suddenly her house phone rang. The answering machine picked up. They were both silent and still. It was Jack calling from his cell phone. He was back from Afghanistan. Listening to his voice, tears rolled out of her eyes.

> *'Hey baby, it's me. I'm back. I'm on my way back to Dallas, and I can't wait to see you. I should be there around eight. I'm in Louisiana right now. I was going to surprise you, but I thought you might be working late, so I hope you're not working tonight. I'll see you when I get there. Call me when you get this."*

The message enraged him. He laughed an evil laugh and looked down at her. He saw she was terrified, and he saw the tears. "He'll be too late." She was shaking like a leaf. Making her look up at him while still holding the pistol to her head, he said, "I'll love you to death." He kissed her lips.

She shook her head, crying. She was still fighting to get away from him, but his weight on her was overpowering. He made her look at him and kissed her again. Suddenly, they heard police sirens. She was relieved and elated, but knew she was still in imminent danger. He could kill her in a panic.

She could still see the rage in his eyes. He smiled down at her chest. He hit her in the head with the pistol. She was unconscious lying on the bed, helpless and exposed. He placed the pistol on her chest and quickly left eluding police.

Many of her neighbors had heard the door being broken down, the two guns shots, the struggle, and her screaming. They called the police as well. The attack only lasted twenty minutes, but it felt like a lifetime to Kate.

Morgan arrived home. Stepping out of the elevator, she saw the kicked in front door. She slowly walked inside and saw the furniture thrown, glass shattered all over the floor. "Kate?" she called out.

Seeing a blood trail from the bedroom to the front door, she looked at the front door and saw a bloody handprint on it. She entered Kate's bedroom and found her unconscious on the bed. "Oh-my-God, Kate! Kate…" she said trying to wake her up. She was terrified. She thought an intruder had raped her. Blood was everywhere.

"Someone help me, please!" she yelled. The police officers stepped out of the elevator and saw the kicked in door. They carefully entered and saw the furniture thrown, the living room completely trashed. Broken glass was everywhere. The officers searched the kitchen with their weapons drawn.

"Miss Johnson? Dallas Police!" an officer called out to her. Police officers were very cautious when arriving to a domestic violence call. They were prepared to find an injured or possibly deceased victim, but in some lucky cases, the victim would be alive.

"Hurry, she's in here!" Morgan called out. The officers entered the bedroom and found her, lying on the bed with a gun on her chest. Her blouse was open and her jeans half way pulled off, Morgan was in a complete panic.

"Ma'am, are you alright?" one officer asked Morgan. The other officer rushed to Kate to check to see if she was alive. She had a pulse, but she was an unconscious, bloody mess.

"I'm her roommate. I just came home from work."

The officer comforted Morgan as the other officer radioed the EMTs to their location. He took possession of the pistol. She had imprints of his fingers and palms on her neck and her arms. There were contusions and abrasions to her face and neck. Her right eye was already swollen. Her hair was a bloody, matted mess. Mascara was smeared underneath her eyes. The officers saw she had sustained blunt force trauma to her head and torso. The EMTs arrived. They loaded her on a stretcher and put her neck in a brace.

Morgan was sitting on the sofa answering the officers' questions. "Who do you think could've done this? Has anyone been threatening her or harassing her?"

"The only person she's been having issues with is her ex-fiancé, Kyle Mowery. She has a restraining order and assault charges against him."

"Do you have his address?"

"No I don't. I just know he works for Haskell, Dean and Thompson Architectural Firm. Is she going to be alright?"

"She's in bad shape, but we're going to get her to the hospital. Do you have an emergency contact number we can call?"

She looked in the address book on the counter. She was shaking. She was so afraid for Kate. She looked for Carole's cell phone number. "I can't find her mom's cell phone number, but she is a professor at UT at Dallas."

One of the officers saw she had message on her machine. He played it and listened to Jack's message. "Who is this?"

"That's Jack, her boyfriend. He's in the Army. I think he's stationed in North Carolina,"

"And there's no way he did this?"

"No, Jack would never do this to her. Kyle wanted her back and was jealous that she and Jack are dating." The EMTs carried her out of the bedroom on a stretcher. Morgan watched them. She was crying. "Can I ride with her to the hospital?"

"Yes, but you know the doctors will not be able to tell you anything since you're not a relative?" an EMT stated.

"Yes, let me grab a few of her things." She ran to Kate's bedroom to grab a change of clothes for her.

"You're both going to need to stay somewhere else until our investigation is complete," a detective said.

"I can't find her cell phone," Morgan said.

"Don't worry about that right now." Morgan hurried to the elevator to ride with Kate to the hospital. She climbed into the ambulance. Kate was still unconscious, but she was on oxygen. Arriving to Medical City Hospital, Morgan was forced to wait in the waiting room as Kate was rushed back into the ICU by the EMTs followed by a doctor and three nurses, getting her vitals.

Two police officers were dispatched to the University of Texas Dallas campus to notify Carole of the attack. They opened the door to her classroom. She was in the middle of a lecture.

"Professor Johnson?" one asked.

She was alarmed to see two officers there. "Yes, may I help you?"

"Would you please step out into the hall with us?"

She looked to her class and then to the officers. "Yes, of course." She walked out into the hall with them. When told what had happened to Kate, her legs gave out and she collapsed to the hard floor below. The officers comforted her. They escorted her to the hospital. She frantically called Matt in Washington D.C., but he was in very important meetings. His secretary assured her he would call her back.

Sitting in the Intensive Care Unit waiting room, Morgan called Christi. "Hey Morgan..." Christi answered.

"Hey, you need to come to Medical City," Morgan said, still crying and shaking.

"Why?"

"Kate has been attacked. When I came home from work, the apartment was destroyed, and she was half naked on the bed. She was covered in blood and unconscious."

Christi felt her heart stop out of fear. She knew who had done this to her. There wasn't a question of doubt in her mind. "We're on our way!" she said. She and Jonah sprinted to their car and drove to the hospital.

Carole and the officers arrived at the hospital. She saw Morgan. "Morgan, what happened?"

"I don't know. I just came home and found her like this."

Jonah and Christi arrived quickly. She jogged to Carole and Morgan. "Where's Kate?" she asked.

"She's still being looked at by doctors."

Jonah was stunned and very angry. He felt responsible. He felt that confronting Kyle in his office was what set him off. His cell phone rang. It was Jack. He stepped away towards the elevators to tell him. "Hey, you're back," he said relieved.

"Yeah, I'm actually almost there. I should be there in about two hours, give or take. Have you talked to Kate?"

"Jack, she's in the hospital. Her apartment was broken into and she was attacked."

Jack was very worried for her. "Is she alright?"

"I don't know. I haven't seen her yet. I just know it's pretty bad. She's in the ICU."

"Who did this?"

"My money is on Kyle, her ex. She's been having issues with him lately. He wouldn't leave her alone."

"What do you mean he wouldn't leave her alone?"

"A few weeks ago, she came from work and he was waiting for her at the door. He tried to talk her into getting back with him, but when she refused, he grabbed her and shook her really hard. She filed charges and a restraining order. Then I went to talk to him. I told him if he didn't leave her alone, he'd deal with me. I'm sorry, Jack, I feel like this is my fault."

"Oh I can't wait to hunt this guy down, Jonah. When I get there, we're going to his office for a chat. So what happened to Kate?"

"Morgan is the one who found her. She said Kate's shirt was undone and her jeans were half way pulled down. There was a loaded pistol on her chest, and she was unconscious."

"Was she raped?"

"I don't know." Jack closed his eyes, hoping and praying she wasn't.

"Let me talk to Morgan."

Jonah walked over to Morgan. "It's Jack. He wants to talk to you."

She took the phone. "Hello?"

"Hey, so tell me exactly what happened?"

"I came home from work, and I saw that our front door was completely kicked in. I saw all the furniture thrown around. Broken glass was everywhere. There was a blood trail from the bedroom to the front door and a bloody handprint on the front door. I called out for Kate, and I found her in the bedroom. Her shirt was open and her jeans were half way pulled down. She was unconscious and covered in blood."

"Do they know if she was raped?"

"They haven't confirmed anything to me yet, but there was a loaded pistol on her chest and bullet holes in her closet." He was growing angrier with every word Morgan said.

After being in the ICU for nearly an hour, a doctor came out to talk with Carole. By now Lauren had arrived. She was comforting Morgan. Carole stood and held onto the doctor's arm. Jonah stood behind her to catch her if she collapsed. "Mrs. Johnson, your daughter has sustained very serious injuries. She has a concussion and four fractured ribs. We ran a CT scan and we've confirmed that she does have internal bleeding in her abdomen. It is serious, and we are going to take her into the OR for emergency surgery to stop it. If things go wrong, do we have your permission to resuscitate her?"

"Yes, of course, please just do everything you can to save her."

"We will." Carole called Matt again. He was at the airport trying to get booked on the earliest flight to Dallas.

Jonah called Jack. He walked down by the vending machines. He answered immediately. "Hey, what's going on?"

"Uh, hey it's very serious. She is going into emergency surgery."

"Why?"

"She has internal bleeding to her abdomen."

"I'm almost to Dallas. What hospital?"

"We're at the ICU in Medical City Hospital on Forrest Lane."

Kate was in emergency surgery. She was given general anesthesia. The chief surgeon made an incision on her abdomen. Finding the leaking blood vessel, he successfully sealed the ends with a suture material. The anesthesiologist stood at her head and monitored her breathing, heart rate, blood pressure and body temperature. She wore an oxygen mask.

An hour after the surgery began; the surgeon came out in his royal blue scrubs. "Mrs. Johnson?"

Carole stood, Jonah stood behind her as her support. "How is she?"

"She did great. We stopped the bleeding. She should make a full recovery…" Carole, Jonah, Christi and Morgan all breathed a sigh of relief. "…We'll have her in her room in about thirty minutes. We'll probably release her tomorrow if there are no complications."

"Can we see her?"

"When she gets into her room, I'll come get you. You and your daughter can be the first ones to see her."

"Oh, thank you God," she exclaimed with tears in her eyes. She hugged Jonah.

Soon she was wheeled back into her hospital room in the ICU. The nurse came out to get Carole and Lauren. They saw her lying in a hospital bed, hooked up to oxygen, and many tubes attached to machines. They were taken aback at her appearance. She looked terrible. She had suffered such a savage beating that she was hardly recognizable. "Oh my poor baby…" she said, crying. Seeing the abrasions on her knuckles, the cut on her hand, she gently held her hand.

She was awakening from the anesthesia. She slowly opened her eyes. Mom smiled at her. "Hey sweetie…"

"Where am I?"

"You're in the hospital."

After talking with her for a few minutes, the detectives were called now that she was awake. They came in and interviewed her. She told them that Kyle was her attacker. Mom and Lauren were stunned. Carole looked at the detectives. "Why was he given bail? She got the restraining order to protect herself from him, why did this happen? He almost killed her," she asked upset.

The detectives assured her. "When we find him, he's going to jail for sexual assault and battery."

Christi and Lauren watched as Kate tried to get out of the bed. She was extremely sore. "He tried to kill her. You should charge him with attempted murder." Lauren said.

"I wouldn't want to be Kyle when Jack gets ahold of him," Christi said. Kate was forced to stay in the hospital overnight. She was given pain medication that made her sleep better.

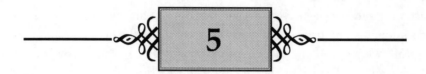

THE SKY WAS painted with colors of blue, purple and orange. The sun was fading into the Texas horizon. The air was cool. Jack was just now arriving into Dallas. He sped down U.S. 75 and found the exit to Forrest Lane. He pulled abruptly into the parking garage of Medical City Hospital. His tires squealed. He jumped out of his truck, barely putting the gear shift in PARK, he hurried into the hospital. He jogged to the elevators and rode up to the floor she was on.

The elevator doors opened. He jogged down the hall and found Jonah and Morgan sitting in the chairs. "Hey, how is she?"

Jonah stood. "She made it out of surgery, but she's still in the ICU. Her mom and sister are in there with her now." he said.

"Is she awake?"

"Yeah, she said Kyle attacked her."

Jack looked to Morgan, who was sitting in the chairs, crying silently. He sat beside her. "Are you okay?" he asked.

She shook her head. "I should've been there for her. I could've stopped him."

He hugged her. "If you had been there, he could've killed you both."

Jonah could tell he was very worried but he was also very angry. He was desperate to see her. They walked away from Morgan. "Thanks for handling the situation for me." They shook hands and hugged.

"It's no problem. I know you'd do it for me."

"Do you know where her ex lives?"

"No, I don't,"

They walked back to the ICU waiting room. They glanced up at the T.V. but that couldn't hold their attention. Minutes later, their eyes were immediately drawn to Carole, Christi, and Lauren as they walked down the hall from Kate's room to the waiting room.

"How is she doing?" Morgan asked.

"She's resting right now."

Christi saw Jack and hugged him. "She's going to be so happy to see you." She turned to Carole. "Carole, this is Jack, Kate's boyfriend. Jack this is Mrs. Carole Johnson, Kate's mother."

She smiled at him. He was everything Kate said he would be. "Hi, I've heard so much about you, Jack. It's nice to finally meet you. Kate described you to a tee."

He smiled. "It's good to meet you too, ma'am. It's unfortunate to meet you under these circumstances."

She smiled. "It's always great to meet the man that's stolen my daughter's heart and made her so happy these last few months."

He smiled. "That's good to hear, since she's stolen mine. You've raised an incredible woman. I'd really like to see her. I promise I won't wake her up, I just really need to see her."

"He just drove straight in from Fort Bragg." Christi said.

Carole smiled at him. "She'll kill me when she finds out you saw her like this, but I know you really care for her, so brace yourself. She's in room 234-A."

"Thank you." He hurried down the hall to her room. Finding her room, he slowly opened the heavy door and saw her sleeping. He was stunned by her injuries. He hardly recognized her. He slowly walked towards her and sat in the chair next to the bed. He gently touched her hand and held it in his.

He looked down at her roughed knuckles. "I'm sorry I wasn't here for you, Kate." he said softly as he gently kissed the top of her injured hand. He looked up at her, seeing the blood matted in her hair, the hand prints around her neck and her swollen eye. Though she looked beyond terrible, he still thought she was the most beautiful woman he'd ever seen.

He sat in the chair, holding her hand in his for nearly an hour. He bowed his head and kissed her hand. "Thank you God for letting her be alright. I don't know what I'd do if I lost her, I love her." he said quietly. He carefully ran his fingers through her hair and gently kissed her cheek.

Letting her rest, he walked to the door and slowly closed it. He walked down the hall and spoke more with her mother. Lauren came back from the vending machines and stood frozen when she saw him. "Wow, who are you?" Lauren asked.

"Jack, this is Lauren, Kate's younger sister. Lauren, this is Jack, Kate's boyfriend." she introduced.

Lauren smiled. "You're her boyfriend? I thought she was exaggerating on how attractive you were, but clearly she wasn't. You're really good looking."

He laughed. "Thanks."

"It was nice meeting you." she said.

Carole, Christi, and Morgan were speechless. "Lauren is much more outspoken and bolder than Kate." Carole explained.

He smiled. "Is there anything I can get for you?" He looked down at his watch and saw it was late. "Have y'all eaten? I'd be happy to go and get you and Lauren some dinner,"

"Oh aren't you sweet? But I'm just fine with food from the vending machines," she said.

He smiled. "We both know that's not healthy. Please, let me go get you both something more substantial to eat,"

Carole smiled up at him. She was appreciative of him insisting to get her and Lauren dinner. "Whataburger sure does sound good right now. I think there is one just down 75-South," Carole said.

"Okay, Whataburger it is," he said. She told him what she and Lauren wanted, but when she tried to pay him, he placed the money back in her hand.

"Jack, please let me pay you,"

"No, Mrs. Johnson, I want to buy you and Lauren dinner,"

She smiled up at him with tears in her eyes. "I'm so relieved to know my daughter has finally chosen a good man instead of…" She started to break down. He kneeled and hugged her. She cried on his shoulder. "…I can't believe he did this to her." She sobbed on his shoulder for a few minutes. After she calmed down, he and Jonah left to get her and Lauren dinner from Whataburger.

"Where'd he go?" Lauren asked.

"He went to Whataburger to get us dinner,"

Lauren smiled. "Is he buying?"

Carole laughed. "Yeah, I tried to give him money for it but he insisted that he pay for it,"

"I like this guy. Kate better not mess this up with her insecurities and trust issues,"

As he drove to Whataburger, Jonah looked over at him and saw how angry he was. "So how was she?"

He shook his head. "I cannot comprehend how a man can do that to a woman. When I get a hold of him, he's going to beg for his life,"

"I'm all for giving him the biggest beating of his life, but let's not do anything stupid," Jonah warned.

"If I had walked in on him hurting her, he'd be a dead man and I'd be in jail."

"I'd bail you out."

"I hope that offer is still on the table after I'm done with him." Jonah saw he was serious. He had never seen him so angry.

They came back with dinner and drinks for everyone from Whataburger. "Jack, you were so right. Those vending machines wouldn't have even come close to this. Thank you so much," Carole said.

He smiled, "It was my pleasure, ma'am,"

"Please call me Carole,"

After dinner, Jonah, Christi, and Morgan were leaving. Lauren decided she wanted to leave to. She wanted to get home and get a shower. "Momma, I'm going to go home. I'll be up here in the morning." She hugged her.

"Okay, sweetheart, I'll see you in the morning."

"Jack, I'll have to interrogate you and embarrass my sister the next time I see you." Lauren said.

He smiled. "I look forward to it. I'm good under pressure,"

As Lauren, Morgan, and Christi walked to the elevators. Jonah noticed Jack was still sitting with Carole. "Jack, are you coming with us?"

"No, I'm going to stay here,"

"Jack, you go on home now. You just drove in from Fort Bragg. I know you must be exhausted," Carole said.

"I'm not tired. I want to stay here. I'll keep you company. You shouldn't be up here by yourself."

She smiled at him. As the hours slowly went by, she went into her room and fell asleep on the pull out sofa. Jack paced the waiting room. He was desperate to talk to her.

Around midnight, Kate finally woke up. She saw her mother asleep on the sofa. "Mom…"

Mom quickly woke up and smiled. "Hi, sweetie, how are you feeling?"

"I'm okay. I'm still just so groggy from the anesthesia." She looked for her purse. "Do you know where my purse is? I need my cell phone to call Jack,"

Mom smiled. "He's here,"

"He's here? What do you mean he's here?"

"He's been here since about eight o'clock and he's out in the waiting room, probably passed out. He came in here to see you earlier."

Mom looked at her and smiled. Kate looked at her strangely. "What?"

"He's a lot more attractive than you let on. You should've seen Lauren's reaction when she saw him. She thinks he's very attractive,"

Kate smiled. "Oh I can only imagine what she said to him,"

"She's going to embarrass you hugely the next time she sees you two together. I'm just letting you know now."

"Do you like him?"

Mom smiled. "Yes, he was very polite and handsome. We talked for a little bit. He told me that I've raised an incredible woman. He even bought Lauren and me dinner from Whataburger and he insisted on staying here with me. He didn't want me to be up here alone."

"He's a good man. I'm in love with him. When Kyle was pulling my jeans down, all I wanted was Jack."

"He cares a lot about you,"

She looked around the room for a mirror. "Do you have a mirror?"

Mom searched her purse. She handed her a compact. She looked at herself in the mirror. "I knew I looked horrible, but I didn't think I looked this bad. I don't want him to see me like this,"

She smiled and tucked her hair behind her ear. "Kate, you still look beautiful. He's desperate to see you and talk with you. He just drove all the way from Fort Bragg to see you. I'll go tell him you want to see him."

"Wait, I need some gum," She laughed as she handed her a stick of gum. She left the room.

He was watching CNN on the TV in the waiting room. He looked up at her. "She's awake and wants to see you."

He sprinted down the hall to her room. She smiled watching him sprint down the hall. Slowly opening the door to her room, he smiled at her. "Hi baby, how are you feeling?"

"I'm better now that you're here." He hugged her. She closed her eyes. Tears ran down her face. Wrapped in his strong arms, finally, she felt safe.

He felt her tears hit his shoulder. "I'm so sorry I wasn't here to protect you, baby." Releasing her, he carefully smoothed them away with his thumb. He looked at her injuries. "I'm so happy to see you, but it hurts me to see you like this."

She smiled. "I'm happy to see you too. When did you get in?"

"A few hours ago, I came in here to see you after your surgery."

"Yeah, I felt you holding and kissing my hand."

"You didn't hear anything I said, right?" he asked, hoping she hadn't heard him say he loved her.

"No, what did you say?"

"Oh nothing, it's not important."

"Do I look terrible?"

"No, baby you're still gorgeous. If I could take all that he did away from you and put it on myself, I'd do it in a heartbeat."

"You really think that I'm gorgeous?" He nodded and smiled at her. Holding her hand in his, he kissed it. "I really missed you."

"I really missed you too, baby. What did the doctor say?"

With tears in her eyes, she said, "I have a concussion. I had to have surgery to stop the internal bleeding in my abdomen and I have four fractured ribs. But I should make a full recovery, it'll be a slow process but it could've been worse. I'm lucky,"

He hugged her, "You're safe with me, Kate. I'll never let anything happen to you." He smiled and gently touched her face. "I was driving like ninety miles per hour to get here to you. I was really worried about you."

They talked for hours and watched TV in her room together. He tried his best to make her feel better. He stayed with her even after she fell asleep. The next morning, the doctor went over her post surgery instructions with her and Carole. They discharged her. She was forced to take a week off from work and she had to go home with someone. She could not drive for a few days.

"You'll come home with me and Lauren," Mom said.

"Is that really necessary?" she asked the doctor.

"Yes ma'am. It is necessary for your safety. You cannot drive or be alone," the doctor urged.

"You're coming home with me. I'm still your mother. Do as I say."

Jack stood to give her a kiss goodbye. "I'm going home and get a shower, but I'll see you later, okay?" She kissed him goodbye. He smiled as he walked to the door and down to the elevators.

Mom and Lauren took her home with them. Kate sat at the breakfast table while holding a new ice pack on her face and ribs, as Mom made her some hot tea. "Momma, I'm going to lie down. I have such a headache," she said.

"Okay, well here is one of your pain pills," she said, handing her a pill and a glass of water.

She took the pill. Mom helped her walk up the stairs, to her old bedroom. She lied down on the bed. She sat beside her and ran her fingers through her hair like she used to do when she was a little girl. "Momma, you don't have to do that. I'm really tired. My head hurts so bad even my hair hurts."

"Close your eyes and get some rest. I love you, Katherine."

"I love you too, Momma." Mom smiled, wiped a tear or two away and slowly closed the door. Kate broke down and cried. She was desperate to hold in her emotions until she was alone. She thought of all that Kyle did to her, the look in his eyes, and the things he said to her. She was stunned someone she knew and at one point in time loved, trusted, and was prepared to marry, could do this to her. She thought about Jack. Thinking of him during the attack motivated her to survive. She wanted him. She needed him. She knew if she was with him, she was safe. Soon, she fell asleep.

Four hours had passed. She opened her eyes and realized she was not in her apartment. She sat up, slowly got out of the bed. She carefully walked downstairs and saw her mother sitting at the table, drinking tea. Mom saw her and gave her a gentle hug. She was very sore.

"Jack called for you a few hours ago. I told him you were sleeping and that you'd call him back."

"How long have I been asleep?"

"Oh about four hours, all of your friends have called too."

She called him. He was over at his parents' house helping his dad on the truck. He heard his cell phone ringing. He looked at the number and noticed it was her parents' number. He answered.

"Hi…"

"Hi baby…"

She smiled, "What are you doing?"

"I'm helping my dad install this part for the truck. How are you feeling?"

"Sore and very tired, what are you doing later?"

"I'm hoping I can see you, why?"

She smiled, "Well my mom has me under house arrest. I feel like a teenager all over again."

"How about I get some food and bring it over and we watch a movie?"

"You really want to come over here to my parents and have a date night?"

"I don't care where we are, I just want to spend time with you."

"I want to spend time with you too. What time will you be coming over here?"

"Oh how's six o'clock? I'll need a shower. I'm covered in black oil and grease."

She smiled, "That might not be such a bad thing."

He laughed, "I'll see you at six, beautiful."

"Okay." They hung up.

He put the cell phone back in his pocket and resumed working with his Dad. "So, how is she doing?"

"She's sore. He really worked her over, but she's a trooper. I'm just relieved that she is okay."

"I'm sorry that happened to her."

"I am too, but feel worse for her ex. After I'm done with him, he'll either have a permanent residence in the ICU or the cemetery."

"I don't blame you, son. Let me know if you need any help."

"I may need an alibi." he joked.

At five o'clock, he took a shower, shaved and got dressed. He went by a fancy restaurant and bought them a fancy meal to bring to her parents' house. He bought a bouquet of pink roses and began to drive to her parents' house.

Carole was still at class and wouldn't be home until after eight o'clock. Lauren was home with Kate, but she had a date later. He pulled into the driveway and walked up to the door. He rang the doorbell.

Lauren answered it. "Hey, are you ready for that interrogation?"

"Sure, after I see your sister."

He walked into the kitchen and saw her sitting at the table. She slowly got up to greet him. "Hi baby."

She smiled. She was wearing a pair of pajama pants, socks and an orange Texas Longhorns t-shirt. "I'm sorry I'm wearing pajamas today, I just didn't want to wear anything tight. I'm still sore."

He smiled and gently kissed her lips. "You look beautiful." She smiled. "Here these should cheer you up." He handed her the roses.

"Thank you. They're beautiful." He kissed her lips.

Lauren walked into the kitchen and saw them kissing. She smiled. She enjoyed seeing her happy. "So, am I going to be able to leave you two alone?" she asked.

She smiled, "Yes. Wow, you look great. Where are you going?"

"Rob and I are going to Red River."

"Oh well have fun and be careful."

"I will, you know me."

"I know that's why I'm telling you to be careful."

"So Jack, let's get this interrogation started." Lauren said.

"Lauren!" she scolded.

He laughed, "No it's fine. I have nothing to hide. I'm an open book. Ask me anything."

"Where are you from?"

"I'm a military kid, so I was born at Fort Hood, but I call Dallas my home. I enlisted here."

"Have you ever been arrested?"

"No."

"Have you ever been married?"

"No."

"Do you have any kids?"

He laughed, "No."

"Do you want kids?"

"Eventually…"

"Like do you want kids right now?"

He laughed, "No not right now."

"When do you want kids?"

"I think after I've been married for a few years."

"Do you care about my sister? Do you see a future with her?"

He looked at Kate and kissed her hand. "Yes I care for her very much. She's an amazing, beautiful, smart woman. And yes I do see a future with her."

"I'm not beautiful, and I won't be for a while. I look horrible." Kate said.

He kissed her hand. "You're still as gorgeous as you were the day we met." He gently kissed her lips.

They laughed and talked. "Well, Kate I'll be home around midnight or so."

"Okay, have fun, be safe."

"You two behave yourselves." Lauren said as she closed the door. Rob, Lauren's date was waiting on the porch for her.

"Oh do you know what I would kill for a bottle of wine?" she asked.

He smiled, "Iced tea will have to do it, since you're still on your pain meds."

She laughed. They ate dinner together in the dining room and watched a romantic comedy in the den. As they sat on the sofa together, her mother's headlights shone through the windows. "My mom is home."

The door opened and closed. "Katherine?" she called out.

"We're in here, mom!"

Carole walked into the den and turned on the lights. "Oh hi Jack, it's so good to see you again."

"It's good to see you too, Mrs. Johnson."

"Please call me Carole."

She visited with Jack for a few minutes. "Oh honey, did your father call?" she asked Kate.

"Yes, he called and said he'd be home tomorrow around noon."

"Okay, great. Well, I'll let you two get back to your evening. I have so many papers to grade." She knew they wanted to talk privately, so she went into the office to finish grading papers.

"I need to lie down." she said. He helped her up to her bedroom. While in her bedroom with the door wide open, they laid on her bed watching TV. She rested her head on his shoulder. Mom kept finding reasons to walk by Kate's bedroom to make sure they weren't doing anything inappropriate. As a strong Christian woman, she wasn't comfortable with him or any man being in her bedroom. He sensed Carole's uneasiness. When she glanced into the bedroom, he would smile and hold up his hands, showing her that they were not doing anything inappropriate. She would smile, wave, and quickly walk away.

Kate laughed, "I can't believe my mom is supervising us. I'm sorry if she's freaking you out." she teased. They laughed.

"It doesn't bother me." He held her hand and kissed each of her fingers. "I wish you'd talk to me about the attack and tell me what all he did. I want to help you,"

She looked up into his eyes. "I'm much better now that you're back."

"You can trust me, Kate. Let me be there for you. I'll be strong for you."

She held his hand. He gently ran his thumb across the top of her hand. "How do I stop feeling violated? When I close my eyes, I still see him and that deranged look in his eyes. I don't want to see him." She looked in his eyes. "I want to see you."

He gently touched her cheek. "You have to let me in. You don't have to pretend with me. I know you must have been terrified, so if you need to fall apart, fall apart. I'll be here to catch you."

She sat beside him, while telling him about how afraid she was when Kyle broke into her apartment, kicked in her bedroom door and threw her against the wall, slapping her and punching her. She told him how he held a loaded pistol to her head, unbuttoned her blouse, and pulled down her jeans. She saw the anger in his eyes. He saw the pain and fear in hers. "You called while it was happening. He heard your message and that made him very angry."

He looked down at her hand in his. It was shaking. "Is that when he had the gun to your head and was trying to rape you?"

She nodded, shaking uncontrollably. "He unbuttoned my blouse, pulled down my jeans, and covered my mouth. He told me the thought of you and I together made him sick to his stomach, and if he couldn't have me, then you sure as hell wouldn't."

He sat up, held her hand, looked in her eyes. "I'm here now, Kate. You're safe with me…" He kissed her hand. "…What can I do to make you feel safe? I'll do anything."

"I feel safe when you're holding me."

He smiled and opened his arms for her to lie in. "I'll hold you as long as you want me to."

She laid her head back down on his chest. "I love being in your arms."

He kissed her head, smelling her shampoo. He loved the way her hair smelled. He loved how soft her skin felt. "There's no safer place for you than with me." She had fallen in love with him. She truly felt secure in his arms. Not just because he was a Green Beret, but because she could feel he loved her, and that made her feel safe. She had never felt so loved, appreciated, and more wanted by any other man. As he watched TV, he looked down at her and smiled. She was sound asleep, holding his hand. He carefully got off the bed and grabbed a pillow and a quilt. He made a pallet on the floor beside her bed. Soon after, he dozed off.

Mom had walked by the bedroom and saw them asleep. She was comfortable and appreciative that he slept on the floor. The T.V. was still on. She turned the T.V. off and kept the door open and the hall light on. She and Matt had never allowed any of Kate or Lauren's boyfriends to sleep over, but she knew he was different. He was special.

Darkness had come. Lauren came home around midnight from her date. Mom was sitting at the breakfast table grading papers with her cup of tea. Lauren walked up the stairs. Walking by Kate's room, she saw Jack sleeping on the floor. She was surprised, so she turned around and walked back down to the kitchen.

"Um, are you aware that Jack is asleep in Kate's room on the floor?"

"Yes, I am," Mom looked up at her and noticed the shocked look on her face. "What?"

"Okay, who are you and what have you done with my mother?"

Mom laughed. "Jack is a respectable young man and I know how much he cares for her. I trust them. I wasn't entirely comfortable with him being up in her bedroom, but the reality is they are both adults, but he was respectable enough to sleep on the floor."

"I hope Daddy sees it the way you do."

Mom and Lauren had gone to bed. In the middle of the night, thunder rumbled and lightning flashed. The rain pounded hard against Kate's bedroom window. She was having a night terror about the attack and began to relive it. She started crying, kicking, and screaming. He woke up and tried to calm her, knowing she was not coherent.

"Get off me Kyle! Let me go!" she screamed and cried. She hit him several times.

"It's okay, baby. You're safe," he repeated several times. Finally, she stopped fighting him. He held her and she cried. Mom and Lauren had heard her and ran down the hall to see what was going on. They saw her crying on his shoulder, as he held her. He saw them and waved to them to go back to bed. He had everything under control.

After she calmed down, she didn't want to sleep. They played cards. "Did I hurt you?" she asked.

"No, I'm tougher than I look," he joked.

She smiled. "I'm sorry."

"You don't have to apologize. I'm here for you any way I can be." A strand of her hair fell over her face. He smiled and moved it. "You are so beautiful."

"How can I look beautiful to you looking like this?"

He kissed her face. "I see beyond that." They continued to talk and play cards. Nearing 3:00 a.m., she finally fell asleep. He couldn't help but notice how beautiful she looked sleeping. He lied back down in the floor beside her bed.

The next morning, Mom walked by Kate's bedroom and saw he was still sleeping on the floor. She respected him for that. She was not comfortable at all with them sleeping together on the bed. She walked downstairs and started a pot of coffee.

He woke up and walked down the stairs. "Good morning, Jack." she said, sipping her coffee and reading the paper. She was still wearing her pajamas and bath robe. She was sitting at the kitchen table.

"Good morning, Mrs. Johnson."

"Oh please call me Carole. When I hear Mrs. Johnson I look over my shoulder for my mother-in-law." He smiled. "How'd you sleep? There's some coffee there if you'd like," she asked. He poured himself a cup.

"I slept alright, but I want to apologize to you about sleeping over. It wasn't my intention to fall asleep here. I know that makes me look very disrespectful, but I want you to assure you that I have the utmost respect for her, your home, and for you and General Johnson. I just wanted to be here for her."

She smiled. "You are by far my favorite of any of the boyfriends my daughters' have had." He laughed. "I realize you and Kate are adults, but as her mother, I appreciate you for not only respecting my daughter, but for respecting me, my husband and our home. Matt and I have never allowed any boyfriends to sleep over especially in their rooms, so thank you."

"You're welcome."

"How about some breakfast?" she asked.

"Sure, what can I make you?" he asked.

She looked at him strangely and laughed. "This is a first, my daughter's boyfriend offering to cook breakfast."

He smiled, "It's no problem at all,"

"Does Kate know you can cook?"

"I haven't had the opportunity to cook for her yet. What's her favorite breakfast?"

"She loves blueberry pancakes and bacon." She showed him where the pots and pans were and where the pancake mix was in the pantry.

She sat at the bar, watched him cook as she sipped her coffee. "So tell me about you."

"Well, I'm twenty-seven. I've been in the Army since I was eighteen. I love sports. I'm a Christian and I come from a military family with strong family and religious values."

"What branch of the military?"

"Army, my dad is a retired major general,"

"Oh so you and Kate have something in common, both generals kids,"

"Yeah, we do."

"And what does your mom do?"

"My mom is a pastry chef. She's trying to open her own bakery/restaurant,"

"Did she teach you to cook?"

He laughed, "Yeah,"

"Have you ever been married?"

"No ma'am. I don't have kids,"

"So what do you like about Kate?"

"There are so many things I love about her. She's compassionate, she's funny, she's sweet, she's family oriented like me. She loves to help people and she isn't afraid to get her hands dirty and sweat."

"You're in love with her aren't you?"

He looked at her and smiled. "Is it that obvious?"

"Yes, by the way you look at her."

He smiled. "I thought I was hiding it pretty well."

"No, sorry to report you weren't. It's not just the way you look at her, it's also the way you talk to her, show concern for her, and the need to see her and be with her."

"You and General Johnson have raised an incredible woman. She's everything I've always wanted. How long have you and General Johnson been married?"

"We've been married twenty-seven years." He was impressed. "How long have your parents been married?"

"My folks have been married for thirty years."

"And you have a brother and sister?"

"Yes, I have an older brother and I have a younger sister."

"I bet you are one protective big brother."

He laughed. "My sister doesn't appreciate that. Maybe I'm too overprotective at times."

While he cooked, she went upstairs to wake Kate and Lauren up. Kate showered and brushed her teeth.

She walked down the stairs and entered the kitchen. She smiled watching him cook. "Good morning."

He turned and smiled at her. "Good morning beautiful, how'd you sleep?"

"I slept okay, how'd you sleep?" She kissed him.

"I slept great."

"I can't believe you're making breakfast. Ooh you're making my favorite."

"Really, it's your favorite?" he asked pretending he didn't know. She poured herself a cup of coffee.

Lauren came down the stairs. "Hey, wow you cook?"

"Yeah, I do."

"So, I hear you slept with my sister,"

"Lauren!" Mom and Kate scolded.

He laughed at the awkwardness.

"I'm just teasing,"

They all had breakfast together. They laughed and talked. Lauren asked him more embarrassing questions and told him embarrassing stories about Kate. Afterwards, Kate walked him out to his truck. "I'm glad you stayed over. Thank you for being there for me and making me feel safe. And again, I'm so sorry for hitting you and kicking you,"

"It's okay you were having a night terror. I knew you weren't coherent. I'll do anything I can to make you feel safe."

The sunlight shone on her face. Her eyes were honey colored. The cool breeze swept through her hair and a curled piece fell across her face. He moved it. "The swelling is going down."

"I still look horrible."

"No you don't. You look beautiful." He gently kissed her lips. "I'm going to head back over to Jonah and Christi's. I'm sure they've called my phone a thousand times looking for me."

"Thank you for breakfast. Those were the best blueberry pancakes I've ever had."

He laughed. "I'm glad you liked them. I'll have to cook for you more often."

She kissed him goodbye. He went back to Jonah and Christi's to change and shower. She walked in the house and back into the kitchen.

"You hit the jack pot of hot boyfriends," Lauren said to Kate.

She laughed. "He is really handsome, huh? But he's such a good guy. He's kind, he's considerate, respectful and he makes me feel so amazing."

Soon after he left, Matt arrived home in Dallas. He hurried to the door and opened it. Holly ran to the door to greet him. "Honey, I'm home."

Mom, Kate, and Lauren were in the kitchen cleaning up the dishes. "Hey! We're in here!" Mom said. He hugged her and saw Kate. He was taken aback by her injuries. She could tell he was angry and hurt to see her like this. He walked to her and hugged her.

"I'm so sorry, sweet pea. He's a dead man."

"Between you and Jack wanting to kill him, Kyle might want to go into the witness protection program," Lauren said. "Maybe you two should team up."

"Who's Jack?" he asked.

"Remember, he's my boyfriend. I've been seeing him for the last few months." Kate said.

"He knows what Kyle did?"

"Yes, he was just here about an hour ago. He came to check on her last night. He drove straight in from Fort Bragg. He stayed over and made us breakfast."

"He stayed over?" he asked curiously.

"Now before you freak out, he slept on the floor in my room. He's a gentleman." Kate defended.

"Matt, he's a very nice young man. You'll really like him. He really cares for Kate," Carole said.

He looked down at Kate. "Does he treat you right, Katherine?" he asked. Her parents always called her Katherine when they were upset, sad, or talking about something serious.

"Yes, Daddy, he treats me very good. He makes me really happy. I know you will really like him when you meet him."

Mom handed him a cup of coffee. "So tell me about him," he said.

"He's twenty-seven. He's been in the Army since he was eighteen and he's a master sergeant. He comes from a military, Christian family," Kate said.

"He has a hot body, and he looks so amazing." Lauren volunteered.

Mom and Kate laughed at his facial reaction. "That's something I don't need to know, pumpkin. So what's his MOS?"

Kate looked at her mother and then back to her father. "…He's a Green Beret." He was surprised.

The doorbell rang. The detective working her case delivered the police report to her parents' home for their records. He intercepted the paperwork. He sat in his office chair and cried reading how he attempted to rape her with a loaded pistol to her head. He kneeled and thanked God for keeping her safe.

A week went by; her injuries had mostly healed. The bruises were fading, but she was still sore. She could conceal the remaining tiny cuts with makeup. They were having dinner at a local restaurant.

"I'm so happy you're back," she said, giving him a flirty grin.

"I'm happy to be back with you." They enjoyed their dinner while laughing and talking. They gently kissed.

Across the restaurant, Kyle and James were sitting at the bar watching them. He was eaten up with jealousy and anger watching them laugh and whisper in each other's ears. He and James approached them. The police hadn't located him yet. He had avoided police by staying with friends. "Hey Kate, you look good," he said.

Her mood instantly changed, she was afraid. Jack saw the fear on her face and knew that this was Kyle. He stood up in his face. "And you must be Jack?" Kyle asked.

"Yeah, I am. I've been looking for you."

"Here I am," he said arrogantly.

"Jack, let's just go," she said, seeing that things were about to escalate.

The restaurant was suddenly quiet, as the patrons watched. "I'm going to teach you a lesson for putting your hands on a woman," he said.

Kyle smirked. "Listen, G.I. Joe, you don't want to fight me, I'm not like the terrorists you're fighting. I'm not a coward."

Jack smiled. "You're not a coward? But you beat up women?" Kyle swung at him, but he blocked the punch and nailed him with two, right and left hooks to the face. Kyle swung again, but he grabbed him by the back of the head and kneed him in the face twice. He then threw him up against the wall and punched him in the stomach. Kyle charged him, but he quickly put him in a head lock and flipped him forward. Kyle was holding onto his shoulders when he stood up and quickly slammed him hard down on the floor of the restaurant. With Kyle pinned beneath him, he swiftly punched him several times with both fists in the face. The patrons couldn't believe what they were seeing. He placed his forearm on his throat and applied severe pressure. Kyle struggled to breathe and tapped his arm.

"Tapping out isn't going to help you here." James and Kate were stunned. His precise hand to hand combat training was swift, effective, and executed perfectly. During the struggle, he had sustained a tiny cut over his eye. "Say you're a coward and you hit women!" he demanded. Kyle squirmed beneath him, but he had enough pressure to completely subdue him.

He applied more pressure to his neck. "I didn't hear you!" he yelled with his adrenaline pumping.

He relented to allow Kyle to talk. "I'm a coward. I hit women." he mumbled.

"Say it louder!" Jack commanded.

"I'M A COWARD! I HIT WOMEN!" he shouted. James was stunned at the extent of his action and anger. He saw the look in his eye and did not want to interfere. Kate had her hands over her face, she was in shock.

"I ought to kill you for what you did to her. You broke into her apartment, pulled out her hair, slapped, kicked and punched her. You put a loaded gun to her head as you attempted to rape her. Had I been there, you would be in a body bag in an unmarked grave. If you come anywhere near her or contact her again, I promise you I will hunt you down and kill you, do you hear me?!" he yelled in a cold, menacing voice.

Kyle's face was red, breathing suspended but he was barely breathing. James saw the determination and distain in his eyes. He was calm and collected. His breathing was controlled and measured. Kyle looked up at him. "Don't kill me."

"Give me one good reason why I shouldn't. Isn't that what you threatened to do to her?" he asked applying more pressure to his throat.

"Jack, I'll make sure he leaves her alone. You have my word." James pleaded. The side of Kyle's face was already swelling. He was barely conscious.

Jack looked around the restaurant. The patrons were stunned, many were afraid. "Are you going to contact her again?" he asked with his arm still on his throat. "Say 'No Master Sergeant'!"

Kyle remained quiet. He glared down at him. "I can crush your windpipe in a second. You'd better say it if you want to walk out of here. You have three seconds to decide. 1…"

"No Master Sergeant," Kyle said quietly.

"LOUDER! 2…" he shouted loudly and angrily.

"No Master Sergeant!" Kyle shouted.

"How does it feel to have someone controlling how much air you get?" he asked.

The police arrived. Three officers rushed in and saw Jack restraining Kyle. One officer interviewed witnesses as the other two separated them. "What's going on?" one asked Jack.

"This guy, Kyle… whatever his name is, was attempting to harass my girlfriend. I believe he has two warrants out for his arrest for assault and attempted rape against her from a week ago."

One of the officers went to check and found the name Kyle Mowery in the system. He had two warrants for his arrest. The officer walked back and confirmed. "Thank you, we appreciate you holding him for us. We've been looking for him." the officer said as he slapped the handcuffs on Kyle's wrist and read him his rights. His friend disappeared into the crowd.

Jack gave his statement to the police. His story was corroborated by all the witnesses. The police asked him to come later to the precinct to sign his statement. He looked to Kate, who was astonished at what she'd just seen. She looked at him, seeing the bloody cut above his eye brow. "Are you alright? You're bleeding," she asked.

He laughed. "Yeah, I'm fine. It's just a cut."

The police escorted Kyle out to a squad car. He was taken to the Dallas County Jail. He was denied bail. Jack looked at the patrons, all staring at him. "Sorry to have interrupted your evening." The restaurant manager approached their table. He said, "I'd like to pay for the damages," as he opened his wallet.

"Thank you, but that's not necessary, sir. We have insurance. And you were just defending yourself," the manager said.

They walked to his truck. He opened the passenger door for her. She looked at him and touched his face. He smiled. "I'm sorry if I scared you. I kind of lost it in there." he said laughingly.

She hugged him in the parking lot. "I could never be scared of you."

"All I could think about was him hurting you and I just lost it."

Arriving back at Jonah and Christi's home, he entered entry code for the gate. He had a key to the house. Jonah and Christi were out for the evening. They entered the house and turned on the lights in the living room and kitchen.

"I know she has a first aid kit here somewhere," she said, searching the drawers. Finding it, she walked to the table. "Sit down, Master Sergeant," she said, with a smile.

"I'm fine."

She smiled. "Don't argue with me, I'm a nurse."

He laughed. "Yes ma'am." He sat down. As she cleaned the blood off his eyebrow with an alcohol swab, he asked, "So was he controlling when you two were together? Did he ever hit you?"

"He was controlling in some ways. I could never hang out with my friends or my sister. I could only see my friends and sister when he let me. Lauren hates him with a passion. But no he never hit me. He loved to humiliate me and degrade me." He saw the pain in her eyes. "I caught him in my bed with one of my bridesmaids."

He was stunned. "Wow, that's cruel."

She laughed. "I threw their clothes, his wallet, keys, and cell phone out of my window and made them leave with only my sheets wrapped around them. I sold my engagement ring and bought me a new mattress, sheets and comforter set."

"I'm sorry he hurt you, Kate. That must have been humiliating."

She shrugged her shoulders. "What doesn't kill you makes you stronger, right?"

"Yeah, you're definitely a strong, beautiful, and smart woman."

"Thanks. So what about you? What happened with you and your ex? I know she sent you a 'Dear John' letter while you were deployed. Did you love her?"

"No, I barely tolerated her."

She laughed. "How long were you two together?"

"I want to say, about three months."

"Why did you still date her if you could barely tolerate her?"

"Our relationship was mainly physical. We had nothing in common. She was nothing like you." She smiled down at him, as she cleaned the cut with alcohol. She blew on the cut to dry it. "Am I being a good patient?" he asked and she laughed.

"Yes, you are, Master Sergeant," she said playfully, as he laughed.

"What do I get for being good?"

She smiled. "Well I don't have any stickers or lollipops, so what else would you like?"

"A kiss…" She bent down and kissed his lips. He wrapped his arms around her as she stood facing him, sitting in the chair. "If we had medics as gorgeous as you, I bet we'd have a lot more self -inflicted injuries down range."

She smiled and kissed his lips again. Closing the first aid kit, she picked up the alcohol swabs to throw away. "Morgan and I are going to talk to our apartment managers and ask them if we can break the lease. We can't stay in that apartment anymore."

He smiled. "I'll go with you to talk to them. We'll go look at apartments together."

She was impressed with him. "Really, you'd do that on the little time you get for leave?"

"Yeah, I want you to be safe, especially when I'm not here."

"You're incredible, you know that?" she asked. He touched her face and gently kissed her lips. He wrapped his arms around her waist. "I miss you when you're gone," she said, as she looked in his eyes and dragged her fingernail down his cheek and neck.

"I miss you too. You're all I think about."

She smiled and kissed his lips again. As he ran his fingers through her hair, they were kissing passionately. They slowly made their way to the sofa and laid back. They were holding each other tight and kissing passionately.

Feeling things between them were about to go to the next level, she gently pushed him back. "I'm not ready to have sex."

"Okay, I understand. No pressure."

"That's it? No pressure? You're not angry?"

"No I'm not angry. I'm man enough to hear the word no." He held her hand and noticed her golden purity ring on her finger.

She knew he was curious as to what it symbolized. She had to tell him. "Okay there's something you need to know about me…" She smiled at him. "…When I was fourteen, I made a vow to God and to my parents that I would remain a virgin until my wedding night, and this ring is my reminder of that vow. Most people call it a purity ring."

He was surprised. "So, you're a virgin?"

"Yes, and I know you want someone you can have a physical relationship with, and I won't do that. So let's end this now because this isn't going to work."

He held her hand. "I can respect and honor your vow. I don't want to lose you or make you uncomfortable. You mean a lot to me, and I want to be with you, no one else."

"You're able to respect this? You're able to be celibate?"

"Yes,"

"I bet you think I'm a freak don't you?"

"No, not at all, I think it's an admirable quality that you value yourself and honor your vow to God. And I will do nothing to try to pressure you to break that vow, but I just have one important question, can I still kiss you?"

She laughed. "Of course you can still kiss me."

He smiled. "Good because that would be cruel and unusual punishment if I couldn't."

"Thank you. I'm stunned you're so accepting about this decision. I really appreciate you respecting me. Kyle pressured me about it every day, especially after we got engaged."

He smiled and then kissed her lips. "I'm not him. I want you to forget all about him. He's your past."

She looked in his green eyes and smiled. "And you're my present?"

"Yes and hopefully your future." He kissed her lips. They lied back on the sofa, kissing. Both knew the boundaries. As the night got later, they relaxed together on the sofa. He held her, as she laid her head on his chest. She fell asleep listening to his heartbeat. He looked down at her, then looked behind him and saw the sofa throw. He pulled it over them, and after a while he fell asleep, also.

The next day, she, Morgan, and Jack went to look at many apartment complexes in the Dallas metroplex. They were looking at a high rise apartment building. It was a two bedroom/two bathroom spacious apartment. It was in a high rise tower, complete with a door attendant.

"So, what do you two think about this one?" the manager asked. "Is it big enough for you two?"

He looked out the window, at the great view of the Dallas skyline as she and Morgan looked around the apartment.

She smiled. "Yes, I love this one. It's a lot bigger than our current one. Do you like it, Morgan?"

"Yeah I love it too."

"Jack, do you like it?" she asked.

He turned back to look at her, Morgan, and the manager. "Yeah, it's really nice. I like that it has a doorman and a heated pool on the roof. You can't beat that. If this is the one you two want, let's go for it."

The manager smiled at them. "Okay, you two will be able to move in immediately. Don't forget to stop in to sign your lease and get your keys before you leave. Welcome to the building."

"Thank you," he said to the woman. The manager left the apartment to go back in the office to draw up Kate and Morgan's new lease. Morgan followed the manager down to her office. Kate and Jack were left in the apartment.

They looked out the window at the view of the Dallas skyline together. "Thank you so much for coming with us," she said to him.

"You don't have to keep thanking me, Kate. I am not doing this with a hidden agenda. I want you to be happy and safe."

"Okay, I'll try to stop thanking you."

He smiled at her and kissed her lips. "By the way, Jonah and I are going to move you both in."

"No, that's not necessary. We can hire a moving company."

He laughed. "Why would you hire movers when you have me and Jonah? Save your money."

They took the elevator down to the office for her to sign the lease. She paid her portion of the $700 security deposit. To break her current lease, she would have to pay $3,567.43. Jack knew she was stressing about how she was going to pay that, so he went and talked with her current apartment managers privately while she was at work and he took care of it with money he had in his savings account. Her cell phone rang. "Who is it?" he asked.

"It's my apartment manager." She answered. "Hello?"

"Kate, I wanted to let you know that we have released you and Morgan from your lease, since we received the funds."

She was confused. "But I haven't paid anything yet." He smiled listening to her.

"Actually, it's already been taken care of. A man came in the other day and paid it all. So you and Morgan are released from the lease," the woman said.

"Really, someone came in and paid the $3,567? Who was it?" she asked very curiously and in disbelief.

Her apartment manager looked at the card receipt. "His name was Jack D. Hamilton."

She was simply stunned that he did that. She looked over at him and smiled. "Thank you for letting me know," she hung up and the smile on her face grew larger and larger.

He noticed her smiling at him. "Are you okay?" he asked.

"You're incredible, you know that?"

"What are you talking about?"

"You paid the $3,567 to my apartment so they would release me from my lease? I can't believe you are doing all this for me, Jack. You didn't have to do that." she said as he drove back to Jonah and Christi's house.

"I know I didn't have to, but I wanted to."

"Why? You don't owe me anything or have to prove anything to me."

"It's my job to make sure you're happy and safe, Kate."

"Most boyfriends wouldn't pay nearly four thousand dollars to get their girlfriend out of her lease and into a new apartment. I'll pay you the money back."

He looked at her, "No, you won't pay me back. I did it out of love and respect. I don't have a hidden agenda. My primary focus is for you to be safe and for you to be happy. If you try to pay me back, I'll break up with you."

She laughed, not believing him, "You'd really break up with me if I tried to pay you back?"

He laughed, "Okay I wouldn't break up with you, but I wouldn't kiss you for a long time."

"We'll see how long that lasts. Don't make threats you can't uphold." she teased. They arrived at Jonah and Christi's. As he and Jonah were grilling out on the patio, she told Christi and Morgan what he did for her. They were stunned. They had fun grilling; drinking wine, and swimming.

Several days had gone by. It was moving day. He, Jonah, and Christi were helping them move into the new apartment. Morgan had to go out of town for a business meeting. She already had her boxes packed, so Christi and Kate were in charge of boxing everything else up and labeling.

Christi noticed that every time Jack would come back to get a box to take down to the truck, he and Kate would lock eyes and smile at each other. "So, how are things between you two?"

Kate smiled, as she labeled a box. "Very well, I'm really happy. I can't believe he's done all this for me. I never thought a man could be this good to a woman. I didn't think this kind of happiness existed."

"He's in love with you."

She smiled, "What makes you say that?"

Christi laughed, "Oh I don't know, maybe the way he looks at you, the way he talks about you, and the way he treats you. Why else would he do all this for you if he didn't love you?"

She hoped he was falling for her, since she was falling for him. "He could just really like me." She labeled the last box.

"You're obviously blind then, if you can't see that he loves you."

"He knows I'm a virgin…"

Christi looked at her curiously. "How did he react?"

"I could tell he was very surprised, but he was very understanding and supportive. He hasn't tried to take it to the next level or pressure me. It's nice to have a man who not only knows the boundaries, but respects them."

"See! That right there proves he loves you! It shows that your connection and relationship is much deeper than just physical."

He walked back in. She and Christi quickly quieted. He looked at them strangely. "Everything okay with you two?" he asked. He picked up the final box.

"Yeah, we're great, just having a debate."

"Debating about what?"

"It's nothing, girl stuff, you know which makeup is the best you know stuff like that. You wouldn't be interested in it." Kate said.

"You're right that's not interesting at all. Well we've got the truck all loaded. Come down with us." he said. He walked down the hall to the elevator with the final box.

Christi began to walk out the door, but noticed her standing in the middle of the living room.

"Hey, are you okay?"

"Yeah, I'm just closing the door on the past."

Christi smiled. She wrapped her arm around her shoulder. "Well, get ready to open the door for the future." They laughed. They turned to walk out. Kate took one final look. She was leaving her past of her and Kyle behind her for good.

"Come on, Kate! The guys are waiting!" she said, holding the elevator. She smiled, remembering Jack was waiting for her. She closed the door and skipped to the elevator. "Are you really skipping?"

"Yes, come on, skip with me!" she said.

"No!"

She laughed. "It's a lot of fun. Come on; let's act like we're nine years old." They skipped through the lobby of the apartment building. She turned in her key to the manager. They continued to skip out to the parking lot. They skipped to the truck. Jack and Jonah looked at them and laughed.

"Why are you two skipping?" Jonah asked.

"Because we're carefree," Christi said.

Jack placed his truck keys in Kate's hand. "This is a historic moment. I've never let a woman drive my truck, so I trust you."

She smiled. "You trust me not to wreck it?"

"I trust you not to wreck it, and if you do I have great insurance."

She laughed. "I'm honored to be the first woman to ever drive your truck. She's a very pretty truck."

He laughed. "Okay, first off, my truck is not a she or a 'her'."

"What if I want it to be a 'her'?"

He looked at his truck. "I don't see how it could be a 'her'." They laughed. She climbed in his truck, put his worn Oklahoma Sooners ball cap on, and smiled at him. He smiled at her. "You look good in my Sooners hat."

She blew him a kiss. Christi looked at her and was shocked. "You're a traitor! How could you wear that?"

Kate and Jack laughed at her reaction. She looked at him with her sunglasses on and blew him another kiss. "See y'all there!" He and Jonah drove the U-Haul truck as she and Christi drove his truck and followed them.

They arrived at the new apartment building. With the key in hand, the apartment was officially theirs. She and Christi started carrying boxes up and unpacking. After an hour, the truck was emptied. She and Christi repeatedly asked them to move the sofas, TV, and end tables to different positions in the living room. Jonah was starting to get irritated. "Pick a spot before I drop it and you live with it where it falls," he said, as Jack laughed.

They moved it up against the wall. "You women are so hard to please," Jonah said breathlessly, sitting on the sofa taking a break.

"I hate moving," Jack said, sweating and taking a drink of his water. "C'mon, Jonah we have to take the truck back." Jonah groaned, as they walked down to the service elevator to the U-Haul truck.

"I think we should order them something to eat, like pizza or wings. They're working so hard." Kate suggested. Christi had ordered them pizza and hot wings. Nearly half an hour later, he and Jonah walked through the door.

"We're back," Jonah said, lying on the sofa.

"Could you two set up her TV?" Christi asked.

She and Kate took a break from unpacking. They unpacked the kitchen, living room, and bedroom. Jack grabbed his tool box, and put her bed frame together. Kate walked in and sat on the floor with him. She handed him the tools he needed. He was surprised she knew the difference in screwdrivers.

"Let's watch a movie," Christi said, pouring Kate and herself a glass of wine.

"No chick flicks!" Jonah and Kate said, as Jack laughed.

"Oh come on!" Christi defended. Jack and Kate cuddled on the sofa together, as Jonah and Christi looked through her DVDs and fought over the ones Christi picked.

"How about we watch a war movie?" Jonah asked.

"No, let's watch a romantic comedy," Christi suggested.

"Let's settle this democratically, we're going to vote. Who wants an action movie?" Jack asked. He, Jonah, and Kate raised their hands.

"And those opposed?" he asked.

Christi enthusiastically raised her hand. Jonah laughed at her. "Ha, you lose."

"Shut up." she said, with a sideways smile at Jonah.

"Kate, you have a nice collection of action movies here. I'm impressed. I figured you'd be the type of girl who watches all that crap Christi watches and cries over," Jonah said. She had many classic action films.

"I have a few chick flicks down there, but I mostly have action movies like all the *Lethal Weapons* and all the *Rocky* movies, and of course war movie classics like *The Dirty Dozen* and *Heartbreak Ridge*," she said.

Finally, they picked a movie. They watched *Lethal Weapon 4*. The lights were off, as they cuddled on the sofas, eating pizza, and drinking wine. After the movie, they went up on the roof and enjoyed the heated pool. Jack and Kate were sitting together on the steps of the pool, laughing at Jonah dunking Christi under and throwing her in the deep end.

She held his hand. "Thank you." He smiled at her. "Thank you for exceeding my expectations on what a real man does and how he treats the woman he's with. I had no idea a man could be this helpful, caring, and honest. You're my knight in shining Kevlar," she teased.

He smiled. "You're welcome. I'd do anything for you." She kissed his lips.

"So were you worried I was going to wreck your truck?"

"No, I trusted you and even if you had, I wouldn't have been that upset."

"How good did I look driving your truck?"

He smiled. "My truck has never looked better." He pulled her into the water. They splashed each other and laughed.

The next morning, it was Sunday. The sun was rising. The sky was clear and blue. The birds chirped. Sunlight peeped into the blinds of her new bedroom. She opened her eyes and stretched. Looking at her clock, she noticed it was seven thirty. She went to church on Sundays, unless she was on duty. She got up, made her coffee, and took a shower. Her cell phone rang, it was Jack. "Hello?" she answered.

"Hi, gorgeous, what are you doing?" He was making coffee.

"I'm getting ready for church, what are you doing?"

"I was thinking about doing the same. It's been so long since I've gone to my parents' church."

"Come to church with me and my family. I want you to meet my dad."

"What domination are you and your family?"

"We're Christians," she said, with a laugh.

He laughed. "I gathered that, are you a specific denomination?"

"We're Baptists."

"Okay, that's what we are, where do you go?"

"We go to Prestonwood Baptist Church in Plano."

He was stunned. "Seriously, that's where my parents go."

She was excited. "Really, that's amazing. So it's likely that I know your parents and they know me and my parents."

"This should be interesting. I've never let my parents meet any of the women I'm dating, but you're special. I know they'll really like you."

"You think so?"

"I know so. I'll meet you there." She was happy he agreed to come to church with her. She was very put at ease that he was a Christian with a strong faith and relationship with God. She knew that with the demands of his job in the Army, he was not always able to sit in the pews inside a church on Sundays, but knew he knew who God was. He believed Jesus is the Son of God and that he died for our sins. Kyle was not a Christian, and he didn't believe in or support church.

He pulled into the church parking lot and saw Carole, Lauren, and Matt standing and waiting for Kate. Carole saw him and smiled, "Jack, I'm so happy you're here." He smiled at her. She hugged him and turned to Matt. "Matt, this is Jack,"

Matt stuck out his hand. Jack smiled and shook his hand. "It's good to finally meet you, son,"

"It's good to meet you too, sir," Kate pulled into the parking lot and was surprised to see him standing and talking with her parents. Her dad and Jack were laughing. She was relieved they were getting along.

She wore a nice floral skirt and top. Her hair was curled and teased. Jack noticed her. Matt looked at his watch, "You're late…"

"I know, I couldn't find my keys," she said, closing her car door.

"Hi, you look amazing." Jack said to her.

She smiled and kissed him in front of her parents. "You do too."

"Mom, Dad, Jack's parents actually go here. Maybe you know them."

"What are their names?"

"Bill and Denise Hamilton…"

Matt smiled, "I know your dad very well. You look just like him."

"I hear that a lot,"

"Meagan Hamilton, is she your sister?" Lauren asked him.

"Yeah, do you know her?"

"Yeah, she's in my young adult Bible study group. We talk and hang out a lot. I can't believe you're her brother. She's always talking about you."

"We should get together and go fishing. Do you like fishing?" Matt asked him.

"Yes sir, I do." They walked up the steps and through the doors. They saw many people standing in the foyer, greeting one another.

He held her hand. "Are you okay with meeting my parents?" he asked.

She smiled and held his hand. "Of course, I'm excited to meet them. Was my dad nice to you?"

"Yeah, he was really nice."

He noticed his parents talking with other older members of the church. "Momma, Dad…" Denise turned and was surprised to see him.

"Jack, I didn't know you were coming to church. I'm so proud of you." she said. She saw Carole. "Oh honey, just hold on a second…" She touched Carole's arm. "Carole, how are you doing? I haven't seen you in a few weeks," Denise said.

They hugged. "Hello Denise, I'm great. How are you?"

"I'm great. This is my youngest son, Jack. I'm so happy he made it to church. It's been so long since he's been here."

Carole smiled at him. "Yes, I've met him."

Denise looked at her curiously. "You have, how?"

Jack and Kate smiled at her. "Momma, I'd like you to meet my girlfriend, Kate Johnson." he introduced.

"…My daughter," Carole said, with a laugh.

"This is your daughter?" Denise asked in shock.

"Yes, she is my oldest."

"She looks just like you, Carole. I'm shocked I didn't notice the resemblance. Hello Kate, I'm so happy to meet you. You are stunningly gorgeous. Wow…"

Kate laughed nervously. "Thank you, Mrs. Hamilton."

"Oh honey, when you say Mrs. Hamilton, I naturally turn and hope my mother-in-law isn't right behind me…" she said, as Kate and Carole laughed. "…Please call me Denise."

He introduced her to his dad. "Wow, son, Lloyd wasn't kidding when he said she was beautiful, you lucky son of a gun." Bill said, slugging him in the arm.

"Dad, this is so not the time for you to be yourself." he said.

"Honey, it's so good to finally meet you. I've heard very good things about you from Jack."

"Hello, Mr. Hamilton." she said, holding out her hand to shake his.

"Mr. Hamilton? What am I old? Oh sweetheart, please call me Bill." He thought she was very beautiful.

The music began to play over the PA system. Everyone was ushering into the sanctuary to get to their pews. Jack and Kate walked ahead of their parents and siblings.

"How wonderful is it that our children are dating?" Denise said to Carole.

"Oh I know. I had no idea he was your son."

"They look very good together. They look happy and I've never seen him like this. He's never let Bill and I meet his girlfriends."

"I've never saw her smile so much before. I met him after Kyle attacked her. He came to the hospital after driving straight in from Fort Bragg. He was really concerned for her."

"I seriously think they're in love."

"Who knows, maybe we'll be in-laws soon." Carole suggested. The pastor stood at the podium and welcomed everyone. The choir stood and sang. They sang three beautiful songs, *In Christ Alone, Victory in Jesus, and God of Wonders.* The pastor stood with his Bible in his hands making a few announcements. They took up the offering. The sermon was over the book of Peter, lecturing, about taking wisdom from elders.

After the service, the pastor approached Jack and shook his hand. "It's good to see you again, Jack,"

"It's good to see you too, pastor."

"How are you doing, Katherine?"

"I'm great, pastor."

He smiled at them. "So, you two are dating? I must say you two look great together. I'm very happy for you both."

"Thank you, pastor. That's so sweet,"

Carole approached them. "Will you two join us for lunch?"

"Who all is going?" she asked.

"Jack's parents and us, please come."

She looked at him. "Do you want to?"

"Sure." They had lunch together. Her parents really liked him. His parents adored her. They all laughed and told funny stories.

A few days later, Jack called Matt and asked if he wanted to go fishing together. He took him out to Lloyd's, who had a private lake on his ranch in Blue Ridge. Lloyd walked out to his truck. "Hey Jack, how are you doing?"

"I'm good, Lloyd. This is Matt Johnson, Kate's father. Mr. Johnson, this is an old family friend, Lloyd Jefferson."

"Why do you keep calling me old?" Lloyd asked.

Jack and Matt laughed. "I don't mean it age wise."

"It's good to meet you, Lloyd." Matt said as they shook hands.

"It's nice to meet you too. Wow, Jack you're already meeting her parents? Good for you, son. I'm proud of you. Now you need to marry her and make some babies."

Jack was absolutely mortified. "Lloyd, you never cease to amaze me," he said shaking his head.

"You've met my daughter?"

"Oh yeah, he brought her out here a few months ago. She's very beautiful and very polite. You and your wife must be very proud."

"We are."

"Father to father, I saw her and Jack kissing out in the field," Lloyd said.

"Lloyd!" Jack scolded. He was uneasy and very embarrassed.

Matt looked at him. "Jack seems to be a good man. I don't mind if he kisses my daughter, as long as that's all they do."

"Oh, Jack is a good boy. I've known him since he was in diapers. He'd never take advantage of a woman."

Jack was extremely embarrassed and uncomfortable. "Lloyd we're going fishing. I'll catch you later and we're going to have a serious talk." he said.

"I look forward to it, son."

"I'm very sorry about that, Mr. Johnson. He's always embarrassing me."

Matt laughed. "You don't have to call me 'Mr. Johnson' or 'sir', you can call me Matt."

Sitting in the boat, they had their lines in the water, waiting for the fish to bite. It was a sunny afternoon with the sun high, the temperature was setting right around eighty-five degrees. Jack wore a pair of jeans, a white T-shirt, and a worn OU ball cap.

"You're an Oklahoma fan?"

He smiled. "Yes, I love them. They've always been my team."

Matt smiled. "I bet yours and Kate's relationship is really interesting in October, huh?"

They laughed. "Yeah, but she has a really good sense of humor about it."

"So I hear you were recommended for OCS[6] in basic but turned it down."

"Please don't take offense to this, Matt, but I wanted to be an NCO[7]. They're the backbone of the Army."

Matt smiled and laughed. "None taken, I was enlisted too before I was commissioned. Did you always want to be in the Army or were you going to do something else?"

"I had the opportunity to play college football, but I decided at the last minute to join the Army instead."

Matt was surprised. "Really, how did your Dad handle that?"

"I didn't tell him until after I had enlisted. I told him the night before I had to report for basic training. He wasn't too happy. I already had my dorm and everything, but I just knew that's not what I wanted to do. Then after basic and Ranger school, I joined SF[8], I think he just accepted that I'm just like him. My mom was furious with me. I got the silent treatment for a few weeks."

Matt smiled. He saw the Green Berets insignia and motto tattooed on his arm. They talked quite a bit about Afghanistan and the Army's progress there.

"So, have you ever been married?"

"No, I've avoided it as much as possible." he admitted, as they laughed.

"Smart man, but eventually, we all do. How long have you and Kate been dating?"

Jack thought. "Nearly five months."

"Is she someone you could see yourself getting serious with or is she just a temporary girlfriend?"

He looked at him. "She is in no way temporary to me. I see myself getting very serious with her."

"Good answer."

"She isn't like any woman I've ever known," he said.

"What do you like about her?"

He smiled, as he thought about her. "I love the way she laughs; I love her eyes and her smile. I love that she is sweet, honest, and caring. She is absolutely gorgeous. Even when she's not all dolled up—she's the most beautiful woman I've ever seen. She's real. There isn't anything fake about her, and I love that I can have an intelligent conversation with her. I love that she loves to help people, and she'll go out of her way to help you or make your day better. I love that she is a Christian and has a strong faith. She told me about her vow to God…"

"How do you feel about that?"

"I respect and support her decision. And I will honor it."

Matt smiled. "I'm glad to hear that, son. I know most young men look at her and see only one thing and that's all they want her for. I'm extremely proud of her for keeping her vow and respecting herself."

"She's an incredible woman, Matt."

"What else do you like about her?"

"We like a lot of the same things and we have a lot in common. She's family oriented just like me. She loves to shoot rifles, hunt, fish, and camp. She's a good shot too. I know I was shocked when I took her shooting."

Matt laughed. "Her mother might be stunned from shock if you told her that you love that Kate is a tomboy. She would always get mad at me for taking her camping, hunting, or fishing. She is also a champion equestrian and barrel racer."

---

[6] OCS- Officer Candidate School.

[7] NCO- Non-Commissioned Officer

[8] SF- Special Forces, commonly known as the Green Berets.

"I did not know that about her. I noticed her love for horses when we came here to shoot."

"When Kate shot a rifle for the first time, she was ten years old and Carole about had a heart attack. Kate and I have always had that special kind of bond. Lauren isn't the tomboy, she's the prissy girl. Kate is a rough, tough, country girl. She loves life."

"When I first met her, she completely threw me when she told me that she loved shooting Colt 1911's and the Winchester 4590 Center-fire. I brought her here and I let her shoot my rifle and a few of my pistols."

"She always outshoots my dad, brothers, and my nephews at Christmas and Thanksgiving. My parents have a ranch in Paris, Texas, so we go up there to play games and shoot. She loves to play football."

He smiled. "You and Carole have raised an amazing woman. I'm lucky to know her."

Matt patted him on the back. "Well, son, your parents raised an exceptional, honorable man. I like you. It's clear you care about my daughter and make her happy, so as long as she stays happy, you have my permission to date her."

"Thank you."

Kate and Morgan were decorating their new apartment, while her dad and Jack were out. She was curious how he felt about meeting her father so soon in their relationship. Of course, they wouldn't have met so early if Kyle hadn't had done what he did to her. She hoped he wouldn't be scared off by her father. Feeling nervous, she picked up her cell phone and called Lauren.

She told her that Jack and their dad were out fishing together. "Are you crazy? You let him go with Dad?" Lauren scolded, in shock.

"Dad seems to really like him."

Lauren laughed. "He would tell you anything you wanted to hear for the opportunity to get your boyfriend alone to threaten him."

"No, I don't think so. They've been gone for a few hours."

"I bet Dad killed him."

She laughed. "Lauren, don't be ridiculous."

"I'm not being ridiculous, I'm serious."

After fishing, Jack drove back into the city. They ate at the Saltgrass Steak House. They talked more. As he reached for the check, Matt stopped him. "It's on me."

"No, Matt, it's on me."

"Just let me pay. Think of it as mine and my wife's repayment for helping Kate with her apartment."

He felt uncomfortable with people thinking he helped her only for the recognition or for the possibility of reimbursement. "I don't want repayment for helping her. I helped her because I care about her. Her safety and happiness are my focus, nothing else matters. I'd do anything for her." he said, as he took the bill from him. He placed his credit card inside the black folder and handed it to the waitress.

Matt realized he was in love with her. "You're in love with her, aren't you?"

He looked at him while taking a drink of his tea. "Shouldn't she be the first to know before anyone else?"

Matt smiled. "You're right, I apologize, Jack. Thank you for helping Kate and for dinner."

"You're welcome, Matt."

The waitress brought back the slip that Jack had to sign. Matt watched him sign. "I'm proud of her. She picked a good man this time."

He laughed. They arrived back to the apartment. She was curious to know how the day went. Her dad gave her a kiss goodbye and shook his hand.

He closed the door and smiled at her. They went into her bedroom for privacy. They were lying on her bed just talking. "Did he scare you off?" she asked.

He smiled. "No, nothing could scare me off," as he touched her face. She looked up into his eyes.

He looked down at her. "You are so gorgeous." He gently kissed her lips.

As his leave time slowly ran down, they were getting closer, falling more and more for each other. They were at a Texas Rangers' baseball game. They were sitting in the stands of the ballpark, talking and waiting for the game to start. They smiled at each other, as they discovered a level of intimacy they never knew could exist in a relationship. She wore a red Rangers' T-shirt, blue jeans and a white Rangers cap. He wore a pair of blue jeans, a blue Rangers T-shirt, and a red ball cap.

Looking at his hand holding hers, she looked at him and smiled. "What's your biggest pet peeve?" she asked.

He thought about it. "My biggest pet peeve is when civilians thank me for my service. It annoys me. I'm not a hero."

She was surprised. "Yeah, but your job is incredibly dangerous. You don't see the difference between your job and that of let's see, a delivery driver?"

"It'd be different if I did it for free and out of the kindness of my heart, but I don't. I get paid for it."

"You'd think with what all you go through you'd get paid more. Doesn't it bother you that Jonah has a safe job and makes millions and you don't?"

"No, I don't do it for the money. Trust me no one joins the military to get rich. They do it for the brotherhood, college opportunity, or just pride in serving their country, or just to blow stuff up."

"Why'd you enlist?"

"I wanted to be a part of something bigger than me. I wanted to have a legacy that meant something. All the men in my family are military, except Jonah, so I always knew this is what I wanted to do. It's the family business. And I get to blow stuff up, so that's a plus."

She laughed. "Do you consider yourself a patriot?"

"Yes I do, but I don't want anyone making what I do more than it is. I don't have a job, I have a mission. I may wear the flag on my arm and I may be serving my country, but I'm fighting to save my brothers. It's all about the man next to you, your buddy, getting him home to his family. Do you know the difference between a job and a mission? Anyone can quit a job, but you can't quit the mission. You have to see it through until it's complete. Lives depend on it. I don't have a job, I have a mission. I'm responsible for eleven lives, men who have wives and children and parents. My mission is to get them home."

"Who knew your sense of duty could be so attractive."

He laughed. "I know I must sound crazy or self-righteous, but I'm not the only one who feels that way. Many of my buddies feel the same way. Especially since 9/11, my guys and I are constantly stopped by people thanking us for our service. I've had a lot of people buy me drinks, but it's not necessary. We're not the heroes. The men we lose out there are the heroes, but civilians don't understand that."

"You're my hero."

He smiled at her. "What's your biggest pet peeve?"

"Oh I have many, but my biggest one would be people who do not go the speed limit, especially on the freeway. I have road rage really bad."

He laughed. "I don't believe it. You're so sweet and innocent. It's hard to believe you have a fiery temper."

She looked at him and smiled. "I have a dark side."

He laughed. "So how is this temper when your precious Longhorns lose?"

She smiled at him. "It's not pretty."

"It's not your fault. It's a scientific fact that Texas fans have more fiery tempers than Oklahoma fans because they've lost so much to OU," he teased. She playfully swatted him. "Hey don't shoot the messenger, I'm just reporting what the scientists have found," he teased.

"Hey who won the first game?" she asked.

He smiled and laughed, "Okay, touché."

"What good and bad habits do you have?" she asked.

"I swear, drink, and smoke cigarettes sometimes. Being out in the desert with twenty other guys, swearing is normal. I've never met anyone in the military who doesn't swear. I drink occasionally, and I smoke when I'm on deployment just to help with the nerves, but when I'm home, I don't smoke."

"I've never smoked, and I never will. I think it's stupid."

"It is, but it does help calm your nerves."

"What good habits do you have?"

"This may sound weird coming from a guy, but I cannot stand a dirty house. I have to have a clean house. My ex used to trash my place, finally I changed my locks."

"What do you mean she'd trash your place?"

"I'd come home from a live fire training mission and it literally looked like a frat party had been there. Dishes would be in the sink with dried food on them, dirty clothes would be everywhere, and the trash was overflowing."

"Gross, she sounds like a slob."

"Oh she was."

"If it makes you feel any better, I'm the same way as you. I cannot stand to have dishes in my sink or anything out of place."

He smiled at her. "What bad habits do you have?" he asked.

She thought about it. "I leave my bras on my doorknobs, I procrastinate about doing my laundry, and I eat A1 Sauce with everything, especially popcorn."

He looked at her strangely. "You eat A1 Sauce with popcorn? How do you eat popcorn with A1 Sauce?"

"Yes, it's phenomenal. I just dip it." She laughed at the way he was looking at her. "You're looking at me like I'm crazy, but you're going to try it and you're going to love it."

He smiled. "Okay, I'll try it."

"Another one of my bad habits, is I love junk food and fast food, like Doritos Nacho Cheese chips, Tex-Mex, and Whataburger. I also love whiskey. I cannot stand beer."

He looked at her in shock. "You don't like beer, but you can handle whiskey?"

"Yeah, I don't know why,"

"You have done something that most people are unable to do."

"What do you mean?"

"You surprise me."

"What was your first impression of me when we met?" she asked.

He looked at her and smiled. "My first impression was that you were shy and insecure. I saw your self-confidence had taken a huge hit and to cope with it, you had a huge wall up and were careful of who you let close to you," he said.

She smiled at him. "You saw all that when we first met? Did you have a psychologist profile me?"

"No, I'm really good at reading people. I told you your eyes told me everything I needed to know." She smiled at him. She knew she loved him. "What was your first impression of me?" he asked her.

"Well, you were so charming, sweet and incredibly handsome and also very confident, I thought you were full of it."

"And am I full of it?"

She held his hand. "No, you've truly delivered all that you said you would." They laughed and talked more as they waited for the game to begin.

After the game, they were walking through the aisles when a rude man grabbed her rear. Noticing the shocked expression on her face, he asked her, "What's wrong?"

"One of those guys just grabbed me."

He looked to the three men, who were still staring at her and her rear. He was annoyed. "Wait here." he said to her. He walked over to the three middle aged men. "Which one of you grabbed my girlfriend?"

"I did. I couldn't help myself."

He punched him one time in the face. The guy fell back into his friends, spilling their beer and was knocked out cold. The other men didn't defend their friend. He walked away.

"I can't believe you just did that." she said.

"Did you really think I was going to let him get away with that?"

They drove back into Dallas. They walked around The Dallas Arboretum and Botanical Gardens. They walked through beautiful roses and pink tulips.

"What is your favorite Biblical scripture?" she asked, holding his hand as they strolled. The sun was shining high. The temperature was cool. The wind was breezy.

"*Isaiah 41:10* [9]."

She smiled. "That's a good one."

"Yeah, I think of that one a lot when I'm on a mission. What's your favorite?"

She held his hand as they walked around the fountain. "Oh I have many, but if I had to choose, I'd choose *Romans 5:8*[10]."

They stood face to face, as the wind blew through her hair. The sunlight made her brown eyes look like honey. He touched her face. "I'm happy God brought you into my life. You're absolutely perfect for me." he said, pulling her up against him as the sun set. "When I'm gone, I look at your picture and all I want to do is be here with you."

She smiled up at him. "I'm happy he brought you into my life. I couldn't have asked Him for a better man." They both felt they were in love with each other, but were nervous to tell each other. He wanted to wait until the moment was right. He knew they hadn't been together that long, but he knew she was the woman for him after their second date where they kissed in the field at sunset.

They stood kissing as her hair fluttered in the wind. They held each other tightly. As they walked back to his truck, he asked, "Are you hungry? I'm starving."

"Yeah, I'm hungry too. What are you hungry for, what's your favorite?" she asked him.

"I'm a soldier, I'll eat anything."

She smiled. "I want to cook for you."

He smiled at her. "I've never had a woman cook for me, except my momma or Marie."

"I promise I won't poison you." They laughed. He picked her up and twirled her around. He wanted to belt out that he loved her right then, but he wanted the timing to be perfect.

---

[9] 'Fear not, for I am with you; be not dismayed, for I am your God. I will strengthen you, I will help you. I will uphold you with my righteous right hand'."- Isaiah 41:10

[10] 'But God shows his love for us in that while we were still sinners, Christ died for us'."- Romans 5:8

"You know what I haven't had in a long time? Homemade chili…"

She smiled. "Lucky for you, I have the Johnson family chili recipe. It's classified above top secret. It's really good."

"Will you make it for me?"

She smiled at him. They arrived at the apartment. Morgan was out of town again for a wedding in Houston. She changed into comfortable clothes. He watched ESPN while she changed. She came out of her bedroom, walked into the living room, and tied an apron around her waist. She was barefoot. Her hair was up in a clip, but falling down around her face and shoulders. He smiled at her.

He smiled. He liked her wearing the apron. Though he made himself honor her vow, she still excited him. He followed her into the kitchen. "Can I help?"

She kissed his lips. "You've heard the expression 'there's only enough room in the kitchen for one chef'?"

He laughed. "Yeah…"

"This is where it applies. I get a little controlling when I cook, so it's best if you avoid that."

He laughed. "Yes ma'am." He wrapped her up in his arms as they kissed passionately in the kitchen for several minutes.

"I'm starving…" he said.

She smiled. "Then let me cook."

He laughed. "Okay, I'll leave you alone." He walked into the living room and watched ESPN.

She browned three pounds of hamburger meat, chopped an onion, and applied the tomato sauce, and the spices to the meat. The smell was heavenly.

Nearly an hour later, the chili was finished. He smiled at the plate she had made for him. "Wow, this looks incredible." he said. She poured him a glass of Texas sweet tea and sat down beside him. He took a bite. "Wow…this is really…amazing. You're an excellent cook."

"Thank you, I'm glad you like it." They enjoyed dinner together. Afterwards, they ate ice cream for dessert with a few glasses of wine while watching a movie on the sofa. They talked, laughed, and kissed like crazy. They were crazy about each other, but knew they had to keep their emotions under control.

Days later, his leave time was up. It was time for him to leave and report back to Fort Bragg. He was at her apartment saying goodbye to her. They were standing in the middle of the living room, kissing passionately. "I wish you didn't have to go."

"I know, I want to stay with you, but I have to go." he said. He kissed her lips. "I'll be back soon."

"You promise?"

He smiled at her. "Yes, I promise." He grabbed his bag and opened the door. She walked with him down to his truck.

"Be safe."

"Always, please don't worry. Be strong for me." he said. She hugged him and kissed his lips one last time. He got inside his truck and drove away.

6

In March, 2003, the Bush Administration accused Iraq dictator Saddam Hussein of having weapons of mass destruction (WMDs). The President gave the dictator forty eight hours to surrender his forces and his weapons to coalition forces.

In the still of the night on March 19, Alpha, Bravo, and Charlie Teams departed from the U.S. Forward Operating Base (FOB) in Kuwait and were flown just on the outskirts of the capitol city, Baghdad, by helicopter, eluding Iraqi radar. A second U.S. helicopter followed the teams for back up, should they be detected. The helicopters landed in a remote desert location. The Green Berets exited the helicopters and quickly established a 360 degree security perimeter until the helicopters departed.

"Move out." Jack said over his radio to his team. They quickly got to a pre-arranged rendezvous location where they were to meet with Intelligence Support Activity operatives (ISA). Alpha Team saw three men dressed as civilians. They stayed in position, not knowing if they were the ISA operatives or ordinary civilians. They were told the operatives would be dressed as civilians. Jack made a bird call, as the signal. If these were in fact the operatives, the Green Berets would receive a signal back.

The operatives drove the team into Baghdad. They had been covertly working in Baghdad for several weeks, gathering intelligence on potential targets, establishing safe houses all around the city, acquiring transportation, fraudulent identification papers, and most importantly exit strategies. They arrived in Baghdad, with no incidences, and were set up in the safe house. They had pinpointed and observed Saddam Hussein's activities and those of his generals and other Baath party officers. They soon realized that Saddam and his commanders frequently met at a local restaurant to discuss policies. They believed information about the WMD programs was also shared.

It was a hot sunny day. Alpha and Bravo Teams were set up on an undercover observation position on the roof of a building, one block away from the restaurant. A convoy of vehicles, including a Mercedes Benz, the type of vehicle Saddam used, pulled up in front of the restaurant.

"Alpha 3, do you have a visual on *The Ace* inside the Mercedes?" Jack asked Jake, who looked through the binoculars.

"Negative, Alpha 1, there are too many civilians," Jake responded.

"Is *The Ace* among those entering the restaurant?" They referred to Saddam Hussein as 'The Ace' incase the line of communication became compromised. Saddam was the Ace of spades in the deck of cards, that every U.S. soldier and Marine carried.

"Negative, Alpha 1, *The Ace* is not entering the restaurant, but I do have visual confirmation on three high ranking generals in charge of the army and the WMD program." Tom replied.

Jack got on the phone with the Air Force. A bomber was on standby circling the city awaiting instructions from the ground team. "This is Alpha 1, three HVT[11]s confirmed. Drop it." he ordered.

---

[11] HVT- High Value Target

The bomber released his ordinance. Two minutes later, the restaurant exploded in a shower of brick, mortar and dust. The explosion rattled the city and gave the Green Berets the perfect opportunity to escape as chaos and confusion from civilians surrounded them. The Green Berets split up, each finding a different way to make it back to the safe house without drawing attention. As each man made it back, they immediately packed up their weapons and gear. Two of the ISA operatives drove the team back out to the rendezvous point in the desert, to their awaiting helicopters. They made it across the Iraq/Kuwait border safely. The Green Berets and the ISA gave U.S. air command exact coordinates for specific military targets, designed to scare Saddam's 400,000 soldiers into surrendering. U.S. forces prepared to initiate 'shock and awe'.

In Dallas, Kate was visiting with Christi at their home. They were in the kitchen making party favors and snacks for JD's birthday party. He was now six years old. "So, have you heard anything from Jack?" Christi asked.

She frowned. "No, I haven't. He's gone right now. I'm sure he's really busy wherever he is."

"Have you emailed him?"

"No, I wouldn't even know what to write him. I don't want to distract him."

"Well, for starters you can tell him you're in love with him." Kate looked at her. "We both know you are, Kate. Don't even try to lie."

"When have I ever said I'm in love with him?" she asked, blushing.

"Oh please, you're both in love with each other. You two look like you're in love when you look at each other, talk to each other, talk about each other. And the way you look at his pictures—you're definitely in love with him." Christi said, studying her body language and facial expressions.

She smiled like she was in love. "I'd like to tell him how I feel in person, not by email."

"What attracts you to him the most?"

She smiled as she thought about him. "Everything, I get lost in his eyes. His smile makes my knees buckle and his personality makes me happy. I love the way he looks at me, holds me and kisses me. When we're together, all we do is laugh and joke around."

They laughed. "Just admit it. You're in love with him,"

She smiled. "Okay, I'm in love with him, but you can't tell anyone. I want to tell him when the moment is right. I'm just scared he won't feel the same."

"Oh trust me, he feels the same," Christi said confidently.

That night, she sat at her laptop. She typed up an email to him. She was going to tell him how she felt for him. She wanted him to know how she felt about him, in case something happened to him.

> *"Dear Jack,*
>
> *I'm writing you this letter to let you know how I feel about you. The thought of you being so far away, fighting and risking your life and not knowing how I feel about you seems wrong. From the moment I first saw you, I knew you were special and different than any man I've ever known. I'm in love with you, Jack. I know I can trust you. When I hold your hand, my heart plummets to the bottom of my stomach. When you kiss me, my body is covered with goose bumps. When I look at you and hear your voice, I get butterflies in my stomach. I've never felt this way about anyone before, which I find extraordinary considering I was about to marry someone. When you're kissing me and holding me, I don't want you stop or let me go.*
>
> *You're the first person I think about when I wake up and you're the last to enter my mind before I fall asleep. Every time I see a soldier in uniform, my heart pounds excitedly, hoping it's you. And when it's not you, I miss you more than I ever have. I'm very attracted to you.*

You're incredibly handsome, sweet, gentle, a Christian. You're smart, strong, and protective. You're a gentleman, and that is a very attractive quality.

I feel so safe with you. I love that you feel it is your responsibility to keep me safe, even when you're thousands of miles away. I don't know where you are, but I think about you constantly and I worry about you. Even though I've fallen in love with you, Jack, I'm scared to let you love me. I'm scared to get hurt again.

I know wherever you are, you are somewhere dangerous, so the last thing I want to do is distract you, but I needed and wanted you to know that I'm in love with you and I miss you. I can't wait to see you again.

Stay safe. Come back to me. I'm waiting for you.

Love, Kate"

She contemplated whether sending him that letter was a good thing. She hoped he felt the same. After reading it to herself, she regretted sending it. She should've waited until he was home, but with his dangerous job, that was never a guarantee he would come home. She felt comfort in knowing that if something did happen to him, after he read her letter, he would know she loved him.

Massive sandstorms halted all convoys in route to Baghdad. Many referred to the sandstorms as like being on the planet Mars. Everything was illuminated in red, which made it impossible to see anything. The storm stalled the invasion for two days. Alpha, Bravo, and Charlie Teams were in largely populated Camp Taji, which was twenty miles north of Baghdad, and was originally used by the Iraqi Republican Guard for chemical weaponry. The U.S. immediately took control, after invading, suspecting that this was the location where the WMDs were being held, but none were found.

After being outside the wire for several days, the Green Berets were finally able to relax. He was lying on his cot, with his rifle close by, looking at the picture of her. He looked at his laptop and checked his email. Seeing he had a letter from her, he was hesitant to read it, after receiving a 'Dear John' from Chelsea. After looking at the subject line: *How I Feel*, he opened it and read. He smiled as he read the entire letter. He was happy. He wrote.

"Dear Kate,

Hi baby, I'm sorry it's taken me so long to talk to you. I'm glad you told me how you feel. I feel the same way about you. I'm in love with you too. I've wanted to tell you how I felt for a long time, but I didn't want to go too fast or scare you. From the moment I saw you, I knew you were the woman for me. I think it's a fair assessment that you had me from hello. I've never met a woman who is as kind, sweet, loving, generous and loyal as you. You're what I've been looking for and at the same time running from. I've never felt this way about anyone else. All my relationships were casual and purely physical. I wouldn't let any of them get close to me, but you stole my heart. There's no way I could ever let you go, baby, even if I wanted to. I'll never try to seduce or pressure you into having sex, even though I've never wanted to be with any woman as much as I want to be with you, but you're worth the wait. I admire and respect you for your decision. I want to be a worthy man. I want to be honorable, but I'll be honest, there are times when it is so difficult to stop myself, but I know God has given me the strength to control myself and not be tempted beyond my ability.

I know you're afraid to let me love you, Kate, but there's no safer place for you than with me. I promise I'll love you better than anyone ever has. I can promise you that I'll never hurt you. I'll never take you for granted. I'll always be here for you.

I'm looking at your picture. It's by my computer. Just looking at you makes me smile and miss home. I can't wait to see you again. Well baby, I'm going to get some sleep. I'm finally able to lie down. I'm so tired. Please don't worry about me. I'm coming back to you. I love you. Bye gorgeous,

Jack"

He sent the email. He looked at her picture and smiled. He was happy and relieved she loved him and that she had said it first. He didn't want to be the first to say it and face rejection.

Suddenly, at 1:21 am, the camp was abruptly awakened and jolted by a grenade exploding. He grabbed his weapon and hurried out of his bunk. Seconds later, another grenade detonated in an officer's tent. Soldiers scrambled to get their weapons, protective gear and their helmets, preparing for direct contact with the enemy.

"I'm hit! I'm hit!" a soldier yelled, panicking. Other soldiers rushed to his side and lifted him onto a gurney, rushing him straight to the infirmary.

The camp was in complete chaos. Cordite and smoke filled the attacked tents, with a hole in the rubber floor. Soldiers applied bandages and tourniquets to the wounded as part of first triage.

A Lieutenant Colonel stood beside his exploded tent in a daze. "Are you alright, Colonel?" Jack asked him concerned. He saw the dazed look on the man's face.

"I saw the tent flap open up and in rolled a grenade. I was waiting for it to detonate, thank God it didn't."

Chaos was everywhere, soldiers turned tables into makeshift gurneys for wounded comrades. Several grenades were missing. Three had been tossed into tents, but only two had detonated. Many thought they had an intruder in the camp. Several armed soldiers searched to find the intruder. Jack and Tom were among those searching for him. They entered a bunker with their rifles locked and loaded. Jack pointed his light on his rifle to a box of live ammunition. They saw an U.S. Army sergeant in uniform, crouching beside a box, hiding three grenades in his gas mask bag.

They were stunned that one of their own had betrayed them. "Stand up with your hands in the air!" Jack commanded.

"Get back!" the sergeant screamed. "I will kill you!"

They continued to point their rifles at him, as they slowly and carefully approached him. Jack aimed his rifle at his head. "Put the bag down and let me see your hands now!" he yelled.

The sergeant would not comply. "I don't want to be here anymore! You're going to have to shoot me!" the sergeant yelled, as Jack and Tom slowly approached him.

Seeing, the sergeant reach inside the bag for another grenade, they shot him twice in the chest, killing him before he could act. Jack reached down grabbed the bag of grenades, and felt for a pulse as Tom stood over still pointing his rifle. They both stood stunned over the lifeless body of a U.S. soldier.

"We're clear and coming out!" Tom yelled over his radio, as U.S. Army Rangers and other infantrymen had their rifles pointed at the bunker. They lowered their weapons, as Jack and Tom stepped out. All in camp were appalled that one of their own betrayed them.

"What happened? Why didn't he surrender?" Colonel Mitchell asked Jack and Tom.

"We told him to put his hands up and step back. He screamed that he didn't want to be here, and then reached into the bag for a grenade. We had to shoot him." Jack said.

Realizing that Jack and Tom were justified in the shooting, "Alright, CID[12] is going to want your statements." Colonel Mitchell told them.

---

[12] CID stood for Criminal Investigative Division. They investigated crimes within the Army.

"Yes, sir," Jack and Tom walked away. After giving their statements to CID, Jack and Tom were cleared of any misconduct. War correspondents present in camp, subsequently found a story out of this sickening betrayal. They asked dozens of soldiers how they felt by the treachery of one of their own. Many soldiers felt justice was done.

They were sitting outside their bunks, smoking cigarettes. It was the only thing that calmed them down. "I can't believe we shot a soldier," Tom said.

"He was a traitor. If he had surrendered, he would've spent the rest of his life in Leavenworth or he would've gotten the death penalty. This time justice was swift."

"So, how's your woman back in Texas doing?"

He looked at him and smiled. "She's good. She told me she loves me."

Tom smiled. "And did you tell her you love her?" Jack looked at him and smiled. "Oh, please don't even deny that you do; it's a waste of time. I've known you for a long time, and you my friend, have fallen in love."

"I've never said I love her."

"Yeah, whatever, Jack. Go practice saying that in the mirror and when you convince yourself, come find me."

He did love her, but he didn't want his team to know. They'd tease him just as Tom was. "We've only been together for like eight months,"

Tom laughed. "You're a really bad liar, Jack."

He rolled his eyes and laughed. "Whatever. I'll see you later."

"Where are you going? You're going to call her and tell her you love her, aren't you?"

"No…" Jack lied.

"You know you're a horrible liar, right?" Tom yelled as he walked away to the MWR tent.

She was getting ready to leave for work. She checked her email to see if he had wrote her back. When she saw his email, her heart began to pound excitedly. She smiled as she read his email. She was relieved that he felt the same way she did. She saved the email and looked at the picture of them together at a Ranger's game beside her computer. She looked at her watch and realized she was almost late. She quickly headed to work. Her friends noticed the huge smile on her face and wondered what was going on with her. "Okay, what's going on with you?" Angie asked.

She smiled at her, "He told me he loves me."

Angie was happy for her. "Do you love him?"

"Yeah, I do."

"Did you tell him?" Angie asked her. She smiled and nodded. They got busy taking care of their patients.

He finally was able to use a phone after standing in line for nearly an hour. He called her. She was at work. Seeing an odd satellite number was calling, she ran to an empty maternity suite to answer. "Jack?" she answered.

"Hi baby, how are you doing?"

She was excited and happy to hear from him. "Hi, I'm good. I'm at work. How are you?"

"I'm good. I got your email."

She didn't know what to say. "I got yours this morning just before I left for work."

"I'm glad I'm finally able to say it. I've loved you since our second date."

"What made you fall in love with me?"

"When I kissed you after you lost that bet, you kissed me back. And then on the Fourth when you promised you'd wait for me. That sealed the deal."

She smiled, "I fell in love with you when you kissed me the first time. Why do you think I kissed you back?"

"Well I'm glad we finally told each other how we felt. I've wanted to tell you for so long, but I didn't want to scare you. Kate, why are you so afraid to let me love you?"

"I'm just scared to get hurt again. I'm scared to give you all of my heart."

"In order to prove to you I'm not like Kyle, I'm going to need you to trust me and give me all of your heart, not just part of it."

"The hardest thing for a woman to trust a good man after she's had a bad one."

"Well you've had my heart since the day we met, so I guess I'll just have to work harder to win all of your heart,"

She smiled. "I'm kind of glad we're apart because if you were here in front of me, things between us could get out of control," she said.

He smiled. "As much as I want that to happen, I couldn't put you in that situation."

She loved that he was honorable. Even though there were times especially when kissing him, her will to remain pure was tested. "I love you, Jack."

He smiled. "I love you too. I wish I could tell you in person."

"It feels good to hear you say it, and it would be nice to hear it in person, but being that we're thousands of miles apart and you're in a war zone, it makes it more meaningful, more memorable. I saw this soldier in uniform walk out of the elevator the other day, and my heart almost stopped. I was hoping he was you. I can't wait to see you, especially in uniform,"

He smiled. "You wouldn't want to see me in uniform right now. I'm covered in dirt and sand. I haven't showered or shaved in a long time."

"None of that would bother me as long as I got to see you. How are things where ever you are?"

"Busy, I'm just getting back to base."

"I need your address. I want to be able to send you stuff."

"Like what?"

"Anything you want, goodies, pictures, movies, books, whatever you need."

"You'd really do all that for me?"

"Yes, of course! I'd do anything for you!"

"Wow, I'm truly a lucky man,"

She smiled. "What are you going to do while you're on base?"

"Eat, shower, and sleep."

She could hear the exhaustion in his voice. She knew Special Forces soldiers rarely got time to sleep. They were always on the move. "I imagine you're beyond exhausted, so if you want to get off here and get some sleep, I wouldn't throw a fit. You should get all the sleep you can."

"I love you. Thanks for understanding that I'm exhausted, but I want to talk to you more than I want to sleep. How are things back home?"

"They're good. I'm at work right now."

He smiled, "I bet you look good in your scrubs,"

"You'll have to find out for yourself,"

"Is it a pretty slow shift?"

"Yeah, it's pretty slow right now." She heard him yawn. She knew he was really tired. "Jack, I love you. I miss you very much. I'm happy you called me, but go take a hot shower, get some food, and get some sleep."

"You really won't be mad if I hang up?"

She laughed, "No, what am I a spoiled teenager? I'm an adult and I know you have an extremely stressful job. I want you to get as much sleep as possible. I want you to be alert and be safe."

"You're amazing,"

"All I ask is that you come back to me."

"I will, I promise. You bring me home." he said. "I love you. I'll try to email or call you before we move out." He gave her his address. "I won't be here very long, so just send it to me and they'll eventually find me."

"Okay, I love you. Be safe."

"I will, I love you too, baby." He hung up. She walked out of the empty maternity suite and continued to work.

Angie, Tess, and Marci noticed the large smile stretched across her face. "What's going on with you?"

"My soldier called." she said happily.

"And judging by the smile on your face, you two had a great conversation." Tess said.

"We both said I love you." They were happy for her.

He walked to the showers and took a shower. He thought of her as the water cascaded on his head and back. He got something to eat. Lying in his cot, he looked at her picture. He missed her. Soon after lying down, he dozed off.

U.S. convoys were under increasing fire fights, so one way to reduce the number of casualties was to not stop and to speed up. Many of the vehicles were experiencing mechanical difficulties, therefore causing them to break down and fall behind. Many were getting stuck in the sand. In the early morning hours, twenty year old Specialist, Leslie Dennison sat nervously in the back of a Humvee with two others from her unit. Like her, many in her unit have never experienced combat. The forty-five soldiers of her non-combat unit were trained and equipped with only the basics of weaponry.

The driver of Dennison's vehicle lost sight of the convoy vehicle they were supposed to follow. She and her comrades were completely lost. Exhausted and disoriented, the driver made a fatal mistake. Instead of going around the city of Nasiriya, as planned, he drove them into the heart of the unsecured city. The city of Nasiriya was a hot bed of insurgents, loyal to Saddam Hussein and eager to fight with coalition forces.

At first it was quiet, suddenly gunfire rang out. As the lost convoy drove further into the heart of the city, gunfire rang out from all sides. Soldiers inside the lead truck, realizing they were in trouble, encouraged the driver to turn around and retreat. The driver attempted, but he could not maneuver the convoy quickly enough. He slowed to help guide the other trucks behind him, but slow driving proved more to be an advantage for insurgents than helpful for the soldiers.

SPC Dennison and the others were trapped in a hail of gunfire inside the Humvee. She desperately tried to shoot her rifle, but it wasn't firing. She was nervous and terrified.

An RPG hit her vehicle, causing her vehicle to slam into another vehicle. Her injuries knocked her unconscious. The convoy was barraged by RPG fire and eventually overran by Iraqi's. SPC Dennison and four others were taken as prisoners. The attack killed eleven soldiers from her convoy. Survivors alerted Special Operations soldiers' of their ambush and reported five missing soldiers, when they arrived back to Camp Taji.

SPC Dennison awoke in an Iraqi hospital. Seeing she was in the hands of the enemy, she tried to keep herself from panicking. She was unsure if they were going to kill or torture her. She thought of her family in South Dakota.

Colonel Mitchell approached Alpha, Bravo, and Charlie Teams who were all gearing up. "A convoy of Humvee's got lost and went into Nasiriya. We've taken casualties but five are missing. Your mission is to find those five soldiers and bring them home."

"Yes sir."

"Nasiriya is not secure. It's a hot bed. You'll most likely meet much resistance and very few friendlies, if any. Watch your six and stay alert." The Green Berets departed Camp Taji and searched for the five missing soldiers from the recent convoy that was attacked in Nasiriya.

That night, Army CW3 pilot Caleb Brown flew his Apache attack helicopter toward Karbala, a key access point to Baghdad. The city of Karbala was protected by an entire tank division of the Iraqi Republican Guard, who were Saddam's best trained and best equipped men. Over the city of Karbala and Baghdad, the Iraqi's still maintained air defense units. Thirty miles from their target zone, Brown and his gunner, Robert Rodrigues flew over the town of Hilla. They were startled by what they saw below them. Many people were walking below the helicopter, hoisting rifles. The time was just after midnight. Suddenly the entire town lit up with anti-aircraft fire. Brown attempted evasive action, but his Apache was riddled with bullets.

"Turn left! Turn right!" Rodrigues yelled to Brown.

Signals and alerts sound louder and louder, as the helicopter spiraled out of control. Brown desperately tried to control the impact of the landing. "We're going down! We're going down!" he yelled over the radio. He managed to crash land. Dawn was approaching. They scrambled from the wreckage and took cover in an irrigation canal, with water up to their noses. The Iraqi Republican Guard scoured the area, and eventually discovered them. Both were knocked in the head with the butt of an AK-47, their hands were bound behind their backs. They were taken to the city of Samarra. The next day the prisoners were displayed on the Arabic television network, Al-Jazeera. Their captors interrogated the soldiers about their missions.

Colonel Mitchell approached Jack and Tom, who were gathering up more ammunition for the team to go back and continue the search for the five missing soldiers. "An Apache was just shot down and the two pilots are now prisoners. We're getting other reports that there are twelve other missing soldiers." he informed.

The teams used intelligence from the citizens to find the Apache pilots and the other twelve missing soldiers. The commanders of U.S. military found Al-Jazeera footage on Iraqi T.V. of soldiers in the Iraqi Republican Army guarding and interrogating the U.S. Apache pilots being interrogated and they also saw deceased soldiers' bodies on display.

Through intelligence from civilians, Alpha, Bravo, and Charlie Teams were outside the Saddam Hussein Hospital. They were told this is where SPC Dennison was being held. "This is Alpha 1, we found the package. The package is in the Saddam Hussein Hospital."

Suddenly heavy gunfire and tracer rounds exploded in the distance. Black Hawk helicopters roared overhead. The rescue operation for twenty year old SPC Leslie Dennison and the other missing soldiers had begun. The Green Berets maneuvered to deliver a solid attack force to breach the perimeter to rescue the American POWs. Dennison was lying in a hospital bed on the third floor. She heard a helicopter overhead the hospital and then heard shouting outside the room. The soldiers' swept down on the Saddam Hussein Hospital. They prepared for enemy contact.

"Clear!" Brad yelled, as they ran up the stairs to the third floor. They reached the third floor and entered a trauma room. They saw medical staff standing around a gurney. Dennison's captors had fled.

"Nobody move!" Jack yelled in Arabic. He pointed his weapon at the medical staff. Many of the Iraqi medical personnel held up their hands and slowly backed away. The team found the young American female soldier lying on a gurney with absolute terror on her face.

"Detain them! Ask them where the captors are!" Jack ordered, as Brad, Tom, and Jake detained the medical staff for questioning. Jack confirmed the young female soldier was in fact SPC Dennison. He knelt down beside her, seeing she was severely injured, and extremely terrified.

"Please don't leave me!" she begged, while sobbing and gripping his hand tightly.

"We're not going to leave you. Jamal and Chase are our docs and they're going to take care of your injuries, okay?"

Jamal and Chase tried to address her injuries, but she was pulling her arm away from them. "No! No! NO!" she pleaded. Jack held her hand, as Jamal was finally able to treat her injuries. She screamed, as they comforted her. "You're okay, it's alright." Jamal said to her, as she cried. Minutes rolled by. The team secured the perimeter and began comforting her.

"Are we clear to head out?" Jack asked Brad.

"Yes, the helicopter is inbound." Brad replied. Bravo and Charlie Teams were outside surrounding the building and blocking off the doors.

"Okay, Leslie we're going to escort you down to the helicopter. You're going home." Jack said to her.

"We're clear. The helicopter has just landed," Tom said. He and three team members lifted her and the gurney up. They carefully but quickly rushed down the stairs to the helicopter.

They reached the helicopter. "You're safe now," Jack said to her, as she gripped his hand tightly. He ripped the American flag off his uniform and gave it to her.

She held it tight into her hand. "Thank you so much!" she said, crying in relief that she was going home.

"You're welcome. Take care of yourself." he said, as he and the others loaded her in the helicopter to take her back to an American base for treatment. He watched as the helicopter quickly gained altitude. Two Green Berets securing the area found other missing U.S. soldiers' bodies in shallow graves behind the hospital.

"Alpha 1, we've found other POWs out here, deceased. How copy?" Trevor said over his radio.

Jack hung his head in disappointment. "Good copy, I'll be right there." He walked to where the deceased and dismembered soldiers' remains were. He knelt down next to the shallow graves and took off his helmet, saying a silent prayer. He saw that the insurgents were horrible butchers.

They notified command stations that they had successfully rescued SPC Dennison but reported there were more soldiers found that had not been as lucky. The deceased bodies were taken back to base to be sent to Dover Air Force Base for proper identification. The families were notified.

Once the Green Berets returned to camp, Jack walked to the Morale Welfare Recreation (MWR) tent and stood in line to call Kate. He found himself missing her, needing to hear her voice. He had not slept in five days, except at snatched times. As tired as he was, he wanted to talk to her more.

She was home, visiting with Christi when her cell phone rang. She saw that it was an overseas number. "It's Jack!" she said excitedly as she quickly answered. "Hello?"

He smiled, listening to her adorable Texan accent. "Hi baby, how are you?"

She immediately smiled and felt the butterflies in her stomach and tingling all over. "Hi, I'm so happy to hear from you. I'm relieved to hear your voice and that you're okay."

"Yeah, I'm okay. It feels good to hear your voice. I've been thinking about you a lot. I look at your picture every minute I have time."

Christi noticed she was lit up with excitement. "I've been thinking about you a lot too. Any news on when you're getting back?"

"No, not yet, why, are you missing me?"

She smiled and laughed. "Yes, like crazy."

He smiled, "I can't wait to see you. I love you."

"I love you too." They talked for half an hour. Just days after the Dennison rescue operation, the Green Berets, along with Army Rangers and Marines finally entered the city of Baghdad. They surrounded the statue of Saddam with their tanks. It truly was a triumphant sight. Saddam's army was rapidly disintegrating. WMDs had not been used, but with Saddam's army all but defeated, many U.S. troops felt that their objective was done. Now, they were anxious to get home.

On April 9, 2003, Saddam Hussein fled the city of Baghdad and went into hiding. The world watched as U.S. Marines wrapped the American flag around the face of the giant green statue of Saddam Hussein. The crowd of civilians was ecstatic that the cruel dictator had fled the city.

A young boy asked the Marines to pull down the statue of Saddam Hussein in central Baghdad. Marines hooked the statue to a tank and began to slowly roll forward. The statue fell to the ground. It was a magnificent scene. The people celebrated the end of the dictator's reign by beating the toppled statue. The Green Berets were amongst the crowd, ready for confrontation, but they watched the people celebrate by dancing, singing, and hugging the American soldiers. Citizens approached the soldiers and hugged them. Children brought all the soldiers flowers and hugged them. Women brought the soldiers food, as men stood in line eager to shake the soldiers' hands and to greet them the traditional Arab way. Many of the soldiers played soccer or football with the children.

Back in Dallas, it was a chilly spring night. She was at work at the hospital. She walked into the break room to get her a cup of coffee. She heard the news anchors from CNN talking about the overthrow of Baghdad. They showed live footage from Baghdad. She looked up and saw the huge green statue of Saddam Hussein fall with the American flag over its face.

At that moment, Marci, Angie, and Tess walked into the lounge for their break and saw her eagerly watching the screen. Iraq had fallen to the United States and its allies. She wondered if he was in Baghdad and if he would be coming home soon.

"Is Jack in Baghdad?" Angie asked.

"I'm not sure where he is."

"How do you not know where he is?" Marci asked.

"His missions and whereabouts are classified." she explained.

"Do you ever get to talk to him?" Tess asked.

"Yeah, he calls me when he gets a free moment. It's not an everyday thing."

"How often do you get to talk to him?"

"Maybe once a month, it all depends on where he is, and if he's able to call me."

Her friends were stunned. "How do you do it? How do you deal with your boyfriend being in combat and not knowing if he's okay and not be able to talk to him? I would think loving a military man would be so hard," Tess said.

She smiled. "No, loving him is so easy. The distance, the worry and being away from him are what's hard to deal with."

"How do you keep yourself from going insane with worry?" Angie asked.

"I keep myself busy with my normal routine. He is the strongest man I've ever met, but I always worry about him and think about him, but most importantly I have faith that he's okay and that he'll come home."

Marci, Angie, and Tess were remarkably impressed with how strong she was. They couldn't imagine their boyfriends or husbands in a war zone and not be completely unglued, but she was calm, cool and collected. She had great faith that Jack would come home. After all, he did promise her.

"You are so strong, Kate."

"To love a military man, you have to be."

Friends and neighbors gathered at the Hamilton home to show support to Jack and his family. They were standing, drinking coffee and watching the television intensely. The Blue Star Mother's Flag hung on the inside of the screen door. Yellow ribbons were tied around the trees in the front yard to remind everyone in the neighborhood that their son was serving in the Armed Forces.

The regime of Saddam Hussein was over, but the hunt for him had just begun. Saddam managed to stay one step ahead of U.S. troops.

Sixty miles north of Baghdad in the city of Samarra, soldiers of the Iraqi army were still holding Apache pilot Caleb Brown and his gunner Robert Rodrigues prisoner. It had been nearly a month since their helicopter was shot down. The two soldiers had been tortured and interrogated for several hours. Brown began to give up hope. He's accepted that he would never see his wife and little son again.

Suddenly, Black Hawk helicopters roared over the building where the Iraqi's were keeping the soldiers. Brown and Rodrigues heard commotion outside their cell. A door was kicked in, as Alpha, Bravo, and Charlie Teams ran through the building. They shot Iraqi's holding weapons and detained those surrendering. Jack, Tom, and Jamal rescued Brown and Rodrigues, along with the remaining captured soldiers. Jamal looked at the soldiers' injuries.

"Are you alright, Chief?" Jack asked him, as Jamal and Chase checked his vitals.

Brown had tears in his eyes as he looked up at him. "Yes, thank God you all are here."

"You're going home," he said. He walked over to personally check each POW. A female staff sergeant of the captured convoy immediately hugged him, and cried out of relief. She had sustained injuries to her face and neck. Jamal tried to tend to her wounds, but she refused to let go of Jack.

She repeated, while hugging him and crying, "Thank you God. Thank you God." Within days, the captured soldiers' were reunited with their worried families.

Back in Dallas, it was 9:00 p.m. On a Friday night, she had avoided going out with her friends in order to talk to him if he called. She missed him. She didn't expect to hear from him every day, but she couldn't help but worry about him. She was in the kitchen making a snack when her phone rang. She leapt across the room to answer it. Her heart was pounding. She was so sure it was him.

"Hello?" she answered. She hoped it was him calling to let her know he was alright, but it wasn't. It was Morgan.

"Hey, we're down here at this bar. You should come out with us."

She could hear loud music and dozens of people talking around Morgan. "No, that's okay. I don't like bars. I'm happy here. I want to be here in case Jack calls."

"Okay, well you know where we are if you change your mind."

"Be careful. Bye." She looked at the clock. It was 9:15 pm. She looked at a picture of her and Jack on her refrigerator door. She opened the refrigerator and got out a pint of chocolate chip ice cream. She turned on the movie *Pretty Woman* and ate the ice cream while waiting for him to call.

Meanwhile in Iraq, Alpha, Bravo, and Charlie Teams were just coming back to their outpost. Walking across the landing pad for the Blackhawk, Chinooks, and Apache helicopters, Jack and Tom carried their M4s and their gear. He reached inside his pocket and pulled out the picture of her. He smiled at it. "So how are you and Kate doing?" Tom asked.

"We're good. I need to call her. I haven't talked to her in a while. If I tell you something, can it remain strictly between me and you?"

"Yeah, sure what's up?"

He looked around for the rest of the team. They were walking alone back to their bunks. "She's a virgin."

Tom was stunned and stopped walking. "Are you serious? No way…"

"Yeah, I'm dead serious. She made a vow to God to remain one until she's a married woman."

Tom looked at him in dumbstruck awe. "So you've been celibate this whole time?"

"Yes and it is the hardest thing I've ever done."

"How do you make yourself stop with a woman like her?"

He laughed, "Trust me it's not easy, but I make myself stop and then I have to leave."

"How long have y'all been together?"

"It will be a year in June."

Tom shook his head. "You're a stronger man than me, Jack. I don't know if I could be celibate that long. So how do you not have sex? You're twenty-seven years old. Explain that to me."

"Well we're deployed a lot, so I do what most guys out here do."

"Good point, okay but what about when we're home?"

"I go to the gym and increase my workout routine. It actually helps a lot with the frustration and stress. You promise you won't say anything to the guys about this right?"

"I wouldn't do that to you."

He walked to the MWR tent and stood in line to call her. It was close to 2 a.m. in Dallas. Finally, after standing in line for nearly an hour, he was able to call her. Lying in her bed, she was suddenly awakened by the phone ringing. They talked for nearly an hour. They laughed, told each other funny jokes and stories about their families and friends.

Weeks later, Alpha, Bravo, and Charlie Teams came back to base. He had a box from her. Tom and the rest of his team were curious as to what she sent him. The box was huge. He tore the tape with his knife and opened the box. The box was filled with numerous goodies. She sent him three boxes of cherry Pop-tarts, several bags of beef jerky, three family bags of his favorite chips, Hostess snacks, Pringles, several books, and movies and about a dozen pictures of them together.

"What all did she send you?" Tom asked.

He smiled, "All my favorite snacks,"

"What are those pictures of?" Brad asked.

"They're of me and her." They gathered behind him as he looked through them.

"She's so hot." Luke said.

He looked up at the clock on the wall. "I'm going to call her. Stay out of my box." He took the pictures to his bunk. Brett, Trevor, Brad, Jamal, and Tom took what they wanted from his care package. He walked to the MWR tent and stood in line to call her. It was 1:00 a.m. in Dallas.

She was working the night shift at the hospital. The maternity ward was quiet and slow. They had three pregnant women in three of the fourteen maternity suites. The nurses had a lot of down time to catch up on paperwork and to visit.

After standing in line for half an hour, he finally got to a phone and dialed her cell phone number. Her cell phone was attached to her waist band of her scrubs. She felt it vibrating and quickly looked at the screen. She saw that it was a satellite phone number. Her heart started racing, her blood rushed through her veins and she felt her eyes moisten. Her friends noticed she was very excited.

"Girls, I'll be right back!" She quickly jogged to an empty maternity suite to talk to him. "Jack?" she answered excitedly.

"Hi baby, how are you doing?" he asked happily. He loved the sound of her voice.

She smiled. "I'm so much better now that I know you're safe. How are you?"

"I'm good. I just got back to base. I got your care package. Thank you for everything. I especially loved the pictures you sent."

She smiled. "I'm glad you finally got it. Jonah told me what all you liked. I'm so glad you called. I've been worrying about you."

"I had to call to hear your voice. I miss you."

"I miss you too. You sound so tired."

"Yeah, I am tired. I haven't slept much since last week."

"Why don't you get some sleep?"

"No, I'm alright, baby. I want to hear your voice more than I want to sleep."

She smiled. "I love you, Jack. You're incredible, you know that?"

"I love the way you say my name. I'm looking at your picture right now. You're so gorgeous. I love that smile. I wish I could see you right now."

She smiled. "I would give anything to see you. Can I ask you something? What makes me so gorgeous to you?"

He looked around the MWR tent and saw the line of soldiers waiting to use the phones had significantly shortened. A few soldiers were playing video games or watching a movie, but most were all getting as much sleep as they could before heading back out. None were paying much attention to him on the phone. He smiled as he thought of her. "You're gorgeous because you have an amazing personality, a great sense of humor, and you're so easy to talk to. You have a compassionate heart and you have these amazing eyes. Your smile is my weakness. You also have an amazing body."

She smiled as suddenly a brash voice shouted out over the hospital intercom. He heard the intercom at the hospital. "Are you at work?"

"Yes, I am unfortunately. I wish you could be home, and we could cuddle on the sofa, watching football."

He laughed. "That does sound pretty amazing. When I get back, what do you want to do?"

She was excited at the thought of seeing him. "I want to spend all my time with you. I want to go fishing, camping, and shooting with you."

"That sounds like a plan. You're incredible, you know that?"

"I'd give anything to be able to kiss you right now, I miss you." she said.

"I miss you too, baby. Don't worry, I'll be home soon."

"You promise?"

He smiled. "Yes, I promise. Well I'm going to go get a shower and then get some sleep. I bet all the guys have picked my care package apart for all they wanted. Thank you so much for sending me that."

"I'd do anything for you, Jack."

"How did I get so lucky to get you?"

She smiled. "I ask myself the same question about you."

"You deserve to be treated right. I want to give you everything you've ever wanted. I wish I could see you every day."

"I'd love to see you every day, but being apart makes our relationship stronger. For most couples long distance dating is what kills their relationship, but for us, it makes our relationship stronger and true. If we can handle being apart for so long and remain committed to each other, we can get through anything. I'm stronger than the girls you've dated. Military life is nothing new to me. Only now I understand what my mom went through when my dad was gone, but I know how to keep myself busy."

He smiled. "You're amazing, Kate." He heard the brash voice come back on the intercom. He knew she was busy. "Well I better let you get back to work. Don't work too hard. Stay gorgeous, baby. I'll be home soon. I promise."

"I'll see you when you get back, soldier. I love you. Stay safe."

"I love you too, bye baby." They hung up.

She smiled as she thought about him, as she walked out of the empty waiting room back to the nurses' station. She still had the large smile on her face. Her friends were eager to know how he was doing. Christi had told them about Kyle attacking her and how Jack rode in like a knight on a white horse and saved her.

"Was that Jack? Are we ever going to meet him?" Angie asked.

She smiled. "Yes, that was him. You'll meet him when he comes back next time."

"Christi said he's in the Army, like a SEAL right?" Tess asked.

She smiled. "The SEALS are in the Navy." she corrected. "He's a Green Beret."

"What's a Green Beret?"

"They're the Army's Special Forces. They are similar to what the Navy SEALs do, but they differ in a lot of ways."

"What does he do?"

"Due to OPSEC, I'm really not at liberty to say. It's classified."

"What's OPSEC?" Angie asked.

"It stands for operation security. I can't tell you anything about what he does or where he is to protect him, his men, and their mission."

"What's he like?" Marci asked.

She thought of him and smiled. "He is very good looking. He's funny, sweet, smart, humble, down to earth, and very strong."

"What does he look like?" Tess asked curiously, since they were all curious. She showed them a picture of her and Jack together on her phone.

"Oh, wow! He's extremely hot!" Marci said. Her friends could see that she was very attracted to him. "He's every woman's fantasy, and he has a high powered rifle?" Marci said, as they all laughed.

"Christi told us what he did to Kyle," Angie said.

"I honestly thought he was going to kill him," she said seriously. "I mean you had to have seen the look on his face when he had Kyle on the ground."

"Well, he loves you, so of course he would go all Rambo on some jerk that put his hands on you." Angie said.

"When I hear his voice, my day immediately gets better. I've never felt this way about anyone, not even Kyle. I'm questioning if I ever really loved Kyle, because he didn't make me feel nearly as good as Jack does." She and her friends talked more about him. Her friends were ready to meet him.

In June 2003, he turned twenty-eight. For his birthday, she sent him a decorated box with all sorts of goodies inside. In the weeks before his birthday, Denise had given her the recipe for her made from scratch double fudge chocolate cake, his favorite one Saturday they met for coffee. She and Kate were getting close. Denise couldn't wait until he made her a part of the family.

She used his mother's recipe and baked the cake inside a Mason jar and sealed it. She decorated the jar with red, white, and blue ribbon. She sent him many movies and books along with many pictures of them together.

Ten days later, he received the box. He cut the tape with his knife. He picked up the jar and was curious as to what was in it. He smiled as he flipped through the pictures of them.

"What did Kate send you?" Tom asked.

He held up the Mason jar full of chocolate cake. The pint of double fudge chocolate icing was also in the box. "I'm afraid to even guess what this is."

Tom looked at it curiously. "What is that?" he asked, carefully examining it as Jack searched through the box to see if there was a card.

"Hey Babe,

Your momma must really like me since she gave me one of her most classified recipes. I knew you'd want a little taste of home on your birthday, so I put it in a jar for you. Happy Birthday! I love you. I miss you, and I think of you every minute. I'm waiting here for you. Come back to me"

He opened the Mason jar and grabbed a plastic fork. He tasted the cake. He closed his eyes in satisfaction. "What is it?" Tom asked.

"My momma's double fudge chocolate cake. She never gives this recipe out to anyone, but she gave it to Kate. That's sayin' something."

"Like what?"

"That she thinks of Kate as family."

Also in June marked that Jack and Kate had been together for a year. On the exact date they met a year before, he managed to get to a computer and have a massive arrangement of three hundred sixty-five pink roses delivered to her at the hospital. She was sitting at the nurses' station updating a patient's chart when six delivery men walked in carrying six arrangements of sixty pink roses. She naturally assumed they were for different patients.

"I have a delivery."

"What are the patients' names?"

He looked at his clipboard. "Katherine Johnson."

She looked up at him in surprise. "That's me."

He sat the vase down and handed her the clipboard. "The man who sent these must really love you or is really sorry for whatever he did," he said. She smiled and she signed for them. Tess, Angie, and Marci saw the six arrangements of roses. She admired the roses, smelled them, and found a card. She opened it and read:

"Baby,

Happy One Year Anniversary! A year ago today, my life changed for the better. I'm excited to see what the future brings for us! There's a rose for each day I've woken up happy knowing you're in my life. I miss you so much, and I can't wait to see you. If there is ever a tomorrow and we're not together, there is something I want you to always remember. You are braver than you believe, stronger than you seem, and smarter than you think. But the most important thing is, even if we're apart, I'll always be with you. I love you so much, Kate. I'll be home soon. I'm coming home to you.

Love, Jack"

Angie, Tess, and Marci read the card. "That has to be the most romantic thing I've ever read."

She smiled, "He is very romantic,"

"I find it extraordinary that you are still a virgin and have a man like this," Marci said.

"Our relationship is so much deeper than just physical. Yes, I'm extremely attracted to him and there are times when I want to, but he's honorable. He wouldn't let me break my promise even if I wanted to. It's so amazing to have an extremely attractive man who not only knows the boundaries, but respects them. He's never pressured me, not once."

"You're a stronger woman than me, Kate."

It was a Saturday morning. She and Denise were having coffee at Starbucks together. "So, how are you two doing?" Denise asked.

"We're great. I really miss him. I hope he comes home soon. Last week, he sent me three hundred and sixty five roses for our one year anniversary."

"Wow, that's incredibly romantic."

"It was the most incredible thing. He had them delivered to the hospital. The card was the sweetest part. He told me the roses represented each day he's woken up happy that I'm in his life."

"You two are so cute together. You both look so happy and so in love. What do y'all have planned when he comes home?"

"Oh, we're going to go fishing, shooting, and just be together. He's so amazing. When we're together, we just laugh at all these stupid things. I've never loved anyone as much as I love him."

"I overheard him tell Bill that he thinks you're the one," Denise said excitedly. She smiled excitedly. She had fantasized about marrying him. "So do you love him enough to marry him?"

She laughed. "I don't think he is ready to get married."

"If he asked you, what would you say?"

"I would definitely say yes, but I don't want to pressure him into asking me. I want him to ask me when he is ready."

"Your mother and I are so ready for you two to get married."

"We'll see what happens…"

He and his team were coming back to the firebase. "Hey Jack, you got another package. It's from your woman."

They all teased him. "Y'all are just jealous she sends me all the good stuff."

He was happy to see her handwriting. She had very neat handwriting. He took out his knife and cut the tape. He opened the box and smiled at all the goodies inside. She sent him several DVDs, snacks, more pictures of them, and some of just her.

Looking through the pictures, he smiled. Needing to see her, he walked to his bunk to try to catch her on the web cam. She was working the night shift, so she was unable to chat with him. He called her cell phone. They talked, laughed, and flirted. Her friends overheard part of their conversation. They were happy to see her so happy, finally.

In August 2003, the week before her twenty-third birthday, he managed to get to a computer and ordered 176 roses. He had the roses delivered to the hospital to surprise her.

On her birthday, she was at work, helping a young mother through her contractions. The florist's main delivery man and four other delivery men arrived on the seventh floor of the hospital carrying huge arrangements of roses. Marci was sitting at the nurses' station.

She saw the massive delivery. "Can I help you?" she asked, thinking the flowers were for different patients.

"Yes, I'm looking for a Katherine Johnson." he stated as he looked down at the name on his clipboard.

Marci smiled in shock. "These are all for her?"

"Yes, ma'am,"

"Let me page her." She knew Kate would be excited and happy to get roses from Jack again. She walked to the nurses' station and saw all the flowers. "You paged me, Marci?"

"They're all for you," Marci said. Kate smiled. There were seven vases of roses. Each arrangement of roses was a different color, pink, red, orange, white, lavender, and yellow.

"Are they from Jack?" Tess asked curiously.

She was stunned at how many there were. She signed for them. Reading at the card, she couldn't help but smile with tears in her eyes. The card read:

> *"Beautiful, there's a rose for every day we've been apart. These past 176 days, I've thought of you and about our relationship a lot. I can't wait to see you. I hope you have a great birthday. I'm sorry I'm not there to take you out to celebrate, but I plan on taking you out for your belated birthday dinner. I love you.*
>
> *Jack"*

They last saw each other on February 18, it was now August 23. 176 days.

"Yes, they're from him. He is incredible," she said, as she smelled the roses. Her friends helped her carry all the vases to the nurses' lounge. They sat them on the tables. Suddenly, she felt her cell phone vibrate on the waist band of her scrubs. The caller ID indicated that the call was from a satellite phone. It was Jack.

"Hello?"

He smiled, listening to her Texan accent. "Hi beautiful, Happy Birthday, how is your day going?"

She smiled. "Thank you, it's really great now that I'm hearing from you. I just got all your roses. They're unbelievable; thank you so much," she said.

"You're welcome, baby. I wish I could give them to you in person."

"I don't think you could carry all these roses all by yourself. The delivery man had three guys with him."

"I'd make several trips. What are you doing for your birthday?"

"Morgan and Christi are dragging me out with the girls. I really wish I could be home in my pajamas, waiting for you to call."

"You should go out. It's your birthday. Who wants to spend their birthday all alone?"

She smiled. "If I could have anything for my birthday, it would be that you were home and we were at my apartment making out. I can't believe you're somewhere on the other side of the world, in a war zone, and you're still able to send me flowers on my birthday."

"No matter where I am, I'll always find a way to let you know that I love you and I'm thinking about you,"

"So you've actually been counting how many days it's been since we last saw each other?" she asked.

"Yeah, I love you and miss you. Is that weird?"

"Weird is not the word I would use."

"What word would you use?"

"Romantic. I love and miss you too, Jack. When I'm with you, I'm complete."

"When I'm with you, I'm home."

"I'm here waiting for you."

He smiled. "Well baby, I have to go. I just wanted to call you to tell you happy birthday and make sure you got your flowers."

"You better keep your promise to me, okay?"

He smiled. "I am. I love you, baby."

"I love you too." They hung up.

The rallying cry for Saddam Hussein had gotten stronger amongst insurgents. The ambushes on American troops were becoming more and more frequent. Army interrogator Todd Torrez was with the Green Berets, trying to locate Saddam Hussein (code name 'The Ace'). Their mission was to find him and arrest him. Torrez had arrested and interrogated over three hundred Iraqis who were loyal to Saddam.

Alpha, Bravo, and Charlie Teams were in northern Iraq, near the cities of Mosul and Tal Afar, near the Syrian border. Their mission was to search for Saddam in the areas given to them by Army Intelligence, but they kept coming up empty handed.

Thanksgiving Day, the teams returned to their outpost, surrounded by barbed wire and numerous armed guards. They walked into the REC room. They heated up their microwavable dinners and drank ice cold water. Jack and Tom sat down at the long table. She had sent him nearly thirty packages of Ramen noodles. "I can't wait to get home and see Paige and the boys. We're going to take the kids to Disney World. What are your plans when we get back?"

He smiled as he poured Tabasco sauce into his noodles. "I plan on spending all my time with Kate. She loves to go hunting, camping, and fishing."

Tom studied his facial expression and body language. "Do you think you and Kate will get married?"

"Maybe, I think so. How long did you wait to propose to Paige?"

"About two years."

"How did you do it?"

"I proposed to her at her parents' twenty-fifth wedding anniversary. I got their permission before I asked her."

They talked more and quickly ate. After supper, he walked to his bunk. He was finally getting a chance to take a shower. He then checked his email and saw many from her. He smiled as he read them and looked at the pictures she had sent him. He emailed her a long letter.

On December 13, 2003, Army Intelligence was informed that Saddam Hussein may be hiding out in a farmhouse in the town of Adwar, ten miles from Tirkrit, Saddam's childhood home. Many American and British Special Operations teams came together and formed a joint task force (TF-121), Jack and his team was among the task force. Their objective was to hunt down Saddam. TF-121 mobilized, after being briefed on the area of the farm house. They were alerted on possible ambush. On this mission, it was simple, find Saddam and take him into custody, alive. It was very important that Saddam was brought in safely. TF-121 was being flown into the area by helicopters provided by the 160th SOAR. The ride over was silent. They were wearing camouflage Kevlar, with their faces painted with green and black paint to obscure their faces. Their rifles were locked and loaded.

The helicopter landed in a field. The team quickly shimmied down the rope and was on alert for enemy contact. Soldiers from other Army infantry divisions provided security for the surrounding area, as the task force swept through the farmhouse.

They found nothing. "Alpha 1, there's nothing here," a soldier reported over his radio.

Jack and Tom were outside, among other infantry soldiers. "Roger, check for secret doors or compartments,"

He checked a few feet from the farmhouse. The search was not over. "Alpha 1, this is command central. How copy?" Colonel Mitchell said over the radio.

"Alpha 1, good copy, go ahead…" Jack responded on his radio.

"We just got intelligence that *'the Ace'* might be underground. How copy?"

"Good copy, intelligence, where did this intelligence come from?" Jack asked.

"An informant in custody, he says that *'The Ace'* is hiding underground. How copy?"

"Good copy, roger. We'll find him. Alpha 1 over and out,"

The soldiers' attentions were drawn to a small hut near the farmhouse. One soldier looked down and noticed something suspicious on the ground. He walked over to it. As he walked on it, he realized that this was an item not supposed to be here. It was a white mat over, a Styrofoam top, covering a 'spider hole'. The soldier and another pulled the Styrofoam top up, as another soldier aimed his weapon down into the hole. They found a man, cowering. They kept their weapons aimed at him.

The man surrendered. "I am Saddam Hussein, the President of Iraq and I am willing to negotiate." he said, while holding his hands up.

The soldiers were all stunned. "Yeah, President Bush says 'howdy'." one soldier said to Saddam. They pulled him out of the hole. His hair and beard was messy and dirty. He looked as if he hadn't eaten in days.

"Hey, we got him! We got *'The Ace'*!" Brad and Jake yelled.

TF-121 all ran to Brad and Jake's location to verify. After verifying they had captured Saddam Hussein, they were ready to celebrate. TF-121 took pictures with Saddam as proof they captured him. Saddam Hussein, the evil dictator who had oppressed his own people for nearly thirty years, was finally in U.S. custody. Jack knew he had to have been thirsty, so he handed Saddam his canteen. He took it and looked up at Jack in surprise, shocked a U.S. soldier would share his water with him. Jamal and Chase looked over his injuries and gave him some crackers to eat.

The news of his capture made headlines around the world. Many world leaders, who either did or did not support the United States in invading Iraq, were relieved to hear of his capture. Many of the citizens of Iraq were thrilled, but the soldiers knew that many of Saddam's loyal Sunni supporters were not happy. This would cause more insurgency.

In the hut Saddam had been hiding in, he had $750,000 in cash in a locker. TF-121 all posed with the near $1,000,000.00 in cash. Arriving to Joint Base Balad, the task force received applause from the many other Army units, for bringing Saddam Hussein in. Tom and Brad had him in handcuffs and escorted him to the Abu Ghraib prison. He was checked out by medical personnel and photographed.

Once Saddam's loyal supporters knew he was in custody, they started targeting the soldiers more and more. Suicide bombers strapped homemade bombs to their bodies and would walk into a crowd of people on the side of a busy street of civilians as U.S. soldiers were on patrol. They would detonate the bomb, killing dozens of innocent people just to kill U.S. soldiers.

It was a Tuesday afternoon in Iraq. The market was busy. Soldiers were on patrol and trying the different food. Jack and Tom were talking with a local fruit farmer. As they talked with the farmer, a suicide bomber shouted "Allah Akhbar!" and detonated the explosion. Shrapnel went flying everywhere. Jack and Tom were four hundred yards away, but they saw civilians down and some running for their lives. Shortly after the explosion, gunfire rang out. Jack and Tom, along with other Green Berets were looking for the gunmen. A boy, close to eleven years old, ran to Jack. He wrapped his arms around Jack's waist and hid behind him, even as he fired his weapon. He knew the boy was terrified. A small girl was sitting beside her mother, who had been killed by the bombing. She was crying as she tried to wake her mother.

Tom and Jamal saw her. Tom looked to Jack. "Cover me."

Jack, Luke, Brad and others fired, giving Tom cover fire. He and Jamal ran to the little girl. Tom cradled her in his arms and covered her, as Jamal checked on the girl's mother.

Jamal looked at Tom. "She's dead." The girl had minor injuries from the shrapnel. He and Jamal carefully carried her back to where the Green Berets were. Jamal and Chase looked at her injuries as Tom rejoined the fight.

One of the insurgents ran down an alley. Army Rangers and Marines chased him. "Tell them to come back, it's an ambush!" Jack urged the others. The Rangers and other Marines urgently tried to get their comrades to come back, but seconds later a second explosion detonated. It was much larger than the previous.

"Command, this is Alpha 2. We have a second explosion in the center of town at the market. Send MED-EVAC and reinforcements, we have an unknown number of enemy combatants." Tom said over his radio. Jack and Tom ran toward the direction of the smoke. The Rangers and Marines were right behind them. There they found their brave comrades, killed by the explosion. Attacks like this happened frequently.

After a long ten month deployment, Colonel Mitchell and his Green Berets returned to Fort Bragg after the successful capture of Saddam. He packed his bags and drove the 1,160 miles to Dallas to see her. He had been given a month of leave.

7

CHRISTMAS WAS TWO days away. He arrived in Dallas, close to midnight. He had been on the road for nearly eighteen hours. He had not stopped. He wanted to get to her as soon as he could.

The stars were brilliant in the velvet sky. The air was cold as the cold wind howled through the trees. He arrived at her apartment building. He buzzed her, but there was no answer. He had not told her he was coming home, he wanted to surprise her. He drove to the hospital. He stepped inside the elevator and pressed the 7th floor button. As the elevator climbed, he could barely stand the anticipation of seeing her. He ached to hold her in his arms, smell her perfume and the scent of her hair, and kiss her.

The doors opened on the seventh floor. He saw a few families waiting and watching TV in the waiting room. He saw a nurse sitting at the nurses' station desk. Her name tag read Marci.

Noticing he was very attractive, she smiled up at him. "Hi, can I help you?" she asked enthusiastically.

"I'm looking for Katherine Johnson, is she working tonight?"

"Yes, she is. Wait, you're Jack aren't you?" she asked, recognizing him from the many pictures Kate had in her locker.

He smiled. "Yes, it's nice to know that I've been talked about."

She smiled. "You're famous around here. I'll page her for you. She's going to be so excited."

"Well, if she's with a patient, I can wait. What time does her shift end?"

Looking up at the clock, she let out a tired sigh. "Her shift ends at seven." She saw the look on his face. It was midnight. "Are you sure you want to wait that long?"

He had just driven over eighteen hours straight. "Okay, go ahead and page her." Marci was excited for Kate. She knew she had really missed him and she couldn't wait to see them together. He tiredly stood and yawned.

She walked out of a maternity suite. She was wearing her royal blue scrubs and white Nike tennis shoes. Her hair draped her shoulders. She looked gorgeous to him. Stunned to see him, she smiled with tears in her eyes. He smiled at her. Running to him, she jumped up into his arms, wrapping her legs around his waist. Throwing her arms around his neck, they kissed in the middle of the hallway of the labor and delivery floor. The families in the waiting room and her fellow nurses applauded and some cried.

He could smell her perfume and the scent of her shampoo. He didn't want to let her go. He had fantasized about this moment for nearly a year. "Hi baby, you look so beautiful,"

"I missed you so much!" she said. Kissing him again, she had a few 'happy tears' streaming from the corners of her eyes. She had worried about him and now he was finally home, in her arms. She was elated. She had dreamed about being in his arms, for so long.

"I'm so happy you're home," she said, as he placed her down. He wiped the tears away and kissed her lips.

"I love you," he said.

She smiled up at him. "I love you too."

Angie, Tess, and Marci approached them. "Kate, go ahead and take your break. I'll take care of your patient." Angie volunteered. She and Angie were close.

"Thank you, Angie. That's so nice of you." She said with relief in her voice.

"So, this is the famous Jack we've heard so much about?" Angie asked.

She looked up at him and smiled. "Oh, yeah, sorry girls, yes this is Jack. Jack, these are my friends, Angie, Tess, and Marci."

They each shook his hand. "Ladies it's nice to meet you."

"It's finally nice to have a face to go with your name. You're all she talks about." Tess said.

She blushed as he looked at her and smiled. "She talks about me?"

"Yes, all the time," Angie said. Marci and Tess agreed and laughed.

"I'm taking my twenty minute break now," Kate said empathetically as she and Jack walked down the hall. They walked towards the elevator.

"Okay, make the most of those twenty minutes with him," Marci teased.

They laughed as they walked to the elevator. He saw how embarrassed she was. "So, your friends are nice."

She laughed. They got in the elevator. "They're crazy."

He pulled her against him. She looked up at him, as they were smiling into each other's eyes. "Every time I see you, you're more beautiful than the last time I saw you."

She made a face. "I look awful tonight."

He smiled down at her. "If this is what you call 'awful', I love it!"

She smiled up at him. "You look really good yourself, Master Sergeant."

He kissed her passionately. The elevator went down to the parking garage. They got to the parking garage and walked to her car. They leaned up against her car in the dark. He pressed his body up against hers. He wrapped his arms around her waist. As she hugged him, she could smell his cologne on his neck. She closed her eyes and enjoyed being in his arms again. They were looking into each other's eyes. He gently touched her face and gently dragged his finger along her jawline. They kissed. As the minutes rolled by, the kissing got more and more passionate.

"I've thought about kissing you for the past ten months." he said.

"I have too. I love kissing you." She gently kissed his fingertips. "So did you miss me?"

He smiled. "Yeah…"

"Did you ever think about me?"

"I thought of you every night, but I can't tell you what I thought about."

"Why can't you?"

He looked down into her hazel eyes. Her soft silky hair ran through his fingers. He smiled at her. "I don't want to make you uncomfortable." His kissed her lips. She closed her eyes, savoring every moment of being in his arms, smelling his cologne, and tasting his kisses. She wrapped her arms around his neck. He pulled her body up against his. His arms were around her waist. They kissed and talked quietly to each other, in the dark parking garage for the remainder of her break.

"You should go on home and get some rest; I'm sure you're exhausted from driving," she suggested.

"That drive gets longer every time I drive it. It never seems to end," he admitted tiredly.

She smiled up at him. "Welcome home, soldier," she said. She kissed him one last time before he let her go.

She ran her fingers down his palm as she walked away; he pulled her against him, kissing her once more. "Don't go, please," he whispered as he kissed her neck.

She closed her eyes and smiled. She loved the way he kissed on her. "I have to. I'll call you as soon as I'm finished with my shift at seven. "

They smiled at each other. "Okay, goodnight, baby. Drive safe going home."

"Text me when you get home. I want to know you made it." she said.

"I will. I love you," he said.

"I love you too. Be careful."

He smiled, watching her walk away. He slowly walked to his truck. She stepped out of the elevator back on the labor and delivery floor. Marci and Angie were talking at the nurses' station.

"Oh-my-gosh, Kate. He is so good looking. How is it that you two have not...?" Marci asked.

She smiled. "It's definitely a challenge, but we know the boundaries and he respects them."

"How long has it been since you two have seen each other?" Tess asked.

"Ten months."

"Wow, do you think you'll get married soon?" Tess asked again.

"I'm not sure."

"So if he proposed, you'd marry him?" Angie asked.

"Duh…" They all laughed. "Do you think I'm crazy? Of course I'd say yes!"

Her shift ended at 7:00 a.m. She tiredly walked to her car and drove to her apartment. After taking a hot shower, she called him. He was still asleep at his parents' house. They did not know he had come home. He knew they would be surprised. Christmas was only two days away.

Hearing his phone ring beside him, he grabbed it and answered tiredly.

"Hi, I'm sorry to wake you up. I just wanted you to know I am home."

He smiled, "What are you doing?"

"I just got out of a hot shower and I'm about to go to bed."

He pictured her wearing a towel wrapped around her wet body, but he forced himself to think of something else. Although she made a vow to God, she also wondered why she was so tempted to be with him. He thrilled her, excited her, and she constantly thought about the two of them together.

"So how surprised were you to see me?"

She smiled. "I was so surprised I cried, and I never cry. My heart about jumped out of my chest."

He laughed. "I wanted to surprise you."

"I'm glad you did."

"What are your plans for today?"

"Well, I'm probably going to sleep until noon, but after that, I have to run some last minute Christmas errands."

"Can I see you tonight? There's some place special I want to take you. I'll pick you up around six, okay?"

She smiled. "Oh, that sounds so great."

"What's your work schedule like on Christmas?" he asked.

"Oh I'm fortunate to not be working on Christmas. So I planned to spend it with my family, at my grandparent's ranch in Paris. What about you?"

"I'll be with my family here, but I'd like to see you. I was actually hoping you'd want to spend Christmas Eve with me and my family."

She was shocked and excited at the same time. "What time does your family usually celebrate?" she asked.

"We have dinner at six."

She laughed. "I'll spend Christmas Eve with you and your family, if you'll spend Christmas morning with me and my family."

He smiled. "You have a deal." They talked for a few more minutes, but both were exhausted.

Later that morning, his parents' walked downstairs in their robes and slippers. They headed into the kitchen. "I wish Jack could be here," Mom said.

Dad peeped out the window and saw Jack's truck. He smiled and looked at her. Her hair was a mess and she was still half asleep. "Sweetheart, you got your wish. He is home!"

She squealed and laughed out of excitement. She and Dad ran up the stairs to Jack's room. Opening the door, they saw him asleep. Smiling with tears in her eyes, she sat on the bed beside him and kissed his forehead. He slowly opened his eyes.

"Hey momma," he said tiredly.

She hugged him. "Hi, sweetheart, I'm so happy you're home! This is the best Christmas surprise I could've asked for!"

Dad smiled. "Okay, Denise, let him go back to sleep. He must've got in after midnight."

"I'm up." he said, tiredly, as he and Dad gripped each other's hands.

"I'm going to make some coffee and start breakfast. What would you like for breakfast?"

He smiled. "It's been forever since I've had your cheese omelets with bacon and hash-browns."

"Coming right up!" as she and Dad walked excitedly downstairs.

He stood and walked to his personal bathroom. He splashed cold water on his face and turned on the hot shower. After showering and shaving, he dressed and went downstairs to the kitchen. He loved the smell of coffee brewing and his mother's cooking. He walked into the kitchen and poured himself a cup of coffee.

"So, what time did you get in last night?" Dad asked, reading the Dallas Morning Newspaper.

"Uh, I think it was nearly two. I stopped by the hospital to see Kate."

Mom looked at him and smiled. "How are you two doing?"

He smiled. "We're great. I'm bringing her by to meet the rest of the family tomorrow evening, but promise me you won't go overboard by showing her my baby pictures or telling her embarrassing stories, okay?"

"I won't. I'm so proud of you for choosing a sweetheart like Kate. We have coffee every Saturday when she's not on shift. We've really gotten to know each other."

He smiled thinking about her. "She is so amazing. I love her."

Mom and Dad looked at him and smiled. "Does she love you?" Dad asked.

"Yes, she does."

Meagan walked tiredly into the kitchen, still in her pajamas and bathrobe. She was surprised to see him sitting at the table with Dad. "When did you get here?" she asked, grabbing him around the neck.

"I got in early this morning."

"Have you seen Kate?" Meagan asked, pouring her coffee.

"Yeah, I stopped by the hospital before I came here." he said.

"Haven't y'all been together for like a year and a half?" she asked. He nodded. "Are you going to marry her?"

He looked at her and smiled. "I can't predict tomorrow, but it's possible."

They all ate breakfast together. He visited with his parents and sister for nearly an hour before he headed over to see Jonah and Christi. As he walked outside and down the walkway to his truck, many of his parents' neighbors saw him. They shook his hand and welcomed him home.

He surprised Jonah, Christi, and JD. He had to tell him what he had asked Santa for Christmas. He and Jack wrestled on the floor. Jack tickled him and JD laughed and squealed loudly. They had picked up where they left off.

"So, what did you get Kate for Christmas?" Christi asked, sipping her coffee.

"I'm not sure what to get her, but she's coming to Mom and Dad's tomorrow and I'm going with her to Paris, to spend Christmas morning with her family."

"Paris? She's French?" Jonah asked. "I didn't know that."

Jack and Christi looked at him, stunned. Jack said, "You never cease to amaze me, Jonah. No, she's not French, and I'm not going to France. Her grandparents have a ranch in Paris, Texas."

"So, how freaky was Mom acting this morning when she saw you?"

He laughed. "She was really happy. So, Christi I need your help. What do I get Kate for Christmas?"

"Buy her some lingerie from *Victoria's Secret*." Jonah suggested.

He laughed. "That's one store I'm never walking into."

"You could buy her perfume, body butters, or lotions from there. You don't have to walk into the lingerie part of the store, they have a beauty part," Christi said.

"What is body butter?" he asked clueless.

"It is butter you put on your body. Duh…" Jonah said.

"Gee thanks, I kind of assumed that, Jonah."

"It is creamy lotion that had a particular taste, like chocolate, whipped cream or peppermint. It's edible." Christi informed.

He laughed. "Okay, no. I will not buy that for her. If she buys that on her own, fine, but I will not buy my girlfriend body butter."

She laughed. "Stop being such a guy! You can walk into combat and have no fear, but you're afraid of *Victoria's Secret*?"

"That is a store for women by women. Men have no business in there." he joked.

"How about you buy her some jewelry?" Jonah suggested.

"I have no idea what she likes."

"How about you buy her a new purse? She'd like that." Christi suggested.

"You expect me to buy a purse? If I won't buy lingerie or body butter, what makes you think I would actually walk into a store and buy a purse?"

"Kate is really easy to buy for. She is really fashionable."

"Again, I'm her boyfriend. Not a friend."

"I would stick with jewelry. You can never go wrong with jewelry." Jonah volunteered.

"Yeah, I think I will. I'll buy her a bracelet, or a watch, or a necklace."

"Or you could buy her an engagement ring." Christi suggested.

"I'm not ready to propose."

"Why not, you love her right?"

"Yes, I do love her, but we're not ready to get married."

Later that day, he drove to a very busy mall in Dallas. He walked into a jewelry store. There were several men looking in the display cases. He looked at jewelry. He smiled at the diamond bracelets, rings, watches, and necklaces. He bought her a beautiful diamond tennis bracelet and a very nice watch, with diamonds on it.

He then walked by *Victoria's Secret*. Seeing many other men dragged in there by their girlfriends and wives, he walked in to the beauty section. He smelled the many perfumes on the shelves. He bought her three perfumes and three lotions. No body butter.

She was shopping with Lauren. "What are you getting Jack?"

"I have no idea. He's a huge sports fan and he loves the outdoors. I just don't know what he likes."

"What if he proposes to you?"

"I don't think he will."

"What would you say if he did?"

"I'd say yes." She bought him an expensive watch, cologne, a few Sooner T-shirts, and ball caps.

After shopping all day, they had a romantic dinner at Reunion Tower. He saw the look on her face as she looked around the restaurant. "Have you ever been up here?" he asked.

"No, I've always wondered what it would be like." she said, admiring the sunset against the skyline. They talked about their families, giving each other full warning about the chaotic, crazy, family members they had. They made plans for the remainder of his leave. They laughed and were comfortable and happy with each other.

After dinner, he drove her back to her apartment. He walked her up to her door. She unlocked the door and turned on the lights. They relaxed on her sofa. Morgan was entertaining her boyfriend in her room. The door was closed.

He smiled at her, tucking a strand of her hair behind her ear. She had a look in her eyes. He leaned in to kiss her. They started kissing more and more. They laid back on the sofa, holding each other close. He was lying on top of her, with one hand in her curly hair.

After a while of passionate kissing, she felt as if things between them would escalate to a level they shouldn't. What scared her was that she wanted to go further with him. Regaining her moral compass, she gently pushed him back.

"What's wrong?"

"I don't trust myself with you. I want more and it scares me that I'll give in." She looked at him. "Have you thought about us?"

He smiled. "Kate, I wouldn't be a man if I hadn't thought about us, but I can control myself out of respect for you."

"I'm to that point where kissing you makes me want more. I find myself wanting to break this vow. I'm scared that I might lose control and ask you to stay with me."

He smiled. "As much as I want to be with you, I wouldn't let you break that vow."

"How can you stop yourself?" He thought of a scripture that he had to remind himself of several times when he's with her.

He laughed. "It's definitely not easy, but I'd do anything for you. God must be giving me the strength to stop because there's no way I could do this without him."

"Thank you for understanding. This really means a lot to me, Jack. I'll walk you to the door."

They walked to the front door. He leaned in to kiss her. He left her apartment and headed to Jonah and Christi's to use Jonah's weight room.

He was benching three hundred pound weights. Jonah walked in from the house. "Hey, what are you doing?" he walked over to spot for him. They talked as they worked out together.

On Christmas Eve evening, it began to snow. The residents of Dallas were excited to have a white Christmas. A rare white holiday really made it feel like Christmas. The city was decorated with wreaths, clear and multi-colored lights and red bows.

She was getting ready to go with him to his parents' house. She had already met his parents, but was a little nervous to meet the rest of his family. She changed her outfits several times. She wanted to give a good impression. He would be by to pick her up at 5:00 p.m. His family served dinner at 6:30 p.m. She looked in the mirror and applied a light layer of lip gloss. She wore a pair of faded blue jeans, a red sweater, and her favorite brown boots. Her hair was curled, and her makeup was flawless.

She had given him a key to her apartment building's main door and to her apartment. At 5:00 p.m., he arrived at her building and unlocked the door. The doorman recognized him.

"Merry Christmas, sir!" the doorman politely and cheerfully said.

"Merry Christmas!" he replied, with a smile.

He rode the elevator up to her floor. He unlocked her door. "Baby?" he called out as he closed the door. He walked into her kitchen, she wasn't in there.

"I'm back here!" she yelled from her bathroom. Entering her bedroom, he saw numerous blouses and pairs of pants scattered all over the bedroom floor. He found her standing in the bathroom, looking nervous.

"Hi, baby." She turned to face him and smiled. "Wow, you look gorgeous."

"Thanks, you look great too." she said, giving him a kiss. He wrapped his arms around her and pulled her up against him.

He smiled as he wiped the layer of lip gloss off his lips. "That stuff tastes weird," he commented as she laughed. "You're nervous aren't you?"

She nodded. "Don't be nervous, okay. My family is normal, for the most part." She laughed. "You've already met my parents, so I don't understand why you're nervous."

"What if the rest of your family doesn't like me?"

"They will…" he assured, with his hands on her face.

"How do you know?"

"…Because they'll see what I see. They'll see that you're sweet, honest, caring, you're beautiful, and funny. They'll see that I love you."

She smiled up at him, looking into his eyes. "I love you too." She put on her coat, grabbed her purse and his gifts. Her gifts were in his truck, along with his parents, Jonah's, Meagan's and JD's. The drive over to his parents' house was silent. He knew she was nervous. He held her hand.

His parents' lived in a neighborhood much like her parents. She saw vehicles parked in the driveway and along the curb in front of the house. The house was decorated in multi-colored Christmas lights that twinkled in the evening sky. A beautiful wreath hung on the front door. He opened the door for her and held her hand as they started up the walkway.

Opening the door, he hung up their coats. "Hey, where's everyone at?" he called out.

Hank ran to him. He jumped on him. "This is Hank. Hi buddy, what are you doing?" he asked as he played with him.

She smiled and kneeled. She petted him and laughed as he licked her cheek. Mom and Dad walked into the foyer. "Hi, you two!" she greeted.

"Hi, Momma, hey Dad," he said, hugging them.

"How are you, sweetie?" Denise asked her, hugging her. He smiled as his parents hug her. He had never brought any of his former girlfriends home to meet his family.

"I'm good, Denise. How are you?" she asked, as Dad hugged her and kissed her cheek.

"We're good. I'm just cooking and making sure everything is ready for everyone to get here."

"Is there anything I can do to help?" she asked as they walked into the kitchen. She tied an apron around her waist and helped his mother prepare Christmas Eve dinner. They talked and laughed as they cooked together. His parents adored her.

Meagan was up in her room getting ready. Jonah, Christi, and JD hadn't arrived yet. He and Dad walked in the den to watch ESPN and talk. Soon, everyone arrived. They were surprised to see Jack. They didn't know he would be home. He introduced her to everyone.

His grandmother hugged him. "Is this your wife?" she asked. She was suffering from Alzheimer's disease.

They smiled at each other. "Not yet. Ma-maw, this is my girlfriend Kate."

Ma-maw smiled. "Oh, she's lovely."

"Thank you." Kate said.

His family served traditional turkey, green bean casserole, homemade dinner rolls, mashed potatoes and brown gravy, with Texas style sweet tea, and pumpkin pie for the Christmas Eve dinner.

Kate, Christi, and Meagan were helping and talking with his mother and aunts in the kitchen, while Jack visited with Dad, Jonah, uncles, and cousins. Bill was the oldest of three brothers. Denise was the youngest of three sisters. He saw her laughing with his aunts. She looked happy.

There was a long dining table with chairs for everyone. A beautiful red Poinsettia was the centerpiece for the table. Special holiday dishes were laid out at each place setting. Kate and Christi were bringing the turkey fresh out of the oven to the table. Jack watched her from the living room, talking with his mother, sister, and aunts. He smiled, knowing that they accepted her and were beginning to love her too.

Everyone gathered to the table as dinner was ready. Standing over their plates, they held hands and bowed their heads. Dad always blessed the food at their meals. He began to pray. "Heavenly father, we come together to celebrate the birth of your son, Jesus Christ. We thank you for allowing everyone to be here safely. We humbly ask you bless this food we are about to receive to the nourishment of our bodies. Lord, thank you so much for keeping my youngest son safe while serving our country. We are so blessed to have him home. Bless all our soldiers serving overseas. Bless their families as they are not able to celebrate Christmas together. Bring each soldier home safely. Bless all our family here today. Amen."

Jack and Kate sat next to each other. They served their plates and ate. His aunts and uncles told her many funny stories involving Jack and Jonah when they were kids. They all laughed.

"So, how long have you two been together?" his aunt asked.

"We've been together for a year and a half," she replied, holding his hand under the table.

"Do you love each other?" his other aunt asked.

They looked at each other and smiled. "Yes, we do," he said. They were all shocked. Mom and Dad were about to burst from excitement.

"What do you do for a living, Kate?" his other grandmother asked.

"I'm a labor and delivery nurse at Medical City Hospital."

They were impressed. "How old are you?" his aunt asked.

"I'm twenty-three."

"Where did you go to college?" Dad asked her, casually.

"Okay stop, before she answers, I want you all to keep in mind that I love her and I do not want y'all to lynch her," he said, teasingly.

"Where'd you go to college, sweetie?" his aunt asked.

The table was silent. The entire Hamilton family was loyal University of Oklahoma fans. She smiled at him. "I went to the University of Texas." Everyone looked at him and laughed.

"I bet y'all love each other during Red River Rivalry," Dad said, with a laugh.

"We're mature about it. I love sports, and yes it is always a morale killer when your team loses, but if you can't handle losing, you shouldn't be a sports fan," she said.

"That's very true." Jonah said.

"She's played basketball and softball throughout school, and she played on the women's basketball team for UT all four years," he informed them all.

"Wow, impressive." Dad said.

"Are you two going to get married?" his aunt asked.

She looked at him. "I can't answer that."

"Thanks for putting me on the spot, Aunt Kim." he said.

"It should be an easy question," Meagan said.

He smiled at her. "Yes, we're going to get married one day."

"Could you be more specific on when?" Meagan asked, taunting him.

"Don't pressure him, y'all. He'll ask me when he's ready," she defended.

"Hopefully you're not waiting forever," Meagan said.

"Let's change the subject," he said, taking a drink of his tea. Each member of the family told her embarrassing stories about him. They were holding hands under the table.

After dinner, Kate and Christi helped clear the table and clean the dishes. "So has your family met him?"

"He's meeting the rest of them tomorrow."

Christi looked at her and smiled. "I've never seen you look so happy and in love, Kate."

She smiled. "I am. I love him very much. He's everything I've ever wanted. By the way, how did JD like the presents we got him?"

They bought him G.I. Joe action figures. "Oh he loved them. He woke us up at five this morning. We didn't get him in bed until midnight, he was too excited."

She looked at JD and Jack playing in the living room. She loved watching them play. She thought he'd be an excellent father one day. His mom walked into the dining room, as she wiped the table down. "Girls you don't have to clean up." she said, wrapping her arms around both of them.

"Oh it's no problem. You cooked, so it's only right." Christi replied.

"Enjoy being with your family, we got this." Kate said to her. His mom really liked her. She smiled at her and thanked her and Christi. Denise walked into the living room and sat next to Jack on the sofa. She noticed him watching Kate as she moved around in the kitchen. "I've never seen you this happy before."

He looked at her and smiled. "She makes me happy."

"Your father and I adore her. She is beautiful, sweet, and she has the cutest accent."

He laughed. "Yeah, she does."

"I like that she helps out."

He smiled at Kate. Seeing the way he looked at her, she smiled and said, "Go get her so we can open presents."

He walked into the kitchen. She was alone and washing dishes. He walked up behind her, moved her hair off her shoulder, and kissed her shoulder. She enjoyed him kissing on her. "You know you don't have to do this, right?"

"My momma taught me to always help prepare and help clean up."

"Yeah, but you're a guest."

"I didn't offend your mom, did I?"

He smiled. "No, not all, my mom loves you."

"I want to help. She's really happy to have you home, so I thought as my gift to her would be to take care of everything here so she can have more time with you."

He smiled at her as he touched her face. "You're incredible, you know that?"

He kissed her lips. She wrapped her arms around his neck, as he pulled her up against him. They were kissing passionately, since they were all alone in the kitchen.

"Jack, are you and Kate coming or not?" Christi asked.

He released her and they walked in the living room. They sat next to each other on the sofa. He looked over at her. He held her hand in his. "You look so gorgeous today." he whispered in her ear.

She smiled at him. "Thank you. You look very handsome. I can't stop looking at you."

He held her hand. He gave her one of his presents. She opened the jewelry case. His family was anxious to see what was inside. She smiled at him and opened the case. Inside sat the beautiful diamond tennis bracelet. She was stunned at how beautiful it was. He fastened it around her wrist.

"Jack! It's so beautiful, I love it! Thank you so much!"

"I'm glad you love it." His female relatives admired the bracelet.

She gave him one of his presents. He opened the watch. "Wow, thank you baby. I love it," he said, as he fastened it on his wrist. It was a nice Swiss Army watch from a jewelry store.

He gave her a set of perfume and lotion from *Victoria's Secret*. She excitedly smelled the perfume and rubbed the lotion on her arm. "Thank you, they smell amazing!" she said.

"Jack, you actually went into *Victoria's Secret*?" Meagan asked.

"And lived to tell about it…" Jonah teased.

They all laughed. "I went into the beauty part. Not the other part." he said.

The women sat at the table, watching Jack and Kate smile, laugh, and whisper to each other. They were sitting really close and holding hands. "Denise, they are so cute together. I've never seen him smile so much in my life," his aunt said.

"Neither have we. He's been like this since their first date."

"Do you think they'll get married?" one of the other aunts asked.

"I hope so. I think she is the sweetest thing," Denise said.

She bought his parents a gift. His family enjoyed seeing them together. After opening presents, Denise sat down next to her on the sofa. "I have something for you."

She handed her a wrapped gift. Kate smiled at her. She tore open the wrapping paper and opened the white clothes box. She was stunned at what was inside. His mother had embroidered KATHERINE on a stocking, just like she had done for Dad, Jonah, Jack, Meagan, Christi, and JD.

Jack was happy she had done that for her. She patted her hand. "I know you're not officially part of the family yet, but I have a feeling he will make you family soon. But we already consider you family and you are welcome here anytime. We love spending time with you. You're everything I want for him and more importantly you're everything he needs. I think you two are a perfect match."

Kate had tears in her eyes. She smiled and hugged her. "Thank you so much, Denise. It's beautiful."

"You're quite welcome, now let's hang it up," She hung it up next to his stocking.

"Did you get Momma's subtle message?" Jonah teased.

Everyone laughed. "Yeah, I got it." He held her hand.

She looked at him and smiled. "I love your family."

"Good, they love you." They visited with everyone a little while longer and then said goodbye to everyone. She hugged his parents. The women in his family thought she was classy, sweet, and respectful. They could tell she had a Southern upbringing by the way she had insisted on helping prepare the meal and clean up.

They arrived back to her apartment. He turned her Christmas lights on and started a fire in the fireplace. She was in the kitchen making them hot chocolate. "Will you watch a movie with me?"

"Depends on what movie you want to watch," he teased.

"Have you ever seen *Dirty Dancing*?"

He laughed. "You remember Meagan my sister, right?" She laughed. "Unfortunately, I've seen *Dirty Dancing* probably a hundred times in my lifetime only because Meagan is my sister." She made a pouty face. He smiled as he tucked a strand of her hair behind her ear. "But I suppose one more time won't kill me."

"Thank you."

"But please don't tell me how hot you think Johnny is, okay?"

She laughed. "He's nothing compared to you."

They cuddled on the sofa and watched the 1987 classic with the fire crackling. They dozed off while watching the movie, but were awakened by Morgan and her beau raiding the refrigerator at two o'clock in the morning. He looked at his watch. "Baby, I should be going."

She looked at hers. "Okay, I wish you could stay."

He kissed her goodbye. "I do too. I love you. I'll see you tomorrow."

She walked him to the door. "I love you too."

Morgan's beau, Michael was also walking to the door. Kate and Morgan had a roommate agreement that men would not sleep over. Jack and Michael walked out of the apartment and to the elevators.

She looked at Morgan. "You looked like you had some fun."

"Oh yeah, I think he's the one." Morgan and Michael had been dating for nearly six months.

Kate walked to her bedroom and crawled into her bed. She looked at the picture of her and Jack together on her nightstand. As she looked at it, she had an alert on her phone. She looked at it. He had sent her a text message.

"I loved you sleeping in my arms."

She smiled and wrote back. *"I know I wish I could've slept in them all night."* They sent each other sweet and romantic text messages until they both fell asleep.

Christmas morning, it had snowed the night before. It was sunny and cold. The undisturbed snow sparkled in the sunlight. Her family gathered together on Christmas morning for breakfast. It was 7:30 a.m. They were driving two hours northeast to Paris, Texas.

They laughed and talked the whole drive. He looked over at her and smiled. He held her hand in his. "I love you."

She smiled at him. "I love you too."

"I want to spend the rest of my life with you." he said.

They smiled at each other. She was about to burst from excitement. "I can't imagine living the rest of my life without you."

Arriving at her grandparents' ranch in Paris, Texas, she saw it had snowed there too. The ranch house roof was covered. There was smoke coming from the chimney. The pastures were covered, as well as the roof of the barn. She saw her parents' car, her sister's, and her aunts and uncles were all there. The sunlight hit the snow and sparkled.

They walked hand in hand up the walkway. It began to snow again. They looked up and smiled at each other as snowflakes fell above them. They softly kissed in the snow. They walked up on the porch and she opened the door.

"Hey, we're here!" she said, as her Grandpa Roy, greeted them.

"Merry Christmas, angel!" he said as he hugged her tightly.

"Merry Christmas, papa, this is my boyfriend, Jack Hamilton."

He and Jack shook hands. "Good to meet you, Jack."

"It's good to meet you too, sir."

Her grandmother saw them. She walked over and hugged her. "Is this Jack, the soldier that stole our Katie's heart?" she asked.

"Yes ma'am, I am," he said to her.

She smiled at them. "Jack, it's so good to meet you. I've heard a lot about you from Kate. I'm glad she finally decided to bring you out here to meet us."

"It's good to meet you, ma'am."

Carole and Matt came to greet them. "Jack, it's good to see you again." Matt said.

"It's good to see you too, Matt." Carole hugged him and then hugged Kate.

"Momma, how long until breakfast?" she asked her mom.

"At least twenty minutes, why?"

"Oh that's plenty of time. Jack and I will be in the barn."

They got their coats on and walked through the snow, hand in hand, to the stables. There were several horses in the stalls. She had three beautiful horses, Blue Bonnet, Crawford, and Sam Houston. Blue Bonnet was her champion barrel racer. She was a beautiful Bay with dark skin and gorgeous black mane. Crawford was a striking buckskin mare. Sam Houston was her champion equestrian horse. He was a black horse with a white diamond on his face.

"These are my horses. If they like you, I'll marry you," she teased.

He laughed. "Which are your champions?"

"Blue Bonnet is my barrel racing champion, and Sam Houston is my equestrian champ."

He smiled at the snowflakes in her hair. He found it amazing that no matter what, she always took his breath away. Even when she wasn't dolled up wearing a pair of jeans and a T-shirt, with no makeup and her hair not fixed, she still captivated him.

They locked eyes. He pulled her towards him. He passionately kissed her as they leaned against the stall. "I'm so happy you're home," she said.

He smiled. He looked down at her big brown eyes. "You bring me home."

After kissing for several minutes up against the stalls inside the warm barn, they walked back in the house. Breakfast was almost ready. She walked into the kitchen, and put on a Christmas apron and helped her sister, aunts, mother, and grandmother prepare the food. He sat in the living room with her dad, grandpa, cousins, and uncles. They talked about football.

"Jack is a big OU football fan," Matt announced.

Her uncles and grandpa smiled. "Does Kate know that?" Corey asked.

They all laughed. "Yeah, she knows. We tease each other about it all the time," he said.

The women were finishing up in the kitchen. Lauren and her Aunt were gathering plates from the cabinet. Kate, Carole, and her Granny were in the kitchen. "Kate, he sure is handsome," Granny said to her.

She watched him talking and laughing with her dad, uncles, and grandpa. She smiled. "Yes, he is and he's a good kisser." she teased.

"Please! He's way more than handsome. I know when I saw him, I stopped in my tracks," Lauren said.

"How did you two meet?" her Aunt asked.

"My best friend is married to his brother, so they introduced us."

"And he's in the Army, right?"

"Yes."

"What did he get you for Christmas?" Lauren asked.

"He bought me this diamond bracelet."

Mom and Granny oohed and awed over the bracelet. "Oh, that is beautiful," Granny said.

"And he also bought me some perfumes from *Victoria's Secret.*"

"What did you get him?" Mom asked.

"I gave him a new watch. I also bought some cologne, and a few OU t-shirts, and new ball caps to give him when we open gifts. He's a big OU fan."

Lauren and Kate walked in the dining room to set the table. Lauren noticed the smile on her face. "You two look really happy together."

"We are happy."

"Do you think you'll marry him?"

She smiled. "Yeah, I think I will."

The women had cooked scrambled eggs, blueberry and buttermilk pancakes, biscuits and homemade gravy, with smoked bacon and sausage, orange juice, and coffee. The table was set with holiday dishes, similar to his mother's. A beautiful pine cone and poinsettia arrangement sat in the middle of the table along with two candlesticks. Her grandfather blessed the food. As they ate, they talked, laughed, and got to know him. They felt comfortable around each other's families. Both came from good, close, Christian families.

"So Jack, what do you do for a living?" her grandpa asked.

"I'm in the Army."

Her grandfather and uncles were impressed. "Really, what's your rank?"

"I'm a Master Sergeant."

"What do you do in the Army?" her Aunt asked curiously.

"He's a Green Beret," Matt said.

"Are you going to make the Army a career?" her grandmother asked.

"Yes ma'am."

"Have you deployed to Iraq or Afghanistan?" Carole asked him.

"Yes ma'am, I've deployed to both."

"What's the action like over there?" her uncle asked.

He never liked talking about combat with civilians. "It seems endless."

"Do you want to marry my sister?" Lauren asked bluntly.

"Lauren!" Mom and Kate scolded.

"What, I'm asking him the question everyone in this room is too scared to ask,"

"No, we're just too polite to ask such a blunt question." Carole said.

"I'd actually like to know if he does," Granny said. The table fell quiet.

He looked at Kate and smiled. "Yes, I do."

Carole and Granny were giddy with excitement. Matt was happy to see Kate smile again. "But I'm not pressuring him to ask me. He'll ask me when the time is right."

They talked and laughed over breakfast. Lauren told him more embarrassing stories about Kate. After breakfast, they opened presents. She gave him the cologne and the OU gear. He gave her another set of perfume and lotion from *Victoria's Secret.* "I couldn't make up my mind," he admitted, when she exclaimed about another set of perfume set.

She opened the diamond watch he had bought. She was shocked. "Jack its beautiful! I love it! Thank you!" she said as he fastened the watch around her wrist.

He liked the gifts she bought him. He also brought gifts for her parents, Lauren, and grandparents.

After having breakfast, opening the presents, and cleaning up the kitchen, they walked around the property in the snow. They walked to the nearly frozen pond, then into the barn. All her horses were in their stalls with coats on their backs.

She kissed and petted each horse. He loved watching her with her horses. He had never seen anyone have so much love and passion towards something, until he met her. "Do you want to ride with me?" she asked.

"Sure." He saddled up Crawford as she saddled up Blue Bonnet. He looked over at her. He saw she had a huge smile from ear to ear on her face. She looked over at him.

"What are you looking at?"

"You, I've never seen anyone look so happy like you do when you're at work or with your horses."

She smiled. "I love my horses, my job and…" She walked towards him and wrapped her arms around him. "…I love you. I love my life."

"I love you too." he said, he kissed her lips. They rode horses through the snow dusted pasture. They visited with her family more, ate apple pie, and drank hot chocolate and warm apple cider. Afterwards, nearly seven thirty that evening, they wanted to head back to Dallas before it was too late.

Opening her apartment door, they took off their coats and hung them up. She turned her Christmas tree lights on. "Will you start a fire in the fireplace? I'm going to change into my pajamas. Then I'll make us some hot chocolate."

Morgan was visiting her family in Wichita Falls. She wouldn't be back until after New Year's. She walked back to her bedroom as he started a fire and lit a few candles around the room. Both were thinking about making love, but knew they couldn't. She walked back in the living room and sat beside him.

He smiled at her soft brown hair framing her face and her big brown eyes twinkling in the light of the Christmas lights. He saw she was still wearing the watch and bracelet and could smell the perfume. "Do you like your presents?"

She smiled and gently kissed his lips. "Yes, I love them. Do you like yours?" He pulled her into his lap, kissing her lips.

"Yes, I do. I love my new watch. Thank you. I'm glad we got to spend Christmas together."

"I am too. I loved being with your family. I couldn't believe your mom embroidered my name on a stocking."

"She loves you."

She smiled down at him. "Well, you know what I love?" He smiled at her. "I love kissing on you. I love being with you. I love looking at you." she said kissing his lips, forehead, and neck.

They held each other tightly, kissing passionately. Finally, they laid back on the sofa, cuddling under a blanket and watched a Christmas movie on the Hallmark Channel. They had dozed off while watching the movie. He opened his eyes and looked down at her sleeping in his strong arms. He gently kissed her cheek. He looked at his new watch and saw it was near midnight. The fire crackled and the Christmas lights provided a soft romantic glow.

"I better get going, baby. It's really late," he whispered in her ear. He wanted to stay with her, but knew if he did, something could happen.

She slowly opened her eyes and sat up. He brushed her bangs out of her face and kissed her lips. She walked him to her door.

"I'll see you tomorrow. I love you."

He kissed her goodbye. She smiled. "I love you too. Drive safe."

After the holidays, it was time for him to report back to Fort Bragg. He drove over to her apartment to tell her goodbye.

"I really hate saying goodbye to you."

He ran his fingers through her hair. "I'll be back before you know it."

"You promise you'll come back?"

"There isn't anything that could keep me from you."

"Say I promise."

"I promise you, Kate. I love you."

She kissed him. "I love you too."

He looked at his watch. "I need to get on the road."

"I'm going to miss you."

"I am too. Be strong for me. Keep your head up and that gorgeous smile on your face."

She smiled and kissed him goodbye. "Be careful. Call me when you get in."

"I will baby. I love you."

"I love you too." He opened his truck door and turned over the ignition. He drove away. Walking back inside, she finally broke. She didn't want to cry in front of him. It served no purpose. She saw no point in crying over something she couldn't change, or making him feel worse. She knew he was a soldier, and this is what he did for a living. He, along with thousands of others, put his personal life on hold to serve his country. She and Morgan talked over a pint of Ben & Jerry's chocolate ice cream.

Immediately after reporting back in, he and his team were deploying back to Iraq. He called her to tell her goodbye. She assured him she would be here waiting for him.

A troubling insurgency had erupted in Iraq. Insurgents had developed a new method on how to kill more Americans by planting improvised explosive devices (IED) under the roadways. The American death toll was rising drastically. Alpha, Bravo, and Charlie Teams were in Fallujah. It was one of the most hostile and deadliest cities.

She stuck to her usual routine. Lauren had met someone and was serious with him. Watching her sister happy and in love with her new beau, she could only think of Jack. She missed him and wondered where he was, what he was doing, and when he would come home.

Churches from all over the country had donated teddy bears and sent them to the troops in Iraq and Afghanistan to give to the children. Soldiers passed out many teddy bears.

He saw a little boy about JD's age walk up and ask for a teddy bear. He knelt down and smiled. He handed the boy the teddy bear. The boy thanked him.

Days later, the Green Berets were driving their Humvees back to their firebase. They were driving past rubble from the explosions the Air Force had dropped at the beginning of the war. He was sitting in the passenger seat in full Kevlar when he saw a little boy with a teddy bear on top of a pile of rubble. The little boy saw the soldiers and placed his teddy bear on top of the pile of rubble.

He wondered what the boy was doing. The boy was marking an IED to warn the soldiers. "Stop the truck." he said.

Sam slowly brought the Humvee to a stop. He kept his eyes on the boy and stepped out of the truck. Luke stepped out of the second Humvee behind his. "What is it?" he asked.

"He's trying to warn us," he said still watching the little boy. He called out to him, "What are you doing up there?" he asked in Arabic.

He walked closer to the pile. The boy became very scared and on edge. "Don't come closer!" the boy yelled in Arabic.

He didn't walk toward him. "I'm not going to hurt you."

"Go back the other way!" the boy yelled.

His suspicions were confirmed. He wanted to climb the pile to talk to him and get him down. If there was an IED up there, he didn't want the boy to accidentally set it off. "I don't want you to get hurt. Carefully climb down to me." he said to him.

"You have to go back the other way. There are more," the boy said.

"I'll leave if you come with me. I'll take you back to your mother."

The boy carefully climbed down. Jack's heart rate was racing. He was so afraid the boy would accidentally set the explosive off. He held the boy in his arms and walked him back to his mother's house. The mother was afraid when she saw Jack holding him.

He took off his sunglasses so the woman could see his eyes. "I'm not going to hurt you or your son. He saved mine and my men's life today," he said to her in Arabic. He placed the boy down. His mother immediately shielded him.

He had studied the Arab culture. He knew the women were treated worse than animals. They were property in their husbands' eyes. He knew Arab women would not talk to soldiers. They were not to speak to any man except the men in their family.

He slowly walked away. He and his team continued on the way back to their firebase. "I can't believe that kid marked that IED for us," he said to Tom.

"Yeah, it feels like we're making a difference here."

"Yeah, if only we could tell who is friendly and who's not."

In March 2004, the city of Fallujah was so hostile that the Marines had to establish a base outside the city. Every time Army Rangers or Marines went into the city, they were attacked by heavy numbers of Iraqi insurgents.

On March 31, 2004, four U.S. contractors with a private military company ignored the Marine Corps commander order to wait for an armed escort. They drove into the heart of the city where they were ambushed. They were killed and dragged from their vehicles. They bodies were beaten and burned. Their charred remains were hung over a bridge crossing the Euphrates River. Jubilant Iraqi's posed with the bodies and the pictures were released worldwide. It was a barbaric act of violence.

Jack and Tom were playing video games. It was their day off, but not anymore. They were given orders to go into the city with Rangers and Marines. This led to the First Battle of Fallujah. The insurgents outnumbered the soldiers and the battle was very bloody. Many Green Berets, Rangers, and Marines were killed. After losing the fight, American soldiers vowed to retake the city with better tactics.

In July 2004, summer had come back to Texas. The air was hot and humid, rain was scarce. The temperatures soared well over one hundred four degrees. He came home to Dallas for only two weeks after six months in Iraq. It was a Saturday afternoon. The sky was blue and clear, the summer breeze was cool and offered relief from the heat. The trees were green.

He and Kate had made plans to drive up to Paris, Texas. She wanted to show him a special place she'd go when she was a young girl. He rang the doorbell. She answered wearing a pair of cut off jean shorts, a brown belt with a gold belt buckle, a white button up blouse and dark brown cowboy boots.

"Hi." she said. Her brown curled hair fell in soft waves past her shoulders. He smiled at her wearing her brown boots.

"You look gorgeous," he said, as he kissed her lips.

"Thank you." They walked to his truck. They held hands as he drove two hours northeast of Dallas to Paris. He drove down her grandparents' dirt lane and parked in their driveway.

He smiled and walked around the truck to open the door for her. She stepped out and they held hands as they walked up to the front door. Granny opened the door. "There's my beautiful Katie!" she exclaimed as they hugged.

"Hello, Granny. How are you?"

"We're doing alright. Hello Jack, how are you? It's good to see you again," she said warmly.

"I'm good. It's good to see you again too, ma'am. How are you and Roy?"

"We're fine, just dealing with this heat. You know Katie, he's a lot better looking than that Kevin."

Granny had always called her Katie. Her face turned bright red. She looked at him and smiled. "Thank you," he said.

"I agree he is a lot better looking. He's nicer too."

"Jack, can I ask you a question?"

He stepped forward. "Yes, ma'am,"

"When are you going to marry her? You know she ain't gonna wait on you forever," she said. He smiled and tried not to laugh.

"Granny, I can't believe you just said that to him!" she scolded, mortified.

"What? I'm just telling him. If he knows you want to marry him, maybe he'll ask you."

"Okay Granny, this conversation is over. I'm going to take him up to the spring. Are the horses in the stables?"

"Okay, darlin' you two have fun. Oh, Sam Houston and Crawford are out in the pasture with the others, but Blue Bonnet is in the stables," she said as she watched them walk to the barn, holding hands.

"I like your Granny," he said as they laughed and walked.

She looked at him and smiled. "I'm glad because it's obvious she likes you too if she's rushing you to propose." They laughed together.

They walked inside the stables. She opened the door, petted her and kissed Blue Bonnet. "How's my girl?" she asked.

He loved to watch her with horses. She looked happy and relaxed with them. He held his hand out. The horse sniffed his hand. She looked at Jack and smiled. "Aw, she likes you. She hated Kyle; she even bit him once."

He patted the horse's neck. "Good horse."

She laughed. "Yeah, that should've been my first clue that he wasn't the man for me. Since my horses like you, I might marry you," she teased.

He had thought about asking her to marry him. "It seems they do like me." He stared at her as she got her reigns, saddle pad, and saddle out of the tack room. "So, was what your Granny said true, or was she just trying to embarrass you?"

"What?"

"That you're getting sick of waiting on me to ask you to marry me?"

She blushed. "I don't want to pressure you. I want you only to ask me when you're ready." She saw the look on his face. "What? Is there a bug on me?" she asked, as he walked towards her slowly. They stood in the stall with the horse.

He ran his fingers through her hair. "No, you're so beautiful."

"I'm so happy you're home."

He pulled her against him. "I am too," he kissed her lips. They stood kissing next to Blue Bonnet.

"Do you want to ride or walk?" she asked.

He looked around. "I'd like to ride, but your other horses are in the field."

She saddled Blue Bonnet up and smiled at him. "Ride with me." She stepped back and motioned the horse. He smiled and got on. Extending his hand down to her, she grabbed it and he pulled her on the horse, behind him. She wrapped her arms around his waist. He held the reigns loosely, as the horse trotted out of the corral. As they rode up the steep hill, they admired the land. She thought of how she and Lauren had loved spending summers here as girls, riding their horses, climbing trees, exploring the woods around the house, and swimming in the creek.

"This is a beautiful property. How many acres is it?" he asked.

"Uh, I think one hundred acres. It's been in the family for years. My great-great grandparents owned and worked this land. They were full blooded Cherokee."

"My great grandparents' were Chickasaw. My grandparents live in Ada, Oklahoma, and they have a pretty good sized ranch too."

"I'd like to meet them soon."

He held the reigns in his hand, with her arms around his waist. He smiled as he could smell her perfume. "Well, we can go if you want. I have all the time in the world. I bet my parents have told them all about you."

They stopped at the top of the hill. He dismounted and tied the reigns to a tree branch. He helped her down, by holding onto her hips. They looked into each other's eyes. The wind swept through her hair. He touched her face and gently kissed her lips. He wrapped his arms around her waist and pulled her up against him. They held each other for several minutes.

He stepped back and looked around. "Where is this spring at?"

She grabbed his hand, as they walked up the trail. "We have to walk this way." They reached the spring. On the banks of the creek, there was a log cabin. She and her sister, used to play in there when they were little. Her father and grandfather had built the cabin to use in the summer for camping and in the fall for hunting. The Oak trees forged a canopy with plenty of shade all around the cabin. The grass was smooth and cool. Wildflowers were everywhere. The sound of the water rushing was relaxing. Green moss covered the rocks along the water's edge. The drop off in the creek created a beautiful waterfall.

"Wow…" he said as he looked around. "The log cabin is awesome. I like that it's secluded."

"This is my favorite place in the world."

He looked at the cabin. "What's in there?"

"There is a fireplace, a table, and two twin beds."

"Can we go in?" he asked. They walked inside. It was a one room cabin. The fireplace was made of rock. Oil lanterns were all over the cabin. There were two twin beds by the window and a large table in the center of the room. He walked around the cabin. They looked at each other and smiled. She sat on the table. He admired her, staring at her tanned legs and the brown boots.

She smiled at him. "You like my boots?" she asked playfully as she modeled them.

He laughed. "Yeah, I do." He walked over to her and stood in front of her. She touched his face. He stood between her knees, barely touching her skin with his fingertips. They looked in each other's eyes. She kissed his fingertips. They longed for each other. He had fantasized about having her nearly every night.

"What are you thinking about?" she softly asked, looking in his eyes.

He smiled. "I'm thinking about something I shouldn't, but can't help."

She smiled up at him. "I am too."

"Tell me what you're thinking."

"I want to give myself to you here, right now." She placed his hand on her chest. Feeling her heart racing, he kissed her lips. She wrapped her arms around his neck. He wrapped his arms around her waist, pulling her closer to him. They were hip to hip as he kissed her.

He could smell her perfume on her skin as he kissed her neck. He barely caressed her body. "Do you want me to stop?"

She shook her head while looking into his eyes and taking shallow breaths. She sat on the edge of the table, with him in between her knees. Gently caressing her smooth, tanned legs, he could feel her body tremble out of nervousness and excitement. Looking into her eyes, he moved his hands up her thighs. As his hands moved, he saw the look in her eyes and realized he was violating her promise.

A scripture flashed in his mind. 1 Corinthians 10:13[13]. He backed away from her. He was upset with himself. "I went too far, I'm sorry."

"It's my fault. I'm sorry I didn't stop you," she said breathlessly. She saw he was upset with himself. He placed both his hands on his head and paced the room.

"No, you shouldn't have to stop me. I should've never started. I want to be honorable. I love you, and I really want to be with you, but..." Looking down at her eyes, he saw she was embarrassed. "...I love you enough to wait. I want you to keep your vow to God."

She smiled up at him. "I love you too, but I know this must aggravate you to some extent."

"I'll admit there are times, like right now, where it is aggravating, but I'm man enough to know when to stop. The last thing I want to do is make you uncomfortable."

"Being with you, I've never felt so comfortable, happy, respected, and loved by anyone." He smiled. They walked out of the cabin and sat on the bank of the stream.

The sun was setting against an orange and violet sky. The breeze was cool and full of fragrance from the wildflowers and wild sage growing. The crickets chirped as fireflies twinkled around the creek. They were holding hands, talking, and enjoying their intimacy. She took her boots off and walked barefooted to the water's edge.

"What are you doing?"

"Come here," she said, wading knee high in the creek. He stood, slipped off his shoes and socks and walked in the water to her. He wrapped her up in his arms and twirled her around. They laughed and splashed each other.

Now the sun had set, so they mounted the horse and rode back down the hill. "I want to show you one more place," she said, holding onto him. The horse galloped through the field of blue bonnets. Her curled brown hair flowed in the wind. They stopped at a pond with lily pads. The banks of the pond had wild sunflowers, dandelions, and daffodils growing all around it.

He saw a knotted rope hanging from a branch beside the pond. Kate and Lauren used to swing from that and drop into the water. "Did you swing from that?"

She smiled at him. "Yeah, I haven't done it since I was a kid." He saw all the wildflowers around them. He picked a daisy and handed it to her. Smiling down at it in her hand, she placed it behind her ear. They got back on the horse as it galloped through the field of wild black eyed Susan's, daisies, and blue bonnets. Arriving back at the stables, he helped her dismount the horse. They were in the stall with Blue Bonnet unsaddling her and brushing her.

He saw the way she was looking at him. "What are you thinking about?" He walked behind her.

She smiled as he pulled herself against his body and kissed her neck and shoulders. "I'm thinking about how I thought love like this only existed in fairytales. You had the perfect opportunity to seduce me and you didn't take it. Any other man would've ignored my vow, but not you. You're different from any man I've ever known."

He smiled at her, "I don't need you to break your vow to show me that you love me. By keeping it, you're showing me that you do. You vowed to wait until marriage, and I want you to give yourself to me on our wedding night."

She smiled up at him, "Our wedding night?"

---

[13] *No temptation has overtaken you that is not common to man. God is faithful and he will not let you be tempted beyond your ability, but with the temptation he will also provide the way of escape so that you may be able to endure it."- 1 Corinthians 10:13

He smiled, running his fingers through her damp curling hair. "Yes, our wedding night. I'm going to marry you, Kate. I want the timing to be right. I want your father's permission and I want to plan a romantic proposal."

"I don't need the most romantic proposal with flowers, champagne, or whatever, and you don't need my father's permission. I'd be happy if you asked me right here."

"I know I don't need your father's permission, but I want his permission. Proposing in a barn with horse manure everywhere is not my idea of romantic."

She laughed. "Depends on who you ask, I guess." She touched his chest and looked up into his eyes. "You know what, I thank Kyle. If he hadn't hurt me like he did, I wouldn't know what a good man feels like."

"And you thought all men were the same…"

"I've never been so happy to be proven wrong." They kissed again and walked out of the barn to visit with her grandparents.

They walked inside the house. Granny and Papa smiled at them. "Jack, do you know how to play Pitch?" Granny asked him.

"Yes, ma'am,"

"Sit on down here and let's play." Papa said to him.

"Did you two have fun?" Granny asked. They sat and played cards over sweet iced tea.

"Yes, we did." she said.

"I love that cabin. My dad and brother would love having that to stay in when we went hunting," Jack said.

"Matt and I built that almost twenty years ago. We've enjoyed many camping and hunting trips in that."

"Kate and Lauren loved it up there. They'd be out climbing trees, exploring the woods and swimming in that creek until dark. They hated to come in," Granny said.

They ate supper and talked more. Her grandparents' could see how they felt about each other. After dessert, they said goodbye and drove back to Dallas. "Did you have a good time?" she asked him, holding his hand.

He smiled at her. "Yes, I had a lot of fun."

A week later, on a Friday night, Jonah and Christi were celebrating their nine-year wedding anniversary. Kate and Jack had volunteered to babysit JD, who was now seven years old. Christi had just found out that she was expecting again. She and Jonah, as well as everyone else in the family, were thrilled.

"Are you sure you two want to watch him?" Christi asked.

"Yes, we'll be alright. Go have fun and celebrate," Kate assured her. JD and Jack were building an Army fort with the Legos in his bedroom.

"Okay, well call me if anything happens."

"Chris, you're only going out for a few hours. I promise he'll be perfectly fine."

She and Jonah walked out to their car. She closed the door and walked upstairs to see what the boys were doing. "What kind of trouble are you two up to?" she asked. He and Jack were laughing.

"Kate, are you my auntie?" he asked sweetly. They looked at each other and smiled.

She smiled at him. "No, honey I'm just your mommy's friend."

"Hey bub, let's go play video games."

"Okay!" He ran downstairs to the living room. They played video games, while she cooked dinner. She was making grilled chicken, green beans, mashed potatoes, and sweet tea.

He walked into the kitchen to get him more orange juice in his cup. He looked at her and smiled. Walking up behind her, he wrapped his arms around her waist pulling her body up against his and kissed her neck and shoulder. He moved her hair over to her other shoulder. He closed his eyes as he smelled the perfume on her skin. "You smell so good, baby."

She closed her eyes and smiled as he gently kissed her neck. She touched his hands as they were around her waist and his fingers were inner-locked in front of her abdomen. She turned around and kissed him. They were kissing seductively in the kitchen.

JD walked into the kitchen and saw them holding each other tightly and kissing. "You are kissing like my mommy and daddy do," he said.

They quickly backed away from each other. "Hey bub, I thought you were playing your game?"

"And I thought you were getting me something to drink?" he asked, folding his arms.

They smiled at each other. "Okay, Mr. Smarty Pants, I'll get your juice. Now go back in there."

JD walked away. He kissed her again and then poured juice into his cup. They ate dinner together. Afterwards, Jack gave him a bath and helped him get his pajamas on. He watched JD brush his teeth and his hair.

She was downstairs cleaning up the kitchen while Jack got him ready for bedtime. "Uncle Jack, will you read me a story?" he asked, as he held one of his favorite toys in his arms. His room was decorated in G.I. Joe.

He smiled. "Okay, pick which book you want me to read." he said.

Sitting in the chair beside the bed, he opened a dinosaur book and began reading to him. After she cleaned the kitchen, she picked up all of the toys before Jonah and Christi came home.

She walked upstairs and listened as he finished the story. Then they said their prayers. "I like when you're home, Uncle Jack. I want to be a soldier like you when I grow up."

He smiled. He didn't want JD to follow in his footsteps. He wanted him to go to college and be successful like Jonah. "Be better than me, bubba. Be like your dad. Good night. I love you." He kissed him on the forehead and turned off his lamp. She walked downstairs before he came out of the room.

"Good night, Uncle Jack. I love you too. Will you be here in the morning?"

Jack smiled. "I'll be here."

As he started to close the door, JD asked, "Will you leave my door open?"

He left the door partially open, with the hall light on. He walked down the stairs and heard her putting away the clean pots and pans. He walked to the refrigerator to get a beer. "He's finally asleep."

She smiled at him. "You're really good with him."

He smiled. "I love that kid."

"I think it's so cute he's named after you," she said.

He laughed. "I have no idea why they named him after me," he said.

"Isn't it obvious? Jonah really admires and respects you. It makes sense that he'd name his son after you. Why do you, JD, and Jonah all have David as your middle names?" she asked.

"Our great-grandfather's name was David Hamilton. He fought in World War II at the Battle of Midway. Every son since him has David as their middle name."

"Is he still alive?"

"Yeah, he's alive and still kicking. You think I'm a handful? Well he's who I get it from."

She laughed. "I'd like to meet him soon."

"He lives in Austin. We can go tomorrow if you want, but I'm warning you now, he may try to steal you from me."

She laughed as he wrapped his arms around her. "That's not possible."

"What's your middle name by the way?"

She smiled. "It's Elizabeth."

He wrapped his arms around her and smiled down at her. "Katherine Elizabeth? I love it."

"It's very old fashioned. Don't make fun of me," she said.

"I'd never make fun of you, baby."

She smiled as he picked up JD's little green soldiers. "When you're gone, he talks about you a lot. He's always asking Jonah when you'll be back. He loves you, and he wants to be just like you."

He smiled at her. "I don't want him to be like me. He should be like Jonah."

"Why don't you want him to be like you?"

"He could be so much better. He could go to college and hopefully play sports like Jonah and make millions of dollars."

"Didn't you have that same opportunity?"

"Yes I did."

"You chose the Army over college, and what if JD has that same mindset?"

"When he grows up and tells me he wants to enlist, I will accept it."

"Really, you would?" She didn't believe him.

"Of course, but I'd call every recruiter in the area and threaten them to not push him through."

She laughed. "I take it your Dad didn't do that when you enlisted?"

"No, he had no idea I enlisted until I told him and my mom. I told them, and then the next day I left for basic training."

"Why did you tell them the night before you left?"

"I knew if I had told him sooner, he would've tried everything to get me out of going."

"How did they react?"

"Oh they were very angry. My dad and I got into a huge screaming match. My mom cried and gave me the silent treatment until it was time to leave. I had my scholarships, my dorm, and even a jersey on the football team, so I understand they were angry and disappointed, but I just realized that wasn't for me."

"Where were you going to play football?"

He smiled, "Oklahoma,"

She smiled. "Do you regret not going to college?"

"No not at all. Enlisting was the best decision I've ever made."

She walked towards him. Standing face to face with him, she smiled up at him. She touched his face and looked up in his green eyes. "I'm much more attracted to soldiers than football players," she joked.

He laughed. "Thanks." He smiled at her as he pulled her against him and kissed her lips. He picked her up and placed her on the counter, and they kissed passionately. They were coming dangerously close to acting on their passions, but he backed away. They walked into the living room to watch a movie. They watched *Pearl Harbor*. Lying on the sofa, with the lights off and a few candles lit, he spread a blanket over them as she laid in his arms. "Are you comfortable?" he asked.

"Yeah, I am. I love being in your arms." He held her hand in his, gently caressing her fingers. As she laid up against his chest, she could feel his heart racing. He kissed her hand. Running his fingers through her gorgeous hair, he lifted her hair off her shoulder and kissed the back of her neck and shoulder. Lying beneath him, she looked up into his eyes. He gently touched her face and kissed her lips. She wrapped her arms around his neck. He looked into her eyes. She ran her fingers through his hair and glided her fingernail gently down his cheek. His dog tags were dangling. She pulled the chain gently down to kiss his lips. As they laid there kissing passionately, the minutes slowly passed. He felt he was losing control. He longed for her. He dreamed and fantasized about having her, but he knew he couldn't. He wanted to be honorable. She deserved an honorable man. He stopped kissing her and looked into her eyes. She looked angelic with her curled hair covering the sofa pillow, as if it were a halo. They wanted each other, but knew one day soon the waiting would pay off.

At that moment, the headlights from Jonah and Christi's Hummer shone through the living room window. They sat up and watched the movie. Then Jonah and Christi walked through the door.

"Hi, ooh candles, what were you two doing?" Christi asked as she and Jonah were curious.

"Yeah, what were you two doing on our very expensive sofa?"

Kate blew out the candles on top of the mantle. "We were just watching a movie. How was your date?" she asked.

"It was good. We had a great dinner and went to a great movie." Christi said.

"That was a stupid movie. She made me watch a chick flick. I would rather watch those old women sell jewelry than to have sat through that gigantic waste of time and money." Jonah groaned, as Jack and Kate laughed at his expression. He struggled to loosen his tie and grabbed a beer. "It didn't even have a plot."

"Oh, it was not stupid. You're just being obnoxious." Christi scolded him.

"Yeah, yeah, yeah, oh y'all are watching *Pearl Harbor*," he said excitedly, as he sat in his recliner. "When a movie makes a woman cry, trust me it's stupid." Jack and Kate laughed.

"Is JD asleep?" Christi asked, as she took off her high heels and her earrings.

"Yes, he's been asleep for over an hour. Jack gave him a bath after dinner." Kate informed them. "So how did you two like babysitting?"

"It was fun." Jack said. They visited with them for a few minutes. They said goodbye and drove back to her apartment. She dimmed the lights and lit candles around the living room. They sat on the sofa to watch a romantic comedy. With his arm around her shoulders, she laid her head on his shoulder.

Throughout the movie, they began kissing more and more seductively. They laid back on the sofa. She touched his chest. Feeling his heart racing and his dog tags, she grasped the chain and gently pulled him down to her. He smiled and kissed her lips. They were kissing passionately while holding each other tight.

After several minutes, feeling she was about to lose control of herself, she stopped kissing him. "What's wrong?"

"I don't trust myself anymore. I'm so in love with you that I want to be as close to you as possible." He ran his fingers through her soft hair. "I'm dying to be close to you," she said.

She looked at him. She could see he was frustrated. He wanted to be with her and had to fight to keep himself under control. "Alright, I'm going to get going."

"I know I must aggravate you we can't be as close as you were with the other women."

Pacing the room, he looked at her. "I love that you're not like the women I've been with. You're you. You mean more to me than anything, Kate. I can deal with the temptation, but what I couldn't deal with is giving in and you regretting it later."

She stood and walked towards him. "I would never regret being with you, Jack. I have to fight to control myself, but it's so much harder than I thought it would be. I love you and I want you to have all of me."

Smiling at her, he ran his fingers through her brown curled hair. "I want all of you too, but I want you to keep your vow until we're married."

"Why?"

"Because that's the best gift you could ever give me." She smiled. Hearing him say that excited her. Her heart wanted to jump out of her chest and run away with excitement. "I can't wait for you to be my wife and the mother of my children."

"Well hurry up and ask me!" she playfully scolded.

He laughed. "Be a little bit more patient with me. I want to do this the right way, the honorable way. I want to ask your father for his permission to marry you. I want to plan a romantic proposal. I want you to have that memory. I've never proposed to anyone before, so I want to knock it out of the park."

"As long as I got you for the rest of my life, I wouldn't care if you proposed to me at Burger King."

He laughed. "I'd never propose at Burger King. It's going to amazing, and it'll be when you least expect it."

"You promise you'll ask me?"

"I promise. I'll ask your father when the time is right."

"My entire family loves you. They think you're perfect for me and that we bring out the best in each other."

"Being with you has made me a better man and a better Christian."

She wrapped her arms around his neck, and he had his hand in her hair. They looked into each other's eyes. She smiled. "I can't wait to be your wife and the mother of your babies."

He kissed her lips. The passion was intense. Then, he quickly released her and said, "I need to go, or I'm going to lose control." She smiled at him and walked him to the door. He gave her a long kiss goodbye.

Days later, they took the afternoon to drive to Austin to see his great-grandfather. He was in his early-90s and was still as ornery as he was in his youth. His hair was still black and he looked great for being ninety-two. His great-aunt Rhonda was his caregiver. She was excited to see Jack. It had been years.

She hugged him tightly. "Jack! Oh it's so good to see you! You're so handsome, just like your daddy. How are your momma and daddy?"

"They're good. It's good to see you, Aunt Rhonda."

"Who is this beautiful woman? You better not be married, because I didn't get an invitation."

He laughed. "No, I'm not married yet. This is Kate, my girlfriend."

She smiled at Kate. "Hello darlin'. I'm Rhonda, Jack's great aunt. How are you?"

"I'm good. Thank you. It's nice to meet you."

"Jack has never brought any of his women friends around the family, so the fact that he's bringing you to meet Dad says a lot."

"I've heard that a lot," Kate said.

Rhonda smiled at Kate then glanced over and saw the way Jack was looking at Kate. "She sure is pretty, Jack. You know Dad is going to try to steal her from you."

Jack and Kate laughed. "Yeah, I've already warned her about that."

They walked in the house. His great grandfather was sitting in a recliner watching a football game. "Dad, guess who's here?"

"Jack!" he said excitedly. He hugged him tightly. "It's good to see you son."

"Hey grandpa, how are you doing?" They resembled each other. Kate looked at the pictures around the living room of him when he was younger and she was shocked at how much he and Jack resembled.

Grandpa saw Kate and stared at her. He looked at Jack and smiled. "Oh, I'm much better now that you brought her. Is she for me?" he teased.

Jack and Kate laughed. "No, grandpa she's <u>my</u> girlfriend. Her name is Kate."

"You lucky son of a gun, had your great grandmother looked like her, I don't know if I would've joined the war," he teased. They laughed. He looked to Kate. "It's nice to meet you, sweetie. You sure are beautiful," he said, kissing the top of her hand.

"Thank you, it's nice to meet you too." They sat and talked. Grandpa told them a lot about the war. He enlisted the day after Pearl Harbor was bombed. He fought throughout the Battle of the Pacific. After the war, he returned to Texas and started a hardware store. Jack's great Uncle is now in charge of the family business. Jack and Kate told him how they met.

"Jack, are you going to marry her?"

He looked at Kate. "Yes, I'm going to."

"What's taking you so long?" he asked. She smiled at Jack.

"I'd actually like to hear the answer to this," she teased.

"I have to work up the courage to ask her father, and I'm a little intimidated."

"Does your father like Jack?" he asked her.

"Yes, my dad loves him. He practically wants to adopt him."

"It seems he wants you in the family, so you better hurry up and ask her. Be bold."

"Her father is also the Army Chief of Staff, so that in itself is intimidating."

"Just don't ask him in uniform. How are Jonah and Meagan? Is Meagan still bringing these knuckleheads around?" Grandpa teased.

"No, I haven't met anymore boyfriends, other than the one I knocked out."

He and Grandpa laughed. "How's Jonah's boy?"

"JD is good. He's growing by the minute."

"He reminds me a lot of you when you were his age."

"I love that kid."

"So have you seen any action over there?" Grandpa asked.

"Yeah, I have."

Rhonda had offered to show Kate the house and all the photographs of Jack when he was little. Jack and Grandpa watched her and Rhonda walk away.

"I think you found a winner, son. Does she know what you do?"

"Yes, her dad was Special Forces."

Grandpa laughed. "So you're dating the boss's daughter?" he teased. He asked Jack more questions about Iraq and Afghanistan.

Rhonda was showing her old photographs of Jack when he was little. "Aw, he was so cute!"

"Yes, he was. Even at seven years old, he had all the girls chasing after him." Rhonda watched her smile. "So, do you love him?" Rhonda asked.

"Yes I love him very much."

Rhonda smiled. "Do you want to marry him?"

Kate smiled. "Yes, I do." Rhonda showed her more pictures of him and told her funny stories. After spending three hours laughing, visiting and hearing the war stories, they said goodbye. They drove back to Dallas.

"So, how'd you like my grandpa?"

"Oh, he was ornery, and I can tell you two were cut from the same cloth."

They laughed. "I told you so. He really liked you."

"What do you want to do on your last night here?"

"I'd like to go fishing out at Lloyd's. You want to go with me?"

"Yeah, I wish we could go hunting together."

"We'll do that on my next leave."

They drove to his parents' house to get the fishing poles and tackle boxes. Then they drove out to Blue Ridge and went fishing on Lloyd's private lake. They left their cell phones in his truck. Sitting in the boat, they fished, talked, and laughed. As the sun was setting, lightning bugs began twinkling, the crickets were chirping. After two hours of fishing, they started packing up. He put the fishing poles in the bed of his truck. She grabbed his hand and pressed her body up against his. They kissed up against his truck.

"I don't want you to leave."

He held her. "I know, baby. I don't want you to leave you, but I have to."

"When you're gone, I feel like a part of me is missing, and when you're home, I feel complete."

He smoothed his finger against her jawline. "I love you, Kate. You're always in my heart and you're always on my mind. You're who I'm coming home to."

They climbed into the truck and drove back to his parents'. They visited with them, and also had cheesecake, sweet tea, and played cards with his parents and sister. He had to leave for Fort Bragg the next day. The next morning, he stopped to see her before he left. They were standing outside next to his truck.

"I wish you didn't have to go."

"I know, but I'll be back soon. I love you."

She looked up in his eyes. He noticed she had tears in hers. "I love you, Jack. Promise me you'll come back?"

A tear rolled down her cheek. He smoothed the tear away with his thumb. He smiled. "I promise. I will come back." She had tears in her eyes. They rolled down her cheeks, and he could feel them hit his shirt. He looked in her eyes, smudged two tears away with his thumbs. "Don't cry. Be strong for me."

She kissed his lips. "I'll be here when you get back."

"I love you Kate." He looked into her eyes. "I will come back."

"I love you too."

He kissed her one last time. "I'll call you when I get in." He opened the truck door.

"Be careful…" He got in his truck and drove away. Twelve hours after reporting in, he and his team were given a mission and deployed to Afghanistan.

IN MARCH 2005, Alpha, Bravo, and Charlie Teams moved into the Pech Valley of Afghanistan, where a fanatical commander deploys a new weapon, the IED. The IED is deadly and very effective for U.S. troops. Followers of the 'Commander Ishmael' videotaped U.S. troops driving through abandoned villages. Jack and Alpha Team were behind Charlie Team in a convoy of Humvees.

He watched the ridges for pockets of entrenched enemy fighters. He grabbed his radio and said, "Guys be alert. Watch for anything suspicious."

"Roger, Alpha 1."

Suddenly the lead Humvee detonated an IED[14]. The Humvee was completely destroyed. The other Humvees stopped as many soldiers rushed to the lead Humvee. Six members of Charlie Team were killed in action. IEDs were not just used in Iraq. They were being frequently used in Afghanistan.

Now June 2005, Alpha, Bravo, and Charlie Teams made it back to their outpost. Morale was low. They lost six brothers. They had a memorial service at the firebase. They finally got a chance to eat a real meal, instead of MREs.

"How are you and Kate doing?" Tom asked him.

"Be proud of me, I've worked up the courage to ask her father for his permission to marry her when we get back."

"Do you think her father will give you his permission? Do you two get a long?"

"Oh yeah, her whole family and I get along great and my family absolutely loves her."

"About what time frame do you want to get engaged?"

"I want to ask her maybe around Christmas or New Year's. I want her to think I'm gone, and then surprise her in front of everyone. I want her to be completely shocked." They talked more about different ideas.

After eating, he saw he had a care package from her. She had sent him all his favorite snacks, razors, shaving cream, the newest video games, and a few books she thought he'd like. She had made him a cake-in-a-jar, for his thirtieth birthday cake. She also sent him pictures of them together. She wrote him a card.

"I love you very much, Happy Birthday! I wish you were home so I could make you a birthday dinner and a real cake. I miss you so much. I'm waiting by the phone and the computer to hear from you. Please be safe, and come back to me"

He smiled. He hadn't spoken to her in three weeks. He walked to his bunk to call her. She was working the night shift at the hospital. Her cell phone rang and she saw that it was an overseas number. She was excited and walked into an empty corridor to speak with him.

"Hey baby, it is so good to finally hear your voice." he said.

---

[14] IED- Improvised Explosive Device

"Oh I'm so happy to hear yours too. Are you okay? Have you received any of the packages I've sent you?" she asked.

"Yeah, I did. Thank you so much. You're a lifesaver. I cannot wait to eat that cake in a jar. I loved the pictures you sent. I'm sorry we won't get to celebrate our birthdays together again this year." he said.

She smiled. "It's military life, part of the job description. Just know that I love you and I miss you very much and I'm here waiting for you."

He smiled. "Hearing that was the best birthday present ever. It made up for the fact that we're thousands of miles apart."

"I can't wait for you to come home."

He smiled. "I can't wait to hold you again. I love you."

"I love you too, Jack. Do you realize that this month we've been together for three years?"

He smiled. "If I was home, I'd go all out for this. I'd have a car and a driver pick you up. I would buy you this amazing black dress and these sexy black heels. I'd wear a black suit. I'd have the driver bring you to Reunion Tower, and I'd hand you a red rose, romance you with dancing, and a great dinner. Then I'd take you for a walk through the botanical gardens."

She smiled. "That sounds incredible, but you left out one very important detail."

"What's that?"

"The best part would be going back to my apartment and kissing like crazy, but the date sounds like something out of a fairytale."

"Yeah, that is the best part. Good, I'm glad you like that plan. You deserve a fairytale."

"I already have my fairytale, Jack. It's you. I love you."

"I love you too. I'm the luckiest guy alive."

She smiled. "And why is that?"

"Because I have you in my life, and I'm going to marry you."

"You'd be an idiot not to." she teased.

"Ouch, thanks. I will marry you."

She missed him. Hearing his voice made her have butterflies in her stomach and just knowing he was in the middle of a war zone made her worry. "Promise me you'll come back to me, Jack."

"I promise."

"Being away from you is so hard, but loving you is so easy."

"I know, baby. Being away from you is hard on me too, but I'll be home soon. I hear that cake-in-a-jar calling my name, if my guys haven't already eaten it."

"I hope they didn't. They don't want me to come wherever you all are."

He laughed. "They know better."

"Okay, be safe. I love you, Happy Birthday."

"I love you too. Stay gorgeous. I'll be home soon." They hung up. He walked back to his care package. He was so ready to eat that cake-in-a-jar, but noticed the lid was off and there were four plastic forks sitting next to it with chocolate icing on them, he looked at Jake, Jamal, Brad, and Marcus. Trevor and Brett were sitting with them.

Each acted normal as if they hadn't eaten his birthday cake. He stood at the front of the room, holding the empty jar, glaring at each of them. "Alright, who ate my damn cake?"

They looked at him as if they were children in trouble. "Jake took a bite first," Brad confessed.

Jake looked at Brad. "We agreed we weren't going to tell him," he said.

"We're sorry, Jack. It was cruel and unusual punishment to look at it and not eat it," Jamal laughed.

"If it's any consolation, it was phenomenal," Brad said.

"I know that's why I'm mad you all ate it," Jack said.

"Do you think she'll send more?" Tom asked. The guys laughed.

"If she does, I'm hiding it so y'all won't eat it." The next day, he and his team were hanging around their outpost. Jack, Tom, Jake were playing cards with Trevor, Brett and other members of Bravo and Charlie Teams. Sam, Jamal, Chase, Mark, and Brad were playing video games.

"So, how are you and Kate?" Trevor asked curiously as he smoked a cigarette and dealt the deck of cards.

"We're great. If I tell y'all something, y'all promise not to make a big deal about it?"

"She's pregnant, isn't she?" Brett asked.

They laughed. "No, she's not pregnant you, idiot!" Jack said, laughing.

"Okay, that's great news. The last thing the world needs is another Jack Hamilton running around." Jake joked, as they laughed.

"Okay so what are what not supposed to make a big deal of?" Trevor asked.

"I'm asking her father if I can marry her when we get back," he admitted.

They were all stunned. Their bottom jaws dropped. "Seriously, Jack?" Brett asked, thinking Jack was just joking.

"You want to get married?" Trevor asked.

"Yeah I do," Jack said as his friends looked at him in surprise.

"Why?" Most asked at the same time.

"I love her and I want to be with her."

"You couldn't pay me to get married." Trevor said. "I'm happy having a different chick every weekend." They laughed.

"You seriously want to be with one woman for the rest of your life?" Brett asked.

"Yeah, I do."

"Have y'all seen a picture of Kate?" Brad asked. "I don't blame Jack for wanting to marry her."

"What does she look like?" Trevor asked. He showed him and Brett her picture.

"Damn, does she have any sisters?" They all laughed.

"Yeah, she does."

In October, Alpha, Bravo, and Charlie Teams were accompanying a Humvee convoy to Kandahar. Their weapons were loaded and ready. They were on alert for insurgents. U.S. convoys had been hit many times with IEDs, and it had claimed countless American lives.

Jack looked out the window for any suspicious activity, when he saw a young man, in his mid-twenties wearing dark clothes and a red and white scarf over his face. He looked closer, and saw the man was holding a video camera and filming as the convoy passed by. The man waved at the soldiers, but he was immediately suspicious. He looked at the front of the convoy, and then back at the man. The man was smiling and waving at the troops. He had a strong inkling that something horrific was about to happen. He picked up the radio and radioed Colonel Benjamin Ryan, who is riding in the lead Humvee of the convoy. "Alpha 1 to Tango 2-1, how copy?"

Colonel Ryan answered him on the radio. "This is Tango 2-1, I read you loud and clear, Alpha 1."

"Colonel, we need to stop, how copy?"

"Good copy, Alpha 1. We can't stop. We have to keep going."

"Colonel, I have a very bad feeling about this. We need to stop and turn around, how copy?" he urged.

"Good copy. What's wrong, Alpha 1?"

"I just saw a kid holding a video camera, as we passed him. He's clearly waiting to videotape something big, like maybe us hitting an IED, we should turn back."

"Negative Alpha 1, this route has been checked."

"Tango 2-1, this is a mistake. We need to stop, get the camera, and question the kid." he urged.

Colonel Ryan was annoyed. He dismissed Jack's concerns about the road and about the male holding a video camera. "Alpha 1, we cannot stop a convoy, just because we saw a kid with a video camera. I do not appreciate my command decisions to be second guessed by an NCO!"

Jack was stunned that the Colonel's pride was in the way of making critical decisions. "Tango 2-1, we're going to get hit!"

"My orders stand, Alpha 1." Knowing that was a bad decision, he began to silently pray to God. Miles down the road he saw another male holding a video camera. The man wore the same dark clothing and scarf as the first one. He had a very uneasy feeling. Suddenly, the Humvee leading the convoy, carrying Colonel Ryan hit an IED.

The truck exploded into flames. Just then as the third truck hit one, so did the fifth truck. The second and fourth trucks were blasted several feet in the air by the explosion. Jack was in the fourth truck. The men were yelling and screaming. Many said prayers fearing death was imminent. The truck landed hard on the ground, and then rolled over on its' side. His head hit the railing of the truck, and he was knocked unconscious. Several minutes later, he regained consciousness. His vision was blurry and his ears were ringing. He slowly moved his head, arms, and feet. He was relieved he was not paralyzed or seriously injured. The smoke was settling. Sand filled the inside of the truck. "Is everyone alright?" he asked loudly, as blood streamed down the side of his head.

He slowly crawled out of the Humvee, covered from head to toe in ash, soot, oil, and blood. His vision was still blurry. He stumbled around. Sand was blasted into his face, taking off skin as oil and blood stained his face. His eyes and teeth were the only thing clean on his face. Soldiers from the two Humvee's behind Colonel Ryan came running up to help. They provided cover fire, during the attack, as twelve armed insurgents tried to ambush the undamaged trucks.

"Master Sergeant, are you alright?" one soldier asked him.

"Yeah, how are Colonel Ryan and Major Hines?"

"They are both KIA. You're in charge now, Master Sergeant."

Jamal saw he was bleeding from the top of his head and inside his ears. "Jack, you're bleeding." he said to him. "You need to let me look at your injuries," Jamal said.

He shook his head in regret. "I have to control the scene." He stumbled unbalanced to the truck to grab a radio. "Control, this is Alpha 1, how copy?"

"Good copy, Alpha 1."

"We have been hit. Launch MED-EVAC. There are numerous casualties and wounded," he yelled loudly over his radio. He gave the exact coordinates as to where they were. Blood streamed down the side of his face and neck. He had a deep gash on his scalp. Jamal tried to tend to his wound, but Jack was trying to control the scene. He ran to both of the charred trucks, looking for survivors and to help the wounded.

He looked in the truck behind him. The smell of cordite, smoke, and fire was overwhelming. He found Major Matthew Hines from Chicago, Illinois slumped over towards the driver. The major and the driver were dead. He and his team found survivors from the charred fifth truck. He ordered his team to apply first aid to the wounded until the MED-EVAC helicopter arrived. Walking up to the first Humvee, he saw Colonel Benjamin Ryan from Cheyenne, Wyoming. His face was covered in blood, and his eyes were closed. No survivors were with him.

"Command central, this is Alpha 1. How copy?"

"Good copy, Alpha 1."

"Be advised Tango 2 and Tango 3 are KIA." he said over his radio as he looked at Colonel Ryan's lifeless body. Tango 1 was Colonel Ryan and Tango 2 was Major Hines. He looked for survivors in the third Humvee. None were there, all killed in action. Thirty U.S. soldiers were killed in route to Kandahar that day.

"Roger, Alpha 1. MED-EVAC helicopter will arrive to your location in ten mikes." One 'mike' is one minute.

"Roger command central."

"Alpha 1, what is the status of the dead and wounded?"

"Thirty are KIA and ten are wounded, how copy?"

"That's a good copy, Alpha 1. MED-EVAC helicopter is in route as is your ride home." A Blackhawk was also in route to pick up remaining troops.

"Roger, command central. Alpha 1 is over and out."

"Roger, Alpha 1." Ten minutes later, the MED-EVAC helicopter approached the site from the East. He and several other soldiers helped load the dead and wounded onto the helicopters, and they were airlifted back to base. Shortly after the helicopter headed back towards the East, the Black Hawk helicopter arrived from the South. The soldiers' returned to base to regroup and held a memorial service for those lost. Morale was low. Jack sat in his bunk, looking at the picture of Kate he always carried. He smiled at it and thought about how close he had come to not being able to keep his promise to her.

A few weeks later, he and his men returned home. They were debriefed and Jack quickly packed and headed to Dallas. He was excited to see her.

It was a cool Friday night. She was at home lying on the sofa, watching re-runs of '*Touched By An Angel*'. She was wearing a pair of comfy, pajama boxer shorts, and a pink tank top. She was barefoot, with a little amount of makeup on her face and her hair up in a messy ponytail, clearly not expecting company. Morgan had gotten engaged and moved out. She moved in with Michael. Kate was very happy for her.

He pulled into the parking lot, excited to see her. The doorman at the entrance of her building recognized him and told him hello. He had the key to her apartment that she had given him. He walked up to her door, he knocked. Curious as to who was at the door, she got up and looked out the peep hole. She was stunned and very happy to see him.

Opening the door, he smiled at her. To him, she looked more exquisite than ever before. "Hi baby!"

She jumped in his arms, wrapping her legs around his waist and her arms around her neck. "I'm so glad you're home!" she said kissing him.

Kissing her lips, he carried her to the sofa and laid her down. "Is Morgan here?"

"No, she moved out three months ago."

"Why did she move out?"

"She moved in with Michael. They're getting married at the end of this month."

"Oh so we have the place to ourselves?"

She smiled up at him. "Yes, all to ourselves, but I have some bad news for you."

He looked at her strangely. "Okay..."

"The five year winning streak of OU beating Texas is finally over."

He laughed, "What was the score?"

She smiled, "Forty-five to twelve..."

He shook his head. "There's always next year."

"You're not as upset as I thought you'd be,"

"I don't care about football right now, how can I be upset when I have you right here?" They held each other tightly and kissed passionately. He smiled down at her. He wanted her. He had fantasized about having her for so long, but he knew he had to honor her promise to God.

She smiled up at him, as she ran her fingernails through his hair. "I love you, Jack."

"I love you too." She looked up into his eyes. Seeing the chain with his dog tags dangling, she gently grasped ahold and pulled him down to kiss his lips. They were kissing seductively and holding onto each other tightly. He looked into her eyes and brushed her hair out of her face. As their passion and desires began to get stronger, they both felt they were losing control. He looked down at her. He knew he had to stop himself.

He stood up. "I can't do this. I mean don't get me wrong, I really want to. I've never wanted to so bad in my life, but we can't. I don't want you to regret anything."

She was conflicted. She wanted him just as badly as he wanted her, but she knew she had to keep her promise to God. He walked to her kitchen to get a glass of water. The scripture about temptation 1 Corinthians 10:13[15] flashed through his mind. He wanted to respect her beliefs and he knew God would help him overcome his physical desire for her.

"How many women have you dated?"

"I've dated a lot."

"How many of them have you slept with?"

"All of them."

She was surprised. "Did you love any of them?"

He smiled. "No, and they didn't love me. Before I met you, I had no intention of having a serious relationship with anyone. I didn't want the distraction. But when I met you, game over. I knew from the moment I saw you that you were special, and I wanted to be with you."

"And these women knew you had no intention of having a serious relationship with them, just a physical one?"

"Yes."

"How do you know you're not a father or don't have any diseases?"

He laughed. "I was very careful to avoid that."

"What's so different about me than all those women?"

He smiled at her. "You're different in every way. You're sweet, beautiful, and you're smart. You're responsible, honest, independent, and I trust you. I know you love me. You take the time out of your busy day to send me care packages seven thousand miles away. I've never had anyone do that for me, except my mom. I've never had a woman care about me or promise to wait for me. When I met you, you changed my mind on what I wanted."

"And what's that?"

He held her hand. "I want to marry you and have a family with you."

She smiled at him. He kissed her lips. She changed her clothes and freshened up. They walked down to his truck and drove to his parents' house. He held her hand as he drove. Arriving to his parents' house, he saw the garage door was open, an indicator that Dad was puttering around in the garage. His parents' cars and Meagan's car were sitting in the driveway. They stepped out of his truck and closed the door.

Dad saw them and walked down the driveway to them. "Hey Dad…" They hugged.

---

[15] *No temptation has overtaken you that is not common to man. God is faithful and he will not let you be tempted beyond your ability, but with the temptation he will also provide the way of escape so that you may be able to endure it."- 1 Corinthians 10:13

"Hey son, it's good to see you." He looked to Kate. "Hello, Kate, you keep getting prettier and prettier." He remarked as he hugged her.

"Oh, thank you." They walked up the walkway to the front door.

"Hey, Mom we're here!" he said, as Hank ran to them.

"Hi!" Mom said, as Dad closed the front door. Mom, Kate, and Meagan sat at the bar in the kitchen and talked, so Jack and Dad snuck out to the garage before supper.

"Son, you look really happy. I don't think I've ever seen you this happy. You better hurry up and marry her before she gets tired of waiting on you."

He had a look on his face that Dad had never seen before. He could tell that Jack had something important weighing on his mind. "I need some advice, Dad."

"Okay, sure, what's going on?"

"I need some advice on marriage."

Dad looked at him in surprise. He smiled and then took a drink of his soda. "You need advice on marriage?"

He smiled at him and nodded. Dad laughed, "Well, it's about time, son. Are you finally ready to get married?"

"Yeah, I am. We've been together for three years. I love her, and I want a family with her. Do you and Mom like her?"

Dad smiled. "We love her, are you kidding? We think she's beautiful, smart, sweet and responsible and honest. She treats you right. We can see you two love each other very much. Why are you hesitating?"

"I don't know. I'm just so used to taking care of myself and my team, not a woman. What if I'm a horrible husband? I'm going to be gone all the time, and I know that eventually that will take a toll on us. How did you and Mom hold things together?" he asked.

"Your mother and I, from day one understood that our marriage was not going to be normal or typical, but extraordinary. You'll cherish the moments you're face to face and not countries apart. Every phone call and every love letter will be special. Your mother and I have had good times, and we've had bad times. We were apart a lot, but it made us even stronger. Marriage is work. You have to work to keep it going."

"Dad, during this last deployment, something happened. It was a close call." He confided in his Dad only about combat.

"Tell me, son."

"We were in a convoy to Kandahar and I saw these two kids holding video cameras, filming us going by. I immediately had a bad feeling about it. I tried to get the Colonel to turn back, but he refused. He kept telling me that I was paranoid. Then his truck hit an IED, and the one behind me hit an IED. My truck was blasted into the air. When we landed, I hit my head on a railing inside the truck. I was knocked out."

"Wow that is a very close call. Thank God you're alive. I worry about you every time you deploy, but finish what you're saying."

"I remember exactly what I was thinking as we were blasted in the air. I thought I was never going to see Kate again. Now that I'm alive and I'm here with her, I want marry her. I feel like if I don't marry her, I'm making a huge mistake. God put everything in perspective for me. I know He wants me to marry her."

Dad wiped his hands with a red rag. "Does she want to get married?"

He smiled as he thought of her. "Yeah, she does."

"Then marry her if you're both ready. Have you talked to her father? You should ask for his permission before you propose."

"I know, I planned on that, but I'm really nervous to ask."

Dad laughed. "Yes, I was nervous too when I asked your grandfather if I could marry your mother. But it shows character, honor, and respect."

Supper was ready. They laughed and talked. His parents could see how happy they were together. He could see how much his parents adored her and how she felt very comfortable with them. After dessert, he stood and kissed Mom on her cheek. "Mom, dinner was amazing as always, but we're going to get going."

"Okay, I'm glad y'all came by. You two look so great together. Kate, I want you to come by and I'll show you his baby pictures."

Kate smiled. "Aw, that would be great. I'm sure he was as handsome then as he is now."

Jack laughed. "Yeah, like that's happening. I may have to do some recon, find those pictures and hide them."

"You should let her see them," Mom said. "Kate, when we get together next week I'll show you the pictures," she said.

"I'd like that a lot," she said.

They said goodbye and walked out to his truck. They were holding hands. He picked her up and twirled her around, as she laughed. "Do you know how happy I am with you? I love you so much," he said. She kissed him.

"I love you too."

Mom and Dad watched them from the dining room window and smiled at each other. "What were you and Jack talking about?" she asked.

He smiled. "He wanted my advice on marriage."

"I hope they get married soon."

It was a cold, rainy Saturday afternoon in November. They were lying on the sofa in her apartment. They were watching a movie and cuddling under a blanket. Lying in his strong arms, she could feel his heart beating. She smiled feeling that their heartbeats matched beat for beat. She turned over to look in his eyes. He ran his fingers through her hair and smiled down at her. He softly kissed her lips. She held his hand tightly as they kissed passionately.

Thunder rumbled and lightening cracked, the rain hammered against the window like nails. Suddenly the electricity went out. They stopped kissing. He searched the kitchen for matches or a lighter, as she gathered up all the candles she could find. She lit the candles as he lit a fire in her fireplace.

He watched her in the kitchen lighting a candle. She glowed in the light. Looking up, she saw he was staring at her. Slowly walking towards her, she smiled at him. Standing face to face, he could see the reflection of the flame in her eyes, he touched her face. She wrapped her arms around his neck. "I love being with you. I'll always be strong for you and I'll always stand beside you."

"You're my heart. You're my strength when I'm tired. You're my home," he said. He gently kissed each of her fingers. She smiled and kissed the palm of his hand on her face. "Dance with me," he said.

She smiled. "We don't have any music. The power is out."

He smiled down at her as she placed her hand in his and wrapped her arm his neck. "I don't sing, but I'll hum, but you're going to dance with me."

She laughed as they began to slow dance to his humming in the candlelight. She smiled up at him. "I love that when you're holding me, I know I'm in the safest place in the world."

"You'll always be safe with me."

"I love knowing you're coming home to me."

He looked in her eyes. "I'll always come home to you. Nothing could ever keep me away from you."

"I love you."

"I love you too, Kate."

She looked into his eyes. She could see the candlelight's reflection in them. "I wish we could make love. I want to feel you in my soul. I need you. I want to be as close to you as I can be."

He smiled down at her. "Everything inside of me wants you and needs you. I love you so much, Kate, but I wouldn't really love you if I took advantage of you, so to prove that I really love you, I'm going to honor your vow."

He kissed her lips. They kissed passionately, as they stood in the middle of her living room with the fire crackling and candles lit all around the room. The rain pounded hard against the windows and her balcony. Thunder rumbled and lightening cracked. She wrapped her arms around his neck, as his were around her waist. As she tasted his gratifying kisses, 1 Thessalonians 4:3-5[16], the scripture that made her decide to remain pure until she was a married woman flashed in her mind. She knew it was God telling her that she was coming too close to breaking her vow.

Pulling away from him and taking a deep breath, she said, "Okay, we should stop before we go too far." He backed away from her. The lightening still flashed across the night sky as the thunder rumbled and the rain pounded. The electricity was still out. With no power, the fire crackling and candles lit, she found abstinence to be more testing than she thought it would be. She never knew a man could make her feel this way. He made her feel beautiful, desirable, aroused and sexy. He was handsome, caring, kind and honorable. He was a strong Christian who overcame his lust and strong desire for her and honoring her and respecting her beliefs. He was a man that desperately wanted her but loved her more to wait for her. She knew she had found the man of her dreams, the man that God had sent her.

"What are you thinking about?" she asked. They sat in front of the fireplace, roasting marshmallows and making Smores.

He looked at her. "Why do you want to marry me?"

She smiled. "I have never felt as safe as I do when I'm with you. I love being in your arms. I'm so madly in love with you that I would have to invent words to describe how much I love you. I want you more than I've ever wanted anything. Our connection is so much deeper and truer than anything I've ever dreamt or thought it could be. You gave me intimacy without having to have sex. You have no idea how much that means to me. I want to marry you, I want a family with you and I want to take care of you. Why do you want to marry me?"

"I need you in my life. I need you to be that stability, that constant factor that I've avoided for so long. You're the only woman in the world that makes me feel this way. You're my heart, Kate. You've had my heart since day one. I want to give you everything. I want to take care of you. I want to protect you. I know I've found perfection. You can handle and respect my career. You're everything I've ever wanted and you're everything I need. When I look at you, I see my children."

She smiled at him. "You're so amazing."

"Isn't it hard to love me with what I do for a living? I mean you're used to a guy being able to take you out every weekend for a date night or being able to go with you to family events and I'm not able to do any of that, except when I'm home on leave."

---

[16] *For this is the will of God: your sanctification: that you abstain from sexual immorality, that each of you know how to control his own body in holiness and honor, not in the passion of lust like the Gentiles who do not know God."- 1 Thessalonians 4:3-5

"No, loving you isn't hard. The distance, the separation, and the sacrifices are hard, but loving you is the easiest thing I've ever done." They made a pallet in the floor in front of the fireplace. They held each other and kissed passionately as the fire crackled beside them. With his strong arms wrapped around her, they talked for hours until she fell asleep.

Finally, the electricity had come back on and the storm passed. The sky was dark and the stars were now visible. Seeing it was near midnight, he looked down at her. She was asleep, holding his hand as she slept against him. He stood up from the floor and stretched. He picked her up and carried her to her bedroom. Pulling the comforters back, he gently laid her down and covered her up. He kissed her cheek and turned off the lamp beside her bed. He quietly left and headed back to Jonah and Christi's.

The next afternoon while she was at work, he called her parents. He had scheduled a meeting with Matt without her knowledge. He was going to ask for her father's permission and blessing, for him to propose. He pulled in the driveway. He stepped out carrying a bouquet of yellow roses, her mother's favorite. He calmly but nervously walked up the steps and rang the doorbell.

Carole answered the door. "Hi, Jack, how are you?" she asked enthusiastically.

He walked in, hugged, and kissed him on the cheek. He smiled. "I'm great, Carole. How are you?"

"Oh, we're doing great. Come on in," she said.

He stood nervously in the foyer. "These are for you," he said, giving her the flowers.

"Oh thank you so much, Jack. They're beautiful."

"You're welcome. I have a meeting with Matt,"

"He's in his office, just right back there. You can go on back. How are you and Kate doing?"

He smiled. "We're great." He walked down the hall to Matt's office. He looked at the pictures of Kate and Lauren on the wall from the time they were babies up until their recent family photo.

Jack entered the office and saw Matt sitting in his desk chair, while on the phone with a friend in Washington D.C. Jack knocked on the office door. Matt was happy to see him. "Jack!"

"Hello, Matt, I didn't realize you were busy. I can come back later."

"No, that's okay. Come on in. Have a seat…" Jack sat in the chair in front of his desk. "…Sam, I'll have to call you back. My future son-in-law just walked in."

He hung up. Matt stood as did Jack. They shook hands and hugged. "Jack, how are you doing?"

"I'm great. How are you?"

They sat down. "I'm fine. Are you enjoying your leave?" The office had many pictures of Kate and Lauren hanging on the wall behind his desk, along with pictures of Matt with the President and the Secretary of Defense.

"Yes, I am."

"Have you seen Kate?"

He smiled, as he thought of her. "Yes, I've seen her. She is more beautiful every time I see her."

"Carole and I have never seen her so happy before."

He smiled, looking at a picture of him and Kate together on the corner of the desk. "I love her very much. She deserves to be happy."

He was nervous and was beginning to sweat. He hoped Matt would give him his blessing. Her parents loved him and felt that they were perfect for each other. "So, what's on your mind, son?" Matt asked nicely. He could tell he had something serious on his mind. He saw how nervous he was.

He took a deep breath. "Well, as you know, Kate and I have been together for three years now and I love her very much. She is the best person I've ever met. I could never hurt her and I can't imagine not being with her. I love your daughter, Matt. May I have your permission to ask her to be my wife?"

He slowly stood and Jack quickly stood. He smiled and stuck out his hand. He said proudly, "Of course you have my permission, son."

He was relieved. He shook his hand. "Thank you. That was nerve racking."

Matt laughed. "I really appreciate you coming out here and asking me for my permission. I know nowadays it seems outdated, but it's rare. It shows respect, honor, and character, and those are the qualities I want in a son-in-law."

Carole walked in carrying two glasses of iced tea. "Honey, you'll never guess what Jack has asked me."

"What? I could tell it was something important."

Matt and Jack smiled at her. "He asked me for my permission to marry Kate."

"Did you give it to him?" she asked excitedly.

Jack and Matt laughed. "Of course I did."

Carole smiled. "Oh, this is so exciting! Welcome to the family!" she said as she hugged Jack.

"Well she hasn't accepted yet," Jack informed.

"Oh, but she will. She's only been waiting three years for you to ask," she said, with a laugh.

"Have you already purchased the ring?"

"No, I wanted your permission first. Now I'm going to go shopping, I hate shopping."

He and Matt laughed. "Have fun." Matt joked.

"I'll drag Jonah and Dad along."

"Yeah, that will be fun. After you ask her, we should get together with your family for dinner."

"Yeah, we should. I'll set it up."

"Do your parents' know that you are going to propose?" she asked.

"My dad does, but my mom doesn't know yet."

"When are you thinking about asking her?" Matt asked him.

"I'm not sure. I don't know exactly how I should do it. I've never proposed before."

"Don't be nervous; she'll say yes," Carole said.

"I hope so. Thank you for your permission."

Matt held out his hand. "Welcome to the family." he said as he and Jack shook hands.

He smiled and proudly walked out to his truck excited about asking her. He drove to his parents' house and visited with his parents and sister while she was at work. He pulled into the driveway of his parents' home. He walked into the kitchen. Mom was looking through her recipes as Meagan was working on homework at the breakfast table.

"Hey Momma, what are you doing?" he asked, sitting at the bar.

She looked up at him and smiled. "Oh, I'm getting rid of old recipes, what are you doing? How is Kate?"

He flicked Meagan in the arm. She elbowed him. "She's good, amazing as ever. I need to talk to you about something important."

He was nervous on how his mother would react. "Okay, what's going on?" she asked curiously.

"How do you and Dad feel about her?"

Mom smiled, "Oh, we adore her. We love her like another daughter, why? Is everything okay with you two?" she asked, scared they were breaking up.

"Yeah, everything is great. I'm really glad you and Dad love her, momma. I really love her too."

"I know. I can see it when you two look at each other."

"I'm asking her to marry me."

She smiled and immediately got excited, but tried to contain it, thinking he was just joking. "Jack David Hamilton, if you're pulling a practical joke, this isn't funny."

Meagan was just as stunned as her mother. He laughed. "Mom, I'm being 100% serious right now." She smiled at him. "I thought you didn't want to get married?"

"I didn't, until I met her. She changed my mind." She began to cry. She was so happy. "Oh momma, please don't cry. I hate it when you cry," he said.

"I'm just so happy for you. I love Kate. She is gorgeous, she's sweet, smart, and she loves you so much." She hugged him tightly. "My baby boy is going to get married."

"Mom, I'm thirty years old. I'm not a baby anymore."

"Well I don't care how old you are, you'll always be my baby boy." she said, dabbing her eyes with a Kleenex. Dad walked in from the garage his hands covered in black oil and grease. He smiled as he knew Jack had shared the news with her.

The next afternoon, Dad, Jack, and Jonah went to uptown Dallas to the jewelry stores. They spent all morning looking at engagement rings. They enjoyed the day together, just doing "guy" things.

They were eating lunch at *Chili's Bar & Grill.* "So, when do you plan to propose?" Dad asked.

"I want to do it at Christmas, if I'm not deployed."

"You should do it at our Christmas party," Jonah suggested.

Dad laughed. "Yeah, dress up as Santa and have her sit on your lap and ask her what she wants for Christmas," he suggested, as they laughed.

He didn't take the Santa Claus getup seriously. After lunch, he, Jonah, and Dad continued their search. They walked into a very upscale, high end Dallas jeweler *Bachendorf's.* The staff was friendly. He looked at the large selections of diamonds. After not finding a diamond or setting he liked, he had a ring custom made for her. He only had a few days before he had to return to Fort Bragg, but once the ring was finished, it would be delivered by armored truck to his parents' house. Dad would keep it secure.

His leave was up. He had to report back. He told his family and Kate goodbye. Shortly after getting back to base, he deployed to Iraq.

One month later, it was Christmas time in Dallas. The city was decorated beautifully. The weather forecast predicted snow during the week of Christmas. Everyone in north Texas was hoping for a white Christmas.

Jonah and Christi were hosting their annual Christmas party. Kate was attending alone, because Jack was deployed on a mission. They had invited family, close friends, and even her parents, Lauren and grandparents.

It was the night of the party. Jonah and Christi's home was decorated beautifully with clear Christmas lights, candy canes and a wreath on the front door. Kate was the first to arrive, she agreed to help Christi. She wore a nice black cocktail dress with black heels. Her hair and makeup looked fantastic. Christi was now in her third trimester of her pregnancy. She was expecting another little boy they planned to name Andrew.

She rang the doorbell. Jonah answered. "Hey, it's my little brother's other half. Woo! Don't you look pretty!" he said laughingly and obviously tipsy.

She laughed at him, as she hung up her coat. "How much liquor have you had?"

"Um, I think I've had three or maybe five glasses. I lost count," he said with a drunken slur.

She laughed as she walked to the kitchen. The house smelled like cinnamon and gingerbread. Christi was wearing her Christmas themed kitchen apron as she put the hor'd'eouvres in the oven. "Merry Christmas, you look amazing!" Christi said as they hugged.

"Thank you, so do you! You're glowing!"

"I can't wait to be back to a size four. I'm so fat."

"No you're not. You're beautiful. I only hope I look as stunning as you when I'm pregnant. The house looks great," she said.

"Thank you, have you heard from Jack?"

She frowned. "No, I haven't heard from him in a few weeks. I wish he could be home for Christmas. I miss him so much."

"I know you do, but maybe he'll only be gone for a little while."

"Let's hope so," she replied trying to get in the Christmas spirit.

Guests arrived and mingled. Waiters circulated, carrying flutes of champagne and trays of hor d'eouvres. People stood and sang along as Christmas carols were played on the grand piano. Kate's parents were laughing with Jack's, as Lauren and Meagan looked at some of the single teammates Jonah invited.

Jonah walked in with Santa Claus. The guests were excited. Seeing Santa brought out the true spirit of Christmas. "Ho! Ho! Ho Merry Christmas!" Santa said, as everyone cheered.

"I didn't know you hired a Santa. This is new," Kate said to Christi, as she drank champagne with Angie, Marci, and Tess while Christi drank orange juice.

"Well, it is a Christmas party. We thought it would be fun to have Santa here."

"I think Santa is so sexy," Marci admitted. The girls gave her an odd look. "Did I just say that out loud?" she asked.

"Ewe, you're attracted to an old guy with a jelly belly and a white beard?" Tess teased, as they laughed.

"I'm attracted to authority figures, like police officers, firemen, military men, and Santa. What is sexier than a man deciding if you're naughty or nice?" Marci asked.

The girls laughed at her. "Only you would turn a sweet children's Christmas carol into something you'd expect to see on the cover of a Santa themed dirty movie," Angie said, as they laughed.

Santa sat in a chair in front of the fireplace while the stockings hung behind him and the fire crackled and popped.

Jonah stood at the front of the room in front of the fireplace and behind Santa. Everyone got quiet. "Okay, everyone, I had enough money to bribe Santa to leave the North Pole early to be here. He can have a few drinks and have a good time before delivering toys to all the children of the world…" as everyone laughed. "…But he wants to know what y'all want for Christmas, so Kate, why don't you go first?" he suggested.

Everyone looked at her. She blushed and laughed out of embarrassment. "No thanks."

"Ah, come on, why not?" he asked.

She laughed again. "Because I'm not a four year old, I'm an adult. Why don't you do it? You're drunk enough."

"Come on, just do it for fun. Where's your holiday spirit? Tell Santa you want Jack home for Christmas." Christi encouraged as she and the rest of her friends escorted her to Santa.

He looked up at her. She reluctantly sat on his lap. Everyone was quiet, as some videotaped and took pictures of her talking to Santa.

"Hi Santa…"

He smiled up at her. "Have you been a good girl this year?" Santa asked, with a deep voice.

Her face was all shades of red from embarrassment, avoiding eye contact with him. "Well you're Santa, shouldn't you know if I have been or not?"

"I don't have my naughty and nice book with me, so I'd have to check. Do you think you've been a good girl?"

She laughed, out of embarrassment. She noticed all of her friends and some of her family members and his were taking pictures. Christi was taking pictures as Jonah recorded her with his video camera.

"Yes, I've been a good girl."

"I'll take your word for it. What would you like for Christmas?"

Knowing Jonah was videotaping her, she decided to give an answer none were expecting. "I would like my boyfriend to stop dragging his feet and propose already," she said.

Bill and Matt laughed out loud, hysterically. She was right. That was not the response they had expected from her. Christi elbowed Jonah and told him to be quiet.

Santa smiled up at her. "Do you love him?"

She smiled as she thought of him. "Yes, I love him very much."

"Why do you want to marry him?" Santa asked with a deep voice.

She had tears in her eyes as she thought of him. She said quietly to Santa, "Because, he's everything I've ever imagined my husband to be. I feel safe with him. When he's gone, I feel like a part of me is missing, and when he's home, I'm complete."

Santa smiled up at her. "I'll see what I can do to get him to stop dragging his feet. Could you get up please? I have a present to give to you."

She stood up, and so did Santa. She looked over at Jonah and Christi and the rest of their friends and family. She noticed everyone was still videotaping and taking pictures of her and Santa. She briefly wondered why. He took off the beard, glasses and the hat. It was Jack! She was still looking around the room. He smiled at her. The flashes from cameras were flashing. She saw the looks on everyone's faces and turned back to look at Santa. She covered her mouth in shock as tears formed in her eyes. She thought he had been on a mission. He smiled at her. Reaching in his pocket, he pulled out a little black box and kneeled in front of her. Their family and friends gasped with excitement. Holding her hand in his, he looked up into her tear filled eyes.

She was shaking with excitement. She had fantasized about this moment for so long. She couldn't do anything except smile. He held her hand and looked up into her glistening eyes, "Katherine Elizabeth, I love you. I want to spend the rest of my life with you. I know with my career, we'll rarely get to see each other, but I promise you that if you marry me, I'll always be faithful. I'll always need and miss you. I'll always love you and I promise to always come home to you…" He smiled and opened the box. "…Will you marry me?"

And without hesitation, she shouted "Yes! Of course I'll marry you!" She threw her arms around his neck. Their friends laughed at her enthusiasm and excitement. He smiled as he took the beautiful three carat sapphire ring out of the box. The sapphire was oval shaped surrounded by sparkling round brilliant diamonds. It was very similar to the late Princess Diana's engagement ring.

He stood. "In ancient times, when a man gave a woman a sapphire, he pledged his loyalty and trust to her. Kate, I promise you that you can trust me. I'll be loyal to you for the rest of my life. I love you so much. Inside the ring, there is an engraving that I want you to look at when I'm gone, and every time you're scared or nervous that I'm not coming back, I want you to read this." He showed her the engraving on the inside band of the ring, *I Will Come Back.*

She smiled with tears in her eyes as he slipped the ring on her finger. He kissed her and hugged her. She had tears drizzling out of the corner of her eyes, as he held her against him.

Their families and friends' applauded and cheered for them. They faced their family and friends. Christi hugged her as Jonah shook Jack's hand.

"Welcome to your engagement party!" Christi said to her. Their family and friends toasted them and yelled, "Congratulations!"

"Let's get drunk!" Jonah yelled. Christi swatted him. They stood with Jonah, Christi, and their parents. She showed their mothers, their sisters, and Christi the ring. They thought her ring was breathtaking and stunning. He changed from the Santa suit.

"So, Kate, were you surprised?" Jonah asked, as they all laughed.

She looked up at him. His arm was around her waist. She smiled up at him. "Yes, I was! How did you all pull this off? Who all knew?"

Their friends all laughed. "Um, everyone here knew," Jonah said with a slur.

"We sent out special invitations to everyone, but you got our regular Christmas party invite." Christi explained.

"Y'all are sneaky. I'm surprised no one slipped," she said.

"Jack threatened most of them with imprisonment at Gitmo or Leavenworth." Jonah teased.

"How much have you had to drink, Jonah?" Jack asked curiously, as Kate and Christi laughed.

Jonah held up three fingers, but said, "I think five or six."

She looked up at him. "When did you get back?" she asked him.

He smiled down at her. "Three days ago. I had to keep my phone off to keep me from calling you or I would've spoiled the surprise. Dad and Jonah had to hide my truck keys and phone so I wouldn't call you or drive to your apartment."

Jonah said, "Yeah, it was not easy babysitting him. I caught him several times attempting to sneak out. But it gave me an insight as to what JD will be like when he's a teenager and I'm trying to keep him from going somewhere." They all laughed.

She smiled up at him. "This was the best surprise I've ever had! When I saw you, my heart about jumped out of my chest."

"I had the same reaction when I first saw you. You look gorgeous."

He smiled down at her and gently kissed her. Jonah and Christi smiled at them. "Jack, that's a gorgeous ring. Why did you buy her a sapphire?" Christi asked.

"I went in with the intention of buying a diamond, but when the salesman told me that sapphires symbolize loyalty and trust. I knew that was perfect." He touched her hand and looked at the ring. "I had this custom made for her." He saw Kate looking at it. "Do you like it? We can take it back to get you a different ring if you don't like this one," he whispered to her.

"If I had all the rings in the world to choose from, this is the ring I would choose. I love it. I've always loved sapphires."

Matt, Carole, Denise, and Bill walked up to them. Her father wanted to see the ring. "Jack, that's one heck of a ring! It looks beautiful on her."

"Oh, Jack, it's breathtaking!" Carole exclaimed.

"Thank you."

Denise hugged Jack and kissed her on the cheek. "I'm thrilled you're going to be part of the family."

"I can't wait to be Mrs. Jack Hamilton," she said looking up to Jack. He smiled and kissed the side of her head.

They mingled with all their friends and family. Angie, Marci, and Tess hugged her and Jack. "You're lucky Marci didn't take advantage of you; she's attracted to Santa." she said, as they laughed.

Jack teased Marci. "You're attracted to old fat guys?"

"Oh shut up!" Marci teased, as they all laughed.

He visited with Jonah and some of their friends. Throughout the party, he smiled, watching her show her engagement ring to her friends. He saw that she was really happy. Her granny walked up to him and Jonah. "Hello Jack."

He smiled and was happy to see her. "Hello, Granny. Well, I finally proposed."

She kissed him on the cheek. "What took you so long to ask her? It's a wonder I ain't dead yet," she playfully scolded him in her strong Southern drawl.

He and Jonah laughed. "I'm sorry, Granny. I had to work up the courage to ask her father and then to ask her."

"Just please don't make it a long engagement for Pete's sake. I ain't got forever," she teased, as they laughed. Around 10:00 p.m. The party began to break up. Guests were leaving and saying goodbye to Christi, since Jonah was intoxicated and asleep on the sofa.

They went back to her apartment. She turned her Christmas tree lights on as he lit a fire in her fireplace, dimmed the lights, and lit some candles. She changed into her pajamas and made them some hot chocolate. After he finished in the living room, he walked into the kitchen. He saw her admiring her ring in the light. He smiled. "I'm relieved you love your ring. I was nervous about getting a sapphire since it's not traditional."

"Actually sapphires are common engagement rings, especially after Prince Charles gave Princess Diana a sapphire engagement ring. I love it, Jack. You picked a very beautiful ring. I couldn't have picked a better ring!"

She wrapped her arms around his neck, as he pulled her up against him, wrapping his arms around her waist. "When do you want to get married? Please say you want to drive to Vegas."

"No, our parents would kill us if we took off to Vegas. I want a wedding here."

"Okay, but please let's make this a short engagement," he suggested.

"Well how short are you talking about?"

"Six months max."

She laughed. "You're joking, right?"

"No, I want to get married as soon as possible so you can move with me to Fort Bragg."

"I've always wanted a fall wedding."

He smiled, moving a strand of her hair behind her ear. She smiled at him. Her smile was his weakness. He knew a fall wedding was what she wanted. He groaned and smiled. "Okay, we'll get married next fall."

She kissed his lips. "Thank you. I know it's not easy for you to remain celibate, and now you have to go ten more months, but you're strong. You're the strongest man I know."

"I don't understand why you need nearly a year to plan for one day. I don't want anything expensive or over the top. I'd be happy with going to the court house, but I know I'm just the groom. My job is to shut up, show up and smile," They talked more about the wedding.

They took their hot chocolate into the living room to cuddle on the couch, while watching Christmas movies. With his strong arms wrapped around her, she pulled his hand up to her chest. He felt her heart racing. "I love being in your arms. I feel so safe."

He ran his fingers through her soft, curled brown hair and tucked it behind her ear. "You'll always be safe with me." Her hair smelled of jasmine and honeysuckle. "I can't wait to marry you."

He kissed her lips. He smiled at her. "I'm sorry it took me so long to propose. I finally stopped dragging my feet." They laughed.

"You're forgiven."

"Did you really not know that was me in the Santa suit or were you messing with me?"

"NO! I honestly thought you were on a mission. Why do you think I started crying?"

He laughed. "I got you good, didn't I?" They cuddled and kissed on the sofa listening to the fire crackle and the Christmas movie playing in the background.

A FTER THE HOLIDAYS, Kate, Jack, Jonah, and Christi went out to Lloyd's to visit and to have a shooting competition. Christi, at full term, was ready to learn how to shoot a rifle. It was a sunny but chilly afternoon in January. They were driving up as Jonah and Christi followed. JD stayed back in Dallas with Bill and Denise.

He held her hand as they drove. He looked down at the sapphire ring. "So are you sure you don't want to go to Vegas?" he teased her.

"No, I want a big Texas fall wedding in our church."

"If that's what you want, it's my job to make you happy."

"You do make me happy and to have our wedding here in Texas with all of our friends and family would make me very happy. I love you."

"I love you too." They pulled into Lloyd's driveway. They stepped out and waited for Jonah and Christi. Nearly ten minutes had passed. They finally saw Jonah's truck pull into the long driveway. Parking behind Jack's truck, Jonah got out and helped Christi slowly step out.

"Hey, Chris, how are you feeling?" Jack asked.

"I'm pregnant, how do you think I'm feeling?"

Jack and Jonah laughed. "She's been a little mean today." Jonah said, carrying his rifle.

"It's your fault." Jack said to him.

"That's what they keep telling me."

Lloyd and Marie opened the door and walked out on the porch. "Hey!" Lloyd shouted. Jonah and Jack unloaded their trucks and walked up to greet Lloyd.

"Chris, I can't believe you're out here. You should be home taking it easy."

"Oh, I'm fine. My doctor said I'm probably going to have to be induced." They walked into the house and visited with Marie. They visited with Lloyd and Marie.

An hour later, Kate and Christi were visiting with Marie, eating some of her famous blackberry cobbler while Jack, Jonah, and Lloyd were three miles away from the house shooting.

"So, Jack, are you ready to be a married man?"

"Yeah, I tried talking her into going to Vegas, but she wants a wedding here this fall."

"Why do women need big weddings? I see no point in it." Jonah admitted.

"Why do women need half the things they do?" Lloyd asked as they laughed.

"How long do you and Kate plan to wait until you have kids?" Lloyd asked.

"I don't know, really. I think we should get married and then in a few years we'll talk about kids."

"I can't wait for your bachelor party. It's going to be awesome," Jonah said to him.

Lloyd and Jack laughed. "Better than yours was?" Jack asked.

"Oh yeah, I've already got things planned out."

"Just don't get me in trouble, or you will be in trouble."

"Oh don't worry, everything is strictly classified and on a need to know basis," Jonah said.

Jack laughed at him. The guys continued to shoot. Lloyd had gotten ahold of some binary explosives. "Jack, congratulations on your engagement, this is officially the beginning of the end."

Jack and Jonah laughed. "I have a surprise for you both." He walked down to the targets and taped a plastic paint can to the target.

"What's in there?" Jonah asked.

"You'll see." He walked back to where Jack and Jonah were standing. "Jack, shoot it."

Jack looked through the scope and smiled. He knew what was in the container. Squeezing the trigger, the bullet met the pain container and BOOM! Jack and Jonah were like kids in a candy store.

"Oh, that's awesome!" Jack said.

Meanwhile, as they guys shot and enjoyed time together, Kate, Marie, and Christi were up at the house talking and laughing over cobbler and tea. "So have you and Jack decided on when the wedding will be?" Marie asked.

"In September or October, I've always wanted a fall wedding, but Jack wants to go to the courthouse or drive out to Vegas."

"Oh Denise would kill him if you two ran off," Christi warned.

"I told him that. He expected me to have a wedding planned in six months. I mean I guess it is possible, but a Texas wedding in June or July would be absolute torture."

"Are y'all going to have a big or small wedding?" Christi asked.

"Not too big, not too small."

"I remember the night he brought you out here to go shooting. I could tell you two were it for each other. I've known Jack his whole life, since he was in diapers, and I had never seen him like that."

"Like what?" Kate asked.

"He looked happy, relaxed and he looked to be in love with you. He's never brought any of the women he was dating home to meet anyone of the family, so when he brought you out here, I knew you had to be the girl that stole his heart. And it's clear you did," Marie said.

"We had our first kiss out in the field. I remember Lloyd and your boys spying on us and whistling when we kissed. How are your boys?"

"Oh they're good. Ryan is now a lance corporal in the Marines, and Jake is a specialist in the Army."

"Where are they stationed?"

"Ryan is stationed at Camp Pendleton and Jake is stationed at Fort Benning in Georgia."

Kate noticed Christi looking pale and that she hadn't touched her scoop of cobbler. "Christi, are you alright?"

"Oh, yeah I'm fine," Christi lied.

She was not convinced. She could see her beginning to sweat, her breathing was concentrated. Christi was having contractions and was in labor. "No you're not. Okay, we need to get Jack and Jonah. We have to get you to the hospital."

"We don't have time,"

"Why?"

"…Because my water just broke."

Marie and Kate sprang into action. "Okay, hold on. I'll get Jack and Jonah!" Marie shouted as she ran out the door to the four-wheeler. Kate helped her very slowly off the bar stool and to the guest bedroom. Her contractions were strong and very close together. Kate knew that she was going to have to deliver the baby herself.

Marie reached Jack, Jonah, and Lloyd. "What's wrong?" Lloyd asked.

"Christi's water broke! We have to get back to the house now!"

Lloyd jumped on the ATV with her as Jack and Jonah jumped in Jack's truck and took off towards the house. Christi and Kate made it to the bedroom. She lied down on the bed as Kate ran to the guest bathroom to get towels and blankets. She found an at home hair-coloring kit and took the plastic gloves out of the box.

She hurried over to Christi to check to see how dilated she was. She was fully dilated. "Kate, I don't think I'm going to be able to wait until the EMTs get here."

She knew she wouldn't. "I know, Chris, but I promise that everything will be okay."

"I'm sorry you have to do this, but I know you can."

Kate smiled. "It's a good thing I'm a labor and delivery nurse."

Christi smiled as she squeezed her hand during an intense contraction. Lloyd, Marie, Jack, and Jonah arrived back to the house. "Christi?" Jonah called out.

"We're in here!" Kate shouted from the guest bedroom.

He opened the bedroom door and saw Christi sweating, crying and breathing hard. "Okay, we need to get her to the hospital," he said.

"Jonah, there isn't time. She's going to deliver here."

"Who's going to deliver the baby?" he asked.

Kate smiled. "I'm at your service."

"You're going to deliver my son? Oh no, I'll get her to the hospital in time."

"She's not going anywhere. It's safer for her and the baby here."

She looked to Jack. He could see Jonah was very worried and starting to panic. "Jonah, I know it's scary, but Kate is right. It's safer for Christi and the baby here. Kate knows what she's doing. Trust her," he assured. He was very impressed with Kate's demeanor and focus. She was calm, cool, and collected as everyone else was panicking. She sprang into action.

Lloyd was on the phone with 911 as Marie was comforting Christi along with Jonah. Jack was trying to be useful, but he had never delivered a baby and wasn't entirely sure he wanted to. The EMTs were twenty minutes away.

Kate looked up to Jack. "You may not want to see this."

"I've seen worse," he admitted.

"I don't want him looking at me down there! Get out!" Christi snapped. Jonah was supporting Christi and holding her hand. She was nearly breaking his hand.

"I'll just be over here," he said walking across the room.

"Okay, Christi, you're crowning. It's time to start pushing," she said.

Christi was crying. "This is not how I imagined this day."

"I know, sweetie, but you can do this. I'm right here with you."

"You wouldn't happen to have any epidural medicine on you, would you?" Christi asked.

Kate smiled. "No, I didn't pack the anesthesiologist."

"Ask Marie if she has any horse tranquilizers?" Christi asked.

"Are you sure you're able to do this, Kate?" Jonah asked. He was scared and nervous.

"Jonah, I do this every day. But if you don't want me to do this, you or Jack can do it and I'll coach you through it."

"I know Kate can do this, Jonah," Jack said. He did not want to deliver the baby.

"I don't want Jonah to do it. He'll pass out. Kate you're doing it!" Christi ordered.

She began to push and scream. Kate coached her. Jack was trying to keep his lunch down. He knew if he looked, he would throw up or possibly faint, and he would never be the same again. He kept his eyes on Kate. He was very impressed with her. He had never seen her so focused yet so relaxed.

After ten minutes of pushing and screaming, Andrew David Hamilton was born. The baby cried out and Kate smiled, with tears in her eyes. She just delivered her future nephew.

"Here he is! He has all ten fingers and ten toes. He looks healthy," she added as she cleaned him off. She placed him on Christi's chest.

Christi and Jonah were elated that he was healthy and safe. Jack looked at her. He was so proud of her. They watched Jonah and Christi kiss their son. He looked down at her. "I'm so proud of you, baby." She smiled. "You were incredible."

She kissed his lips. "Thanks."

The ambulance arrived and loaded Christi and the baby up. Jonah looked at Kate and walked over to her. He hugged her. "Thank you, Kate. We're so lucky to have you. I owe you."

"You don't owe me anything, Jonah. I'm just glad I was able to help."

"What'd you name him?" Jack asked.

"Andrew David."

"It's a good name," Jack said.

Lloyd and Marie were oohing and awing over the new baby. Christi was fine. The EMTs told Kate she did great, and one asked if she had ever considered being a paramedic. Jack called his and Jonah's parents as Kate called Christi's parents and told them that she had the baby, and they were being taken to the hospital. They drove to the hospital to see the baby.

They entered Christi's hospital room and saw her and Jonah looking down at the baby. Jonah stood up, cradling the baby in his arms. He slowly walked towards them. "Hey Andrew, meet your Uncle Jack and Aunt Kate."

"I don't know if I should hold him or not. I've never held a baby," Jack said, nervously.

"Oh, it's easy. Just pretend he's a football or a bomb." Jack laughed.

He placed him gently in his arms. Kate smiled at him holding the baby. She pictured him holding their son or daughter one day. He looked at her. "Am I doing this right?"

She smiled and touched the baby's hand. "Yes, you're doing great." She looked to Jonah. "He looks just like you, Jonah." she said.

"Thanks. Yeah, I know he's a handsome little guy. Do you want to hold him?"

She smiled. "I'd love to." She gently took him from Jack. She walked over to Christi. "How are you feeling?"

"Oh I feel much better now. Thank you for delivering him. I'm sorry you had to do it, but…"

"I was happy to do it."

Christi smiled at her holding him. "You're now an Aunt," she said to her.

"I love my little nephews."

"Oh did you call my parents?"

"Yes, Jack, and I called them. They are going to pick JD up from school and bring him here." She placed Andrew back into Christi's arms so she could nurse him. She and Jack hugged Jonah and left.

As they walked down the hallway, he looked at her and smiled. She noticed the smile on his face. "What? Why are you smiling at me like that?" she asked.

"You looked amazing holding my nephew."

She smiled. "Well he's already a good looking little guy."

"How soon after we get married do you want to have kids?"

She smiled up at him. "After we've been married for a few years, how soon do you want kids?"

"I was thinking the same thing."

"We have to decide when we're getting married."

"Yeah, too bad you don't want to go to the Dallas County Courthouse and get married."

"I know you don't want a big wedding…"

"If that's what you want, then that's what we'll do. I love you and it's my job to make you happy."

"You do make me happy." They went over the calendar with his parents and her mother. The wedding date was originally going to be October 7, but it was quickly discovered that was the day of Texas and Oklahoma play at the Cotton Bowl in Dallas, the worse day for a wedding especially in Dallas. Both families agreed that the date had to be changed. The wedding would be on Saturday, October 28, 2006 at their church the Prestonwood Baptist Church in Plano, Texas.

In early February 2006, he was in his apartment, watching a baseball game on TV and enjoying a pizza and a beer. His cell phone rang. He looked at the screen and saw it was his commanding officer, Colonel Mitchell.

He quickly answered the call. "This is Alpha 1."

"Alpha 1, we depart for Afghanistan in five hours."

"Yes sir." He was ready. He always had a bag and his gear packed. He called her cell phone.

She saw he was calling. "Hello hubby."

He smiled. "Hi baby, I just wanted to hear your voice and tell you I love you. I'll see you real soon."

She knew he had a mission. "Please be careful and come back to me."

"I'll always come back to you baby." He could hear her crying. "Please don't cry, baby."

The tears rolled down her cheeks. "I'm sorry. You have no idea how scared I am when you're gone. Like you said, it's not easy saying goodbye and then not knowing if you're coming back or not."

"I will come back. I promise. I love you, Kate."

"I love you too."

"Be strong for me, baby. I'll be thinking about you every second."

"Think of me only when you're safe. Promise me you'll come back."

"I promise you I will. I love you."

"I love you too. Bye, Jack." He hung up. He and his team immediately boarded a C-130 aircraft and deployed to Afghanistan.

She, Christi, and her mother began planning the wedding. Over the next few weeks, they decided on a venue for the reception, she picked her colors, and she and Christi went to register for wedding gifts. The guest list had been finalized and over two hundred invitations had gone out.

In Afghanistan, the Green Berets were going on multiple raids, sometimes a dozen raids in one night. By early 2006, the U.S. was preparing to cut troops in the south of Afghanistan and shift focus to the insurgency in Iraq. The Taliban used its safe havens in Pakistan to regroup. They expanded their operations to Kandahar.

Colonel Mitchell and his Green Berets were in Kandahar. Suicide bombings that were popular in Iraq were now being used in Afghanistan, after insurgents saw how effective it was. U.S. and coalition forces were losing ground to this large enemy force. This was the teams' fourth combat deployment to Afghanistan.

On September 3, 2006, NATO ground forces moved from the Penjawi Valley to the Arghandab River across from a cluster of villages. Their target was a white school house that Taliban had taken and used as a key fighting position. Operation Medusa was about to commence. The stakes were high. If Medusa failed, NATO failed. After air strikes continually pounded the enemy for two days, it was quiet. At dawn, the NATO troops were given the order of crossing the river. Many were apprehensive as to what waited for them on the other side. It was quiet until gunfire from all around them rang out. The NATO troops returned fire.

"Tango, one, Tango one, we are in a ****** of trouble here." a Canadian soldier said over his radio.

Nearby, Colonel Mitchell received word that the Canadians were in real trouble. Colonel Mitchell and his team knew the Canadians would come to their aid, so they didn't hesitate to go to their aid.

Flying in on Chinook helicopters, Colonel Mitchell stood to look at his three teams of seasoned warriors. "By God, if they want a fight, we'll give 'em one."

After several hours of intense combat, the Canadians were taking heavy casualties. The Green Berets devised a plan to take a tall hill overlooking the white school house. They swept the area for land mines. They placed a small element on top of the hill and established close air support.

In addition to his three Green Berets teams, Colonel Mitchell commanded sixty Afghan National Army soldiers. As he stood with his war hardened warriors in front of the sixty Afghans, he gave them a pep talk. "The enemy of your country has returned. This is going to be a very dangerous mission, but you have to decide right now, are you lions or are you sheep? If you're a lion, you'll willingly join me and my men and fight them until the death, but if you're a sheep, you're free to go without judgment."

Not one of the Afghan soldiers moved. They looked at Colonel Mitchell. The leader of the Afghans stood. "We want to be lions."

The Green Berets were glad to hear that. They charged into the firefight on a three sided ambush. "Red smoke marks enemy target, over!" Jack yelled over his radio to two Apache pilots who were inbound.

"I need cover fire!" Tom yelled. Gunfire surrounded them, RPGs were fired constantly.

"I need a vehicle prepared to move him safely, over." Jamal said as he struggled to save a wounded NATO soldier.

The Green Berets and the NATO troops were locked in a fierce firefight with no end in sight. "This Alpha 1, I'm coming from that ****** tree line!" he yelled over his radio to Colonel Mitchell. "Contact west, two hundred meters. Dismounts, small arms and RPGs!" he yelled.

"I'm amber on ammo, green on water. How copy, over?" a NATO soldier said over his radio.

Colonel Mitchell had to make a command decision. He and his men could stay and die, or retreat and live to fight another day. "Break contact!" he ordered. He hated to give the order. Hearing the order over their radios, Alpha, Bravo, and Charlie Teams retreated. Colonel Mitchell looked to Jack. "I know you never like to retreat, but this was the smart thing to do."

"You don't have to justify anything to me, Colonel. I'm getting married next month. Kate will kill me if I don't come back," he teased, as he and the Colonel laughed.

Coalition and U.S. troops retreated and regrouped. Colonel Mitchell's truck was shot to pieces. It would take days to repair. Several days later, Alpha, Bravo, and Charlie Teams and the Canadian troops go back on the offensive.

The pilots of the Apaches and Black Hawk helicopters were providing air support. "Request clearance to fire." the pilot said.

"We got a bird two hundred meters out." Jack yelled. "Oscar, level the building." he told the pilots.

"Ok, understand." The pilot fired his weapons. Jack called in more air strikes allowing his team to advance. The Canadians made their final push. Operation Medusa was a success, but the cost was high. Nineteen Canadian soldiers were killed in action.

After an eight month deployment, Alpha, Bravo, and Charlie Teams were going home. Jack and Tom were sitting at the base waiting to board the aircraft to head back to Fort Bragg, eating sunflower seeds, and drinking water. "Hey, so the wedding is next month, are you ready?"

He smiled. "Yeah, I'm ready."

"How's the wedding planning going?"

"From what I read in her emails, it seems, her mother, and my mother have planned the biggest wedding Dallas has ever seen. The guest list is up to two hundred. I don't even know two hundred people."

They laughed. "Well you have your parents, siblings, grandparents, aunts, uncles, and cousins. Then you have the distant relatives and friends of the family."

He shook his head. "I tried to talk her into going to Vegas to get married, but she didn't want to."

"She wants the big wedding?"

"Yeah, I see no point in it. Why spend so much money on one day?"

"You're so clueless. You're about to get married and you have yet to figure out how women think. Women are long term thinkers. Kate is planning a big wedding, full of detail. Remember, they all dream and plan this day from the time they're three years old. She wants that day to be perfect and beautiful so when you two have kids, she can tell them about it and show them pictures. At least that's the way I see it."

He walked away to call her from the satellite phone. She, her mother, and sister were looking at bridal gowns in an uptown Dallas boutique. She was upset that she still hadn't found the dress she wanted, but the bridesmaids gowns had already been decided on.

She looked at her cell phone and saw an overseas number. "Jack?"

He smiled hearing her adorable Texan accent. "Yeah, baby it's me."

"I'm so happy to finally hear from you."

"What are you doing?"

She smiled. "I'm looking at wedding gowns with Mom and Lauren."

He smiled. "I can't wait to see you in one. Have you found one yet?"

"No not yet."

He could hear in her voice that she was bummed. "Well, baby you'll look gorgeous in anything."

"Thank you babe, I love you."

"I love you too. Hey, I'm saving my leave for the wedding and honeymoon, so I'm hoping you will come out and see me, after I get through debriefing and have time off. Can you get a weekend off of work?"

She smiled excitedly. "Yeah, I have a lot of vacation time saved up. I can't wait to see you."

"I'm excited too. My friends' and their wives want to meet you. I'll call you when we get back to Bragg and let you know the dates. There will be an open ticket waiting for you at DFW, fly out here to Fayetteville. I'll be at the airport."

"Okay, I love you."

"I love you too. I'll see you when I get back."

"Okay, be safe. I'll see you soon, master sergeant."

He smiled. "I love you, baby."

"I love you too." She hurried home. The next day she put in a tentative request for a weekend of vacation time. Her boss approved it. She packed and waited for him to call.

Seventy-two hours later, Colonel Mitchell and his men returned to Fort Bragg to their awaiting families. He arrived at his apartment and called her. "Hey, I'm back."

She smiled. "Ok great, I'm all packed. I can't wait to see you!" They said goodbye after talking for over an hour.

She caught a taxi to Dallas/ Fort Worth International Airport. She boarded her flight to Fayetteville, North Carolina. He was waiting for her at the airport. She was walking out of the terminal and eagerly looking for him.

He smiled as she searched the crowd for him. He jogged toward her. "Kate!"

She smiled and ran to him. He picked her up and twirled her around as she wrapped her arms around his neck. They kissed in the middle of the crowded terminal. "I'm so happy to see you!"

"I've missed you so much, baby. You look gorgeous. How was your flight?" he carried her bag for her.

"It was good, I'm happy to finally be with you," she said, as they walked out to his truck.

They drove to his apartment. He got her bag out of his truck and they walked up to his door. "This is it."

He opened the door and turned on the lights. "Wow, it's definitely a bachelor pad." she said, as he laughed. He had a 50" plasma TV mounted on his wall, a bench press in the living room with a black leather sofa. He didn't have a table, just two barstools at the bar to the kitchen. He had a king sized bed and dresser.

"It's not much, I know. But I'm rarely here. Are you comfortable staying here? Don't worry, I planned to sleep here on the sofa, but if you want to stay at a hotel, I won't be offended."

She walked to him, wrapping her arms around his neck. "I'm with you, I couldn't be more comfortable."

He kissed her lips. "I'm so happy you're here."

"I'm so happy to be able to see you and kiss you. Oh, before I forget, I have your birthday present." she said.

He smiled. "I bought you something too." He walked back to his bedroom and brought out a small wrapped box.

She sat on his sofa and opened it. It was a beautiful small, gold heart-shaped locket. "Oh Jack, it's gorgeous. Thank you so much."

He fastened it around her neck. "You're welcome." She kissed his lips.

She smiled. "Happy Birthday, babe," she said, handing him a wrapped box.

He smiled. "You didn't have to get me anything."

"I wanted to." He opened the box. It was autographed football by legendary Dallas Cowboys quarterback, Troy Aikman. She also gave him an Oklahoma football jersey.

"Thank you. I love you," he said.

"You're welcome. Guess what I'm making you?" she asked.

"What?"

"Your momma's double fudge chocolate cake."

He smiled. "I can't wait. What do you two talk about when you have coffee?"

"It's classified. I'd love to tell you, but once I told you, I'd have to kill you."

He laughed. "I'm glad you and my Mom get along so well."

"Your parents are so sweet. She showed me all of your baby pictures."

"Oh no…" he said.

She jumped up into his arms, wrapped her legs around his waist. He smiled up at her. "I can't wait to have a little boy that looks just like you."

He kissed her lips. They held each other tightly and kissed passionately. He walked to the sofa and sat down. Later that night, he took her out to a romantic dinner in Fayetteville. She told him about the wedding. They would be married at their church.

"Where do you want to go on our honeymoon?" she asked.

He smiled. "That's what I'm looking forward to,"

"I am too. Where have you always wanted to go?"

"It's not where I want to go; it's where you've always wanted to go. It's my job to take you on the honeymoon of your dreams."

"I don't care where we go, as long as I'm with you," she said.

When they came back from the restaurant, he made up the sofa so she could sleep in his bedroom. She wondered as she unpacked whether sleeping in his apartment was such a good idea, but it was comforting to her that he was willing to sleep on the sofa. They cuddled on the sofa and watched a movie together in the living room. She looked down at her watch and saw it was near midnight.

"Do you mind if I take a shower?"

He smiled at her. "Baby, you don't have to ask me if you can take a shower. My house is your house."

She stood up and walked into the bathroom. She opened the cabinet and got out a towel. She liked that he was neat and clean. She was prepared for his house to be extremely dirty, like a man lived there, but was surprised that it was moderately clean. She turned on the shower. The steam from the hot water fogged the mirrors. Towel drying her hair, she got dressed in her pajama shorts and brushed her teeth. She opened the door and walked in the living room. He looked up at her.

"Hi." he said. He was extremely attracted to her. He stared at her hair that was wet and curling, her tanned legs and bare feet with crimson painted toenails.

"Hi, I just wanted to come kiss you goodnight," she said leaning down to kiss him.

He smiled. "Goodnight baby." He saw she was wearing one of his Oklahoma Sooners t-shirts.

"So I borrowed one of your t-shirts, I hope you don't mind,"

He smiled. "You look really good in crimson. You look better in my shirts than I do." She leaned down and kissed his lips. "I'm glad you're here." he said.

She sat in his lap. "I am too. Thank you for lending me your bed."

He touched her wet hair. "You're very welcome. I love you. You're so gorgeous."

She kissed his lips. He wrapped his arms around her. "I love you too." He placed his hand under her shirt and touched her back. They were kissing passionately.

She stood up and proceeded to walk down the hall to the bedroom then she paused. She walked back into the living room. He looked up at her.

"Thank you for respecting my beliefs and for being a gentleman and a Christian. I really appreciate you."

He smiled. "I'd do anything for you."

Kissing him goodnight, she said, "Goodnight. I love you."

"I love you too. Goodnight. I'll be out here if you need me." She walked back to his bedroom, closed to door and laid down. She could smell his cologne on the pillow cases and the sheets. She longed for him. She fantasized about being with him.

He was lying on the sofa watching a movie. He walked into the bathroom and smelled the scent of her body wash. His bathroom smelled of jasmine, honeysuckle and sea salt. Closing his eyes, he loved that scent. He wanted her. He walked back to the sofa.

"Lord, keep me strong. I want her so bad, but I want to be honorable. She deserves an honorable man. I'm relying on you for strength." He dozed off watching sports shows.

The next day, he showed her around Fort Bragg. The post fences were lined with 'Welcome Home' posters by the families. The post was getting ready for a Fourth of July concert and post wide barbecue. She met Janet. She was very impressed with Kate. She could see how much she and Jack loved each other.

A friend of his owned a helicopter business. He had arranged to have them taken up in a helicopter for an air tour. He looked over at her, with the headphones over her ears and her sunglasses on her face. "What do you think?"

She smiled at him. "It's incredible! There is one thing I want you to take me to do."

"What's that?"

"Sky diving, I've always wanted to do it."

He was shocked. "You really want to go sky diving?" She smiled and nodded her head at him.

"I'll see what I can arrange." he said, over the headphone.

They went to a local skydiving company in Fayetteville. Fourteen thousand feet up in the air, they were preparing to jump out. Tom, Jake, and Brad agreed to go with them. Tom checked his parachute, since he was very experienced. She was attached to him. She wore a black flight suit and goggles. He smiled at her. "Are you sure you want to do this? This is your last chance to back out."

She smiled. "I'm not scared."

"Are you ready?" he asked her. She was nervous. Standing against him, Tom hooked her up to his parachute.

As the doors opened, her curled hair fluttered as she looked down. Holding his hand tightly, she turned to look at him. "I just want you to know in case we die, I love you," she said.

He kissed her. "I love you too. We aren't going to die. Are you ready?" Before she could answer, he saw the green light and jumped. She screamed. Tom and the guys on board laughed. They were falling against an orange, blue, lavender sunset. She opened her eyes and was amazed at how beautiful it was up there. Finally reaching the ground, he quickly released her from the parachute. Her hair was a mess. She began to walk funny. She sat on the ground and kissed it. She had never been so happy to be back on the ground.

Seeing her kiss the ground, he laughed. "So, 'Miss I'm Not Scared of Anything', what did you think?"

She smiled. She took off the goggles and helmet. "It wasn't that bad, but I'm never doing that again for as long as I live."

He laughed. "I'm glad you tried it though."

Tom, Jake, and Brad drove up on the four wheelers. Jack and Kate walked toward them. "So, how did she do?" Jake asked, drinking a Pepsi. They laughed at her appearance. Her hair was still a mess.

"She did great," he said.

"Kate, did you like it?" Tom asked.

"I prefer being on the ground more," she admitted, as they laughed in response. After having supper at a romantic restaurant in Fayetteville, they were lying on the sofa, watching *Sports Center*. She could see he was really interested in the show. The sports announcers were talking about his beloved Oklahoma Sooners and their ranking in the NCAA polls.

She touched his cheek and gently dragged her fingernails down his jawline. "How many kids do you want?" she asked.

He smiled down at her. "I don't know, I guess two or three. How many do you want?"

She smiled. "I'd be happy with three, only because they would be your children."

She kissed each of his fingertips as he watched his show. He looked down into her eyes and smiled. She straddled him, wrapped her arms around his neck, as he ran his hands up the back of her shirt. They were kissing seductively and holding each other tight. He picked her up and carried her to his bedroom. He laid her on his bed, kissed her lips and neck. He pulled his shirt off over his head. She smiled up at his pectorals, rippling stomach and muscular arms. She noticed the scars from the shrapnel injuries before he met her. She gently touched the scars. Her touch thrilled him. He looked down at her. She kissed the scars. He kissed her lips. His dog tags dangled down with the black silencers on. He smiled as she pulled him down to kiss her. They were both aroused, wanting each other. As he kissed her neck, she softly moaned. He gave her a long seductive kiss.

"Please marry me now…" he said. She smiled. "…I can go find my chaplain and we can get married tonight in the chapel and still have a wedding with our family and friends."

"Our parents would be very hurt and upset if we eloped," she said.

"They'd never know. We could get married tonight in the chapel here on post and still have the big wedding in next month with everyone. No one would know, but at least we'd be husband and wife tonight…" Seeing the look on her face, he realized he was being selfish. "Okay…I'm being selfish, I'm sorry. I just wish we could get married now. It's getting harder and harder to stop myself from going too far."

She smiled up at him. "I can't wait to marry you, but I want to do things the right way. I don't want to elope as if we're two teenagers forbidden to be together. I love you, Jack, and I know what you're going through. I want to be with you just as badly as you want to be with me."

Lying beneath him on his bed, she had to fight her urge to have him. His passion and desire for her grew stronger. She looked so angelic yet at the same time seductive. He thought about the scripture where God would not let him be tempted beyond his ability. The doorbell rang. He groaned as he slipped his shirt back on and walked to the door. He answered the door.

He answered the door. Tom, Jake, and Brad were there. "Hey, do you and Kate want to come play some pool with us?" Tom asked.

"Sure, we'll meet y'all there." They met his friends' at the pool hall just outside the gates of post.

"Hey, there they are," Tom said. Paige and Jenny had come with Tom and Jake to meet her. The women were introduced and began talking.

"So, how is your sexual frustration?" Tom asked him privately.

He looked at him. "I just have one more month to get through, but it's getting harder and harder to stop myself. I wish she'd just let the chaplain marry us while she's here."

"I commend you, man. There aren't a lot of guys who would remain celibate for four years."

"Don't remind me how long it's been…" he said. Tom laughed. He watched her talk and laugh with Jenny and Paige. They wanted to see her engagement ring. He smiled watching her show them. "…but she's worth it."

An hour went by. They enjoyed playing pool, talking, and drinking a few beers. Other women had joined the pool game. Brad, Marcus, and Jamal were single. Luke came down to the pool hall and joined the game.

"So Kate, how'd you really enjoy skydiving?" Paige asked.

"I loved it, but I'm never doing it again." Paige and Jenny laughed.

"What else are you two going to do while you're here?" Jenny asked.

"We're going to go shooting at the range tomorrow," Jack said.

They were surprised. "Have you ever used a gun before?" Jamal asked.

"Of course I have. I own a Colt 1911," she replied.

"She's a really good shot too. She's shot my SCAR rifle."

"I loved it. I want one of my own."

They adored her Texan accent. They laughed. "You're a Texan for sure aren't you?" Luke asked.

"Yes, I am. Thank you," she said, with a smile.

"Where'd you go to college?" Tom asked her.

"I graduated from the University of Texas."

The guys were shocked. Tom looked at Jack and smiled. "You must really love her to marry a Texas grad."

"I do really love her," Jack said. "But I've gotten her to wear OU stuff."

They all talked, laughed and got to know each other. As Jake, Tom, Brad, Luke and Jack were playing pool, an attractive woman approached Jack. "Will you teach me how to play pool?"

"Sure," he said nicely, with the best intentions.

Tom and Jake could see that this woman was trouble. Jack, being a nice guy, didn't see anything wrong with it. "Okay, you have to lean over the table with the pool stick in between your thumb and index finger," he said keeping his distance.

The woman intentionally pretended to not know how to stand. "Am I standing right? Can you show me?" He stood behind her to show her. She rubbed her body up against his. Tom and Jake watched, shaking their heads.

"How much do you want to bet a fight is going to break out?" Jake asked Tom.

"I hope not. It'll be pretty ugly." Tom said, drinking his beer.

"But you got admit it would be awesome to see a chick fight."

Kate saw him standing behind this woman. She could see the woman flirting with him by touching his arm and smiling at him. The woman constantly stroked his arm. Kate was uncomfortable and noticeably upset. Paige and Jenny saw the look on her face.

"Excuse me. It's getting really stuffy in here. I need some fresh air," she said nicely. She walked outside to get some fresh air. She felt flushed. Seeing him and that woman instantly reminded her of how she walked in on Kyle and one of her bridesmaids having sex in her bed. She felt humiliated all over again.

Tom walked out to talk to her. She was sitting on the bench outside, looking at her engagement ring. "Are you okay?" he asked her.

She looked up at him and wiped tears away. "No, I'm not. Tell him I'm checking into a hotel near the airport and I'm going back to Dallas."

"I'll get him, so you two can talk."

"No I'm just going to go." She hailed a taxi. He ran back inside.

Jack saw him and looked around for Kate. "Hey, where's Kate?"

"She said she's checking into a hotel and going back to Dallas."

He dropped the pool stick and ran outside. He saw the taxi beginning to drive away. He ran to it and banged on the window. The driver stopped the car. "Friend of yours?" he asked.

She opened the door. "Could you wait for a minute?" she asked the driver, as she got out.

"What the hell is your problem?" he asked.

She slammed the door. She was angry with him. "What's <u>my</u> problem?"

He was angry with her. "Yeah, what's your problem?"

"I'll tell you what my problem is, Jack. I flew all the way out here to be with my fiancé and I see you teach some slut how to play pool, when it's obvious of what she's really after."

"What are you talking about?"

"I may be a lot of things, but stupid is not one of them. She was touching you and rubbing herself all up against you. How would you feel if I let another man hit on me, touch me, and rub against me in front of you? You wouldn't like it would you? You humiliated me!"

"So, let me see if I can wrap my head around this, you asked my best friend to tell me that you're leaving me, all because I taught a woman how to play pool and she was flirting with me?"

"Do you really want to get married?" she asked him.

He was stunned. "Kate, you're really overreacting and blowing this whole thing way out of proportion. Yes, I want to get married. I made a commitment, and I don't run from my commitments."

She started to cry. "I've already been made a complete fool of once. I won't let it happen again, Jack."

He was upset with her. "When are you going to realize I'm not Kyle? I'm not going to hurt you! He left you! Not me! He hurt you! Not me! I am so sick of you comparing me to him!" he shouted at her.

"What if I wouldn't have been here? Would you have slept with her? I know it's been so difficult for you to not have sex. So if you want to have unfulfilling sex, then go home with her!"

"I don't want her. I want you." He shook his head. "So, this is it? Our wedding is next month, and we're done over something this stupid?"

She took off her engagement ring and placed it in his hand. "I can't marry someone I can no longer trust. I'm sorry Jack."

He was stunned, looking down at the ring. "Yeah, well I won't marry someone who can't see the difference in me and her ex. I won't be punished for the mistakes he made."

She was crying. "I'm going to get my stuff and go stay at the hotel near the airport. I'm going back to Dallas."

He was upset. "Yeah, well maybe that's for the best. Have a nice life, Kate."

Tears rolled rapidly down her cheeks. "Goodbye Jack." She got back inside the taxi and they drove off. He kicked his truck several times in anger. He quickly got in and followed the taxi to his apartment. He wasn't going to lose her. The taxi brought her to his apartment building. She paid the driver, while still crying. She opened the door and saw him pull in and park.

He walked towards her. He saw she was a complete mess. "I could've gotten your key from your landlord." she said.

"Janet wouldn't have given it to you. I'll let you in," He unlocked the door. She walked to the bedroom and began to pack. He got a beer out of the refrigerator and sat on the sofa. He could hear her crying. It was killing him to hear her cry and to know that he was losing her. He walked back to his bedroom and watched her fold her clothes and zip up her bag. She looked up at him, with tears and black mascara smeared on her cheeks.

"Kate, you know I love you more than anything, and I would never intentionally hurt you like Kyle did. You know that you're the only woman on this planet that I want. I've respected you and your vow to God. I've never given you a reason not to trust me. But tonight, you proved to me that you don't see me, you still see him. I can't be with someone who lives in the past. You can't punish me for the mistakes he made. I want to be your future, but you won't let go of what he did to you…" He held her ring in his hand. "…I want you to have this. I gave it to you and if you don't want it, go sell it and buy something nice. I'm sure it'll buy more than just a new mattress and sheet set."

He laid the ring on the bed and left the room. She looked at the picture of her and him on the dresser as she held her engagement ring. She knew if she left him, it would be the biggest mistake of her life. She laid down on his bed and cried. He could still hear her crying. He stood up and walked into the bedroom.

Seeing her lying on the bed with her face buried in his pillow, he carefully climbed on the bed and held her. He kissed her head and her shoulder. "Talk to me, baby," he whispered in her ear.

She looked up to him. He smudged a tear away. "I know you could hurt me and that scares me."

"You should know by now I would never hurt you. I need you to trust me, like I trust you or this will never work."

"I'm just so scared of being hurt again."

"I'll never hurt you."

"The hardest thing to do is trust a good man after you've had a bad one."

"You need to let go of him and what he did to you. If we're going to move forward, I need you to see me for me, not what Kyle did and what I might do. Our marriage will never last if you're constantly comparing me to him."

She was crying. "I have let go of him and what he did to me, it's just when I saw you with that girl, and it just brought all of it back. It scared me."

"I'm sorry I engaged her. I should've walked away once she began flirting with me, but Kate, you should know by now that there isn't a woman alive who can compare to you. Nothing will ever change how I look at you or how I feel about you…" He touched her face and wiped a tear away with his thumb. "…Will you forgive me?"

"I'll forgive you, if you forgive me. I'm embarrassed at how badly I overreacted, do you still want to marry me?" she asked.

"I forgive you." He said. He kissed her lips. "Yes, I still want to marry you. I'm sorry I humiliated you. Please don't ever take this off again," he slipped her engagement ring back on.

"Never…" she said, as she kissed his lips and wrapped her arms around his neck. As they were kissing, thunder rumbled, and it began to rain. Lightening flashed across the dark sky and the rain pounded hard against the windows. He smiled at her dark curled hair draping her shoulder. She looked angelic, and at the same time seductive. He wanted her more than he ever had before, but couldn't bring himself to violate her vow.

He saw in her eyes that she wanted to give in and that made him feel dishonorable. "This may sound funny coming from me, since I'm a man, but I think we should stop. It's getting harder and harder to stop myself."

"I know what you mean. When you're kissing me, I just want to give myself to you." He tucked a strand of her hair behind her ear. She smiled at him. "I'm blessed to have a man like you, who respects my beliefs and who cares about what I want."

"I know most guys would be doing everything they could to get you, but I don't want to be like most guys. I love you and I do care about what you want. I know how much your promise means to you…" He looked at her purity ring behind her engagement ring. "…And knowing how much this vow means to you, I couldn't take advantage of it."

They ate supper and drank a few glasses of wine. It was late. They laid on the sofa holding each other and watching a movie. Soon they fell asleep together. They spent quality time together that week. They had almost given into their desires, but they were strong enough to resist each other. The long weekend had gone by too quickly and it was time for her to fly back to Dallas. He took her to the airport. She checked in and they walked to the security check point.

"I'm really glad you came to see me, baby. I'm going to miss you."

"I'm going to miss you too."

"I can't wait until next month."

"I can't wait either."

"We could've eloped this weekend, but no you didn't want to." he teased.

She hugged him tightly. "I love you."

He breathed her fragrance in and closed his eyes. He loved how her hair smelled, her perfume and the way her skin was soft and smooth. "I love you too."

The final boarding call for her flight was announced. She looked at the gate and saw the agent taking boarding passes. "Now I know how you feel when you leave me in Dallas." she said to him.

He hugged her and kissed her goodbye. "You better go before you miss your flight."

"If I miss my flight, I'll get to stay one more night with you."

He smiled, "I have to go back to work tomorrow."

She kissed him one final time. "I love you."

"I love you too. Have a safe flight, baby. Call me when you land."

She smiled and nodded. She turned and walked away. She felt a knot in her throat and tears immediately formed and ran down her cheeks. She hated to leave him. She didn't know when she'd see him again. Once she returned to Dallas, she, Carole, and Christi were at a bridal boutique looking for her wedding gown. The wedding colors were mocha and pale pink. The bridesmaids' gowns were beautiful mocha, tea length dresses.

She was in a dressing room as a bridal attendant laced up a dress. She wore an off the shoulder ivory gown. The bridal attendant pushed back the drapes and she stood on a platform in front of mirrors. Mom's eyes glistened, and a smile graced her face. She thought of Kate as a baby, a toddler, a preschooler, a child, a pre-teen, a teenager and a young woman—now a woman about to be a man's wife, not just any man—Jack, who proved that not only would he protect her, but he would also defend her.

Kate studying her mother's expression, asked, "Mom, what do you think?"

"Oh sweetie, if this is the gown you love, let's get it, you look absolutely beautiful."

She turned to look at herself in the mirror. Mom noticed that instead of a smile, there was a disappointed frown. "Don't you like this gown?" she asked.

"I like it, but…"

Mom smiled and tucked a strand of her hair behind her ear. "But you don't love it?"

"No, I don't. This isn't the gown I've always imagined I'd wear."

"It's okay we still have time." They went to another bridal boutique in Dallas. As she was browsing the gowns hanging, she stood frozen staring at the mannequin wearing a beautiful ivory gown. It was covered with beaded crystals and pearls on the bodice, with a chapel style train.

Christi noticed her expression. Walking over to her, the gown caught Christi's eye also. "Oh wow, that is gorgeous."

She smiled. "It is. I can't stop looking at it."

The bridal attendant smiled. "Would you like to try it on? We have it in your size." she said as she unlaced the bodice.

She smiled. "Yes, I would." The bridal attendant escorted them to the sitting area in front of three dressing rooms as three other attendants took the gown off the mannequin. Champagne was presented to them. Each had a glass, then a second.

She stepped out of the dressing room. Mom, Christi and Lauren were speechless. She smiled at herself in the gown. "Oh-my-gosh, I love it!"

"I think that's the winner of them all," Lauren said.

Mom stood and walked up to her, getting a closer look at the gown. "I love it. You look so beautiful."

"Jack is going to be blown away," Christi said.

"You think so?" she asked, admiring herself in the gown.

"Oh, definitely, you look amazing."

She looked at her mother's face. Mom smiled proudly, holding back the tears. "You look absolutely gorgeous, honey."

She smiled. "Thank you, Momma…" Mom gently touched the veil, as the bridal attendant fluffed the train of the gown. "…I love this dress, I can't wait for him to see me in this!" she said admiring herself in the dress. Mom bought the gown with the matching shoes and a cathedral style veil that would flow down the train of the gown.

She walked outside to call him. He answered. She smiled, hearing his deep voice. "Hey guess what, I found my dress!"

He could hear the excitement about the wedding in her voice. "Send me a picture of you in it."

"No, you can't see me in my dress until the wedding."

"Why?" he asked, with a laugh.

"It's bad luck! Plus, it's tradition."

"That makes no sense. Next you're going to tell me that I can't see you after the rehearsal."

"No, you can't."

"Explain to me why I can't see you."

"It's bad luck."

"I don't believe in luck. I have faith."

She laughed. "I have faith too, but you know our mothers are going to make sure we do everything traditionally."

"What are you doing after this?" he asked.

"Christi and I are going trousseau shopping."

"What's a trousseau?" he asked.

She smiled and wanted to laugh. "It's something for the wedding."

They talked for a few more minutes before she had to go back in. Afterwards, she and Christi went trousseau shopping.

A few weeks later, it was finally October. He was on a short leave in Dallas. Jonah was beginning to plan his bachelor party. They were playing video games in an unusually quiet house. Christi was out helping Kate and her mother complete the list of things needed to be done with the wedding coordinator. JD and Andrew were at Jonah's parents' house.

"I'm excited about this bachelor party. It's going to be awesome. There is going to be some amazing entertainment there."

"Yeah, I know you're going to be disappointed, Jonah, but I don't want any strippers."

Jonah looked at him seriously. "What the hell is the matter with you? That's like a guy code. The entertainment isn't for you. It's for the rest of us."

They laughed. "Then why is it called a bachelor party?" Jack asked.

"Because that's how we get away with it with our wives. If they knew that strippers were really hired for all the married men, then none of us would get to go. Think of it as a 'code name'."

Jack laughed.

"I can't believe you don't want a traditional bachelor party. I've been looking forward to this for a long time. Throwing you an awesome bachelor party is the job of the best man and not to mention my birthright, since I am your brother."

"I appreciate you wanting to do that, but I don't want Kate to feel uncomfortable and I don't want to do anything that might jeopardize my relationship with her."

Jonah shook his head. "How would she feel uncomfortable if she's not there? Here's you some free advice on marriage. What your wife doesn't know can't hurt you. She doesn't have to know about any of it."

They laughed. "Jonah, please respect this."

Jonah groaned. "Okay, then what boring idea did you have?"

"I was thinking we'd all just go to a Rangers' game. I looked at the schedule and on the night before the wedding, they'll play the Red Sox here."

Jonah rolled his eyes. "That certainly is boring. You're killing me, Jack." Jack laughed at him whining like a child. "Fine, I'll get us all tickets to a great game," Jonah said reluctantly.

"Thank you." They joked around while playing video games.

The leaves were turning to red, yellow and brown. The air was crisp and cool. Fallen leaves blanketed the sidewalks. Jonah surprised Jack and Kate with tickets to the OU/Texas game at the Cotton Bowl in Dallas. He also bought tickets for him, Christi, and JD. Jack, Jonah and JD wore their favorite Oklahoma t-shirts, as Kate and Christi wore their Texas t-shirts. They enjoyed the game together, but sadly Oklahoma lost to Texas, 28-10.

A few weeks later, it was a Friday night, the night before the wedding. The rehearsal dinner was being held at *Truluck's Steak and Seafood* on the corner of Maple and McKinney Avenue in Dallas, the same restaurant where he brought her on their first date. They drove to the restaurant together in his truck.

He looked over at her. "You look very beautiful tonight."

She smiled at him. "Thank you, you look very handsome."

"So one more day until we're married, are you sure you want to marry me? I have a lot of flaws and bad habits." he teased.

She smiled at him. "Yes, I'm definitely sure I want to marry you. I love you and all your flaws and bad habits. Are you sure you want to marry me? I'm told I'm quite the handful."

He laughed. "It's nothing I can't handle." They walked into the restaurant. Their parents and the bridal party were there. Dinner was served. The families and friends enjoyed telling funny stories about when they were younger. They had a great time laughing with family and friends. Many of Jack and Kate's good friends from high school and college flew in for the wedding and were invited to the rehearsal. Toasts were made. Kate had a few glasses of wine.

After dinner, he walked her to the limousine Christi had rented for the bachelorette party. Her bridesmaids and close friends were climbing inside. "Where are y'all going?" he asked.

"It's classified. It's on a need to know basis," Christi playfully snapped at him.

"I do need to know."

"We are aware what most men do at bachelor parties, so you shouldn't worry about what we're doing." Christi said.

She smiled up at him. "Where are you and the guys going?"

"We're going to a Rangers game."

"Oh how boring." Lauren teased.

"I wish I could go. Take me with you." she quietly begged.

"No, you're coming with us." Christi said. They were talking in front of the limo full of tipsy bridesmaids.

"So are we really doing this? We're really getting married? I'm going to be Mrs. Jack Hamilton?"

He smiled and touched her face. The cool Texas breeze swept through her hair. "Yes, we're really doing this. You're not getting cold feet are you?"

She smiled. "No, they've never been warmer, but I'm just afraid you'll back out at the last minute."

"No, I'd never back out. I'm marrying the most beautiful woman in Texas. You're going to be happy, appreciated, and loved every day. I love you."

She kissed his lips. They were holding each other and kissing with the headlights of the limousine shining on them.

Christi looked down at her watch. "She's going to make us late." She lowered the partition and climbed over the driver. "Excuse me." she said as she pressed firmly on the stirring wheel and honked.

Kate jumped. Jack tried not to laugh. "Kate! Come on!" she yelled.

"Christi that's not funny!" she said.

"Come on, we're going to be late! You'll see him tomorrow!"

She looked back up at Jack. "You better go before she gets out and pulls you in." he said.

"I love you."

"I love you too. I promise you that I'll be at the altar at six o'clock waiting on you."

They kissed goodbye a final time. She walked to the limousine and climbed in. He walked to Jonah's truck and climbed in. They were trying to beat traffic to the Arlington Ball Park, but no matter what time of day you travel in Dallas, there's always traffic.

They attended a playoff game between the Boston Red Sox and the Texas Rangers in Arlington, Texas. They were seated behind home plate at the Ranger's Ball Park in Arlington.

"So are you ready to be a married man?" Bill asked, taking a drink of his Coors Light beer.

Jack wore a red Rangers' T-shirt and a ball cap. He sat between Matt and Bill. "Of course, I am. It's about time. I was about to take her to Vegas." He took a drink of his Coors Light beer.

"Your mother would have killed you." Bill said as he and Jack laughed.

"And I would've killed you for robbing me the joy of walking my first born daughter down the aisle and giving her away." Matt said. The guys talked and enjoyed the game.

She was at her bachelorette party on Northwest Highway in Dallas. Christi and her bridesmaids took her a male strip club. She was beyond uncomfortable. Carole and Denise were purposely excluded from this little outing.

She snuck away to the bathroom to call him. He looked at his cell phone and saw she was calling. The fans were screaming. The baseball themed music began to play as the Rangers took the field. He walked away from his seat to the empty corridor to talk to her.

"Hi baby."

She could hear the fans cheering and the music in the background. "Hi, can you sneak away?" she asked.

He laughed. "I wish, but I came with Dad, Jonah, and your Dad. My truck is at the restaurant. What are you doing?"

She smiled and laughed out of embarrassment and uncomfortableness. "At a male strip club, I want to leave, but if Christi found that I've called you, she'd kill me."

He laughed. "So it was in deed a classified mission?"

"I wish I was with you at the game. Are they winning?"

He smiled. He loved that she loved sports. "Yeah, they're winning. It's a good game so far. So, you're getting lap dances from male strippers?"

She laughed. "Well, Christi, Lauren, and Meagan told them I'm a bachelorette, so yeah."

He laughed. "Did you enjoy it?"

She laughed. "No, it was the most embarrassing experience of my life."

"More embarrassing than leaving Jonah and Christi's without your stuff when we met?"

She was surprised he remembered that. "I wasn't embarrassed."

He laughed. "Yeah you were, especially when I came out thinking you had locked your keys inside."

"I really want to see you right now. Come kidnap me and we'll spend the night together." She joked.

"Your dad would have me shot if he caught me trying to sneak into your bedroom window."

"Well you're trained to survive, evade, resist and escape. I'm sure he'd uphold the Geneva Convention if you were captured."

He laughed. "I'm not taking that chance. We'll see each other tomorrow evening. We can make it."

"I really want to see you."

He smiled, thinking of her. He longed for her the way she longed for him. "I really want to see you right now too, baby, but you know if we saw each other, we'd go too far. Are you scared about tomorrow night?"

"Scared about the wedding?"

"No, are you scared about the wedding night?"

She smiled. "No, I'm not scared of you. I can't wait. I'm so excited."

He was relieved. "I am too."

"I love you, Jack."

"I love you too, baby. Hearts are going to break all over Texas tomorrow..."

"And why is that?" she asked.

"...Because I'm marrying the only gorgeous woman in Texas."

After the bachelorette party, they all went home. She was in her old bedroom of her parents' house. She was in her pajamas, sitting on her bed looking at pictures of her and Jack together.

Mom knocked on her door. "May I come in?"

"Sure, Momma..."

"Well, everything is set for tomorrow. It's going to be very beautiful and romantic. I was just wondering if you had any questions or concerns about the wedding."

"No, I think everything is great."

She sat on the bed with her. "Do you have any questions or concerns about the wedding night? I want you to know that it's perfectly natural for you to be scared or nervous."

She blushed. "I'm actually excited but a little nervous."

"What are you nervous about?"

"I'm just a little nervous that I won't be what he's been expecting all these years."

Mom smiled. "Oh honey, you shouldn't worry. Making love is a sacred, beautiful thing. It's the joining of two souls. He loves you so much. You shouldn't be nervous."

"I just want tomorrow night to be what I've imagined it to be."

"It will. Your father and I are very proud of you for your choice to refrain from having a physical relationship until you're a married woman." Her eyes began to get misty. "You've grown up into a beautiful woman and we love Jack." She and her mother spent an hour talking.

10

Saturday morning, October 28, 2006 arrived! The long awaited and highly anticipated wedding day was finally here. The sun was rising in the clear blue Texas sky and the birds were chirping. The morning news weather forecast predicted that it was going to be a beautiful autumn day. The trees in Dallas were golden, red, and brown. Colored leaves were everywhere. The air was cool and crisp, the perfect fall morning.

Her parents were downstairs having breakfast, sipping coffee, and reading the newspaper, trying to have a relaxing morning before a very busy and emotional evening. Kate and Lauren were still asleep in their rooms.

Matt said, "I can't believe she's getting married today. It seems like only yesterday we brought her home from the hospital, took her to kindergarten and then we watched her graduate from high school and college. Where did the time go?" he asked. He smiled and they both remembered her as a little girl.

Carole smiled, as she sipped her coffee. "I actually looked through her baby book last night. It's crazy how fast time flies."

Kate was just waking up. The sunlight peeped through her white silk curtains hanging in her old bedroom. She laid there thinking and listening to the birds' melody. She was thinking about the day. She walked into her bathroom and took a shower. She dressed in a pair of blue jeans and a light sweater. She put her hair up in a messy bun until her hair appointment.

She walked downstairs to eat breakfast and talk with her mom and dad. "Good morning." she said cheerfully. She kissed each of them on the cheek and hugged them.

"Good morning, sweet pea. How did you sleep?" Daddy asked her.

She poured herself a cup of coffee. "I slept great. It's been a long time since I slept here." She put sugar and milk in her coffee.

"You look beautiful. I can't believe you're getting married today," Mom said.

"I'm so excited." Mom handed her a plate with bacon, toast, and a cheese omelet.

After an amazing game that went into extra innings and the Rangers claiming victory over the Red Sox, Jack walked inside his parents house after finishing his usual ten mile run. Running helped clear his head. He wasn't nervous or scared to get married. He felt confident and ready, but he wondered was he being fair to Kate? After all their marriage would hardly be normal or typical. He would always be gone. He would always place his team and their mission ahead of his marriage. They would go months without seeing each other and weeks without talking. But he knew that Kate was aware of what they would have to sacrifice. He walked into the kitchen and a made of pot of coffee for everyone. He then walked upstairs to shave and shower. Before stepping in the shower, he sent her a text message.

'Today is the day! I love you so much. I'm going to make you happy, keep you safe, and give you everything you've ever wanted. I'll meet you at the altar at six…"

She smiled as she read it. She replied with: *"Today I'm not only marrying the man of my dreams, but my best friend. I promise I'll always be here waiting for you. No matter how long you're gone."*

Receiving her text message, he smiled and was once again reminded that she was the woman for him.

He walked downstairs to make himself a bowl of cereal and read the Dallas Morning Newspaper.

His mom and dad were just waking up also and were coming down to start breakfast. They walked into the kitchen in their pajamas and robes. "Good morning," Mom said as she kissed the top of his head.

"Mornin', I made y'all some coffee."

She smiled at him. "Oh, thank you." She poured herself and Dad a cup.

Dad sat down beside him and read the pages he had already finished. Mom looked at him reading the paper and eating his cereal. She sat down beside him. "So, are you nervous about today?" she asked him with a smile.

"No not really." He and Dad continued to eat and read the newspaper. Mom left them alone, knowing this was how men dealt with stress.

Kate, her mother, Denise, her bridesmaids, and close female relatives had brunch at a premiere Dallas restaurant. She gave each bridesmaid a gift.

It was now five o'clock. The ceremony was exactly an hour away from beginning. The bridal party descended on the Prestonwood Baptist Church in Plano. The ceremony would take place in the Faith Chapel. Carole, Christi, and the bridesmaids had their gowns on and they helped Kate get hers on. Carole laced the corset of the gown up for her. She reached for a long black box she had laid on the dresser.

"Mom, what's that?" she asked, as the bridesmaids gathered around her and her mother.

"My great-grandmother gave these to my grandmother on the day she married my grandfather. And my grandmother gave them to my mother when she married my father. When my mother gave these to me, on the day I married your father, I hoped I would have a daughter to give these on her wedding day. Now that day is here, and I'm giving these to you. Hopefully if you and Jack have a daughter one day, you can give her these on her wedding day," she said, choking back tears.

She had tears in her eyes, as she opened it and showed her a string of real pearls that has been in the family for many years. Her grandmother and great-grandmother stood beside Carole.

"Oh Mom your pearls…they're beautiful!"

Carole fastened it around her neck. "This will be your something old,"

She admired the necklace in the mirror. The pearls matched her gown perfectly. She hugged her mom. "I love it."

"You look so beautiful. My little girl is all grown up," she said, fighting back tears.

She smiled at her. "Thank you, Mom."

Jack and the groomsmen had their formal uniforms and suit on. Jonah, his best man was wearing a black tuxedo. They and were in a private room, while they visited and waited until the ceremony began. His groomsmen were Jonah, Tom, Brad, and Jake. JD, now nine, was a junior groomsman. He wore a black tuxedo. He would stand with Jack and Jonah. Both Bravo and Charlie Teams came as well as Colonel Mitchell and his wife, Miranda.

The pews quickly filled with guests as it drew closer to 6:00 p.m. The wedding planner made sure everything was in order at the chapel. Her team was taking care of the reception site.

Jack, his great-grandfather, his grandfather, Bill, Jonah, and the groomsmen waited for the ceremony to start. "You want a shot of whiskey?" Jonah asked Jack.

"Yeah, make it two. My nerves are getting to me."

Pouring him a shot of *Jack Daniel's Tennessee Whiskey*, he said, "You face death daily in combat with your men, but you're nervous about getting married?" Jonah asked.

He took the shot. "Most men would say getting married is facing death," Grandpa joked, as they all laughed. Jonah poured him another shot.

The photographer had already taken photographs of the guests, the flowers, and the pianist. He came into the room to take a picture of the waiting men's group. It was ten minutes until six o'clock. "Well, it is ten minutes until six, are you ready, Jack?" his grandfather asked. His grandfather was a retired Army chaplain and would be conducting the ceremony. A Korean War veteran, he would be in uniform also.

He stood and checked himself in the mirror to make sure his uniform, medals, and ribbons were in order. "I'm ready, grandpa."

He looked to his mom, who had just slipped into the room. "You look so handsome," she said with a proud smile.

"Thanks, Momma. Have you seen Kate?"

"I haven't seen her since the ladies brunch this afternoon. She looks radiant and very excited."

He smiled and took a deep breath. "Jonah, you have the ring right?" he asked for the third time.

"Yes, you asked me five minutes ago. Yes I have it."

"You have a tendency to lose things."

The guests were seated. They walked into the foyer of the chapel where people had been standing mingling before going in to be seated. While waiting, he saw Matt waiting outside the bridal suite.

He looked at him and smiled. He walked over to him. "Matt, thank you for giving me your blessing, I promise I'll make her happy and keep her safe."

He stuck out his hand. "I know that. Why do you think I gave you my blessing?" They shook hands. "Today we become family," he said.

The chaplain, Jack, Jonah, and the groomsmen stood beside the two beautiful Mahogany double doors. Matt was standing outside the bridal suite, as Christi, Lauren, and the bridesmaids were inside with Kate.

Bill offered his arm to Denise. Then he escorted her down the aisle. Many soldiers, friends of his, had flown into Dallas from all over, for the wedding. They were also in uniform. Matt and Bill had invited several of their friends who are either retired or still active duty. The wedding was a true military wedding.

Inside the chapel, hundreds of candles in candelabras flickered with fall colored rose wreaths. Candelabras were lining the outside walls. Beautiful red, orange and pale pink rose decorations were on the end of each pew. The lights were slightly dimmed. The candlelight provided plenty a soft glow. It was a very beautiful, intimate, and romantic. The guests were in complete amazement. There were huge beautiful arrangements of red, orange, and pale pink roses with English Ivy, red and orange berries, on each side of the altar. With thousands of fresh cut roses, the sanctuary smelled heavenly.

Jack, Jonah, and JD followed the chaplain into the chapel. Mom and his grandmothers smiled at him and Jonah.

"Bub, did I hear you like one of the flower girls?" Jack asked him.

JD turned around and gave Jonah a bad look. "Dad, you said you wouldn't say anything!" he scolded Jonah.

Jack and Jonah laughed quietly. "Are you going to ask her to dance with you at the reception?" Jack asked.

"No because she'll have to meet my parents, and I'm not ready for that yet."

Jack smiled. JD looked at his tuxedo and then back up to Jack in his uniform. "I want to have a uniform like yours one day. I want to be like you." They smiled for pictures. Denise was snapping many. She was so proud of him. He looked very handsome in uniform.

The bride was ready. She was wearing the pearl necklace from her mother for her 'something old'. Her wedding gown was her 'something new'. She had 'borrowed' pearl earrings from Christi and she was wearing a baby blue garter for 'something blue'.

Her hair was beautifully curled and left down. The veil made it more dramatic. Her makeup was flawless. The bridesmaids, along with Carole and Kate were still inside the bridal suite. She was sipping some water and chewing gum. She did that when she was nervous.

"You look gorgeous. I've never seen you look more excited and happy," Lauren said.

"Thank you. Have you seen Jack? I can't wait to see him in his uniform."

"Yeah, I saw him earlier. His hotness level is raised to a thirty," Lauren said. Kate laughed. She handed Kate her bouquet.

Her bouquet was a cascade style made of pale pink roses, English Ivy trailed down the middle of her dress. Her veil was cathedral style with lace edging and hand embroidered crystals. It trailed with the train of her gown. Her wedding gown was a strapless princess style. An ivory satin gown, it was made of bridal matte satin and was hand embroidered with silver threading adorned with seed pearls and crystals. The train was a chapel style train; a magnificent and gorgeous gown.

The bridesmaids' gowns were beautiful tea length, A-line, strapless, mocha dresses, with light pink colored Shawls. Their hair was curled and swept up. Their bouquets were of pink and orange roses, with an ivory ribbon tied together in a beautiful bow, with the strings of the bow trailing down.

All of the guests were seated. The chapel was nearly packed.

Matt knocked on the door to the brides' room and opened the door. "Wow, look at you." he said to Kate. She, Lauren, and Carole smiled. "No woman has ever looked so beautiful."

"Thank you, Daddy."

"Ladies, it's time," he said. The bridesmaids gathered their bouquets and shawls and exited into the empty hallway.

Carole was starting to get weepy. He stared at Kate and smiled. Though she was a grown woman, he could still see the six year old in pig tails, who wanted his attention every minute. "I can't believe you're getting married. I remember the day you were born. I remember holding you and knowing that one day I would have to give you away. I'm so proud of you, sweet pea."

She had tears in her eyes. "You're the greatest father a girl could ask for."

"I'm proud to have Jack as my son-in-law. He's a good man, and I see how happy he makes you."

She smiled. "Yes, he is a good man, and I love him very much. He's going to take care of me, and I'm going to take care of him. So you don't have to worry about us."

She stood. He walked toward her and hugged her. "Here's the penny for your shoe," he said handing her a 2006 shiny penny. She put it in her shoe. "Don't forget to spit out your gum. You don't want to give it to him when you kiss." he advised. She laughed and spit out her gum.

The groomsmen were waiting in the hallway outside the chapel for the bridesmaids. The bridesmaids and the two flower girls walked out and waited for Kate and Matt. The bridesmaids and groomsmen paired up as the bride and her father entered the hallway and stood behind Christi.

Carole pulled the blusher veil over her face, kissed her cheek, and then walked to the front of the bridal party to be escorted down the aisle by an usher. As the double doors to the chapel slowly opened, the violinists softly played Pachelbel's Canon in D major as the bridal party started down the aisle. The flower girls were admiring Kate in her wedding gown. She looked down at them and smiled. The flower girls' dresses were beautiful, long, ivory colored poufy gowns, with a big bow in the back. They each had a headband wreath of fall colored rose buds on their heads.

She looked up at her father, who was smiling at her. The bridesmaids and groomsmen slowly walked down the aisle and then each stood on opposite sides of the altar. Christi slowly walked down the aisle. She smiled at Jonah and at Jack. She could tell that Jack was really happy this day was finally here. The flower girls walked slowly down the aisle, taking turns tossing out the rose petals. The guests murmured at how adorable they were. Rebecca, the wedding planner, carefully fluffed the train of Kate's gown to drag beautifully. As the flower girls reached the altar, Millie, the pianist, played the Bridal March. The chaplain lifted his hands, signaling everyone to rise in honor of the bride and her father.

Matt stood tall in complete military dress as he walked her down the aisle. The guests were captivated by how beautiful she was. Jack was amazed. He and Kate smiled at each other and kept eye contact. When they reached the altar, the music stopped. The chaplain opened his Bible, and the guests were seated.

"Dearly beloved, we are gathered here today in the presence of God, family and friends for the purpose of uniting Jack David Hamilton and Katherine Elizabeth Johnson together as husband and wife. Who gives this woman to be married to this man?" the chaplain asked.

He looked at Matt, whose eyes were filling with tears, as he held her hand tightly. This was the moment he had been dreading ever since Jack asked for her hand in marriage, nearly a year before. Actually, he had been dreading this moment for the past twenty-six years. Though, he knew Jack was the perfect man for her, he wasn't ready to let her go. He looked down at Kate. She smiled up at him. He saw her beautiful smile and wiped a tear out of his eye. "Her mother and I do," he said proudly.

He smiled at her and then he smiled at Jack. He gently kissed the top of her hand and turned to face Jack. "She's all yours now. Take care of her. She's one of a kind," he said quietly to Jack.

"I will." They firmly shook hands. Then he gave Kate's hand to Jack. He sat down beside her mother, who quickly grabbed his hand. Jack, Kate, Christi, and Jonah carefully walked up the steps to reach the chaplain. Jack and Kate stood beside each other, hand in hand, as the chaplain smiled at them. He continued with the ceremony.

"Jack and Katherine, you have come here today to create a covenant of marriage through our Lord. As you stand here before each other, God and all these witnesses, you are promising Him as well as each other, you will be committed to these vows every day, on good days and on bad days for the rest of your lives until death. Marriage is a wonderful and idyllic experience and when a husband and wife can work together with the Holy Spirit, it is one of the most beautiful experiences any human being can have. A man shall leave his father and mother and hold fast to his wife, and they shall become one flesh. A marriage without our Lord is doomed to fail, but if you keep the Lord in your marriage, nothing can break what He has joined together, not even the Devil."

They faced each other, holding hands. "Jack repeat after me. I. Jack David Hamilton…" the chaplain read the vow.

They smiled at one another, looking into each other's eyes. Her eyes were glistening. "I, Jack David Hamilton, choose you Katherine Elizabeth Johnson to be my wedded wife…" he repeated after the chaplain.

"…I promise to love, comfort, and be true to you all the days of my life." She smiled up at him as he said the vow to her.

"Katherine, repeat after me. I. Katherine Elizabeth Johnson…" the chaplain read the vow.

She held his hand tightly and smiled up at him. "I. Katherine Elizabeth Johnson, choose you Jack David Hamilton to be my husband…"

"I promise to love, comfort, and be true to you all the days of my life…" the chaplain said.

They looked into each other's eyes, and she said, "I promise to love, comfort, and be true to you all the days of my life."

"The rings please…" the chaplain asked. Jonah handed him the ring.

He held her hand and smiled at her. "I give you this ring, Katherine, as a symbol of my solemn vow to you and to the Lord. And with this ring, I thee wed." He slipped the ring on her finger.

Christi gave her the ring. The chaplain asked her to repeat the pledge. She held his hand and looked up at him. "I give you this ring, Jack, as a symbol of my solemn vow to you and to the Lord, and with this ring, I thee wed." She slipped the ring on his finger. Engraved inside his ring were the words, *I'm Waiting for You.*

The chaplain smiled at both of them. "Jack and Katherine, now that you both have confirmed this covenant to each other and to the Lord, I bless you in His name. But I also have a forewarning for you both. Even as you stand before Him now, there are no challenges, no controversies, or conflicts testing your promise to each other today. You may feel confident that issues will never come between you. I can assure you that challenges, controversies, and conflicts will come. It is in that moment for you to remember this commitment that you've made to each other and to the Lord today. You will need courage and patience, kindness, love, and most importantly, you will need Faith in Him, always. From this moment on, you are now one in Christ. Though you'll be separated by great distances and great lengths of time, it will be easy to be led astray, but remember these vows and always trust in the Lord. Let Him guide you through, for He is the way, the truth, and the life. Let us pray…" Everyone bowed their heads. "…Heavenly father, we come to you today to ask that you please bless this man and this woman. Please bless the joining of two families, bless the children born into this beautiful union. Please keep this man, this woman, and their marriage strong as they will be separated by a great distances. Please keep this man strong and safe when he goes off to war. Amen." Jack and Kate looked up, into each other's eyes and smiled. "Now, by the virtue of the power vested in me and by your mutual faith in the Lord our God, I now pronounce you husband and wife. Son, you may kiss your bride," he said, closing his Bible.

They looked at each other. He slowly raised her veil. He touched her face and gently kissed her lips for several seconds. They turned to face their families and friends. The chaplain smiled at them. "I am proud to present to you Master Sergeant and Mrs. Jack Hamilton."

Their guests quickly stood and applauded. The pianist played the recessional music. Christi gave Kate her bouquet as they walked down the aisle to stand in the receiving line, to greet their guests. She met his friends from high school and the Army. She met Colonel Mitchell and his wife. He met many of her friends from college and extended family members. The wedding party and most of their guests had gone outside to wait. They held hands and walked to the doors.

The chapel doors opened. Birdseed and orange, red, and pale pink rose petals were tossed at them. Their family and friends laughed and cheered, as they rushed to the limousine. Arriving at *The Adolphus Hotel* in downtown Dallas, they stepped out of the limousine and walked into the hotel, to the ballroom to their reception. As they were walking through the lobby, customers along with the staff applauded them.

As they entered the ballroom, their guests greeted them with applause. The musicians began playing the music. Their guests enjoyed the appetizers and the cocktails. They found their name cards on elegant and calligraphic seating cards on round tables. The ballroom looked magnificent and very romantic. There were hundreds of cinnamon and pumpkin scented candles flickering, with hundreds of fresh, fall colored flowers, and beautiful elegant tables and place settings. The tables were covered with silk ivory linens and mocha colored napkins with gold napkin holders. Beautiful ivory and gold china rested on brown thatch plate chargers. There were huge bouquets of fresh red, orange, and pale pink roses with ivy and four ivory colored, lit candlesticks were set in the middle of the centerpieces. The ballroom looked absolutely gorgeous. It was very intimate and romantic.

Carole and Denise visited with all the guests and friends from old and new. Bill and Matt talked and laughed with friends of theirs that were retired or active duty. They drank champagne and watched as Jack and Kate hugged their relatives and friends. Jonah and Christi and some guests danced. JD chased one of the flower girls around the dance floor. Meagan and Lauren flirted with some single men who were friends of Jack's.

Dinner was served. Jack, Kate, Christi, Jonah, and the rest of the wedding party sat at the long, elegantly decorated head table. He turned to Jonah sitting next to him. "Promise me that you won't embarrass me. Better yet give me your speech, I want to proofread it."

Jonah gave him a sarcastic smile. "Now I take offense to that. Have I ever embarrassed you?"

He looked at him. "Are you kidding me? Uh yeah, you've embarrassed me a lot."

"Name one time I've embarrassed you."

He looked at him in surprise. "Really, you want to play this game?"

"Yeah, tell me one time when I've embarrassed you."

"The day I met Kate, you told her that I thought she was gorgeous and that I should ask her out in front of her, case and point."

"And had I not done that, we might not be here." Jack was speechless. "See, I have a method to my madness."

Jack shook his head. "Give me your speech."

"I didn't write it down. I'm just going to wing it."

He rolled his eyes. "Oh no, this is going to be embarrassing. Keep in mind, my CO and many of my friends, including my team are here. If you embarrass me, I'll put you in a head lock later."

"Will you just trust me?"

Every guest was served their meal of choice. Champagne and wine glasses were filled. Jonah stood and clanked his glass to get everyone's attention. The room was silent.

"Remember what I said," Jack warned.

Jonah looked at everyone. "He's threatening me." Everyone laughed. "I've always been proud of my baby brother. He's definitely a handful and it seems we were always side by side getting into trouble. He's my partner in crime, my sidekick. He had the opportunity to play college football, but turned it down to serve his country instead. I remember the day he came home and told our parents, Meagan, and I that he had enlisted in the Army. I've never seen him so sure of something, so dedicated, and so determined to succeed as he was when he left for the Army. He loves the Army and serving his country. He's a warrior. The many medals and ribbons on his chest prove he is a brave, dedicated, faithful soldier. He goes where he's needed and doesn't complain about missing birthdays, funerals, weddings, anniversaries, or other important family events. He accepts that it's part of the job. I'm proud of his service. I'm thankful for it…"

He looked down at Jack. "…I'm also proud of him for choosing a good woman to share his life with. She is a very sweet, beautiful, and caring woman. And most of all, she loves him and can put up with him and the demands of his life. He had found the woman that God wanted him to be with. When he leaves, he asks me to watch over her for him. I take that responsibility very seriously. I was honored when he asked me to be his best man. He's not just my brother, he's my best friend. My wife and I helped him plan the proposal, many of you were actually there at our Christmas party when he dressed up as Santa, and surprised her by proposing…"

Many guests laughed, as Jack turned red from embarrassment. "…Jack, you knew I was going to embarrass you a little bit…" he said.

Jack looked up at him, shaking his head and laughing. "…But I'm happy he finally found a woman who loves him for who he is, who will be faithful to him, who can handle and respect his career, and who most importantly, will always be waiting for him when he gets home from war. Jack, I think you've come as close to perfection as you can get. Kate, welcome to the family, and now if you get the urge to choke me like my wife, Jack, and Meagan do, you'll fit in just fine…" Everyone laughed, including Jack and Kate. "…So, to Jack and Kate, I love you both and may God bless this union." he said, hoisting his glass in the air to toast.

Everyone lifted their champagne glasses and toasted Jack and Kate and applauded Jonah's speech. He sat down beside Jack. He and Jack looked at each other. Jack laughed and stuck out his hand to him. "Good speech, man." he said as they shook hands and continued to eat.

The reception songs were a wide variety. Jack and Kate were on the dance floor, dancing, and holding each other close. "You look absolutely gorgeous tonight."

She smiled. "I've never seen you in uniform before, and you look very handsome." She looked at his left hand and smiled at his wedding ring. "Do you like your ring?"

He looked down at it. "Yeah, I do."

"On the inside of your wedding ring, I had something engraved for you, something I want you to know if you ever doubt me."

He touched her face. "Oh yeah, what's that?"

She smiled up at him, with her arms around his neck. "I'm waiting for you."

"I love you."

"I love you too." They kissed and continued to dance on the dance floor. They cut the cake, danced, and talked with their guests. It was time for her to throw the bouquet. A sea of single women gathered onto the dance floor as she stood on stage. She had taken her veil off shortly before the reception. She had a French bustle on her gown so her train wouldn't get in her way.

Jack smiled as he watched her tease the women by pretending to throw it. She finally tossed the bouquet and Lauren caught it. Everyone cheered for Lauren. Now it was time for Jack to take the garter off. She sat in a chair in the middle of the dance floor with their guests around them. As he slipped the garter off many friends of his whistled, her face was red with embarrassment. He kissed her as the guests cheered. Many single men huddled onto the dance floor to catch the garter. He flipped it backwards and one of his friends from Fort Bragg caught it. He and Lauren were introduced and forced to take a picture together. The wedding was beautiful. The reception was stunning, romantic and fun.

It was near ten o'clock when Jack and Kate said goodbye to all of their guests. Their guests again threw rose petals, as they jogged to the elevator to go up to their honeymoon suite for the night before beginning their honeymoon the next day. They would fly to Oahu, Hawaii. Stepping out of the elevator, he picked her up into his arms and carried her down the hall to their suite. Finding their room, he opened the door with the key and carried her across the threshold of the suite. Dozens of candles flickered. Rose petals were scattered all over the bed and floor. A bottle of Dom Parignon champagne chilled in a bucket of ice.

She was amazed. "Wow, this is incredible," she said. They walked out on the balcony of the room. They could see the lights of the surrounding suburbs of Dallas metroplex. The sky was dark as velvet. The stars were bright. The fall breeze was cool and crisp.

He stood behind her and wrapped his arms around her waist and kissed her neck and shoulders. She smiled. Her curled hair fluttered in the cool Texas breeze. He could smell jasmine and vanilla in her hair. Turning to face him, she smiled. He touched her face. The moonlight shone on her skin and hair. "Those eyes put these Texas stars to shame," he said.

"Are you always this quixotic with women?"

He smiled down at her. "Only with you…" She wrapped her arms around his neck and kissed his lips. She pulled him by the hand back into their room, closed the door and the curtains. He pulled her against him and kissed her lips.

He walked over to the light switch and dimmed the lights. He changed out of his uniform as she changed out of her gown in the bathroom. Standing in the mirror wearing the trousseau, she looked at herself. She wasn't nervous or scared, she was excited. She had waited and fantasized about this moment for the last four years. Sitting at the foot of the king sized bed, he waited for her. She opened the bathroom door and stepped out. He was stunned. "Wow, you look…amazing," he said.

She smiled down at him. He stood and admired the trousseau. She was extremely attracted to him shirtless. He had rippling abs, strong, solid pectorals and big muscular arms. He held her in his arms. "Are you nervous?" he asked.

She smiled up into his eyes. "No," she said softly.

He kissed her lips. They stood kissing in the middle of the suite. She wrapped her arms around his neck. He picked her up and laid her gently on the bed. He gently kissed her neck. He smiled down at her. Seeing his dog tags dangling, she gently grasped the chain and pulled him down to kiss her.

"I'll be as gentle as I can be."

"Tonight, soldier you're mine." she softly said. He smiled and kissed her. He made slow love to her. This was the moment they both had been wanted, fought against, and fantasized about for the longest time. It was everything they wanted, dreamt it would be, plus more.

The next day, they arrived in beautiful Hawaii and were taken to their hotel. They received the traditional Hawaiian leis around their necks. She wore a jean skirt, black flip flops and a white blouse, with her sunglasses and pink and red lei. He wore a pair of shorts, tan flip flops, and a brown T-shirt, a white OU ball cap, sunglasses, and blue lei around his neck.

After checking in and receiving their room keys, they hurried to the elevators. They were alone in the elevator, holding each other tightly and kissing, as the elevator slowly rose to the tenth floor.

Their room was 1445. He swiped the key card and opened the door. They were both stunned. A champagne bottle was cooling in an ice bucket. "Oh, this is so beautiful!" she said. He put their bags in the closet. They walked out on the balcony to look at the ocean view. "Okay, this is paradise, and we're never leaving." she joked.

He looked at her, smiled and wrapped his arms around her waist. They watched the waves' crash onto the beach. The sea gulls swooped through the air. He turned her around to face him. They kissed on the balcony as waves' crashed onto the beach. The ocean breeze swept through her hair.

He picked her up and carried her to the bedroom. He closed the door and the curtains. He pulled her against him and kissed her lips. They made sweet married love.

The next afternoon they ventured out on the island of Oahu. They sunbathed on the beach and played in the water. She knew he had a fascination with World War II, and knew he would want to go see Pearl Harbor and the memorials for the battleships USS Oklahoma and Arizona.

As they were touring the USS Oklahoma museum, she saw the look on his face. He looked like a kid in a candy store. He loved military history, especially Pearl Harbor and the battles of the Pacific.

After touring the memorial, they went hiking up in the hills of the island. She had her bikini on underneath her tank top and shorts. They discovered a secluded waterfall flowing into a sapphire blue lagoon, surrounded by island plants and beautiful flowers.

"Wow, this is absolutely breathtaking," she said.

He saw that behind the waterfall was a cave. "Look, there's a cave…" She looked at him and smiled. "Let's go check it out." They got in the water and swam to the waterfall. The water was warm.

They looked to each other. She stared up at him and kissed him as the water from the falls cascaded down on them. He wrapped his arms around her and picked her up.

"Where you lead me, I will go. I'll always stand strong beside you, no matter what. I'll always be here waiting for you." she said.

He smiled. He touched her face and her wet hair. "You're the breath in my body, the blood that's in my veins. You're my strength when I feel weak. I know I can always trust you, count on you for support, and I know you'll always be faithful to me."

She looked at the waterfall and then back into his eyes. "Have you ever made love under a waterfall?" she asked, giving him a flirty smile.

He smiled. "No, but I like to try new things." They made love underneath the waterfall surrounded by beautiful island flowers.

After an incredible week of honeymooning in paradise, they returned to Dallas. They moved to Fort Bragg. It was hard for her to say goodbye to her friends and family. Her life now revolved around his life, where he was stationed. She knew what she was giving up, the sacrifices she was making, her past and starting a new chapter. Now, they would travel this journey, military life, together. It would be difficult—they accepted they would be apart more than together. She would worry about him and praying he would come back to her. She knew the reward was greater than the sacrifices. She finally got him.

Shortly after moving to Fort Bragg, they moved into their house on post. It was a modest three bedroom house with spacious rooms, a fireplace in the living room, and a large kitchen. They had fun moving in, throwing the Styrofoam chips at each other. They enjoyed the typical married things like shopping for furniture, cooking together, having date nights. They were comfortable, happy, and madly in love.

After setting up house, she got a job at the post hospital in labor and delivery. She missed Lauren, Christi, Angie, Tess, and Marci, but quickly made new friends. Jenny, Jake's wife and Paige, Tom's wife, accepted her and they got along great.

I T WAS A Monday morning in mid-November. Thanksgiving was right around the corner. Jack and his team sat in the briefing room with Bravo and Charlie Teams, as Colonel Mitchell walked in. They saluted him.

"Alpha, Bravo, and Charlie Teams are needed in the Korengal Valley. You'll fly out in ten hours."

"What's the mission sir?" Jack asked.

"The Taliban won't give up in Korengal Valley. Since the conflict in Iraq began, we have very little troops in Afghanistan to stop the insurgency. This will be a long deployment, gents."

The team was dismissed after the briefing. They were set to depart in ten hours. He already had vital paperwork drawn up. He went to the Judge Advocate General Corps (JAG) office and had his last will and testament written and named her as his sole beneficiary. He had named her as his Special Power of Attorney [17] (SPOA). That document gave her the ability to ship, remove, and receive household goods, personal baggage, and other personal property, to accept delivery of household goods, to title his name with any state or government agency, to obtain Department of Defense (DOD) identifications cards, to pay bills in his name, and to access his W2 and Leave and Earning Statements (LES) from Defense Finance and Accounting Services (DFAS).

He had named her as his sole beneficiary on his Service-members' Group Life Insurance (SGLI) and as his next of kin, should anything happen to him shortly after their honeymoon. He also had a Military Advance Medical Directive written up, designating her as healthcare proxy, giving her the power to make health care decisions for him when he was no longer capable of making them for himself.

When he arrived home, he put the thick stack of paperwork on the dining room table. He looked around their house at their furniture, the wedding pictures on the wall as well as others from when they were dating. He walked to their bedroom and saw her robe lying on the chair. He picked it up and could smell her perfume. He began packing the things he needed for the mission.

As he waited for her to get home from work, he cleaned his rifle. He knew she was going to be upset. He had to compose himself to remain calm. Now he understood what his married team members felt when saying goodbye. They wanted to stay with their families and at the same time they knew they were needed in the defense of their country.

She walked through the door and saw him cleaning his weapons at the kitchen table. "Hey honey."

"Hi, how was work?"

"Good. I missed you today." They kissed. He picked her up and carried her to the bedroom. She lied beneath him.

He looked down in her eyes. "I got my orders today."

---

[17]   The special power of attorney (SPOA) was the single most important document to any military spouse. Without that, it was nearly impossible to do anything using the service members' name.

She had a knot in her stomach and could feel her heart pounding. She knew she had to show him she could be strong, even though she was terrified inside. Swallowing her fear and braving it with a smile, and asked, "How much time do we have before you leave?"

He looked at his watch, "We have three hours,"

She smiled up at him, "Then let's make them last," They kissed seductively and held each other tight. They made love, cherishing every moment. They were both aware that this could be the last time they make love because of the dangers of his job. Neither one would allow themselves to think those thoughts.

Two hours later, they were lying in bed holding each other while wrapped up in the bed sheets. Savoring every moment they had together, he lied on his stomach as she gently dragged her fingernails up and down his back.

"I'm going to miss doing this for you," she said.

"I'm going to miss it too. It's an amazing stress reliever,"

She kissed his back and shoulders. He turned over and they kissed passionately. "I'm going to miss you so much." she said as he kissed her neck.

Straddling him, he kissed her chest. "I'm going to miss you too, baby."

She looked down into his eyes, "Promise me you'll come back. I need you to come back to me."

Noticing her eyes were moistened, he touched her face and ran his fingers through her hair. "I promise you I'll come back." They kissed. She had to fight to keep her tears at bay. Looking at the clock on the night stand, he looked back down into her eyes. "I need to take a shower and get ready." He stood and headed toward the bathroom.

"Want some company?"

He looked back at her, shirtless and with that crooked smile she fell in love with when they first met. "Come on." She followed him into the bathroom and they took a hot steamy shower together. The hot water cascaded down on them while they made love one last time. The mirrors were fogged from the steam.

Afterwards, they both dressed. He picked up the thick stack of paperwork. He handed them to her. "I need you to keep these in a safe place."

Reading '**LAST WILL AND TESTAMENT OF JACK DAVID HAMILTON**' she suddenly felt sick to her stomach. Tears immediately formed in her eyes. She was shaking. Her heart felt as if it had been dropped from the top of the Empire State building, but she forced herself to appear strong and composed. Most American women didn't have to deal with reading over their husbands' will and having a special power of attorney or healthcare proxy written, but American military wives had to. This was part of the job description they all hated, but each one knew it's better to be prepared than not at all.

He saw the look on her face. He could see the fear and the worry in her eyes. He wrapped his arms around her and looked down in her eyes. "I don't want you to worry about me. I'm going to be fine, just like I always am. You're strong. I know you'll be okay." His hands were on her face, as she looked up in his eyes. He saw the tears forming.

She knew she had to be strong. He needed her to be strong. "I'll be strong for you, just as I have been since I met you. I don't want you to worry about me. You just focus on coming home," she said bravely.

"I'll be thinking about you every minute," he said.

Tears drizzled down her cheeks. "Think of me when you're safe." He smoothed her tears away with his thumb. "I can't have anything happen to you,"

"Nothing is going to happen to me. I promise. You're always in my heart and you're always on my mind."

"I'm going to miss you so much. This house will feel so empty without you here," she said with as strong of voice as she could.

"I know baby, I'm going to miss you too, but I'll be home as soon as I can." He pulled out his wallet and held the picture she had given him, when they first started dating. "I'm carrying you with me always. You bring me home."

He walked out to the garage to get the gear he needed. She helped him get the last few things he needed. With bags and gear in hand, he opened the front door but paused before leaving. He looked back at her, wearing his favorite Oklahoma Sooners football t-shirt and a pair of short shorts, he dropped his bags and kissed her once again. She wrapped her arms around him tightly.

Smelling the scent of her perfume on her neck, he closed his eyes and said, "I love you. I will come back." She kissed his lips, as tears ran down her face. They stood kissing passionately in the doorway.

"I wrote this for you." she said handing him an envelope. He smiled down at it. "Read it when you're missing me."

He kissed her goodbye. "Bye gorgeous. I love you." he said as he folded the envelope and put it in his pocket.

"I love you too. Be safe. I'll be here waiting for you." she replied, watching him walk out the door.

Alpha, Bravo, and Charlie Teams headed to the airfield to be taken by a C-130 to the nearest U.S./NATO base in Afghanistan closest to the Korengal Valley. They boarded the plane. The pilots steered it down the runway. He looked at his team. Most were sleeping or reading a book. He remembered the letter she gave him was in his pocket. He pulled it out and opened it. He read:

"Dear Jack,

If you're reading this, you're likely headed for danger somewhere and I'm here missing you terribly. I'm counting down the days until you're home again. I can't wait to throw my arms around your neck and tell you how much I love you and how much I've missed you. Saying goodbye to you is absolute torture. I'm terrified that kissing you goodbye will be the last time I kiss you. I'm terrified telling you I love you will be the last time you hear it. When I'm in your arms, I feel your heartbeat against me, and I smell your cologne. I have to make myself let you go. I'm terrified I'll never get to tell you goodbye. I love you so much. You showed me what true love is like and how a real man loves a woman. You proved to me that you're nothing like all the other men I had dated in the past. I love that I can tell you anything and you'll be honest and you'll always find humor in it. I love that I can depend on you. I love that you value my opinion on things, even the unimportant things like what you should wear or what you should order. There are so many things that you do that I love. I love how when you get out of the shower, the bathroom smells like menthol and mint. I love that your clothes hanging in the closet smell like you. I love waking up to your dog tags clanging together in the mornings when you're getting ready. I love how when you get up, you always make my coffee for me and pour it in my favorite thermos or cup. I love how if there are clothes in the dryer, you'll fold them and put them away. I love that you do housework without me having to ask you. I feel like we're a team, and I know I can always count on you for anything.

When I first talked to you on the phone when Jonah was trying to set us up, your voice made my body have a reaction. You excited me. I love your voice. It's so commanding, sexy, and strong. I will never forget the reaction my body had when I saw you in person the first time, I felt warm, and I felt my heart stop. The way you looked at me, you made me feel like I was the only woman in the world you wanted. I knew the first time I kissed you that I wanted to be your wife. You're everything I've ever wanted in a man. I love you for so many reasons. You're: charming, exceedingly handsome, smart, kind, gentle, strong and generous, humble, the best lover, my protector, and my best friend, but my favorite feature is that you have God in your heart. I love your eyes. I get lost in them. I love your smile. Your smile nearly makes me come unglued. I'm very attracted to you. I love the way you look, the way you touch me. I'd give you anything to feel you touch my face right now. I miss you so much, Jack. God blessed me by sending you into my life. I believe he designed you just for me. He knew I was running from love after what I had went through previously, so he guided me to run to you. When I found you, I found Love.

Before our wedding night, I had to fight the hunger to have you each time you touched me, kissed me and held me. Every inch of my body wanted you. I never knew how powerful seduction, desire, and lust were until I kissed you. I wanted to feel you in my soul. When we finally made love, you were so gentle, caring, attentive, loving, and masterful. I could feel how much you loved me. I could see it in your eyes. I love making love to you. I miss you so much right now, but I'm strong. I'll be strong for you no matter what. I know how much you love serving your country and I'm so proud of you. I'm always waiting for you. Time could never change the way I feel about you. I know you'll keep your promise, and you'll come back to me.

I promise you that I'll always love you, and I'll always be faithful to you even if you're gone for a year. I promise you, Jack, that no matter how difficult your career in the Army is for us, I promise to never ask you to choose between me and the duty you have to your country. I've accepted our life and our marriage will never be normal, but always extraordinary. We'll cherish the moments we're face to face and not worlds apart. We'll cherish each phone call, love letter or email, hug, and kiss as if it were our last. With you being in combat, I am terrified that I'll lose you, and I'll have to carry on without you somehow. If I lost you, my world would end, and my heart would be shattered. I love you so much, Jack. I cannot wait until we start a family together. You're going to be an amazing father, Jack. I love you so much. I don't want you to worry about me; I'm tough. You concentrate on coming home to me. I need you more than you know, Jack.

Like a wave out on the ocean, I know you'll always come back to me. I'm here for you, always.

All my love, Kate"

He smiled as he folded up the letter and looked at her picture. He missed her more and more as he stared at the bent photograph of her, that he's carried all these years. He thought of their life together, especially the idea of starting a family with her.

She was sitting alone in their quiet house. She had to find something to keep her busy. Walking into the laundry room, she folded clothes. In the load of clothes, she found another one of his favorite Oklahoma Sooners t-shirts. Bringing it up to her nose, she could still smell his cologne. Tears rolled down her cheeks. Now that he was gone, she could cry.

Twenty hours later, the team arrived in Kandahar, Afghanistan. They would be taken by Chinook helicopter to their remote outpost, Firebase Vegas. The terrain of the valley was rugged and lush. They valley was commonly referred to as the 'Cradle of Jihad'. Soldiers tried to work peacefully with the local villagers, but in the 1980s, these locals joined the Mujahideen or the warriors of Islam, to fight the Soviets. The difficult task for U.S. troops would be weeding out the insurgents among these villagers. The Korengal Valley was one of the deadliest spots for all U.S. troops in Afghanistan.

After arriving and unloading their equipment, their firebase came under enemy fire. The remote outpost was surrounded by dozens of enemy fighters, armed with RPGs and small arms.

"Tom, are you good?" Jack asked, taking cover beside Brad on the opposite of the ridge. He could see Tom reloading his weapon.

"Yeah just another day at the office," Tom replied over bullets ricocheting off trees, rocks and equipment.

The heavy and constant fire from the enemy lasted well into the night. The monkeys were screeching, the noise was very unsettling. Finally, around 2:00 am, the gunfire was silenced. The Green Berets surveyed the damage and got a head count of who was injured or dead. One of Jack's close friends from Bravo Team, Jason Erickson, from Springfield, Missouri was killed in the attack. The soldiers renamed the firebase in their fallen brother's honor.

For the first three months into the deployment, the Green Berets at Firebase Erickson were attacked every day by RPGs, mortars and small arms fire.

He was lying on his cot in his bunk late at night looking at a picture of her. He missed her. He missed hearing her voice. He wondered what she was doing, what she was wearing, how her day was going. Suddenly, he heard a scream. It sounded like a woman's scream. He jumped up, grabbed his rifle, and sprinted towards the location of the screaming. He found Tom, Jake, Marcus, Jamal, and Brad, along with members of Bravo and Charlie Teams laughing hysterically at Eric and Luke.

"What are y'all doing?" Jack asked, wearing a sleeveless muscle shirt, his dog tags and ACU pants.

"Look…" Tom said putting a small box in his face. Inside the box was a giant camel spider, crawling around inside trying to escape.

"What's wrong with you?" Jake asked him, noticing the rifle in his hands.

"I heard a woman scream, and I ran as fast as I could to see what was going on."

They all laughed. "That was Luke! He screams like a little girl," Jake said as he, Brad and Tom laughed.

"That's not funny! Jack, tell them that's not funny," Luke said.

"That's messed up!" Eric said.

"Get it out of here. Get some sleep." Jack said.

The next morning, most of the team gathered for breakfast. Jack had an idea. To get back at Jake, Tom and Brad for pulling a camel spider prank and scaring him nearly to death, Jack, Luke, and Eric had organized their own prank.

Jack and Luke were sitting at the table reading sections of the Army Times newspaper with Jake, Jamal, Brad, and Marcus on the opposite side. Eric slowly walked up behind Jake and motioned for all sitting at the table to be very still and quiet. He carefully put a large camel spider on top of Jake's head. He was wearing a Boston Red Sox ball cap. Eric sat down beside Luke and acted normally.

Tom walked in with his protein bar and stopped dead in his tracks. "WOW! Don't move!" he yelled at Jake. Jake looked around the table trying to figure out what Tom was freaking out about. Tom grabbed a bat and stealthily approached Jake. The rest of the team watched hoping Tom would whack Jake with the bat.

"Tom, what is wrong with you?" Jake asked, alarmed.

Tom stealthily approached Jake wheeling the bat in his hands. "Sssh, don't move. You'll make me miss!"

Jake was very alarmed. He thought Tom was having a psychotic break. "What do you mean 'make you miss'?"

"Sssh, just trust me," Tom said.

"Tom…" Jake said. Tom slammed the bat hard on Jake's head. He missed the spider. The spider jumped onto the table. Jake began to scream like a little girl.

"That thing was on my head, and y'all didn't tell me!" Everyone belted out a hysterical laugh. Jack and Luke had tears coming out of their eyes, they were laughing that hard.

"That's what you get!" Luke said.

Jake grabbed the bat from Tom. "Here, how do you like it? You jerk!" he proceeded to whack Tom with it.

"I tried to kill it."

"You're just lucky it didn't bite me." Jake said as he kept touching his hat to make sure it wasn't still there. The morning between warriors and brothers started off very comical. The incident was recorded on video by Sam and Mark. They showed the video to Bravo and Charlie Teams, even to Colonel Mitchell. Everyone watched it over and over, laughing hysterically.

During the week of Thanksgiving, Kate flew home to Dallas to be with their families. She didn't want to be alone. She knew that he would miss Christmas, New Year's, and Valentines' Day. Being with their families, she found she missed him even more. When she looked at Bill or Jonah, she immediately saw him. They laughed, talked and shared funny memories involving Jonah and Jack.

She took her glass of wine out on the patio and looked out in the scenic backyard. She sat in the deck chairs and wrapped her cardigan around her. Denise knew what Kate was going through, as did Carole. Denise walked out on the patio and sat beside her.

Kate was crying. She quickly wiped her tears away. "You don't have to hide your tears from me, sweetie. I know what you're going through. I'm here for you to vent to and cry to."

She smiled. "It's never easy not having him home for the holidays, is it?"

Denise smiled, "No, it's not," They hugged.

After the holidays, she was keeping everything together. She knew that she had to be strong for him. She kept to her usual routine of running every morning when she wasn't on duty. Running helped keep her stress level down. Being a military wife to a Special Forces soldier, she sure had a lot of stress. She worked full time. She had formed friendships with Paige, Miranda, and Jenny. They went out together to eat and visit. They all shared about their lives while their husbands were deployed.

She stayed in touch with her family and friends back home. She waited by the phone and computer, day and night for him to call, but he rarely did. She emailed him, but she rarely received an email from him. At nights when she was really lonely, she'd replay their wedding video just to hear his voice.

One Friday morning in January, Carole called her at home. She was home cleaning that day. "Hey sweetie, are you busy?"

She was happy to hear her mother's voice. "Oh, hey Momma, I'm just cleaning. It's my day off. I'm trying to stay busy while Jack is gone. How are you?"

She had something to tell Kate. "Actually, I'm calling because I have something to tell you."

She could hear the seriousness in her mother's voice. "Okay, what's going on?"

"About a week ago, I went to my OB/GYN for my annual exam. Doctor Ashton found tumors on my uterus. We had a biopsy done and he tested the tumors. It turns out that they are malignant."

Kate could hear her pulse throbbing, her heart racing, sweat beading on her face and chest. She felt as if she had the wind knocked out of her. "What?" she asked with her voice cracking and tears rolled down her face.

"I have uterine cancer, Katie."

She was crying. She could hear her mom crying also. Her mother was only fifty-three years old. "So what do we do now?"

"I had an appointment with my oncologist in Dallas, and we went over my treatment options. He seems to think that removing my uterus it the best option. The surgery is on Thursday at seven in the morning."

"I'm coming home! I'll be on the next flight out!"

"I don't want you to worry about me, sweetie. I'm going to be fine. I just wanted to let you know."

"I'm still coming home, momma."

"Okay, that's great. I can't wait to see you. I miss you and our talks."

She was crying. "I love you, momma."

"I love you too, sweetie. Now stop that crying. I've got God on my side. That's all the strength and protection I need."

She wiped her tears. "How are Dad and Lauren taking the news?"

"Lauren reacted the same way as you are now. And you know your Dad, he never likes to show how he's feeling but I can tell he is petrified."

"I am too."

"If my Lord needs me, Katie, you shouldn't be scared for me. I've raised you better than that. I know my Lord will take care of me."

"Don't talk like that, momma."

"Kate, I need you to prepare yourself for the worst and pray for the best."

"I don't know what I would do, Momma if I lost you."

"You'd go on living and taking care of you and your husband."

Wiping the tears from her face and trying to breathe. "Well I need to call the hospital and let them know, and I need to email Jack."

"You shouldn't let him know what's going on while he's deployed. His stress level needs to be low. If you tell him, he'll worry about you."

"You're right. I'll just tell him I'm coming back to Dallas for a visit."

"Tell my favorite son-in-law that I love him, miss him, and I hope he's doing okay."

She smiled. "Okay, momma I'll tell him."

"I love you, Katherine."

She knew when her parents called her Katherine it was a very serious matter. "I love you too, momma."

As she hung up with her mom, the phone rang again. She saw it was a satellite number.

She breathed a sigh of relief. "Jack?"

He smiled, listening to her adorable Texan accent. "Hey baby, it's me." She smiled and tried to hide that she was crying. He could tell she was upset and had been crying. "Baby, what's wrong?"

"I'm so happy to hear from you. I was really starting to worry," she said sniffling, with a tremor in her voice. She tried to make herself stop crying and act normally. The last thing he needed to do was worry about her.

He had never heard her like this. He was immediately worried. He knew something was wrong. "Baby, what is going on? Are you alright?"

"Yes, I'm fine. I'm just missing you. I haven't heard from you in a while, and I've been worried."

He remained silent, listening to the words and the tone in her voice. "Uh, I'm going to take a week off from work and fly home to Dallas to see my parents and yours," she said.

"And you're sure you're alright?" he asked again.

"Yes, baby. I'm fine. I just need to get away." She reserved herself to be brave and not burden him with the news of her mother's cancer. He had enough to worry about with dodging bullets, RPGs, IEDs, and losing friends in combat. She didn't want him to lose focus or worry about her.

"I just got all your emails. I'm sorry I haven't been able to call or email lately. I haven't been near a computer or a phone, but I'm back on base now, and we can Skype. I can't wait to see you. I've missed that gorgeous face, those eyes, and that killer smile."

She smiled. "I can't wait to see you either."

"Log onto Skype right now please, I want to see you."

She smiled. "I'm a mess. I've been cleaning, and I look awful."

"It's impossible for you to look awful. I need to see you. You're beautiful no matter what."

"Okay, give me five minutes."

"Okay, I love you."

"I love you too." They logged onto Skype and talked for close to an hour. They really missed each other, but no matter how lonely they were, they were true to each other. They had a private moment together. He was in his bunk with the door closed. That was the only romance they had while on deployment.

Later that day, she confided to Paige and Jenny. "I'm flying home tomorrow to Dallas."

"Is everything okay?" Jenny asked.

"No, my mom has uterine cancer."

They were stunned. "Oh my goodness, we're so sorry!" Paige exclaimed, hugging her.

"Did they catch it in time or is it terminal?" Jenny asked.

"Her oncologist seems to think removing her uterus is the best option. The surgery is Thursday. "

"Did you tell Jack?"

"No! I don't want him to be distracted. I'll tell him once he comes home." They continued to talk.

She requested a week off and flew home to Dallas to be with her mother. Arriving in Dallas, she stepped out of the terminal and made her way to baggage claim. During the flight, she thought of Jack and of her mother. The two most important people in her life were facing danger, of course in different circumstances, but she knew her world would end if she were to lose either one of them.

As she picked up her bag, she saw her Aunt Tina, her mother's sister, waiting for her. "Hey sweetheart, how are you doing?" she asked.

"I'm still shocked, but I'm optimistic. How's Momma?"

Tina smiled. "Oh you know your momma, she's always reassuring everyone that she's fine."

"Is my Dad here?"

"Yeah, he got in earlier this week. He's been waiting on her hand and foot. He'll carry her around the house so she doesn't have to walk."

Kate smiled. "It's incredible after being married for so many years they're still madly in love with each other."

"How is Jack? Is he home or is he gone?"

"He's gone. I miss him so much, and I can't wait for him to be home."

"When are you two going to try to have a baby?"

She smiled. "We've only been married for four months. It's kind of soon isn't it?"

"No not for us. We're all so excited for you and Jack to have a baby."

They drove to her parents' house. Kate saw Lauren's car parked in the driveway. She opened the door to her aunt's car and looked around at her parents' house. Dad came to the front door, opened it, and smiled at her. "Sweet pea…"

She smiled at him. "Hey Daddy…"

"How was your flight?"

"It was okay. How's Momma?"

"She's good. She's upstairs resting." She walked up the stairs to her parents' bedroom. She opened the door and saw her mother sleeping with her reading glasses on and a book halfway opened and pressed on her chest. She smiled and slowly walked towards the bed. Taking off her shoes, she laid down next to her mother.

Mom woke up and saw her. "Hi sweetie, when did you get here?"

"A few minutes ago…"

"I'm happy to see you, honey."

She smiled with tears in her eyes. "I'm so happy to see you, momma."

"Why are you crying, baby?"

She broke down. "I'm just so scared to lose you, momma."

"Oh honey, I'm not going anywhere. I promise. I'm going to beat this. But if I can't, I've taught you better than that. I know where I'm going when I die, so you shouldn't worry."

"I would be lost without you."

"No you wouldn't. You're a Christian. God wouldn't allow you to be lost. Besides, you have Jack, and he'll always be your compass. How is he doing?"

"I talked to him yesterday. He seemed so tired and so busy, but he found time to call me."

"I'm so blessed to have him as a son-in-law. I couldn't have picked a better man for you. He's every mother's dream."

"He is so amazing, momma."

"I know. He loves you so much. When are you two going to give your father and me some grandbabies? I can't wait to be a grandma."

Kate laughed. "Well that's odd to hear you say. Most women would dread being a grandma."

"No not me. They say grandchildren are the sweetest gift in the world. That you get to spoil them more than you did your own children, and then you send them home to their parents." They laughed. She tucked a strand of Kate's hair behind her ear. "I hope you and Jack have a big family."

"I would be happy with three."

"Oh, that would be sweet as Heaven. You're going to be an amazing mother."

"I have the most amazing mother, so I only hope I could be like you."

They talked, laughed, and cried together for hours. The next few days, Kate, Lauren, Tina and Matt took turns taking care of her. It nearly drove Carole nuts to stay in bed.

Matt and Carole were in their bedroom talking late at night. Everyone was in bed. He looked at her. "I'm scared." she said. She finally broke down and cried on his shoulder. He held in his emotions and held her tight.

"I know you're scared, sweetheart. I am too. When you're weak, I'll be strong. When you let go, I'll hold on. When you need to cry, I'll dry your eyes. I'll love you through this. I'm not going to leave you," he said.

She looked in his eyes. "You've made my life so wonderful. I remember the first time I saw you. I knew by the way you looked at me that I'd marry you."

"I remember arguing with you to marry me. You wanted to call it off."

She laughed. "I wouldn't have. I just wanted to see if you'd let me go."

He smiled. He was scared to lose her. "I'd never let you go, Carole. You've always been so strong. You're an excellent wife, an incredible mother, and I can't thank you enough for taking care of everything during my many deployments through the years. You've raised two beautiful, smart, kind women, and now it's time for you to let me be strong for you. Rely on me for strength. I'll never leave you." She smiled. They hugged, cried, and talked.

Kate was sitting up looking at photo albums she and her mother had made together in her old bedroom. Jack called her cell phone. She smiled seeing he was calling. "Hello, master sergeant."

He smiled, hearing her voice made him relax and happy. "Hi baby, how are you doing?"

"I'm good. I'm in Dallas."

"How is everyone?"

She smiled. "Everyone is good." she lied. "Guess what Momma and my aunt were asking me today."

"What?" he asked.

"They want to know when we're going to have a baby."

He was excited about starting a family, but he was nervous and apprehensive too. "I'm excited to have kids with you, but are you really ready for that?"

She smiled. She wanted children with him, but she wasn't ready. "Truthfully, no I'm not. We just got married four months ago. I want to be married for at least three years before we have a baby. I can't wait to be the mother of your babies, but I just want to enjoy newlywed life with you. I've barely had you home since we got married."

He breathed a sigh of relief. "You have no idea how happy I am that you feel that way. I'm not ready either. Just out of curiosity, when you say babies, how many babies are we talking about?"

"I'd be happy with two at the most four."

"How about we meet in the middle and agree on three kids?"

"Okay, three kids." She let out a tired sigh. "I'm so tired."

He could sense she was holding back. He knew there was something seriously wrong and he couldn't help but worry about her. "Baby, I may not be there physically for you but I am always here for you to vent to."

"I'm okay, just a little overwhelmed. I have to be Super Woman and keep everything together so you don't have any stress on you."

"Baby, you're not a very good actress. You're an amazing nurse, and an amazing wife, just not a great actress. I know you. I know when something is wrong. You can tell me. You don't have to carry the weight all by yourself. I'm here for you. We're partners."

"I don't want you worrying about the vehicles, the house, or me. I want you to focus and come back alive. I can handle everything. It's just there are times I feel weak, and I wish you were here, but your love keeps me strong. I'll get through this."

"I know this isn't easy, Kate, and I'm sorry that I'm not there to help you through whatever it is you're going through, but I love you so much. I miss you beyond words. I can't wait to see you and hold you. Did you bring your laptop?" he asked.

"Yeah, I brought it."

"Log onto Skype. I need to see you," he said.

She logged onto Skype. They were so happy to see each other. "Wow, there's the most gorgeous woman in the world."

"Hi, wow you look amazing. Hurry up and come home."

"Oh, I wish I could. I'd be on the next flight home if we could come home, but maybe in a few weeks."

"How is it over there?"

"Oh, it's the same as it always is. I'm ready to get home and relax with you."

"Who says you'd be relaxing?" she asked, giving him a flirty grin.

He smiled. "Okay what would I be doing?"

"I'd put you to work for a few hours."

He smiled. "I wouldn't complain." They talked and laughed for a long time. Seeing him made her feel better. He was happy to see her. He loved how her soft brown hair draped her shoulders and framed her face. He loved her big brown eyes. At that moment, he'd trade anything in the world just to be able to hold her, smell her, and kiss her. She still excited him. He wanted her. He missed making love to her. They had a private moment together.

Later that week her mother had her surgery. Kate, Lauren, Matt, and other immediate family members were at the hospital in the waiting room near the vending machines. Jack's parents even showed up for support. His parents had kept Carole's diagnosis a secret from him also. Their pastor was there also, holding his Bible and praying with them.

She was holding Denise's hand as they waited. Jack called her cell phone by satellite phone. "Hello?" she answered excitedly.

"Hi baby, how are you doing?"

She composed herself to tell him about her mother. She couldn't lie to him anymore. "I'm at the hospital with my family."

"The hospital, is everything alright?"

"My mom found out she has uterine cancer, so today she had surgery to remove her uterus. She's still in surgery. We're all in the waiting room."

He felt terrible that he was gone when she needed him the most. "Is this why you were crying when I called you earlier this week?"

"Yeah, I thought I did a pretty good job of hiding it."

"I'm sorry I'm not there for you, baby. You know if I could hop on a flight, I'd be there. How are you doing?"

"I know you would be, Jack. I'm okay, I've prayed a lot and our pastor is here. But I'd be better if you were here."

"I know I wish I could be there for you, but I know your mom is going to be fine. She's the strongest woman I know. For crying out loud, she gave birth to you, and you are no cupcake."

She laughed. "Yeah, Momma says I was her stubborn baby. She was in labor with me for almost seventy-two hours."

"Well, see that proves what we already know…"

"Oh, really and what is that?"

"…That you're stubborn as a mule…" She laughed. "…But you're very beautiful, sweet, and compassionate. You're independent and stubborn as all get out and you mean everything to me."

"I love you, Jack. How are you doing?"

"I'm alright. I'm ready to come home to you."

She smiled. "I am too."

As they were on the phone, the surgeon came out in scrubs with Carole's chart. "Hold on Jack, the surgeon just came out."

Matt stood, as Kate and Lauren rushed to his side. "Mr. Johnson, your wife is out of surgery, and she did great. We are confident that by removing the uterus, the cancer shouldn't return, but we got it out just in time. We'd like to keep an eye on her for the next few days. Once released, she needs to take it easy the first two weeks, then she needs to stick to an exercise routine, a healthy diet, and monthly appointments for exams. She should make a full recovery in two weeks. I'd like her to follow up with her doctor in three weeks."

Matt breathed a sigh of relief. "Thank you, doctor."

"Can we see her?" Kate asked, as she and Lauren were desperate to see her.

"She isn't in recovery yet, but she will be soon. I'll have a nurse come out and get you both."

She put the phone back to her ear. "Momma made it out of surgery just fine." Kate told Jack.

He breathed a sigh of relief. "Well that's awesome."

"I'm so relieved. I've been praying for her nonstop. Thank you, Lord."

She laughed as a few tears escaped down her cheek. He longed to see her. "I would give anything to see you and hold you right now," he said.

"I would give anything to see you. I can't wait for you to be home."

"I know I miss my gorgeous, sexy wife."

"I miss you too."

"I wish I was home right now. I just want to touch you and hold you."

"I do too. I love you so much."

"I love you too, baby."

"I'm so relieved the surgery went good."

"I am too, baby. How long are you staying?"

"I leave in four days. Now she's going to make a fuss about us taking care of her. How are you doing?"

"Oh, I'm good. You know it is one hundred and twenty degrees out here, the scenery is beautiful and the accommodations are amazing. It's the vacation everyone dreams of," he joked.

"No, you don't have me there, so it's not a vacation."

"You're right. If you were here, I could ignore everything else." he teased.

"That's probably not the smartest thing."

He laughed. "We should take a vacation together when I get back."

"I agree. You need some R&R."

"You're my R&R." He looked at his watch. "Well baby, I need to get off here and go to the TOC. I'll Skype with you later tonight, okay?"

"Okay, please stay safe and come back to me."

"I promise you I will come back. I have to. I have the most gorgeous wife in the world waiting for me."

"You know I am."

"I love you, baby. Tell your mom I'm relieved she's alright. And for the record, don't keep things like this secret from me again. I can handle whatever is going on back home. As long as I know you're safe, I can handle anything."

"I'm sorry. I just didn't want to distract you."

"I know, your motive was to protect me, and I appreciate that, but I want to know all the important things going on with our families, okay?"

"I love you, Jack."

"I love you too." They hung up.

Her mother's recovery went well. She exercised more, kept her check-up appointments with her doctor and maintained a healthy diet. At her mother's insistence, Kate returned to Fort Bragg. Lauren returned to work in Houston, but Matt maintained his schedule from the house in Dallas. He would return to Washington D.C. once he knew she was alright.

Now, August 2007, after ten months in Afghanistan, Colonel Mitchell and his men returned home unexpectedly to their wives and children. Kate was in Dallas visiting with their families and celebrating her twenty-seventh birthday at her favorite Tex-Mex restaurant, El Fenix.

She wore an orange, halter top dress and brown cowboy boots. She wore a turquoise necklace and earrings. Her hair was loosely curled and her makeup was perfect. She was happy to be back in Dallas with their family and friends. She was laughing and enjoying visiting with her parents, Jack's parents, her sister, Jonah, Christi, and Meagan and her friends from her old job.

"So, Kate any news on when you and Jack are going to have a baby?" Angie asked.

"No, not yet, we want to be married for at least three years before we start a family."

"Do you know when he'll be home?" her aunt asked her.

"No, I never know when he'll be home. He surprises me."

"How is he?" Jonah asked.

"I talked to him a week ago. He sounded really good, just really tired." She looked down at her engagement ring and smiled. "He'll be home soon," she had to reassure herself. She couldn't be weak.

"What are your plans when he comes home? Is he getting a lot of leave time?" Bill asked.

"We were talking about taking a trip overseas, but we'll just have to see."

"That sounds great. You two definitely need a vacation together." Denise said.

"Yeah, we've only spent three weeks together since we've been married."

"That must be so hard." Tess said.

"It is, but you know it doesn't help to wallow about something I can't control or that he can't control. I'm just so excited when he comes home."

"I bet he'll be home soon." Meagan said.

"Yeah, I hope so."

"How is work at the post hospital?" Marci asked.

"It's busy, but it's such a sweet place to work. Every day I see these Army guys there when their wives give birth, and it's a priceless moment. The looks on their faces are so incredible and so rewarding. I find myself daydreaming about when Jack and I have our own child, hopefully he'd be there when I go into labor."

After dinner, the waiter and the owner brought out her very elaborate cake. The restaurant sang 'Happy Birthday' to her. She was embarrassed. She looked at the lit candles. "Make a wish!" Carole said to her.

"I'm just going to tell y'all what I wish since I know it can't come true anyway, not for a while. I wish Jack was home." She blew out the candles. As the smoke billowed up from the candles, she felt someone standing behind her. She turned and immediately smiled with tears in her eyes. It was Jack!

"Jack!" she yelled, jumping into his arms and kissing his lips. He wrapped his arms around her and held her tight. He was still in uniform. Their families and friends were teary eyed and happy to see them together. The restaurant gave him a standing ovation and applauded his homecoming.

He smiled and closed his eyes at the scent of her perfume. He loved the way she smelled when he held her. "Hi, baby. Happy Birthday; you look gorgeous."

"I missed you so much."

"I missed you too, baby. I'm happy I was able to surprise you. I was so afraid someone was going to accidentally slip and tell you."

"I'm so happy you're home!"

After arriving home from deployment, he caught his flight from Fayetteville to Dallas. Christi and Carole had emailed him and let him know where Kate was going to be. He greeted his parents and Kate's. His mom and dad were teary eyed. They were so elated he was home safely. He sat next to her. Their parents' watched as they whispered in each other's ears and gently kissed and smiled at each other.

After visiting for a little while, they stood and said goodbye to everyone. Jonah had lent him one of his trucks. "Don't wreck my truck." he warned.

"Yeah, I'll go do that right now. How many accidents have I had?"

"There's always a first time."

They walked out to Jonah's truck. She grabbed his hand and looked up in his eyes. He kissed her lips. Wrapping her arms around his neck, he pinned her up against Jonah's truck and kissed her passionately. "Do you know how much I've missed kissing you?" she asked.

"I've missed you so much."

"What do you want to do now?"

"I have a surprise for you."

She smiled. "Can you tell me?"

"Not yet. Where's your stuff?"

"At my parents' house," He drove to her parents' house. "Why do I need my stuff?"

"You'll see, no questions, please." They arrived at her parents' house. She unlocked her parents' door. Holly greeted them. He played with Holly as she hurried upstairs to get her stuff.

"Do you have enough clothes for four days?"

She smiled. "I take it we're going away for the weekend?"

He smiled. "I'm not telling you anything yet."

"Where are your clothes?"

"The backseat of Jonah's truck, he picked me up from the airport earlier today."

They walked hand in hand out to his truck. He drove north. Nearing the state line, she looked at him. "We're going to Oklahoma?"

He smiled at her. "Will you please just let me surprise you?" They entered Oklahoma. They were driving up in the Kiamichi Mountains of eastern Oklahoma. He arrived at the Eagle Creek Escape cabins. He got the key from the front desk and the map on how to get to their secluded cabin.

The sun was setting. The wildflowers were in full bloom as the crickets and the bull frogs sang sweet serenades. He parked in the driveway of a beautiful cabin. "Oh Jack, it's so beautiful."

He grabbed their bags and held her hand as they walked up the walkway to the door. He unlocked the cabin, opened the door, and turned on the lights. "Wow, this is absolutely gorgeous." They looked around the cabin. There was a King sized bed in the bedroom. The refrigerator was stocked with fresh groceries in the full kitchen. There was also a Jacuzzi on the back porch, overlooking a beautiful lake.

They stood on the back porch looking out at the water. He wrapped his arms around her as they stood looking out at the scenery. "I want you all to myself this weekend," he said, as he kissed on her neck and shoulder.

She smiled and closed her eyes. "You're going to be a busy boy."

"Put me to work." he whispered. She turned and kissed his lips. He picked her up. She wrapped her legs around his waist. Laying her down, she smiled up at him, at his strong arms, and his rippling abdominal muscles. He climbed on top of her and kissed her lips. They kissed passionately.

He laid on his back. She kissed his shrapnel scars. "Are there any new scars that I need to kiss?"

He smiled. "No." They made gratifying love for hours. They savored every moment of being together. They loved each other like there was no tomorrow. After an exhausting weekend of making love, they returned to Dallas to say goodbye to their families, and they flew back to Fayetteville.

Now late September, a month after an incredible, mind blowing weekend away in the beautiful Kiamichi Mountains of Oklahoma, Kate had discovered she was late. She did not tell him what was going on until she knew for sure. She suspected she was pregnant. On Sunday, they went to church on post. She hadn't told him that she had missed her period. They attended adult Bible study together and were active in their church. After church, they drove home. He watched football in the living room.

"I'm going to go to the commissary, is there anything special you want?"

"No, I'm good."

She kissed him goodbye, grabbed her car keys and drove to the commissary. While in the commissary shopping, she could not bring herself to be near the fresh meat, seafood, or poultry. The smell was just too much. Soon, she found herself in the feminine products aisle. She saw the many pregnancy tests on the shelf. There were so many choices. She had never taken one before. She just wanted a basic pregnancy test. Looking at the labels, the accuracy and how soon the hormone is detected, she tossed one in her shopping cart.

Arriving home, she noticed he wasn't home. She figured he went to the store or was at the range with Tom, Trevor and Brett. She placed the pregnancy test on the counter and stared at it. She decided she wasn't going to take it. As she put up the groceries, she thought about how excited she was and at the same time how terrified she was.

He came home and saw her unloading the dishwasher. "Hey baby."

"Hi, where'd you go?" she asked.

He kissed her. "I went to the range with the guys. I got my list of confirmed kills today."

"Oh yeah, how was it?"

"I have 200 confirmed kills."

"Wow, that's impressive," she said. He could tell she had something on her mind. He noticed the pregnancy test. Picking it up, he looked at her curiously. "Do you think you're pregnant?"

She smiled. "I could be. I've missed my period."

He was excited. "Well, let's take this and find out." They hurried to their master bathroom. He sat on the edge of the bathtub as she took the test. "How long do we wait?"

"Two minutes."

He watched as she nervously shook. He studied her facial expression and body language. "I know we agreed to wait until we've been married for three years and we've only been married for almost one, but are you going to be upset if you're pregnant now?" he asked.

She looked at him. "No, I won't be upset. I'll be happy, but I really just hope I'm not."

He smiled. He held her hand. "Everything is going to be fine."

She kissed his lips. "Are you ready to find out?"

He smiled. She picked up the test off the counter and held it flat in her hands. She smiled and looked at him. "What's the verdict?"

She had tears in her eyes. She looked up at him and smiled. "It's positive."

He smiled excitedly as he hugged and kissed her. She had tears in her eyes. "Yes! I love you. Okay, let's call our parents!" he said. They called their parents and siblings. The news of the pregnancy thrilled their families and friends.

They had gone to hear the baby's heartbeat and find out her due date. She was due mid-May. When they both heard the heartbeat, they were amazed. He looked at the screen in shear dumbstruck awe. He looked back at her. She was glowing. Their love life was busier than usual. They celebrated the start of the family by going to Las Vegas. They rented a spacious hotel room at the Bellagio Hotel. They went to numerous shows, shopping, and to many restaurants. After four days, they returned to Fort Bragg.

The leaves were turning. The summer breeze now turned crisp and cool. She was working. It was near 2:00 p.m. He was just informed of a mission. He wanted to tell her goodbye in person. He drove to the hospital. He saw her friend Nicole at the nurses' station. "Hey, where's Kate?"

"She's in with a patient."

"I need to talk to her now."

She hurried into the patient's room. "Kate, Jack is here."

"Okay, I'll be right out."

A few minutes later, she came out into the hall. She smiled at him. "Hi, what are you doing here?"

"I need to talk to you privately."

"Okay, let's go in here." They went into a corridor in the stairway. "What's wrong?"

"I have a mission." She knew she had to put on a strong front. He needed her to be strong and brave. She forced herself not to get emotional, though pregnant that was very difficult.

"When do you depart?" she asked, feeling the growing lump in her throat as she talked. She felt as if someone was applying pressure to her throat.

He looked at his watch. "In an hour…" He saw her eyes were misty. He wrapped his arms around her waist and pulled her against him. "Be strong for me, baby."

She looked up into his eyes and wrapped her arms around his neck. "I'm always strong for you."

"I love you so much. I'm going to miss you."

"I love you more and I'll miss you more."

He smiled, "That's not possible." He kissed her lips. They kissed passionately in the private corridor for several minutes.

She looked up into his eyes. "Promise me you'll come back."

He smiled and touched her belly. "I promise you, Kate. I will come back."

"We'll be here waiting for you to come home."

He smiled. He looked down at her belly and kneeled. "I have a feeling you're a boy, so you take care of her." he said to her belly.

She smiled. "You're so cute. You're going to be an amazing daddy."

"I love you baby."

"I love you too. Be safe."

"I will. I'll see you when I get back." They kissed goodbye. She watched him walk down the hall to the elevators.

In mid-October 2007, they had been married for a year, but unfortunately had only spent very little time together since their wedding. They didn't even get to celebrate their first anniversary together. It was hard on them, but they knew they had to be strong for each other. They knew their love would get them through. Not celebrating anniversaries together was part of the lifestyle. It was in no way ideal, but it was reality.

Alpha, Bravo, and Charlie Teams deployed back to the Korengal Valley in Afghanistan. They were unsuccessful in talking peacefully with the locals. They receive intelligence that the village closer to the Green Beret outpost was harboring insurgents, who have attacked and killed many U.S. soldiers.

Operation Rock Avalanche was launched. The operation targeted the village. The U.S. gunships destroyed the village. After the attack, soldiers found that many of the casualties were women and children. The soldiers tried to make amends by evacuating the wounded for proper care in a U.S. hospital. The radio operators learn over their radios that the angry villagers have sided with the insurgents and were planning a revenge attack.

"Bravo 4, Bravo 4, this is Alpha 1. The enemy is pushed up on the high ground, my southwest."

Bravo 4 and two other scouts were on a mission hunting insurgents when Taliban fighters attack them. "Bravo 4 is hit!" a soldier yelled over his radio. "They pushed him over the hill!"

Both Alpha and Bravo Teams rushed to the scene. They discovered Bravo 4 Robert Russo, from Providence, Rhode Island had been killed. The other two scouts from Bravo and Charlie Teams were seriously wounded.

"Where's his weapon? Did they take it?" Jack asked, searching the brush for Russo's weapon.

Two days after Bravo 4 was killed, Alpha, Bravo, and Charlie Teams were returning to their outpost from patrol. A shot was fired really close to the soldiers. Then thousands of bullets were shot. Jack saw one of his men fall to ground. He ran under personal heavy fire to get to him. As he approached the soldier, he helped him get back on his feet. He then noticed one of his men was missing. Two Taliban fighters were carrying him off.

He took out his knife and stabbed one of the fighters in the side, nicking the heart. The other dropped the soldier and ran away. He held the badly wounded soldier in his arms. He had been shot six times. Blood trickled out of his mouth. He carried the soldier to Jamal.

Jamal desperately tried to stop the bleeding, but there was nothing he could do. The soldier died in Jack's arms. Jamal looked at him and shook his head. "Damn it!" Jack yelled.

They went back to their firebase and had a memorial service for those lost. He walked into his bunk and called her via Skype. She was at home, on her day off. It was nearly midnight in Afghanistan. "Hey baby, how are you doing? How's the baby?"

She smiled. "We're good. I went to the doctor yesterday. I had a sonogram yesterday."

"Any news yet if it's a boy or a girl, I'm really hoping it's a boy."

"No, not yet, we won't know that for a while."

"I wish I could be home with you right now."

"I do too, but you're needed out there. I don't mind sharing you as long as I get you back."

He smiled. "You'll always get me back."

"I love you, Jack."

"I love you too. Happy Anniversary, baby,"

"Did you get the care package I sent you?"

"No, I haven't gotten anything yet."

"Oh well I sent you all your favorites."

"Did you send me a cake-in-a-jar?"

She smiled. "Yes, just keep it classified so your guys don't eat it."

"Oh I know I can't trust them with my packages anymore."

She saw he was tired. She knew he wasn't getting as much sleep as he should. "You look so tired."

"I am. I'm ready to come home."

"Why don't you get off here and go take a hot shower, get something to eat, and then get a good night's sleep?"

He smiled. "You're always watching out for me, aren't you?"

"Someone has to."

"I love you."

"I love you too."

"Take care of yourself. Mail me a copy of the sonogram."

"Okay, I will."

"Bye baby."

"Bye," as they disconnected their web chat.

The Taliban maintained a strong hold over Musa Qala, a city of 20,000 people. On December 8, 2007, under the cover of darkness, Chinooks fly over the city. Members of Alpha, Bravo, and Charlie Teams captured a cell phone tower overlooking the city.

As the sun began to rise, the enemy opened fire. Families evacuated, fearing for their lives. The soldiers pushed down the hill. Members of Alpha, Bravo and Charlie Teams entered one of the mud wall structures. Two Taliban fighters turned a corner. One was shot, but not dead. The soldier's rifle jammed, but his buddy finished the job. The other fighter fled. The soldiers moved further into the compound when they spotted another fighter in a doorway. They opened fire just as the fighter raised his weapon.

The fight for Musa Qala lasted for two more days. Before the Taliban gave up the last major city, Afghan National Army troops rolled into town and raised their flag above Musa Qala. The city bounced back. Citizens came forward to talk with soldiers.

After three months in Afghanistan, Alpha, Bravo, and Charlie Teams returned to Fort Bragg. Kate was at work at the post hospital. He went by their house to unload all of his gear. He looked around the house and noticed everything was still the same as it was when he left, besides new pictures on the walls.

He drove to the hospital, got in the elevator and rode up to the fifth floor to Maternity and OB/GYN. He saw her good friend, Nicole. "Hey is she busy?"

"I think she's on her lunch break, let me go check." Nicole said, walking down the hall to the nurses' lounge. She found her eating a light salad and drinking a bottle of water, while glancing over a magazine. She walked back down the hall. "She's in the nurses' lounge."

He smiled and calmly walked down to the nurses' lounge. He saw her slowly eating and reading a magazine. He carefully walked up behind her, wrapped his arms around her. "Hi baby," he whispered.

She smiled, jumped up into his arms. "Wow, you look incredible. You're glowing,"

"I've missed you so much. Welcome home, soldier," she kissed his lips.

"I've missed you more." he whispered. They were all alone in the nurses' lounge and kissing very passionately.

"When does your shift end?"

She looked at her watch. "Two hours."

"I can't wait that long." He let her go and gently touched her stomach. She was barely showing. He kneeled down and looked at her belly. She smiled down at him as he gently kissed her belly. "You've never looked more beautiful or happy."

He kissed her lips. "I'll meet you at the house in two hours and we'll pick up right here," kissing his lips again.

"Okay, I love you."

He left and headed home. Her shift ended at 7:00 p.m. She hurried home to see him. She looked throughout the house for him, but found him in the garage. She walked out in the garage.

"Hey baby,"

"Hi, what are you doing?"

"I was bored waiting for you to come home,"

She walked over to him. They kissed passionately. He picked her up and carried her to their bedroom. He carefully laid her down. They were holding each other tight and kissing passionately. They undressed. He smiled at her little baby bump showing. He kissed her stomach. They made sweet love until late into the night.

Everything was perfect. They were so excited about starting their family, but on a cold, rainy early January afternoon, all would change. She was working at the hospital. All of her friends and doctor friends were excited for her and Jack. She was twenty weeks, five months.

As she was taking care of a patient, she felt a sudden pain in her abdomen. She was doubled over and then blood gushed from her down her leg. The patient was concerned for her when she saw the massive amount of blood all over Kate and all over the floor. She started to feel weak. Her heart was beating rapidly and she found it difficult to breathe. It was difficult for her to walk. She felt as if her feet were made of cement. Her vision was blurry and she felt extremely dizzy. Staggering out into the hallway, blood was soaking through her scrub pants and smearing all over the floor.

Nicole looked up and saw her. She had never seen Kate look so disoriented. "Kate?"

She fell to the ground. Nurses and doctors rushed to her side. "Kate, what do you want me to do?" Nicole asked, frantic.

"Call Jack…" she managed to say. She was starting to have a seizure and was going into shock. She was lifted on to a gurney and rushed into the ICU. Nicole ran to Kate's purse and dialed Jack's cell phone number.

He was in the weight room working out with Jake and Tom. "So, how is Kate liking being pregnant?"

"She's so happy and excited. We heard the heartbeat again last week. It was incredible."

"What do you want, a boy or a girl?" Jake asked.

"I hope it's a boy. We're supposed to find out soon." Jack said, as his cell phone rang. He saw it was Kate. "Hi, baby." he answered.

Nicole was trying not to cry or panic. "Jack, its Nicole from the hospital, I need you to meet me at the ICU right now. Kate is being admitted."

He could hear the seriousness in her voice. "The ICU, what's happened?" Jake and Tom stopped working out and were curious.

"I don't know. She started to have a seizure, difficulty breathing and there was blood everywhere. She told me to call you just before she was taken away."

"Okay, I'm on my way." He hung up. He looked to Jake and Tom.

"What's wrong?"

"Kate had a seizure and can't breathe. They took her to the ICU." He hurried to his truck and drove quickly to the hospital. He was very worried for her and their baby. Tom and Jake quickly ran out to their vehicles and followed him to the hospital. He was driving extremely fast.

Arriving at the ICU, he saw a nurse working the nurses' station. "I'm looking for Kate Hamilton."

Looking at the computer screen, the woman said, "She's in room 4." He jogged through the waiting room doors and found ICU Room 4. He opened the door. She was lying in the bed, hooked up to a fetal monitor, oxygen, a blood pressure cuff, and heart monitor. She smiled at him. She was happy to see him, but scared she might be losing the baby. She was still in severe pain.

He kissed her lips. "Hi baby, what happened?" he noticed her bloody scrubs in the chair beside her.

"I don't know, I have this horrible pain in my stomach, and then I saw blood gushing out of me. Then I guess I blacked out. I woke up here. I'm scared, Jack. I hope the baby is okay."

He hugged her. "Everything is going to be fine."

"I'm in the ICU. Obviously everything is not fine," she said nervously.

They waited for the doctor to come in. Finally, the OB/GYN on duty walked in holding her chart. "Hello, Mrs. Hamilton, I'm Captain Pratt. So, we've ran some tests and what we've determined is that you had what we call a PA or placental abruption. In most cases, bed rest is the only treatment we can suggest…"

"Oh, thank God that's all it is," she said, breathing a sigh of relief.

"…Unfortunately Kate, yours is a severe case. More than half of your placenta has separated from the uterine wall. You have lost a significant amount of blood and the baby isn't getting any oxygen."

"Okay, so what do we do now?" Jack asked concerned.

"This is a serious situation. From the fetal monitor readings, the baby is in severe distress, and if we don't act now, Kate's life is in danger."

"What do you mean if we don't act now?" Jack asked.

"We need to do an emergency cesarean right now."

"Are you serious? She's only five months pregnant." Jack asked.

Kate was in disbelief. "Yes, I'm afraid this is a very serious situation. I'll have a nurse bring you a pair of scrubs." the Captain said.

He left the room. Jack paced the room with his hands on top of his head. He looked over at her and the shocked look on her face.

She had tears in her eyes. "Why is this happening? I did everything right. I avoided the X-ray machines, I ate right, and I exercised."

He held her hand and kissed it. "Baby, this is not your fault,"

The nurses came in and wheeled her into the operating room. Captain Pratt pulled him out into the hall. "Master Sergeant, this is a very dangerous situation. The baby hasn't received the sufficient amount of oxygen for quite some time and I'm sorry to tell you that the baby probably won't make it. Your wife's life is in critical danger. I need to know if things go wrong, do we have your permission to resuscitate?"

"Yes of course, you do everything possible to save her."

As he talked with the doctor, Tom and Jake arrived with other members of the team. "Jack?" Tom said.

"I can't talk right now. I'll talk to y'all in a little while." He followed Captain Pratt into the OR. He wore the pair of scrubs and a face mask. Her hair was pulled into a hair cap. He held her hand tightly as he watched the doctors perform a C-section. This was a very dangerous situation. She had lost a dangerous amount of blood. The baby had not received sufficient oxygen.

They got the baby out quickly, but it didn't cry out. It was a little boy. He was fading fast. They cut the umbilical cord and rushed him to the Neonatal Intensive Care Unit (NICU).

"It didn't cry out," she said as tears ran rapidly out of the corners of her eyes.

"Kate, I'm not going to lie to you. It doesn't look good for him."

"It's a boy?" Jack was trying to be as strong as he could be. He held her hand tightly. "I want to see him," she said.

"Unfortunately, Kate you can't right now." Captain Pratt said to her.

"I'll go see him." he said to her. She looked up at him, as tears rolled down her face. A nurse escorted him down to NICU. He was led to an incubator and inside was a very tiny baby, hooked up to many tubes. He was stunned and could barely tolerate to see him like that. He looked to a nurse. "Can I touch him?"

The nurse nodded. He placed his hand inside the hole and barely touched his hand. He had tears in his eyes. He could handle a lot of things, bullets, bombs, RPGs and IEDs, but not seeing his child like this. "Hey bubba, it's your dad." Just speaking to him, he broke down and cried. After crying for several minutes, he pulled himself together and walked back to her room.

"Did you see him? How is he?" she asked. She noticed he had been crying.

"Yeah, baby, I saw him. He's not looking too good right now."

"I want to see him." As a nurse, she knew their son wouldn't survive the first twenty-four hours, but for the first time in her career, she hoped her training and her 'gut' were wrong. Soon, she was wheeled in a wheel chair down to the NICU. They looked over their son. He could barely tolerate seeing him like that, but he knew she wasn't going to leave. He had to endure it. He had to be strong for her. She smiled as tears ran down her cheeks while carefully holding him in her arms. "He's beautiful."

"Yeah, he is."

"He looks just like you. What do you want to name him?"

"I don't know. You pick."

"What about Tyler David?"

He had tears in his eyes. "That's perfect."

She looked over at him. She had never seen him cry before. "Do you want to hold him?" She gently placed him in his arms. He kissed his forehead. He had called their parents and let them know the situation. Naturally, they were very concerned for her and the baby.

Four hours after delivery, little Tyler perished. They were naturally devastated. He held her in his arms as she screamed and sobbed. Once she calmed down, he walked to the hospital waiting room where he found all of his team members. Even members of Bravo and Charlie Teams and their wives were there. Colonel Mitchell and Miranda were there also.

Tom saw him and shot straight up. "How's Kate? How's the baby?"

He had tears in his eyes. "We had a son. We named him Tyler David."

"Oh, so the baby is okay?" Paige asked relieved.

He wiped his tears. "No, he…uh…he passed away ten minutes ago."

They were all shocked. "Oh my god, Jack, how's Kate?" Miranda asked.

"She's devastated, but I need to get back in there to talk with the doctors." Paige, Miranda, and Jenny hugged him. He walked back to the hospital room. He saw her sobbing almost uncontrollably. He touched her shoulder and sat beside her.

Captain Pratt entered the hospital room. "Mr. and Mrs. Hamilton, I am so deeply sorry for your loss. I've brought you some pamphlets with information on support groups here on post, and I've also brought you discharge forms. I would like you to take two weeks off from work to just rest and heal up."

"What about our son?"

"What about him?"

"I'd like to bury him."

"Oh, of course, we'll take care of everything. Just let us know what funeral home you prefer." Captain Pratt stood and just before exiting, he looked back at them. He felt terrible for them. "Again, Master Sergeant and Mrs. Hamilton, you have my deepest sympathies and condolences."

"Thank you." Jack said, wiping his tears. Captain Pratt left the room. She tried to keep her emotions in, but she couldn't. She was devastated. With her hands over her face, she sobbed. He hated to hear her cry. He knew there was nothing he could do to make her feel better. He stood beside her on the bed and leaned down and wrapped his arms around her.

He walked down the hallway to the restroom. He called his parents and told them that the baby had passed away. He also called her parents. After talking with his parents and in-laws, he punched the bathroom wall several times. He was very angry, very devastated.

The next day, she was discharged from the ER. He wheeled her out of the hospital in a wheel chair. Paige had brought her a change of clothes. He opened his truck door and carefully placed her inside. "What about my car?"

"I'll come back and get it." The drive home was silent. He was upset. He was really looking forward to being a father, and he knew how excited she was. Arriving home, he opened the door to the truck and carried her inside. He carried her to their bedroom and laid her down on the bed. She turned her back to him. She didn't feel like talking.

"Do you need anything?" he asked. She shook her head. "Do you want me to keep you company?"

"No, I just want to be alone."

"I'll be outside if you need me. I'm here for you, baby." He barely shut their bedroom door. As he walked down the hall, he could hear her crying. Sitting on the back porch, he bowed his head, and prayed. "Lord, I know you know what's best for us. I'm trying to understand this, but I don't. We were so excited and now we're devastated. Help me understand your reasoning."

The team's chaplain and the funeral director arranged for them to bury their son in the post cemetery. They had a marker made for him. Colonel Mitchell and all of Alpha, Bravo, and Charlie Teams attended the small graveside service, as well as Jack and Kate's family members. The marker read:

Tyler David Hamilton
January 23, 2008
3lbs, 8 in and 3 oz.
1:54 p.m.-5:54 p.m.

The chaplain gave an uplifting sermon. After the service, they went home. She locked herself in their bedroom. He tried to open the door, but he couldn't. He was alarmed. "Babe, open the door please." He didn't hear an answer. "Kate, seriously baby open the door."

She unlocked the door. He opened it and saw her climb back in the bed. He laid down beside her and touched her hand. He knew she was very angry and very hurt. "I'm here for you baby, just please don't shut me out."

She touched his face and hugged him. "I need you to help me through this," she said.

He was relieved. He wanted her to need him. He kissed her head as he held her. "I'm right here. I'll love you through it."

"I can't believe we had a boy. I was hoping it was a boy." Tears rolled down her cheek. "I can't believe I lost him. I wanted him so bad."

"I know you did, baby. I wanted him too."

"I just don't understand why. I ate right. I exercised. I didn't drink, smoke, or do drugs. I'm married. I just don't understand what the hell happened." She was angry and heartbroken.

"I don't know what happened, baby, but it was not your fault,"

"I was working too hard. I should've cut my hours back."

He kissed her hand. "Baby, please don't blame yourself. You did nothing wrong. You took care of yourself."

"I'm sorry, Jack."

He touched her face and caught a tear with his thumb. "You don't have to apologize. It's not your fault, but the doctor said in a few months we can try again."

"Will you divorce me if I don't want to have any more children?"

"No, I would never divorce you."

"I know you want kids, but I just don't think I can go through this again."

He knew she was just angry. "I understand. What can I do for you?"

She cried. "Will you hold me?" He opened his arms and she sobbed.

He had called Tom and Paige. He asked Paige to stay with Kate while he and Tom went back to the hospital to get her car. On the drive, Tom looked over at Jack. "Are you okay? You know if you need to talk, I'm here."

He looked over at him. "It's Kate we need to worry about." They arrived at the hospital parking lot. He parked beside her car. He handed his truck keys to Tom. He walked over to her car and unlocked it. Opening the driver's door, he saw a bag from Babies R Us. He opened the bag and saw the baby clothes she had bought over the weekend. He pulled an Army themed onesie and held it. He had tears in his eyes. He kneeled down, covered his face, and cried. He finally felt comfortable to grieve. Tom also kneeled and placed his hand on Jack's shoulder. "I'm here for you, buddy."

Paige was at the house consoling her. The news of the baby's death was heartbreaking for their families and friends. Everyone was supportive for Jack and Kate. Paige and her friends came over during the days, while she was recovering. They brought casserole dishes of prepared meals so she wouldn't have to cook.

Nearly two months later, she was still very hurt and angry after losing the baby. Looking for a way to cheer her up, he found an Irish terrier breeder near Fort Bragg. He went by and spoke with them. He found an adorable male Irish terrier. "I think my wife will love this one, how much for him?" he asked the man. He and the man worked out a bargain. He bought the puppy for her and went to the pet store to buy a collar and leash. He hoped she would like the puppy.

She was at home, deciding on what to cook for dinner when he walked in the door. "Hey, I have a surprise for you?"

She smiled at him. "What did you get me?"

"Close your eyes." She did. He picked up the puppy and held it to her face. She opened her eyes and was excited.

"Oh, Jack! He's so cute!"

"I'm glad you like him. He's for you."

He watched her play with him. He hadn't seen her smile in so long. "What should we name him?"

"You pick?"

She noticed he had bought him an OU themed collar. She looked up at him and smiled, "Well since he's got an OU collar, we should name him Boomer,"

He laughed, "I like it." He petted him. "I'm glad you love him. I feel better now knowing that you have a watch dog looking out for you."

"I went to the doctor today."

"How did that go?"

"I made the decision to get on birth control."

"I thought we were going to make that decision together?"

"It's my body and I made it. I don't want to get pregnant again."

"What kind of birth control, the pill?"

"No, it's an IUD."

"What's that?"

"IUD stands for intrauterine device. It goes inside my uterus and prevents me from getting pregnant for up to five years."

He was shocked she made this decision without talking to him about it. "Are you telling me that we're not going to have kids for five years?"

"Right now, yeah that's what I'm telling you." He knew he had to give her time to grieve. She was still angry and hurt. He also knew he couldn't force the issue. It had to be a decision they made together.

She walked into the kitchen and looked through the pantry, deciding on what to make for dinner. "What would you like for dinner?" They cooked dinner together.

Later that week, he was at the range with Trevor and Brett. "How are you and Kate doing since...?" Brett asked.

He was still upset about it. "We're as good as to be expected."

"I'm so sorry, man," Trevor said.

"How is Kate dealing with it?" Brett asked.

"She refuses to let herself think about it. I'm worried about her. Now she's talking about possibly not having kids for five years. I know she's just angry and hurt, she doesn't mean that."

"Why five years," Brett asked.

"It's what she wants."

Their cell phones all went off. They had a mission. They were to report to the airfield for immediate deployment to Afghanistan in thirty minutes. They slipped their weapons back in their holsters and quickly left the range. He pulled into the driveway and unlocked the door.

He quickly packed his gear, his rifles, and ammunition. As he was walking through the living room to the front door, he stopped and looked around the house one last time. He played with Boomer. He wished he could tell her goodbye, but there was no time. He grabbed a notepad from the desk and a pen and wrote her a goodbye note.

> *"Baby,*
> *I got my orders. I'm sorry I wasn't able to give you a kiss goodbye, but I love you very much, and I'll be thinking of you. Remember, I'm carrying you with me. You keep me alive and bring me home. Take care of yourself baby. I love you. I will come back.*
> *P.S. I already fed Boomer and let him go out.*
>
> *Jack"*

He walked out the front door and got back in his truck. He drove to the airfield and parked his truck. They quickly boarded the C-130 with all their cargo and equipment and departed for Afghanistan. They left the week before Valentine's Day.

She came home from work at 7 pm. She noticed his truck was gone. She walked into the kitchen and sat her purse down. Boomer ran to her and greeted her. She played with him and then saw Jack's note. She stood frozen as she read it. With her heart pounding, she was shaking with tears in her eyes. He was gone. She didn't get to make love to him, help him pack, kiss him and tell him goodbye.

Paige found the same note left by Tom. She ran up on Kate's porch and knocked on the door. Kate rushed to the door and saw the look on Paige's face. "So, I'm guessing you got the same note?"

They hugged. They had become the best of friends. They went shopping together. All the wives got together during deployments for weekly dinners and several glasses of wine. They were each other's God send.

Twenty hours later, the team arrived in Afghanistan. They arrived to their established outpost Firebase Bronco in the Nuristan province of south-eastern Afghanistan. The sun was shining. The temperature soared well above one hundred and twenty degrees. They settled into their bunks and unloaded their equipment. The outpost was armed by a handful of Green Berets. In all there were sixty U.S. soldiers and fifteen Afghan National Army soldiers.

Weeks after being in country, the Green Berets had engaged the Taliban numerous times. The Taliban were becoming more coordinated and tactful in their attacks on the outposts.

It was 2:00 a.m. Afghanistan time. He settled in his bunk for the night. He picked up his lap top and logged onto Skype. He called her. She was at home on her day off.

She heard him calling. She rushed to the computer and answered his call. He smiled when he saw her. "Hi, baby."

She smiled. "Hi, what are you doing?"

"I'm just about to get some sleep. I just wanted to talk to you and see how your week is going."

"It's pretty usual. I ran this morning, I had coffee with Paige, and now I'm cleaning. The adventurous life of an Army wife." she teased.

"Are you doing okay?" he asked.

"Yes, I'm fine."

He could see that she wasn't. "Have you made an appointment with the chaplain to talk with him about the baby?"

"No."

He knew she needed to talk to the chaplain. "Why not, we agreed that you need to."

"Well I've changed my mind. I don't want to go. I don't want to talk about it. I'm over it," she lied.

"You can't possibly be over something like that?"

She was starting to get angry with him. "Can you please just drop it and let it go? It's over. I have no other choice but to move on and get past it."

"Baby, there's no shame in getting help."

She was irritable. "You know I think we should get off here before we have a fight."

"I'm only trying to help you, baby. I'm not meaning to rub salt in your wounds. I just want you to be okay."

"And I'm telling you that I am. There's no explanation why we lost him, so why dwell on it? All I can do is move on." she snapped at him.

"Okay, I'm sorry I brought it up. How are things at work?"

"The usual, Lauren's birthday is next Friday. We're going to Vegas to celebrate. Meagan is going too."

"You really think jetting off to Vegas is what you should be doing right now?"

"I'm going to see my sister and your sister, what's the big deal?"

"Oh I don't know, it's Vegas, and I'm not entirely too comfortable with you all going without me or at the least without Jonah to protect you three."

"Are you telling me I can't go?"

"I'm not telling you can't do anything, Kate. I would feel better if you didn't go right now."

"Do you think I'm going to get drunk and sleep with someone? I'm just going to see my sister and yours."

"It's Vegas. Y'all will be drinking and partying and being vulnerable to guys. It's not smart, and I would be worrying about you. Why can't she celebrate her birthday in Dallas?"

"It's my sister's birthday. I want to have fun. I deserve to have fun. I have had a stressful couple of months."

"So you're going to go regardless of what I think?"

"I think your concern is misguided. I'm an adult. I can take care of myself. I'm not going to get drunk and party."

"Then why go? That's why people go to Vegas, to drink, party and gamble."

"I just want to be with my sister and Meagan. I want to have fun and act my age."

"Do what you want, Kate. It's obvious my opinions don't matter. You're being selfish and unreasonable. You went to the doctor and got put on birth control without talking to me about it."

"I'll still make time to talk to you, if that's what you're worried about. And it's my body, my decision. If I don't want to have another baby, that's my prerogative."

"No, it's no longer just your decision. I would've supported you if you had come to me and we talked about it like we planned, but what pisses me off is you made this decision without me. If you go to Vegas, I won't call you."

"What decisions am I allowed to make without you, Jack? You're gone more than you're here. I'm used to handling things on my own."

"No, you did this specifically to get back at me. I think in a way you blame me for what happened."

"I just don't want to have another baby, Jack. If you want a baby, get a new wife. I'm not getting pregnant again. And, are you seriously trying to make me choose between a weekend in Vegas with my sister and yours and our marriage?"

"It should be an easy choice, Kate. Keep in mind you're living with your choice. I'm sorry you have a husband that cares what you do and is just looking out for you. And for the record I don't want a new wife, I want you to stop being so damn angry at the world. He was my son too, Kate. I wanted him just as bad as you did."

"No you just want me to be at home and have no life. I've given up everything to be with you. I've left my family, my friends, and my job. I deserve a weekend of fun with my sister. You're never home with me, so am I not supposed to have fun?"

"Oh, you poor baby; we should throw you a pity parade. I seem to remember you saying you could handle my career. What, now you can't?"

"If you loved me, you'd realize that I need a weekend away."

"I'm not saying you can't have a weekend away. I'm just not comfortable with you going to Vegas while I'm deployed." He was angry with her. "When we got married, it stopped being just about you or me. It's about us, Kate. I don't know why you are so determined to go to Vegas, but do what you want. You know I don't need this added stress and worry when I'm over here. It distracts me, but hey as long as you have your fun, nothing else matters, right?"

"It's one weekend, Jack."

"I can't believe how selfish and immature you're being. Why are you suddenly like this?"

"Well I'm going to do what I want."

He was angry with her. "You usually do, don't you? You don't care or value my opinion. You've made the decision that we're not going to have kids for five damn years without even talking to me. Now you're going to go to Vegas regardless of what I think. I don't have time for this. I called to talk to my wife, not a twenty-seven year old who wants to rediscover her youth and act stupid. If you go, I won't be calling you."

"It would be nice for my husband to just say 'have fun, beautiful and be safe'."

"I don't know any man who would be comfortable with his wife running off to Vegas to party while he's on deployment. You find me one married man who's fine with that, and then maybe just maybe I'll see your point, Kate."

"Why can't you just call me when I'm in Vegas?"

"Because I don't want to hear some guy in the background trying to pick you up or you wasted beyond the point where you can't even walk or talk."

"I wouldn't do that."

"Everyone does that in Vegas."

"I wish you'd trust me."

"I do trust you, but I am not comfortable with you going to Vegas without me. So are you going to go or not?"

"I've already told my sister I would."

He was stunned. "Bye Kate. It's nice to know what your priorities are. I'm on the other side of the damn world doing my job, and if what goes on out here isn't enough, now I have to worry about my wife in Vegas, drunk and disoriented. Thanks for the extra stress." He disconnected the call. He was angry with her.

She sat at the computer. She felt terrible for arguing with him, but she did promise Lauren that she would go. She hoped he would call back and they would make up. She waited for several minutes, but it became apparent that he wasn't going to call back. She was so frustrated, she broke down into tears.

He left his bunk and went to the weight room to lift weights and do some push-ups and sit ups.

Over the next few weeks, she was growing increasingly worried about him. They hadn't talked since their argument. She had sent him an email apologizing and that she wasn't going to Las Vegas, but it went unanswered. She was desperate to tell him she was sorry for how she talked to him. He had time to call and email her, but he was still angry with her, so he didn't.

She sat at the computer and typed him a second email.

> *Dear Jack,*
>
> *This is my second email. You were right. I was being selfish, immature and unreasonable. I'm so sorry for how I was acting. I should've respected your opinion. I told Lauren that I'm not going. My marriage matters more to me than a weekend in Vegas. I'm so sorry for adding more stress to you, I'm such an idiot. I love you so much. I'm worried about you. I wish you'd call me. I hate fighting with you. I'm desperate to hear your voice and just know you're alright. I've went and talked with the chaplain. You were right, it was helpful to talk to him and let some of my anger and sorrow out. I just don't like admitting I need help. I'm still angry that I lost the baby, but I need to take care of me and get help when I need it. Please email me or call me when you can. I love you. I miss you. I'm here waiting for you. Please talk to me.*
>
> *Love you forever. Kate*

He checked his email and saw he had two unread messages from her. He was still angry with her. He logged off his computer and went to sleep. She stayed up past 3:00 a.m. hoping he would call her, but he didn't. She went to bed every night and cried herself to sleep.

The next afternoon, Denise called her to see how she was doing and if she had talked to Jack. "Hi Kate, how are you doing, sweetie?"

"Oh I'm okay. How about you? How's Bill?"

"We're great. Have you talked to Jack lately? How's he doing?" she asked.

"No I haven't."

Denise could hear in her voice that something was wrong. "Honey, is everything okay?"

She tried not to cry. "I don't know. He won't talk to me."

"What do you mean he won't talk to you?"

"We had a fight a few weeks ago. It was a stupid fight. I wanted to go to Vegas with my sister and Meagan for my sister's birthday. I told him about it and he told me he didn't want me to go. We just fought about me going. I should've just accepted he didn't want me to go. I cancelled my plans with my sister and Meagan, and I've sent him several emails apologizing and begging him to call me or email me, but he hasn't."

Denise knew the pressures of holding everything together while her husband was deployed. She had said hurtful things to Bill while he was on deployment and then regretted them later. She knew what Kate was going through. She could hear the sincerity in her voice when she admitted she was wrong and that she loved him.

"Do you want me to talk to him?"

"No. That would just make things worse."

"Well, I know he loves you. He's just being stubborn like his father. I bet he'll call you in the next few days."

She hoped he would. Six weeks had gone by and they still had not talked and resolved their fight. She had sent him three more emails apologizing to him and begging him to talk to her, but each email went unanswered. She was hurt. She wondered if their marriage was in trouble. She was so upset that she had lost six pounds. She didn't know what to do. It's not like she could go to Afghanistan and confront him. All she could do was wait and hope he'd call or write her.

It was midnight in Afghanistan. He tiredly walked into his bunk and opened his laptop. He saw he had five emails from her. He read each of them. He began to type an email, but after writing *Dear Kate* he deleted the words. He looked at the blank screen and thought about what he wanted to say to her. He began to type.

> *Kate,*
>
> *I really haven't had any desire to talk to you. I've been too angry and I knew if I did talk to you that I would say something I'd regret, so it's been best for me to just ignore you. I'm okay, so you can stop wasting your time worrying about me. You should've gone to Vegas, that way you can tell me if it was worth our marriage or not. We'll talk when I get back.*

She checked her email. Her heart began to pound excitedly when she saw she had an email from him. Reading it, she sat shaking from fear. He had never been so harsh or so blunt with her. Though she was relieved to know he was okay, she also felt ashamed of herself. Tears rolled down her cheeks as she turned off the computer and continued to clean the house. She was so upset that she ran to their bedroom and put on her jogging clothes and went for a five mile run. She knew she had put their marriage in a difficult place and now she had to figure out how to fix it, if she could fix it.

Her friends and family could sense something was seriously wrong with her. She avoided their phone calls. She began working the overnight shifts more. She was losing weight. Her friends at the hospital wondered if she was eating. She hadn't sent Jack anymore emails after the one she received. She honestly didn't know what to say to him, so her best course of action was to do nothing.

Now May 2008, it had been eight weeks since they've spoken to each other. She thought of him and their marriage every day. She still hoped he would talk to her, but every day she was met with disappointment when her inbox showed no new emails from him. All that showed was the one she received from him. She made a decision to not check her emails anymore. If he didn't want to talk to her, then she wouldn't talk to him. It was a childish course of action, but the silent treatment has always been an effective tool in love and war.

She sat at a table in the hospital cafeteria eating alone. Her good friend Nicole saw her. "Hey Kate, may I sit with you?"

She smiled. "Sure Nicole."

Nicole sat down. "Kate, is everything okay? The past two months you've been real distant."

"Yeah, everything is fine. I just have a lot on my plate." she lied.

"You know you can talk to me. I know what you're going through." Nicole's husband was also in the Army and away on deployment.

To keep herself from bursting into tears, she made herself laugh. "I'm fine, I promise. Every deployment presents new challenges, but I'm fine."

"Are you and Jack having problems?"

Nailing the issue right on the head, she could feel her façade crumble away. She had to look away to avoid crying. "No, we're fine." she lied.

"Are you sure?"

"Nicole, it was good to talk with you, I have to go." She excused herself to a restroom and cried privately.

In June, Colonel Mitchell allowed an embedded reporter from the New York Times to interview his men. Her name was Rachel. She was in her late twenties and looked remarkably a lot like Kate. She had an instant attraction to Jack. He was a strong, handsome, Green Beret carrying an M4 assault rifle and was in uniform every day. He couldn't deny an attraction to her, simply because she reminded him so much of Kate.

Over a few days of her being present in the camp, they spent a lot of time together talking and laughing. Tom and the rest of the team had noticed a serious change in him. Usually, all he talked about on deployment was getting back to Kate, but in the last two months, they hadn't heard him mention her name hardly at all. He was very distant from his guys. Tom sensed that he and Kate were having marital issues. He was stunned to watch him and Rachel flirt with each other.

Her assignment was to write an article on how Special Forces soldiers and their families cope with frequent deployments, but instead of interviewing members of Alpha, Bravo, or Charlie Teams, she found more of a story spending quality time with just Jack. They both flirted with each other like crazy. They had a lot in common and they talked a lot.

It was his thirty-fourth birthday. He was sitting outside smoking a cigarette alone and thinking about Kate. He was spinning his wedding ring. He took it off and looked at the engraving 'I'm Waiting for You'. He wondered should he call her and make up with her or should he continue to ignore her to prove his point.

Rachel walked in to the Rec Room and saw Tom and Jake sitting at the table looking at car magazines. "Hey have y'all seen Jack?"

"No."

"Oh, well do you know where he might be?" she asked. She wore a pair of jean shorts, cowboy boots and a tank top. The soldiers found her attire to be unprofessional, and it was hard for them to take her seriously.

Tom looked at her. "You realize he's married, right? When men wear a ring on their left hand it generally means they're married."

"Yeah, I know he's married."

"I think it's time you packed up your little interview gig and went back to the states. It's clear what you're really out here for."

Jake looked at him and wanted to laugh, but didn't.

"And what is that supposed to mean?" she asked.

"Can I be totally honest with you and you not burst into tears and pull all that female crap?" She looked shocked. "I'll take that as a yes. You're one of those women who get off on what we do out here. You're attracted to the hero/protector type of man. You think we're a bunch of playboys and you like the prestige. I think your little interview gig is a front. You go from outpost to outpost sleeping with single soldiers and maybe even some married ones. You take advantage of the fact that we're away from our wives and girlfriends. Frankly, I think you're a slut. If you were really out here for a story, you wouldn't be dressed like this, you would act professional and you would interview more than just one person. Would you like me to tell you about Jack's wife? Let me just put it to you this way, you aren't even close to measuring up to her. You've got some major competition, and I'd say she has a head start since she's married to him."

She was so speechless that she just walked away. She walked outside and found Jack sitting on the picnic table, looking at a picture of Kate.

"Hey…" she said.

"Hey, what's up?"

"Oh you're buddy Tom just called me a slut."

He looked at her in disbelief. "That doesn't sound like him."

"He did. He accused me of going from outpost to outpost and sleeping with single and married soldiers."

"Do you want me to talk to him?"

"Yeah, would you? That would be great." She watched him smoke a cigarette. "Are you thinking about your wife?"

"Yeah, I am. Today is my birthday."

"Happy Birthday, how young are you?" she joked.

"I'm thirty-four."

"Wow, you're only five years older than me. What does your wife normally do for you on your birthday?"

"If I'm deployed, she'll send me a big box of my favorite snacks and a cake-in-a-jar of my mom's double fudge chocolate cake recipe."

"And if you're home?"

"She'll cook for me, bake me a real cake and let me watch sports all day."

"How long have you been married?"

"Two years in October."

She could hear the stress and tension in his voice. "I know it's none of my business, but are you happy with her?"

He didn't know how to answer. "I haven't been lately."

"What happened?"

"We lost our baby and after that everything changed. I think in a way she shut down."

"I'm so sorry, are you two going to try to have another baby when you get back?"

"I don't know. She says she doesn't want to have another baby."

"Well, you deserve a woman who can give you as many kids as you want."

He looked down at her. He was attracted to her. She was beautiful, nice, and smart. She had a good career. He tried to ignore his attraction to her, when he looked at her, he saw only Kate.

She touched his hand. "This is going to be out there, but I find you really attractive and we seem to really connect. I was hoping you'd want to hook up later tonight? Just for one night, no strings attached. No one has to know."

He was shocked. He instantly thought of Kate and how he promised her he'd never hurt her. "Uh, I'm flattered but no. I'm married."

"Come on, just one time. It's been a long time for me and you look like you could use a little distraction from everything out here. It's your birthday, so let me do something for you." Seeing his reluctance, she kissed his lips in hopes to sway him.

Tom had walked out and saw them kissing. He was stunned and naturally thought the worst of Jack. He thought that Jack was going to start an affair and throw his marriage with Kate away.

He pushed her back. "I told you I'm married." He couldn't deny that he was tempted, but there wasn't any way he was going to risk his marriage.

She laughed. "I don't want you to leave your wife and marry me." She groped him. "I just want to have some fun."

He was beyond uncomfortable. He wasn't this type of man. He was honorable. He pushed her back again. "Rachel, I'm not the type of man who cheats on his wife."

"I can tell you're attracted to me, Jack. I see the way you look at me." She tried to kiss him again, but he moved away.

"I'm more attracted to my wife."

She was stunned that he had turned her down. "I cannot believe you're turning me down. I thought this is what you wanted."

"No, this is not acceptable. I think you should leave."

"Lucky for you, I'm here for the next two weeks."

"That privilege will be revoked once I inform my chain of command on your behavior and your proposition."

She took his honorableness and refusal as code for her to try harder. He walked away to his bunk. Tom marched in. "I need to talk to you now." he demanded.

He had never seen Tom so angry. "Okay, what's going on?" he asked.

"Whatever is going on between you and Rachel, you need to end it now. I can't believe you would throw everything you have with Kate away over an argument."

"Let me stop you right there…" he interrupted. "There is nothing going on between me and Rachel. Yes, Kate and I are having a bit of a rough patch, but I would never jeopardize my marriage especially with a girl like that."

"I just saw you two kissing. You're walking a dangerous thin line. You're one step away from having an affair."

"She kissed me. It was in no way mutual."

"I'd hate to see you ruin your marriage just for a woman who promises you a great one night stand."

"I'm not going to have an affair, Tom. I love Kate, and I would never do that to her."

"What is going on with you and Kate?"

"Tom, I appreciate your concern, but my marriage is between me and Kate, and it's none of your business."

"Hey Jack, you got a package from Kate." Luke said.

He walked into the Rec Room and saw the box sitting on the table. He took it back to his bunk. Cutting the tape with his knife, he opened it and saw she had sent him another cake-in-a-jar with his favorite inside. She had also sent him razors, shaving cream, and other toiletries. She sent him more pictures of them together and a heartfelt love letter in her handwriting.

Later that night, he was in his bunk looking at the picture of Kate he always carried. He heard a knock at his door. "Come in." He thought it was Tom or one of the guys. He was surprised to see Rachel.

"Rachel, you need to leave. This is very inappropriate."

She smiled at him shirtless and still wearing his ACU pants and combat boots. Her attraction to him escalated. "I just wanted to apologize to you for how I acted today. I was way out of line and very inappropriate. Are you still going to talk with your command?"

"Yes, I have to. Your behavior and proposition was completely inappropriate and unacceptable. I have to tell my command to protect myself, my marriage, and my career, but I do accept your apology. Now please leave."

She sat down on his bed. "This bed is comfortable." He felt extremely uncomfortable. She saw the picture of Kate in his hands. "Is that your wife?"

"Get out."

"I'll leave after you tell me why you won't sleep with me. I've never been rejected before. I usually have guys chasing me around the corner and down the block, but you are the first guy to ever reject me even though I know you're attracted to me."

"I can't and won't do this. I love my wife."

"I commend you for being faithful to your wife, but how do you know she doesn't have affairs while you're gone? Why shouldn't you be able to have some fun if she is?"

"You don't know her."

"She's a woman, isn't she? She gets lonely when you're gone for long periods of time."

He stood in front of her. "Rachel, I want you to leave now,"

She stood up and touched his hand. "Are you really playing this hard to get? I know you want me." She pulled her shirt over her head.

Wrapping her arms around his neck, she said, "I bet I could change your mind." She kissed him. This time he did not resist her. She fondled him.

Tom walked into his bunk. "Hey, we're watching…" he stopped seeing Jack and Rachel kissing. He quickly pulled away from her. "Sorry to have interrupted."

He saw the look on Tom's face and walked past her and walked outside. "Tom, wait!" Tom was angry with him. He shoved him against the wall. "What the hell is your problem?" he asked, shoving him back.

"You were going to sleep with her weren't you?"

"No, I wasn't."

"I just walked in on you and her kissing and her top was off! I saw the look on your face, Jack. You've crossed a line, and you can never go back. Are you prepared to lose everything you have with Kate for a one night stand? Because I promise you, you will lose Kate."

"I'm not dealing with this, Tom. From now on, we're on a professional level, no longer a friendship."

"Yeah, I won't be friends with someone who cheats on his wife."

"I haven't cheated on Kate."

"Yeah you did. You know you being a strong Christian you should look up what Exodus 20:14 says. In case you've forgotten, it's that you shall not commit adultery. You should tell Kate."

He walked away from him to his bunk. She was sitting on his bed, looking at his pictures of him and Kate. "You need to leave. I can't do this. I won't do this. I love my wife. Get the hell out of my bunk now."

She laughed and rolled her eyes. "Fine, I'm tired of chasing you. It's too bad. You look like you would've been really great." She slipped her shirt back on and walked out. He slammed the door.

He looked at his computer. He had a picture of Kate beside his computer. He saw his Bible beside his bed on a milk crate serving as a make shift nightstand. He picked up his Bible and read Exodus 20:14. He cried as he felt conviction. He knew he was in the wrong. He had been tempted by another woman and failed to get himself out of a potentially compromising situation. Though he hadn't pursued the woman and adamantly professed his love for Kate, he didn't stop her when she kissed him. He prayed and asked God for guidance.

After praying for nearly an hour, he felt God tell him to talk to Kate. He opened his lap top and saw the five emails she had sent him. He read them. He logged onto Skype and called her. She was home, cleaning. She had to do something and not be left to just sit and think. She saw he was calling her. He saw she was logged on. It was midnight in Afghanistan.

She ignored the call. He typed to her: *Please talk to me baby. I've been an idiot. I'm sorry. I love you.* He called her again. She looked at the screen and contemplated whether she should answer. She wanted to talk to him, but he really hurt her. She felt God tell her to talk to him and forgive him.

She answered the call. He smiled at her. "Hi, baby."

"Hi."

"How are you doing?"

"I'm fine. How are you?"

"I'm missing you so much. I'm so sorry for being a jerk and not talking to you for so long. I'm an idiot."

She could see he had been crying and something was going on with him. He looked nervous to talk to her. "Jack, what's going on?"

"What do you mean?"

"You've been crying, you're talking fast, and you're nervous."

"I need to tell you something…" He felt conviction. He knew he had to tell her the truth. He didn't want to be like Kyle. "Baby, I don't even know how to start,"

She knew it was something bad. "Just tell me, Jack."

"Okay, there's this reporter here. Uh…her name is Rachel."

"I don't care what her name is! Have you slept with her?" she snapped at him.

"No, baby I haven't. I wouldn't do that to you." he said seriously.

"What have you done with her?"

He covered his face. He knew this was going to destroy her and their marriage. "Earlier today she asked me if I wanted to hook up with her just one time. I refused. Then she kissed me. I pushed her away and told her I'm married and I walked away. Tonight, I'm in my bunk lying here. She knocks on my door…"

She knew something bad happened. "Go on…"

"…She came in and still tried to get me to sleep with her. She took off her shirt, fondled me and we kissed."

She had tears rolling down her face. "Where did she touch you?"

"Below my belt…"

She could feel her heart break. "Were you attracted to her? Did you want to sleep with her?" She saw the look on his face. She saw he <u>was</u> attracted to another woman. She was stunned. She covered her mouth as tears streamed more frequently down her face.

Hearing and seeing her cry made him feel even worse. "Baby, I don't want to make you feel worse."

"Just tell me, Jack. Were you attracted to her?"

"Yes, I was." He saw the look on her face. "I'm so sorry,"

"Is she still there in camp?"

"Yes, unfortunately she is."

Desperate to hold her emotions in until after they got off the phone, she felt they were surfacing on their own. "Maybe you should go sleep with her, and let me know if she was worth our marriage. I have to go, Jack."

"No, baby, please don't go. Talk to me."

"I have nothing to say to you right now."

"I know I've messed up, but I still love you, and I don't want to lose you."

He could see her shaking. "Maybe you should've thought more about me and less about her and we wouldn't be in this situation. I need time to think. I need to figure out how to process this because I never in a million years thought you would ever hurt me and betray me especially like this. Go sleep with her, Jack. At least you won't have to be celibate for four years to be with her. She's guaranteeing you one night." She was crying, but bravely trying to keep her feelings inside, but she was failing to. "When you come home, this house will be empty, and I won't be here."

"Kate, I love you and I want you. I don't want to be with anyone else."

"We both know that's a lie."

"I will do anything to fix this. I will go AWOL to come home to you. I will get out of the Army if it meant that I didn't lose you."

"You love the Army."

"I love you more."

She wiped her tears. "No, you don't. You've broken my heart. As if ignoring me for two months didn't break it enough, but admitting you kissed another woman, letting her touch you, and that you saw her breasts and wanted to sleep with her, you've shattered it. You are just like Kyle. Goodbye, Jack. Happy Birthday,"

"No wait, Kate. Don't leave. I love you." She disconnected the call. He bowed his head. "Lord, help me. I messed up and I'm sorry. Please don't let me lose her. I need her."

The alarm sounded. The shouting of yelling 'Incoming, Incoming, Incoming...' had every man scrambling to battle stations. He grabbed his weapon and several boxes of ammunition. He threw on his battle gear. He had to put his shambled marriage aside and focus on surviving.

The outpost was in Nuristan province of Afghanistan. The outpost had forty-eight U.S. Special Forces and only twenty-four Afghan National Army soldiers. The base had close air support. The remote outpost and its observation posts were surrounded by two hundred, heavily armed Taliban guerilla fighters. The outpost was taking heavy mortar fire and heavy RPG fire. Much of the equipment was damaged.

He and Tom were fighting side by side. "Where's the SAW?" he yelled.

Tom handed it to him. "Where are you going?"

"I'll be right back." The outpost was very close to being overrun. He climbed the watch tower and fired at the sea of enemy fighters. Seeing Jack firing and killing many enemy fighters, a fighter fired an RPG at him.

"RPG, Jack! Get down!" Tom yelled. He saw the man shooting the RPG. It was coming straight for him. He jumped from the twenty foot tower. The tower exploded. He landed on his back, on top of a Humvee. Tom ran to him. "Are you alright?"

"Yeah, that was a long way down." They were under heavy personal fire. The fighters broke through U.S. lines. It was now very dangerous to rely on air support since now the fighters were now inside the base. The fighters entered the main base before artillery and Kiowa air support arrived in their aid.

After the attack, the soldiers surveyed the damage to their camp. Nine U.S. soldiers were killed and twenty-seven were wounded, including Jack. He had shrapnel injuries from the RPG explosion that he was lucky to miss. Four Afghan National Army soldiers were killed. This was a well-coordinated attack.

As Jamal patched up his injuries, Jack thought of Kate. Jamal saw he was lost in thought. Most of the team members knew about the Rachel incident. Luckily the communications tower was not hit in the attack, so they still had the ability to connect to the internet and call their families. He logged onto Skype and called her. She didn't answer. He called repeatedly, still no answer.

He decided to leave a message. "Hey baby, I know you don't want to talk me. I wish you would. Hearing your voice would make this day better. I want you to know Kate, that I love you very much. You're the best person in my life, and I know I don't deserve your love or forgiveness, but I am really sorry about what happened. I never meant to hurt you, baby. Please email me or call me when you get this. I love you. You're my heart and my home."

He went and talked with Colonel Mitchell. He told him about Rachel. He confessed everything. She was sent back to Kandahar and then home to the states.

Kate was at home, lying on the sofa watching their wedding video. She was crying listening to them exchange vows. She prayed. "Lord, help me. I don't know what to do. I love him, but he really hurt me. Help us get past this. Please help me forgive him. I miss him so much. Please keep him safe. I would be devastated if something happened to him."

If only she knew she almost lost him in the base attack. The soldiers at the remote outpost held memorials for their fallen brothers. It was nightfall; the stars were visible. He and Tom were sitting outside on the flight pad by a few dozen feet from their air craft smoking cigarettes. "Does Kate know you were injured?"

"I don't think she'd care at this point. I told her about Rachel. Things are really messed up, Tom. I don't know what to do."

"What was going on with you and Kate before the Rachel incident?"

"It was stupid. I should've just let her do what she wanted to do and we wouldn't be where we are now. We were arguing about her going to the chaplain and talking about losing the baby. Then she told me that she was going to go to Vegas for her sister's birthday weekend. I told her that I wasn't comfortable with her being in Vegas without me and especially while I'm on deployment. I told her I didn't need the extra stress and worry. You know, I could picture a couple of guys trying to take advantage of her, getting her drunk, and taking her back to their hotel, and I couldn't handle that."

"I understand that."

"I told her that if she went that I wouldn't call her again."

"So, she went?"

"No, she sent me an email telling me she was sorry for upsetting me and that she didn't go to Vegas."

"So how long has it been since you've two talked?"

"Before the Rachel incident, it was just two months."

"So are you two over, or are y'all going to try to work it out?"

"I want to work things out, but I'm afraid she may want to call it quits."

She had shut down after talking with him. She didn't accept any phone calls. She kept herself busy. She didn't check her email. It hurt her not to talk to him, but hearing his voice and thinking about him and that woman was too much.

Tom had called Paige and asked her to go by Jack and Kate's to check on her. She went to the house and opened the front door. She found Kate packing up all her things in big brown boxes. The wedding pictures and all the others had been taken down. She looked rough. Paige saw how swollen her eyes were. The house was trashed and there were empty whiskey bottles on the table and coffee table. "What's going on Kate?" She ignored her. "Sweetie, what's going on? Why are you packing your things?" Paige saw she was heartbroken. She was crying as she taped up a box.

"It's over and I'm leaving." she said.

Paige was stunned. "Oh my-gosh, sweetie, what happened?"

She shook her head and walked away to the bedroom to finish pulling all of her clothes out of the closet and dresser drawers. Paige followed her. "Kate, talk to me."

"I really can't talk about it, Paige, but it's over. I want out. I'm going back to Dallas."

Paige was stunned that Jack and Kate, the last two people you'd ever suspect to have problems in their blissful marriage, were in fact calling it quits. Paige hugged her as she sobbed on her shoulder. She called Tom and told him what was going on with Kate.

In Afghanistan, Jack was in the weight room. He was lifting weights, doing push-ups, pull-ups, and sit-ups. Tom walked in and saw him. He had just finished talking with Paige.

Jack was very frustrated, angry, hurt, and upset. All he could think about on his down time was getting home to her so he could fix their marriage. "What's up?" he asked, lifting weights.

"Oh, I just talked to Paige."

"Did she go check on her?"

"Yeah she did…"

He sat up from the weight bench. "And what's going on?"

"I don't know how to say this, but she was packing up all of her things and the wedding pictures were taken down. Paige said she's never seen the house look so trashed and she looks terrible. Paige suspects she hasn't eaten in days. There were empty whiskey bottles everywhere."

Jack felt as if a dagger had stabbed him in the chest. He was hurt. Not only did she want to leave him, but it was unbearable to know she wasn't okay and that <u>he</u> caused it. At that point he thought about jumping on a C-130 cargo plane, going AWOL, and getting home to her.

"Well it looks as if my marriage is officially over. I've ruined everything. I'm stuck out here. I can't fix anything from here. She won't take my calls or answer my emails. What do I do?" Tom felt bad for him. "How could I have been so stupid? I've hurt the one person in this world I swore I would never hurt. I betrayed her."

"You had a moment of weakness, and you confessed to her about it. At least you told her."

"I should never have been weak in the first place. I was angry at her and that anger caused me to be weak and stupid."

Jake walked over to Tom and Jack. "What's going on?"

"If you guys don't mind, I think I'm going to work out alone."

"Yeah, I'll talk to you later," Tom said.

Jake wondered what was going on. "What's going on?" he asked Tom quietly as they walked back to the TOC.

"He and Kate are over."

Jake was shocked. "Is this all over what happened with him and Rachel?"

Tom nodded. "I knew that girl was trouble."

Jake had a confession to make. Later that evening, he walked to Jack's bunk and knocked on the door. Jack was sitting on his cot looking at his favorite picture of Kate. Jack noticed him and quickly put the picture away. "What's going on?"

"Can this be off the record and strictly between friends?"

He looked at him curiously. "Yeah sure, what's up?"

"I know what you're going through, Jack."

"You know what I'm going through with what?"

"I know what you and Kate are going through because Jenny and I have been there…" He looked at him. He knew he couldn't deny it. "…On my third deployment, Jenny and I were having marital issues and money problems, a bad combination. Anyways, on my third tour, I got involved with this nurse. At first it was a harmless flirtation, but it quickly got very physical, very. It went on for almost two months, and finally the guilt caught up to me and I ended it."

"Did you tell Jenny or did she find out?"

"No, I manned up and I told her the truth. I admitted everything that happened. I nearly destroyed her and our marriage. She wanted to divorce me and take the girls from me, but I couldn't lose my family."

"But you and Jenny act so happy…"

"Yeah, we do, but we have to work extra hard to stay that way. The damage I caused can never be erased, but I did regain her trust, her respect, and eventually I got my family back. I regret it every day. I ask for forgiveness every day. It was definitely not worth it."

He was stunned. "How did you convince Jenny to stay with you?"

"Oh, I didn't convince her. I had fully accepted that I had caused this, so I have to live with it. But I remember I had moved out of our house and into an apartment in town. I was living off of Pork & Beans and Kool-Aid and Styrofoam plates and cups. She came over and we had a long talk. She told me that when we got married, we vowed to stay together for better and for worse. We were at our worse. She told me that she forgave me for being unfaithful and that she still loved me. Then she saw I was eating Pork & Beans. She laughed and told me to come home and she'd fix me a real dinner."

"That's great for you man, I never suspected that."

"Jenny and I are very private people, but when I heard about what happened with you and Rachel, I thought maybe my story could help you. So does Kate know everything?"

"Yes, I told her everything. I couldn't lie to her."

"How did she take it?"

"She was devastated. Apparently she's packing up her things and wants to leave. It seems like we're done."

"Hopefully we get home soon so you two can work things out."

"So, how did you and Jenny work things out?"

"It took a long time. We had weekly counseling sessions with the chaplain. I worked every day to make Jenny see me as the man she used to see, the man she married, and make her fall back in love with me."

"I think that's what I'm going to have to do with Kate, but if Kate isn't willing to work things out, I may have to just accept that I gambled with my marriage and I lost everything."

"I don't think so. I think Kate is just angry, hurt and scared. I know Kate. She is a lot like Jenny. When that woman looks at you, it's obvious that you're her hero."

"Not anymore…" He and Jake continued to talk.

In October 2008, their second wedding anniversary was approaching. She was miserable. She could hardly eat. She confided in Lauren about what happened. Lauren was stunned. She swore Lauren to confidence. She and Jack hadn't talked since his birthday.

The Green Berets were still in the Nuristan province. It was midnight. He was sitting in his bunk looking at the pictures of him and Kate. He got on the internet and ordered four dozen pink roses and had them delivered on the day of their anniversary, the 28th.

On their anniversary, she called in sick. She was packing up more of her stuff. Most of her stuff was boxed up in the garage. She had movers coming at the first of November to move her back to Dallas. The doorbell rang. She wondered who could be at the door. Opening the door, she was surprised to see four delivery men each holding a vase of twelve beautiful hot pink roses.

"Are you Mrs. Kate Hamilton?"

"Yes…"

"These are for you. Please sign here."

She signed for them. She took each vase and placed them inside. She read each card. The first card read: *"I Jack David Hamilton chose you Katherine Elizabeth Johnson as my wedded wife."*

The second card read: *"I promised to love you, comfort you and be true to you all the days of my life."*

The third card read: *"I gave you that ring as a symbol of my solemn vow to you and the Lord."*

The fourth card read: *"And with that ring, I thee wed. I love you so much baby. I'm so sorry I've hurt you. Please talk to me."*

She was crying. He had just recited their wedding vows. She looked at the computer and then back at the cards.

Logging onto Skype, she called him. She didn't know why she was, but she felt something inside her guiding her, steering her. It was nearly midnight in Afghanistan. He was lying on his cot, looking at her picture and thinking about her. He saw she was calling. His heart nearly leapt out of his chest.

He answered. He was so happy to talk to her. He hadn't heard her voice in so long. "Hi, baby."

Seeing him, immediately brought tears in her eyes and a knot in her chest. She felt heartache, and at the same time, she felt everything she had felt every time she had seen him before, warmth, joy, happiness and extreme attraction. But though she loved him with all her heart, she was very hurt also. "Hi, I just got your flowers and the cards."

"Did you like them?"

Wiping the tears from her eyes, she smiled, "Yeah, they are beautiful."

He knew he had severely hurt her. He broke his promise. But he was determined to set things right and win her back. "Much like my beautiful wife, I'm so happy to talk to you. Happy Anniversary baby, I know I've made some monumental mistakes, but I love you so much. I can't lose you baby."

She was crying. "Jack, I'm moving back to Dallas. I'm trying to get my old job back at Medical City."

He was shocked. "I know you're mad at me. I know I've hurt you and damaged our trust, but why are you throwing away our marriage?"

"I didn't throw it away. You did. I don't know what else to do."

"We could work this out. I don't want to lose you, Kate."

"I don't think we can, Jack. The trust has been shattered. I never thought you could ever betray me or disappoint me, but you have."

"I'm disappointed in myself, but I promise I can work to get your trust back. I'll do anything."

"I just need to be alone and think about things."

"That's not the answer. We're apart more than together. We need to be together. What if we took a vacation somewhere, just the two of us? We can go anywhere in the world you want to go."

"I don't think so."

"Kate, I love you. I'm so sorry for what's happened. If I could go back in time, I'd change that. I wouldn't make that mistake. I'm willing to do anything to save our marriage."

She wiped tears from her cheeks. "I love you too. I'll always love you, Jack. And I'll always be here for you, but this isn't going to work."

"Have you filed for divorce?"

"No, I want to try living in Dallas and see how things go."

"Are you going to start dating other guys?"

"No, I have no intention of dating anyone. I just need time to think."

He had tears in his eyes. He felt as if someone was standing on his throat and kicking him in the chest. "This is killing me you know that? Losing you is killing me."

She was crying also. "This is killing me too, Jack, but you'll be okay. I'm easily replaceable."

"No you're not, Kate. You're irreplaceable."

"We need to do this to see if we both want different things."

She saw the tears in his eyes. "I know what I want. I want you. I want to stay married and have a family with you and grow old with you. What do you want?"

"We can't always have what we want."

He looked at her brown curled hair frame her face, her big brown eyes. "You're so beautiful. I'm truly the biggest idiot in the world to have ruined what we had. I'm sorry, Kate."

"I know you're sorry, Jack, but no matter how many times you apologize or how many pink roses you have delivered is going to change or make me forget what happened."

"Please don't leave me."

She was crying. "I wish I could stay but I can't."

"I guess I'll rent a hotel room when I come home. How are you getting back to Dallas? Where are you going to live?"

"I have movers coming next week. I'll put my stuff in storage in Dallas and stay with my parents until I can find a place."

"Your parents are going to hate me."

She smiled. "No, I won't let them."

"Your dad may kill me."

She smiled. "No, I won't let him."

"My parents are going to be so angry with me. I'm a failure. I'm so sorry I failed you, Kate. I never meant for any of this to happen."

"No, you're not a failure, Jack. I'll always care for you and love you, but let's just end this amicably and try to be friends."

"I don't want to be your friend, baby. I want to be your husband."

She wiped her tears. "In life, you have to realize it's not always what *you* want but what is. For example, I don't want you to be attracted to another woman. I don't want you kissing and seeing her half naked, and I definitely don't want another woman to touch you, but I have to deal with what is. I know you were angry with me and that is part of the reason you participated in this. You wanted to get back at me and you succeeded."

"I would do anything to take it back."

She wiped her tears. "I know, but you can't, Jack." She looked up at the clock. "I have to work. I need to get off here and get ready."

"Please don't go."

"I have to, Jack."

"Wow, we got married two years ago today and on our anniversary you decide to divorce me."

She smiled with tears running down her face. "I haven't decided whether I want to divorce you yet. I just want to be separated. Thank you for the beautiful flowers and the very sweet cards. Stay safe."

That was the first time since they've met she hadn't asked him to promise her he'd come back to her or told him she loved him. He wiped his tears. "I love you, Kate."

"You know I love you too, but I don't want to say it. I need to get used to not saying it."

"I'm coming home to you."

She smiled. "I won't be here. Bye, Jack." She disconnected the call. She immediately broke down. She didn't have to work. She only told him that so he wouldn't see her break. Staring at a blank screen, he was devastated that he had lost her. He grabbed his Bible and began reading it for strength. There was no way he'd get through losing her without God's help. She cried on their bed until she fell asleep.

She rescheduled the movers for later in the month and picked up more hours at the hospital, she would need extra cash to pay her expenses. She had made up her mind that she was only living off her salary, not his. She still paid their bills, but she was saving her money. She was desperate to leave that house. The memories of them making love in every room after moving in, cooking together, cuddling on the sofa and watching a movie and bubble baths together were just too much for her.

Three weeks later, Alpha, Bravo, and Charlie Teams were headed home. He was desperate to see her and talk her into staying with him and working things out. After twenty hours in the air, the plane finally landed on Fort Bragg. He hurried off the plane. The teams had to be debriefed. After being debriefed, he sprinted to his truck and drove to the house they had made their home. He saw her black 2008 Ford Fusion car parked in the driveway. He was relieved she had not already left for Dallas. He didn't know what he was going to say to her. He pulled in and parked in the driveway. He saw their American flag bolted to their house.

He sat in his truck and looked at their house. "Lord, I'm begging for your help, I've really messed up. If there's any way for Kate and me to save our marriage, please I'm begging you to allow her to forgive me. It's going to take a miracle after what I've done for her to see that I love her. I want her. I want her to see me as the man I used to be. She never saw any bad in me. Lord, please help me."

He was nervous about how she would react to seeing him, what she would say. He knew he had to face it and take it like a man. He wanted her back. He stepped out of his truck and walked up to the door. He unlocked the door with his key. She was moving the numerous taped up boxes to the garage. He heard her struggling in the hallway near the garage. He watched her carry a heavy box into the garage. She saw him and stood frozen. He smiled at her. The butterflies in her stomach stirred up, she was insanely attracted to him, like always. His smile made her heart pound excitedly.

"You're back." she said. She wore a pair of shorts and a sleeveless shirt. She was barefoot. She had barely any makeup on and her hair was pulled back in a messy bun. Like always, she always took his breath away. All he wanted to do was hold her, kiss her and make love to her.

"Yeah, I just got in. How are you doing?" He smiled at her hair falling down against her neck and shoulders. He was very attracted to her.

Boomer ran to him and started jumping up on him and licking his hands. He was so happy.

"I'm okay, I guess," she said.

He walked towards her. "You look beautiful."

She smiled. "Thanks." She avoided eye contact with him. She knew if she looked into those eyes, she'd surrender.

"Can we talk?"

"What do we possibly have to talk about?"

"I want to talk about us." She turned and folded her arms across her chest. "Please Kate. Please just give me five minutes."

"Okay…"

"I don't blame you for hating me. I hate myself. Though I did not sleep with her, I feel guilty and ashamed for even thinking about it and letting my guard down. I love you so much. I can't imagine living without you. I want you and only you for the rest of my life. I'm begging you to please forgive me and give me a second chance."

She looked down. Tears rolled down her cheeks. He slowly walked towards her. He was desperate to touch her. "Kate, you're my heart and my home."

She looked at him. "Do you have any idea how badly you've hurt me? I gave you everything. I trusted you. I believed you when you told me that you'd never hurt me like he did. How do we move forward from here, Jack?"

They stood face to face. He touched and held her hand. Feeling his touch, she wanted him, but wasn't going to forgive him that easily. "I know I've hurt you, and I know it's going to be a long road, but I'm willing to work very hard to win your trust, your love, and your respect back. I'll prove to you every day that I'll never make that mistake again."

She looked up in his eyes. He tried to hug her, but she hit his chest. He looked in her eyes, the pain he had caused. He tried to hug her a second time, but she hit his chest again. He wasn't going to give up. She hit him repeatedly until he wrapped his arms around her and held her against him. Smelling him and feeling him, she surrendered and wrapped her arms around him. She cried on his shoulder. He smelled her hair, honeysuckle and jasmine.

"I need you. I can't let you go." he whispered against her hair. She continued to cry as he held her. "I love you so much, Kate."

He hugged her tightly as he kissed her head. She looked up at him. "I love you too."

Seeing the tears run down her cheeks, he touched her face and smoothed the tears away with his thumb. She looked at his lips and then back up into his eyes. She wrapped her arms around his neck, stood on her tip toes and kissed his lips. They held each other tightly and kissed passionately. He pinned her against the garage wall and pressed his body up against hers. She jumped up in his arms and wrapped her legs around his waist. She took off his worn Oklahoma Sooners cap and placed it on her head. She smiled down at him and said, "Welcome home soldier."

He kissed her lips and then her neck. She closed her eyes as she held him. She was relieved he came back to her. He carried her to their bedroom. He kicked the door closed, leaving Boomer on the other side in the hallway. Laying her down on the bed, his dog tags hung and clanged together. She smiled up at him while pulling the chain of his dog tags down to her.

"Tonight, soldier you're mine." They kissed. The sun was setting. The stars were visible against a periwinkle sky. They were kissing passionately and holding each other tight, under the sheets.

She kissed his shrapnel scars. They made fulfilling, enticing love. Afterwards, they laid in bed wrapped up in the bed sheets and holding each other. She laid on his chest, listening to his heartbeat.

"What are you thinking about?" he asked running his fingertips down her bare back.

She looked up at him. "I'm just happy you're home." He brushed her curled hair out of her face. "I love you, Jack."

"I love you too, baby." They laid in bed and talked and laughed for nearly an hour. She changed into a pair of gym shorts and one of his Oklahoma Sooners T-shirts. She never wore her Texas shirts anymore. They went into the kitchen. She began to make them something to eat for dinner. They ate dinner together, drank a bottle of wine and cuddled on the sofa while watching a movie. She fell asleep with his strong arms wrapped around her. He looked down at her and smiled. He kissed her head and covered them with a sofa blanket. He silently thanked God for helping him. He vowed that he would never put his marriage at risk again. He and Tom talked and fixed their friendship.

13

IN MAY 2009, American and Afghan commandoes launched a daring pre-dawn strike. Their target was an open-aired drug market in central Helmand Province. When they entered, they expected to be met with heavy resistance but it was quiet. Tom was unnerved by the lack of enemy fire.

"Something isn't right here, Jack." he said.

"I know it's too quiet."

"It's way too quiet. Something is up." The calm disappears in a barge of gunfire and mortar rounds. U.S. Special Forces were taking heavy fire.

"I'm coming in next to you, Sam," Brad said on the roof of the building.

The rural area had been under Taliban rule for nearly a year. The insurgency had thrived from the money made from the booming opiates business. This market was the heart of the narcotics trade. Insurgents were firing from inside buildings. Bullets were whizzing by the soldiers as they collected the drugs. The street value for the opium taken by the U.S. soldiers was nearly $4,000,000.

After the raid, Special Forces soldiers returned to their firebase. Jack walked back to his bunk to call her. She was home, on her day off. She was cleaning and had their wedding video on, just to see him and hear his voice.

He was able to log on to Skype and video chat with her in his bunk. She answered excitedly. "Hi Master Sergeant…" she said giving him a flirty smile.

He smiled at her. "Hi baby, wow you look gorgeous. I wish I was home."

She was happy to see him. She smiled. "I wish you were too. How are things over there?" She could see the exhaustion in his eyes.

"I'm tired. I hardly get any sleep here. I'm so ready to come home."

"Yeah I am too. There are a lot of things around here that need fixing." she suggested.

He laughed. "I'm just your personal handyman?"

"Yeah, didn't you get the memo?" she asked. He laughed. She always made him laugh. That was one of the many things he loved about her.

"How's Boomer?"

She smiled. "Ornery as ever, I can tell you picked him. He loves to chew on my bras and drag them all over the house."

He laughed. "I guess you'll have to break that habit you have of hanging them on the doorknob."

They talked. She told him funny things that had happened at work. "I'll be home soon, baby. We should take a trip somewhere, anywhere you want to go. Start planning it now."

She smiled. "I think a trip to Key West would be amazing."

He smiled. "I'd love to see that bikini body again."

They laughed. "Oh when you get home, you'll see more than that."

He smiled. "Show me now." They had a private moment together. While they were talking, the camp came under attack by RPGs, mortars and small arms fire. She could hear the explosions and the gunfire.

He saw the look on her face. "Jack, what's happening?"

His demeanor immediately changed. As drained and exhausted as he was, his adrenaline kicked in. He knew he was needed. "Baby, I have to go."

"No, please don't go." She heard the loud alarm and a man on the intercom of camp yelling *"INCOMING! INCOMING! INCOMING!"* as mortars fired into camp.

Seeing the worry and panic on her face, he said, "I'll call you when I can. I love you Kate."

Shaking with fear and in shear shock, she managed to say, "I love you Jack. Come back to me."

He hung up. Millions of thoughts raced through her mind. She was terrified that their conversation would be their last. Did she tell him she loved him enough times? Did she tell him she missed him enough times?

He found his team and saw them firing at insurgents trying to invade the camp. The outpost was surrounded by three hundred enemy fighters. The small outpost was very close being overrun. "Where's the 50?" he yelled, referring to the .50 caliber machine gun while, running to his team.

A soldier got on top a Humvee and fired the 50 caliber machine gun at the insurgents. Many dropped to the ground. An insurgent threw a grenade at the Humvee, the grenade exploded, nearly killing the soldier.

"Fire the grenade launcher!" Jack ordered. Brad and Tom fired the Milkor M114 Grenade Launcher. He shot the M249 Squad Automatic Weapon (SAW). He realized that the only way to have an advantage would be to get to higher ground and use his rifle. He climbed the watch tower and used his XM2010 Enhanced Sniper Rifle. The insurgents were met with his rounds. Other snipers joined him on the watch tower. He climbed down to find his team. Finding Tom and Brad, he fought alongside them.

Thirty-five year old sergeant Gavin Brown from Houston, Texas, fought alongside Jack and his team. Receiving a gunshot wound to the abdomen, he screamed, falling over holding the wound. Jack grabbed him, covering him from further enemy fire.

"Jamal get over here NOW!" he yelled, holding the sergeant's head in his lap.

Jamal and Chase administered treatment. "Am I going to die?" the soldier asked him.

He looked to Jamal who nodded his head. Jack chose to lie to this soldier. "No, you're going to walk out of here. What part of Texas are you from?" he asked, recognizing his Texan accent.

"I'm from Houston, how'd you know I'm from Texas?"

He smiled. "I'd recognize a Texas accent anywhere. I'm from Dallas." Sergeant Brown was trying to breathe normally and not panic. Mortars were still exploding and gunfire surrounded them. Jamal tried desperately to stop the bleeding.

"My wife Laura and I have been married for ten years, yesterday. We have three boys."

Jack smiled. "Wow, ten years and three boys? I bet they are as strong as you. What are their names?"

Sergeant Brown had tears rolling out of his eyes as he bled profusely. "Adam, John, and Luke, I love my boys. What about you?"

"I'm married, but no kids yet." Jack replied.

"Don't wait too long."

Seeing he was breathing erratically, Jack tried to keep him calm. "Well you hang on here. Don't give up. Stay with me."

"I don't think I can hold on anymore. Master Sergeant, will you do me a favor?"

Jack looked down at him with the soldier's head on his lap. "It'd be an honor, Sergeant."

Sergeant Brown pulled a folded envelope from his chest pocket, with his wife's name on the front with their address. "Will you give my wife this letter? Tell her I love her and my boys. Tell my boys that I... fought hard." his voice cracked as tears rolled down his cheeks.

He had tears in his eyes as he held the blood smeared envelope in his hand. "Yeah, I'll give it to her, and I'll tell them." Mortars were still exploding all around them. Gunfire and the whistling of RPGs were constant. A few minutes later, Sergeant Gavin Brown, of Houston, Texas, died in Jack's arms.

Jamal reached up to feel Brown's pulse, there was none. Jack still held him, as if he was still with them. "Jack, he's gone," he said.

He had to keep his emotions under control. His team needed him to be squared away. He nodded. The body was taken. Looking down at his hands, he noticed they were covered in Brown's blood. He picked up his rifle and rejoined the fight. He wouldn't think of Brown, his wife and their three boys. Now, he had to focus. The fire fight between the insurgents and U.S. soldiers lasted well into the morning hours. Finally, just as the sun was rising, it stopped. The fire fight had killed twelve soldiers.

Days went by, Kate had not heard from him yet. The base attack had temporarily cut off communications. As she was driving home from work, she got a flat tire. She pulled over. Realizing she did not have a spare, she reached inside the car to grab her cell phone. Instead of calling her husband like most women would do, she had to call roadside assistance and wait. She put her cell phone inside her purse and accidentally closed her door. The car locked.

She felt a cold breeze. The sky was turning dark. A severe thunderstorm was rolling in. She tried to open her door, but it was locked. Her keys were still in the ignition and running. Locked out, she had no shelter and no way to call anyone. The rain began to pour down on her.

Beyond frustrated and scared, all she wanted was him home. She worried about him. She had just heard his base getting attacked and had not heard from him since. Her hair and clothes were soaked. Dealing with the daily demands of the job as a full time nurse and as an Army wife, she felt frustrated, helpless and overwhelmed nearly every day. Frustrated that she had to carry the load on the home front alone, which some days didn't seem so hard, but when she hadn't heard from Jack and was very worried for him, it was extremely hard. But she found comfort that there were thousands of other military wives in her life boat, like Paige and Jenny.

She was soaked waiting for roadside assistance. Finally, the nice man arrived forty minutes after she had called. He changed her flat and unlocked her car. She was soaked and very cold.

Three days after the attack, communications had been restored. He had time to Skype with her. He went into his bunk, opened his lap top and called her. She was at home sick with a cold from being stuck out in the pouring rain. She was lying on the sofa, with Boomer in her lap, watching their wedding video wrapped up in a blanket and her pajamas. Her laptop was open and sitting on the coffee table. Seeing his picture appear on her computer screen, she breathed a sigh of relief.

"Jack, are you okay? I was so scared."

He smiled. "Yeah, baby. I'm okay. I'm sorry you had to hear that." He noticed she looked sick. "Are you okay? You look like you're sick."

"I have a cold. I got a flat tire the other day and I stupidly locked myself out and it was pouring down raining. I was soaked and cold, but I handled it," she said proudly.

"Did you change it yourself?"

"No I didn't have a spare, so I had to call Roadside Assistance to help me."

He felt bad he wasn't there for her. "I'm sorry, baby. I should've been there for you. I'm sorry I don't have a normal eight to five kind of job. You deserve that."

"I have the best husband in the world. Granted, it would be nice sometimes for you to have a normal job, but I'm so proud of you. Being a soldier is who you are. I married you fully knowing that you are a soldier and I could never let you give that up."

"I wish I was there to take care of you, to make you chicken noddle soup and give you medicine. But even though you look like Rudolph with that red nose, you are still so gorgeous."

"Aren't you sweet? I'm really glad you're okay. I couldn't sleep. I was so worried."

"I know. I would give anything to hold you and touch you right now."

She smiled at him. "You would get sick too."

"I wouldn't care. It'd be worth it."

"I can't wait to feel you again."

"Have you decided on where we're going to go when I get back for vacation?"

"Yeah, I looked at this incredible beach house in Key West,"

He laughed. "I can't wait to see you in a bikini." She smiled. "How long would you want to stay?"

"I think five days is perfect."

"Great, well when I get back, we'll book it and take a second honeymoon. I love you, baby. I miss you so much." He smiled at her.

She held back the tears in her eyes. "I love you and miss you too. Don't worry about me. I've got everything under control." He could see she was stressed, tired, and overwhelmed, even though she tried to act like she had everything under control. She didn't want him to be stressed about trivial things like the vehicles, the bills, or the house. Holding down 'their fort' was her job. His job was to complete his mission and come home. But though she tried to act as strong as she could, she forgot that he could read people very well.

"I know this deployment is difficult and I know you're stressed, but I'll be home soon, baby. Hang in there for me. Be strong for me."

She smiled at him. "I'm strong for you. You look amazing, Master Sergeant," she said.

He laughed. "I probably don't smell amazing," he joked.

She laughed. "I'd ignore it as long as I got to touch you and kiss you. You have no idea how much I miss you."

"I miss you just as much, baby," he said. "I miss the way the shower smells like your body wash. I miss watching you get ready in the mornings. I miss holding when you sleep. I miss your cooking. I miss the way your hair smells. I miss your perfume."

She smiled at him. "I miss how when things break, you can fix it. I miss knowing if I screw up the TV settings, you'll fix it. I miss doing your laundry and cooking for you. I miss cuddling with you on the sofa watching movies or sports with you. I miss tripping over your boots and gear. I miss the way the bathroom smells like your body wash and shaving cream. I miss hearing you whistle cadences when you're shaving. Don't laugh at me, but I spray your cologne on your pillow every night so I can sleep."

He smiled. He looked at her tease her curled hair as it fell down onto her shoulders. She noticed him smiling at her. "What are you smiling at?"

He smiled. "I'm just smiling at you. God must really love me since he gave me you."

She smiled. "I can't imagine my life without you, Jack. You've always been there for me, a shoulder and my protector."

"I'll always be here for you baby. I'm not going anywhere. I'm sorry you have so much to deal with. You're an incredibly strong, independent woman. How can you deal with my career, your career and all that you face while I'm gone? I'm truly in awe of what you take care of. You work a full time job. You take care of our house, our bills, the maintenance on my truck and your car, our taxes, me and whatever I need. I know my career adds more stress on you and makes your life harder, baby, but I'm so proud of you and happy you're my wife."

"Jack, you wanted a woman who was strong and independent and who could handle your career without asking you to choose, someone who could handle the stresses and demands as well as the rewards. Yes, this deployment has been a little rough, but it's nothing I can't handle. I could never ask you to choose between me and the Army. I love being your wife and I'm so proud of what you do. Loving you is not hard. It's the easiest thing I've ever done."

He smiled. "I really appreciate you taking care of everything while I'm gone. I love how organized and meticulous you are with our finances. You take a tremendous weight off my shoulders and I never tell you enough that I love you and I appreciate you."

"Thank you, it's nice to hear that. I love you so much."

"I love you too baby. I can't stop looking at you. Just looking at you makes me wish I was home."

She smiled. They had a private intimate moment together. He missed her. They both longed for each other. "I wish you were lying here next to me, with your head against my heart."

She smiled. "I would sell a kidney just to be with you."

He laughed. "I wouldn't let you sell a kidney." They talked until it was nearly 2:00 a.m. in his time zone. He mailed the letter to Sergeant Brown's widow, after she had been properly notified her of his death.

Weeks later, Alpha, Bravo, and Charlie Teams were driving through a valley, off a road, trying to avoid IEDs. Taliban fighters were burying IEDs in the roads, so when American convoys would pass, they would hit an IED. It was a deadly strategy. Jack and Tom were riding side by side in battle gear. They drove to a local village. This village was friendly some times when Americans came through. Jack and his team stepped out of their trucks and began to walk towards the villagers. The sky was clear and blue. It was scorching hot that day. The temperature was over 120.

As the team walked towards the villagers, Chase stepped on a landmine. The force of the blast amputated his right leg and left arm. Jamal, Jack, and Tom rushed to him as the others provided cover fire and swept the area for more landmines. Chase was screaming. His face and upper body was badly burned. He was going into shock. Racing against time, Jamal quickly applied a tourniquet to his right leg as Jack applied one to his left arm to stop the bleeding. If they didn't stop the bleeding, he could bleed to death before getting to a hospital. Jack radioed the Air Force Para-Jumpers (PJs) to medically evacuate (MED-EVAC) him via helicopter. "They're coming, buddy. Just hold on." he said, holding him.

"What happened?"

Jack looked up at Tom and Jamal. He never liked to lie to his men. "Chase, you stepped on a landmine."

"I can't feel my arm or leg."

He looked down at him as Jamal quickly took his vitals. "I know man, but help is on the way." He couldn't tell him that his leg and arm had been amputated.

The PJ's arrived at the point of injury (POI). Jamal gave one of the PJ's Chase's vitals. Marcus, Luke, and Eric helped load Chase onto a gurney and hoist him up into the helicopter. The PJ's allowed each member of Jack's team to say a quick goodbye, fearing he wouldn't make it.

The leader of the PJ's and Jack shook hands. They were good friends. "Hey, take care of him for us, will ya?" Jack asked.

"You got it." Jack rushed back to his team as the leader of the PJ's quickly climbed back into the helicopter. The helicopter lifted off and rushed towards the nearest base with a hospital. The Air Force Para-Jumpers and Special Forces considered each other brothers. There was a strong comradely.

Arriving back to their outpost, all three teams reflected and were worried about Chase. They gathered in the briefing room and sat in the chairs around a long table. He stood in front of the men.

He wore his worn Oklahoma Sooners baseball cap and held his bottle of water in his hands. "Alright, guys. I know we're all concerned about Chase. I'm keeping in contact with the hospital and the PJ's did get him there and he was alive. They gave him a blood transfusion aboard the chopper. But I do not know if he made it out of surgery. I think right now would be a great time for us to have a moment of silence to pray for him and his family. He is a good buddy, a great brother, and soldier."

They stood. Most were wearing their favorite ball caps. Tom and Jack, of course were wearing their worn Oklahoma Sooners and Alabama caps. They took off their caps and were silent for a few minutes.

As Jack was walking to his bunk, Mike stopped him. "Hey you got a package from Kate." He handed the box to him. He walked to his bunk and opened the package. She had sent him all his favorite snacks, books, movies, and boudoir pictures she had professionally taken. He was stunned. He looked to his laptop, opened it, and logged on to Skype.

She was home on her day off. He smiled when he saw her. "Hello beautiful, wow it's so good to see you after the day I've had."

"Hi, did you have a bad day?"

He stressfully rubbed his head. "Yeah, I did."

She smiled. "I'm sorry. I'm just glad you're safe."

"You are so beautiful. I just got your package and your pictures are incredible. I love them. I'm going to have to keep these in a safe spot so my guys won't see them."

She smiled. "I was nervous how you would react."

"I love them. They make me want to go AWOL to see you. Was the photographer a man or a woman?"

She laughed. "She was a woman."

"Okay, good. I don't want any other man knowing what I have waiting for me at home."

"You don't have to worry about that. I want and need only you."

He flashed that sexy little grin to her. "You need me?"

"Yes, I do. I love you."

"I love you too, baby. How's everything back home?"

"Oh everything is good."

"I can't wait to get home. For our anniversary, I've got something pretty amazing planned."

"I want to celebrate at home, specifically the bedroom. We won't leave the bedroom for a few days."

He smiled. "Okay that sounds so much better than what I had planned." She laughed. "I miss you so much."

"I miss you too, Jack." They had a private moment together. They really missed each other. They talked for nearly an hour.

Chase made it through surgery. He retired from the Army and lived prosperously in South Dakota with his wife and daughters.

Colonel Mitchell and his Green Berets returned to Fort Bragg in July 2010. The U.S. Army had pulled out of the Korengal Valley. They were given a month of dwell time. Jack had just turned thirty-five.

Arriving home, he saw her black Ford Fusion; they bought together, in their driveway. He pulled in and parked beside it. The house looked the same, except for maybe the pink tulips planted in the yard. Their American flag was still mounted on the post to the house. He unlocked the door with his key.

He opened the door and saw everything was the same. He saw a calculator, the stack of bills and the ledger that she recorded all their bills in. He appreciated how organized and meticulous she was with their finances. He loved that she was also a saver like him, not a spender like Chelsea. He saw the pamphlet of the beach house she wanted to rent in Key West, Florida on the kitchen table. It was an amazing beach house at a surprisingly reasonable rate.

He walked to their bedroom. He heard water swish and felt the steam from the hot water from the bathroom. She was in a hot bubble bath with her headphones on, and her eyes closed. She had lit lavender scented candles around the room to help her relax. He smiled at her as he walked to the edge of the tub. He sat beside her arm and he gently touched her.

She opened her eyes and was very happy and very surprised to see him. She was covered in bubbles. "Hi! I didn't even hear you come in."

He kissed her lips. "I noticed. How are you?"

"I'm much better now that you're home."

"I've missed you."

"I've missed you more."

"Show me how much you've missed me."

She smiled up at him and pulled him into the tub. They laughed and kissed. Bubbles were all over their bathroom.

Covered in bubbles, he carried her to the bedroom. He laid her down on their bed as they were kissing passionately. "Happy belated birthday, honey what would you like for your birthday?" she asked.

He kissed her knee. She smiled at him. "I have what I want right here."

His dog tags were dangling. She grasped the chain and pulled him down to her, she smiled up at him and said, "Tonight, soldier you're mine." He smiled and kissed her lips. He struggled to take off his soaked, soapy clothes. They held hands as they kissed. They made passionate love.

Finally, they were lying in bed, wrapped up in the sheets. They were exhausted. He woke up in the middle of the night, thinking the love they had just made was all a dream, until he looked down and saw her lying there with his strong arms wrapped around her. She was sound asleep. She looked peaceful and angelic. He closed his eyes and kissed her head. It felt good to wake up to the reality he was home in bed with his beautiful, faithful wife and not on a cot nearly 7,000 miles away, wanting and missing her.

When he went to sign out for leave, she went to her OB/GYN and asked Major Stephenson to remove her IUD.

"So, are you and Jack trying to get pregnant?"

"Yeah, I think we're finally ready to try again."

Once it was removed, she sat up. "So, about how long should I wait to conceive?"

"You don't have to wait. It returns quickly. So just be as you normally are and it'll happen when it happens."

"We're going to Key West today, so I'm hoping I'll get pregnant while on vacation."

"Good luck. I know you and Jack will be amazing parents."

"Thanks." she said. They finally took their much needed getaway to a beach house in Key West. The ocean water was light blue. The beaches were white. The beach house was a three bedroom home, with a large kitchen and a wrap-around porch. They spent five days in paradise. They swam, wrote each other's names in the sand, took funny pictures, as well as posed shots. They made love on the private beach several times. They toured the town and tried numerous restaurants.

On a normal Friday night, a few weeks after their little second honeymoon, they were getting ready to go out for a special dinner. They tried to have as much normalcy as most married couples, with dinner-and-a-movie weekly, home cooked dinners every night, and breakfast every morning. They spent as much time together as possible.

She was wearing a sexy black cocktail dress and stunning black pumps. He was tying his black tie. He watched her get ready. He smiled as she carefully covered her lips with red lipstick. Her hair was curled and her makeup was flawless.

She walked up to him and asked him to fasten the heart shaped locket he bought her years before, around her neck. She lifted her soft curled hair as he fastened the clasp. He kissed the back of her neck and her shoulder. "You look beautiful, baby." He pulled her up against him.

"Thank you." She could smell his cologne and body wash. He smelled of Old Spice. "You smell incredible. Do you like my dress?"

He smiled. "I love it. You make the dress look amazing."

The sun had set. The stars were visible. The cool wind provided relief to the hot summer night. They went to a nice restaurant with waiters in tuxedos, white cloth linens and tea light candles on the table. The waiter handed them each a menu. He poured each of them a glass of red wine. They ordered. He knew she had been looking forward to a real date night with him for so long, but all he could think about was getting her home. He watched her big brown eyes dance in the candlelight glow. Her soft brown curled hair draped her shoulders. Her skin was radiant and looked scrumptiously soft.

Their meal finally arrived. Their waiter had refilled their wine glasses. After dinner, he touched her hand. She smiled at him as she softly drew a heart on his hand with her fingernail.

He smiled at her. She could tell he was thinking about something. He was lost in thought. "What are you thinking about?" she asked.

"I'm thinking about getting you home."

She smiled. "We haven't had our dessert yet."

"They don't have anything here I want. I know what I want."

She smiled at him. "And what's that?"

"I want you."

She looked around the restaurant and saw their waiter hanging out at the bar. She looked back at him. "Let's go home." He knew by the look in her eye and the way she was touching his hand what she was thinking. He paid the waiter. They walked out of the restaurant hand in hand. He drove quickly to their house.

Walking through the front door, they closed it and were kissing up against it. She untied his tie and threw it on the floor. She kicked off her high heels. He took off the sports coat to his suit. They slowly made their way to their bedroom. He picked her up and carried her to the bed. Laying her down, he unbuttoned his shirt.

"I'm sorry our date night was cut short," he said.

She smiled up at him. "This is perfect." He kissed her. Kissing and holding each other tight, they made love for hours. Afterwards, she talked him into watching her favorite movie *Fried Green Tomatoes* in their bedroom. They were cuddled up in the sheets, eating rocky road ice cream and drinking red wine.

"I've watched this with you so many times I've lost count, but there's something I haven't been able to figure out, do they really barbecue that guy Frank?" She laughed. "Seriously, I've never really figured it out. They let you think they did, but did they really?"

"Yes, they barbecued him and fed him to that Alabama sheriff that came looking for him."

"Damn he ate like four plates of barbecue." She laughed.

Lying in his strong arms, she kissed his hand. He looked down into her eyes. "Are you ready to have a baby?" she asked.

He smiled down at her. He touched her cheek, moving a strand of her curled silky hair off her face. "Yes, when you are."

"I'm ready," she said.

He smiled. "Are you serious?"

She smiled as she straddled him. "As a heart attack…" They laughed. "Yes, I'm serious. I'm ready to start our family. I want three kids, two little girls and a little boy. I want a son that looks and acts like you."

He smiled up at her and kissed her hands. He touched her soft, smooth hair. "Our daughters will be beautiful just like their mother."

She smiled. "And our son will be handsome, sweet, stubborn and strong just like his daddy." she teased, as they laughed together.

He laughed. "Listen to the pot call the kettle black. You are way more stubborn than me. So if our child is stubborn, he or she inherited it from you."

"As long as our son has your good looks, I don't care. If I can deal with you, then a miniature version won't be anything I can't handle."

He looked up into her eyes and kissed her lips. He was excited that she was finally ready to have another baby. She smiled. She kissed his chest and stomach muscles. "Tonight, soldier you're mine."

He laid her down. His dog tags were dangling. She looked up into his green eyes. Gently grasping the chain, she smiled pulling him down to her to kiss his lips. They made love again. After hours of passionate, intense lovemaking, they laid exhausted, wrapped up in the sheets. He held her in his arms.

"You're really ready?" he asked. "If you're not ready, don't think you have to get pregnant to make me happy. I'm very happy with you, just the way things are."

She smiled slowly dragging her fingernails down his arm. She loved how fit he was. "I'm really ready. I want a part of you here with me, when you're gone. This house gets really quiet, really boring and really lonely when you're gone."

"I just want you and the baby to be safe. Last time, I was really afraid I was going to lose you too."

She kissed his lips. "You won't lose me." He kissed her lips.

"So, do you still have that IUD in?"

She looked up at him and smiled. "I went to my OB/GYN just before we left for Key West last month and had her take it out."

"So you decided last month that you're ready to have a baby?"

"Yeah, it wasn't fair that I got that IUD put in without discussing it with you, so I apologize, Jack. I was wrong to do that."

He kissed her lips. "I love you. Thank you."

They kissed passionately. "I'm going to take a hot bath." She got up and walked into their master bathroom. The water turned on. She poured bubble bath into the water. She lit the little candles surrounding their tub and dimmed the lights. After pulling her hair up into a messy bun, she got in.

He walked into the bathroom and sat on the edge of the tub and smiled at her. She smiled up at him.

"When you smile at me like that, I'm easily manipulated." he said.

She smiled. "Good to know."

"And I just gave you ammunition to use it against me, didn't I?" He smiled. He grabbed her arm and kissed the top of her hand, then her wrist. "Do I make you happy?"

She moved closer to him. "Yes, I'm beyond happy."

"What's beyond happy?"

"Blissful." They kissed passionately. She pulled him in with her. He was covered in bubbles and she laughed hysterically.

"Oh it's payback time."

"You wouldn't do anything to the mother of your future children." He tickled her. Water and bubbles were everywhere.

It was the night of her thirtieth birthday. He was planning on taking her out for a special romantic dinner. She noticed while getting ready to go out with him that she had missed her period. She became very excited, but didn't want to tell him until she knew for sure. He took her to a romantic restaurant in town and then home to make love, eat ice cream in bed, and cuddle while watching a movie, her choice of course.

The next afternoon, she came home from work early and immediately laid in the bed. She fell asleep in her scrubs and Nike tennis shoes. Boomer jumped up on the bed with her and cuddled up with her. He came home a few hours later. He called for her, but when he walked into their bedroom, he saw her sleeping. He noticed she had been sleeping a lot more than usual. It was unlike her to sleep so much. She was an energetic person, always going and barely stopping long enough to eat. She was a very proactive and busy person.

He untied her shoes and pulled them off and covered her up with a blanket. He looked down at her sleeping. He leaned down and kissed her cheek. He and Boomer went into the living room. He ordered a pizza and watched sports highlights on TV while she slept.

About ten o'clock that night, she finally woke up and was famished. Noticing she had fallen asleep in her scrubs and it was dark outside, she realized she had not made dinner for her and Jack. She immediately jumped up and went into the kitchen. He saw her. "Hey baby, did you have a good sleep?"

The overwhelming smell of garlic, sauce and cheese filled her nose and she stopped. Suddenly she did not feel so well. "What is that smell?" she asked.

"I ordered a pizza earlier. You want some?"

She covered her mouth and hurried into the bathroom. She vomited. He walked to the bathroom door and stood there. "Hey, open the door." She opened it, turned towards the sink and splashed cold water on her face.

He watched her. "Hey, could you be pregnant?"

"I doubt it. I think I'm just coming down with the flu or something from work."

"We've been practicing a lot to have a baby. You've been sleeping a lot, and you're more in the mood than normal."

She looked at him and smiled. "Well, it's because I have such an amazing, sexy, strong husband, what woman wouldn't be?" She kissed his lips.

The thought had entered her mind briefly, but she kept dismissing the possibility. She didn't want to get her hopes up about being pregnant and then not be.

He smiled at her. "How about I go get you something from Burger King?" he asked.

"Aw, thanks babe, but I don't have much of an appetite. And the thought of a greasy hamburger meat makes me want to throw up more."

"I think you should make a doctor's appointment."

"Okay, I'll call Major Stephenson tomorrow and make an appointment."

"I bet you're pregnant. I hope you are." He was hoping she was pregnant.

The next morning, she called her OB/GYN, Major Daphne Stephenson. She made an appointment at the post hospital for later in the week. She bought a home pregnancy test from the commissary. She waited until he went to work before taking it. After taking it, she was almost caught off guard when the results appeared instantly. +POSITIVE. She was excited, scared, and happy at the same time. She hid the pregnancy test and tried to act as if nothing was going on. She wanted to be 100% sure before she told him, their family and friends.

The day of her appointment with Major Stephenson finally arrived. She sat nervously on the exam table with a gown on. The door opened. The Major smiled. "Hello Kate, how are you doing? How was Key West?"

"I'm great. Key West was absolutely beautiful and very relaxing. How are you?"

"I'm not too bad. How is Jack doing?"

"He's great."

"Is he home or gone?"

"He's home. I'm happy he's home for a little while."

"So, what's going on?"

She took a deep breath. "Well, I took a home pregnancy test and it was positive. So here I am. I want my blood drawn so I'll know for sure if I'm pregnant or not."

"We had your IUD removed a little over a month ago, right?" Major Stephenson said looking at her chart. "Have you had any symptoms?"

"I've missed my last period. The first day of my last period was July twentieth. I've noticed nausea in the mornings and had the actual morning sickness. I've noticed that certain smells bother me more and Jack says he's noticed I've been sleeping a lot."

"Okay, well I'm going to send you to the lab to have your blood drawn. I should have the results back in an hour." She went to the lab and had her blood drawn.

With an hour to waste, she drove to the Post Exchange and looked around. She soon found herself in the baby section, looking at the many cribs, the adorable bedding sets for boys and girls and the little clothes. She daydreamed about what hers and Jack's child would look like.

Then she went back to the waiting room. The nurse called her name and she walked back to the exam room. Major Stephenson reentered the room carrying her chart. She smiled at her.

"Congratulations are an order. You're definitely pregnant!"

She was in bliss and couldn't wait to tell him. She knew he was going to be so excited. Major Stephenson gave her prenatal vitamins and sent her to the imaging center on post to have her first sonogram taken. She held the sonogram in her hands and smiled. She couldn't wait to see his reaction. She was due April 24, 2011.

Later that evening, she made a big meal for them. He and his team were doing a live fire training exercise in preparation for a mission. She lit candles around the room and on the table. She put on soft romantic music. She had a wrapped present for him. She was dressed up as well, wearing a sexy black cocktail dress and black high heels. Her hair was curled and makeup flawless.

He walked through the front door. The house was spotless and the smell of delicious food filled his nose. "Hey baby, I'm home!" he said.

She smiled and stepped into the foyer. "Hi, how was your day?" she asked.

"Good, wow, you look amazing. Where are we going?"

She wrapped her arms around his neck and kissed his lips. "Why would you think we're going somewhere?"

"You're all dressed up."

"Can't a girl dress up for her hard working, handsome husband?"

He noticed she was acting strange. He smiled. "Okay, what do you want and how much is it?"

She laughed. "Jack David, you automatically assume I want something. I just felt like looking nice."

He laughed. "You ain't foolin' me, I know how women work. Every man knows when his wife puts on a sexy black dress and black heels she wants something expensive. So, what do you want?"

She wrapped her arms around his neck. "I have everything I could ever ask for right here."

He kissed her lips. "Well I'm glad to hear that. You look like you're feeling better. What did the doctor say?"

"She said everything looks really good."

He opened the refrigerator door and grabbed a bottle of water. "What are you cooking? It really smells good."

"I'm making chicken Fettuccine Alfredo, garlic bread and vegetables and your favorite double fudge chocolate cake," she said, opening the oven door.

A big smile spread across his face. "Wow, it looks so good. Is it almost done?"

"Yes, but in the mean time I have a present for you."

He smiled at her. "Is it you?"

"No, that's later." She handed him a small wrapped box.

He suddenly wondered what month and date it was. "What month is it? It's not our anniversary, is it?"

She smiled. "No, it's not our anniversary."

He laughed and breathed a sigh of relief. "Okay, crisis averted."

"Ha, you're so funny."

"If it's not our anniversary or my birthday, why are you giving me a gift?"

She wrapped her arms around his neck and smiled up at him. "Because you're my amazing husband and you work so hard and I just wanted to do something nice for you."

"Is this one of those tricks where you put something you want in the box and pretend it's for me?"

She laughed. "No, it's for you. Just open it."

He tore the wrapping paper and opened the box. He smiled down at the sonogram. He looked at her and smiled. He could see the glow on her face and wondered why he hadn't noticed before. He held the sonogram and saw their baby. "You're going to be a daddy."

He smiled as he gently touched her stomach. He looked down into her eyes and smiled. "Thank you." he said.

"I love you."

"I love you too."

They hugged tightly. "I can't believe I'm going to be a daddy." She smiled, smelling the cologne on his neck, feeling his heartbeat against her body. "When are you due?" he asked, touching her stomach.

"I'm due April 24th." They smiled at each other. She could tell he was very happy and excited.

Dinner was finally ready. The cake was cooling on the stove. They ate dinner together. After dinner, he was watching a show in the living room. She caught his eye. She was standing at the stove. Her hair was draping her shoulders. She was spreading the fudge icing over the cake. He admired her.

After she was finished icing the cake, she licked the butter knife. He watched her. He walked towards her and pulled her against him. "I'm jealous of that knife."

She laughed and kissed him. They stood kissing passionately in the middle of the kitchen. "Can I have my other present please?" he asked. She pulled him by the hand to their bedroom. She dimmed the lights and lit the candles around their bedroom. They celebrated the start of their family by making slow love.

The next morning, she woke up and he was not beside her. She walked around the house and looked in the garage. The coffee pot in the kitchen was on, with a full pot already brewed. She poured herself a cup of coffee, toasted a bagel and made a fruit salad. She heard the garage door opening. He pulled in and parked. She walked out in the garage and smiled at him. He smiled at her as he walked to the cab of his truck.

"Hey, where'd you go?"

"I just went to the PX." He opened the door and pulled out Pampers' Swaddlers Newborn diapers, baby bottles, a few Army themed onesies and bibs, and pacifiers.

She smiled. She thought he was so adorable. "I see you went shopping."

He smiled. "Yeah, I couldn't help myself."

"I love you." she said, as she wrapped her arms around him. "You are so cute." She kissed him.

It was October. Summer was officially over and autumn was here. The leaves were red, orange and golden. The air was crisp and cool, perfect temperature for an expectant mother.

He had saved up his leave time. They decided to fly to Dallas to tell their families and friends about the pregnancy in person. She was barely showing, but she able to conceal with flowing shirts that were tight on her breasts, but loose on her belly. They would announce the news at her parents' when both their families had gathered for dinner. They were in bliss. Their love life was very busy.

"How do you think everyone will react?" she asked.

"I can picture our moms screaming and our dad's smoking cigars in celebration. Hopefully no one will have a heart attack."

"Well I'm an RN. I know what to do."

He looked at her and touched her hand. "You have never looked so happy or so gorgeous."

She held his hand. "I'm happy every day I wake up because I'm married to you."

They landed in Dallas at Love Field Airport. They rented a car and drove across town to her parents'. They parked in her parents' driveway. They happily walked up the walkway to the front door. Pushing the door open, she yelled, "Hello?"

Lauren was coming down the stairs when she saw Kate and Jack. "Kate! Jack! It's so good to see you!" she said hugging them. "Kate, you're glowing! Have you been tanning?"

Kate smiled. "No."

Lauren was unsuspecting. "Well you look amazing. Jack, you're still as good looking as you've ever been." They laughed.

Carole heard Jack and Kate and walked into the foyer. "Kate!" she said wrapping her arms around her and hugged her. "I've missed you so much."

"I've missed you too, momma."

She hugged him. "Jack, my favorite son-in-law, how are you doing? It's so good to see you."

"It's good to see you too, Carole."

"Momma, where's Daddy?"

"Oh he is in his office."

He walked to Matt's office. "Hey grandpa, what's going on?" he asked.

Matt smiled. He didn't catch the slip of the tongue. He hugged him. "You look good, son. How's the Army treating you?"

"It's busy, but good."

"Good. How are you and Kate doing?"

"We're great."

"Where is she?" he asked.

"Oh she's in the kitchen with her mom and Lauren."

He and Matt walked into the kitchen. "Sweet pea, you look gorgeous."

"Isn't she glowing?" Lauren asked.

Carole smiled. "Yes, you are. What's going on with you?"

"I'm just so happy." Kate said. The doorbell rang. It was Jack's parents, Jonah, Christi, and Meagan.

Jack answered the door. Bill and Denise hugged him tightly. Jonah and Meagan hugged him and teased him. Kate greeted them and hugged them. "Kate, you're glowing! You look absolutely stunning." Denise said as she hugged her.

"Thank you. Being married to Jack makes me glow," she said.

The evening air was superb. The men were on the deck talking and enjoying a few beers before supper. Carole was cooking a fancy, four course meal in celebration that Jack and Kate were home. The families were now complete.

Kate and Denise were peeling potatoes as Meagan and Lauren were setting the twelve seat dinner table. "So, Kate, how are you and Jack?" Denise asked.

Kate smiled. "Oh we're beyond great."

"I saw this adorable baby the other day and it made me start thinking about how yours and Jack's child will be a very good looking little thing, when you decide to have one."

Kate felt flushed.

"Oh I know. I catch myself doing the same thing when I see babies. I can't wait to be a grandma," Carole said.

"Have you two talked about having another baby?" Denise asked.

"Yeah, we've talked about it, but we're just enjoying our married time together. We rarely see each other for long periods of time."

"Well it'll happen when you're ready." Denise said.

"I'm ready to be a grandma. I'd like this house to be filled with toys and nothing but cartoons on." Carole said. "I have to stop myself from buying those precious baby clothes."

Kate walked out on the deck and saw Jack sitting in a chair with a beer in his hands. He saw her. He quickly got up. They went into a private room. "Are you okay?"

"Yeah, I'm just a little flushed."

"Why?"

"My mom and your mom were talking about how ready they are for us to have a baby."

He smiled. "Do you want to tell them now?"

"No, we'll wait until dinner." She looked up at him. She had a look in her eye and he knew what it meant. She kissed his lips and pulled him upstairs to her bedroom.

He wrapped his arms around her waist and pulled her up against him. "I love you."

"I love you too." They kissed passionately up against the door to her bedroom. "We've never had sex in your parents' house. What if your Dad catches us?"

She laughed. "You worry too much." They quickly got dressed and walked out of the room. He walked back out on the deck. She went back into the kitchen to see if she could help her mom with anything. When she entered the kitchen, she saw the roasted chicken and peppers. She suddenly felt very nauseous. She quickly hurried to the bathroom and closed the door.

"Is she okay?" Denise asked.

She and Carole walked to the bathroom door and knocked. "Sweetie, are you okay?"

They heard the faucet water running. "Yeah, I'm fine."

"Go get Jack," Carole said.

Denise walked out to the deck. "Jack, Kate just got sick. She's in the bathroom."

He quickly hurried to the bathroom and knocked. "Baby, you okay?"

"Yeah, I'm fine. Ask my mom if she has any Saltine crackers and some ginger-ale?"

"Yes I do sweetie." Carole said. She went to the kitchen to get the crackers and to pour her a small glass of ginger-ale. She brought it to Jack.

"Baby, let me in." he said. She unlocked the door and he slipped inside. She was sitting on the edge of the tub, with her head in her hands. "You okay?" he asked, handing her a few crackers.

"No, I'm so nauseous. When I saw that chicken, I just got very sick."

He turned the faucet on and put a washcloth under the cold water. He put the washcloth on the back of her neck to cool her off. "Do you want to go?"

"No, I want to have dinner with our families. They never see us." She looked up at him. "Do I look like crap now?"

He smiled, moving her hair out of her face. "No, you look beautiful."

She ate the crackers and drank small sips of the ginger-ale. After a few minutes, she began to feel better. They came out of the bathroom. She walked back into the kitchen and he walked back out on the deck.

He sat next to Matt and Bill, drinking a beer. "Is she okay?"

"Yeah, she's fine."

Bill looked through the patio door at Kate laughing with Christi and Meagan. "She looks really happy. How are things with y'all?" he asked.

He looked at her and smiled. "Everything is really great."

Jonah laughed. "I've never heard a married man say that before."

They all laughed. "You know the saying, happy wife equals happy life?" Bill replied. They talked about football, the Army, and planning a hunting trip later that week.

Supper was finally ready. Everyone sat at the dinner table and held hands to bless the food. Matt stood at the head of the table. "Heavenly Father, we ask you to use this food to the nourishment of our bodies. Thank you Lord, for allowing my gorgeous daughter and my amazing son-in-law to come home and spend time with their families, we really have missed them. Lord, we are ready for a new baby in this family, so whenever you decide to bless all of us with that, we'll be eternally grateful."

"Thanks Dad, that was subtle." Kate said as they all laughed.

Seeing everyone drinking wine, except Kate, Denise wondered why Kate wasn't drinking. "Kate, would you like a glass of wine?" Denise asked, offering to pour her a glass.

"No, she can't drink!" Jack said protectively, taking the wine away.

Denise and Carole suddenly got a suspicion Kate was pregnant. Putting together her random sickness and by his protective demeanor. "Why can't she?" Matt asked.

"Because I've already had a few beers, so she needs to drive later." he lied.

"You two could stay here for the night until you slept it off." Carole suggested.

"It's just not a good idea." Kate said.

"So Jack, I was asking Kate have you two talked about when you're going to have a baby." Denise said.

Jack smiled at Kate. "I'm sorry, I didn't mean to sick your mother on you."

"I really think you two should have one soon. We're all ready for a grandbaby." Carole suggested.

"I don't understand why y'all have to keep us waiting forever. It took y'all forever to get married, and now I'll probably die waiting for another grandbaby." Bill scolded with a thick southern drawl.

Jack and Kate held hands under the table. She looked at him and smiled. "How about April 24th?" she asked.

The table fell silent. "How do you know it'll be April 24th?" Jonah asked. Their parents' were on edge. They were hoping she was pregnant.

Kate and Jack smiled at each other. He kissed her hand. "…Because that's her due date."

"I'm pregnant!" she announced. Their parents and siblings were ecstatic! They laughed at their mothers' and sisters' jumping around in shear giddiness. Carole and Denise hugged Kate. Matt and Bill hugged him and shook his hand. Matt had tears in his eyes, as he kissed Kate's cheek. Everyone congratulated them.

"Well it's about time!" Lauren said hugging both of them. "I'm going to be an aunt!"

"How far along are you?" Carole asked.

"I'm almost four months,"

"Why'd you wait so long to tell us?" she asked.

"We wanted to make sure everything was good before we told everyone," she said.

"Do you know if it's a boy or a girl?" Meagan asked.

"No not yet."

"What do you want?" Christi asked.

"We want a healthy baby." he said.

"Yeah, everyone wants that." Christi said.

Kate looked at him. "I'd like another little boy."

"Well I'm excited for you both. You'll be excellent parents. My grandbaby will be as good looking as me." Matt said as everyone laughed. "I personally would love a grandson to take fishing and hunting with me, but if it's a girl, I can still take her to do those things. I took Katherine."

"Why do you want a boy?" Lauren asked.

Kate looked at Jack and smiled. "I want a little boy to look exactly like Jack, talk like him, and act like him."

"Oh, you're asking for trouble," Jonah said.

Everyone laughed. "Jack, what do you want?" Carole asked.

He looked at Kate. "I'd like a little girl."

"Let me guess to look like Kate?" Jonah asked.

"Yes, she's gorgeous. Of course I'd want my daughter to look like her." The women smiled as Jack and Kate gently kissed. "That might not be a good thing in sixteen years, when she is old enough to start dating. I'll run all the boys off with my SAW rifle." he said as Bill, Jonah, and Matt laughed. "Y'all think I'm kidding, but I'm not." he declared. Everyone laughed.

"Isn't he cute?" Kate asked, kissing his cheek.

"So what is she craving?" Denise asked.

"Milk and cereal, I'm always going to the commissary to get more milk and more cereal. In one week, she went through four gallons! I think it would be cheaper to buy a dairy cow and put it in our backyard."

Everyone laughed. "Oh there's an old wives tale saying that if a woman craves dairy during her pregnancy, it meant she was having a girl and if she craves spicy foods and meat, she was having a boy." Carole said.

"Looks like you're having a girl," Jonah said.

"As long as Kate is safe and the baby is healthy, I'm fine with either a boy or a girl," he said.

"I hope it's a girl. I want her buy her adorable bows and dresses for her to come to me for advice with her boyfriends." Lauren said.

Jack laughed. "As long as that advice is don't date, I'm fine with that." They all laughed.

They enjoyed being home with their families and close friends. For their fourth anniversary, he took her to dinner at Reunion Tower and for a stroll through the botanical gardens. The news of the pregnancy made everything perfect. Carole and Denise were already buying baby clothes and buying baby furniture for the nurseries at their homes, for when they could babysit.

Jonah had bought Jack, Kate, himself, and Christi tickets to the OU/Texas game. He and Jack wore their Oklahoma t-shirts proudly. They were getting ready to head to Dallas for the game.

Jack walked into the bedroom and saw her pulling a Sooners t-shirt over her head. "You're wearing an OU t-shirt?"

"Yeah, is that okay?"

"You are aware of where we're going and what today is?"

"Yeah, we're going to the game."

"And you still want to wear an OU shirt?"

"Yeah, are you okay?"

He was amazed. "Did you hear that?" he asked seriously.

"What are you talking about?" He motioned her to be quiet. "Jack, I don't hear anything,"

"You didn't hear that loud crack in the planet since I've converted a Texas graduate to an Oklahoma fan?" he teased.

She swatted him. "You had me thinking something really happened." They laughed and wrestled on the bed. He tickled her. "Stop, you're messing up my hair and you're going to make me pee on myself!"

Christi couldn't believe she was wearing an OU t-shirt. "I don't know you anymore. Did Jack brainwash you or something?"

"I love both teams."

"In this rivalry, you can't ride the fence." Christi said. They arrived at the Cotton Bowl Stadium in Dallas. The Texas State Fair was going on. They took funny pictures in front of Big Tex, a famous landmark at the fairgrounds. They enjoyed the game. Oklahoma defeated Texas, 28-20.

"Our Sooners won," she said to him. He laughed and kissed her head.

After spending a long, great week with their families, they had to say goodbye to their families and catch their flight back to Fayetteville.

Arriving back to Fort Bragg after the week in Texas, he was promoted to First Sergeant. They announced to their friends that they were expecting, though most of them suspected.

It was a Monday afternoon in November. She had an ultrasound appointment. They would find out the sex of their child, hopefully. He went with her to the Imagining Center on post.

"What girl names do you like?" she asked him.

"I'd like to name her something that means something."

"Okay, like what?"

He thought about it. "I like the name Liberty, what do you think about that?"

She laughed, "Liberty, as in the statue?"

He smiled. "Yes, I think that's an awesome name. We could call her Libby for short. What do you think?"

She tried not to laugh at him, but couldn't help it. "Are you being serious?"

"Yes, I'm being very serious."

She laughed again. "Don't make me laugh. The baby is right on my bladder, I'll pee all over your new truck." He had just bought another black 2011 GMC Sierra.

"I really like that name. Don't you like it?"

"I like it, babe,"

"What names do you like?"

She smiled, as she thought. "I like the names Abigail, Gracelyn, or Olivia."

"Okay, what if we have a boy?" he asked, as he parked at the ultrasound center.

"I like the names Payton, Jasper, or Connor. What names do you like?"

He smiled. "I love the name Maverick." he said.

She smiled at him. "I like that too, but let's agree that the middle name should be a family name."

He shook her hand. "You have a deal." They walked into the office and sat in the waiting room. They both flipped through magazines until they were finally called back.

She laid down on the table and lifted her shirt. Her adorable 'baby bump' was bulging. "Do you have any names picked out?" the technician asked.

They looked at each other and laughed. "We're still debating." he said. The sonogram tech squeezed warm gel onto her abdomen and placed the transducer to her belly. The heartbeat began to beat loudly over the speakers.

"Is the baby's heartbeat supposed to be that fast?" he asked. He didn't want anything to happen like during her last pregnancy.

She smiled. She thought it was adorable how concerned he was. "It's a good strong heartbeat. Now, if you look at the screen mounted on the wall, you'll be able to see your baby," the tech said.

They looked up at the screen and were amazed. They were holding hands tightly watching the baby move around. They watched the baby suck its thumb for several minutes. He was amazed. He smiled up at the screen. He was excited to be a father.

"Okay, do you want to know the sex, or do you want to be surprised?" the tech asked them.

They looked at each other and smiled. "We want to know."

The tech smiled looking at the screen. "You're having a girl."

She smiled and immediately had tears in her eyes. He smiled at her and kissed her hand. "She's beautiful just like her mom." he said quietly, as he looked at the screen.

"She's strong like her daddy," she said.

"Don't you mean 'stubborn'?" he asked.

She smiled. "No, I mean strong." They kissed.

After the appointment, he took her out for a romantic dinner. Then they went to a local Babies R Us store and bought a crib, changing table, dresser and rocker for the nursery. She was dying to register. He could see how excited she was, so he was a good sport and tagged along. After registering, buying the nursery suite, they called their families and friends to let them know they were having a daughter, but were still undecided on a name.

It was a chilly afternoon. She came home from work. She saw his keys, cell phone, and wallet on the bar next to their house phone. She heard him in the nursery. Walking in, she saw him putting the crib together. He looked up and saw her.

"Hey gorgeous, how was work?"

She smiled. "It was good, but my feet are killing me. What are you doing?"

"I'm putting the crib together, so you won't have to worry about doing it when I'm gone." he said, looking at the directions, with his tools scattered on the floor. She smiled at him, paying close attention to the directions. She walked into their bedroom to change out of her scrubs. She had thought about the big possibility that Jack would have to miss the birth of their daughter, if he was called to combat.

He walked in their bedroom and saw her looking at their wedding picture and other great photos of them together. He knew what she was thinking about. Holding her hand, he pulled her towards him. "What if you're gone when I go into labor and you miss the birth?"

"I hope I'm here, but if I'm not, you know our moms will be here, so you shouldn't worry."

"I want you to be here, I mean of course I want our moms to be here, but I really need you more than I need them."

"Kate, I know. I want to be here more than anything, but I can't stay behind. My team needs me out there."

She was upset. "Are they always going to come first? I need you more than they do. I'm having your child."

"I know you do, baby. Please don't start an argument over something I can't control. Right now I'm home with you. Let's not think of what could or could not happen."

"I just don't know how much longer I can be your consolation prize. You don't want to be home with me. You want to be in combat. It's like you live for killing Al-Qaeda or something. What are you going to do when you kill all of them? You won't know what to do with yourself."

He knew she was just upset but she was starting to hit nerves with him. "Well that's what I do for a living, Kate. I am not a banker or a real estate agent who can have normal paternity leave. This isn't even a fair argument. You know that when my team is deployed, we are gone until the mission is complete. Why are you being this way?"

"Call me crazy but I just want my husband home with me when I'm giving birth. I think every normal woman, every normal wife wants that. I'm tired of always being alone."

"We don't have a normal marriage, remember?" He didn't take her seriously when she was upset. He knew Kate. He knew these were just her hormones. "If I'm called to go, I have to go. I have no choice. Are we really fighting over this? Do you think it doesn't bother me that I may have to miss the birth of my first child? It does. It bothers every man to miss something like that. But we look at it like this is what we do. It may not be fair. It may not be right, but it is part of the job description. You and the baby mean everything to me. I'd do anything to stay until after you had the baby, but it's not in my hands."

She had tears in her eyes. "I'm just scared to go through this without you."

"I know you're scared, baby. It's a possibility that I'll deploy before the baby is born and I'll unfortunately have to miss it, but it's also a possibility that I'll be home. I don't know, but right now I'm home with you so let's just enjoy it." He hugged her. "You and the baby are the two most important people in my life. If I was to lose just one of you, I'd be lost."

"You won't lose us." They hugged tightly. They kissed passionately and made love for over an hour.

They laid together in bed, wrapped up in the sheets. He touched her belly and felt the baby kick. "Wow! That was crazy!"

She looked at him and smiled. "What?"

"She kicked."

She smiled. "Yeah, she does that all the time."

"Does it hurt?"

"No…"

He kissed her belly. "Daddy loves you." he whispered to her belly.

She kissed his lips. "Your daughter and I are hungry."

"How about I make dinner tonight?" he asked.

"I'm craving milk and cereal."

He laughed. "Is there anything else you'll eat?"

"Ooh no, I would love some Mexican food. No salsa or Pico de Gallo."

"Is that code for me to go get you some Mexican food?"

She laughed. "You're catching on, very good, First Sergeant."

They got dressed, walked into the kitchen. She wore his favorite Oklahoma Sooners T-shirt and a pair of his workout shorts, since her shorts no longer fit. Her hair was a curled, teased mess. He tied his shoes and grabbed his wallet, sunglasses and keys off the bar. She sat at the bar eating a bowl of fruit. "I'll be back in a minute," he said.

"Okay hurry up. I'm starving."

He laughed and closed the door. He got in his truck. "I love that woman." He started his truck and left to get her food. Twenty minutes had passed. He walked in the door carrying her food. She excitedly waited for him to open the white Styrofoam plate. He noticed the look on her face. "What is it?"

"There's Pico de Gallo and salsa."

"I specifically told them no salsa." He saw the look on her face. She looked as if she was going to vomit. "Are you not going to eat it? I can scrape all the Pico de Gallo and salsa off."

She smiled. He was kind enough to go get her food. The least she could do was eat it without complaining. "I'll eat it. Thank you for getting it for me." He scraped the salsa and Pico de Gallo off. "I might as well take an antacid now."

He laughed. "So my Mom was asking if we had picked out a name yet."

"We need to."

"She came up with a fair way to pick a name," he said.

"Okay, how?" she asked as she ate the fruit salad.

"We pick our absolute favorite names and put them in a bowl. Then we draw a name, and that'll be the name we go with."

"Okay, we'll do it after dinner."

"I just want to have a name picked before I leave again. That way, if you have her when I'm gone, I'll at least know what my daughter's name is."

She looked at him and smiled. "I'll let her know how much her daddy loves her."

"But if I'm called, you're always in my heart and you're always on my mind."

"And you're always in mine." After dinner, they each picked their absolute favorite girl's name, complete with a middle name and put them into a bowl. They both agreed that her middle name should be a family name.

"What name did you pick?" he asked.

"I picked Gracelyn Rose. My grandmother's name is Rose. What about you?" she said.

He smiled. "I picked Liberty Belle. My great grandmother's name was Belle."

She let him draw a slip of paper out of the bowl first. "So, what's our daughter's name going to be?" she asked.

He looked down at the paper and then smiled at her. "Liberty Belle Hamilton…" He smiled. "…My little Libby," he lovingly rubbed her belly. They laughed, he tickled her. They got themselves some ice cream and watched a romantic comedy in their room before bed. As she laid in his strong arms, she began to gently drag her fingernails down his chest. He looked down at her, into her eyes. She straddled him, slipping her sexy white laced teddy from *Victoria's Secret* over her head.

"Tonight, soldier, you're mine." He smiled. He leaned forward to kiss her neck. Her arms were around his neck, as she leaned her back. The ends of her long, wild curled hair nearly touched the bed sheets. He made her look at him. He brushed her bangs out of her face and looked into her eyes. "You are so gorgeous."

She smiled, as she softly kissed his neck, shoulder and pectorals. She gently kissed each of his abdominal muscles. They were kissing passionately, as he made love to her. Afterwards, they were lying underneath the sheets, holding each other. He ran his fingertips up and down her bare back, as she drifted off to sleep with her head lying on his chest listening to his heartbeat. He could smell the jasmine in her hair and the smell of honeysuckle on her skin.

The next afternoon, he drove to the mall and bought a recordable book for his daughter. While she was at work, he sat in the nursery and recorded his voice by reading the book. He also bought many other children's books and recordable DVDs. He sat in the nursery and recorded himself reading the many books to her.

She came home for lunch. She saw his truck sitting in the driveway and walked inside. "Hey I'm home." she said hanging up her purse.

"I'm in the nursery." he said. The nursery was looking good. They painted the walls pink and put up butterfly themed wall border. The crib furniture was white. They had LIBERTY in flowered letters on the wall behind the crib.

She walked in to the nursery and saw him sitting in the glider with a book on his lap. "Hey, what are you doing in here?" she asked.

"I'm just thinking."

Seeing the book on his lap, she asked, "What's that?"

"I bought a book and I recorded my voice on it for her, so when I'm gone, I can still read to her and she'll know my voice. Here, I want you to play these for her when I'm gone too."

"What are they?" she asked, holding about twelve DVDs in her hands.

"They're videos of me reading to her."

She began to fear for him. She had nightmares at night about him. She was terrified for him. They made dinner together and watched a movie in their bedroom over their favorite ice cream, chocolate chip cookie dough. They made love very passionately; for she had a feeling he would be leaving soon.

After making love, he watched ESPN on their bedroom TV as she laid on his chest, listening to his heartbeat. His arms were wrapped around her. Soon after, she drifted off to sleep. He continued to hold her until he fell asleep.

In the middle of the night, his cell phone rang. He was told he and his team had a mission. He departed in two hours. He hung up the phone, looked over at her, sleeping peacefully. He smiled and gently kissed her cheek. He got out of bed, got dressed and began to pack. She awoke to his dog tags clanging together, bags zipping, the closet doors opening and drawers closing.

"What's going on?" she asked.

He looked at her, while packing. "I have a mission."

She pulled her robe on and tried to hold back her fear for him. "How long will you be gone?"

He zipped his bags. "Until the mission is complete, will you be alright?"

She smiled bravely. "Yeah, I'll be fine. I don't want you to worry about me."

He pulled her against him, as she silently cried on his shoulder. Tears streamed from her eyes onto his shirt, like bullets. He felt her tears. "I'll be home before you know it."

She looked up in his eyes, as her tears drizzled down her cheeks. "Promise me, Jack. Promise me that you'll come home to us."

He caught her tears with his thumbs and kissed her lips. "I promise I'll come back to you, baby."

"I'll be here waiting for you to pick up where we left off." she said.

"Smile for me and be strong for me. I'll be back soon…" He reached in his pocket and showed her the picture she had gave him years before when they first started dating. "…I'm carrying you with me always. You keep me alive and you bring me home."

She hugged him and kissed him, as they were standing in the middle of their kitchen, holding each other tightly. "I love you, Jack."

He smiled down at her. "I love you too baby." He looked at her growing belly, touched and kissed it. "Daddy loves you, Libby," he whispered.

"Here I wrote this for you." she handed him a white envelope. He smiled and put it in his pocket. The team would send a truck to come get him. The team didn't have time to drive their personal vehicles to the compound. The truck would take them to the airfield and they would immediately deploy.

He picked up his bag. The truck was waiting on the curb with him. Tom walked down his driveway to the truck.

"Bye baby. Take care of yourself."

"I love you."

"I love you too." He walked to the truck and got in. The truck quickly drove away. The teams and their much needed equipment boarded a C-17 cargo plane in the middle of the night. It lifted off into the dark horizon. He looked at her picture for hours, and read the letter she had given him.

> *Dear Jack,*
>
> *Once again, if you're reading this, you're on your way somewhere dangerous for who knows how long and I'm here missing you and praying for you. This house already feels different. Without you here, it doesn't feel like home. I miss you so much. I miss your laugh, your smile. I even miss tripping over your boots. I know I complained about that a lot, but I wish they were here to trip over. I miss washing and folding your uniforms, seeing your gear everywhere, and you cleaning your weapons at the kitchen table. I'm looking around the house and it feels like you're still here. I almost expect you to come through that door and we pick up where we left off. Your time at home with me is never long enough, but it's enough because I let you know how much love you, how much I miss you when you're gone, that I'm waiting for you and we make love like ten times a week. I miss hearing your dog tags clang together.*
>
> *I love you so much Jack. You're an amazing husband and you're going to be an extraordinary daddy. Our daughter is going to be spoiled rotten by you. I can't wait to see you with her. I promise to read her that book you bought for her every night. She'll know who you are. I have pictures of you and me all over the nursery. She will love you and have you wrapped around her little finger. I'm counting on you to keep your promise and come back to us. We need you.*
>
> *I love you so much, Jack. I'm here waiting on you. Stay safe.*
>
> *Come home to me"*

Twenty hours later, the team landed at the Bagram Airbase in Afghanistan. The aircraft was unloaded and the team was briefed on their mission and their objectives. A week into deployment, they had been engaged by the Taliban several times. In his bunk late at night, he sat and thought about what he wanted her to know if something were to happen to him. He got out a piece of notebook paper and wrote her a letter. Afterwards, he taped the letter at the top of his foot locker.

Tom knocked on his door. "Hey, Mike says there is something we need to see in the TOC."

"Alright, I'll be right there." Jack said. The team met in the TOC for briefing on the area they were going to. They were going into the Swatalo Sur Mountains, twenty miles west from Kunar's provincial capital city, Asababad.

14

IT WAS A cold December 12th night. All team members except Sam were going out on this mission. He would stay behind and monitor the TOC. He wanted to go out with the team, but knew Jack needed him in the TOC. Bravo and Charlie Teams were given another assignment.

Alpha Team quickly ran toward the helicopter, carrying their rifles in full battle gear. Sam approached the helicopter. "Watch your six. I got ya covered from the air." he said.

"See ya when we get back," Jack said.

With the team aboard a stealthy Blackhawk helicopter, they lifted off and gained altitude. Dressed in camouflage Kevlar with their faces painted green and black, they were to blend in with the darkness. He and his team were sitting quietly armed with an arsenal of weapons. He refused to let himself think about Kate and the baby while on a mission. It was too much of a distraction to him. He had to be completely focused on his men, their mission, and getting back alive. Their mission was to hunt down and eliminate a small group of locals, who had aspirations of creating a regional Islamic fundamentalist prominence, called Ahmad Shah, commonly known as 'Commander Ishmael' and kill them. The area was under heavy Taliban control.

Using the darkness as cover, the helicopter flew in and landed at the team's established landing zone (LZ-Charlie). He and his team quickly exited and established a secure perimeter around the helicopter allowing the helicopter to depart. They had intelligence suggesting that a small number of insurgents were operating in nearby mountains and were terrorizing locals in the village at the base of the mountains and forcing men to join them and aid them. They were sexually assaulting and brutally beating women and young girls.

Once they located the terrorists, they would deliver a solid attack, eliminating the threat. They looked through night vision binoculars, looking for anything in the darkness. "Anyone got anything?" he whispered over his radio.

"That's a negative, Alpha 1," Tom replied.

"Alright, let's head out." They used the darkness to move closer on the village below. The village was smaller than what they were used to seeing. "Spread out. Keep small. Kill shots only, use your silencers." Jack ordered.

Each man panned out to look for these wannabe terrorists. Brad and Jake were moving stealthily when they saw two men with AK-47s talking outside a building. "Two targets armed with AK's." Brad quietly said over his radio.

Jack and Tom stopped where they were. "Take them out, head shots only." Jack ordered. As one of the terrorists walked back inside the building, Brad fired, killing the one remaining outside. He and Jake quickly moved to retrieve and hide the body in the brush. They took the man's weapon and ammunition for additional ammunition. When the second man reappeared, he knew something was not right. He wondered where his friend could have gone. He was looking around and shouting the man's name in Arabic. Tom fired one shot at the man, but as the man fell, he had pulled the trigger on his rifle, alerting the entire village that visitors were present.

"Our cover has been blown!" Jack yelled, as more men with more rifles came out. He, Marcus, Brad and Luke were separated from Tom, Jamal, Mark, Eric, and Jake.

Sam was back at the firebase inside the TOC, monitoring the radio transmissions. He was ready to send re-enforcements to the team's location if they needed back up.

The terrorists began firing all around them. Jack realized he and his men were severely outnumbered. Intelligence suggested it was a small group, consisting of thirty men. The reality was that numbers were severely understated, more than two hundred.

Back at Fort Bragg, Kate, Paige, and Jenny were all talking over dinner. They got together a lot during missions, it helped get them through. They relied on each other. No other woman knew better about what they were going through than each other.

She was at the end of her second trimester. Paige and Jenny were beginning to plan her baby shower. "It's going to be so amazing to see him as a Daddy. To be honest, I never pictured Jack as a husband or a father." Paige admitted.

"Oh I know. I remember him saying that he would never get married and never have kids." Jenny said. "And then he changed. He was different after he came back from Dallas after he met you."

Kate smiled. "He told me the minute he saw me, I changed his mind on what he wanted."

"You two look so perfect together."

"I miss him so much. I hope he's here when I go into labor."

Paige touched her hand. "But if he's not, you have us. We'll be here for you. We take care of our own."

"What's the name you're naming her again, Justice or Independence?" Jenny asked, as they laughed.

"We're naming her Liberty Belle Hamilton."

"Well, it does sound cuter, the more you say it, Liberty Belle Hamilton." Paige repeated three times.

"I'm sorry, it just sounds like something you'd name a battleship," Jenny said, as they laughed.

Kate looked at the picture of her and Jack together on the bar. "I really miss him."

"They'll be home soon, just keep being that strong pregnant Army wife," Paige said as they laughed.

"How do you two get through this with children? Were Tom and Jake home when you had your kids?"

"Jake missed Riley's birth, but came home ten months later. He was home for Rachel's birth, but he missed the whole first year of her life also."

"Tom was home for both of our boys' births. Of course my boys were born in the late 90s. There was no war like Iraq and Afghanistan going on." Paige said.

"How do you do it? How do you keep it together with kids?"

"I've found it's easier with kids. The kids keep you busy. You don't have so much free time. The boys and I have a routine. You have to have a solid routine…" Paige said.

"A bottle of wine is a must." Jenny admitted. They laughed.

"I don't drink that often," Kate said.

"Once you have that baby, you will." Jenny teased. "Trust me, when you have kids, the waiting isn't so bad anymore because you're constantly busy with changing diapers, chasing toddlers everywhere. Time flies once you have kids."

"I'm nervous about the possibility that Jack could miss the birth and the whole first year." Kate admitted.

"Unfortunately it's a fact of military life. But you shouldn't worry because you have us to help you." Jenny reassured. She was thankful for having friends like Paige and Jenny.

In Afghanistan, after only a short period of time on the ground, the team was met with heavy enemy fire such as RPGs and small arms fire. They returned fire. After an hour of fighting, Jack requested emergency extraction seeing as they were highly outnumbered. The time was 2430 ZULU. (12:30 a.m.)

"Sam, I need gunships on station ASAP! Have them roll in hot!" Jack yelled to Sam, giving the coordinates.

"Roger, Alpha 1, how many hostiles?" Sam asked. He was worried for the team. Those were after all, his brothers.

"Close to two hundred, it's the whole damn village. Attack from direction west, clear it hot!" Jack yelled.

"Roger, Alpha 1." Sam said. Colonel Mitchell was behind Sam in the TOC listening to the radio transmissions. Sam looked to Colonel Mitchell. "They need air support and they need it now, sir,"

Colonel Mitchell got on his phone and ordered an air strike. "Roll in strike package Bravo against large number of enemy combatants. I authenticate Tango Whiskey. Time is 2430 ZULU." The pilots and crew were grabbing their gear and sprinting to the aircraft. They listened over their radios. "This will be a dangerous close fire mission." Colonel Mitchell said over his radio to other stations. "Attention all aircraft this is a dangerous close fire mission. Nine man Green Beret team is on the ground."

Marcus had been shot in the thigh and the arm. Jack rushed to him and applied a tourniquet onto his thigh. An RPG was fired at Jack. "RPG!" a soldier yelled.

Jack saw it coming straight at him and Marcus. He dove on top of Marcus, they slid down a hill. The RPG exploded within feet of Luke and Brad. The explosion sent shrapnel pieces into Luke's face. He couldn't see anything. Brad had shrapnel in his leg and back. He was protecting Luke. Luke had given him his rifle and sidearm.

"Alpha 1, ETA for gunships and MED-EVAC is five mikes." Sam informed Jack. He couldn't help but be worried for his team.

Minutes were referred to as mikes. The rest of the team was cut off and under even heavier enemy fire 800 yards away. "Alpha 1, we are pinned down! We won't make it to the extraction point!" Tom yelled over his radio.

He wasn't leaving any of his men behind. It was his job to get them all safely back to their families. "I'm going back for the rest of the team," he told Marcus.

"Jack, an air strike is coming! You'll never make it back!"

He pulled the map out of his pocket and handed it to him. "If I'm not back in five mikes with the rest of the team, you direct the helicopter here to this clearing for extract. Do not wait for me! Get out or we'll be overrun!"

Rounds were ricocheting off rocks and trees. They could hear the fighters getting closer and closer. The nine man team was separated, surrounded and outnumbered. "You're crazy! You'll never make it!" Marcus yelled.

He took off in the direction of his pinned down team. Each team member was close to him, as brothers. He knew they needed him. He wouldn't leave anyone behind. He lived by a code: **never leave a comrade wounded on the battlefield, never leave a man behind**. They would all go home together.

As he got closer to his team, he came under heavy fire. A round struck him in the right leg. Despite the pain, he kept going. His adrenaline was pumping. His heart was pounding so loud he could hear it instead of just feel it.

He fired at enemy fighters as he ran through them to get to his team. He called out to Tom. "Alpha 2, I'm coming for y'all. Hold your fire to the north!" he yelled as rounds ricocheted past him and mortars exploded around him.

"Copy Alpha 1…" He looked to the men he had with him. "Hold your fire to the north. Jack is coming." Tom had been shot in the shoulder. Eric had been shot in the chest. He was killed in action (KIA). Jake had been shot through the neck. He was KIA. Jamal was tending to the wounded, though he had been shot multiple times in the shoulder, stomach and thigh. Mark was severely injured from an RPG explosion.

Reaching his cut off and severely wounded team, he saw he had two dead team members and three critically wounded. He loaded Tom and Jake onto his back and grabbed Eric's pant leg to drag him. "I'll stay with Mark." Jamal said, still doing what he could to treat Mark's wounds. He was disoriented, barely coherent. His breathing was erratic. Jamal was doing all he could to keep him calm and apply tourniquets.

"I'll come back for you both." he said to Jamal. He was trying to keep Mark calm. He took off carrying three brothers to safety. He had five mikes until the air strike. Two mikes had already passed by. He ran the 800 yards under heavy small arms fire. Tom couldn't believe what Jack was doing. He couldn't believe Jack could carry two men on his back and drag another, while injured and under personal heavy fire. Jack laid them down.

"I'm going back for the rest of the team!"

"Jack! The air strike is two mikes out!" Marcus yelled.

"I have two mikes! Change the extraction point now!" Tom grabbed the radio from Marcus and changed the coordinates for the extraction point to the clearing Jack had shown Marcus on the map.

As he ran the 800 yards back to Mark and Jamal, he was shot in the chest and back. Despite the pain, he kept going. His indomitable spirit wouldn't let him stop. He carried Jamal on his back, and cradled Mark in his arms, he ran as fast as he could.

50 yards from the original extract point, he tripped over a downed tree. Three insurgents attacked him. He fought all three off by his precise training. A fourth fighter attempted to take Jamal, who was lying on the ground. He had lost a lot of blood and was getting weaker and weaker. Jack grabbed his side arm and shot the fighter. He again threw Jamal on his back and again cradled Mark. He pushed himself to get his team to the new extract point. With his heart pounding, his adrenaline pumping, he had never been so determined or so focused in his life. He was bringing all his men home.

Reaching Tom, he grabbed the radio and told the pilots, "Nine man team waiting for emergency extraction, north of green smoke!" he yelled over the radio. He ran to the clearing, now the new extraction point. It was 50 yards from his team. He threw three canisters and green smoke quickly rose in the darkness. He had less than two minutes to get his beleaguered team to the new extract point before the air strike. He reached his team. All were accounted for. He had two men killed and five severely wounded men.

"Jack, the gunships are going to roll in hot and they are thirty seconds out!" Tom said.

"I have time." he lied to himself. He was either going to succeed or die trying to save his men and himself. But in his mind set, failure was not an option.

Throwing Jamal and Tom on his back, he cradled Mark in his arms. He ran as fast as he could to the extract point. He laid them down and gave Tom and Jamal each a weapon and an extra magazine of ammunition to defend themselves and their new position until he returned. Two helicopters were coming, a MED-EVAC helicopter and an Apache armed with hell fire missiles carrying Navy SEALs and more Green Berets.

He went back for Marcus, Jake, Eric, Brad and Luke. He threw Marcus and Brad on his back and dragged Luke and Eric by their arms. He was in severe pain. The MED-EVAC helicopter was approaching. He reached the new extract point as the helicopter was coming in to land. He had to go back for Jake.

"I have one more man," Jack said to the pilot as he loaded Jamal, Marcus, Brad, Luke, and Eric into the helicopter.

"Negative, we have to go now! Let's get the hell out of here!" the pilot said to him.

"NO! You can wait two mikes! I'm not leaving without my men!" Jack demanded. He ran back for Jake.

The helicopter was getting ricocheted by rounds. The fighters were getting closer. Tom and Brad defended the helicopter. "Oh my God, we're going to get hit," the pilot said to his crew. The gunners were firing to cover the helicopter.

"Just give him two more mikes." Tom said, firing his weapon.

"He'll be back. He doesn't know how to fail," Brad said.

As he reached Jake and loaded him onto his back, an enemy fighter snuck up behind him and swung his rifle at him. He laid Jake down and charged him, tackling him to the ground. He pulled out his knife and stabbed the fighter twice. He threw Jake over his shoulder and hurried to the helicopter. Reaching the helicopter, he loaded him into the helicopter. With all his men aboard, he realized there was no room for him. He completed the mission. All of his men were accounted for.

An attack force of fifteen fighters descended onto the MED- EVAC helicopter. "Get out of here!" he yelled to the pilots. Seeing he would be left behind and was severely injured, Tom and Brad jumped out of the helicopter just as the helicopter lifted off the ground. They wouldn't leave without him.

"What are you two doing?" he asked them.

"We're not leaving you without any backup," Tom said.

The helicopter lifted off with the rest of Alpha Team. He watched the helicopter take off under heavy fire. He turned to Tom and Brad. "Kill as many as you can." He grabbed the classified documents out of his pocket and burned them. They prepared for combat with their knives. Suddenly, as if God had answered their prayers, the Apache helicopter and the Blackhawk helicopter carrying re-enforcements was inbound, carrying eight Navy SEALs and eight Green Berets. The gunships began firing at the area where the enemy fighters were.

"Oh thank you, God!" Jack exhaled. They were relieved when they saw the helicopters and began to have faith that they'd make it out of this skirmish. That hope was shattered when both the Apache and Blackhawk were hit by RPG-7 rockets. They watched helplessly as the helicopters spun out of control. Black smoke billowed out of the aircraft. The pilots desperately tried to maintain in control, but both helicopters crashed down into the valley…

The MED-EVAC helicopter arrived back to base. The injured Alpha Team members were each rushed into surgery. Mark died aboard the MED-EVAC helicopter, as did Jamal. Colonel Mitchell was taken by Blackhawk to the base hospital, which was a fifteen minute flight from the outpost. Sadly, Marcus and Luke died in surgery. Their injuries were too severe and each had lost seventy percent of their blood. Six of the nine man assault Green Berets team had been killed in action in the ambush. Jack, Tom, and Brad were the only survivors.

There Colonel Mitchell was briefed on the status of his team. He had six members KIA and three missing. The pilot of the MED-EVAC helicopter told him that three members remained in the Swatalo Sur Mountains, under heavy fire.

The next day, it was a sunny but chilly December 13th afternoon. Kate was visiting with Paige and Jenny. They were sitting on the front porch of Jenny's house sipping coffee, enjoying the beautiful winter day. They were laughing about funny things their husbands did, but the laughter quickly silenced when they noticed an unmarked government vehicle slowly drove down their street. All gasped and sat frozen, praying the car would pass them by and not stop in their driveways. Their hearts pounded, their minds raced to the recent memories of their husbands and they held their breath. They watched as the vehicle pulled into Jenny's driveway. Their hearts sank, but who's life would be forever changed?

The team chaplain and a Casualty Notification Officer (CNO) stepped out dressed in their Army formal uniforms. The CNO carried a briefcase. The chaplain carried his Bible. They walked purposefully up the walkway to the porch. Every military wife knows what it means to have men in formal dress uniform come to their home.

Jenny stood bravely. "Are you Mrs. Jacob Brigham?"

She nodded while shaking uncontrollably. Paige and Kate held their breath. Jenny was shaking. "Mrs. Brigham, the Secretary of the Army regrets to inform you that your husband, Sergeant First Class Jacob Riley Brigham was killed in action yesterday, December 12, 2010 at approximately 2440 hours."

She brought her hands up over her mouth and fell to her knees on the hard porch. She screamed. Kate and Paige rushed to her and held her. She sobbed hysterically. Paige and Kate were crying too. "I'm very sorry for your loss, Mrs. Brigham."

The chaplain held her hands. "He died for his brothers and for his country."

"How did he die?" she asked as Paige and Kate held her.

The Casualty Notification Officer composed himself professionally. "He was shot through the neck. He died instantly."

Jenny shook her head and sobbed. Paige and Kate were crying with her and holding her. "I was so stupid...I was so stupid to believe he'd come back." she sobbed.

"No, sweetie, you aren't stupid. We all believe that." Kate said. As she held her friend, now a grieving widow in her arms, she began to worry for Jack. Where was he? Was he in danger? Would he come back?

In the unforgiving mountains of Afghanistan, the helicopters carrying re-enforcements was just shot by RPGs. The three team members watched helplessly as the pilots fought to keep the helicopters under control, but both quickly crashed in the valley. The three men carefully made their way to the helicopters to check for survivors. All on board were killed, including the pilots. They took their fallen comrades weapons and extra ammunition as well as the canteens for hydration.

They had just witnessed many of their friends die and there was nothing they could do to save them. The sudden 'hit in the gut' reality was that they were on their own. Jack got on his radio. "Sam, the birds were just shot down!"

Sam's stomach dropped. "Roger, Alpha 1. Are there any survivors?"

Jack looked at the helicopter. "Negative. Launch CRT[18]."

"Affirmative, what's the status of your team, Jack?"

"Six were med-evacuated out. Tom and Brad are with me. We've got at least a hundred on our asses! Send whatever you have, how copy?" He gave him their new coordinates.

All three were badly injured but still able to fight. "Roger, sending Charlie Team now, ETA to your location twenty mikes."

He could hear the fighters getting closer and closer. "Negative, we don't even have ten mikes! They're right on top of us! We're about to be overrun!"

---

[18] CRT stood for Casualty Recovery Team

His radio was badly damaged. Sam could hear him talking and the gunfire in the background, but the static was garbling it all up. He couldn't understand.

"Jack, please repeat, over…"

"Sam, do you copy?" he asked. The radio went dead. He took the radio's ear piece out of his ear and threw it on the ground. It was useless. He looked to Tom and Brad.

"Colonel, the birds were shot down. I've lost radio contact with Alpha 1." Colonel Mitchell was in disbelief.

"We're on our own. Kill as many as you can," he said, as he distributed the last of his water in his canteen to Tom and Brad. He was extremely thirsty, but he shared what little he had left with them. He knew the likelihood they'd survive was slim. He knew it wouldn't be long before the enemy would discover them and kill them.

"Jack! They're coming up on this side!" Tom yelled. He ran back and forth to defending their position from all sides. An hour into the fight, forty insurgents outnumbered the three Green Berets. The fighters were heavily armed. Jack was on his last magazine. He fired the last of his ammunition. He had one grenade left. He pulled the pin and threw it. "GRENADE!" he yelled, covering Tom and Brad.

As the smoke cleared, an enemy fighter charged them. Brad aimed his M9 Berretta and pulled the trigger. After firing two shots, he was out of ammunition. "I'm out!" he yelled.

Jack tackled the fighter and fought him with his bare hands, no weapon. Killing the fighter, three more charged Jack. He fought as hard as he could, but was struck in the back of the head with the butt of a weapon. He fell to the ground, unconscious. Tom and Brad fought the insurgents, until they were subdued in the back of the head with the butt of a rifle.

"Take their ID chains off," the leader said. He knew the U.S. military used tags to identify its members. The insurgents searched Tom and Brad and found their dog tags. Jack's tags were also taken off him. The others were hit in the back of the head with the butt of a rifle, each knocked unconscious. The insurgent leader looked at each of the dog tags he held in his hand. He read:

HAMILTON, JACK D.

MERRITT, THOMAS M.

ROBERTS, BRADLEY M.

One insurgent found Kate's picture and handed it to the leader. Holding Jack's tags and the picture in his hand, he watched the three soldiers being carried down the mountain. He threw the tags down into the blood saturated sand. The photograph blew into bushes, near the last known location of Jack, Tom, and Brad.

At the bottom of the mountain, the insurgent leader ordered that the three soldiers be put into the bed of a pick-up truck to be driven across the border into Pakistan to trade them for more weapons from Al-Qaeda in Pakistan.

Dawn had approached. The sun was rising over the two charred remnants what was two stealthy aircraft. The Casualty Recovery Team (CRT) was dispatched to the crash site of two helicopters crashing in the valley of the Swatalo Sur Mountains. Charlie Team, along with a search and rescue team was dispatched to the mountain valley. They hoped to find the three members of Alpha Team. The deceased SEALs and Green Berets' bodies and the classified material aboard the helicopters were recovered. The downed aircrafts were destroyed by fragmentation grenades.

Charlie Team arrived to Jack's last known location. They discovered numerous ammunition casings, a canteen and three sets of dog tags lying in the blood saturated sand.

"Be advised, three sets of tags have been recovered," Brett said as he held the tags in his hands. It was quiet in the mountains.

"Affirmative, what are the names on the tags?" Colonel Mitchell asked. Sam and Mike were present in the TOC.

"HAMILTON, JACK D., MERRITT, THOMAS M., and ROBERTS, BRADLEY D." he read over the radio. Sam's stomach dropped. He tried to maintain his composure. He knew six members of the team were killed. He couldn't help but worry and naturally assume the worse had happened. He assumed Jack, Tom, and Brad were savagely butchered and buried near the ambush site.

"Copy that." the Colonel said. He looked to Sam. "What was the last radio transmission you received from Jack?"

"That 'they were right on top of us. We're about to be overrun.'"

A Charlie Team member searched the twigs and found the photograph of Kate in the bush, near where Jack was knocked unconscious. He picked it up and turned it over. He saw the personal message on the back that read: 'Come back to me'

"I found a photograph here," he said as he handed the photograph to Brett.

Brett looked at it. He recognized Kate. He read the back of the photo. "Be advised, we have also recovered a photograph of a woman. There is a personal message on the back of the photo," he said over his radio.

"Copy that. Bring the tags, the canteen and the picture home with the deceased." Colonel Mitchell.

"We have not located the three missing team members." Colonel Mitchell looked up at Sam. He was noticeably upset. As of now he and Mike were the only remaining Alpha team members.

Jack, Tom, and Brad were in the bed of the truck, being driven through the desert-mountains, still in and out of unconsciousness, with a tarp over their bodies. Their hands and feet were bound with rope. The driver slipped across the border into Pakistan, to a compound in Abbottabad. The compound had walls fourteen foot high, surrounding the entire compound. It was a heavily guarded fortress.

Two armed men approached the drivers. "What are you doing here?" one asked, clutching an AK-47.

"We have trade for more weapons," the driver informed.

The two men were curious. "Show us," the other armed man ordered.

The driver and passenger stepped out of their truck and lifted up the tarp. "Our leader wishes to trade these three American soldiers for more weapons and money."

The two armed fighters looked at the soldiers, seeing that they were still alive and considered the trade. The soldiers were carried into the compound and were taken down into the dark basement. The fighters bound their hands behind their backs with their feet stretched out in front of them. Jack regained consciousness as the insurgents were tying him up. He kicked the man in the face and broke the bonds around his wrists and attempted to free the other two, but was jabbed in the ribs by a wooden object. The soldiers fought back, but were quickly overpowered.

Charlie Team arrived back to the firebase. They handed Sam the personal effects they had found. Sam held Jack's tags and the picture of Kate in his hands. Colonel Mitchell looked over the evidence recovered from the scene. He held the blood stained dog tags of his fallen team and the photograph. The photograph was bent, torn, and stained with dirt and blood.

A task force made up of U.S. Army Green Berets, Marine Corps Force Reconnaissance, Navy SEALs and Air Force commandos from a base in Kandahar, Afghanistan was immediately sent out to the firebase to search for the missing soldiers. They used intelligence from local civilians, but found nothing but empty leads.

The Army officially notified the families of the fallen Navy SEALS and Green Berets soldiers on board the helicopter. The Army also declared Jack, Tom, and Brad as Missing in Action (MIA). Paige and Kate worried for their husbands. Every member who had gone on the mission had been killed besides Jack, Tom, and Brad. At this point, no news was good news.

It was a cold wintery December 14th afternoon. The funerals for Jake, Luke, Eric, Marcus, Mark, and Jamal were held on post at the chapel. The families all elected to have the fallen team laid to rest together in Arlington National Cemetery. This morning was the morning of Jake's funeral.

Paige and Kate consoled Jenny and her daughters at the post chapel. They wore black dresses and black high heels. They cried listening to the music and the chaplain read the obituary. They looked at the flag draped coffin and the Army photo of Jake on an easel. Paige and Kate were terrified that their husbands shared the same fate as the others. Jenny sat next to his parents and their daughters. She and her daughters were sobbing.

After the services, Paige and Kate headed home as Jenny and her family were driving to Washington D.C. to bury Jake. She pulled her car into the driveway next to Jack's truck. She looked at his truck and smiled. She opened his truck door and smelled his scent. She closed her eyes as tears quickly streamed down her face. She was very worried for him. She walked into the house.

Children were playing outside. The moms were talking inside, as their kids played. Suddenly, wives looked out their windows and saw a government vehicle entering the neighborhood. They all watched intensely as they prayed and held their breath, praying the vehicle would pass their homes. When the car would pass, they would breathe a sigh of relief.

The vehicle pulled into the Hamilton residence and parked behind her car. The chaplain and the Casualty Notification Officer (CNO) stepped out in their formal uniforms and walked up the walkway to the front door. She was still wearing her black dress, but had taken off the black heels. She needed to hear his voice, so she put in their wedding video and sat on the sofa. Hearing his voice, she cried. She watched the video when she needed to hear his voice, which lately had been every night. She was extremely worried for him, especially since six members of his team were dead.

The doorbell rang. She assumed it was Paige. Looking out the peep hole, she stood frozen in shock. She saw the two men in full dress uniform. Fearing he was dead, she felt a knot in her throat nearly cutting off her oxygen. She struggled to breathe and think. Gently touching her stomach, she could feel the baby kicking. With tears in her eyes, she swallowed her fear and said out loud, "Lord, please be with me and give me strength, especially for our daughter."

She opened the door with an expression of hope and heartbreak on her face. "Are you Mrs. Jack Hamilton?" The CNO asked her.

She was shaking with fear. "Yes."

"The Secretary of the Army regretfully informs you that your husband, First Sergeant Jack David Hamilton, has been reported as missing in action. He and two others lost contact near the Pakistani border on December 12, 2010 at approximately 0100 hours. Ma'am, I express to you and your family my deepest concern for his well-being. Here are his personal effects, his foot locker, his dog tags, and this photograph of you. The dog tags and the photograph were recovered at the scene."

He placed the blood stained tags and the badly creased, stained photograph in her hands. Tears were rapidly rolling down her cheeks. She saw probably *his* blood, dirt, and sand dried on the articles. He brought Jack's foot locker into the living room.

The chaplain saw she was shaking and her desperation to hold in her emotions until they left. He had counseled Jack and Kate after he was put in a near compromising situation with a war correspondent. He also counseled her through the devastating loss of their child.

"Kate, would you like me to stay with you? I could pray with you and call your families if you need me to."

Tears streamed down her cheeks. She was shaking. Her voice was cracking. "No thank you chaplain. I just need to be alone."

"Do you need me to call your doctor?" he asked concerned.

She shook her head as her face had turned very pale. "No." she cried.

"I'm at the chapel if you need me."

The two men turned and walked away. Closing the door, she belted out a loud scream of anguish, fear and heartbreak. They walked across the street to the Merritt residence to inform Paige. Michael and Sam, Tom's sons, were throwing a football to each other in the front yard. They noticed them walking up the walkway.

Looking up to the mantle above their fireplace, she saw their wedding picture beside it. She took his Army picture off the mantle and pressed it to her heart. She screamed his name, sobbed and prayed to God. She touched his foot locker and opened it. She saw his uniforms neatly folded. She could smell his scent on the clothing. She touched the extra ammunition magazines, pictures of her and him together. Noticing the envelope taped up inside, she pulled it off. The front of the envelope read: *Katherine Hamilton.* She opened the envelope and read the letter he had written her.

> *"Katherine,*
>
> *If you're reading this, I broke my promise and I'm not coming home. I'm up here with God and I'm looking down on you now. I'll always be with you. I'll always be a part of you. I need you to know, Kate, you were the best thing that ever happened to me. I'm so happy I married you.*
>
> *Before I met you, I had no interest in marriage, but when I saw you, you changed my mind. There isn't a day that goes by where I do not stop to thank God for bringing you into my life. I carry you in my heart and soul, next to God.*
>
> *I won't be there for the birth of our little girl. I hope she looks just like you. I hope she's like me in some ways. I hope she's a good person, a good friend who stands up for her friends and for what's right. I'm relieved to know that you'll have her, the last piece of me with you. I'm sorry I won't be a part of her life like I wanted. I was looking forward to being home when she was born. I know she'll be beautiful. I know she'll be kind, hopefully smart just like you. You're going to be an amazing mother, Kate. I couldn't have found a better woman to have a family with. Promise me you'll tell her how much I love her every morning and every night. Be sure to play those videos for her every day and every night. I want her to know my voice, even though she'll never know me. That's my biggest regret, is that I was too busy serving my country to be the husband and father I should've been. She is my greatest accomplishment, my pride and my joy. Every day, tell her how proud I am of her and that I'm watching over her.*
>
> *I still have your picture with me. It's pretty worn. I've kept it since you gave it to me after we met. It's beside me as I write this to you. I miss you so much.*
>
> *I need you to tell my parents that I love them very much. They are the greatest parents a guy could ask for. Tell Mom I love her very much. Tell Dad that I don't regret following in his shoes by serving my country. Tell him that I'm proud to be his son. He taught me everything about being a soldier and being a leader. Tell Jonah that I love him. He promised me that he would look after you and Liberty for me. I want him to be her replacement father, the man she goes to when she needs anything. He owes me that. Tell Meagan that I love her. Tell JD and Andy that I love them. Tell JD I want him to go to college. I don't want him be like me. I want him and Andy to have a few of my medals and my pistols. Dad can have my rifle, but I want you to keep my wedding ring, my uniforms, medals and dog tags.*
>
> *I don't want you to grieve for me forever, Kate. One day you're going to meet someone else and I want you to allow yourself to be happy. Hopefully, he won't be like me. I hope he'll*

spend every minute with you and protect you, like I wanted to. I hope he's a good man, a good husband and is the father I always wanted to be to Liberty. When that day comes, I do not want you to feel guilty for loving him or that you're somehow being unfaithful to me, because you're not. I hope you keep me in your heart and think of me and what we had often. I'll have your past but I'm man enough to acknowledge that he'll have your future. You and I will be together in your dreams. I want you to be happy and be loved every day.

As far as the funeral goes, I'd like to be buried in the Dallas Fort Worth National Cemetery. I want my casket closed and I want to be in my formal uniform. I'd also like Liberty to have a college savings fund created and a portion of my life insurance to go towards her education. I want her to be able to go to the best university in the country and not worrying about money.

It's time to say goodbye. It's time to let me go and live your life. My life was filled with everything a man could ask for. I served my country and gave my last full measure of devotion. I loved and married a beautiful woman and had a beautiful child. You kept your promise to me, baby, you always waited, I'm just sorry I let you down by breaking mine. Promise me one more thing, promise me that you'll move on and be happy. Put this letter away and never read it again. I love you so much and I'm sorry.

I'm with you always. You're always in my heart and you're always on my mind.

Love, Jack"

She screamed and cried in anguish as she read the letter. Boomer ran to her side. She buried her face into him and sobbed. Miranda, Colonel Mitchell's wife, had rushed over after hearing the news. She comforted her as she cried. She asked her to call her parents. Miranda picked up the phone and dialed her parents' phone number. Her dad was working in his office at home there in Dallas. Mom was out running errands and Lauren was at work.

When the phone rang, he looked at the phone and saw it was Jack and Kate's number. He quickly answered the phone. "Hey sweetheart, how are you doing?"

"Hi, this is Miranda Mitchell. I'm a friend of your daughter's."

His first thought was something had happened to Kate, like early labor. "Oh my God did something happen to her or the baby?" he asked worried.

"No, no they're okay. I'm Colonel Mitchell's wife, Jack's commanding officer. He has been reported as Missing in Action."

He heard Kate sobbing in the background with Paige. They were both comforting each other. He was stunned and speechless. There was a knot in his throat preventing him to breathe. "May I talk to her?" he asked with his voice shaking.

She handed Kate the phone. "Daddy, Jack is missing in action."

"Are they sure?"

She was still sobbing. "I'm holding his tags and the picture of me he always carried with him. There is dried blood on them."

He began to get tears in his eyes and a pain in his heart. He knew that neither Al-Qaeda nor the Taliban held prisoners very long and frequently executed their prisoners and broadcast it on live television. "I want you to come home. You need to be with family." he urged.

"Dad, this is my home. This is where he was with me last. I don't want to leave. Can you tell his parents? They deserve to hear this in person."

With the tears in his eyes and the pain in his heart, he felt like he had just been sucker punched. "Yeah, sure honey. I'll do it."

Carole pulled into the driveway. He heard her car door close and saw her walk up the walkway to the front door. She unlocked the door. Still stunned about the news with tears running down his face, he kneeled on the floor and prayed for Jack. Cheerfully walking into his office, she saw him kneeling and praying. "Honey, are you alright?"

He stood. She saw the seriousness and heartbreak in his eyes. "Jack has been declared as Missing in Action. Kate was just notified."

She immediately covered her face and began to cry. He hugged her. "I need to be with her right now." she said.

"We'll fly out tonight, but she wants us to notify Bill and Denise first."

Tears ran down her face. "Okay, well let's go." He changed clothes. She called Kate and was so heartbroken when she heard Kate crying hysterically. They drove over to Bill and Denise's home.

Arriving to the Hamilton home, they stepped out of their car and walked slowly up the driveway. They were nervous to tell their close friends that their youngest son was missing in action. The American and the Army flags were hoisted proudly. They fluttered in the chilly breeze against a clear blue Texas winter sky. Ringing the doorbell, they waited. They noticed the 'Blue Star Mother's' flag next to the doorbell. Carole looked back at the yard and saw the yellow ribbons tied around the hickory tree.

Bill opened the door and was happy to see them. "Hello, how are y'all?" he cheerfully asked.

He hugged Carole and shook Matt's hand. "Hello Bill, how are y'all?" Carole asked as Denise came to the hallway.

"Oh we're doing alright." Denise said. They walked in and sat on the sofa. "Do y'all want some coffee or tea?" Denise asked. She sensed they had some serious news.

Carole looked at Matt. She could see he was nervous about delivering heartbreaking and terrifying news to their closest friends. "We came to tell you something very serious." he said, as they sat down together in the den.

"Is everything okay with Kate and the baby?" Denise asked worried.

"Yes, they're fine. Bill… Denise… there is really no easy way to say this, and the fact that we're family makes this even harder to say…" Matt said, as he started to get emotional.

"Okay, Matt, you're scaring us. What's going on?" Bill asked nervously.

"…About an hour ago, Kate was notified that Jack has been declared as Missing in Action."

Bill and Denise's faces lost color. She covered her mouth and shook her head in shock with tears immediately rolling down her face. Denise buried her face into Carole's shoulder and cried. "Are they absolutely sure? I mean he could just be taking longer than expected to get back to base." Bill stated, not wanting to believe it.

Matt looked at him and saw he was devastated and in disbelief. "Bill, they found his tags and they gave them to Kate."

Denise sobbed. Carole held her, and she also cried. Bill was in shock. He had tears in his eyes, looking at her sobbing on Carole's shoulder. He walked outside to the patio, to think and to get some fresh air. He felt as if he was being smothered. He stood facing the pool with his hands on top of his head, crying.

Matt stood behind him. "I'm sorry that I had to come tell you. I'm here if you need me."

Bill was trying to hold his emotions in, but tears were rolling uncontrollably down his face. "I'd rather you and Carole told us, than complete strangers. How is Kate?"

Matt looked down at the ground. He knew his friends were in unimaginable torment. "She's devastated and scared. Her friends are with her now."

"If he's a POW, we don't have much time. Those animals execute their prisoners." Bill said panicking.

Matt placed his hand on his shoulder. "Bill, right now, they have the SEALS, Marine Force-RECON and other Green Berets teams looking. The only thing we can do is to wait and think positive."

Bill turned to him with tears in his eyes. "Will you pray with me?" They both knelt on the ground, bowing their heads. Matt put his hand on his shoulder.

"Lord, please watch over my son. Keep his body and mind strong as he is in the hands of animals. Keep his faith in you strong. Remind him that his family loves him very much. Please Lord let him come home to his family. I beg you Lord." Tears streamed down his cheeks.

Denise rushed upstairs. Carole quickly followed. "Denise, talk to me." she said as she watched her frantically packing her suitcases.

"I'm going to demand answers. They have to tell me more than this. I'm his mother." she said panicking.

"Honey, this is all they know. I promise you that they'll tell us more when they know more." she assured her.

Meanwhile, Meagan came by after work. She sat her purse down next to the coat rack. Seeing no one in the den or kitchen, she walked upstairs.

"Carole, he's my baby. How do you function, not knowing what's happened to your child? I'm going to find out what's happened to my son even if I have to catch a flight to Afghanistan."

Meagan overheard her mother. She saw her mom and Carole hugging in her parents' room. She stood in the doorway. "Mom, what's going on? What's happened to Jack?"

Carole walked towards her. "He's missing in action."

Meagan was in shock, as tears immediately formed in her eyes.

"My head is spinning. I need to be alone just for a moment, to lie down and to pray." Denise said.

Carole and Meagan walked downstairs to make Denise a cup of tea. "I can't believe this is happening. If he's dead, he won't even know his own daughter." Meagan said, sobbing.

"We have to think positively even when we feel there is no hope. We have to have faith." Carole encouraged. Meagan nodded her head in agreement, while sobbing. They hugged, cried and prayed together.

Jonah walked in the house, and heard Carole and Meagan talking in the kitchen. He was cheerful until he saw Meagan sobbing. He immediately thought Jack had been killed. "Meagan, what's going on? What's happened to Jack?" he asked shaking and his voice cracking.

She rushed to him, hugged him and cried on his shoulder. "He is missing in action."

He was in shock. Seeing the fear, the worry and the heartbreak on their faces, he realized that this was real, not a dream. Stumbling backwards, he quickly sat down in one of the breakfast table chairs and tried to hold his emotions in. "Where's Mom?" he asked with his voice cracking.

"She's lying down for a few minutes." Carole said.

Bill and Matt saw him through the patio window, sitting in the chair, with his hands covering. Bill walked in and patted him on the shoulder. Jonah looked up at him. He stood and hugged him tightly. "What do we do, Dad?"

Bill looked down at him as tears formed in his eyes, also. "All we can do is pray and wait, son."

Denise slowly walked down the stairs. She was holding his Army picture, pressing it against her heart as she cried. Bill quickly hugged her as they cried together.

"Who is with Kate right now?" Jonah asked.

"She has her friends with her now." Matt said.

"Denise and I will go out there tonight. We'll stay with her until after she has the baby. She doesn't need to be alone." Carole said.

"I'm going with you. I promised him that I would look after her." Jonah said.

Back at Fort Bragg, she was lying on their bed, sobbing. She looked up at their closet and walked over to it. She looked at his formal uniforms, his black dress shoes and his civilian clothes. She saw his numerous Oklahoma Sooners football t-shirts and ball caps. She touched his favorite one and pulled it off the hanger. She held it up to her face, smelling his cologne. She laid on their bed and sobbed into it for hours. Neighboring friends stayed with her until their families could get there.

Bill, Denise, Carole, Jonah, and Christi flew out that evening, to Fort Bragg. They hailed a taxi from the airport in Fayetteville, North Carolina. They arrived at their home around 9:30 p.m. One of the neighbors answered the door. After the introduction, they went into their bedroom. Carole went straight to the bed, sat down and folded her arms around her. She held onto her mom and wept. Finally, she raised her head and hugged Denise also.

By the second day, all the Hamilton and Johnson families had arrived to Jack and Kate's home. They reserved rooms at the post hotel. For them, Christmas was put on hold. None could celebrate without knowing whether he was alive or dead.

Bill and Matt went on to Washington D.C. to find out more information from some of Matt's contacts inside the Department of Defense.

Jack, Brad, and Tom's whereabouts were still unknown. Numerous Special Ops teams had all came to the same conclusion, that they were no longer in Afghanistan, most likely in Pakistan, if they were still alive. They were bound and gagged in the basement of a compound in Abbottabad, Pakistan. They had been beaten, tortured and interrogated for days. Jack's injuries were serious. He had lost a lot of blood from his injuries sustained the night of the ambush and from the torture. He had a deep gash on top of his head from the stock of the rifle hitting him when he wouldn't talk to the interrogators, days ago. Blood had dried in his hair and on the side of his face. His uniform was covered in dirt and blood.

The basement was dark, dusty and very cold. They were still wearing their blood stained uniforms. They knew their families' had most likely all been notified that they were missing in action. The door to the basement squeaked as it opened. They heard numerous footsteps walking down the stairs. The light came on. Five armed insurgents stood in front of them, as the soldiers' glared up at them.

An interrogator, with a British accent squatted in front of Jack. "We're going to have a doctor look at your injuries."

"You might as well let me die, because I'm not telling you a damn thing!" Jack said, he glared up at the man.

"You realize by not cooperating, it will cost one of your men here, his life. Do you want to be responsible for getting them killed? You should cooperate."

Jack glared up at the interrogator and his masked gunmen. "My name is Jack Hamilton, First Sergeant in the United States Army, serial number 35867982." he repeated, the same as the weeks before, when interrogated.

"We have ways of making you talk…" The soldiers remained quiet. "…Americans are the guardians of freedom and the protectors of the innocent…" the interrogator said laughing. He was taunting them. "…Do any of you believe in Allah, or as you call him God?" he looked at them.

The soldiers refused to look at him. "Do any of you have wives or children?" he asked again. Jack thought of Kate and his unborn daughter.

"Your women will likely move on and forget all about you. Your children will too, because you are nothing to them." This was a torture and brainwashing technique. It took the prisoners minds off being focused and non-responsive to emotional thoughts of their families. Repeated tactics could weaken the soldiers. All Special Forces soldiers were required to go through SERE (Survive Evasion

Resistance Escape) training, which prepared them for the possibility of captivity. They knew the enemy would use extreme torture and mind games.

The man squatted down, with his face level with his. "If you want to go home to your families, you need to cooperate." he said in a calm voice.

Jack glared up at him. One of the men removed the gag from his mouth. "I'd rather die than help you." he said, covered in sweat and blood. Another insurgent punched him in the face. He spat out the blood. His hands were tied behind his back. Other insurgents hit them with wooden objects. One grabbed Brad by his collar and held a seriated knife to his throat.

An older man walked down into the basement and saw his men beating the soldiers. He held up his hands and shouted in Arabic "Stop!"

The others stopped to address him. The man's face appeared in the light and the soldiers were stunned. They were face to face with "Geronimo" himself. He was the mastermind of the 9/11 attacks and countless other attacks on other countries.

"I want these prisoners kept alive. We can use them." he said to his followers. He hoped the soldiers' would release vital information on other Special Forces teams near the Pakistan border. Their objective was to make one talk, even if that meant torturing and/or killing the other two.

Women dressed in Burkas came in and applied wet wash cloths to their wounds. They wiped the blood from their faces and provided them with very little food and water. The insurgents left, as did the women.

"We need to figure out a way to get out of here. Lord, show us the way out!" Jack prayed as he looked around the room.

A physician came to the compound and was escorted down in to the basement. He was alarmed to find three American soldiers, bloody, beaten and half starved. He examined Jack. He was very uncooperative. He didn't want the doctor to touch him. The doctor asked for men to hold him down as he treated his gunshot and stab wounds. He would have to dig the bullets out of him. It took seven insurgents to hold him still.

The doctor removed his gag. "You might as well let me die because I'm not telling you anything!" he yelled. "Lord, give me the strength to get out of here. If it is your will that I be with you in paradise, I will not complain! Prepare my place now Lord!"

"Do not let your hearts be troubled. Trust in God; trust also in me. In my Father's house are many rooms; if it were not so, I would have told you. I am going there to prepare a place for you"- John 14:1-2

The doctor opened his bag and pulled out surgical equipment. He cleaned the wound. He dug into his body. He screamed. The doctor pulled the round out of his chest. He cauterized the wound.

"Lord, don't leave me! Give me the strength to hold on! I will not fear anything for you are with me!" he shouted over and over. An insurgent punched him, knocking him unconscious. The doctor was able to finish treating him. The women bandaged him up while he was unconscious. Brad and Tom fought the doctor also.

The torture had intensified because the soldiers had continually refused to talk. An insurgent was beating him. "If I live, I live for the Lord and if I die, I die to the Lord! So whether I live or I die, I belong to my Lord!" he shouted in severe pain.

"If we live, we live to the Lord; and if we die, we die to the Lord. So whether we live or die, we belong to the Lord."- Romans 14:8

The others tried to break their bonds and help him, but the ropes were too tight. One insurgent grabbed Brad, by his shirt collar and held a knife to his throat. They placed him and Jack face to face.

"Tell us what we want to know or we'll kill him!" the interrogator demanded.

He saw the fear in Brad's eyes, as they made eye contact. Brad saw he was conflicted. "Jack, don't you dare! Don't tell them anything!" he commanded.

Seeing the tears in Brad's eyes, accepting he would never see his family again, he looked up to the insurgents, making the hardest decision any human being can make. "I swore an oath, death before dishonor. I will not betray my team, my country, or my faith."

Tom and Brad were relieved that he did not tell them anything. The interrogator and the insurgents were shocked. "Then we will kill him!"

"Jack, tell my parents I love them and don't tell them how they killed me."

Jack had tears in his eyes. "Goodbye brother. Go with God. I will see you soon." he said to him.

The masked insurgents made Brad kneel in front of a video camera on a tripod. The leader read a prayer to Allah from a piece of paper, justifying the slaughter of an American soldier.

Brad looked into the camera. He knew what was about to happen. With tears in his eyes, he said, "I am an American soldier! I love my country! I pledge allegiance to the flag, of the United States of America, to the Republic for which it stands, one nation under God…" Brad yelled. They hung their heads, as Brad continued to scream the soldier's creed and the Pledge of Allegiance. With one swift, violent swing, Brad was gone. The slaughter made Jack and Tom vomit. They were beyond angry and lunged at the insurgents, though tied up.

Looking at their friend's lifeless body, Jack scooted over in severe amounts of pain to Brad's body. He cried as he took Brad's family watch off, with his wrists still bound. Brad had always worn his family heirloom watch, as a good luck charm. He had pushed the watch on his upper forearm, under his shirt sleeve. Fortunately, their captors had not discovered it. His grandfather had worn it in the jungles of Vietnam and his father worn it in the hot sun of Desert Storm and in Somalia and after the September 11th attacks, Brad's father had given the watch to him.

"Rest in peace, my brother." he said, as he cried looking down at the body. He looked at Tom. "We'll give this to his parents."

Once, when the women had unbound their hands, so they could eat, he searched his pockets and found her letter. He read it and cried as he read that she promised she would be waiting for him. Searching for her picture, he realized it was gone. He had lost it. He knew he had to survive. He was going to be a father. He had to hold on and find a way back to her.

Christmas had come, but neither the Hamilton nor the Johnson family could celebrate. Carole, Meagan, Lauren, and Christi were all out shopping for groceries. Both her mother and Denise tried to sway Kate from working at the post hospital, but she needed that escape.

It was a Saturday afternoon, Denise was home with her. Looking around the house, she could tell how happy they were by all the photographs of them everywhere. She felt the love and happiness in their home.

Looking at the picture of them on their wedding day, Denise knelt in the hallway. She prayed to God. "Lord, please be with my son. I know he's alive. I pray that you keep his faith in you strong, keep his mind and body strong and that you never let him give up hope. Tell him his family loves him and are waiting to have him home. Please bring my son home, Lord. I vow to never ask you for anything again if you please bring my baby home." she pleaded.

Kate was lying on their bed watching their wedding video and crying. Boomer was by her side. Denise heard her crying and praying. She also heard Jack's voice.

"Lord, please don't take him from me. Give him back to me. I love him so much. I feel in my heart that he's alive. Please bring him home to me. Thank you so much for bringing him into my life, but I need him in it for the rest of my life. Not just part of it. I want forever with him."

Denise barely knocked and slowly opened the door. She smiled at her. "May I come in?"

"Please…" she said gathering up the numerous wadded up Kleenex's around her. Denise looked at the TV and saw she was watching the wedding video again. She sat on the bed with her. "…I watch this when I need to see him or hear his voice again." she said, as tears ran down her face.

"I understand…" She looked up at the screen. "…I remember hearing him say that he'd never get married because he didn't believe there was a good woman out there who would or could handle his career. Then he found you. I remember the day I first heard him say your name and I knew…" she said as her voice cracked. She was choking back tears. "…I've never heard him so happy or so excited. Then when I finally got to meet you, I saw by the way he looked at you that he loved you." Denise said.

She touched her stomach and could feel the baby kicking. She noticed the sapphire engagement ring. She broke down into tears remembering the engraving he put on, '*I Will Come Back*'.

Denise quickly hugged her. Sobbing on her shoulder, Kate said, "I'm terrified of what he may be going through. I'm terrified that he'll never come home. I'm terrified that I'll have to raise her alone and she'll never know him. Mostly, I'm terrified that I'll never get to say goodbye."

They cried together. "The Lord will guide us all through this fog and he'll never leave us to grieve alone, but we have to trust Him."

"I don't this to be it. I want forever with him." she sobbed. They hugged and cried for nearly an hour. Denise stayed with her until she fell asleep. She smiled at her as she ran her fingers through her curled brown hair much like her mother does. She thought about the day she and Jack were married. She silently thanked God for bringing her into Jack's life. She was appreciative how devoted Kate was to her son, even though the possibility of him being alive was slim.

It was a Monday morning. Kate was working her normal shift. She was in the delivery room with a woman. The woman's labor had progressed very quickly. Her husband was out doing a training exercise on post. The woman continually expressed her worry that she would have the baby without her husband.

Suddenly, the husband came running into the delivery room carrying a dozen pink roses and was in uniform. He made it in time for the birth of his daughter. Kate wrapped the baby girl in a pink blanket and handed her to the woman. She stared at the new family. She was overcome with emotion that she had to leave the room. She quickly rushed into the ladies room and cried. She missed Jack beyond words.

The baby shower had been planned months ago by her friends at work. Now that he was missing, Christi and her mother thought it would be the perfect way to take her mind off the stress. Kate was relieved and thankful that her mother, Denise, Lauren, Meagan, and Christi were there. She steeled herself to make it through this day. This baby shower would give her a break from the terrifying reality of Jack missing in action and would give her a time of normalcy again.

Every once in a while she and Paige's would lock eyes. They were thinking the same thing. They gave each other a slight smile of encouragement and forced their thoughts away from their missing husbands, a near impossible task. They focused on the task at hand, getting through this day. Neither of them would let their minds drift to that black pit of despair.

The ladies at the shower knew the circumstances regarding Kate and Paige. They were sensitive and all tried to remain cheerful for Kate and Paige. Every woman there tried to give her the normalcy that she so badly wanted again. They laughed, told funny stories, shared advice, and adored over the adorable gifts. She would occasionally glance to their wedding picture and his Army picture on the mantle. She had to force herself not to cry in front of everyone. It was a difficult challenge.

The baby shower was fun and interesting. She actually laughed, but she looked up at the mantle and saw the picture of him staring down at her. She had tears in her eyes, but tried to be pleasant and cheerful for her guests. There times where she would excuse herself, lock the bathroom door and cry privately. She received a lot of gifts from their family and friends.

After the shower, she and Christi were in the kitchen drinking punch. "How are you holding up?" Christi asked.

"I'm trying to hold it together, but truthfully I'm miserable. I have nightmares about him every night and those are just nights where I actually sleep."

"You know I'm always here for you, right? No matter what time a day or night. If you need me, I'm just a phone call and three hour flight away."

She smiled at her. "How are JD, Andy and Jonah doing?"

"The boys' grades are slipping. I think they're worried about Jack and also about Jonah. Jonah has really taken this badly. He drinks a lot and sleeps a lot. He's thinking about leaving basketball and getting a normal job."

"Jack wouldn't want him to be like this. And I know he wouldn't want him to give up basketball. He was always so proud of Jonah."

"I've tried to tell him that, but he won't listen. He's consumed with grief and anger."

"I don't know why he'd be consumed with grief. Jack is missing, not dead." she declared. She refused to let her mind go to that place. "If I let my mind think about planning his funeral, I'll lose it. I refuse to even entertain the thought that he's dead. I'm going to have faith that he's alive, until God lets me know that he has Jack in Heaven with him, I'm going to have faith that my husband will come home. I feel God telling me to hold on. I wait by the phone in the middle of the night, hoping somehow he found a phone and would call me to let me know he's coming home."

Christi dabbed her eyes with a Kleenex. "I'm sure he'll do that."

"It's funny what you miss about a person when they're gone. I miss watching him shower and work out. I miss watching him shave and hearing him whistle cadences while he does it. When I see an OU sticker on a car, I instantly think of him. He loves OU."

Christi laughed. "Yeah, he does."

"But most of all, I miss just knowing and feeling him next to me in bed. If I had a nightmare he'd pull me against him and hold me for the rest of the night. Being in his arms is the safest place on Earth for me."

Christi had tears in her eyes. "It sounds like you had a fairytale."

She smiled. "<u>He</u> is my fairytale."

Weeks turned into months with no updates on his whereabouts. Bill and Matt traveled again to Washington D.C. to talk to some of their Army contacts who worked closely with the Central Intelligence Agency (CIA), the commanders of the Green Berets and the Navy SEALs. They were meeting with the director of the CIA at the Pentagon and the Secretary of Defense.

"Do you have any operatives in Afghanistan or Pakistan?" Bill asked.

"I am unable to confirm or deny." the CIA director said brashly. He was a tall man in a navy blue suit.

"Why not, we have proper clearance?" Matt asked.

"I can't divulge classified material on a classified operation." he said.

Bill was on edge. The stress, the frustration and the fear that Jack could be dead was affecting him. He hardly ate or slept. He drank *Jack Daniel's Tennessee Whiskey* when the reality that Jack might never be found got to be too much.

"Come on Vic, we've known each other a long time. Can you please just give us something?" Matt asked.

The CIA director looked at the Secretary of Defense. "What I will tell you is that we have sent several Special Ops teams out looking for your three soldiers and we've found nothing. None of us are optimistic that your three boys are coming home. They were probably captured, executed, and buried somewhere near the ambush site."

"You can't say for sure that they are dead without remains." Bill stated.

"There is really nothing more that we can do here." He stood and buttoned the overcoat to his suit. "Good day, gents. My secretary will call you a taxi if you need one."

"Sit down." Bill commanded.

"Excuse me?"

"You heard me. Sit down."

"Mr. Hamilton, there is nothing the United States can do."

"My son has given everything to this nation and you're not going to help bring him home? He's fought, he's bled and nearly died and for what? For you to give up on him?" he said angrily. "…Show me what my service and my son's has purchased! This is not the America I nor my son has fought for! We never leave a man behind!" he said angrily in the hallway of the Pentagon. Many high ranking officials stopped and stared as he stormed out.

Matt asked to have a meeting with the President of the United States, joined by other joint chiefs of staff from the Navy, Air Force and Marine Corps generals, all knew him on a personal friendly level.

He stood at the front of a conference room at the White House, in front of an illuminated map. On the projector, the border of Afghanistan and Pakistan was enlarged. "Months ago, we received confirmation that three Green Berets soldiers were missing in action. They were last seen in the Swatalo Sur Mountains of Afghanistan. We now assume that they are prisoners of Al-Qaeda. Dozens of SEALs and other Green Berets teams have gone out trying to find them, but we get nothing. We believe they have been taken into another country and are being held for ransom, most likely in Pakistan."

The generals were confused. "Matt, if the SEALs and other Green Berets teams have searched for these missing soldiers over the past few months and have found nothing, maybe we should declare that they are deceased instead of as missing in action." a four star Marine general said.

Shaking his head adamantly, Matt responded, "No, we can't ever declare that they are deceased without remains. We must confirm one hundred percent whether they are dead or alive, so their families will have closure and peace." They talked about the different scenarios but ultimately the decision was left with the President and the Secretary of Defense.

The families of the missing soldiers were all trying to stay positive and rely on their faiths. Kate's mother and Denise tried to talk her into taking a leave of absence from the hospital, but she refused. By working with patients, she was able to concentrate on others instead of Jack. Though working in an Army hospital was torturous for her too, seeing soldiers with their wives hold their newborns. She feared Jack would never be able to do that.

Jonah had sunk into depression. As a result, Coach Riley benched him when the Mavericks entered the playoffs. Tuesday night, the Dallas Mavericks were in San Antonio playing the Spurs.

Jonah was benched by Coach Riley in the first half. He had been noticing something serious had been bothering him for several weeks.

As he walked through the sea of ESPN reporters, trying to get to the locker room, he was asked, "Jonah is there a reason why you're playing so horribly and were benched?" a reporter asked.

"Do you think you're at risk for being traded next season?" another asked. He ignored the reporters criticizing questions.

"Jonah, sources have confirmed that your brother is currently missing in action in Afghanistan. Could this be a reason why you're playing so horribly?" a reporter asked.

He glared at the reporter as ESPN cameras and microphones were all around him. "Yes, my brother is missing in action! My family and I are going through a difficult time right now. I hope our fans will understand." he announced, as he began to get tears in his eyes.

Many reporters began writing quickly on their notepads. "How long has he been missing?"

"No, you aren't going to use my brother, to sell your stories. I would appreciate it if everyone would respect my family's privacy and not hound us for more information." he retorted, as he pushed past them. He walked into the locker room. He saw his teammates and coaches standing around. They stared at him in shock. They couldn't understand why he had not told them that Jack was missing. He apologized, but he just couldn't talk about it.

Jonah and Christi family had tied yellow ribbons around the trees in their yards, and also at his parents' home, since they were away. Friends and neighbors of the Hamilton's did the same.

Outside Jack and Kate's home, friends and family had tied a yellow ribbon around the Spanish Moss tree in the front yard, laid flowers, flags and posters with "Praying for Jack" written across them. Across the street at Paige and Tom's home, the same memorial was beneath their tree.

It was past midnight in Dallas. Bill couldn't sleep. He walked into the den and poured himself a drink. He popped in the DVD of Jack and Kate's wedding. As he watched them exchange vows, he mourned for his son.

Kate was now in her third trimester. She was in the nursery, folding many pink clothes and tiny baby socks. She had pictures of him all over the nursery. She remained confident that he would come home. After all, he did promise her. She wanted Liberty to know her daddy. She had the recorded book he had bought in the nursery. She planned to rock her to the sound of his voice, having faith he would come home.

Denise, Meagan, Christi, Carole, and Lauren were still visiting with her and would stay for the birth. "Hey, how are you doing?" Meagan asked as she and Denise entered the nursery, carrying hot chocolate from Starbucks.

"I'm okay."

Lauren picked up a baby blanket with the name Liberty Belle embroidered on it. "I love her name. It's so cute, so American."

She smiled up at them. "Jack is the one who thought of it. He loved it." she said, as she held the picture of her that he always carried with him. She rocked in the rocking chair.

Denise and Meagan smiled at her. "He promised me that he'd always come home to me, and I know he's trying. I know he'll come back to me and to Libby." she said.

"What's this?" Lauren asked picking up the recordable book.

"Here, let me have it. I can't risk it accidentally getting deleted." Lauren handed her the book. She opened it. There was a note.

"To Liberty, so you'll always know my voice. Love, Daddy"

His voice immediately began playing over the speaker. Denise closed her eyes and took steady deep breaths. Hearing his voice, she wanted to break down.

"He bought this for her. He also made her dozens of DVDs of him reading to her. He wanted her to know his voice,"

Meagan started crying. "He's already such a great father." She looked at the picture of her and Jack on the table next to the rocking chair in the nursery. Smiling at the picture, she touched her stomach as their daughter kicked. She was holding on tight to his promise that he would come back.

Now April 2011, Jack and Tom were still bound in the basement of the large house. They were sitting in the dark and the freezing cold of the night. They were given one tiny glass of water every other day, with very little food.

Sitting in the dark, Jack began to think of his daughter. "My daughter will be born soon and she'll never know me," he said.

"We can't give up hope, Jack. Let's pray together." Tom encouraged. He looked at him and they began to pray together. They prayed for God to get them through this hellish nightmare and to get them safely home to their worried families. They prayed for each other's families. As they were praying, the insurgents came in and attacked them. They fought them off. Tom was dragged out of the room to another room for interrogation.

"Leave him here!" he commanded.

"Jack! Jack! Don't tell them anything!" Tom yelled from the other room.

"Tom! Be strong!" he yelled. A rope was tied around his wrists and lifted him off the ground, hanging by his arms.

The interrogator came back in guarded by a handful of insurgents armed with AK-47s. "Are you ready to talk now or continue praying to your fictitious God?"

"Where's Tom?"

"He's enjoying more of our accommodations in another room. Are you ready to talk now?"

He looked straight ahead and shouted, "I am an American soldier! I am a warrior and a member of a team! I serve the people of the United States and live by the Army values! I will always place the mission first! I will never accept defeat! I will never quit! I will never leave a fallen comrade!"

The interrogator laughed and lit a cigarette. Suddenly he was punched in the face. Jack snarled down at him. "How many times are you going to scream that? Is that what they brainwash you with to commit murder?"

"I'll scream it until you give up trying to extract information from me."

"The American military is evil. They convince you to kill without mercy."

Jack laughed. "You're an idiot."

The insurgent punched him. "You hide behind your precious flag claiming that you defend freedom and democracy when all that follows you is a river of blood, the blood of my people."

"I don't hide behind my country's flag, I defend it."

"You know they think you're dead, right? Your commanders think you are dead." Looking at his wedding ring, he smiled. "They've told your wife you're dead. I'm sure she has another man in your bed right now, forgetting all about you. American women are whores who do not know their place."

"Oh I'd love nothing more than to kill you right now, but you're safe with me up here." he said.

"You are very arrogant. Are you from Texas? You act like a cowboy."

Jack ignored him, as the man lit a cigarette and smoked. "You got one of your men brutally executed for not cooperating. Are you going to continue to ignore me?"

He kept quiet. The torture and interrogation continued for hours. He could hear Tom screaming the Army Values, the Soldier's Creed, and even the words to God Bless America.

With Jonah on the bench, the Mavericks were NBA Champions. Their final opponent was the Miami Heat. After the best of six games, the Mavericks won their first ever NBA Championship. Coach Riley ordered Jonah to speak with a psychologist about Jack.

Sitting alone in the dark on the sofa in his mansion, Jonah looked down at the championship ring. "Jonah, are you in here?" Christi called, looking for him throughout the house.

He quickly wiped his tears away. "Yeah, I'm in here."

"Why are you sitting in the dark?" she asked, turning on the light and sitting beside him.

"I'm just thinking." He had a bottle of Jack Daniel's Tennessee Whiskey in his hand. It was half empty.

"Are you thinking about Jack?"

"Yeah, I was just thinking about something he asked me a few months ago after he found out they were having a girl."

"What did he ask?"

He had tears in his eyes and his voice began to crack. "He asked me to promise him that if anything happened to him that I would raise his daughter, be her father."

Christi smiled. "He asked you that because he loved you and trusted you. You're a great father and he knew that if his daughter needed you, you wouldn't let her down. You'd do everything for her."

He tried to contain his emotions, but he was unable to. He began to cry. Christi had never seen him like that.

She held him. "Jonah, I know it seems hopeless but we can't give up on him. He could be alive and he could come back."

JD, now thirteen and Andrew, now six years old. overheard their parents talking about Jack. They were scared that their Uncle Jack was dead. They were both very close to their favorite uncle. Walking back to his room, JD looked at all the gifts his Uncle had ever brought him and the pictures of them together at Rangers, Maverick and Cowboys games. He wanted to be like so much like Jack.

"I miss him. He's not just my brother, but he's my best friend. He was always so brave. He wasn't afraid of anything. He always had my back, and I had his. I'll raise his daughter for him. I'll let her know what a hero he was and how much he loved her and wanted to be with her." Jonah said, sobbing.

"I know you miss him. We all do, but I still have faith that he'll come home." Christi said.

On April 18, the CIA and the U.S. Army became aware that the Taliban were releasing live footage to the Arabic Al- Jazeera television network. The footage showed two men on their knees with black hoods over their heads, their hands bound behind their backs. It was clear that they were prisoners.

Matt and many of the Joint Chiefs of Staff viewed the video, along with the CIA director at the Pentagon in Washington D.C. One insurgent dressed in all black pulled out a long seriated knife. He pulled the black hoods off the prisoners. They squinted at the sunlight and saw the video camera. Jack glared into it, as he worked through his worn bonds. He knew what was about to happen.

"There they are!" Matt said with relief. He studied them, seeing the signs of torture in their eyes and on their faces. "There is your confirmation that they are alive. Permission to assemble SEAL Team six?" he asked the Secretary of Defense.

The mission was granted. He called the commander of SEAL Team 6 and informed him of the situation.

"We sacrifice these infidels to the glory of Allah. He gives us justice!" the lead insurgent said reading from a written prayer.

Jack and Tom recited the Pledge of Allegiance[19].

The insurgent jerked Tom backwards by his hair and held the knife to his throat as the leader continued with the long written prayer. With just seconds before they were to execute Tom, Jack broke through the worn rope around his wrists and grabbed the man holding the knife to Tom's throat. He instantly killed the man.

The video was still recording. Matt and the other members were watching this live. An insurgent charged him, tending to Tom who was still bound. He grabbed the man and threw him into the tripod. The video lost feed.

With six dead Al-Qaeda fanatics around them, he quickly unbound Tom and grabbed the weapons and ammunition left on their captors. They heard insurgents coming and screaming in Arabic. They locked and loaded and were ready to open fire. Three insurgents came in and were stunned that they were loose.

They opened fire. The insurgents fell to the floor. They took the ammunition, knives and grenades. They ran down the hallway.

Other insurgents on the street heard the gunfire and came running into the house. Jack and Tom heard more coming. They immediately stopped and prepared for combat. Five insurgents turned the corner, holding AK-47s as the soldiers opened fire and killed them. They took the extra ammunition. They got to the bottom of the stairs and were close to the alley of the house. Their plan was to make it out of the house and hide out until it was clear, to get back to a Forward Operating Base (FOB) in Afghanistan. They believed that they were still in Afghanistan.

Just as they entered the alley, Jack was shot in the back of the leg by a stray round. He fell to the ground. He rolled over and quickly killed the insurgent who shot him. He got up and tried to run without putting too much pressure on that leg. Falling to the ground, he bled profusely. He tore his uniform sleeve and applied a tourniquet. He was too far behind Tom and knew he would slow him down. He heard more insurgents coming.

Tom turned to see that he was not with him and was way behind. "Jack!" he yelled.

He waved him off. "Get the hell out of here! I'm hit. I'll just slow you down!"

Tom ran back to him. "I'll carry you!"

"No, I'm giving you a direct order, Tom! Get the hell out of here while you still can!"

"No, you're crazy! We never leave a man behind." Tom said, trying to throw him over his shoulder.

"Go or I will shoot you myself!" Jack said, pointing the rifle at him.

Tom stood frozen and saw that he was serious. "You really expect me to leave you here?"

"I'll hold on as long as I can. You alert the SEALs where I am, and confirm that Geronimo is alive and here. Trust me, they'll come. Don't let me down, Tom. Put the mission first." he said, in severe amounts of pain.

Tom realized that he has to obey him. He was his first sergeant and NCOIC[20]. "When you see Kate, tell her that I will keep my promise and that I love her and Liberty."

Tom looked toward the escape route and then down at Jack. "I'll be back for you. I promise."

"Don't let me down, Tom. <u>Go</u> before they come!"

Tom headed for his escape route. He made the hard decision and left him behind. Jack watched him run to the compound walls, as he sat on the ground, bleeding profusely from his leg.

---

[19] "I pledge Allegiance to the Flag of the United States of America, and to the Republic for which it stands, one nation under God, indivisible with Liberty and Justice for all."

[20] Non-Commissioned Officer in Charge

As Tom went out of sight, the insurgents found him and dragged him back down to the basement. His body was shutting down due to the malnourishment, loss of blood and poor circulation. They beat him unmercifully. They tied him up by his wrists to a pipe on the ceiling of the basement. They gagged him again. They proceeded to whip him and cut him.

"Geronimo" removed the gag as he stood in front of him, beaten and bloody. "You made a very stupid mistake killing my men."

Jack looked down at him. He had a deep bloody cut over his left eye, as blood trickled down his face. "Your boys weren't very well trained in hand to hand combat." he taunted.

He struck Jack across the face. Jack glared down at him and spat blood in his face. He glared up at Jack as he wiped the blood from his face.

"You Americans are so arrogant. This is why you always lose. You lost in Vietnam, in Somalia, Iraq and now in Afghanistan. This is our war. Not yours."

"It became our war when you murdered three thousand American civilians on 9/11."

"We do not differentiate between civilians and those who wear military uniforms. All Americans are to be killed. You are the infidels, the godless creatures. You allow your women to be whores."

"You and your followers use women and children as shields from U.S. troops. We follow the rules of engagement. We do not murder innocent civilians like you do."

Geronimo laughed. "You are the only military in the world that believes there are rules in war. You are losing this war! This is a Jihad!"

Jack glared down at him. "I'm not a coward like you! For ten years you've been hiding from us!"

"You are a careless leader. You led your men into an ambush where many died. You got one of your men killed in here for not cooperating. Did they have wives or children? You failed them."

"If I weren't bound, I would do the world a favor and end you." he said as he spat blood at him. Blood splashed on Geronimo's face. He wiped the blood away.

He was beaten even more. "Answer me when I call to you, oh my righteous God! Give me relief from my distress… be merciful to me and hear my prayer!" he shouted over and over. The insurgents beat him harder and longer, since he was shouting out Christian biblical verses.

"Keep me safe, Lord… For in your name I take refuge!" he called out to God.

An insurgent struck him across the face. "Infidel!" he shouted, as Jack tried to hold on. The images of Kate entered his mind. He pictured her face, the way her hair fluttered in the breeze, the twinkle of gold in her amber eyes. He had to survive to keep his promise.

He shouted louder with passion and in pain. "I pledge allegiance to the flag of the United States of America and to the Republic for which it stands…one nation under God, indivisible…with liberty and justice for all."

The interrogator tried a different tactic. The torture and intense interrogation stopped. He tried talking to him as a friend. He wanted to gain his trust. He continually tried to have 'small talk' with him, but Jack just glared at him.

"So what do you think about America's economy, crazy isn't it?" he asked. He looked at his bound hands. "You know you must be in extreme discomfort, I could free your hands if you'd like."

He smiled. "If you free my hands, I'll cut out your heart. You're safe with me bound."

The interrogator laughed. "You're always the American warrior out to kill anything that threatens his precious flag and country. Would you still protect America if you knew the politicians were corrupt? That they make back door deals with terrorists, war lords and child smugglers and traffickers?"

He continued to ignore him. "I would guess that you are from Texas. What city in Texas are you from?" The interrogator noticed his wedding ring. "I see you're married, what's your wife's name? Do you have any children?"

Jack really hated that man talking about Kate. He glared at him. "Isn't it clear that you aren't getting any information from me? So why not kill me?"

"I haven't been given that order, but trust me I'd love to."

The CIA had surveillance on a courier that they believed to be the personal courier of Osama Bin Laden. Two American operatives, disguised as Pakistanis, followed him to a compound with high walls and heavily guarded.

They had surveillance on the compound from a mile away in an apartment building. They noticed that the women and children never left the compound. The children were home schooled. They burned their own trash and slaughtered the many goats they had in the courtyard for food. They were suspicious that someone needed that much privacy. The operatives had surveillance photos on a man who paced the courtyard religiously. They nicknamed him the "Pacer". Few thought they had discovered Osama Bin Laden's location, but many debunked that theory.

Two CIA operatives living in an apartment across the way from the compound noticed a man running from the door of the compound, carrying a rifle. He looked disoriented and famished. They called the station chief back in the States and reported what they were seeing. They couldn't tell if the man was American or Pakistani. He was covered in dirt and dried blood. His clothes were nearly black.

One operative ran outside to intercept him. They could interrogate him for intelligence on who was inside the compound. Tom saw the operative running towards him. He raised the rifle and spoke in Arabic to stop.

The man lifted his hands. "Are you an American?" the operative asked him. Tom was silent. "I'm here to help you…"

As the man got closer to Tom, he saw that Tom was wearing an American military uniform, blackened from blood, dirt and sand. He showed Tom his ID and credentials for the CIA. "Let me help you. I'll get you home to your family."

Tom realized the man's credentials were legitimate. "My team leader is still inside. I won't leave him behind. I need to contact the Pentagon."

The operative escorted Tom back to the safe house. The other operative inside was briefed on the three Green Berets who went missing back in December of 2010. "Where am I?" Tom asked them.

"You're in Abbottabad, Pakistan. Who are you?" one asked, giving him a plate of food. Tom looked at it. Even though he was very hungry, he couldn't bring himself to eat it knowing Jack was not able to eat.

"I'm Sergeant First Class Thomas Merritt, U.S. Army Special Forces." The operatives had heard this name before. They were briefed on the mere possibility of captivity by the Taliban months ago, but did not think those three soldiers would still be alive today.

They wrote down his name. "Why were you in that compound?"

"My team and I were ambushed in the Swatalo Sur Mountains in Afghanistan on December 12, 2010. My team leader, myself and one other was taken prisoner."

"There are two more soldiers inside?"

"No just my team leader."

"Who's your team leader?"

"First Sergeant Jack David Hamilton." An operative wrote Jack's name down on a notepad.

"Who's the other soldier?"

Tom looked at him. "Sergeant Bradley Roberts…he was executed."

"Who's inside that compound?"

"Geronimo." The CIA operatives were stunned. They just got the confirmation they had been eagerly trying to get. One operative called their station chief. They told him about Geronimo being inside the house and about two Green Berets were who were prisoners of war, one of which was still in captivity.

In Washington D.C., Matt was sitting as his desk when the CIA director sprinted into his office. "I have news for you regarding your three missing Green Berets!" he said panting.

Matt dropped his pen. "What do you have?"

"Two of my operatives in Pakistan found a man running from this compound we found in Abbottabad, Pakistan. He is a Special Forces soldier named SFC Tom Merritt."

Matt's heart nearly burst. "So you found them?"

"Yes, he claims that his team leader, First Sergeant Jack David Hamilton is still inside the compound with, are you ready for this? …Geronimo."

Matt dropped his cup of coffee. "Geronimo?"

"Yes, SFC Merritt is with my operatives now." He and Matt sprinted back to his office to get the operatives on the phone. The operatives handed Tom the phone to speak with Matt.

"Hello?" Tom answered.

"Identify yourself."

"Sergeant First Class Thomas Michael Merritt, U.S. Army Special Forces. My serial number is ********."

With his serial number verified, Matt closed his eyes and thanked God silently. "This is Lieutenant General Matt Johnson, Army Chief of Staff. How are you doing, son?"

"SERE training was harder, sir. Launch SEAL Team 6 for rescue of First Sergeant Jack Hamilton and to apprehend or kill high valued target Geronimo. I say again, Geronimo is alive."

Matt was stunned. At first he did not believe him, thinking that the psychological, emotional, and physical trauma had made Tom mistaken someone else for Osama Bin Laden also known as "Geronimo". "You're telling me that you've actually seen Geronimo with your own eyes?"

"Yes sir. Be advised Sergeant Brad Roberts has been executed and my team leader First Sergeant Jack Hamilton is still a POW."

"Why is First Sergeant Hamilton still a POW?" Matt asked.

"He ordered me to leave him behind and to continue with the mission. I need a SEAL team to come to my location and I will assist them in the rescue of Hamilton and the killing of Geronimo."

"Is he injured?" Matt asked concerned.

"Yes sir, he needs medical attention." Tom said.

"Okay, you're coming home, soldier." Matt said.

"Negative, sir, I won't leave my team leader behind. I'll meet up with the SEALs and head out with them." Matt smiled, as he listened. He knew Tom was going to disobey the order to come home.

The CIA could not confirm that "Geronimo" Osama Bin Laden was in fact alive in Abbottabad, Pakistan. Matt was still trying to gather more information on Jack's location, working nonstop. The Navy SEALS were given the assignment, unclear on the identity of the high valued target was. Many speculated that it was Geronimo, but none were certain.

15

ON THE EVENING of April 21st, Kate was lying in bed, thinking about him and trying to be strong for herself and for Liberty. Boomer was always by her side. He could feel her pain. Her mom walked in the room to get the dirty laundry. "Hey, where would you like to go for dinner tonight?"

She wiped her tears with a tissue, and she looked at their wedding photo on the nightstand. "I'm not hungry."

"Honey you need to eat. Jack would want you to take care of yourself." Mom reminded.

"Okay, I don't feel like eating anything heavy. I'm feeling a little nauseous today."

"I can always get you a good salad from the Olive Garden." Mom said, as she helped her stand up from the bed.

She walked into the bathroom to take a shower. Mom was looking through her closet to pick her clothes. Suddenly her water broke. "Uh Momma, can you come here?" Mom walked into the bathroom and touched her shoulder, as she stood very still in the middle of the bathroom. "My water just broke." she said.

Mom excitedly hugged her. "Oh this is so exciting. I've got to call your father and Denise." as she ran to get the phone. She called Matt in Washington. As soon as he could, he would catch a military flight from Andrews Air Force Base to Fort Bragg.

She started to cry. Mom walked back in and saw her sitting on the edge of the bathtub, with her head in her hands. Mom kneeled down and touched her shoulder. "Momma, I don't want him to miss this. It'll break his heart." she sobbed.

Mom hugged her. "Honey, he would understand. His only concern is you and Liberty. He wants you both to be safe and healthy."

"I wish he was here. I need him here, and so does Liberty. She deserves to know her father. I don't think I can do this without him."

"You have me here." Mom wiped her tears with a tissue. "Remember the Lord gives us strength and courage to do the things we have to do, even when we think we can't."

Mom hugged and cried with her. Bill and Jonah knocked excitedly on the door. Mom helped her walk to the door. Jonah carried her to the truck and gently placed her inside with Christi, Denise, and Carole. They arrived at the post hospital. She was immediately taken up to labor and delivery. The nurses checked her cervix and determined she had progressed to a five. They admitted her, hooked her up to the fetal monitor and blood pressure cuff.

All the nurses on call were all friends' of hers. They were sensitive and aware Jack would not be there. Gina, Kate's friend was her nurse. "Hey Kate, it's finally time."

She smiled and tried to relax. "Yeah, it is. I'm ready to see her."

"What are you going to name her?" Gina asked.

She held the picture she had brought of her and Jack on their wedding day. She smiled at him. "We're naming her Liberty Belle."

"That's a unique name. How did you come up with that?"

"Jack did. He loved that name and that's what he wanted to name her."

Gina smiled at her and Mom. "That's so beautiful." and then walked out in the hallway.

Four hours into labor, the contractions were starting to get more and more intense. She was trying to be as strong as she could and make it through, but she was starting to get tired. She buzzed her nurse. "What do you need, sweetie? More ice?" Mom asked.

She stiffened up when a contraction came on. She held her mom's hand and took deep breaths.

"Okay, breathe, just breathe." Mom coached, as she ran her fingers through her hair. "Are you sure you don't want the epidural?"

"I don't want it." Sweat and tears were drizzling down her cheeks. The pain was getting unbearable. Trying to relax, she put her arm over her eyes and cried.

Major Stephenson came in and checked on her. "Okay, you're now six centimeters dilated."

Mom walked down the hall to let Bill and Denise know her progress. Kate picked up the picture of her and Jack. She smiled with tears in her eyes, as she touched the picture. "I know you're alive and you're trying really hard to come home to us. I know you're excited to meet our daughter. I love you so much, Jack. I'd give anything to have you home right now. I pray for you every moment. You're in my heart and I'm still here waiting for you. I'll never give up." she said, as she began to cry.

The contractions were getting more and more intense. She tried to get some sleep, but was unable to. She constantly thought about Jack and what he might be going through. Morning finally arrived. She had watched the sun rise, she hardly slept. Her nurse checked her cervix again and she was fully dilated.

Their immediate family members were all in the waiting room, sleeping in the waiting room chairs. JD and Andy were in Dallas at Christi's parents. Matt's military flight from Andrews Air Force Base had just landed at Fort Bragg. He caught a ride to the post hospital. He rushed into the waiting room and saw Bill, Denise, Jonah, Christi, Meagan, and Lauren, all sleeping. He sat down and rested for a while, also.

It was now time for her to start pushing. Major Stephenson scrubbed up. After thirty minutes of pushing, she became exhausted. "Come on honey, you can do it." Mom encouraged.

She cried out. "I can't do it anymore!" she screamed. She was crowning.

She pushed again. "Okay, Kate, one more big push should do it. Come on, you're very close." Major Stephenson said, encouragingly.

"Do it for Jack." Mom said to her. She took a deep breath, tightly clutched her mother's hand and pushed as hard as she could. The baby cried out, as Mom and Major Stephenson laughed. Mom cried out of relief. Liberty Belle Hamilton was born on April 22, 2011 at 7:32 a.m.

She laid back and exhaled. She was sweating and exhausted, but happy. She was now a mother and Jack was a father. Whether he'd ever get to see and meet his daughter was all up to God. "Oh Katherine, she's gorgeous!" Mom exclaimed as the nurses cleaned the baby up and placed her on her chest.

Major Stephenson stood at Kate's side and patted her arm. "You did a great job, Kate. She looks very healthy. I'm proud of you and I know Jack would be too."

Tears ran down her cheeks, as she kissed Liberty's forehead. "Hi sweetie, I'm your mom. I've waited a long time to meet you."

"She has your eyes." Mom said, dabbing her eyes with a Kleenex. She touched Liberty's tiny hand.

She looked up at her mom with tears in her eyes. "She has Jack's nose and his toes. I've never loved anyone this much! He would be so proud of her."

Then, the nurses took Liberty to the scale to weigh her, get her height and vital statistics. Liberty weighed seven pounds, ten ounces. She was twenty-one inches long. She had a full head of dark brown hair and brown eyes. The nurses put a diaper on her. Gently swaddling her in pink baby blankets, they brought her back to Kate. She kissed Liberty's forehead. "Your daddy and I love you so much."

Mom wiped her tears with a tissue. "I'm going to go tell everyone that she has arrived safely and healthy and that she's so beautiful." She walked to the waiting room. As she walked into the waiting room, everyone was awake. Matt stood and smiled at her. She hugged him and kissed him. "We are grandparents!" she announced to Matt, Bill, and Denise.

Kate smiled down at Liberty. "Sweetie, I know you're probably wondering where your daddy is. I wonder that myself, but I'm not going to lie to you. I told myself that I was going to tell you the truth. No one knows where he is, or when he's coming back. He loves you so much and he desperately wants to be here with you…" she said, as tears slowly ran down her cheeks. She looked at her gorgeous daughter sleeping. "…You are the best parts of your dad and me. When I look at you, I see him."

Liberty rested her head on her chest, as she sang a lullaby. Her parents, Bill and Denise came into the room. Denise was crying. "Oh Kate, she's gorgeous." She kissed Liberty's head and touched her tiny little hands. Kate gently placed her in Denise's arms. Bill and Denise looked down on her. Carole and Matt also held her.

She needed to call the American Red Cross to notify Jack of the safe arrival of their daughter. Though he was missing in action, she still wanted that to be the first message he received when found. She provided the operator his full legal name, rank, social security number, branch of service, date of birth and his military unit address in Afghanistan.

Lauren, Meagan, Jonah, and Christi came into the hospital room. "Here she is, our gorgeous little Liberty." Matt said, kissing her forehead.

"She looks just like Jack." Jonah said proudly, as Christi smiled and wiped her tears away.

"Yes, she does look like him, but she's gorgeous like her mommy." Denise said, as she handed Bill a cup of coffee.

"I can't wait to hold her, and then one day she'll call me 'auntie'." Meagan said, as she, Christi and Lauren giggled with excitement.

Denise looked up at Bill with tears in her eyes. "I just wish Jack could be here. He'd be so proud of her."

He hugged her, and she broke down and cried on his shoulder. Matt looked at everyone standing there and wished he could say something about the developing events in Washington D.C. and in Pakistan. But he had to keep military information secret for now.

Jonah held Liberty in his arms. He looked down at Kate and smiled. "She's gorgeous. Jack would be very proud." She smiled watching the family gush over Liberty.

Two days later, Kate and Liberty were discharged from the hospital. Matt flew back to Washington D.C. Meagan and Lauren flew back to Dallas to go back to their jobs. Bill and Denise, along with Christi, Jonah, and Carole stayed a few more days after the birth. Carole planned to stay as long as Kate needed her.

Kate was rocking Liberty in the nursery. She just finished nursing. Liberty was asleep on her chest. She looked at the pictures of Jack on the dresser and then she saw the recordable book on the table by the glider. She opened the book and his voice began to play. Tears formed in her eyes and streamed down her cheeks as she listened to his voice reading the book. She thought about the day she and Jack first met, how she was instantly attracted to him and couldn't stop looking at him or thinking about him. She smiled at how determined he was to get her to go out with him. She smiled about when they went shooting at the ranch and they shared their first kiss. She thought about the moment he had told her he loved her and wanted to marry her. She remembered how excited he was to learn he was going to be a father.

She laid Liberty down gently in her crib and sat back down in the glider and wondered where Jack was. She couldn't let herself think about the possibility he was dead. She <u>knew</u> he was alive somewhere and that he was trying to get home to her. She knew he would keep his promise. She began to pray quietly. "Lord, I know you have a plan for each of us. You have a reason for everything that you do and that we are not to question you. We're only supposed to trust in you. You brought Jack and me together. You knew we needed and completed each other. I love him so much. I'm incredibly blessed to have him as my partner and as the father of our daughter, but I need him back, Lord. I know you can make miracles happen. You already gave us one miracle, and she's sleeping right here, but please I beg you, please grant me one more miracle and have him come home alive. I promise to never ask you for anything else. I will love you Lord regardless of my husband's fate. Please give me the strength to get through each day and please give me the wisdom to explain to our daughter what happened to her father when she's older, if your will is that he is to join you in Heaven. Amen."

She wiped her eyes and continued to rock in the chair. She wanted to be able to be there if Liberty needed anything. Mom peeped into the nursery and saw her sitting. She was lost in thought. Closing the door, she looked up at the pictures of Jack and her on the wall. She saw some photos from when they were dating, photos from their surprise engagement party and their wedding. She saw many from just ordinary days in their blissful marriage. She saw and felt the love in their home.

In Afghanistan, Colonel Mitchell received her American Red Cross message. He went into his office and personally called her. "Mrs. Hamilton?"

"Yes, Colonel…" Her heart and stomach immediately dropped. She hoped he had good news for her. "Have you found him yet?"

"No, ma'am, we haven't, but we're still looking. I just received your Red Cross message. How are you and the baby?"

She had tears in her eyes. She was met with disappointment that Jack still had not been found. "We're fine."

"Boy or girl?"

"A girl,"

"What'd you name her?"

"Jack and I decided to name her Liberty."

"Is she healthy?" he asked concerned.

"Yes, she's perfect. She has Jack's nose and his toes."

"As soon as we find him I'll let him know she arrived safely and that she's healthy. You have my word."

"Thank you, Colonel. I appreciate that."

It was the morning of Friday, April 29, 2011, as the world watched Britain's royal wedding of Prince William and Katherine Middleton, The President of the United States assembled his top advisors one last time, on the decision to raid Osama Bin Laden's compound in Pakistan. He was presented the evidence of the huge possibility of Bin Laden's presence and the confirmation that Special Forces First Sergeant Jack Hamilton was held as a prisoner of war inside that compound.

"Mr. President, have you reached a decision on Operation Neptune Spear?" one asked him.

The President was tense. He took a brief moment of silence, weighing his decision. Lives were at stake. He looked back up at them. "Let's do it." he said boldly.

On Sunday May 1, in Jalalabad, Afghanistan, a task force of U.S. Navy SEALs with Tom accompanying, lifted off from the U.S. base. Under the cover of darkness, two stealthy Blackhawk helicopters and two stealthy Chinooks traveled undetected into Pakistani airspace, flying low. Tom and the strike teams were aboard the Black Hawks.

The United States did not notify the Pakistani government of the operation, due to the fear of comprising the mission.

The strike force wore camouflage Kevlar, with their faces painted black and green. Their M4 rifles nestled between their feet. The team leader just received confirmation on their target identity. He was suddenly excited, but professional. He announced over the radio. "Gents, I just received confirmation on our target. It's Geronimo…"

All team members looked up and some shouted out in excitement and slapped hands with the man next to them. They had been waiting for this mission for ten years. This was the mastermind behind the September 11th attacks and many other vicious attacks around the world on the United States and its allies. "…This is a kill mission. No captives. We are rescuing Green Berets First Sergeant Jack Hamilton from captivity, so let's get our game faces on."

The mission's objective was to rescue the American POW and to take down HVT (high valued target) Osama Bin Laden. The helicopters approached the compound, just after midnight. One helicopter malfunctioned and accidentally clipped the compound wall. Landing hard in the yard of the compound, the SEALs knew they had just made their presence known but were determined to complete the mission. The President and his closest advisors, including Matt saw the helicopter mishap on live video feed. The mood was immediately tense.

Jack was awake, thinking about Kate and the baby. He heard the helicopter clip the wall. He wondered what was going on. He recognized the sound of the helicopter and knew there was no way the Pakistani military had acquired such a stealthy helicopter.

This team of nearly twenty-five commandoes was divided into three teams. Team #1 was assigned the mission of killing Osama Bin Laden. Team #2 was assigned the rescue of Jack, and Team #3 was assigned to gather intelligence and evidence. The assault teams departed the helicopters. Each team member had their assignment and each had a camera on their helmet, documenting their mission. The President and his staff were in the Situation Room watching the mission unfold through the team's helmet cameras. The mood was tense and nervous. The last thing anyone wanted was a repeat of the failed U.S. Special Operations mission in Mogadishu, Somalia.

The teams' entered the compound and shot anyone holding a weapon. Both teams shot many males on the first floor. As Team #1 swept up to the second floor, suddenly two young girls jumped out in front of the SEALs. One team member grabbed both of them in his arms and took them out of the line of fire.

Tom and Team #2 swept the hidden passageways of the house. They found a tunnel to a make shift basement. Minutes passed, he heard the gunfire and the screaming of women and children. He knew by the sound of the rifle that the SEALs were here.

He could hear the gunfire was getting closer and closer. Tom and three SEALs shot the guards guarding the door to the basement. They busted the door down. "I'm an American! Don't shoot! Don't shoot!" he yelled with his hands bound in front of him.

Three SEALs and Tom ran to him. He was blinded by their flashlights. "You'll be happy to know your Sooners won the Fiesta Bowl." Tom said to him.

"Tom?" he asked in disbelief. He couldn't believe he came back.

"I told you I'd come back for you." Tom said.

He laughed out of elation and relief. "I've never been so happy to see your ugly face."

Tom laughed. "Yeah, it's good to see yours again. Are you able to walk?" Tom asked, as the three SEALs untied him and helped him out. They whisked him off to the helicopters. He was checked over by a corpsman aboard the helicopter. His numerous wounds were treated. He had lost a lot of blood. He was given an IV for hydration and a blood transfusion.

Team #1 was on the third floor engaging targets. They found Bin Laden in a bedroom with two of his many wives. One of the women picked up a weapon and charged the SEALS. They subdued her with a shot to the right leg. As his wife fell to the ground, Bin Laden reached for a weapon on a nearby table, but two team members shot him twice, once in the chest and the other in the left eye. He was dead. The house was filled with dead Al-Qaeda men, terrified women and children.

The team put Bin Laden's body in a black body bag and quickly loaded him aboard the helicopter. Team #3 began to sweep the house for intelligence and evidence. They gathered valuable information on the Al-Qaeda terrorist network. They collected notebooks, journals, laptops, hard drives, videos and other personal effects.

"**For God and country… Geronimo! Geronimo! Geronimo is dead!**" the leader of Team #1 announced over his radio.

CIA director confirmed and relayed to the President. "Geronimo EKIA[21]." The President and his staff were elated that Bin Laden, the most wanted terrorist for the past ten years, had been killed with no American casualties. The Situation Room quickly became a celebration room, but the mission was not complete. The SEALs had to recover the POW and get out without alerting the Pakistanis.

The leader of Team #2 confirmed over his radio. "POW is recovered and alive." The President and his staff celebrated the successful rescue of Jack. Matt knelt and thanked God for Jack's rescue. He now had to get to Fort Bragg to personally deliver this miraculous news to Kate in person.

He was aboard the helicopter with Tom and other team members. Many of the SEALs on board knew him and were happy to see him again. A Navy Corpsman tended to his wounds.

"So, have you gone home?" he asked Tom.

"No, they tried to make me, but I didn't go."

Jack looked at him strangely, as he smoked a cigarette to calm his nerves. "Why didn't you go?"

"Because I would've violated our code, we never leave a man behind."

"Have you at least called Paige to let her know you're alive?"

"No, I put the mission first."

He smiled and playfully shoved him, like men do. "Tom, you're my best friend."

"You're my best friend too."

"I can't wait to get home. I'm going to be a daddy soon." he said.

The helicopter lifted off and headed back to base. All of FOB Tillman were happy to see Jack. Colonel Mitchell and Sam were very happy to see him. Colonel Mitchell shook his hand and hugged him. "Your daughter has arrived safely and she's perfectly healthy. Kate is also healthy."

He smiled. "Thank you, Colonel." He looked rough. He had dried blood, dirt, and sand all over him. His hair and beard had grown. All that was visible on his face were his eyes and teeth. He took a shower for the first time in five months and shaved. Tom gave him a 'high n tight' haircut with the clippers. He looked like him again, just with more battle scars.

"Where are the guys at?" he asked, looking for Marcus, Luke, Mark, and Jamal. He didn't know that they had died after arriving to the base hospital. Tom, Sam, and Colonel Mitchell looked at him.

---

[21] (Enemy Killed in Action).

"They didn't make it, Jack." Sam said. He was angry, dumbfounded, and sad. He couldn't help but feel like a failure. He felt responsible that the operation had bad intelligence and that six members of his team had been killed.

"Jack, there wasn't anything more you could've done." Tom said. He kneeled on the ground, covered his face. Tom and Sam comforted him. Alpha Team had been a team before 9/11. They were closer than brothers.

Sunday, May 1 2011 at 11:35 p.m., President of the United States, Barack Obama stood up at the podium at the White House for a speech announcing the Al-Qaeda leader, Osama Bin Laden was dead!

"Good evening, tonight I can report to the American people and to the world, that the United States has conducted an operation that killed Osama Bin Laden, the leader of Al-Qaeda, and a terrorist who is responsible for the murder of thousands of innocent men, women and children. It was nearly ten years ago, when a bright September day was darkened by the worst attack on the American people in our history. The images of 9/11 are seared into our national memory, hijacked planes cutting through a cloudless September sky, the Twin Towers collapsing to the ground, black smoke billowing up from the Pentagon, the wreckage of Flight 93 in Shanksville, Pennsylvania, where the actions of heroic citizens saved even more heartbreak and destruction. And yet we know the worst images are those that were unseen to the world, the empty seat at the dinner table, children who were forced to grow up without their mother or their father, parents who would never know the feeling of their child's embrace, nearly three thousand citizens taken from us, leaving a gaping hole in our hearts. On September 11, 2001 in our time of grief the American people came together. We offered our neighbors a hand, and we offered the wounded our blood. We reaffirmed our ties to each other, and our love of community and country. On that day, no matter where we came from, or what God we prayed to, or what race or ethnicity we were, we were united as one American family. We were also united in our resolve, to protect our nation and to bring those who committed this vicious attack to justice. We quickly learned that the 9/11 attacks were carried out by Al-Qaeda, an organization headed by Osama Bin Laden, which had openly declared war on the United States and was committed to killing innocence in our country and around the globe. And so we went to war against Al-Qaeda to protect our citizens, our friends, and our allies.

Over the last ten years, thanks to the tireless and heroic work of our military and our counterterrorism professionals, we've made great strides in that effort. We've disrupted terrorist attacks and strengthened our homeland defense. In Afghanistan, we removed the Taliban government which had given Bin Laden and Al-Qaeda save haven and support. And around the globe, we've worked with our friends and our allies to capture and kill scores of Al-Qaeda terrorists including several who were apart of the 9/11 plot. Yet, Osama Bin Laden avoided capture and escaped across the Afghan border into Pakistan. Meanwhile, Al-Qaeda continued to operate from along that border, and operate through its affiliates around the world. And so shortly after taking office, I directed Leon Panetta, the Defense Secretary, to make the killing or the capture of Bin Laden the top priority of our war against Al-Qaeda. Even as we continue to broader our efforts to disrupt, dismantle and defeat his network. Then last August, after years of pain staking work by our intelligence community, I was briefed on a possible lead to Bin Laden. It was far from certain and it took many months to run this thread to ground. I met repeatedly with my national security team as we developed more information about the possibility that we had located Bin Laden, hiding within a compound deep inside Pakistan. And finally last week, I determined that we had enough intelligence to take action, and authorized an operation to get Osama Bin Laden and bring him to justice.

Today, at my direction, the United States launched a targeted operation against that compound in Abbottabad, Pakistan, where a small team of Americans carried out the operation with extraordinary courage and capability. No Americans were harmed. They took care to avoid civilian casualties. After a fire fight, they killed Osama Bin Laden and took custody of his body. For over two decades, Bin Laden has been Al-Qaeda's leader and symbol. He has continued to plot attacks against our country, our friends, and our allies. The death of Bin Laden marks the most significant achievement to date in our nation's effort to defeat Al-Qaeda. Yet his death does not mark the end of our effort. There is no doubt that Al-Qaeda will pursue attacks against us. We must and we will remain vigilant at home and abroad. As we do, we must also reaffirm that the United States is not and never will be at war with Islam. I've made clear just as President Bush did just shortly after 9/11, that our war is not against Islam because Bin Laden was not a Muslim leader. He was a mass murder of Muslims. Indeed, Al-Qaeda slaughtered scores of Muslims in many countries, including our own. So his demise should be welcomed by all who believe in peace and human dignity.

Over the years, I've repeatedly made clear that we would take action within Pakistan if we knew where Bin Laden was. That is what we've done, but it is important that our counterterrorism cooperation with Pakistan helped lead us to Bin Laden and the compound where he was hiding. Indeed, Bin Laden had declared war against Pakistan as well, and ordered attacks against the Pakistani people. Tonight I called President Zardari and my team has also spoken with their Pakistani counterparts. They agree that this is a good and historic day for both our nations. And going forward, it is essential that Pakistan continue to join us in the fight against Al-Qaeda and its affiliates. The American people did not choose this fight. It came to our shores. It started with the senseless slaughter of our citizens. After nearly 10 years of service, struggle, and sacrifice, we know well the costs of war. These efforts weigh on me every time I, as Commander in Chief, have to sign a letter to a family that has lost a loved one, or look into the eyes of a service member, who has been gravely wounded. So, Americans understand the cost of war. Yet, as a country, we will never tolerate our security being threatened, nor stand idling by when our people have been killed. We will be relentless in defense of our citizens, and our friends and allies. We will be true to the values that make us who we are. And on nights like this one, we can say to those families who have lost loved ones to Al-Qaeda's terror, that justice has been done.

Tonight, we give thanks to the countless intelligence and counterterrorism professionals who've worked tirelessly to achieve this outcome. The American people do not see their work, nor know their names, but tonight they feel the satisfaction of their work, and the result of their pursuit of justice. We give thanks for the men who carried out this operation, for they exemplify the professionalism, patriotism, and imperiled courage of those who serve our country. They are a part of a generation that has born the heaviest share of the burden since that September day. Finally, let me say to the families who lost loved ones on 9/11, that we have never forgotten your loss, nor waivered in our commitment to see that we do whatever it takes to prevent another attack on our shores. And tonight let us think back to the sense of unity that prevailed on 9/11. I know that, as it does, that time has frayed, yet today's achievement is a testament to the greatness of our country and the determination of the American people. The cause of securing our country is not complete, but tonight we are once again reminded that America can do whatever we set our mind to. That is the story of our history, whether it's the pursuit of prosperity for our people, or the struggle for equality for our citizens, our commitment to stand up for our values abroad, and our sacrifices to make the world a safer place. Let us remember that we can do these things not because of wealth and power, but because of whom we are one nation under God, indivisible with Liberty and justice for all. Thank you. May God bless you and may God bless the United States of America."

That same night, Matt, the Casualty Notification Officer, and the team's chaplain returned to Fort Bragg. They were to deliver the news that Jack and Tom had been successfully rescued to Kate and Paige. Carole was still there with Kate helping her out with Liberty. Everyone else had gone back to Dallas. Paige was over at Kate's visiting with her. She was helping her fold a load of laundry, as Carole was cleaning the kitchen.

Paige and Kate relied on each other when they needed to cry, vent, yell and pray. They were sitting on the sofa in the living room. They had just watched the President's speech and were stunned that Osama Bin Laden had been killed. They felt justice had been done, but still feared for their husbands. Neither of them had given up hope.

"That was the mission Jack wanted so bad."

"Oh I know. Tom always talked about how they all wanted the mission to kill Bin Laden."

Matt, the chaplain, and the Casualty Notification Officer arrived at Jack and Kate's residence. Matt smiled at Jack's black 2011 GMC Sierra truck sitting in the driveway. He smiled at the OU and U.S. Army decals in the windows. He was happy that Jack <u>was</u> going to get to drive that truck again.

They knocked anxiously on the door. Looking at the clock, she saw it was almost midnight. "Who could that be at this hour?" Carole asked. Boomer was on alert.

Liberty just had her second feeding for the night and was asleep in the bassinet in the master bedroom. Kate walked to the door and looked out the peephole and saw her father standing with the Casualty Notification Officer, and the chaplain standing under her porch light. She immediately got a knot in her stomach and began to cry, thinking that they finally found Jack's and Tom's remains. "It's the CNO, my father, and the chaplain."

Carole walked beside her and held onto her shoulders. She looked at his picture on the mantle. "Lord, give me strength." she whispered.

She opened the door, and saw the huge smiles stretched across her father's, and the chaplain's faces. "They're alive!" Matt exclaimed. "They're coming home!"

She and Paige were in shock. "Really, where are they?!" as she and Paige cried.

"They're in Germany right now getting completely checked out and then they'll be on the next flight here." the Casualty Notification Officer explained.

She and Paige hugged and cried together. Paige hurried across the street to tell her sons that their father was alive and coming home. Carole and Matt hugged. Kate hugged him tightly and cried tears of joy on his shoulder.

"They couldn't kill him. He's the toughest son of a gun I know. He's built like a tank." he said. She smiled. "Where's Libby?" he asked.

"She's sleeping." As Kate was crying and hugging her mother, the phone rang. "Hello?" she answered.

Jack smiled as he listened to her adorable Texan accent. Tears formed in his eyes and his voice cracked. "I thought I'd never hear your voice again." he said.

She closed her eyes as tears drizzled down the corners of her eyes. She smiled and let out a breath of relief. "Jack, oh thank you God, are you okay?"

"Yeah, I'm okay, baby. I'm coming home. I got your Red Cross message, how is she?"

She was crying. "She's so beautiful. She looks so much like you."

He had tears in his eyes. She could hear him crying. He was devastated that he missed the birth of his first child. She could feel his disappointment, and regret, as he tried not to cry. "Jack?"

"Yeah I'm here, baby." he said, as his voice cracked and held back his tears.

"I love you so much." she said.

He smiled. "I love you too."

The tears rolled down her cheeks. "We're here waiting for you. Hurry home!"

"I can't wait to see you." he said.

She smiled. "I can't wait to see you either." They talked for a few minutes before the doctors came into administer tests on him and Tom. The doctors tended to their numerous injuries and checked their vital signs. They were given antibiotics for the infection of their wounds, nutrition and both sat down with an Army psychologist and chaplain. Matt called Bill and Denise to give them the news. They were ecstatic and very emotional. The family's pastor came and prayed with them, thanking God that he was coming home.

Arriving to Fort Bragg at 11:30 p.m. seventy-two hours after being rescued, the plane slowly rolled on the runway. They saw their families. He saw Kate. He had never wanted to hold her so badly until that moment. Nearly all of Fort Bragg anxiously stood hoisting flags and 'Welcome Home' posters. The door to the plane lowered to the ground.

She excitedly waited to see him. Her heart was pounding, she couldn't stand still. She was desperate to see him, touch him, and kiss him. He stepped out. She smiled and felt her heart stop. He smiled at her. They sprinted towards one another. Reaching him, she jumped into his arms and wrapped her arms around his neck. He twirled her around. He looked up into those big beautiful hazel brown eyes. Her curled brown hair fluttered in the breeze. Looking down at his crooked smile that made her weak in the knees, she kissed him. She had tears streaming down her face.

"I never thought I'd see you again! I love you so much!" he said.

Her face was buried in his neck, as she cried out of joy. "I love you too! I knew you'd come back!"

"I promised you I would." They kissed and hugged tightly. "You look so beautiful. I missed you so much." he said.

"I missed you too. I'm so happy you're home!" she exclaimed.

He smiled, as he looked into her eyes. They kissed again. Then they walked toward their waiting and emotional families. "I want you to meet someone very special." she said. Her mom was holding Liberty tightly in a pink camouflage baby blanket. He was stunned. Kate took Liberty and smiled at him. "Meet your daughter."

She placed her in his arms. He had tears in his eyes, and big smile on his face as he held his daughter. He kissed her forehead. "She's so beautiful and so tiny," He closed his eyes and kissed her forehead again. He touched her tiny fingers. She grabbed ahold of his finger. With a tear in his eye, he kissed her chubby cheek. She opened her eyes and looked up at him. "Hi, baby girl. I love you so much. You're just as beautiful as your mommy." he said to her. He could feel her little heart beating.

He gently placed her in Kate's arms. He hugged his parents, brother, and sister. JD and Andrew hugged him tightly. Denise was crying and kissing him. "I never stopped praying for you baby. I knew God was taking care of you." she said crying.

"He did take care of me, momma."

He looked at Bill. He saw the emotional smile, filled with pride, relief and gratefulness. "I'm so proud of you, son."

He hugged Matt, Carole, and Lauren also. As he was wrapped up in his family's arms, he saw Jenny, Jake's widow, and their daughters. He walked towards them. "Jenny…"

She smiled while crying. "I'm so happy you came back safely."

"Jake was an outstanding soldier and one of my best friends. He loved you and the girls so much." He had tears in his eyes. "I'm sorry I failed to bring him home."

She hugged him. "Jack, if it hadn't been for you, he probably wouldn't have made it home the first time."

He also saw Brad's parents standing holding an American flag. He had tears in his eyes. He approached them. Mrs. Roberts had tears running down her face, as her husband held her. He reached inside his pocket. "Mr. and Mrs. Roberts, I brought this back to you and to your family, in hopes of giving you some comfort. Brad wanted me to tell you that he loved you both very much. He was a dedicated soldier, and he always put the mission and our lives above his own. I want to express to you my deepest condolences. He saved my life numerous times. He was a good brother, a great warrior and one of my best friends."

He placed Brad's family watch in Mr. Robert's hands. Mrs. Roberts cried and hugged him. "Thank you, Jack. Our son always had high praises for you."

After an emotional reunion with family and friends, Jack, Kate, and Liberty arrived at their home on post. He parked in the driveway. "Oh it feels good to be home again." he sighed. They walked inside. Boomer was so happy to see him. He and Boomer wrestled in the floor. She nursed Liberty in the nursery and laid her down in her crib. Liberty would be up at 2:00 a.m. to feed again. He looked around the house. Everything was exactly the same as when he left. She quietly walked out of the nursery and barely closed the door. There were baby monitors in every room.

She walked into the living room and found him looking at their wedding picture and his Army picture on the mantle of the fireplace. She walked up behind him and wrapped her arms around his waist. She kissed his back. "Are you hungry or thirsty?"

"No, I ate on the plane."

"Are you alright? Do you want to talk about anything?" she asked, quietly.

He turned to face her. "No, I'm okay. I'm just really tired." She smiled and kissed his hands. He wrapped his arms around her waist and pulled her against him. "I've missed you."

"I've missed you more."

"The sex may not be very good, like it usually is. I'm just… overwhelmed right now."

She put her finger over his mouth to make him stop talking. "All that matters to me is that I can see you, touch you, and know you're home. I don't care how good it is."

She smiled and gently pulled him by the hand to their bedroom. She dimmed the lights and lit a few candles. "I have something that belongs to you."

She walked to the nightstand drawer and pulled it out. She picked up his dog tags and walked back to him. He smiled. She put them on him. He looked down into her big brown eyes. He couldn't believe he was home with her, finally after five months in captivity, he was home. He tried to make himself wake up, thinking this was all a wonderful, vivid dream, but it wasn't a dream. It was finally reality.

They were standing in the middle of their bedroom, kissing and holding onto each other tightly. He kissed her neck.

"Tonight, soldier, you're mine."

He smiled. "You are so beautiful." She noticed all his gunshot wounds, and healing bruises. He saw the look on her face. "Don't look at them."

She gently touched the bullet wounds, the stab wounds. Tears rolled down her cheeks. "What did they do to you?"

He held her tight. "Don't cry I'm home with you. I'm back." She kissed his lips, neck and his shoulders. She gently kissed his pectorals and abdominal muscles. She kissed each scar, cut and bruise. He brushed her hair out of her face and looked into her eyes and kissed her lips.

They made love. Tears slowly drizzled out of the corners of her eyes, as she was so happy to have her husband in her arms again. Tonight, she knew he was safe. They were kissing passionately and holding onto each other. They looked into each other's eyes, by candlelight.

She kissed his sculpted arms, the palms of his hands. He ran his fingers through her curled hair and kissed her neck. She dragged her fingertips down his bare back. She could feel the scars on his back.

It was close to 2:00 a.m. It was time for the next feeding. They walked into the nursery. She sat in the rocker and nursed her as he watched. She noticed him looking at her. "Why are you looking at me like that?"

He smiled. "You look so happy and I've never seen you look this beautiful before."

"I have an amazing life, I love my life. I have you and now we have Liberty. How could I not be happy?"

"You're an amazing mother, baby. I'm so proud of you."

She looked up at him. "Thank you. That's the nicest thing you could ever say to me."

After nursing, burping, changing and rocking Liberty back to sleep, she gently laid her back in her crib. Then they went back to bed. They were lying in bed, holding each other with only the sheet over them. She was lying on his chest listening to his heartbeat, as he dragged his fingertips up and down her bare back.

"I can't believe you're really here in my arms. I've dreamed of this since the night you left." she said.

He kissed her head. "Every day I would pick a different memory I had of you, and I'd replay it over and over in my mind. I would picture every detail of your face and body, until I could see you standing in front of me. I honestly thought I'd never see you again."

She looked up into his eyes. "I love you so much." He kissed her lips, as she straddled his lap again. Wrapping her arms around his neck, they were kissing passionately, while holding onto each other. He looked into her eyes, brushing her hair out of her face. They made love for the third time. Exhausted and drained hours later, they soon fell asleep.

She awoke and saw he was not beside her. Looking at the alarm clock on the nightstand she saw it was close to 4 a.m. She slipped her robe on and walking down the dark hallway, she found him standing in Liberty's room, watching her sleep. He was so proud of her. He was so proud to be a father. She slowly approached him and wrapped her arms around him, and smiled at him and then down at their sleeping daughter.

"She is so beautiful like you." he whispered, kissing the side of her head.

She smiled up at him. "She's strong like you."

He kissed her. They walked back to their bedroom. "How was the delivery? No complications?"

"No, other than it was the most pain I've ever experienced in my life, but she's extremely healthy."

"What time was she born?"

"Uh, it was seven thirty in the morning." They lied back down in the bed. He held her against him. "We should get some sleep. She'll be getting up for her next feeding soon."

"Can I keep you both company?" he asked.

She smiled up at him. "Of course you can keep us company."

Liberty woke up at six o'clock. She showed him how to change a diaper. He watched her nurse. She was a great mother. After she nursed her, he sat in the rocking chair in the nursery, rocking Liberty to sleep while she took a shower. Walking back in the nursery, she found him asleep with her asleep on his chest, listening to his heartbeat. She smiled, as she picked her up and laid her back in the crib and covered him with a blanket.

Weeks after returning home, Jack, Sam and Tom drove to Arlington National Cemetery where the team was buried. They visited each grave. Jack still carried enormous guilt for how all died, especially Brad. As they stood over their headstones, Jack read:

BRADLEY MICHAEL ROBERTS
STAFF SERGEANT
U.S. ARMY SPECIAL FORCES
FEBRUARY 15, 1981
MARCH 17, 2011
BRONZE STAR & PURPLE HEART
OPERATION ENDURING FREEDOM- AFGHANISTAN
OPERATION IRAQI FREEDOM
LOVING SON, BROTHER AND FRIEND

JAMAL MARTIN FIELDS
SERGEANT FIRST CLASS
U.S. ARMY SPECIAL FORCES
PURPLE HEART & BRONZE STAR WITH VALOR
JANUARY 13, 1979
DECEMBER 12, 2010
OPERATION ENDURING FREEDOM-AFGHANISTAN
OPERATION IRAQI FREEDOM
LOVING SON, BROTHER, SOLDIER AND FRIEND

JACOB RILEY BRIGHAM
SERGEANT FIRST CLASS
U.S. ARMY SPECIAL FORCES
SILVER STAR WITH VALOR & PURPLE HEART
MARCH 2, 1975
DECEMBER 12, 2010
OPERATION ENDURING FREEDOM-AFGHANISTAN
OPERATION IRAQI FREEDOM
LOVING FATHER, HUSBAND, SON, BROTHER AND FRIEND

LUCAS BRIAN RICHARDS
SERGEANT
U.S. ARMY SPECIAL FORCES
PURPLE HEART & BRONZE STAR
NOVEMBER 12, 1977
DECEMBER 12, 2010
OPERATION ENDURING FREEDOM-AFGHANISTAN
OPERATION IRAQI FREEDOM
LOVING SON, BROTHER AND FRIEND

MARCUS ALLEN WILLS
STAFF SERGEANT
U.S. ARMY SPECIAL FORCES
PURPLE HEART & BRONZE STAR WITH VALOR
JULY 5, 1980
DECEMBER 12, 2010
OPERATION ENDURING FREEDOM-AFGHANISTAN
OPERATION IRAQI FREEDOM
LOVING SON AND BROTHER

ERIC DANIEL DAVIS
STAFF SERGEANT
U.S. ARMY SPECIAL FORCES
PURPLE HEART & BRONZE STAR
SEPTEMBER 10, 1979
DECEMBER 12, 2010
OPERATION ENDURING FREEDOM-AFGHANISTAN
OPERATION IRAQI FREEDOM
LOVING SON AND BROTHER

MARK ELLISON BRIGGS
SERGEANT FIRST CLASS
U.S. ARMY SPECIAL FORCES
OCTOBER 12, 1979
DECEMBER 12, 2010
PURPLE HEART & BRONZE STAR
OPERATION ENDURING FREEDOM-AFGHANISTAN
OPERATION IRAQI FREEDOM
LOVING SON

Jack kneeled and cried. "I'm sorry I couldn't save you, brothers. I tried."

Tom had tears streaming down his cheeks, listening to Jack grieve. Placing his hand on his shoulder, he said, "You did all you could, Jack. You were a strong leader. They died while doing what they love. They died as warriors." Tom said.

"You can't blame yourself for their deaths. You went back in to get them and they know that." Sam said. Each took a swig of *Jack Daniel's Tennessee Whiskey*, the team's favorite drink. They toasted their fallen brothers and said their goodbyes. Walking back to the car, they looked back at the peaceful, quiet cemetery. Jack looked at each gravestone. He could see of their spirits, in full battle gear with smiles on their faces. He knew they were in a better place. They made the drive back to Fort Bragg.

Months went by. Jack, Kate, and Liberty were living as normal as possible at Fort Bragg. He had increased his routinely workouts to deal with his frustration about not being able to return to combat. He had weekly sessions with the chaplain. She was working at the hospital, as Liberty went to the post daycare center.

She was at work, discharging a patient. "Hey, how is Jack doing?" her friend, a fellow nurse, Nicole asked her.

She smiled at her. "He's doing so great. He's working out like four times a day. He wants to return to combat, but they won't let him yet, so he's frustrated about that."

"I can't believe he wants to go back after what he went through." Nicole said.

Kate knew that combat is what Jack knew. He had been a soldier before they met. She knew how hard he worked and how much he loved being a part of a combat team. "It's who he is. Combat is all he knows. I know he's happy to be home with me and Liberty, but I know he is missing being part of a team and in combat. I know that sounds weird. He has two families, the Army and his team and then he has me and Liberty."

"Why doesn't he just retire? He's been in for like twelve years, right?"

"He's been in for close to eighteen years. He enlisted right out of high school. I don't think retirement is an option for him. He's still physically and mentally able to do it."

"He wouldn't retire for you and Liberty?"

"I'll never ask him to. I promised him when we were dating that I would never ask him to choose between me and the Army."

"Wow, you're stronger than me. I'd be forging my husband's signature on those retirement papers especially after what all has happened."

"He's worked too hard for his career to end like this. He's just thirty-seven."

"Would you be happy if he retired?"

"Well yeah, I mean I would, but I know it would be the hardest decision of his life."

"How is parenthood? How does he like diaper duty?"

She thought about Liberty. "Oh he loves being a dad. They have their own special relationship, their own special bond. He gets up with her a lot, and it is just so heart melting to watch him fall asleep rocking her in her room. He doesn't change very many diapers unless they are pee-pee ones." They laughed.

"Aw, I'm so happy for you and Liberty. Is she trying to crawl yet?"

Kate laughed. "She moves like a little worm."

Jack was just walking in the door from running ten miles. Boomer rushed to him. He petted him. Sweating, he wrapped a towel around his neck as the phone rang. "Hello?"

"Hello is this First Sergeant, Jack David Hamilton?" the voice asked.

"Yes it is."

"Please hold while I connect you to the Oval Office." He was connected to the Oval Office.

"Hello?" a man's voice asked.

"Hello?"

"First Sergeant Jack David Hamilton?"

"Yes."

"It's a pleasure to talk to you, Jack. This is the President."

Jack was stunned. The tiny hair on the back of his neck stood up. "Hello Mr. President, how are you?"

"I'm fine, thank you. I can tell you were not expecting a phone call from me were you?"

Jack laughed. "No, Mr. President, I wasn't. I just walked in the door from running ten miles, so I apologize for sounding out of breath."

"Wow, ten miles? That's impressive."

"Thank you, sir."

"It is my esteemed pleasure to inform you that I have approved that you be awarded the Congressional Medal of Honor. You will be the first living recipient since the Vietnam War."

The Congressional Medal of Honor was the highest military decoration a service member can receive. It was only given by the President of the United States.

He was disappointed, but he acted honored. "Oh…thank you sir, but I'm sure there are more soldiers who've done much more than I have to deserve that award."

"Jack, I've read the report of what happened in Afghanistan and how you went back in under personal heavy fire to get six of your team members. That's heroic. You received severe injuries, but your indomitable spirit never let you turn back or give up. I've also read the reports of what you and two of your men faced in Pakistan. You went above and beyond the call of duty, Jack. You do deserve this medal. Your country is proud of you, son."

After the conversation of a lifetime, Jack stood in the middle of the kitchen thinking. He thought of his actions in Afghanistan when he and his team were ambushed. Lost in thought, he could hear the gunfire, he could see the RPG hitting the helicopter filled with re-enforcements explode and crash in the valley. He remembered being tortured and beaten, almost to death. He remembered the look in Brad's eye just before he was executed. He knew it was likely he'd have post-traumatic stress disorder (PTSD) from this last mission and the five months as a prisoner of war, but he would never admit it to anyone.

The phone rang. It startled him and brought him back to reality. Looking at the caller ID, he saw it was Bill. "Hey dad, what's going on?"

"Hey son, how are you doing?"

"I just got a phone call from The President. He informed me that I'm being awarded the Congressional Medal of Honor."

Dad was so proud. "Wow, son, I'm so proud of you."

He was disappointed. He hesitated. "Dad, I don't want it."

Dad was stunned. "Why? It's the highest decoration you can receive."

"I know, but I didn't earn it, so therefore I don't deserve it."

"Son, I know I've taught you to be modest and humble, but you did earn this. You charged through heavy enemy fire to retrieve six of your men and then you got each one to safety. You received numerous life threatening injuries, but you still got all of your men out. You were a prisoner of war for five and a half months. You were tortured every day and you helped one of your men escape. You put yourself in incredible danger of being killed."

He was irritable. "Dad, I got my men killed. One was butchered right in front of me. I really don't deserve it and I sure as hell don't want anyone calling me a hero, when I'm not." he said angrily.

"You saved your men. You went back in and got them out. You made a heroic decision."

"I'll never be able to go back to combat. I'll spend the rest of my career telling people my story and I don't want to do that. If I wanted to be a recruiter, I would've changed my MOS. I enlisted to be a warrior."

Dad heard his frustration and irritability. "Son, I respect your feelings, but you're being awarded the highest military decoration this country has and its being awarded to you by the President, as much as you don't want it, you have to accept it. Your mother, Kate, Libby and I are all so very proud of you."

Kate walked in the door with Liberty, and saw him on the phone. He smiled at them. "Dad, can I call you back?" as he hung up. "Hi baby, how was work?"

She smiled as she wrapped her arms around his neck and kissed his lips. "It was good, but I found myself wishing I was here with you."

They smiled at each other. "I love you." he said.

"I love you too. How was your day?"

"It was alright. I ran ten miles and did two hundred push-ups and one hundred sit ups."

She smiled. "Yeah, I can tell." She got the feeling he was not telling her something. "What's wrong?"

"Nothing is wrong. I'm just worn out."

"Jack, I've known you for a long time, so I can tell when you're holding something back."

He frowned. "The President just called and told me that I'm going to be awarded the Congressional Medal of Honor."

She smiled at him, as she got Liberty out of her car seat. "The Congressional Medal of Honor, baby that's great!"

"No it's not, babe. It means the end of my career in combat. They'll want me to go on tour and tell everyone my story and encourage people to enlist. I don't want to do that. I enlisted to be a warrior, not a recruiter. I won't be their poster boy. I'm not trading my rifle for a damn microphone."

Seeing he was really upset, she wrapped her arms around his neck and kissed his lips. "Everything is going to be fine. Do you have any idea how proud I am of you?"

"I wish I could refuse this medal. I'm not a hero and I don't want anyone calling me that."

"You are to me. You're my knight in shining Kevlar."

He smiled. "Only you can call me that." He looked at Liberty and smiled as she played in her jumper. "Hi Libby, how was your day at daycare? Hopefully it was better than my day." he asked her as they sat in the floor and played, as Kate started supper.

She knew he wanted to return to combat so badly. She worried very much for him and she hoped he'd never return to combat, but she knew how much he loved his job. She promised to never ask him to choose between her and his duty to his country.

In November 2011, The President invited Jack, Kate, his parents' and siblings, her parents, and many politicians and past Congressional Medal of Honor recipients from WWII, Korea, and the Vietnam War to the White House for the ceremony of presenting and awarding the Medal of Honor.

They were in a very elegant ballroom, with the American, Navy, United States Marine Corps and the Army flags draped behind the podium as a backdrop. Jack, like Bill and Matt and many others was dressed in his formal uniforms. Kate wore an elegant Navy blue dress and high heels.

He was standing up on the stage with the President and an Army Chaplain. "Let us pray, all mighty and merciful God, in whom we place our trust. We invite your Holy presence, as we gather as a nation to honor the extraordinary actions above and beyond the call of duty rendered by Army Special Forces First Sergeant, Jack David Hamilton, an American soldier, patriot and hero. Our hearts forever resonate with the noble theme of heroes proved in liberating strife, and more than self their country loved, and mercy more than life. May our remembrance of Jack's combat actions in the Swatalo Sur Mountains of Afghanistan on December 12, 2010 and his actions as a prisoner of war in Abbottabad, Pakistan, inspire all Americans with great pride and humility that we have selfless warriors like Jack living among us today. We also remember all of our armed forces and those who stand in harm's way across the world. As we celebrate this special day with Jack and his family, may we remember in prayer all military families who await the safe return home of their loved ones. Amen." the chaplain said.

He stepped away from the podium, as The President stepped towards the podium. "Good afternoon everyone, please be seated. On behalf myself and the First Lady, welcome to the White House. Thank you chaplain for that beautiful invocation, of all the privileges that come with serving as President of the United States, I have none greater than serving as Commander in Chief of the finest military the world has ever known. And of all the military decorations that a President and a nation can bestow, there is none higher than the Congressional Medal of Honor. Today is particularly special, since the end of the Vietnam War; the Medal of Honor has been awarded nine times for conspicuous gallantry in an ongoing or recent conflict. Sadly, our nation has been unable to present this decoration to the recipients themselves because each gave his life, his last full measure of devotion for our country. As President, I have presented the Medal of Honor three times to the families of our fallen heroes.

Today, therefore marks the first time in nearly forty years, that the Medal of Honor recipient for an ongoing conflict, has been able to come to the White House and accept this recognition in person. It is my privilege to present our nations' highest military decoration, the Medal of Honor, to a soldier as humble as he is heroic, to Green Beret First Sergeant, Jack David Hamilton."

The audience cheered for Jack. The President smiled at him, as the expression of pride and gratitude filled his face. "I think anyone who meets Jack; they'll see humbleness, integrity, pride, character, loyalty and patriotism. As a little boy, he grew up watching G.I. Joe and wanting to be just like his father, retired Major General and Special Forces soldier William David Hamilton. Jack was raised to love and serve God and to love and serve his country. He embodies the true American patriot spirit. It is people and families like this all over the country that make America the greatest country in the world. They are what make our military the greatest and most powerful military in the world. This is a joyous occasion for me, something I've been looking forward to. The Medal of Honor reflects the gratitude of the entire nation. Today, we welcome the family and friends who've made Jack into the man he is today and we congratulate them on what a fine job they did. He has conducted nearly hundreds of missions to the Middle East since 9/11. He has come to terms to losing comrades in battle…" He told about what happened in the mountains and then what happened as he was a prisoner of war. He then turned towards Jack. "…On behalf of a grateful nation, for gallantry and extraordinary heroism at the risk of life above and beyond the call of duty, I present to you, First Sergeant Jack David Hamilton, the Congressional Medal of Honor."

The audience cheered and applauded him and gave him a standing ovation. Many of the men Jack had served with cheered loudly. The President fastened the medal around his neck and shook his hand then hugged him. He had been given another Purple Heart for his injuries. "Do you feel comfortable saying a few words?" The President whispered in his ear.

"Yes sir." He walked up to the podium. He looked down at his parents, Kate, and siblings. He saw pride on their faces. He started to get tears in his eyes, as he looked at Kate. While in captivity, he started to wonder if he would ever see her face again. "Thank you, Mr. President. Thank you everyone for being here, but I…" he looked down at Kate. He saw the pride on her face as she smiled up at him. "…I honestly do not consider myself a hero. I never have. I'm no one special, I'm just a soldier and I did what any other soldier would've done in my situation. My team members were my brothers and when your brothers are in trouble, you go back for them, no matter the danger. I did what I was trained to do. The real heroes are those… I failed to bring home alive to their families. The only way I can accept this medal is if it's not for me, but for our brothers who are not with us today. This is their medal. They gladly gave their lives not just for this country, but for the man, that brother, next to them. It's important that we never forget them, their sacrifice or their families. Thank you."

The audience applauded and gave him another standing ovation. The President shook his hand and posed for a picture. As Kate looked proudly up at him shaking the President's hand, with the Medal of Honor around his neck, she had tears in her eyes and a proud smile stretched across her face. He kissed her gently and then hugged her. Bill and Matt were very proud. Kate, Denise, and Carole dabbed their eyes with Kleenex's.

After the ceremony, Jack and Kate met and greeted several people who were excited to meet him. Tom, Paige, and their sons were there. Tom and Jack hugged. Tom had been awarded the Distinguished Service Cross for extraordinary heroism and was also given a Purple Heart. In Jack's entire military history career, he had received seven Purple Hearts for battle injuries.

"I want to get out of here." he said quietly to Tom.

"I hear ya." Tom said, with a laugh.

After talking with many members of Congress and other Medal of Honor recipients from World War II, Jack and Kate drove to Arlington National Cemetery to visit the team's graves. In full dress uniform, he stepped out of the vehicle and opened the passenger door for her.

The cemetery was preparing for Veterans Day. Each grave had flags either planted by loved ones or by the cemetery grounds keepers. The autumn air was crisp and cool. The leaves were golden and brown. The sky was clear and blue. It was a beautiful autumn day.

They checked in at the cemetery, the guards saw the Medal of Honor around his neck, they immediately saluted him. He returned a salute as he and Kate walked through the thousands of rows of graves.

"So, what'd you think about the ceremony?" he asked her. They held hands as they slowly glanced down at the graves.

"I thought it was amazing. I'm so proud of you. I loved your speech. It was very humble, very you."

"I personally think they are making way more of this that it actually is."

"No they're not Jack. You did an extraordinary thing. You risked your life so many times for your team. I know you thought of each of them as your brothers and you all had been through a lot together, but you did a heroic act."

Finding the seven graves, they stood over them. The leaves crackled beneath their feet, the cool autumn air swept through her hair. She saw the look on his face and held his hand tighter. "Do you want me to give you a few minutes alone?"

He looked at her and smiled. "Thanks." She walked away and looked at other graves of soldiers who were killed in action in Vietnam, Iraq and Afghanistan. She looked at the birthdates and realized how young some were. She soon found herself at the tomb of the Unknown Soldiers. The Army guard was pacing back and forth in full military dress with a rifle, known as The Old Guard.

He kneeled down and prayed and cried over his fallen teammates. Watching him grieve, she knew he would never tell her about the night he lost all but two of his men nor would he tell her about his captivity. She wasn't sure she wanted to know what he faced. She saw the scars, the wounds and that was enough truth for her. But with as much as he went through, he never broke his promise. He came back to her.

He stood and proudly saluted each one and walked towards her. She smiled at him as he walked towards her. The Army guard quickly saluted him. He returned a salute.

He kissed and hugged her, as the fall leaves fell around them, in the middle of the cemetery filled with white granite grave stones and thousands of American flags. "I want to find my best friend from high school's headstone."

"What was his name?"

"Mark Thompson, he and I enlisted together and he was stationed at the Pentagon. He was killed on 9/11."

She was stunned. He had never told her that. "Oh Jack, I'm so sorry." The leaves crackled beneath the shuffle of their feet as more fell from the branches. They walked the rows of grave stones until they ran across Mark's stone.

Mark Charles Thompson
June 18, 1974
September 11, 2001
Staff sergeant
U.S. Army
Gone but never forgotten

"Let's go home." he said smiling at her.

They turned and walked back towards the gates. They arrived back at their hotel room and he began writing a letter.

> *"Dear Mr. and Mrs. Roberts,*
>
> *I know there is nothing that will or could ever ease your sorrow, your heartbreak and your loss, but I want to give my sincerest condolences for the loss of Brad. He was not just a member of my team, but through many of 'our life and death situations', he became a brother to me. He saved my life so many times. Not a day goes by where I do not think of him. In the last few minutes of his life, he asked me to tell you that he loved you both very much. He wanted you both to know that he fought like a warrior should fight. He showed no fear when facing death. He died, not just for his country, but for his brothers. Enclosed is something that very few receive, it is given for conspicuous gallantry and valor in the face of great personal danger, the Medal of Honor. It was awarded to me by the President and though I was ordered to accept it, I will not keep it. Your son's death still haunts me to this day. He was a true warrior, the true hero and it would only be right if your family had this medal. He earned it, I did not. Your family is in my prayers every night and though I know this gesture does not ease the pain of losing Brad, but knowing he was the real hero will ensure his legacy, his cause, his sacrifice will be remembered forever. I was honored to lead such an exemplary soldier.*
>
> *Sincerely with abiding respect,*
> *First Sergeant, Jack Hamilton"*

He enclosed the medal and a picture of Alpha Team together inside the letter and mailed it to Brad's family in Laguna Beach, California. Brad also received the Bronze Star with valor and many other awards for his bravery, all of course were presented to his parents.

Brad's mother, Beth, walked in her California home with the stack of mail she had just retrieved. Noticing a package from Washington D.C, she opened it and held the Medal of Honor in her hands. Seeing a letter and a photograph in the envelope, she held the photo, smiled with tears in her eyes at her son. She opened the letter, read it and cried. Brad's father, Dan, walked in from the backyard and saw her crying over the letter and photograph.

"What's wrong?" he asked rushing to her. He saw the Medal of Honor lying on the kitchen table.

"Jack sent us this letter and picture along with the Medal of Honor he was awarded."

Stunned by the generosity, Dan held the medal while reading the letter. He smiled at the photograph of Brad and the team posing with their weapons. Jack and Brad were standing next to each other.

"Now that's a hero." he replied, as Beth leaned her head on his shoulder as they looked at the photograph. Though they appreciated the incredible gesture, they returned his Medal of Honor to his and Kate's home on Fort Bragg. They also sent a heartfelt letter back to him, expressing that it was their wish that he keep it simply because he did earn it.

After the ceremony at the White House, Jack continued to serve in the Army. He was presented the option to retire, but wasn't ready to do so. After careful review of his medical records and psychological tests, he was able to return to combat. He was now the Non-Commissioned Officer in Charge (NCOIC) of Bravo Team.

A year had passed since the Medal of Honor ceremony. He was home for six months dwell time. Liberty was almost two years old. She had long, gorgeous wavy brown hair like Kate and big green eyes like Jack. She was the apple of their eyes. They were ready to add to their family.

It was a Friday afternoon, in October. He was at the gym working out. Liberty was at day care. Kate came home early from work. She suspected she was pregnant. She had bought a pregnancy test on her way home. The results of +POSITIVE appeared instantly. She smiled. She placed the pregnancy test next to his razor in their bathroom.

She went to pick up Liberty from daycare. She came home and started on dinner. An hour later, he came in the door. "Daddy!" she said excitedly, running to him and jumping in his arms.

"Hi Libby!" he swooped her up in his arms, tickled and kissed her belly. She belted out a happy laugh. "I love you so much."

"I love you, Daddy."

He sat her down and she continued to watch Sesame Street on the TV. He walked into the kitchen and saw Kate unloading the dishwasher as dinner was cooking on the stove. "Hi baby."

She looked at him and smiled. "Hi, how was your day?" she asked, wrapping her arms around his neck and kissing his lips.

"It was good. How was yours?"

"It was good." He noticed she was glowing. After all their years together, she still looked as beautiful as she was the day they met.

He grabbed a bottle of water from the refrigerator. He walked into the bedroom and then in their bathroom. As he washed his hands, he noticed the pregnancy test next to his razor. He saw the result of +POSITIVE and smiled. He walked into the kitchen and smiled at her.

"What?" she asked.

"You look very beautiful."

"Thank you."

"You're glowing. I haven't seen you look like this since you were pregnant with Liberty, right after you found out." She smiled up at him.

"Oh maybe it's my lotion."

"I found the pregnancy test. So baby number two is on the way?"

"Yes."

"Thank you…"

"For…?"

"…For having my children."

"Well it was a team effort. I wouldn't have been able to do it without your participation."

He laughed. They kissed in the middle of the kitchen. "I hope it's a boy." she said.

"Why? You don't think Libby would want a sister?" he asked.

"I want a little boy to look like you, act like you, and talk like you."

"You want two of me?" he asked, laughing.

"Of course, you're just so handsome, sweet, strong, kind and very funny." He helped her get dinner on the table and they ate. Afterwards, she gave Liberty a bath, combed her beautiful hair and he came into her room to read her a story. He loved reading to her. She laid her head on his chest. She fell asleep listening to his voice. He laid her down and kissed her puffy cheek. He covered her with her Hello Kitty themed comforter. He touched her hair and smiled. Kate peeped in her bedroom and saw him kneeling down to her. She smiled watching him kiss her goodnight. He turned off her lamp and smiled at her.

They walked to their bedroom. "How are you feeling?" he asked.

"I feel amazing."

"How far along do you think you are?"

"I bet I'm seven weeks."

They laid down in their bed. He ran his fingers through her hair. "You look incredible, you look so happy."

She turned over and looked at him. "I am happy."

He placed his hand on her stomach and kissed it. They started kissing each other and holding onto each other. They made passionate love. Afterwards, they were lying in the bed, wrapped up in the bed sheets. He lied on his stomach as she gently dragged her fingernails up and down his back.

"I love when you do this."

She kissed each of his scars, his shoulders. She gently massaged his back and shoulders. He turned over and looked up at her. She had their sheet wrapped around her chest. Her curled hair was wild. He ran his fingers through her hair.

"Do you know how much I love you?" she asked.

He smiled. "No, I don't."

"Yes you do," They laughed. He tickled her and they wrestled around.

A few days passed, she went to Major Stephenson and found out her due date would be June 19. She had a sonogram taken. The announcement thrilled their families and friends. He was so excited.

Four months later, they were going to the imaging center on post to find out if they were having a son or a daughter. "So, what names do you like for a girl?" she asked.

"How about Truth or Justice?" he teased. They laughed.

"Please tell me you're joking."

"Yes baby, I'm joking. I don't know. What names do you like?"

She smiled. "I love the names Olivia, Kimberley or Grace."

"What about boy names?"

She smiled. "I'll let you pick the name if we're having a boy."

"I still like the name Maverick."

She smiled. "I think that's the perfect name for your son."

The sonogram technician called her name. She had an adorable baby bump showing. She lied on the table and pulled up her shirt. He smiled at her belly. He was praying for a boy.

"Do you have any names picked out?"

"We've decided on a boy's name, but we're still thinking about girl names." she said.

"What's the boy name you've picked?" the tech asked.

"Maverick David…" he said proudly.

"Aw that's so adorable." She placed the transducer on her stomach. The baby's heart beat played over the speakers. They saw the baby moving and sucking its thumb on the screen.

"Do you see that thing right there?" the tech asked, pointing to the corner of the screen.

"Yeah, it's a boy…" he said excitedly.

Kate and the tech smiled at his excitement. "Yes. It looks like Mr. Maverick David is having a good time in there." the tech said.

He smiled hugely. "Yes!" he said as he jumped up and down.

Kate smiled at how happy he was. "He'll be just as handsome and strong as his daddy." she said.

He smiled at her. "Don't forget stubborn."

"No, I'll fix that." she teased.

He was so happy. "Oh Heaven help us if he's anything like me."

"He will be."

He looked at her and kissed her lips. Their parents were thrilled and excited that they were having a son. Jack, Kate, and Liberty went home to Dallas to see their families. Christi, Lauren, and Meagan planned a very adorable baby shower. They celebrated Liberty's second birthday.

"Daddy, will you help me?"

"I sure will." They sang happy birthday to her. She got embarrassed and hid behind him. She made a wish. Denise and Carole loved watching him with Liberty. Meagan and Lauren spoiled her. Jonah loved to give her horsey rides. Carole was very proud with how nurturing and loving Kate was as a mother.

Now June, she was full term. She had only gained twenty pounds during this pregnancy. Liberty was so excited to be a big sister. It was his birthday. She and Kate were making him a birthday cake using his mother's recipe for his favorite double fudge chocolate cake.

"How are you feeling baby?" he asked, dipping his finger in the batter.

"Fat and hot, I have to walk sideways just to get through the door. And I constantly feel like I'm in a sauna."

He laughed. "You're not fat, baby. You're beautiful."

"I helped momma make your cake, daddy." Liberty said to him.

He swooped her up in his arms. "Do you know how much I love you?"

She smiled. "This much?" she asked opening her arms as far as they'd go.

He shook his head and smiled at her. "No, I love you more than that."

"How much?" she asked.

He opened his arms as far as they'd go. "Wow…" Liberty said. She had a very soft voice.

Paige and Tom came over for cake. They were going to babysit her when Kate went into labor. They were laughing and talking, while eating cake. Around 7:30, she had taken Liberty to bed.

Tom and Paige visited until 8:30. She excused herself, she was exhausted. After Tom and Paige left, he walked into their bedroom. He smiled at her sleeping. He climbed in the bed with her and held her. He could smell the jasmine in her hair. Soon he drifted off to sleep. He had a long day also.

At 10:30 p.m. she woke up suddenly. She hurried into the bathroom where her water broke. He was still sleeping. "Jack…Jack…" she said calling him from the bathroom.

Finally he woke up. "Yeah, baby what's wrong?"

"It's time. My water broke."

He ran into the bathroom. "Are you okay? What do I do?"

"Yeah, call Paige and Tom. Ask Paige if she can come here and stay with Libby." He quickly got dressed. He called Paige. She would be right over.

He and Kate took off to the hospital. "How cool would it be if he shared the same birthday as me and Dad?" he asked.

She was taking deep breaths and exhaling them slowly. "Yeah, that would be neat." They arrived at the post hospital. She was admitted and sent up to labor and delivery. Her labor was progressing very quickly. After only being admitted for an hour, she was ready to push.

After pushing for only fifteen minutes, Maverick David Hamilton cried out. He was born at 11:45 p.m. He weighed eight pounds, ten ounces and was twenty-two inches long. Major Stephenson placed him in his arms. He shared his birthday with him.

"Hi bubba, welcome to the world…" he said. He looked at her. She was lying back, relaxing. "…This is the best birthday present ever."

She smiled. "Happy Birthday…"

Maverick had a full head of light hair like Jack. He laid Maverick on her chest. He kissed her lips. "Thank you, baby, I love you so much."

She kissed his lips again. "I love you too."

Major Stephenson smiled at them adoring their son. She knew he had missed Liberty's birth, so she knew this was a monumental experience for him. The nurses swaddled Maverick and placed him in her arms. "He looks just like you." she said as she nursed him.

He smiled and kissed the side of her head. He called their parents. His parents' were so happy that Maverick shared Jack and Bill's birthdays. Bill was born June 9, 1949. Jack was born June 9, 1974 and now Maverick born June 9, 2013.

Two days later, they were discharged from the hospital. Their families were on their way to see Kate and the new baby. Paige and Tom were the first to see him. Liberty was excited to meet her baby brother. Boomer was curious about the new baby.

"Oh he is so handsome." Paige said.

"Yeah, he gets that from me." Jack teased. Tom laughed.

"Just what the world needs is another Jack Hamilton running around." Tom teased. Jack and Kate laughed. Paige and Tom left. Liberty settled down for a nap. Kate was exhausted, but she knew she couldn't sleep. She was in the nursery, nursing him and rocking him. He was in the kitchen cleaning up, so she wouldn't have to later. The doorbell rang. It was Colonel Mitchell and his wife, Miranda.

"Hey Jack."

"Hello sir. Hello ma'am."

"Congratulations and happy birthday." the Colonel said, slugging Jack in the arm.

"Thank you, sir. He's perfect."

"What'd you name him?" Miranda asked.

"We named him Maverick David."

"Aw, that's adorable. How's Kate?" she asked.

"She's great. She did amazing."

"Where is she?"

"I think she's feeding him. Let me go check." He walked to the nursery and barely opened the door. He saw her asleep in the rocker, with Maverick on her chest. He knew she was tired, so he didn't wake her. "She's sleeping with him right now."

"Oh well then we won't bother her, but we do want to see him." Miranda said.

"I promise to call you when they're both awake." he said. Other neighbors had brought casserole dishes of food for them. He was surprised. He didn't know that people did that. The refrigerator was quickly filling up with comfort food.

An hour later, she awoke from her nap and carried Maverick into the living room. She sat in the recliner and rocked him. She heard him in the kitchen. "What are you doing?"

"Hey baby, I'm just cleaning up the kitchen and trying to figure out where all of this food is going to fit in our fridge."

"What food?"

"Most of our neighbors have brought us casserole dishes of something."

"Oh that's nice."

"Are you hungry? I'll make you something to eat."

"No, I'm okay thanks." He sat on the sofa and folded laundry while watching a baseball game.

She smiled at him folding. "You look adorable folding clothes."

"I figured I'd help you out with some things." She noticed he had cleaned the kitchen, mopped and swept the floors, vacuumed the living room, and even dusted. Now, he was folding laundry.

"You did all this just in the short time I napped?"

"Yeah, it wasn't that hard."

"I was going to do it."

"I wanted to do it for you. You're tired, baby. You just gave birth. Let me help you out around here. Oh by the way, the Colonel and Miranda came by. They wanted to see Maverick, but I told them to come back later."

They cuddled on the sofa as Maverick and Liberty slept. Soon, their families had arrived. They were so eager to see Maverick and Liberty. Bill held him in his arms. "This is the best sixty-fourth birthday present a man could ask for."

Denise and Carole took a picture of Jack, Bill, and Maverick together. Three generations all born on the same day. Bill and Matt were ecstatic to play with the new baby. Meagan and Lauren loved holding him. Their families stayed for a few days. One afternoon, Colonel stopped by the house. Jack answered the door.

"We have a mission. We fly out in three hours."

He could see Jack was reluctant. "Roger, I'll meet you and the team at the rendezvous point in an hour."

She came to the door. "Colonel, what's going on?"

"I'm sorry to have to do this to you, Kate."

"Thanks, Colonel. I'll see you in an hour," he said.

The Colonel walked away. He closed the door. She was stunned and a little angry, but mostly worried. "You're not going." she said to him.

"Baby, you know I have to go." She was terrified. Their families wondered what was going on. He walked over to his parents. He kissed his mother on the cheek. She went into their bedroom and slammed the door.

"Where are you going?" Denise asked.

"I have to go." He went out into the garage to pack. Jonah walked out there with him. He watched him pack. "Do me a favor, Jonah…"

"Sure, I'd do anything for you. You just name it."

"If anything happens to me, I want you to take care of my family. I want you to raise my kids like your own."

"Sure, man. I'll do that."

"You promise?"

"Yes, I promise." After packing, he walked into the house. He knew she was upset. He saw his mom holding Maverick in her arms.

"Where's Kate?" he asked.

"I think she's in the bedroom." He walked into the bedroom and saw her sitting on their bed. She had tears rolling down her face.

He kneeled in front of her and touched her face. She looked in his eyes. He smudged a tear away with his thumb. "I love you so much. I know this is not easy for you, especially now that we have kids, but I really appreciate you being strong for me, baby. You're the strongest woman I know. I know you'll make it."

"I'm so scared for you. I almost lost you last time. I need you, Jack. Our kids need you."

"I know, baby, but I promise you I will come back."

"What if you don't? We have two children. What am I supposed to do if I lose you?"

"You won't ever lose me, baby. I promise."

He kissed her lips and hugged her. He felt her tears drop onto his shoulder. He knew she was terrified for him. "I need to take a shower and get ready to go. Do you want to join me?" he asked, giving her a crooked smile.

She smiled. "Don't I always?" she asked. They walked into their bathroom. He turned on the shower. The hot water created steam onto the mirrors. They stepped in the shower together. They were kissing passionately.

"I love you." he said.

"I love you too." They made love, for possibly the last time. He got dressed and packed his personal bag. He said goodbye to his family and in-laws. He held Maverick in his arms and kissed his forehead. "I love you so much bubba." He was starting to get tears in his eyes, so he placed him in Carole's arms.

He picked up his bags and threw them over his shoulder. He, Kate, and Liberty walked out to his truck.

He kneeled down to talk to Liberty. She was wearing a pair jean shorts and a red tank top. Her hair was down and fluttering in the wind. She was starting to look more and more like Kate every day. When he looked at her, he always smiled because she looked just like Kate.

"I love you, Libby. Be good for you momma and be her little helper, okay? I'll be home soon."

"Where are you going, Daddy?"

He looked up at Kate and then back down to Liberty. "Sweetie, I have to go help the good guys fight the bad guys."

"Will you come back?"

He picked her up and held her tightly. "Yes, I promise I will come back."

"I'm going to miss you, daddy." she said. She was starting to cry.

He felt his heart breaking. "I'll miss you too sweetie."

Kate was holding back the tears. She didn't want Liberty to be as upset as she was. She had to remind herself that Jack, even though he was a husband and father, he was still a soldier and soldiers go where they are needed, when they're needed. She frequently had to remind herself that as the soldier's wife, her job was to hold things down at home and be strong. She had to be strong for their children.

As he held Liberty tight in his arms, he looked at Kate. She smiled at him. He kissed her lips. "I promise I'll come back, Kate."

She smiled. "I know. We'll be here waiting for you."

"I'll call you when I can. I love you so much, baby."

"I love you too, Jack." He sat Liberty down. She ran back in the house to be with her grandparents. "I have something for you."

"What's that?" he asked, loading his bags in the back of his truck. She handed him the picture of herself that he always carried with him and that he lost in Afghanistan after he was ambushed.

"It seems this is your good luck charm and I wouldn't want you to go away without having it."

He smiled. He held it in his hands. Looking in her eyes, he watched the tears roll down her cheeks. "I'm carrying you with me. You keep me alive and bring me home." He opened his wallet and put the picture inside, but he pulled out a letter that was badly worn and stained.

"What's that?"

"This is the letter you wrote me just before I left for a deployment right after we got married."

She smiled. "I can't believe you kept it."

"I read this a lot when I was a POW. It kept me going. It was my motivation to get home to you."

She wrapped her arms around his neck. She looked up in his green eyes. "Please come back to me, Jack."

He wrapped her up in his arms tightly. The scent of her shampoo and perfume filled his nose. He closed his eyes and buried that scent deep in his memory, for when he was missing her, like he always did on deployments, he would remember how she smelled. "I promise you I will. I love you baby."

"I love you too."

"I have to go."

"Be safe." He kissed her one last time. They kissed for several seconds. He opened the door to his truck and backed out of the driveway. He waved just before he was out of sight. She waved back. He was gone.

She was on maternity leave for the next six weeks. She had to find a way to stay busy, but knew having a newborn and a two year old, working a full time job, taking care of a house and paying the bills, would keep her plenty busy. Once maternity leave was over, things were really tough and really busy for her. With Maverick's feedings every three hours, changing diapers, feeding Liberty and getting her to daycare, and working a full shift, she was exhausted after cooking dinner and cleaning up the house and doing laundry. Though she was extremely stressed and tired, she forced herself to be strong and hold it together. He was counting on her to be strong.

Late at night, he called. She was lying on the sofa, half asleep. Dinner had been cooked, leftovers stored in Tupperware in the refrigerator, kids were fed, bathed and in bed. Toys were picked up. The laundry was folded and put away. The kitchen was clean. "Hello?" she answered tiredly. She was enjoying the silence and the relaxation.

Listening to her voice, he couldn't help but smile. "Hi baby, how are things going?"

She breathed a sigh of relief. "It's good. I'm holding everything together."

"You sound like you're half asleep, did I wake you up?"

"No, I was just dosing. How are you?"

"I'm good. I'm ready to come home."

"Yeah, I am too. I miss you."

"I miss you too. How are the kids?"

"They're good. Maverick is not letting me get hardly any sleep."

"Oh does he have cholera?"

She laughed. She knew he meant colic. "You mean colic?"

"That's what I said."

She laughed. "No, you said cholera. Thank you for the laugh, I needed that."

"You sound tired baby."

"I am, but don't worry about me and the kids. We're fine. Maverick looks just like you and Libby asks about you every morning. She prays for you every night."

"I miss you all so much."

"We miss you and love you too. I'm so tired."

"If I was home, I'd give you a break. I'd pay for you to go to the spa and spend all day there while I took care of the kids."

"I'm okay. I go back to work in a few weeks. I'm not looking forward to that. I was going to talk to you about possibly quitting and staying home with the kids' full time."

He was stunned to hear her talk about quitting. "Baby, you love your job."

"I know I really do, but I love my kids and husband more."

"It's your decision, but I'm against you giving up what you've worked so hard for all these years."

They talked about ordinary things, they laughed as she told him funny things Liberty has said or done.

As the months went by, she continued to work at the hospital in labor and delivery. Maverick and Liberty went to the post daycare. She missed him desperately and worried for him. It was October 28, their wedding anniversary. They had been married for seven years. It was 4:00 p.m. She felt her cell phone vibrating on her waist band. She saw it was an overseas number. She quickly answered. "Jack?"

"Yeah baby, how are you doing?"

"I'm much better now that I know you're alive and safe."

He laughed. "I'm okay. Happy Anniversary, baby I love you so much."

She smiled. "Happy Anniversary, I can't believe you remembered."

"Of course I remember. I married the most beautiful woman in the world, how can I forget that?" he teased. "How are the kids?"

"They're good. Libby loves daycare and Maverick is now on baby food and he's starting to jabber."

"How are you doing with working and being a full time mom?"

"It's hard, but I wouldn't have it any other way. I really miss you. Liberty really misses you. She's always asking me when you're coming home."

"I really miss you and the kids too, baby."

"Where are you?"

"I can't say over an open phone line."

"I can't wait until you come home."

"Oh I know I can't wait either."

"I love you, Jack."

"I love you too, baby. Are you at work?"

"Yeah, I get off at five."

"I wish you were at home so we could Skype. I need to see you."

"If you can give me an hour, I'll be home then. I really want to see you."

"Unfortunately I don't have an hour, baby."

She was bummed. "I'd give anything to see you right now, Jack."

"I know I'm feeling the same way."

They talked and laughed for a few more minutes. "Well baby, I have to go. I love you so much."

"I love you too. Come back to me."

"I'll always come back to you. Give the kids kisses from me. Tell them I'll be home soon."

"Okay, I will."

"Stay gorgeous, baby."

"I love you. Be safe." He hung up. He walked out of his bunk and saw Tom lifting weights. "Hey, how are Kate and the kids?"

"They're good. How are the boys?"

"Michael is in his second year of college and Sam just graduated high school."

"Are you upset you missed Sam's graduation?"

"Yeah, but Paige recorded it all for me. I know it's not the same, but at least he knows I would do anything to be there."

"Kate said Libby loves daycare and that Maverick is on baby food."

"Yeah, I bet he's getting big." Tom said.

When she arrived home after picking up the kids from daycare, she began to start dinner for her and Liberty. The doorbell rang. "Maybe it's Daddy!" Liberty screeched in excitement. She ran to the door.

She knew it wasn't. She walked with Liberty to the door. She opened the door and saw two men, one carried a huge bouquet of pink roses and the other man carried a box from a local bakery. She took the flowers and the box inside. She opened the box and was stunned. He had arranged to have a local baker recreate the top tier of their wedding cake. Though he knew that was the traditional for the first anniversary, he wanted to do something special for her. She looked at the huge bouquet of pink roses and saw there was a note.

The note read:

> *"After seven years of marriage, you're still as beautiful as you were the day we met. I love you very much and every day I thank God for giving me such an amazing woman to be my wife and the mother of my children. I miss you so much, baby. I'll be home soon and Happy Anniversary. Kiss the kids for me.*
>
> *Yours forever,*
> *Jack"*

She fed the kids, bathed them, read them a book and tucked them in. She finally got the chance to relax. She cleaned up the kitchen and picked up the hundreds of toys scattered all over the living room, dining room and kitchen. After the house was picked up, she sat on the sofa eating a piece of cake and watched their wedding video. She fell asleep watching the video.

After nine months on deployment, Jack and his team arrived back at Fort Bragg. It was mid-afternoon, she was still at work. Liberty and Maverick were in daycare. He arrived home and unlocked the door. He saw the house was clean, except for a few toys lying around. He saw the stack of bills on the kitchen table, a calculator and their ledger for bills. He looked at it and smiled.

He unloaded his gear into the garage and unpacked his bags. He decided for ole-time sake, he'd go to hospital and surprise her like he always did when they were dating. He arrived at the hospital and got in an elevator. Stepping out of the elevator, he saw many nurses. He looked for her.

She came out of a patient's room. He smiled at her. She still took his breath away. He was surprised to see that she was down to her pre pregnancy weight before Liberty. She looked amazing. He walked up behind her. She was writing down the patient's blood pressure. "Excuse me, could you help me? I'm looking for the most gorgeous woman in the world." he said.

Recognizing his voice, she quickly turned around, smiled up at him and jumped into his arms. She kissed his lips and held him tightly. "Hi baby." he said to her.

"I missed you so much." she said. Other nurses smiled at them. He was wearing his ACUs.

"I missed you too."

Her shift ended and they went to the daycare to pick up the kids. Liberty was very happy to see her daddy. She ran to him and jumped into his arms. "I missed you, Daddy."

"I missed you too."

"I love you." she said. The daycare workers were tearing up.

"I love you too." They walked to Maverick's class. He was now almost ten months old. He had been trying to walk. Maverick saw Kate, Liberty, and Jack. He was crawling. "Wow, he's crawling."

Maverick crawled towards Jack. Kate and Liberty were shocked. Jack felt his heart melt. He hurried to him and picked him up. "Hi bubba, I missed you so much." he said, kissing him.

The Hamilton family was now complete and together again. They went home. She started supper as Jack played in the floor with Liberty and Maverick. He loved being home. He loved being with his family again. After dinner, he helped her give them each a bath. He read her a story as she rocked Maverick to sleep in the next room. His room was decorated in Army camouflage, helicopters, tanks and soldiers. Liberty's room was very girly. She had Hello Kitty everywhere.

She laid Maverick down in his crib and covered him with a blanket. She closed the door to his room. Jack slowly walked out of her room and closed her door. It was just after 8:00 p.m.

She walked into the kitchen to clean up from dinner while he took a shower. She was happy he was home. He walked out of their bedroom, shirtless and in a pair of gym shorts. He walked up behind her and moved her hair off her shoulder. He pressed himself up against her and kissed her neck and shoulder. "That feels so good." she said.

"Kissing on you feels good." She turned around and kissed his lips. They were kissing passionately up against the sink full of dirty dishes. After all their years together, she was still extremely attracted to him. She loved how strong he was and how he still looked amazing.

She grabbed him by the hand and led him to their bedroom. He closed the door. He pulled her up against him and kissed her lips. They made it to the bed. He was on top of her. "I love you so much, Jack." she whispered in his ear as he kissed her neck.

"I love you too." He looked down at her and smiled. She straddled him and kissed his lips. He rubbed his strong hands all over her back and through her long, curled hair. He kissed her neck. She kissed each of his abdominal muscles and all of his battle scars on his torso. They made love. As they lied in bed holding each other, they began to talk about their future.

"You want to hear something crazy?" he asked, twisting a strand of her hair around his finger.

"What?"

"I'm actually considering putting in my papers for retirement."

She was stunned. "That is crazy! I never thought you'd retire."

"I'm almost thirty-nine. I have a wife and two kids I need to be here for. So you'd be okay with it if I retired?"

She smiled up at him. "Well yeah I'd be okay with it, but don't think you're going to not be busy, I'll put you to work three sometimes four times a day." she teased, straddling him with their bed sheet wrapped around her chest.

He smiled up at her. "I love working for you. I can be on duty round the clock for you."

"That's good to know, but right now there is a mission that requires your expertise and amazing skills." as she kissed his chest.

"I'm all yours." They made love until the early hours of the morning. The next morning, he called his Dad while she was at work and the kids were at daycare.

"Hey son, how are you doing?"

"I'm good."

"How are Kate and the kids?"

"They're amazing, Dad. Maverick crawled to me."

"You'll always remember that."

"Yeah, I know. Are you busy? I need to talk to you about something."

"Yeah sure I have all the time in the world."

"I'm thinking about putting in my papers for retirement."

Dad was shocked. "Really, you want to retire?"

"Yeah, I'm ready to put the Army behind me and move forward with my family. I don't want my kids growing up without me and hardly knowing me when I come home."

"I completely understand that, son. What are you going to do when you get out?"

"I was thinking that you and I could start a car restoration business there in Dallas."

Dad smiled. "That would be amazing to do. It'd be a good business."

"Yeah, it would. I love being in the Army, but I'd love for us to have our own business, something we can hand down to JD, Andy and Maverick one day. Plus I want to be able to see my family whenever I wanted, not when I could."

They talked more about retirement and starting a business together. He filled out the retirement forms and drove to Colonel Mitchell's office. "Hey Jack, how are you doing?"

"I'm alright, sir. I just wanted to drop these papers off to you."

Colonel Mitchell was saddened to hold Jack's retirement papers in his hand. "You're ready for retirement?"

"Yes sir, I've given twenty one years and I'm ready to move on with my family."

"You were a hell of a soldier, among the bravest and the toughest I've ever had the privilege to command."

He shook his hand. "Thank you, sir."

"Are you sure you don't want to be promoted to Sergeant Major and become an operations analyst? You'd be home with Kate and the kids."

Jack laughed. He knew Colonel Mitchell was going to do everything he could to keep him on active duty. "No sir, it's time for me to walk away. I love being in the Army, but I know when to walk away."

Colonel Mitchell stood and shook his hand. "You have nothing more to prove, Jack. Good luck."

"Thank you, sir."

"We're going to have a big retirement ceremony for you."

"I appreciate that sir, but I didn't have a ceremony when I enlisted, I see no point in having one when I retire."

He cleaned out his locker in the team's lounge. His retirement was approved. After enlisting at the age of eighteen, right out of high school, he retired at the age of thirty-nine, after twenty-one years of faithful, loyal service. He and Kate used his terminal leave to look for a house in Dallas. They bought a beautiful five bedroom, three bathroom home close to their parents. The house had a large, gourmet kitchen, large bedrooms and a spacious backyard, complete with an in ground pool and barbecue pit.

They moved back to Dallas and he, Dad, and Jonah started a car restoration and dealership together. It was making very good money. He enjoyed working with his brother and father. She resumed working at Medical City Hospital.

Years had passed by. They were enjoying civilian life. Finally, they had a normal marriage. He had a normal life. He was able to see her and the kids every night, go to school plays, ball games and take her out on their anniversary and her birthday. They were happy, they were comfortable. Their marriage had survived some of the toughest lessons and challenges. They had their share of problems, but they were great partners, great friends and great lovers.

One sunny Saturday afternoon in the summer, they were having a barbecue at their home. They invited their parents, siblings and close friends over. He was in charge of marinating the meat. He stood on the patio, looking out at the backyard at JD, Andrew, Liberty, and Maverick, playing tag and chasing Boomer.

She was inside making the salad and the Texas style sweet tea with her mom, Lauren and Denise and Meagan. Christi and Jonah were sitting at the patio table. Bill and Matt were sitting in patio chairs talking and laughing with Jack as he cooked.

They had a great dinner, pool side. They laughed and talked. Jack, Jonah, and Bill's car restoration business was really doing well. After dinner, the guys and Liberty played football. Liberty, Jack, Maverick, and Matt were against Jonah, JD, Andy, and Bill. Kate and the women were sitting at the patio table, watching them play and talking.

As the women talked around her, she couldn't take her eyes away from watching him play with the kids. She knew after seeing him with JD when they were dating, that he would be an incredible father. And he was. He loved to play with their kids and his nephews. She smiled at Maverick running next to him. He was now four and a half and Liberty was almost seven. He had blondish brown hair and green eyes like Jack. He and Jack were very close. They loved going to Rangers' games together. He loved to show him how to play sports.

She smiled at Liberty chanting "Daddy! Daddy! Daddy!" as he hoisted her up on his shoulders.

He looked over at her, and saw her staring at him. He smiled at her. She smiled back at him. He had kept his promise. He overcame impossible and overwhelming odds, but his indomitable spirit wouldn't let him stop. It kept him going, pushing him to make it back to her. He kept his promise that he would come back.

The End

Biography

J ESSICA JASPER-RING IS from Peggs, Oklahoma, a small northeastern town. She is married to a U.S. Army sergeant, who has completed three combat tours to Iraq and Afghanistan. She and her husband are the parents' of two young girls. Being a military spouse, she knows the challenges and stresses today's military families face.